Blood-Borne Series

~BOOK ONE~

A Midnight Bloom

C.R. QUINN

Designed by C.R. Quinn
Cover created by C.R. Quinn and Tony Leone
Photo art provided by Nuttarit from
www.freedigitalphotos.net

Printed in the United States of America

Library of Congress
ISBN-10: 0615989780
ISBN-13: 978-0615989785

A Midnight Bloom

To John, who read and wanted more,
and to Twin who cried.

Chapter One

Brianna

My life had few surprises. I changed the batteries in the smoke detector every six months, picked up the dry cleaning on Tuesdays, and every day I would wake up hating the fact that I was Brianna Lewis. It was partially my fault, though. It wasn't like I did anything about it. I had made the choice to marry Sam Lewis when I was young and stupid, and he had made sure I would never find my way out. Manipulation and violence were powerful tools, and I was effectively beaten down. Many times, literally.

It was a perfectly ordinary April Sunday morning in Connecticut, meaning grey skies and threatening rain. But despite being overcast, I loved that it was Sunday because it meant I was allowed to leave the house to go to church and sing with the small choir.

The choir loft was located in the back of the church, and my view was obstructed by the large piano in front of me so I rarely knew what was going on during the service. I tried to listen, truly I did, but like most Sundays, my mind began to wander…

The racing river was freezing, and I was gasping for air as my head popped up out of the water for a brief second, just long enough for him to see me. My handsome prince in tight black jeans dove in after me and pulled me back to shore. His well-defined muscles were clearly visible through the wet T-shirt that I desperately clung to as he laid me on the ground.

His dark eyes desperately searched my face while his hands pulled and petted my wet hair. Unable to restrain himself any longer, he pressed his cold lips to mine, making my heart race. Barely able to catch my breath, I opened my mouth and allowed his tongue to enter. His hands began to explore the curves of my body, finally grabbing my thighs and pulling me up to straddle his waist. His passion soared as did my need for him. I arched my head back to give him what he wanted. He kissed my neck and seductively licked his favorite spot to drink from.

He ripped my shirt open and I saw that his fangs were extended. This was it. This was what I needed - the passion, the initial sting of pain followed by a rush of euphoria. He brought his head back down to my neck and pressed my breasts firmly against his chest. I felt the slightest nip at my neck and then...

"Bri?"

What the hell?

"Hey zombie girl, the service is over," Renee said as she hit me in the arm with a hymnal. "You didn't even get up for the last song. Are you okay?"

"Uh...yeah," I stuttered and bent down to grab my purse, suddenly realizing that my imagined lover's shirt wasn't the only thing that was wet. Unbelievable! I was going to hell. How could I let my imagination run rampant? And in church? I guess that's what happens when you read too many vampire novels and your husband is a piece of shit, especially lately.

While Renee continued to bark in my ear, I glanced down at my watch. Already 11:03. Fantastic. Not only did I lose consciousness during church, the service went longer than usual. Sam would be furious. I was surprised my phone wasn't vibrating from my purse.

Crap! My cell phone was in my car. Stupid, Brianna. Stupid, stupid. So not only had I not called my husband at exactly 11:01, I wasn't answering my phone. Without waiting for my best friend, who was oblivious to the fact that I wasn't listening to her, I raced down the choir loft's stairs to the bathroom. Once inside I ran into the first stall, latching the door quickly behind me. Seconds later Renee and her four-inch platforms came clomping into the bathroom and paused on the other side of my stall.

"So, looking at my watch," she began in her typical sarcastic tone, "I see that it is now 11:06 a.m. Since you practically slid down the stairs, I'm assuming you're panicked about not making your required 11:01 phone call to your darling husband. He probably thinks you're having an orgy on the pulpit. Damn you're a slut."

"Renee! We are still in church!"

"You started it."

"Did not!" I snapped back.

"What the hell are you doing in there anyway? You're certainly not peeing."

"What are you, the pee police?" However, she was right; I wasn't peeing. Instead, I was trying to quietly wipe away the guilt from my underwear. "I got my period during the service. I'd rather not have to drive home like this." It sounded plausible enough.

"Your period? Sam must be furious. I know he practically counts the days until you're ovulating again."

Sadly, she was right on both accounts. Sam had been furious when my monthly bill showed up a couple of weeks ago. And he'd bought one of those drug store ovulation kits so he could find out for himself when I was most likely to get pregnant. He stopped trusting my calculations, but that was because I lied to him most of the time. It wasn't that I didn't want to get pregnant. I just didn't want *him* to get me pregnant. The truth was I desperately wanted a baby. But it wasn't fair for me to bring a child into the nightmare I had created for myself.

After cleaning up as best I could, I swung the door open, practically catching Renee in my arms. I forced a smile, but she reached up and wiped away the tear running down my face.

"I'm sorry, I meant it as a joke," she said, the sarcasm stripped from her voice. "Once again I place my large platform shoe in my mouth. Still love me?"

"Of course I do. How could I not? You keep me sane. And although it shows how stupid he really is, Sam thinks you're a good influence."

"It shows he has good taste. Besides, I'm sure he knows I'd kick his ass if he tried to 'prevent' me from seeing you."

"I wonder if you'll ever learn how air quotes are really supposed to be used."

"Bri, they're my 'signature.' They make me stand out."

"They make you look like..." Renee pursed her lips and cocked an eyebrow at me, "...like...my darling best friend."

"More like only friend."

"That, too," I laughed, but then reality sunk in. "I've got to get out of here and call Sam. I'm surprised he hasn't come barreling into the building." I joked, but it had happened once before. Thankfully Renee had been with me which meant he didn't make a scene. Sam was under the impression that Renee didn't know how violent he was with me. Sam actually thought Renee liked him. But it was all an act, one that allowed me to have someone take care of me when I needed it and didn't judge me.

"Text me when you get home and let me know you're okay. I'm planning on going out tonight, but if you need me, I'll rush over. My mother declared that she has found my soul mate, but seriously, who sets up a date on a Sunday?"

Renee was extremely attractive, and looked no more than twenty-five, even though she was thirty-one, like me. Bitch. Her thick red hair hung just to her shoulders and had that natural waviness that women spent hours trying to create. But if that wasn't enough, her small hips and waist gave way to D-cup breasts, the perfect proportions in most men's eyes. And yet, she was still single. And not from lack of trying on her mother's part. I'd begun to suspect that she was staying single to spite her mother. No one ever forced Renee to do anything. Ever.

As we left the tiny bathroom and made our way to the back parking lot, the butterflies in my stomach grew to the size of birds. I could almost hear Sam screaming into my voicemail from here. It didn't matter that it was the minister's fault I was late. It didn't matter that I'd left my phone in the car. All that mattered was that I was late. We'd had the argument endless times, with me always on the losing end. But perhaps today would be different. Maybe Sam would get hit by a semi-truck.

"Okay, kiss me, I'm gonna run to my car," I said turning to Renee. "Wish me luck."

Southerners could never leave others without some sugar and although I had spent almost fourteen years in Connecticut, I was still a good Southern girl. While I hugged Renee and kissed her cheek, I saw a man leaning up against the light post on the corner with his arms crossed tightly in front of his chest. He was tall, on the slim side, but I could tell even through his thin leather jacket, that he worked out. His black skinny jeans must have cost a small fortune, but they were nothing compared to his Italian-looking, possibly cashmere, black V-neck sweater. His jet-black hair was cut short against the sides, but had thick wavy curls on top. Yummy. The only thing not black were his silver aviator sunglasses, not that he needed them on a day like today. No doubt his expensive sunglasses were hiding his seductively dark eyes that matched everything else about him. Oddly enough, he was staring at me. Stranger still, he looked pissed.

I straightened up and looked behind me to find the person he seemed irritated with, since it obviously couldn't be me. I didn't even know the guy. But after scanning the parking lot I realized that Renee and I were the only ones left. I turned back around to see that Mr. Tall-Dark-and-Pissed-Off was still staring at me, but now he had pushed himself off the light post and taken a couple of steps towards us.

Following my gaze, Renee's eyes widened when she noticed the stranger staring intently in our direction.

"Ex-*cuse* me," she said with extreme attitude. "Do we have a problem here? If you haven't noticed, this is a church, not some creepy dating service. Why don't you just go back to your little black-clad cult and leave us alone before I kick your ass."

Grabbing my arm, Renee pulled me toward my SUV but I couldn't help looking back at Mr. Stalker. Although his firm stance had not changed, I could see the slightest curl of his lip develop into a wickedly cute crooked smile. Melt my heart.

"Hey! Snap out of it!" Renee said abruptly, pulling me from my hypnotized state. "Might I remind you that you probably have an irate idiot screaming into your phone right now? Sam could be speeding around that corner at any moment and see you ogling creepy hottie guy over there."

"I'm sorry, I couldn't help myself. His bravery on wearing men's skinny jeans alone intrigues me, and those sunglasses and the leather jacket…I mean how can you resist that bad boy smile?"

I placed my arm around Renee's shoulder and turned her around so that she too could experience that heart melting smile. But he was gone, vanished. Where could he have gone in the two seconds I was able to tear my eyes away from him. I felt my stomach drop, and suddenly a wave of sadness washed over me.

Renee snapped her head back around and said, "Considering I don't see a smile, let alone a person around, I'd say you've officially lost it. Creepy guy is gone, be thankful, and get in your car. You have bigger problems to deal with right now."

Ignoring my friend's warning, I frantically began looking around for a glimpse of a black jacket, a flash of light reflecting off his sunglasses, anything. What was wrong with me? Some creepy, though incredibly handsome man gives me a smile, and now I was depressed that he disappeared without sweeping me off my feet and carrying me off into the sunset.

Okay, I've been reading way too many romantic novels.

"Re, you're right, I know. I'm just delaying the inevitable," I said and fished around in my purse for the key remote to my dark gray SUV.

"I'm serious, Bri, text me if you need me. Maybe I could even break my record of an eleven-minute date." Although she had a smile on her face, the concern in her eyes was obvious.

"Maybe it would be good for you to actually get to know someone of the opposite sex," I teased. "I may just punish you by *not* interrupting your date tonight."

The familiar tight lipped, slow inhalation of breath, and widening of her eyes always warned me that she was about to blow up. I'd seen that expression for almost ten years and it still felt good that I could get under her thick skin.

"Brianna Marie Morgan Lewis, don't you even kid about not calling me if you need help. You know I'm scared shitless about what will happen when you get home and that there's nothing you'll let me do about it," she shouted as her eyes became glassy with tears. "You have no idea how helpless I feel. Being your friend isn't easy, Bri. It can downright suck sometimes, especially when you say crap like that."

"I'm sorry, sweetie, I was just kidding. I didn't mean to make you upset. I will let you know if I need help. I promise," I lied. I hated doing it, but if I called her every time I needed help she'd never leave my house. She deserved a life too.

"All right, then. I love you," she said with a sigh. After a quick peck on my cheek, she ran across the parking lot to her beat up red sedan that surprisingly matched her hair. I sometimes wondered if that was why she bought it.

Well, it was time to face the music, however horrible it might be. I looked at my watch and it was nearly 11:30. My heart jumped into my throat. I unlocked my SUV, hopped up into the driver's seat and started the engine. Before I checked my messages, I pressed the button for my favorite feature, the heated seats. It could be July and I would still press that button. I was always just a little cold.

As the warm leather seat began to envelope my legs and back with its comforting heat, I took my cell phone from the cup holder and saw that I had missed fifteen calls. Only fifteen?

Putting the SUV in gear, I sped out of my parking space while telling my car to check my voicemail. Seconds later the lovely voicemail lady announced, "You have one new message."

That can't be good.

"Bri Bri, this is your husband..." - pause - "Sam." Really? No shit. "It is now 11:20 need I say more." Click.

Short, to the point, really bad news for me. The shorter the message, the angrier he was and that meant trouble. Well, I'd taken it for almost fourteen years, did I expect him to change? Fat chance.

"Call Sam," I said to my cell. Interestingly enough Sam's phone went right to voicemail which meant he was now ignoring me. This was good for me, well kind of. I really needed to get to the grocery, and if he had answered, he wouldn't have allowed it. I was already in trouble, and the consequences would be the same whether I made the stop or not.

After hearing the beep for his voicemail, I said into the microphone, "Hi honey it's me, I'm so sorry about not calling. The service went late today and I left my phone in the car. And then Renee just talked my ear off afterwards and I didn't want to be rude." Obviously, I wasn't going to tell him about my stalker so I continued with, "I have to stop by the grocery. We're out of so many things. I'll be home right after. Love you, bye."

I should win an Oscar. My Southern upbringing taught me how to sound like an angel on one end of the phone while flipping you off on the other. It was a gift, one few women up North possessed.

Rolling through the stop sign at the next corner, I turned left to head to the grocery rather than going home. I realized I had an hour of Brianna time, an hour that would be filled with wild imaginations about my new fantasy lover. Maybe you know him - tall, thin, dark wavy hair, vintage aviator glasses. Hmm, maybe that's all he would have.

Chapter Two

Brianna

My cheeks were flush as I pulled into the local grocery store parking lot. I was barely two minutes down the road before I was dreaming about being naked on the beach with Mr. Stalker. I was pathetic, but at least I knew it.

Sundays in Connecticut were often quiet, well at least in my little corner. Most people were either in church, or inside because of the cold. So having the only sound in the parking lot coming from my black spikey heels wasn't anything new. But suddenly the click-clacking of my heels was drowned out by a deep, thundering roar coming down the aisle next to me. Instinctively I turned to my right to see an exquisite jet-black Aston Martin Vanquish pulling into a parking space across from where I was standing. To me it was one of the most beautiful cars ever made, but what the heck was it doing here?

Then I saw him. *Him!* Mr. Stalker was sitting in the driver's seat still hiding behind his silver aviators. Slowly he stepped out of his car in a movement that had its own seductive soundtrack playing in the background. If his hair had been longer, it probably would have been billowing behind him in slow motion.

"Uh, hi," I stuttered, sounding like the village idiot. Real smooth, Brianna, maybe tomorrow we could graduate to three letter words. Unfortunately, his cute crooked smile from earlier had disappeared and he just stood there, staring at me, saying nothing. "Awkward. Well, bye."

Completely crushed that he didn't instantly fall madly in love with me, I picked up my pace and rushed into the grocery. Now I was thoroughly embarrassed. I avoided the looks of my fellow shoppers as I entered the store. They too noticed Mr. Stalker's killer car and had all started gathering in the front window of the store for a better look. So in turn they were looking at me wondering how the elusive Mrs. Lewis knew this dark stranger.

"Lovely day, isn't it, Michael?" I said as I passed the store's owner. Michael Bazzuto was one of the few people who didn't know my husband that well, and only because Sam hated grocery shopping. So thankfully I was always allowed to go by myself, but only to Bazzuto's Market.

"Good afternoon, Mrs. Lewis, do you know that man in the black car?" Michael said, gesturing to Mr. Stalker who was still standing by his car and now talking into his cell phone.

"Actually, I don't," I said loud enough for those shoppers around me to hear. "I was just admiring his car."

"Of course you were, that's an Aston Martin. You don't see those very often and boy is it a beauty." Quickly he turned around to the small group of people peering out the main store window as he said, "Folks let's go about our business. It's rather rude to be staring at a customer as he walks into the store."

Walks into the store?! Turning so fast I almost broke my ankle, I grabbed a cart and proceeded to run down the first aisle I could get to through the crowd of people trying to disperse. Continuing down the aisle, Renee's voice was screaming in my head, 'You've lost it! You've actually lost it.' Why in God's name was I running down a grocery aisle to get away from someone who obviously wasn't interested in me in the slightest?

Just then, out of the corner of my eye I saw a dark shadow cross in front of the aisle. When I turned around, I fully expected to see Mr. Stalker, but there was no one there. I was beginning to see medication in my future. Now I was imagining things.

Shaking it off, I pushed the cart down the rest of the aisle to the meat section and selected some chicken and a steak. There was nothing like a good piece of meat to ease your husband into forgiveness. Looking ahead of me I noticed another black shadow turning down an aisle a few feet ahead of me. I couldn't explain why, but I knew this black shadow was my stalker, I could feel it. With both hands, I grabbed my cart and pushed it toward the aisle the last shadow had disappeared down. When I rounded the corner, of course, I saw nothing. Now I was just pissed off. This creepy asshole had me thinking I was crazy, and people in the store were beginning to stare.

"Brianna Marie, pull yourself together," I whispered to myself.

After a deep breath, I headed down the aisle trying to forget about stalkers and shadows and instead take an interest in marinades. While I debated between teriyaki and chipotle, I could hear footsteps approaching me from behind. It was him, I knew it was him. I could almost feel his dark presence around me.

"Listen asshole," I said as I whipped around, "follow someone else you creepy bastard."

The young stock boy with pimples covering his face was as red as Renee's hair. "I...I'm s-sorry ma'am. I saw this drop out of your cart when you went around the c-corner," he stuttered and held out my favorite lip gloss.

"Ohmygod, I'm so sorry. I..I thought you were someone else."

I ripped the lip gloss from his hand, tucked my tail between my legs, and headed straight for the register. I needed to get out of here.

Thankfully there were no lines at the register and within minutes I was handing the cashier my credit card. Out of the corner of my eye I saw Michael Buzzuto speaking sternly to the young stock boy. The cashier handed me my credit card and small bag of groceries before I bolted toward the front door of the store.

"Mrs. Lewis, wait, can I talk to you?" Michael said from behind me.

Not missing a beat, I kept walking to the door and said, "Sorry, Michael, I have to run. By the way, you've got quite a young man there. He deserves a raise or a promotion or something."

I was practically yelling the last part through the door closing behind me. I couldn't get to my car fast enough. I needed the soft warm leather retreat of my SUV to calm down and bury my embarrassment.

Before pulling away, I wanted to see if the culprit of this fiasco was still here, but no such luck. The shiny black car was gone, along with its mysterious driver. Asshole. I needed to get home and have my head on straight before the shit storm named Sam came down upon me.

Chapter Three

Cameron

"Cameron, do you or do you not have her in your possession?" Victor's raspy, although groggy, voice echoed through my car.

"I do not," I replied tentatively. "She is going to be a little difficult to obtain. She has been surrounded by people since I found her, and now she seems curious."

"Interested ladies have never been a problem for you in the past. How is she any different?"

"I cannot explain it, Father, she is simply...different. Have Jazlyn take care of this one, she is on the East Coast as well. She could easily grab her and be done with it." I knew that I was pushing my maker, but this case truly had me uneasy. I could not explain it to myself, let alone to him.

"Cameron, you are my favorite child, and I would certainly grant you a pardon on this if I were able. However, Eris requested you specifically. Now I need you to gather his daughter and deliver her to the Facility as you have the others."

"Yes sir. I will gather and deliver her as promised."

"Good boy. Next time, could you please wait until a decent hour? It is still morning here, and you know I prefer to sleep until dusk."

Of course I knew. That was why I decided to call him at this hour knowing full well the time difference between the East and West coasts. I was hoping he would be too weary to argue with me and assign Jazlyn to this case like I so desperately wanted. But I knew very well why I was chosen, I was the best Gatherer out there. And Brianna Morgan, or Brianna

M. Lewis as it said on her driver's license, was important. However, I was not privy to why.

"Father, I apologize. I will call you once I have gathered her, but know it may be a couple of days." The words left a sour taste in my mouth. The Gatherers had never waited more than twenty-four hours for one of my cases. Because Brianna's father had hidden her all these years, she most likely knew nothing about what she truly was. That made my job more difficult. She might just be the assignment that broke my streak and made me lose my wager with my sister of sorts. "I am sure that Jazlyn will never let me live it down."

"As is her right. You have been baiting her for almost two years now. Maybe this assignment will bring some life back into you."

"You know that is impossible."

"You are a vampire, child, anything is possible. Call me when you have her."

As I disconnected the phone, I realized that Victor was right, I had become a robot, but that was how I survived. Having no emotions or attachments was how I *had* to do this job. Not that it was really a job, more of an obligation. When your maker, or father as our coven referred to Victor as, orders you to do something in the best interest of our race, you could not say no. You merely found a way to push through the hurt.

My first year as a Gatherer was nothing like this. I made a connection with each and every hybrid. I held them when they cried, soothed them when they were scared, and bedded them if the need arose. However, the problem with making a connection meant I always had to break it once I delivered them. Whether I spent two hours or two days with one of them, the tears they shed when I left them alone in a new world ripped my heart out, at least what was left of it. The women I had taken to bed were always the most difficult to part with. Not that I was in love with them, it was as simple as having shared an intimate moment with someone. But in the end, it became too hard. I found it was easier to find them, gather, and deliver. Nothing else. It was hard at first but after a while I convinced myself that it was my duty to turn my back on them and go onto the next one.

Brianna, however, was different. It was not because of her powerful lineage, though that certainly made her unique. There were other reasons. I was taken aback when I first saw her through a window at her home this morning. Feelings were stirring within me, and it angered me. I had not meant for her to catch me outside of the church, but my mind had been elsewhere. I found myself thinking about a woman in ways I had not in many, many years, and after only a few glances. I was pathetic and weak, and again it made me angry. Teasing her around the grocery store gave me a little pleasure. But when she yelled at a young man thinking it was me, I knew it was time to leave.

When her dark gray SUV passed my hiding place, I realized it was time to go back to work, even if it was in the shadows for the next few hours. I assumed she was returning home, and there were plenty of side roads for me to hide my car and get a few hours of sleep. I never needed much, but not having fed for several days had weakened me, and there was not a blood contact in the area. I needed this assignment over with and get as far away from Brianna Lewis as possible. There was a nagging feeling that if I did not separate myself now, I would be unable to leave her again. That alone had me scared for the first time in almost three hundred years.

Chapter Four

Brianna

I pulled into my garage and parked in my designated bay. We had a four-car garage, but only one space was mine. It even had its own sign: *Reserved for Brianna M. Lewis*. The other three signs of course read *Reserved for Samuel A. Lewis*. It was only one small humiliating aspect of my life with Sam.

Walking into the house I gave a mocking smile as I passed my little parking sign. Brianna M. Lewis, as my husband insisted on, meant Brianna Marie Lewis. But to me it meant Brianna Morgan Lewis. After I married Sam, he insisted that I sever ties with my family. I was his, which meant dropping my maiden name and everyone that went along with it. It was heartbreaking. My grandfather rarely referred to me as Brianna Lewis because he hated Sam and was not shy of showing it, which was another reason I rarely saw him. Every couple of years I was able to visit when a "cousin" or "aunt" died, but I was beginning to run out of fake relatives.

Once in the house, I shoved the meat into the fridge and reveled in the silence. Sam wasn't home! He was probably playing golf, or getting drunk, possibly both, which meant I had some time to myself before the chaos.

Ooh, but what to do? A nap. That's what I needed, just a quick, quiet nap. Slipping my heels off, I padded down the hall and made my way to my sanctuary, the study. It was the one room that was mine. No Sam, and no cameras. Oh yes, there were cameras in my house. Well Sam had to monitor me while he was at work since apparently I couldn't be trusted.

I opened the door to my study that welcomed me with warm red walls covered in part by cherry wood bookcases almost reaching the ceiling. Sinking my feet into the plush carpet, I couldn't decide whether I wanted to stretch out on my white couch, or my favorite spot - the window seat. It was the width of a full-size mattress and the cushion was almost as thick. It was covered in red and white pillows, and fluffy warm blankets which created the perfect reading area. I spent hours propped up on those pillows, covered in blankets reading with the large bay window slightly open for fresh air. Rainy days were my favorite. Give me a gloomy day and a good book and I was as content as a pig in shit. As long as Sam knew I was in here, he left me alone.

After a few years I had a bathroom built inside the room so that I rarely had to leave except for meals. Unfortunately, as the years went by, the small bathroom became a place where I could clean myself up after Sam let loose on me. I had all the supplies needed to heal from our scuffles: antibiotic ointments, bandages, gauze, ice packs, heat packs, etc. I always healed quickly compared to most people, but that was just on the outside. The inside was a completely different story.

Climbing up onto the window seat, I opened the bay window just enough to feel the cool breeze curl around my fingers. I pulled my favorite two pillows from the assortment and wrapped my best blanket around my body. Curling up like an infant it was only moments before I was fast asleep…

"Brianna! Brianna, love, please wake up!"

I opened my eyes ever so slightly to see my lover sickened with worry that I might be dead.

"Cameron, stop shaking me, you're going to make me sick," I said.

Barely waiting for me to get my last word out, he crushed his lips against mine. I could hardly breathe since I had just been pulled out of a freezing river, but I could have cared less. He came for me, despite the loyalty to his family and the threat of death, he came for me. And now, I had lost my shirt since he literally ripped it in half and threw it on the ground beside him.

Cameron began to comb his fingers through my soaked dark brown hair which was only a shade lighter than my almost black eyes. A feature that was rarely missed by anyone I met, and one that was certainly not missed by Cameron as he stared intensely into them, as I did his that were almost identical in shape and color.

My breasts began to heave with my quickening breath knowing the moment was drawing near. Cam squeezed my right breast tightly as he began to kiss me down my neck. When he reached his favorite spot, I tilted my head back for a better angle. Although the bite would sting at first, the resulting pleasure I would feel was more than worth it. I put my left arm around his neck to anchor myself for the big moment, well the first big moment. The second was definitely stirring under his pants and would be coming for me momentarily. He nipped at my neck with his extended fangs and ripped open my pants. His hand traveled down between my legs...

Are you freaking kidding me?! God dammit, what did it take to get laid in a dream nowadays? The sound of the garage door opening woke me from my latest indiscretion, and I knew I only had moments to make myself presentable and absent of the smell of pheromones. Hubby was home, and in no way did I want to encourage him. After a terse hello through my study's bathroom door, Sam left and I performed a quick scrub down and changed back into my slacks and blouse from church.

One of Sam's biggest pet peeves was a woman who walked around her house in sweatpants. To him it meant she didn't have respect for her home or herself. Therefore, Sam's wife was to always look her best. Even jeans could be grounds for an argument. There was the rare occasion when he would lift his rule when I was ill, or when I worked out. How kind of him. The jackass. You'd think he was raised by Miss Porter herself, but he was born in a two-room single trailer where his mother wore nothing but sweatpants and oversized cartoon T-shirts. When she passed away, he had the trailer demolished so that no one could ever link him to her, like anyone cared.

As I padded out into the hallway, I was surprised to see how late it had gotten. A storm was coming in so the sun had set, but I couldn't believe I had slept the afternoon away.

"Sam? Sam honey, where are you?" Marco? Marco? Where the hell was the Polo?

"Bri Bri, could you join me in the kitchen? We need to have a little talk," Sam said in a low, authoritative tone.

Only two people in my life called me Bri Bri, and I hated it. My mother had always called me that, and my husband quickly fell into step. Both users called me Bri Bri because they knew it made me feel like a child, which was their reasoning for using it.

When I walked into the kitchen, Sam was leaning over the granite island, arms splayed and tense as they held him up. His salt and pepper hair was cut short, almost military style, and thinning in the back. He was only thirty-seven, but you'd think he was in his late forties. He was average height, but had kept his broad shoulders from his high school football days, and worked out to keep his middle-aged spare tire at bay.

"So, how was your little excursion today?"

"Sam, you know it wasn't an excursion. Church ran late, and I had to run to the grocery store. Speaking of, I bought a great sirloin for dinner. Would you like me to make some broccoli or baked potatoes?"

"Neither. I just want some pasta and red sauce. We can talk while you cook."

The man could be presented with the culinary cuisine of the world's best chefs and he would send it all back for a bowl of spaghetti and red sauce. And by red sauce, I'm not even talking about the high-end marinara stuff since it had flavor, and that was bad. The generic tomato sauce he made me buy truly looked like thick fruit punch, hence why I always opted out of his favorite meal. Looked like I would end up with a bowl of cereal.

While I grabbed the pasta and sauce from the pantry, I could feel Sam's eyes on my back. "So, did you go golfing? Kind of a gloomy day for it," I said lightly as I passed by him, smelling the alcohol radiating from his skin.

"I met Jimmy for a quick nine and then we stayed in the clubhouse for a while." The club always had to stock extra scotch when Sam and Jimmy came back for the season. "Speaking of Jimmy, Gayle called him this afternoon with the funniest story."

Gayle Davis, Jimmy's wife, was the biggest gossip in upper Connecticut. She had an entire network of spies that called each other all day long spreading vicious gossip amongst the other housewives. I was not part of that network since I was oftentimes the subject of the gossip.

"Really? How is Gayle?" I asked as I dumped the red viscous fluid loosely called tomato sauce into a pot and began boiling the water for Sam's spaghetti.

"Oh she's fine. Apparently, a stranger was driving around in some fancy car terrorizing the town. He finally stopped into Bazutto's where Gayle was shopping. And guess who she saw?" Shit, shit, shit, I thought. "You. Can you imagine my surprise to know that my little Bri Bri was fraternizing with a terrorist?" He paused, waiting for me to answer, but I stayed silent. "Do you have an explanation?"

Of course I did. Gayle was an evil, over dramatic bitch content on making my life a living hell. Slowly I began to stir the sauce with a wooden spoon trying to form a better answer.

"Sam, honey, did Gayle tell Jimmy what kind of car it was? It was an Aston Martin, actually an Aston Martin Vanquish. You just don't see those cars every day. This random guy pulled into a parking space as I walked by. He got out, I said 'nice car' and kept walking. I bought some chicken and a steak and the receipt is in my purse if you'd like to check it."

"Gayle said you couldn't keep your eyes off of him and practically stalked him around the grocery store."

"Well then Gayle is full of shit!" I shouted. Crap. I'm a dead woman. Not only did Sam not tolerate me talking back to him, I was never allowed to swear. Sam moved from the island to stand directly behind me. My entire body tensed as I prepared for the blow I knew was coming. "I was just admiring the car, Sam. I swear I didn't do anything else."

Sam encircled me with his arms and pressed his forehead into the nape of my neck.

"Promise?"

"Yes, I promise."

He kissed my neck and pulled his arms away. "Let's eat in the living room tonight, maybe there'll be something on TV. And remember to mix the pasta in with the sauce before you put it in my bowl. You know I can't stand it when it's just sitting on top."

I nodded nervously. How did I come out of this one? Looking covertly behind me I saw Sam walk into the living room that opened from the kitchen. Hearing Sam flip through the channels helped me relax since it put some distance between us. As I drained the pasta, I noticed he had settled on racing which would hopefully keep him occupied while I mixed his majesty's dinner correctly.

But a minute later I was startled when I heard Sam say behind me, "Let me help you with that."

"That's okay, honey, I've got it," I replied, not wanting him near me, but Sam came to my side anyway. While I continued to stir his sauce, he suddenly hit the end of the wooden spoon causing hot tomato sauce to fly in my face.

I screamed, taking several steps back and feeling the edge of the island up against my back while my hands frantically wiped the burning sauce off my skin. Completely distracted, I didn't see Sam's wide-open palm come down until I felt my left cheek explode in pain. The force behind Sam's slap caused the right side of my face to slam against the granite countertop and cut my eyebrow completely open. My face throbbed with pain as thick, warm blood flowed into my eye and mouth as I slumped to the floor.

I tried to push Sam away as he dragged me to the opposite wall. He slammed me up against the pantry doors causing the two elongated handles to plunge into my back. Clumsily he unzipped his pants and tried to arouse himself with his right hand while he held me up by my throat with his left and began to squeeze.

In a panic, I pulled at his hand around my throat, seeing the sick smile on his face as he got off on my pain. He ripped my blouse open and reached back with his right fist and jabbed it into my stomach, causing me to completely topple over. Catching me in his arms, he dragged me into the living room and unfolded me onto the couch.

Barely conscious, and finding it difficult to breathe, I tried to prepare myself for what was coming, because unfortunately I knew. Weakly I held the waistband of my slacks, but Sam easily slapped my hands away, ripped my pants open, and pulled them down as far as his patience allowed. A moment later he crawled on top of me and penetrated me deeply and painfully. Again, and again, pounding, endless pounding. I looked wildly around for anything that I could focus on until he was done tearing me apart from the inside out.

It was at that moment when I saw them. Outside the window about two feet above the couch cushion I saw what looked like two dark eyes staring back at me. I kept staring at those eyes almost seeing the faintest outline of a face, but nothing I could recognize.

Tears streamed down my face as Sam's thrusts became unbearable. I screamed at him to stop, but he responded by slapping me in the face and pounding himself inside of me. I looked back up at the window, searching for the eyes to focus on once again, and saw that their owner had pressed his fingertips up against the windowpane. Clumsily I put my hand up to the glass. With our fingertips pressed together, the stranger's face began to take form, but in the same moment my pain became so excruciating that the scene around me began to blur until I was completely covered in darkness.

Chapter Five

Cameron

Vampires do not dream while they sleep, not that I could call it sleeping. It was more like recharging one's body, energy, and strength. Older vampires required little sleep; however, many chose to always be at their strongest and sleep during the day. A new vampire required more recharging since the body was in such flux from the vampire blood. Sunlight for a new vampire was lethal, but faded with age. Along with age also came enhanced abilities and powers. Every vampire was unique because powers were determined by any special abilities one had as a human, as well as the powers that were inherited from their maker.

However, even the most pathetic vampire had strength, speed, and healing abilities, but the weaker the maker, the weaker the child. Your stature in the vampire community was mainly determined on your lineage and your age. Some covens consisted only of members who were created by their maker, or as we referred to it as being Turned, whereas others let anyone join as long as they could pay for the privilege.

I was part of the Warrior coven, the defenders of our kind. When our maker, Victor, was human, his strategic military skills were unsurpassed and were only heightened when he was Turned more than two millennia ago. Victor sought out only those who possessed certain skills he felt would enhance his coven. Every one of my sixty-two siblings had been chosen for a specific skill or talent, except for me. I was Victor's accident. But despite his moment of weakness, Victor ran his coven like a well-oiled machine. He had no tolerance for any of his children breaking the rules. Those who did were killed. It was that simple.

The Gatherers, on the other hand, were not a coven but a group of vampires charged with aiding in protecting those affected by the current unpleasantness, the hunting of our children, commonly known as hybrids. Being Victor's favorite son, he urged me to be first in line, although there was little needed. As soon as I found out that Jazlyn was looking to join the Gatherers, I was determined to always be a step ahead of her.

Although Jazlyn was the closest to me in age, and at times we were close, there were only three other Warriors I considered my true siblings. Devin, Alexander, and Jared ranged from 530 years of age to 26. My brothers were fierce soldiers, and Victor refused to lose them to the gathering effort. Do not misunderstand, Jazlyn and I were great Warriors, but we were better strategists and less blood thirsty. All of which were essential qualities of a Gatherer, and to date I was the best. A title Jazlyn desperately wanted to take away from me.

While recharging in my car, I was suddenly roused by the sound of my sister's ringtone. Not opening my eyes, I found the phone and hit the button to talk. "Darling sister, what do I owe this honor?"

"Don't try and butter me up." Jazlyn's deep voice made every word she said seem sexual; another perfect trait for a Gatherer. "I heard Father gave you a secret case."

"Not secret, just delicate."

"Who is she?"

"How do you know it is a woman?"

"Because you wouldn't risk losing our wager for a guy. You only have a few hours left."

My eyes flew open to find the clock on the dash of my car displaying that it was seven o'clock. Thankfully one of the best gifts a vampire possessed was Projection - the ability to transport one's body to another location. The only drawback was that you had to know where to Project yourself. I could not simply think about Brianna and be whisked to her, more so I had to picture exactly where I wanted to go. Without an explanation I hung up on Jazlyn, centered my thoughts on the woods at the edge of Brianna's property, concentrated on the image in my head, and pushed. Projecting was not necessarily pleasant. It felt like you were ripping your body apart and then slamming it back together in a matter of seconds. It took even the most powerful vampire a few weeks to master landing without completely falling over.

In the blink of an eye, the back of Brianna's house was in front of me. The large bay window that belonged to her study was dark and a small spark of worry hit the bottom of my stomach. Suddenly my phone rang from my pocket and I answered it quickly.

"Jazlyn, not now. I have to..." but I was interrupted by the sound of a woman screaming. I rounded the corner where lights were shining through the tall windows of the home's living room. Jazlyn was yelling in my ear through the phone, demanding to know what was happening.

"Quiet! There might be an intruder," I growled at her. "I am going to try and get a better look."

Carefully I peered through the windows and quickly saw Brianna being held up against a tall cabinet, her face covered in blood. I could see her attacker and with conflicted emotions I was grateful that he was not one of our adversaries, but furious that the piece of slime was her husband.

"Jazlyn, I have to go."

"Cameron, is it Elaina?"

"No, it is her husband, I have to stop this."

"Cameron you can't! You know the rules, we cannot interfere. It'll expose us, Victor will kill you."

Unfortunately, she was right. I could not interfere in human matters, it was law. As I looked back at Brianna's face dripping with blood, shock and terror in her eyes, my anger exploded in my body. This had to end, I had to end it.

"Cameron, are you listening to me? You can't interfere. Father will never forgive you. He'd rather let her die than have us exposed."

What? Let her die! No, no I could not let that happen. "Goodbye, Jazlyn."

As I hung up on Jazlyn, I could hear her screaming into the phone and again I knew she was right. Was this hybrid's life worth my death?

From my view at the window, I looked up just as Brianna's husband ripped open her blouse and planted his fist into her stomach causing her to completely collapse into him. He carried her into the living room and over to a couch located directly in front of the windows, and in turn directly in front of me. As he carelessly threw Brianna's limp body down on the couch, he straightened himself to admire his work and he was almost at my sight line. The second before his eyes met mine, I panicked and quickly stepped several feet back.

I watched while he began his assault on her. Anger and shame filled me as I hid in the dark following my father's precious rules, watching an innocent woman be stripped of all dignity. I could only see the top of the man's head moving forward and back, but I knew he was violating her. He might be her husband, but what he was doing to her could not be construed as anything but rape.

An unexplainable feeling flooded over me. I needed to see her. With great control, I Projected my spirit to the window and tried to find an angle where I could see her. Panic and pain filled her eyes which she could barely open because of the swelling and the blood beginning to clot over them. I Projected more of myself to where my eyes completely formed their shape, and with every ounce of my being I willed her to look up at me.

In that moment, her eyes met mine. Shame overwhelmed me as she continued to look into my eyes while her painful assault continued. Losing all concentration, my Projection was thrust back into my body knocking me to the ground when she screamed so loudly I thought for sure the windows would shatter. Losing sight of her caused utter panic within me and I rushed up to the window.

Brianna's tear-streaked face found my eyes again, and without thinking I placed my hand on the window. I wanted to touch her, hold her, anything but be on this side of the glass. Brianna's limp arm slowly rose to the window and streaked the glass with her bloody fingertips. Whatever was left of my heart crumbled into a million pieces. Her hand stayed with mine only for a moment before it fell away. About to pound through the glass into the room, I noticed she was still breathing and realized she must have lost consciousness. It was probably a blessing.

For an hour I sat and stared at the blood-streaked window pane in front of me. I was angry at myself, Victor, and of course Brianna's husband. Once the bastard was finished, he simply got up and left. He left her there, bloody, half-naked, and unconscious as though she was some pitiful whore. I kept imagining how I would kill him. This monster did not deserve to live after what he had done, and I suspected this was not the first time he had done this to her. I wanted to go back to the window to see her, but I felt that I should give her some privacy.

Jazlyn began calling every ten minutes after I hung up on her. She left several messages, but I did not listen to them. I did not want any distractions from my current state of wallowing. But there was one caller I could not ignore.

"Father."

"Cameron."

Silence.

Jazlyn had sold me out to Victor. Depending on what my sister had told him, he could be thinking of the most efficient way to dispose of his former favorite son. After what seemed like an eternity I finally said, "I do not possess her."

"And?"

"She lives."

"Then why do you not possess her?"

Why? Because she has been beaten and raped and degraded by her son of a bitch husband who I so desperately wanted to kill at this very moment, and I let him do this to her because of *your* god forsaken rules! However, "She is injured," was all I could say. I was an unbelievable coward.

"And the husband?"

"He lives as well," I growled.

"Good. Then all is intact. How long do you think it will take for her to heal enough to travel?"

"It could be a couple of weeks or more, some of her injuries are quite severe."

"Fine then, you can come back for her. There is a case in Massachusetts that you can handle in the meantime."

"NO!"

Another deafening silence. I was unsure if it was from shock or anger on Victor's part. What was wrong with me? I was practically signing my death warrant. I had never defied my father, let alone screamed at him in the same breath. He was waiting for me to break the silence, so I pushed my anger deep down so that I could finish this conversation in a respectful and orderly way, and still get what I wanted. I could not leave Brianna unprotected like this.

"I am sorry, Father, I did not mean to raise my voice. Please forgive me. I am merely thinking of the woman. Both you *and* Eris have made it clear that she is a priority and must be gathered before any of Elaina's minions find her." And because I cannot bear being away from her while she is in the same house with that bastard.

"Interesting."

Interesting? He was going to force me to leave her. Knowing him, he would have Jazlyn come and take my place, which would be a nightmare. She would give Brianna little sympathy or compassion. Brianna needed special attention, she was so fragile and weak.

Stop!

Taking a deep breath, I looked down and saw that I had pulled up several large chunks of the lawn, and I was now covered in grass and dark rich dirt.

"Very well, you shall stay," Victor finally said. "Watch over her and take her as soon as you can. But child, do not forget your duty," he said as his voice took on a sudden seriousness. "You will not interfere, and she cannot be taken while in the sight of her husband."

"It will be more difficult than I thought."

"I am sure you will think of something. No one surpasses your abilities when you have your head about you. Do you understand me?"

"Yes Father…perfectly."

"Good. I will want frequent updates, and if I do not get them, I will send Jazlyn after you. Goodbye, child."

"Goodbye…" - click - "…Father." He was not pleased with me, but he had not threatened to kill me either. That was a good sign. Although the suggestion of Jazlyn joining me was a little hint that I better stay in line.

As I tossed my phone back on the ground, my eyes shot up to the window at the sound of a soft muffled moan coming from inside the house. Slowly Brianna's bloody hand came up and over the couch cushion. Tightening her grip, she slowly pulled herself up, gently catching her head in her right hand. The cut on her right eye was swollen and still dripping with blood. Cautiously she turned her body away from the couch and pushed herself to a slumped but standing position. Her ripped slacks slid down her legs onto the floor as she walked out of them. Finding the island in the kitchen, she pulled herself along looking as though she might collapse at any moment. When she reached its end, she rested for a moment before taking several steps to the hallway where I completely lost my view of her and scrambled around the corner of the house hoping to see where she might have gone.

Looking up and down the house, no other lights came on. What if she had collapsed in the hallway? Or tried to climb the stairs and fell? Would she go to her husband's bed? Did she have a spare room where she could rest? I needed to know where she was going to sleep so that I could watch over her.

While standing in front of the large bay window of her study the entire room was flooded with light while Brianna held herself up on either side of the doorway. I should have looked away because she was standing there only in her undergarments. If she were to look straight ahead, she would see me pressed right up against the window, staring at her like some sick stalker. But in a way I wanted her to. Perhaps if she saw me, maybe I could get her out of the house and to a hospital. But just as I thought she might look in my direction she stumbled toward a small bathroom located to the left of her, and closed the door.

For the next forty agonizing minutes I heard the water turn off and on, drawers slam, yelps of pain, weeping, moans, vomiting, more water running, more weeping, and finally a door creaking open. When she finally exited the bathroom, she was donning a white robe that had small smears of watered-down blood on the collar. Her face was clean, but the cut above her right eye was bleeding through the gauze she had taped over it. She barely had enough energy to walk, but surprisingly she made her way to the large cushion in front of the bay window. In front of me. Losing all my nerve, I took a small step back.

She climbed up on the cushion and raised the center window completely open. A cool breeze swept across her face causing her to close her eyes and allow silent tears to gently flow down her face. As if the breeze took the last ounce of her energy, Brianna collapsed on the cushion, her left hand dragging itself down against the window screen. The sight of her was heartbreaking. I let this happen to her. I watched and did nothing. I had to be responsible for her now.

I knelt to the ground, bringing my face eye level with her hand that was pressed against the window screen. I desperately wanted to hold her fragile hand and stroke it until she fell asleep. What had changed? Twenty-four hours ago, I was perturbed that I was made to drop everything for Brianna M. Lewis. A puny hybrid who had been hidden away by her powerful father. Why was she so important? No one would tell me, and it began to gnaw my insides raw. I hated being told what to do, how to do it, but not why. After all the frustration and anger I had felt earlier, it had all changed in a matter of moments.

I could see her breath settling into an even rhythm as sleep began overtaking her body. Her left hand was still pressed up against the screen of the large window, flinching slightly in response to her dreams. Victor's voice was ringing in my head telling me not to interfere, but losing all control I slowly raised the window screen, being careful not to rouse her. Once her hand was free from the screen, her fingers unfolded before me.

Her palm looked so small and soft, and unable to stop myself I gently rubbed my index finger in a small circle around the inside of her hand. Suddenly her fingers enfolded my hand in hers. I quickly looked at her face thinking she had awakened, but her eyes were swollen and closed. Carefully I turned her hand over and gently kissed each finger. I could taste the saltiness of blood mixed with the sting of disinfectant on the tiny scratches on her knuckles.

"Never again," I whispered. "I will sacrifice my life for you if I have to."

It was true. And at this rate, that might come sooner rather than later.

Chapter Six

Cameron

After the attack, Brianna slept for two days in her study, only waking a handful of times to use the small bathroom. Her husband only checked on her the morning after the attack, merely checking her pulse and thanking her for cleaning up the mess from their scuffle. He was not an intelligent man. Brianna would not have been able to do that in her condition. While she slept, I took the time to scrub the counters and floors, even choosing to burn her torn and bloody clothes in the gas fireplace. When she woke, I wanted there to be no reminders of what she went through.

For two weeks I watched over her. During the day I stayed close by, hiding in the woods or retreating to my car. And by night I watched her sleep, taking care to cover her with blankets when they would fall off from her flailing about in her dreams. I had also resorted to animal blood, which was anything but pleasant. However, it had been four days since I fed because her husband, whose name I discovered was Sam, demanded that she no longer retreat to her study but lay by his side in their bed. The first night she spent with him I stayed at the bottom of the stairs listening for any signs of Brianna in distress. The last three nights, however, I hid within the shadow of her armoire in their bedroom. I stood in the corner watching her, and of course watching him, daring him to give me any excuse to rip his head off.

Victor received his updates every other day even though there was nothing to update him on. Brianna's injuries were healing, quicker than I would have expected, but that was most likely because of the strong vampire blood that was lying semi-dormant in her body. Every morning for the last week Brianna had asked permission to go out and run errands but was denied each time because her face was still swollen and bruised. But even through the darkness of last night I could see that the only evidence of the brutal attack was a scabbed over cut above her right eye.

This morning started just as the others had, Sam's alarm clock went off at 6:05 a.m. and I instantly Projected myself outside their bedroom door. I had been waiting for the day that Sam would finally give her permission to leave the house so that I could follow her and find a way to talk to her. I could have just as easily taken her against her will, but I wanted to do it right, ease her into this gently. I could not just walk up to her and say, "Hello, my name is Cameron Burke. I am a Gatherer here to take you to a holding facility on the other side of the country because you are a human-vampire hybrid. We are trying to protect you from being killed or experimented on by a group of rogue vampires. And, by the way, I have been watching you for almost two weeks and I am willing to lay down my life for you although I cannot figure out why." That could be a little overwhelming for her.

Jolted back into realty, I heard Brianna's voice break the morning silence. "Sam, I have officially been in the house for two weeks. I finished the last book in my stock pile two days ago, and I'm going…I'm just going crazy. My eye is a thousand times better, and I just want to go to the bookstore, and maybe grab lunch with Renee. I haven't seen her and she's starting to worry."

I could hear Sam grumble and sigh. Finally, he said, "Fine. You can go to Roger's shop for your books. Where were you thinking of going to lunch?"

"Just to the little café next door to the bookshop. I'll come home right after."

So enthralled in their conversation, I was just able to Project myself into the next room when Sam walked out of their bedroom and made his dissent down the stairs. This would be my chance. It had seemed like an eternity since I first came to Connecticut for this assignment, and now I was filled with excitement at the prospect of being able to take her away from here.

I looked out the window just in time to see Sam pull out of the garage and head down the driveway. With Sam gone, I could slip into town as well. I needed to do a little shopping for some new clothes because I had only brought enough for one day since I had planned to have Brianna on a plane in less time. Not that my clothes smelled, I did not perspire, but I wanted Brianna to see me in something other than the same clothes she had seen me in two weeks ago.

I also needed to prepare my approach. Following her in the Vanquish would draw too much attention, she knew my car. The town was small enough that it should be relatively easy to find the bookstore she was going to and meet her there. This way we could have a calm and informative conversion. Shortly thereafter, if all went well, she would never return to this house or the monster ever again.

Chapter Seven

Brianna

It had been two weeks of hell, filled mostly with pain, crying, and trying to read with only one good eye. One day I cried for nearly two hours, angry and depressed at being such a coward. Once I began to think lucidly and move about the house, sights and sounds from that awful night would flash into my head. Some things I remembered seemed absolutely real, where other moments I couldn't explain. For instance, I remember the exact moment my eye hit the edge of the kitchen island, but couldn't remember cleaning up the mess afterwards. I knew Sam hadn't cleaned anything since he'd thanked me for removing all signs of our "incident."

My dreams had become more vivid the last two weeks as well, and always had the same leading man - my black-clad stalker. Whether it was the pool, the beach, the kitchen table, wherever, the man and the name would always be the same. Cameron, or Cam as I would scream in ecstasy, with the deep, dark eyes. Boy I sounded like a slut. And where did that name come from? I'd never known anyone by that name, and couldn't remember it from any of the books I had read.

But sex wasn't all I dreamt about, I swear, although it was probably the majority. You always dreamt about what you didn't have. Well, I had a big house and a nice car, but I didn't have love. There wasn't someone lying next to me rubbing my back to help me fall asleep or kissing my neck to wake me up the next morning. Sex with Sam was always rough and passionless. The only time I had any kind of reprieve was when I was pregnant. Sadly, I could rarely carry a baby past the first trimester. Each miscarriage was a painful reminder of the choice I made so many years ago to seek security rather than love. Since then, I've always felt I needed to face the consequences of that choice, even if that meant having a cut on my eye and two hematomas on my back.

But I would not rain on my own parade today, I was getting out of the house. I would finally get to spend time with my best friend who ecstatically accepted my lunch invitation before the words were out of my mouth. We'd talked during the past weeks, but seeing each other was so much better. Plus, she said she had some news for me that had to wait until we were together. It was going to be a good day, and it was certainly way overdue.

I left the house a rebel in a pair of worn jeans, soft black shirt, and sneakers. My outfit was super simple and comfortable, and slightly too big since I'd lost ten pounds the last two weeks. As soon as I opened the door to my favorite little bookshop, Books 'n' Such, the smell of new books brought a huge smile to my face. The short bald owner, Roger Wilson, looked up from his latest gossip magazine.

"Well, if it isn't the gal who keeps me in business, how are we today, Mrs. Lewis?"

"If I'm keeping you in business, then why don't you ever call me by my first name like I've asked you to do a zillion times?"

"It's a sign of respect, *ma'am*, and if any of the other stuck-up women in this town heard me call you anything but Mrs. Lewis, you know as well as I do that by the end of the day the entire town would know that we've been having an illicit affair for the last three years and that we even vacationed together in Bermuda," Roger said in his flamboyant way. If I was allowed to have a gay husband, it would be him. "Are you stocking up today? A bunch of new stuff came out since the last time you were here. I started keeping a list of things you might like."

"Thank you, my darling, you're the best! But you know that already," I said giving him a little peck on the cheek before walking toward the shelves. After five minutes I already had seven books in my arms. "Roger, I'm going to need to borrow your delivery truck in order to get outta here."

I could hear Roger laughing at me from the front of the store and then quiet down when a high-pitched chime announced a new customer coming into the shop.

"Can I help you find anything today?" Roger asked in a sultry voice.

It must be a man, and he must be cute. The gentleman politely said that he was just browsing, and in my mind I could hear Roger's heavy sigh. With a smile I looked back down at my list to find the next title and was so engulfed in looking at the shelf in front of me I didn't even notice the man come around the corner.

"Good afternoon."

Screaming like a little girl, my books went flying in the air and thudded on the floor around me. Roger came running around the corner, his magazine rolled up in his hand.

"Roger…Roger, I'm sorry, he just startled me and I freaked out," I shouted, holding my hands up to Roger as the man in question immediately knelt down and began picking up the books that were strewn all over the floor.

"Whew! I thought I was going to have to ruin my magazine. I haven't even finished it yet," Roger laughed and then walked back to the register.

Feeling completely embarrassed, I knelt down to help the gentleman pick up my books as I said, "I am so sorry. I can't believe I did that, I am so embarrassed that I…"

Holding three of my books in his hand he looked up at me and in that instant my entire body went numb. The eyes! I was face to face with my stalker and looking right into the eyes that I had been dreaming about for almost two weeks. The blood drained out of my face and I started to sway forward. He caught me by my shoulder, but my heavy head fell onto his chest. It was hard to breathe and my head was spinning. Why was he following me? How did he find me here? And why did I feel so comfortable?

Slowly the man leaned his head down near my ear and whispered, "Are you all right?"

I nodded and began taking in his intoxicating scent of autumn leaves and fresh rain. Just then my cell phone rang loudly. I scrambled over to my purse and dug through it to find my cell phone before it went to voicemail. It was Sam's ringtone, I had to find my phone, I-HAD-TO-FIND-IT!

Just as it rang for the fourth time, I wrapped my hand around my phone and pressed the center button. "Hello! Sam?"

There was a brief pause before he answered, "Where are you?"

"I'm in the bookstore. Sorry, I couldn't find my phone. My purse is just too big I can never find anything when I need it. Is everything okay?"

"Yes, fine. I thought that since you're already in town that I would meet you for lunch."

"What a sweet thought, but I'm already meeting Renee. She'll actually be here in a few minutes," I said nervously while pacing around the alcove and picking up the remaining books on the floor.

"Perfect, I'm right around the corner."

What!? Ohmygod, ohmygod, this wasn't happening, not today!

"Oh…that's great. I'll see you at the café then," I responded, hoping that I sounded somewhat convincing.

Sam hung up before I could say goodbye, not that I really cared, my brain was in panic mode. I looked up to my handsome stalker who was staring very intensely at me. I shoved the books into his arms and ran, ignoring Roger's call after me as I bolted out of the store. Standing on the sidewalk, I was taking in big gulps of air when I felt a cool hand take my arm.

"Brianna? Brianna, are you okay?"

I turned around seeing that it was my stalker holding my arm. I wretched it from his grip, afraid someone would see him touching me.

"W-What did you call me?" He didn't answer. "How do you know my name?"

"I will explain everything," he replied, and reached for my hand. "My car is right down the road…"

"You are going to get me killed," I said panicked and took a step back.

He opened his mouth to say something, but over his shoulder I saw Sam coming up the sidewalk. Panic stricken I did the first thing that came to mind.

With a big smile I said loudly, "Oh sure, I know where that is. Just follow this road all the way down until you hit Trumbull Street. Then you'll take the next left and it's the third grey building on your right. You can't miss it."

At first my stalker's eyes were full of confusion, but a second later he thanked me and headed across the street.

Sam was on me in an instant. "Who was that?" he asked, grabbing my arm and pulling me down the sidewalk.

"Sam, I don't know who he was. Just some guy who was lost."

"It seemed like you knew him."

"I didn't. I just gave him directions. Could you please let go of my arm, people are watching."

Sam didn't let go, but he softened his grip as he said, "And what are you wearing?"

I looked down at my casual outfit knowing this was probably the last time I'd be allowed out of the house for a while. "I'm sorry, Sam. I just wanted to be comfortable."

He sighed heavily and led me into the café. As we stepped inside, I looked down the sidewalk just in time to see my stalker walking back across the street towards to bookstore. He was wearing his aviators now, but even with them on I could tell his dark eyes were staring back at me.

Chapter Eight

Brianna

Saying lunch was awkward was an understatement. I thought for sure that Renee's eyes were going to fall out of her head when she saw Sam sitting next to me. He was truly oblivious to the fact that Renee loathed him; she was almost as good of an actress as I was. When Sam finished his meal apparently the entire lunch date was over. With barely a word goodbye to Renee, Sam pulled me out of the cafe and escorted me to my SUV, giving me only fifteen minutes to get home and wave at the spy cameras.

After pulling away from the curb I called Renee, and she picked up on the first ring. "What the hell was that!?"

"Sweetie, I'm sorry. He ambushed me."

"I almost had a freakin' heart attack when I saw him there. Then I fell asleep when he started talking about Ross IBA's.'"

"Roth IRA's, honey."

"See, I was sleeping! And how come you didn't respond to my signal so we could go to the bathroom and talk."

"Was that what that was? I thought you'd developed a facial tic or something."

"Ha ha, very funny. So seriously, how are you? You look…decent."

"My back is still a little bruised, but my eye is much better."

"You can still see the cut, though."

Really wanting to change the subject I said, "So what's your big news?"

"See, that's what makes me mad. I've been saving the news because I wanted to tell you in person, and then Mr. Stupid Shits has to ruin it."

"Stupid Shits? Now that's a new one," I laughed. "So tell me now, I've been dying to know."

"But it's not the same."

"Sweetie, I'm sorry, but I'm rushing home as it is. His leash is tight today."

"I hate him."

"I know you do, but that doesn't change the fact that you can tell me your news. Come on!"

"Okay, okay! Well do you remember that guy?"

"What guy?"

"You know, the guy my mom set me up with."

"Yeah, yeah, I remember. You were going to break your record."

"Right, well I did break my record, I've been seeing him ever since."

"What! Ohmygod, Renee, that's wonderful!"

"I know, right? He's really great, his name is John and he just moved here a couple of months ago."

"What does he do?"

"Well, um, he's...a..." She mumbled the rest.

"Renee, I couldn't hear you, I'm in the car..."

"He's a doctor, all right!" she screamed into the phone.

I couldn't help myself and broke out into uncontrollable laughter. "Oh, that is priceless. You of all people land a doctor."

"Fuck you," she replied and hung up on me. Two seconds later my phone rang again.

"Mrs. Stupid Shits speaking."

"Love you," Renee said apologetically.

"Love you, too."

"The next time Sam comes to lunch uninvited I'm gonna punch him in the junk."

I laughed. "I will pay to see that."

"And then I'm gonna punch you in your woman junk for making me have to spend time with him."

Ah, all was right in the world.

Thirteen minutes later I was sitting in my SUV screaming at my parking sign in the garage. Something inside me snapped. *Reserved for Brianna M. Lewis*. Brianna M. Lewis, Brianna-M-Fucking-Lewis! I hated her! I truly, truly hated her! I started banging on the steering wheel and screaming at the top of my lungs, "I hate you, I hate you, I hate you."

At first, I meant myself, and then I meant Sam. I wasn't even allowed to enjoy an hour with my girlfriend. I couldn't even go and get a book, a book! But knowing I only had a few minutes left, I pushed myself out of the SUV and flipped off my sign as I passed by it. I ran into the front foyer and waved to Sam's little camera to let the bastard know I was home.

Afterwards I walked back down the hall to my study, needing a place to center myself. Once inside the room I slumped against the door and slid down to the floor. My first day out of the house had been so disappointing. While I sat on the floor, something in the corner of my eye caught my attention. Sitting invitingly on top of the desk was a stack of new hardcover books tied beautifully with a red satin ribbon.

I just stared at them, wondering where in the hell they came from. But after a few minutes I finally stepped over to the desk and slowly untied the big red bow. I took the first book and turned it over in my hands, and then I picked up the second and third and suddenly it hit me. These were the books that I'd shoved in my stalker's arms. These were from him, they had to be. But why? How did he know where I lived? Tears began to roll down my face uncontrollably, I couldn't help it. It was the nicest, although creepiest, present anyone had ever given me. But how did he get in here?

I quickly looked over to the window and saw that it wasn't open, and nothing else was out of place. If he'd come through the front door, Sam would have seen him on the cameras. My mind was reeling. I wasn't sure whether to be grateful or petrified. A part of me was almost thrilled that I had an admirer, but then I was also freaked out that he knew where I lived and could get into my house. I stacked the books back on top of each other and tied the ribbon back around them. I wasn't sure what I was going to do, so I decided not to do anything, at least for now.

I went into the living room and began flipping through the 700+ channels on my satellite TV. I sat there for hours, unable to watch a show or a movie for more than fifteen minutes. I wasn't allowing myself to relax, and I couldn't stop thinking about my stalker. Instead of being scared that he broke into my house and left me a gift, I kept thinking about the moment when my head was buried in his chest. His arm held me so gently and his voice was so soft. I could remember every detail about him. The dark wavy hair that matched his eyes, smelling of fall, and oddly he was a little cold. Usually men were so warm, but he was different. Everything about him was different. He also didn't seem so pissed off now and I wondered what had changed.

Outside it was getting dark and the clouds were rolling in. While looking out the window I noticed three smudges on one of the panes. I propped myself up on my elbows and slid my fingers across the streak trying to figure out what it was. As I wiped my fingers down the glass a second time, I noticed that the streaks were the same width as my fingers.

Then it hit me. It was my blood that stained the window. My blood, that Sam had made me bleed. I had finally had enough. Leaving the TV on, I ran down the hall into my study and grabbed my new books in their pretty red ribbon and cradled them in my arms as I ran up the stairs to my bedroom to pack. I didn't have a lot of time because Sam could be watching and he would be speeding home. Once in my bedroom I grabbed a big duffle bag and began throwing armfuls of underwear, bras, and socks into it. From the closet I grabbed a few pairs of jeans, some T-shirts and a sweater. The duffle bag was getting full so the toiletry list needed to be short and practical. So I grabbed the basics: toothpaste, toothbrush, deodorant, soap, shampoo, and honeysuckle lotion. Okay so the last item wasn't practical, but it was my favorite scent.

With the bag over my shoulder, I ran downstairs with my books in hand, grabbed my purse, and headed out to the garage. I was running out of time and had to get out of here. My garage door was opening as I jumped into my SUV and tossed my things in the passenger seat. A few seconds later the SUV was in gear and I slammed on the gas.

Just as my SUV cleared the bay door, a pair of headlights blinded me a second before the other car plowed into my side. The smoke from the airbags had barely dissipated when Sam was pulling the dented door open and screaming at me, but I couldn't understand what he was saying because of the ringing in my ears. I held onto the steering wheel while he grabbed my shoulder, but his pull was too strong and my grip failed, spilling me out onto the driveway.

Sam grabbed my hair and pulled me across the driveway, tearing the skin off my back. The pain made me scream and wrench my legs up, digging my heels into the ground. My change in balance caused Sam to fall backwards and me to topple down on top of him. With him momentarily in shock, I slammed my heel into his groin and scrambled toward the house. Once inside, I ran down the hallway at full speed into the kitchen where there was a phone. I would call 911 and…and…and then, what? I didn't know what to do, my head was throbbing, I couldn't think. I grabbed the phone anyway and moved towards the stairs to the second floor.

When I reached the first step, Sam tackled me from behind causing my head to slam on the stairs. I could feel the cut above my eye reopen and bleed down my face. Sam grabbed me around the throat and lifted my face to his.

"You whore, you fucking whore! You thought you could just run away from me? I will kill you before that happens, do you understand me? I-will-kill-you."

With barely a whisper I responded, "Then you'll have to kill me."

Just then, the front door exploded behind Sam's shoulder causing him to drop me on the stairs like a ton of bricks. There was a tall, slim, dark figure standing in the doorway heaving breath like a mad animal.

"Who the hell are…" but Sam was cut off when the dark figure flew at him in the blink of an eye, grabbed his shirt, and flung him across the room. Sam's face held pure terror, something I'd never seen. Suddenly the dark figure rounded on Sam and began punching him mercilessly. Then in a graceful move, the figure grabbed Sam by the throat and held him three feet off the ground with one hand. My jaw dropped. This just wasn't possible. Then in the next moment Sam was flung across the room again, hitting the corner buttress next to the stairs causing his body to fall limply on the floor. The dark figure rushed over to Sam and placed his hands on either side of Sam's head.

"No, don't!" I screamed.

Suddenly the dark figure froze and looked me in the eye. It was him, my stalker.

"Why not?" he growled at me. "Do you love this man?"

"N-no."

"Then why?" he snapped and allowed Sam to slump back down to the floor.

"I…I don't…I don't know." But I did know. Sam should be the only monster in the room.

My stalker paused for a moment, waves of anger radiating from his body. "Fine then. But we must go," he said and took a step toward me, but I flinched away. "Brianna, the police could be here at any moment, and we need to get out of here before then. Do you trust me?"

"N-no, but you're right, I need to get out of here."

Before I could protest, he picked me up, ran through the hole that used to be the front door, and carried me to the black Aston Martin waiting in my driveway. He slid me easily into the passenger seat and shut the door before he raced to the driver's side. I couldn't believe I was sitting in this car. Oh crap, I couldn't believe I was bleeding all over this car. This was a crime. Of all things to be worried about I was whining over ruining his car.

Seconds later he was sitting next to me and we were barreling down the winding back roads when he rolled down both windows. I tried rolling mine back up, but it didn't work.

"Hey, could you roll up my window, it's freezing."

Without saying a word, he turned the heat up in the car, but didn't roll up my window. I didn't push since there was still a tremendous amount of anger behind his eyes. His grip on the steering wheel was so tight I thought he might rip it right off the column. Knowing that look quite well, if he needed the windows down, then so be it.

"Look, just drop me off at my friend's place, she doesn't live far from here," I said softly, testing the waters.

"I need to take you to a hospital."

"No, they'll ask too many questions, and I have no I.D. with me. Just take me to my friend Renee's apartment and..."

"I really think you need to see a doctor first."

"TakemetoRenee'srightnow!" I shouted, surprising even myself. Taking as deep of a breath as I could, I calmly said, "I'm sorry. Please just take me there. I'm not going to a hospital."

"Fine," he replied through his clenched teeth.

"Take the next left," I said pointing to the road up ahead. "Thank you, by the way."

"I am sorry it got that far. I should have been there sooner."

"Well, anyway, thank you." I let another few moments of silence stretch between us before I said, "I don't even know your name."

With a hint of a laugh, his lip curled into a delicious crooked smile. "My name is Cameron."

I stared at him, a blank expression on my face, unable to move. The only thing I was able to say was, "You're shitting me, right?"

Chapter Nine

Brianna

For the remaining ten minutes of the drive, we rode in silence since I was completely shell shocked by my rescuer's name. Cameron. I kept thinking back on our few encounters trying to think of when he might have given me his name. Hell, I was hoping that at some point he'd worn a nametag. It was just way too eerie that every dream I'd had for two weeks had him as the main character, and I was calling him by his *real* name.

I had demanded that Cameron take me to Renee's, but did I know what I was going to do once I got there? Hell no. What about tomorrow, and the next day, and the next? My head was spinning and it was making me nauseous. At one point I thought about hanging my head out the window since it was still open, but Cameron was driving so fast I thought for sure a low hanging tree branch would rip it off my body. I was freezing, bleeding, anxious, confused, and of course in pain, a really bad mix.

After instructing Cameron to take the next right, I realized Renee's was less than a minute away. How in the hell was I going to explain Cameron? Bleeding wounds, no problem. Tall, dark, handsome stranger, not so much. Looking over at him from the side of my eye I could see that he was still very tense, grinding his teeth even. Boy he was beautiful, even in his moody broody I-almost-killed-someone state of mind. I really wanted to run my fingers through his hair and down his neck, and ever so gently rub my thumb just underneath the collar of his shirt.

"Snap out of it!"

"Excuse me?" Cameron answered, breaking his tense silence and looking over at me completely confused.

"I...I'm sorry, that was uh...meant for me." Oh just kill me now. I sounded like such a fool. Thank goodness we'd pulled into Renee's apartment complex. "Renee's is the first unit on the left. There's usually a visitor's spot in front."

But of course tonight when I could have used a close parking space they were all taken. Cameron found another spot a few units down and my stomach churned at the length of the walk. Before I knew it, he was at my side, opening the door and helping me unbuckle my seatbelt that I was fumbling with. When his hand gently brushed mine away, I noticed that it was still cool like in the bookstore. It seemed odd, and I had no idea why I was focusing on it.

"Brianna, let me carry you," he said as he took my arm and started to pull me up to him.

"No," I responded too quickly. Surprisingly I saw hurt in his eyes and a pang of guilt hit my stomach. "I'm sorry I really want to walk on my own two feet. I need to start doing things on my own."

"Very well, but hold onto my arm."

"Deal."

I had won again. He might look like a bad boy, but he was kind of a pushover. But after only taking a few steps away from the car, my knees faltered, sending me to the ground. Without missing a beat, Cameron caught me and pulled me back up, placing his arm around my waist to hold me steady. It was sweet really. He was still letting me walk, although my feet were barely touching the ground. It was very, considerate? Yes, considerate. Something I didn't have that much experience with.

Once we got to Renee's door, I rang the bell and a few seconds later Renee was standing in the doorway looking utterly terrified at my appearance. Not even waiting for an invitation, I fell into Renee's arms and pushed my way inside.

"I'm so sorry, Re, I didn't know where else to go," I cried, finally, and like a freight train what happened tonight hit me all at once. I could have died. If Cameron had been delayed another minute I would be dead. "It was just so horrible, *so* horrible and I thought he was going to kill me and..." Seeing movement to my left I realized Renee wasn't alone and a concerned gentleman began to walk toward me. "I'm so sorry, I should have called or something."

"Jesus, Bri, stop your nonsense," Renee chided as she pulled me over to a chair in the living room. "Um Bri, this is John, you know, *Dr.* John. John, this is my…really messed up friend Brianna Lewis."

"No, not anymore!" I shouted, feeling the anger rise up from my stomach. "I am *not* Brianna Lewis anymore; she is dead, gone, left in that miserable house. I'm going back to Brianna Morgan. I never want to hear that man's name with mine ever again."

Shaken by my outburst, Renee didn't know what to say. It was a total first.

"Well, Brianna Morgan, I'm Dr. John Ryan and you look like you could use some stitches." Dr. John held out his hand and I shook it gently. He was roughly 5'11", stocky like a rugby player with light brown hair and very blue eyes.

"Dr. John Ryan?" I said a little surprised. "Were your parents big Tom Clancy fans?"

He chuckled. "No, actually, but I hear that a lot. But unlike the other John Ryan, I am a medical man and we need to get you looked at."

"Sorry, Dr. John, that one already tried to get me to a hospital," I said pointing over to Cameron who was still hovering in the doorway. "Oh, sorry, this is Cameron. Cameron, this is Renee and Dr. John." Cameron gave a curt nod and didn't seem at all uncomfortable with the fact that Renee was gawking at him. "I was just hoping I could get cleaned up, and then figure out what to do next."

"Bri, are you insane?" Renee began. "Look at yourself! You can barely move and you're covered in blood. Just let John take you to the ER and you'll be…"

"Renee, I'M NOT GOING!" I had never shouted at Renee in my life and the hurt in her eyes nearly killed me. "Look Re, Sam is going to come looking for me. I need to clean up and then get out of here. I just hope you can understand."

Renee opened her mouth to argue but Dr. John stepped forward to diffuse the situation. "Brianna, how about I take a look at that cut on your eye and I'll do as much as I can here," he said gently before turning to Renee. "Sweetheart, do you have any gauze pads and disinfectant?"

Angrily Renee turned on her heels and bolted into the bathroom located just inside her bedroom. The next few minutes were filled with banging and slamming of drawers.

I felt Cameron's cool fingers brush the side of my arm as he knelt down beside me. "Excuse me, Dr. Ryan, you may also want to examine her back.

Brianna, may I?" I nodded and allowed him to gently lift my shirt up enough to show Dr. John the raw bloody skin on my back.

"Ouch!" Dr. John said after a high-pitched whistle. "Is that…gravel?"

"Asphalt, actually. Sam dragged me up the driveway."

Cameron took in a deep breath through his teeth and held it. I looked up at him and noticed that his eyes were closed and his jaw tight. In that moment I couldn't explain why, but I needed to ease his pain. I could see the anger radiating from within him, and my heart ached. Doing the only thing I could think of to calm him, I gently pulled his hand into mine, loving the coolness of his skin. In an instant his body relaxed and he opened his eyes.

"It's okay. It's over."

Cameron squeezed my hand in response and gave me a silent nod.

"Uh, Renee?" Dr. John said while taking a step toward the bedroom. "I'll need a set of tweezers as well." Instead of answering, Renee simply slammed another drawer.

"Dr. Ryan, thank you," Cameron said extending his hand. "I appreciate you looking after Brianna."

"No problem and please just call me John," he replied and shook Cameron's hand.

"Can I call you Dr. John?" I said with a hopeful smile on my face.

"You can call me Dr. John when you let me be your doctor. Right now, I'm just your friend's boyfriend who's going to pick asphalt out of your back while trying not to ask too many questions. So no, you have to call me John."

I smiled in response. This guy was great. He was perfect for Renee and I'd only known him for five minutes.

Shortly after, Renee came stomping out of the bedroom, arms crossed against her chest. "I put everything I have on the bed. Let me know what else you'll need and I can go and get it."

"Thank you, my friend. I know I'm asking a lot from you, but please just trust me."

Renee turned in a huff and we followed her into the bedroom, except for Cameron who respectfully stayed in the living room. A few minutes later I was splayed out on Renee's bed facedown while Dr. John painfully removed dirt and rocks from my back. As they worked, I relayed the night's activities between yelps of pain. Thankfully by the time I was done reliving the nightmare of the evening, Dr. John was finished and slathering on an ointment claiming pain relieving powers. Well let's hope so. Once my back was cleaned and bandaged up, Dr. John did what he could for my other injuries. While putting the finishing touches on my eye, his cell phone vibrated which caused Renee to groan. He was on call at the hospital's ER and apparently they were slammed.

I had ruined their date night, and I felt horrible. Renee rarely had a date she voluntarily went on, let alone a boyfriend. It warmed my heart to think that she'd finally found a man she could spend more than ten minutes with. Plus, he seemed smitten with her, too. But unfortunately, duty called and Renee escorted him out to his car.

Gritting my teeth, I pushed off the bed over to the clothes that Renee had set out for me. Having recently lost weight, I could actually fit into the small set of burgundy sweats draped over her vanity chair. I stepped into the soft velour pants, pulled them up to my waist and tied the drawstring to secure them. It felt wonderful to be in something other than slacks, and these particular sweats were thoroughly worn and smelled of fabric softener. Getting the T-shirt on, however, was laughable. It was a white baby doll shirt that caused my back to scream with pain as I tried to pull it on. The collar of the shirt got stuck around my face with one arm hanging through one sleeve while the other was pinned inside.

"Re?" I mumbled through the shirt. "Renee, can you help me? I'm...uh...a little stuck." I heard the door open and turned to see Cameron standing in the doorway. He quickly averted his eyes when he noticed I was standing in front of him in my bra.

"I apologize, Brianna, I heard you asking for help," he said still looking at the floor. "Renee is outside with Dr. Ryan."

"Well, since you're here you might as well make yourself useful. It feels like I'm ripping my back open."

I'll admit I whimpered a little when he walked over to me with his crooked smile. He pulled my bent arm out of the sleeve and lifted the entire shirt over my head. I guess we were starting from scratch.

"Lift your arms as best as you can," he said softly.

I did as he asked and he guided both my arms through the sleeves and then pulled the shirt over my head and down my waist. Most guys would have stared at my breasts or at least tried to manage an accidental boob graze. But Cameron didn't.

"Cameron, we need to talk," I said while he helped me into the hooded jacket.

"Yes, Brianna, we do. We need to discuss where we will be going."

"I'm sorry, what?" I replied as I zipped up the jacket and took a step back. "What do you mean, where *we* will be going? Look, Cameron, I am truly thankful for what you did for me tonight, but my life just got really complicated and…"

"I have been sent here by your father."

"My…my father?"

"Yes. Your father sent me to find you and take you to a safe location."

Still trying to take in what Cameron was saying, I simply stared at him, opening and closing my mouth trying to figure out what to say. Finally, "You have the wrong the woman. I've never even met my father. I can't even tell you his name, and since he's never cared about me for one moment in my life, it's hard to believe that he would start now. You must be looking for someone else."

"Brianna Marie Morgan, born September 15th to Shelby Joann Morgan, and until recently, father unknown."

"Wha…how do you know my birthday? Jesus, Cameron, you're scaring the crap out of me. You show up out of the blue and start stalking me. Then you're bursting through my door and almost kill my husband. And now you're telling me the father I've never met is suddenly interested in my safety? Why now? I haven't been safe for fourteen years. What makes me so goddamn special now!?"

"Brianna, please sit down. I will explain everything, but I need you to stay calm and keep an open mind," he said as he gestured to the bed.

Narrowing my eyes at him, I sat down on the corner of the bed and folded my hands in my lap. By the seriousness of his face, I knew what he was going to tell me wasn't good. Also, the fact that he closed the door and positioned himself in front of it meant the news may cause me to make an escape.

"Brianna, your father is concerned about you because you are…"

"What are you guys doing in here?" Renee said as she barged into the room.

Cameron turned around to face Renee and talked to her so quietly that I couldn't hear what he said. But suddenly Renee's eyes glazed over and she left the room. Confused, and slightly afraid, I said, "What did you say to her?"

"I just told her we needed a minute to talk."

"And that actually worked?"

"Yes. May I continue?" I nodded and he continued with, "Brianna, you are…unique."

"Unique?" I said, raising an eyebrow at him. That was it? I was unique?

"Yes, exactly, you are unique. The reason you do not know your father is because he too is unique, and because of his…uniqueness, there are those out there who would want to find others who also had his unique…"

"Will you stop with the unique crap? Seriously, you're giving me a headache."

"This is not going how I had planned."

"I hope not. I can't imagine you practiced that speech."

"Brianna, this is difficult for me to say."

"Just spit it out. I'm a big girl. I can take anything you throw at me."

"I am not so sure about that."

"Try me."

"That is what I am trying to do."

"Try harder."

"I just need a moment to figure out the best way to explain this."

"Sorry, you have exactly five seconds before I'm out that door." Waiting only three, I rose from the bed and headed toward the door. As I reached for the doorknob, Cameron took my shoulder and turned me to face him. "Cameron, either tell me the truth or I'm out of…"

"Your father is a vampire," he said abruptly. "You are half vampire, a hybrid." He paused for a moment. "And I…I am a vampire."

I stepped back to the bed, sitting down when I felt the mattress rub up against the back of my legs. "Wow. So, what? Am I dying or something? Because the truth must be really, really bad if you're going to try and feed me that load of crap."

"Brianna, I am telling you the truth. Your father is Eris, one of the most powerful vampires in existence, and if our enemies were to find you…"

"Stop it! Just stop it! This is ridiculous. Look, you need to go."

In an instant Cameron disappeared, leaving nothing but a shadow of black mist where he stood. Then a second later the same black mist brushed against my face as he cradled me in his arms. He tilted my body at an angle and reared his head back, opening his mouth wide. When his face returned to me, he was displaying two long and sharp looking incisors.

"Brianna, look at me. I. Am. A. Vampire."

The image of Cameron's blazing black eyes and dagger-like teeth were burned into my mind as the world around me faded into complete darkness.

I guess I couldn't take what he threw at me after all.

Chapter Ten

Cameron

Thinking back, I could have handled the situation differently. Projecting at Brianna and extending my fangs was absolutely the worst idea I had ever had. I was ashamed of myself at what I had done. In my career as a Gatherer there was only one other occasion where I needed to give a hybrid a little display of what I was. Brianna was a completely new challenge for me. My entire uniqueness analogy made me want to thrust my head up against the wall. But when Brianna began snapping back at me, I became flustered. Brianna Morgan, formerly Lewis, definitely still had some fight within her.

Realizing I was still holding her, I placed Brianna on the bed and covered her with a blanket. Plans needed to be made to get her to the Facility. There was still no way I could get her on a plane in her current condition. The only option was to drive and that within itself was a horrible one. It would take almost a week to get to San Francisco and we were delayed as it was. Victor was losing patience as I am sure was Eris. This case was a total failure. I was a total failure.

I brushed away a thick strand of dark brown hair from Brianna's face. She was absolutely beautiful, even with a swollen and gashed eye. Since being Turned I had had no particular interest in any woman, human or vampire. That was until now. Of course, now being the most inopportune time. My feelings for her were clouding my judgment which was dangerous. I had never needed to contend with my feelings because they were buried deep down inside me, practically unreachable. But now it seemed as though a faucet had been opened, and emotions I had not felt in three hundred years were flowing through me like an uncontrollable river. How did anyone function like this?

I needed to focus on getting Brianna out of here. That was imperative. Leaving Sam alive created enormous risk. He could identify me as the intruder and possibly even claim that Brianna had been kidnapped. If that was the case, that meant law enforcement would be tracking us, yet another reason why flying would be difficult. I bent down to Brianna one last time and brushed my fingers down her face. She did not flinch which meant she was deep into unconsciousness, leaving me with ample time to set my plan into action.

Reluctantly I left the tiny bedroom and stepped into the living room where Renee sat still affected by the Glamour I had placed on her. Glamour was another useful tool where a vampire could alter a human's thoughts, memories, and even intentions.

Renee looked up as I entered the room. "Were you able to convince her?"

I had told her that I had been sent by Brianna's family because she was in danger. I needed to convince her to come away with me since I was the only one who could protect her. Nothing of which was a lie.

"Yes, Renee, I was able to convince her to come with me." Now that was a complete lie. "Unfortunately, she has passed out. I need to make arrangements for our trip, would you be able to monitor her while I am gone? It should only be an hour or so."

"Of course," she replied and stood from the couch. "And Cameron, thank you. Thank you for getting her out of that house. You've done something she never allowed anyone else to do." I could see the tears filling her eyes. "I can't tell you how grateful I am."

Unable to accept the gratitude, I gave her a quick nod and headed out the door. The first thing I needed to do was to get a different car, which would be difficult for me. I loved my car. I had owned it for only a few years, but within that time it was the only constant in my life. Besides, it was an amazing ride and able to perform at speeds that most vehicles could not. It was one of my only indulgences. Even from this distance I could see its beautiful sleek dark lines, and my stomach sank a little.

But my sports car was not practical for a cross-country journey. Not only because of the lack of room, but because it was covered in Brianna's blood. My blood lust had cooled over the centuries, however, when I carried Brianna from her house, the blood from her back had drained onto my arm. After closing her car door, I could not resist licking my arm clean. The smell alone was intoxicating and I could taste Eris's power. No wonder she was a priority. If Elaina's coven was to find her, they would drain her dry, or at least keep her alive in order to produce the powerful serum. Even with one taste it was hard to resist the urge for more, especially after only having animal blood for the last two weeks. I felt terrible having to drive with the windows down, but it was the only way I could restrain myself from licking the blood from her face. She might have found that odd.

Roaring my car to life, I put it in gear and sped out of the apartment complex. I called my brother Jared in San Francisco because he would be able to access our emergency logistics network. Exchanging cars with another vampire in the area was not the ideal solution since they would quickly recognize the scent of blood in the car. I needed someone who could erase my car's existence.

"Call Jared," I said to my cell phone and within seconds my youngest brother was on the other line.

"What up, bro."

"Jared, I need a car."

"But you already have a car."

"Thank you for pointing that out, little brother. I need to dispose of the Vanquish and get into something else immediately."

"So the golden child has himself in some deep water and he looks to his younger, wiser, and extremely more handsome brother to get him out of it."

"I am not sure about the handsome part, but you definitely have the younger part correct. I will explain everything later, but for now I need a car. Preferably something common that will not bring attention to us, but has plenty of room. I may have to drive my hybrid to California."

"Dude! Dad's gonna be pissed."

"Jared…"

"Okay, okay, working on the car now. Let's see who's closest to you." Hearing the speed typing on the other end, I continued down the desolate streets of the small New England town. "So who's the hybrid?"

"I am sure you will find out soon enough. I doubt I can keep this secret for much longer."

"Well big bro, you are in luck, there's a network contact about twenty minutes from where you are. It's a dealership, so there should be plenty of cars to choose from. I'll contact him now and have everything ready for when you arrive. I'm texting you the location. But before you go, who exactly is gonna tell Jazlyn that you've given away *her* car?"

Ah, the wager. When it was made, my arrogance got the better of me. Not only did we agree to pay $50,000, but I threw in my car which I knew she desperately wanted. She could easily buy one of her own, but she wanted mine since she knew how much I loved it. It appeared that my luck was changing after all.

"Well, it certainly will not be me. So the ball is in your court, little brother."

"Hell no! That bitch is crazy."

"I just got your text, thanks again, Jared."

"Call me if you need anything else. Did you want me to update Dad?"

"No, I will. Eventually."

"What about Alex and Devin?"

"They are home already? I thought they would be away for weeks with that mess in Phoenix." My two other brothers had been sent to investigate a situation in Phoenix where dozens of hybrids had been found tortured, murdered, and then left in a public area.

"They got home last night. Apparently, they didn't find anything but the bodies. The Trackers said it was just a dump job, so they sent the Warrior team home until they picked up the scent again. Do you want me to tell them what's going on? You know they're gonna ask, especially with the way that Jazlyn is flaunting her victory around."

"Fine, tell them. I may need their help at some point."

After quick goodbyes, I told my GPS where I needed to go, and within twenty minutes I was pulling into a high-end used car lot. Being almost 8:00 p.m., the business was deserted except for a middle-aged man feverously typing at a small desk inside the dealership. He saw my headlights as I pulled in and met me outside.

"Good evening, sir, I'm Cal Murphy, your brother Jared contacted me. I'm almost done with your paperwork, I just need to get the tags, and you're all set." The gentleman was straight to the point, no questions. He was a perfect contact for vampires, especially those on the run.

"Thank you. Do you have the car pulled so that I can transfer a few things while I wait?"

"Absolutely, sir. It's the black SUV right over there. Your brother requested something common, and well, you can't throw a rock without hitting one of these babies." Looking past me, he said, "I know it's not like what you're used to driving, but it is fully loaded, leather seats, entertainment package…"

"Cal, you do not have to sell me on the car. It is fine." A little rough on the gas mileage, but Brianna would definitely be comfortable. That was more important, especially with the length of our drive.

"Just give me ten more minutes, and I'll have everything ready for you." And Cal was off.

I turned back to my car, giving it one last look. I should be ecstatic that Jazlyn would not be its new owner, but it was depressing to think I would never be behind her wheel again.

Cal worked his magic and in less than ten minutes I was back on the road driving to Renee's. I was not used to driving such a large vehicle, but Cal was right, the optional luxury packages made quite a difference. Excitement came over me as I realized that within the next hour Brianna would be sitting beside me as we began our long journey together. I just hoped she was as excited about it as I was.

Chapter Eleven

Brianna

A thick gray mist completely surrounded me, making me feel like I was floating. I knew I was dreaming, but why in the heck would I dream about this? Maybe the bonk on the head was worse than I thought.

In front of me an even thicker black smoke moved toward me and I couldn't help but stretch my arm out in front of me, letting it curl around my fingers. Suddenly the smoke pulled itself in like it was being sucked through a vacuum and then began taking the shape of a man. I watched as the eyes, nose, and mouth developed along with a high forehead that gave way to long, dark brown hair. The materializing man was roughly my height and was wearing long sweeping red robes.

"Bri-an-na," he said in a thick foreign accent, Italian maybe.

"Um...yes, that's me. And you are?"

"In time, my Bri-an-na, but now you must wake, mia figlia."

"Why?" I asked. The dark gray mist began to surround me while depression, anxiety and fear enveloped me as if the mist was all my suppressed emotions being forced back into me. "I don't want to, it's too much. I...I'm scared of what'll happen when I wake up."

"I know you are, but it must be," he said, his red robes billowing behind him as he raised his hand and gently brushed my brow. "You are important to our future, mia figlia. You must take this first step."

"No! Who are you?" I screamed at him.

"Awaken, Bri-an-na," he commanded with a sudden thunder clap of his hands...

With a shallow intake of breath, I opened my eyes. Not moving a muscle, I tried to focus and concentrate on my surroundings. Suddenly the sound of a horn made me realize that I was in a car, but whose? Had Sam found me?

At that moment, a low familiar voice said as he laid on the horn again, "New York, what a God forsaken place. No matter what time of day, everyone drives like a maniac."

"Cameron?" I said, turning toward the driver. I was relieved to see him versus Sam, but I was still a little uneasy.

"Oh, Brianna, did I wake you?" Cameron said looking over at me, his face stricken with guilt. "I apologize. Driving in New York City gets me a little, how shall I say, frazzled?"

"New York City?" I said bolting upright in the car and looking out the window. The night was pitch black because of the pouring rain but was still illuminated with thousands of lights from the city and the cars around us. "What the *hell* are we doing in New York City?"

"Brianna, I told you I needed to get you to a safe place. There was no way I was going to be able to get you on a plane in your condition, so we have to drive."

"Whoa, hold it right there. Yes, you said that you needed to take me somewhere safe. I, however, didn't say I was going."

"Brianna, there really is no choice in the matter," he said. "You have to go to San Francisco." He turned to face me again this time his eyes blazing with authority. The intensity in his eyes brought back a flood of images from earlier that evening. It was almost impossible to process them as they flipped quickly through my mind. Then suddenly I saw Cameron's face hovering over mine with the same intense emotion in his eyes before he reared his head back to uncover a set of fangs extending from his mouth before saying, "I am a vampire."

Shocked back into reality, I turned to look out the window, watching the rain stream across the glass. My heart was pounding so fast I thought it would burst through my chest. Finally finding my words, and a little courage, I continued looking out the window as I said, "So, you're a…"

"Vampire."

"And my father? He's a…uh…a vampire, too?"

"Yes, he is," he replied gently.

"So, that makes me…one, too?"

"No, you are not a vampire."

"Oh, thank God!" I said, turning to face him.

"You are half-vampire. We call your kind, hybrids."

"My kind? You can't be serious. In no way have I ever been a vampire, or half-vampire, whatever. I'll send a steak back if it has even the slightest amount of pink in it. I'm obviously not strong or fast, so you must have it wrong."

"Brianna, I am not wrong. I have tasted the power within your blood, it is extremely…"

"What?" I interrupted loudly and frantically began feeling around my neck for bite marks. "You've tasted my blood?"

"Brianna, I did not bite you," Cameron retorted with slight annoyance. "Some of your blood dripped on my arm while I was carrying you out of your house. I just wanted to test it, to make sure we were correct."

"And?"

"Like I said, I tasted the vampire within you. Your father's power is very evident, which is why you are in danger."

I didn't understand his statement, but I also didn't want to dwell on it.

"So, where are you taking me again?"

"I am taking you to San Francisco where we have a holding facility for hybrids."

"And what do they do there?"

His matter-of-fact attitude made it seem as though he'd been asked these questions many times before. "We train hybrids how to protect themselves against other vampires. We also test for their given powers, and depending on their abilities, many are then activated."

"What do you mean by activated?"

"You see, Brianna, a hybrid's vampire blood remains relatively dormant until one is near other vampires or is activated. The amount of power that a hybrid's father possesses determines how dormant the vampire traits will be. Some may heal quickly from injuries, others may be extremely fast or strong, it all depends. Some hybrids exhibit no real vampire traits at all.

"A hybrid is only able to come into his or her full powers by drinking the blood of a vampire, which is what we refer to as activation. If possible, the blood of the biological father is preferred since it will make the hybrid's powers stronger and more solidified."

"I have to drink someone's blood?" Okay, that's gross. My stomach started churning. It didn't help that I hadn't eaten in a while.

"It is not as bad as it sounds," Cameron said, laughing lightly under his breath.

"Well maybe not for you! You're a vampire for crying out loud. Of course you wouldn't mind drinking someone's blood." I took a breath and changed the subject. "How long do I need to stay at this hybrid hotel?" When Cameron didn't answer I felt a lump form in my throat. "Cameron?" I said, prodding him again. "How long?"

"Indefinitely," he whispered.

"W-what? What do you mean indefinitely?" He didn't answer. "Cameron!" My shallow breath quickened and I could taste the bile rising in my throat. I couldn't breathe. Cameron began saying something, but I couldn't make it out with my ears ringing so loudly. "Stop the car!"

"Brianna, please calm down," he said, reaching over for my hand.

I batted his hand away and began trying to open the door, the window, anything. But nothing worked, as if the child proof mechanisms had been engaged. And well, I was acting like a child, but I needed to get out of this car.

"Brianna, stop! I am pulling over, just please stop trying to open the door."

Cameron pulled to the breakdown lane and once he placed the truck in park, I was able to open the door. Stumbling out into the cold rain, I tripped my way over to the guardrail in front of me and vomited over the side. Every bit of fear and anger came out and it was hard to distinguish the tears from the rain as both streamed down my face.

Cameron had come around the SUV and tried to soothe me by rubbing my back, but I yelled at him to leave me alone. My anger was slightly misdirected at him; he was simply the messenger. It wasn't his fault I was a…a hybrid? As the thought of what I was occurred to me, another fit of sickness consumed me. I wasn't sure exactly what I was more upset or scared about – the fact that vampires actually existed or that I was half one myself.

After another few minutes my stomach stopped retching enough for me to stand. I looked to my left to see that Cameron was standing only a foot away from me. For a while we just stared at each other not knowing what to say. I was drenched, but I wasn't about to get back in the SUV.

"Look Cameron, I'm sorry," I said as my lip quivered from the cold, and my nerves. "I need some time to think about this. I'm sorry you came all this way, but I just can't do this right now."

"Brianna, this is not a game. I have to get you to San Francisco. It is the only way you will be safe," he said. Even through the rain his dark eyes blazed into mine.

"You keep saying that, but look at what you're asking me to do?" Cameron's face changed to confusion as his thick curls fell long and wet into his eyes. "I've just escaped one prison, and now you're asking me to go into another? I can't rush into this. I *did* that already, and look where it got me. Fourteen years of hell with Sam. I need to know everything I'm in for before I do this. And either you accept that, or we say goodbye right here and now."

At the mention of Sam, recognition replaced Cameron's confusion. He licked his lips and sighed deeply. Finding his resolve, he nodded and opened the passenger side door of the SUV. "I did not think of it that way. If you get back in the truck, we can come up with an option that works for both of us, okay? I just want to get you out of this rain." Cameron could see my reluctance so he stretched out his hand and said, "Please?"

With a sigh I took his hand and let him help me up into the passenger seat. I was sopping wet and extremely cold. I watched Cameron as he walked to the other side of SUV, but instead of going to the driver's side door he opened the backseat door and got in. I looked back to see him digging through a duffle bag and pull out a couple of dry shirts.

"Hand me your jacket," he said, definitely not taking no for an answer. Quickly I unzipped the hoodie and handed it back him, shivering in my little white shirt. Cameron looked up as he handed me a blue long-sleeved button up shirt. "You can wear this until your jacket dries out."

I thanked him softly and put my arms through the sleeves. It was incredibly soft for a man's shirt, and it smelled new, which was disappointing. I was hoping it would smell like him.

As though he could hear what I was thinking, Cameron handed me his leather jacket - the one I had seen him in that first day. "Take my jacket too, just in case," he said.

Like he needed to ask me twice. I took the jacket and laid it across my lap while I finished buttoning up my shirt. Out of the corner of my eye I could see that he was changing his shirt as well. Feeling completely mischievous, I tried to catch a glimpse. What can I say? I needed to make sure my dreams of him were accurate. It was purely for verification reasons. Just as I turned my head enough to be able to see him, his eyes were looking into mine with one eyebrow raised and a daring smile on his face.

"Enjoying the view, Ms. Morgan?"

Giving him my best I-don't-know-what-you-mean look, I simply replied, "Actually, I was just wondering why you would change your shirt back there if you were just going to have to get back out in the rain." Well, the thought had merit.

And as he had done in Renee's bedroom, he disappeared leaving a cloud of black mist and in the same moment appeared in the driver's seat with the same mist floating around him.

"Okay, you need to stop doing that. At least until I can come to terms with all of this."

"Certainly," he smiled. "So, we need to come to an agreement on how we proceed from here. What is it you need in order to make your decision?"

What I needed was a pair of dry pants.

"I need to go to my grandfather's," I said as I reached underneath the jacket and pealed the sweatpants down my legs and threw them in the backseat with the hoodie. "He's the one person I trust, and it's the only place I can go where I can just...think."

"All right. Where does he live?" he said as he pulled up the SUV's GPS system on the main console.

"North Carolina," I answered weakly. "From here it's probably only another ten hours, even less if you're a fast driver. Plus no one will be on the road. We'll make it there in no time."

He sighed, shook his head and asked, "How long will you need?"

"I don't know," I replied. "Maybe a couple of weeks?" I heard him take in a fast breath and hold it. "I'm sorry, Cameron, I just don't know. It could be less, it could be more. I'll know when I know, that's all I can give you."

He nodded silently, and put the SUV in gear while I entered my grandfather's address into the GPS system.

As we descended further down the highway, I looked over at him and said, "Hey Cameron, what happened to the Vanquish?"

He didn't answer, unless you counted his extreme acceleration as a response.

Chapter Twelve

Brianna

So here's what I found out, it's all true. All the books, movies, and myths were all true in some fashion. vampires' strengths and weaknesses differed from book to book mostly because vampires were just as different. Many authors and screenwriters were either vampires themselves, or were somehow acquainted with one. No one story had the entire truth, but if you put them all together, you'd get pretty close. I assumed that the vampires kept a few trade secrets to themselves; for example, that there were thousands of hybrids like me. Although Cameron was more than willing to talk about my hybrid-ness, I wasn't interested. I wanted to know all there was about vampires. I had always been obsessed with vampire tales, and now I knew why.

The ten-hour drive turned into a six hour one because Cameron drove like a maniac, but I guess you're allowed to speed if you have vampire sight. I slept through most of it, though Cameron endured my endless questions whenever I would wake. So far we'd covered how one was turned into a vampire - by being almost drained of blood then drinking from your maker. Yuck. We also discussed eating habits and the great debate over human blood versus an animal's. Then we discussed his coven called the Warriors, which consisted of his maker, Victor and sixty-two siblings of which his favorite brothers were Devin, Alexander and his wife Kyla, and Jared, although there were a few others that he tolerated including his competitive sister Jazlyn. He had tried to tell me about my vampire father, but I wanted nothing of it. So he began naming all sixty-two Warriors until I fell asleep again.

When I woke, it was just after 4:30 a.m. We were in the mountains of North Carolina which were absolutely breathtaking with their blankets of trees and mist which were now hidden by the pitch black of the early morning. I'd grown up here for the most part, and I knew almost every inch of the back roads we were now spiraling up. Though Cameron's driving speeds were scary, I was happy to know we were close. The trip was beginning to take its toll. My body ached all over and I longed to be curled up in my childhood bedroom with the two narrow French doors that opened to the wraparound porch.

"Cameron," I yawned, "do you sleep?"

He let out a small laugh. "So we are on to sleeping habits?"

I gave him a little laugh myself. "Yeah, I guess so. That's all I can think about right now."

"I do require some sleep from time to time, especially if I have been in the sun for days at a time, used an excess of vampire powers, or if I am in need of blood."

"Do you have a coffin?" I blurted out, unable to help myself.

Thankfully he laughed at my question. "No, I do not require a coffin. However, my brother Jared requires a room without windows since he can still be burned by the sunlight."

"Really? How come it bothers him and not you?"

"Jared is still young which is why he burns. The sun sensitivity becomes less with age, but it takes centuries to become completely unaffected. I still have to cover my eyes if I am weak."

"Inta-resting," I replied, thinking about that first day with him wearing his sexy silver aviators. Just then, the GPS instructed us to turn left onto Morning View Lane. Only a few more minutes and I would be home, safe. "So, how old are you, exactly?"

"In human years or vampire years?"

Well, I'd never thought of it that way. "Human years."

"I am thirty-three in human years."

"So that's how old you were when you were Turned?"

"That's correct."

"Okay then, how about in vampire years?"

"I have spent 268 years as a vampire."

Doing the math in my head I looked over at him and said with a big condescending smile I said, "So you're really 301? Damn, for an old man you're looking pretty good."

"I may be 301, but I am in *very* good shape for an old man."

Not taking my eyes off of him I said in my best Southern accent, "Mr. Cameron, I do declare you are flirtin' with me."

If he'd been able to, he'd be blushing. He dropped his voice and began to say, "Would that be…"

"Cameron, look out!" I screamed.

Cameron slammed on the breaks and the SUV screeched to a halt, burning the road with rubber as we came inches from hitting a man standing in the middle of the road with a shotgun pointed at our windshield.

"Now ya'll know you ain't got business up here, so ya might as well turn on back."

As I opened the door to the SUV, I felt Cameron's arm try to pull me back in, but I stood on the truck's running board and yelled, "Oliver Lee Morgan, you crazy old coot, put that friggin' gun down before someone gets killed! Is that anyway to treat your only grandchild?"

My grandfather slowly lowered his gun and squinted up at me. "'Lil Bri, is that you? What in tar nation are ya drivin' up here at this hour?"

"It's a long story, Daddy O, and I promise I'll tell ya everythin'," I replied, hearing my accent begin to sink back in. "Now can we pull up to the house, or are ya just gonna blow us to smithereens?"

"Well a course, sugar, go on up. I gotta call off the boys," he said as he walked toward my side of the car. Stopping suddenly in his tracks he looked up at me with disapproving eyes. "Brianna Marie, where in the hell are your britches?"

Now completely mortified, I realized that Cameron's leather jacket had slid off my legs when I stood up out of the truck. I was standing in front of my grandfather *and* Cameron in nothing but a shirt and panties, which the shirt really didn't cover. Taken completely off guard, the only thing that came out of my mouth was, "Ummm…well…ahh…"

After recovering from my humiliation, I sank back into the SUV and directed Cameron to my grandfather's house. Daddy O had gone down to talk to "the boys" who were the neighborhood rednecks that monitored the traffic on these mountain roads from the comfort of their homes. Just because they were a bunch of good ole boys, didn't mean they didn't have the latest in surveillance equipment. Because many of the roads were basically loose gravel mixed with tar, they could hear a car coming from miles away. If they didn't recognize the car, they could notify you with plenty of time to get your gun. And yes, they absolutely knew everyone's car, so it was best to notify them if you were having guests. A lesson I was just reminded of.

Once Cameron parked the truck in the driveway I turned to the backseat and grabbed Renee's burgundy sweatpants, which were thankfully dry enough to put on. But then I suddenly realized I didn't have a single thing to my name.

Noticing my sudden solemn mood, Cameron said, "As soon as you get some rest we will purchase you some clothes, and any...personal items...you may need."

I simply nodded and bit my lower lip. With a sigh, I pushed open the door and stepped out of the SUV.

"'Lil Bri, go on in the house. You'll catch cold wearin' nothin' butchya drawers out here," my grandfather said as he trudged down the gravel driveway.

I looked at Cameron and said, "We've gotta keep the whole hybrid thing between you and me, okay?"

"Of course. I will let you catch up with your grandfather. I need to call Victor and update him on our situation," Cameron said as he stepped from the SUV and walked towards the woods in front of the truck.

I turned around to face my grandfather as he closed the space between us. "First of all, Daddy O, I wasn't just wearing my drawers, I had a shirt on. Second of all, get your glasses checked, I have pants on now. Happy?"

"Well, sugar, I'm just happy to see ya. But I gotta ask, who died this time?"

Taking a second, I responded, "Brianna Lewis, I guess." Daddy O quirked his eyebrow. "I left Sam."

"Well that's the best news I've heard in years," he said putting his arm around me.

"Ooh, be careful, Daddy O," I said pulling his arm away. "I'm a little banged up back there."

Daddy O stopped and straightened quickly. "Do I wanna know?"

"Probably not," I replied, shaking my head and looking down at the ground. "But my friend Cameron got me out before it got too bad."

"Well let's getcha inside, and your…friend…can find his own way in."

While we laughed, we walked up the front porch steps to the small country house of my youth. The one level ranch-style house was built on a steep slope that didn't allow for a usable backyard, but it was suited perfectly for a wide wraparound porch and a back deck that was almost as big as the house itself. Most of my time was always spent on the deck looking out at the mountains rising up against the famous Carolina blue sky.

"Welcome home, sugar," my grandfather said as we stepped inside the house.

I could hear Cameron coming up the stairs on the front porch, so I turned to my grandfather and said with eyebrows raised, "Please be nice."

Daddy O gave me a harrumph as he put his gun in the corner. I opened the screen door to let Cameron in, taking note that he seemed almost shy walking into the house.

"Cameron, this is my grandfather Oliver," I said while Daddy O turned to meet Cameron. "Daddy O, this is my friend Cameron."

Suddenly Daddy O turned his back on us, grabbed his gun, locked a shell into the barrel, and pointed it at Cameron.

"'Lil Bri, you stay behind me," he said as he grabbed my arm. "And you, get the hell outta my house!"

"Daddy O, stop it! What are you doing?"

Cameron put his hands up in front of him, palms out wide. "Brianna, it is fine. I will go back to the car."

"You can go farther than that you blood sucking sumabitch!"

I was utterly speechless. Cameron stood in the doorway like a statue; he seemed just as shocked as I was.

"Just put the gun down," I said breathlessly, stepping in front of Cameron. "How do you know what he is?"

Daddy O slowly lowered the gun, his face filled with worry and fear. "He's not the first blood sucker I've seen, sugar. You can always tell by them eyes a theirs," he said and looked directly at Cameron. "Are you like the others?"

"The others, sir?" Cameron said, putting his hands down. "When have there been other vampires?"

"All her life," my grandfather said in a distant voice.

"So you knew what she was?"

"More like what her daddy was."

I felt like I was watching a tennis match looking back and forth between Cameron and Daddy O. This day was unbelievable. And now I'd learned that my grandfather had lied to me my entire life. Frankly, I'd hit my limit and threw my hands up and walked to my bedroom. I just wanted to go to sleep and hopefully wake up with a new life.

Cameron was dressed immaculately in fitted black tuxedo tails and a brilliant white vest, his jet-black hair in severe contrast to his high white collar and bowtie. We were dancing in a spectacular ballroom flooded with candlelight coming from the large candelabras surrounding the room and the incredible crystal chandeliers hanging above. The golden light reflected off a wide diamond encrusted bracelet that surrounded my wrist covered in an opera-length ivory glove. My long ivory empire-waist dress billowed slightly around me as Cameron spun me around the dance floor.

"Shall we go out onto the terrace, love," Cameron whispered in my ear.

"I would love to," I replied, brushing the back of my gloved hand down the side of his face and giving him a soft kiss.

I put my arm through his and he escorted me out through the wall of opened doors towards the expanding terrace outside. As we passed through the doors, I caught my reflection in the glass. My dark hair was piled high on my head, held together with a small crown while the neckline of my dress was scooped low, exposing the roundness of my breasts. I looked spectacular, very My Fair Lady-esque.

Cameron led me to a secluded corner of the terrace that overlooked the beautiful gardens of the estate. Standing behind me, Cameron wrapped his arms around me and began softly kissing the back of my neck. He moved his lips from my neck to my shoulder, brushing his opposite hand across my breasts.

"Ow, Cam, did you just bite me," I said, turning my head to see him. "That hurts, you know."

Looking at me with his adorable crooked smile he replied, "It will only hurt for a second, my love."

"What?" I said startled, my smile suddenly dropping from my face.

"Just stay still, or else the skin will tear," he said as he held me tightly against him and with a sudden growl Cameron extended his fangs and bit into my neck...

"No!" I screamed, bolting upright in my bed. My hand flew to my neck as I gulped in the cool morning's air.

"Brianna!" Cameron shouted as he charged into my bedroom through the French doors located to the left of my bed.

"Get out!" I screamed at him, still affected by the images of my dream.

Just then the door on the opposite side of my bedroom flew open and my grandfather burst into the room.

"'Lil Bri! You okay?" Daddy O said out of breath from running down the hall.

"Get out! Both of you," I yelled looking back and forth between the two of them. Neither one of them moved, as though they were daring the other to leave first. "Now!"

Finally they both backed out the way they came as I violently tugged the comforter up and over my head. I desperately wanted to go back to sleep, but I was terrified of dreaming again. So instead, I grabbed the phone located on the nightstand next me and dialed Renee's phone number. She would be sick with worry, but what was I going to tell her? Certainly not the truth.

Chapter Thirteen

Cameron

After Brianna threw me out of her room, I walked back out on the balcony that wrapped around the majority of the house. The sun had broken over the horizon a couple of hours ago, and I had positioned myself outside her room as to not upset Oliver Morgan. Brianna was doing surprisingly well considering everything she had gone through in the past twenty-four hours. I was, however, worried about her sleeping habits. She whined and flinched violently from her dreams throughout our trip, though she did not seem to remember having them. However, this last dream seemed to have shaken her, though she did not seem willing to share why.

Still standing to the side of her door, I could hear her talking to Renee, trying to relay as much information as she could. Since it appeared that she would be occupied for a while, I wanted to take this opportunity to talk to her grandfather, who obviously knew a little more about Brianna than he had ever let on.

I walked around to the front of the house and found Oliver sitting in a rocking chair drinking his morning coffee.

"Good morning, Mr. Morgan," I said, trying to be as respectful as possible. He looked up in my direction, and continued to drink his coffee. "Sir, I am afraid that we got off on the wrong foot."

"Nope, yur feet are fine. It's yur teeth I'm worryin' about," he replied.

"Mr. Morgan, I can assure you that I am only here to protect Brianna. I would never let anything happen to her by my hand, or anyone else's."

"Well, it looks to me that yur word isn't that great."

"Yes sir, you are right. Her current condition is unacceptable, but your anger should be directed at her husband."

"She thinks I don't know all he does to her, but Renee gives me an update every now and again." Getting up from his rocking chair Oliver headed towards the front door. "Can I getcha some coffee?"

"No sir, I do not drink coffee."

"Do ya drink anythin'? Well besides...you know what."

"No sir."

"Well, come on in. I need a second cup, and you can tell me whatcha doin' with my grandbaby."

I followed him inside through the small dining room that led into the kitchen and watched as he poured himself another cup of coffee. Finally he sat on a stool at the island located in the center of the open kitchen.

"'Kay, so get talkin'," he said, looking at me over his mug.

"From your earlier statement, I am assuming that you know Brianna is half vampire." Oliver shrugged slightly and nodded. "May I ask how you came to know?"

"Nope," he responded flatly. "Don't trust ya enough yet. So how's 'bout you tell me your interest in my granddaughter."

"In my world we would call her a hybrid, and like Brianna, most do not know what they truly are. In the past we let our children live their lives as humans, only taking in those that exhibited powers that might be a danger to others. Then about four years ago we started hearing that hybrids were being found dead. At first the covens merely dismissed the deaths, but when the hybrid death toll exceeded a hundred in only a couple of months, we knew they were being targeted."

"No offense...uh...what's yur name again?"

"Cameron Burke, sir."

"No offense, Mr. Burke, but I hope this story gets better."

I smiled awkwardly as I replied, "Unfortunately, not really, Mr. Morgan. As the number of murdered hybrids increased, we discovered signs that they were being experimented on prior to death. It was determined that we needed to collect all the hybrids we knew about for their own safety. So a group was formed called the Gatherers who travel all over the world to find hybrids and bring them to a holding facility we have built where we train them in combat and all aspects of Vampirism. I am the Gatherer that was assigned to collect Brianna and bring her to San Francisco."

Oliver stayed silent for a moment processing the information. He carried his coffee mug over to the kitchen sink and dumped its remains down the drain as he asked, "Do you know who's takin' 'em?"

"Yes we do," I answered. "A coven headed by a vampire named Elaina."

"So yur takin' 'Lil Bri to San Francisco so that she'll be safe."

"Yes, sir."

"Then whadaya doin' here?"

Victor had asked me a similar question when I talked to him earlier. "Brianna said she needed time to think, and made me bring her here."

"And ya listened?"

"Yes, sir, she was very adamant."

"And did ya take those other hybrids wherever they wanted to go?"

I shifted my weight uncomfortably as I replied, "No…sir."

"Well, she must have some pull on ya then," he said with a humored smile.

"She is very important."

"To you?"

"To our race and to her father."

"Her *father*," Oliver replied with disdain. "With the exception of givin' me my grandbaby, that *man* has done nothin' but bring heartache to this family."

"Sir, would you care to explain? Brianna became very resistant once I told her that her father had sent me."

"I'm sorry, but I can't do that," he said shaking his head and getting off his stool. "That's Bri's sorrow to tell, not mine. If she ain't told ya, I don't feel comfortable doin' so." And with that he left the kitchen.

"Mr. Morgan," I began as I followed him into the living room, "I would like to purchase some clothing for Brianna since hers were lost when we left. Where could I go for her?"

"Well, probably yur best bet is in the next town over, 'bout twenny minutes west. Lots of frufru stores over there, go knock yurself out," he said as he walked toward his bedroom.

"Does this mean I can stay in the house from now on?"

Oliver merely laughed.

Chapter Fourteen

Brianna

The first hour of my conversation with Renee consisted of a lot of hysterical lecturing and screaming on her part. Mostly, she was worried about my injuries, but also about me being swept away in the middle of the night. I assured her that I was fine and that Cameron had taken me to my grandfather's. Oddly enough she seemed to think that Daddy O had actually sent Cameron for me, so I just let it go. It was definitely a much better explanation than anything I'd come up with.

As I started to say goodbye she interrupted with, "Ohmygod, I forgot to tell you. John called me a couple hours after you left because he stumbled across a chart that had the name Sam Lewis on it, and he thought that he might be the Sam. I told him it was totally Sam, and he said Sam was admitted to the ER in pretty bad shape."

I felt the blood drain from my face as she said his name. "Did he say anything? Were the cops there?"

"Yeah. John said he heard one of the cops say there was an intruder."

"Did they say anything about me?"

"Not sure. John couldn't get close without looking suspicious."

"Tell him thanks for everything he did for me. And Re, he's really great."

"I knew you'd like him," she said, but suddenly became quiet. "I just wish you were here to get to know him better."

"I know, sweetie," I said, feeling the tears welling up in my eyes. I had to lie to her, and it killed me. "I'll be home soon. It'll be like I never left."

"You better be home soon. Just call me when you can, okay?"

"I will, I promise."

After I hung up the phone, the tears crested my lower eyelids and streamed down my face. I wasn't crying because we'd been apart for twelve hours, I was crying because I had no idea when I was ever going to see her again. My life got turned upside down and I couldn't tell her a thing, not a goddamn thing.

Rolling onto my back, I flinched a little from the pain, but noticed it wasn't as sensitive as before. Slowly I pulled myself out of bed and walked over to my bedroom door where a full-length mirror hung. I unbuttoned and dropped Cameron's shirt to the floor and pulled the back of my white shirt up as far as I could manage. Turning my back to the mirror, I gently pulled at the tape around the large bandage and pulled the gauze back enough to look at the road rash underneath. It was already looking better. What was it that Cameron had said? The degree at which vampire traits were dormant depended on the power of your father. He'd said my father was really powerful, and I'd always healed really quickly. Could it be because of my father's blood?

Ugh, my father. I learned at a very young age not to bring him up in conversation, or ask questions about what he looked like or why he was never around. I had Daddy O and Mama Jo, and that's all I needed. At least that's what I told myself whenever I would start thinking about what my father was like. Well, now I knew. He was a horny vampire who turned my real mom crazy and left me to deal with her.

Not wanting to think about it any longer I placed the bandage back over my wounds, picked Cameron's shirt off the floor, and placed it on the bed. Through the opened French doors, I could hear a car pull into the gravel driveway, and assumed Cameron had come back. I'd heard him leave while I spoke to Renee and wondered where he'd gone off to; almost fearful he wouldn't come back. But the hope of Cameron coming through the door was diminished by the sound of a female voice giving a high-pitched hello.

Quietly I opened the door and took two steps in the hallway thinking I would catch a glimpse of Daddy O's secret girlfriend, but instead I stopped dead in my tracks when I saw a tiny, overly made-up woman with bobbed blonde hair standing in the foyer.

"Mama," I said shaking with butterflies. My mother, Shelby Joanne, not to be confused with Mama Jo, stood frozen in the foyer giving me a disconcerted look.

"Bri Bri? What are you doing here?" she asked with a hint of annoyance.

"I left Sam."

"Really," she replied, almost laughing. "How can that be? That would require someone with a spine, and you, Bri Bri, have never had one of those."

"Well it's true," I countered back, feeling like I was a child. I had never learned how to fire back at my mother and always sounded pathetic when she would begin with the insults.

"And now you've come here," she said walking toward me, "to live off your grandfather? Is that it?"

"No!"

Daddy O moved in between us to try and break up the argument. "Shelby Jo, let's not do this now. Bri's always welcome in my home for as long as she wants. But right now, she needs rest, not fightin'."

"That's right," my mother quibbled back, "go on and defend her like you always do. Just don't come cryin' to me when she bleeds you dry, which is probably why she left Sam. Is that what happened, Bri Bri? Sam run outta money?"

I suddenly felt sick to my stomach and weak in the knees. Breathlessly I said, "No, it's because…"

"It is because she met me," Cameron said as he stood in the doorway with two large shopping bags looking fierce in his dark clothes and shiny aviator sunglasses.

"I'm sorry," Shelby responded as she turned to Cameron. "You are?"

Cameron stepped into the house and put the shopping bags down. "Cameron Burke," he said, taking off his sunglasses and extending his hand. "You must be Shelby."

Cameron barely finished what he was saying before my mother started screaming frantically and falling over herself trying to crawl away from him. Daddy O was the first to move to try and calm her down, but his efforts were futile as soon as Cameron also stepped forward to help. My mother began flailing about, hitting my grandfather in the head and chest. Cameron pulled Daddy O out of the way and grabbed my mother's wrists, holding them tightly in order to restrain her.

"Are you here for her," she shouted at Cameron. "Are you? Are you here for Bri Bri or me?"

Cameron's shock and confusion reflected my own, but his grip on my mother didn't lessen.

"Take her! Just take her! I'll do anything, just take her with you, I don't wanna die," she sobbed. "I kept my promise, I never went back. Please, don't kill me, please don't kill me. Just take her…she means nothing to me. I stayed away like I promised."

Cameron looked down on my sobbing mother in disgust and took her face between his hands.

"Shelby, look into my eyes," he began and she quickly looked up at him, "you came to your father's house today, and no one was home. You will get in your car and forget that you saw anyone here today. When you return home, you will realize what a horrible mother you have been to your only child, and you will pray for her forgiveness because she is truly a gift. Starting today you will do anything to make up for your behavior her entire life. Now go," he growled at her.

Like a robot, my mother rose from the floor and walked out the door to her car as if none of us existed. Cameron followed behind her and watched out the screen door as she drove away. My grandfather still stood in the middle of the living room; disbelief chiseled into his already deep wrinkled face. My knees were weakening under me, so I placed both hands against the arm of the couch to hold me up as the deep sobs came up from my heaving stomach. Hearing the awful sounds radiating from me, I clamped my hand over my mouth to try and hold it in, but the pain was too great. My stomach kept clenching and releasing, making it hard to breathe. I knew my mother didn't really care for me, but I didn't know I was "nothing" to her.

From the corner of my eye, I saw Cameron pick up the two shopping bags in one hand and then walk over to my side. With a gentle nudge, he pulled me into his side and walked me down the hall. I buried my face into his chest, not caring about ruining his shirt. He led me to my room and quietly closed the door behind us. Lowering me to the corner of the bed, Cameron dropped the shopping bags and grabbed a tissue from the box located on my nightstand.

"Well, I'm gonna need a few more than that."

Cameron reached behind me, grabbed the entire box of tissues, and placed them on my lap. I laughed at first, but my laugh turned back into sobbing. Cameron knelt in front of me and placed his hands on my knees.

"I'm sorry," I said, feeling completely embarrassed at my blubbering. "You shouldn't have to see this."

"Brianna, you have no reason to apologize," he said softly. "Your sorrow is yours to own and how you react cannot be judged by anyone. Although I will admit that seeing you weep like this utterly destroys me."

Surprised by his statement, my sobbing came to an abrupt stop. He cared about me. While I sat here wallowing in my own self-pity, there was a man, vampire rather, sitting here caring for me.

"What did you do to her?"

Taking another tissue from the box, Cameron brushed away the stray hairs that were stuck to my face and began dabbing the tissue to absorb the tears. "I did something called a Glamour, do you know what that is?"

I nodded. "Yes, at least from books. You basically put a spell on her or something?"

"Close, it is not a spell per se, more like influencing one's mind," he said as he finished cleaning my face and placed his hand on top of mine.

"Did you mean what you said? I mean, about me?" I asked, feeling embarrassed as I said it.

"I meant every word."

Suddenly feeling uncomfortable from the intensity of his stare, I looked over his shoulder and pointed to the two large shopping bags sitting on the floor behind him. "So, what's in the bags?"

"A little bit of everything," he replied as he pulled the bags next to him. "I purchased some clothing for you. I was unsure of what you prefer to wear, so I went very basic. And in here," he said opening up the second shopping bag, "there are toiletries, some books, and some…" he cleared his throat, "…undergarments."

He was definitely adorable, and a fast shopper. Heavens, it would have taken me hours to purchase that much stuff.

"Cameron, I don't know what to say. Th-hank you, I'll find a way to pay you back."

"Brianna, this is my gift," he replied and stood up in front of me. "I think you should rest."

Not wanting to argue, I pushed myself towards the top of the bed and tucked my legs under the blankets while Cameron pulled them over me. I still felt like a scared child and I didn't want to be alone. As he took a step toward the door I said, "Cameron, would you mind staying with me? Just until I fall asleep?"

"Of course. Where would you like me?"

Now that was a loaded question. I wanted him on top me, but that may be a little forward. Boy, I just couldn't get my head out of the gutter. Finally, I patted the space next to me and Cameron obliged by climbing on top of the thick comforter.

Turning away from him, I backed myself up until I felt the side of his body touching mine. I pulled my legs up so that I was in full fetal position and didn't flinch when Cameron's cool hand began brushing my hair.

"Can I ask you something?" I said sleepily.

"Anything."

"Is this the first time you've bought books for me?"

"No."

"Did you leave those books in my study?"

I could hear the hesitation in his breathing and when he finally answered, "Yes."

"How did you get in without Sam noticing?"

"I Projected in," he replied. "May I ask, how Sam would have noticed me in the house? He was with you in the café."

"Sam has cameras in every room except my study. Wait, how did you know where my study was?"

"Brianna, I am your Gatherer. I've been watching you. I saw you sitting in that room many times so I knew exactly were to Project. And I will answer any additional questions you may have, but for now, you need to sleep."

Something in the back of my mind was bothering me, but Cameron's soothing strokes made my eyelids heavy.

"You'll be here when I get up?"

In a distant part of my waking mind I heard him say yes, but I was already slipping into a much needed sleep. There would be plenty of time for answers. Cameron hadn't told me whether or not Victor had allowed him to stay, but his continued presence led me to think that Victor had granted it and I was grateful. For years I had wanted to be on my own, but now I was thankful that I wasn't. As the nightmare of Sam ended, a new chapter was beginning. A chapter that hopefully involved a vampire name Cameron.

Chapter Fifteen

Brianna

I slept for three glorious hours. I woke up to find Cameron still next to me, and oddly enough he was sleeping. I remembered him saying he slept when he needed blood or had been in the sun too long. Hopefully it was the latter. Being Cameron's meal right now was not how I needed to close out the day. He was very peaceful, and dare I say dead-looking because he was so still. But even now he was gorgeous and looked right at home lying on my bed.

The bed rocked as I got out of it, but Cameron didn't wake. I walked around to the front of the bed where he had deposited the shopping bags and began quietly looking through the clothes he'd purchased. When he said that he'd bought me clothes, I had a sinking feeling I would find a bag full of ill-fitting mismatched items. But to my surprise, I found designer jeans and slacks, sleek sexy blouses and ultra-soft cotton shirts, even several sets of bras and underwear. Adding to my shock, everything was my size. Had he gone through my underwear drawer when he left those books?

Picking through the clothes again I pulled out a pair of jeans and a soft black shirt in the name of comfort. With Cameron out cold, I decided to change in the room instead of lugging the clothes across the hall to change in the bathroom. I turned my back to him and peeled off my shirt and sweatpants, throwing them in a pile across the room to wash later. The soft jeans and T-shirt made me thankful for the wealthy vacation community in the next town over that required high end shops. It was nice to have clothes that didn't remind me of my former life.

Giving Cameron one last glance, I left the room and padded down the hall. My stomach was growling since I hadn't eaten in more than twenty-four hours, and I felt nauseous from the hunger. Daddy O looked up from his book and took off his reading glasses as I stepped into the living room.

"Hey, sugar, yur lookin' better already," he said getting up from his recliner. "'Bout earlier, I didn't know Shelby Jo wuz comin' over. I woulda tol' her to stay home if I knew. I just wish…"

"Daddy O," I interrupted, "let's just forget about it."

He nodded. "Let's get some food in ya, then."

"Actually, I was thinking I'd make you dinner."

"Now 'Lil Bri, I'll have none a that."

"Well if you have all the stuff, I'll make you smothered chops and biscuits," I said with a smile.

"Well don't let me get in yur way," he responded, almost pushing me toward the kitchen. There was one thing I knew for certain, and that was Daddy O couldn't resist when I made Mama Jo's pork chops with gravy and biscuits.

A few minutes later I was standing at the counter seasoning the meat when Daddy O tried to make a retreat back into the living room.

"Where do you think you're goin', old man? There are some things we need to discuss, dontcha think?"

He headed back into the kitchen where he pulled out his stool from underneath the island. It had always been his favorite spot because he could sit and watch Mama Jo flit around the kitchen making dinner.

"You're right, sugar, I guess it is time for the big talk. Well, when a man and a woman love each other, they do certain things together…"

"Daddy!" I yelled, not wanting him to go any further. I think I'd puke if he said the word sex. "I've been married for fourteen years, I know what happens."

"Yeah, but there was no love there. I want to make sure you know what happens when there is."

"That's not what we're talking about right now and you know it," I said, moving to the pantry to gather the biscuit mix. "How long have you known I was…that I had…V-vampire blood in me?" Saying it out loud was more difficult than I had imagined.

"Since you were born, sugar."

I dropped the box of biscuit mix onto the floor, covering the area in white dust.

"'Lil Bri, maybe it's best that you sit down."

"No, I need to keep moving. Just keep going," I said and began wiping up the mess from the floor.

"You know things with yur mama were never very easy, especially between her and Jo. Well, one night she just up and left, not a word to me or Jo, and we didn't hear from her for a couple a years. Then one day outta the blue she come knockin' on our door lookin' like she was gonna pop you right out on our doorstep. That much I think you know."

I nodded and began measuring my ingredients for the biscuits as he continued, "Well, she was actin' crazy and goin' on 'bout how she wuz chosen, and how we had ta protect the baby. And that the baby was her way back in. A course none of us knew what she was talkin' 'bout, but she wouldn't stop sayin' it. She sounded like one a those crazy people ya see on TV."

As Daddy O relayed his story, I kept my back turned realizing that even before I was born Shelby was using me to get something. Angrily I grabbed a cookie sheet from underneath the oven and began violently scooping the dough onto the pan as I gestured for Daddy O to continue.

"Well, one night Jo had gone ta bed early, and I heard Shelby talkin' to herself in her room. When I went in to check on her, she was babbling on about how she needed to get back and how you wuz gonna be her ticket in. So I asked her where she needed to get back to and she said she needed to get back to yur daddy, back to the vampires. A course I just thought she was talkin' crazy again, but then she started sayin' how as soon as you were born she was takin' ya to California so that yur daddy could make ya both vampires, and she just kept goin' on an on about it.

"Needless to say, it scared me to death. I wasn't scared about the vampire stuff, cuz that wuz just nonsense, but I wuz scared about her takin' ya away. So after calmin' her down, I went in and woke up Jo and told her that we needed to get Shelby Jo some help and take care a her baby. And well, we did just that."

"Okay, but if you thought that the vampire stuff was nonsense, what changed your mind?" I asked as I pulled out Mama Jo's famous cast iron skillet and turned on the stove to start cooking the pork chops.

"After that night, yur mama…"

"Could you please stop calling her that," I snapped back. "After today, I only have one mama and she's dead, God rest her soul."

"Yes, darlin'," he replied comfortingly. "Jo has always been yur mama and you were always her daughter, but Shelby Jo is yur mother too even though she don't act like it sometimes. Without her you wouldn't be here, and with all her faults, I'll always be grateful for that."

"So after that night, *Shelby*..."

"Yes, *Shelby Jo*, must a thought I believed her cuz she would talk ta me 'bout you havin' powers, and how you'd be stronger and faster than any other kids around, and how beautiful you'd be, especially yur eyes."

"My eyes?" I asked, looking over my shoulder at him confused, and then jerking back to my pan when my hand was burned by a bit of grease.

"Oh yeah, she always talked about how you were gonna have eyes like them, vampire eyes; big, round, and black, and she wuz almost right too. You'd just been born an I wuz holdin' ya, and you opened yur eyes. You just looked at me with those big round dark eyes, no cryin', no nothin', just lookin'. Yur eyes were exactly how Shelby Jo described 'em, 'cept maybe they weren't black, but so brown they almost looked it."

"Is that why there aren't pictures of me until I was almost three?"

"Well, no, we just didn't have a camera," he chuckled.

Laughing a little myself I took the chops out of the pan, and began making the final part of the dish, the gravy, which was the best part of the meal.

"But you told Cameron that other vampires had been after me."

"Every now an then, one of 'em would come up to the house sayin' they knew Shelby Jo and heard that she'd had a baby and wanned to see ya. I still didn't believe the whole vampire stuff, but somethin' kept tellin' me not to let them in. An after a while I started noticin' that they all had them black eyes, kinda like yours. Jo and I would always tell 'em that we hadn't seen Shelby Jo in years, and didn't even know she had a baby. And by an act a God, when they'd come around you were either sleepin' or were away from the house, except one time."

"One time?" I asked over my shoulder.

"You were 'bout five I guess, and Jo an I were doin' work out in the yard and you were runnin' around playin'. We didn't even see the man come into the yard. I was around the back of the house, and I heard Jo scream so I came runnin'. And there you were in that blood sucker's arms while he was sucking on your neck. I screamed at him and both Jo and I ran toward him. He dropped ya to the ground and started comin' after us. He grabbed Jo by the throat and hit me so hard I fell like a sack a flour. When I looked up, he was bendin' down like he was gonna bite Jo's throat. I couldn't believe what

I was seein'. I kept thinkin' there was no way this could be happenin'.

"Then suddenly he started screamin', dropped Jo to the ground, and disappeared into thin air. And there you were, standin' and holdin' one a Jo's big knives from her silver servin' set and it was drippin' with blood. You weren't scared or nothin'. I remember you just dropped that knife on the ground and asked if you could have a cookie."

I paused for a moment, staring blankly at my grandfather before saying, "I'm a sociopath."

Daddy O put his hands up, scrunching his thick gray eyebrows together. "Now come on, 'Lil Bri, I didn't say that. That was the day we found out that vampires were real, and that you weren't scared of 'em. But that was also the day I realized that Shelby Jo wuz right about everythin' 'cept for some reason them blood suckers wanned you."

The buzzer from the oven startled me as it went off, telling me the biscuits were done. I couldn't believe what he was saying. Why didn't I remember stabbing a vampire with a big silver knife at age five? Most people wouldn't forget something like that.

"Well dinner's ready. I'm going to wake up Cameron," I said leaving the room.

We Southerners were experts at changing the subject at a moment's notice. Daddy O didn't make any objection as I fled the kitchen to my bedroom, I'm sure it had something to do with hot chops and biscuits. As I approached my bedroom door, I started debating whether or not it was a good idea to wake a vampire. But I wasn't able to test it because when I entered the room Cameron was already gone; the French doors left open and bringing in a cool night breeze.

"Cameron," I called quietly as I walked out the doors onto the balcony. Not hearing a reply, I walked around to the front porch. "Cameron?"

Had he left me already? I felt so pathetic even thinking about it, but just as the sinking feeling began in my stomach, I heard his voice call from behind me.

"Brianna?"

I turned quickly around and found him standing there in front of me, right where I had been seconds earlier. "How did you get th…never mind. I was coming to get you for dinner."

"Thank you," he said with a soft smile, "but I have already…eaten."

"You did? But…oh…um…I get it. Duh! Sorry, still getting used to…uh…anyway. Well, then just come and enjoy the company," I said offering him my hand.

In a formal gesture he bowed in front of me and kissed my hand. "I would be honored."

Humored by his action, I squeezed his hand and pulled him inside.

Dinner was definitely interesting. My grandfather sat at the head of the table, Cameron and I on either side while Daddy O told story after embarrassing story about my childhood. When Daddy O announced he had a story from Brianna, the teen years, I got up and declared that dinner was officially over. I picked up both my plate and Daddy O's and headed toward the sink, but was stopped by Cameron who insisted on cleaning up. Normally I would have argued and insisted on cleaning the dishes myself, but this time I let him. I was too tired to be hospitable.

"Well 'Lil Bri, I'm gonna hit the hay early tonight," Daddy O said as he got up from the table and headed out of the room.

"It's 8:30. Never in your life have you gone to bed this early," I said, giving him a skeptical eye.

"Bri, I'm an old man," he replied, walking past me with a Cheshire cat smile, "I need lots a sleep."

Shaking my head, I turned back and headed into the kitchen in time to see Cameron drying his hands with a dishtowel.

"You're done already?"

With his crooked smile he shrugged and said, "Vampire."

I couldn't help but laugh. It felt good too. "I was thinking about going for a walk, would you like to join me?"

"Certainly," he replied, but then ran from the kitchen and back seconds, yes seconds, later with a black sweater coat in his hands. "The evening has turned cool. You may need this."

He held the sweater coat out and helped me pull it on. It was soft and warm, and perfect for a cool evening walk with a vampire. Yep, it would take a while for that to sound normal.

"Shall we?" I said, gesturing to the front door.

As we stepped down the porch steps he asked, "How are you feeling?"

"My eye still hurts," I replied. "But my back looks much better. Must be all that great vampire blood from my rotten ass father."

"Despite your feelings towards him, I am happy that his blood is helping you heal. It has been difficult seeing you injured."

I blushed as we walked across the driveway to the road. "So, where did you go...to ah...eat?"

Cameron dipped his head slightly as he spoke, "Just into the woods. There are quite a few deer around here."

"Do they taste good?" I asked like an idiot.

"They taste terrible," he laughed lightly. "Did you sleep well?"

"Yes, thank goodness. No weird dreams, just dead sleep," I said and then almost slapped myself in the mouth at my choice of words. "Cameron, I wanted to thank you again for what you did today...you know with my...er...with Shelby."

"No one should ever talk about their child like that."

"Ha, my mother has always talked about me like that," I said, kicking a rock down the street, pretending it was Shelby's head.

"When I left, I heard you talking to Oliver, were you able to get any information?" he asked, but I didn't answer. My silence seemed to worry Cameron, making him stop and put his hands on my shoulders. I could feel his stare, but I couldn't bear to look up at him. "Brianna, there is nothing you can say that will shock or anger me. You can trust that anything you say to me I will keep in the strictest of confidence unless it threatens your life. Please, just tell me."

Still looking down at the road I muttered, "I killed a vampire." Now it was Cameron's turn to be silent, so I finally looked up. "I thought you said I couldn't shock you."

"Honestly, I did not think you could. How...when did you kill a vampire?"

"Apparently when I was five." The shock on Cameron's face grew as I continued, "Daddy O said that this vampire came into our yard and started drinking my blood. Then he attacked Daddy O and Mama Jo and I stabbed him with a silver knife. And then he vanished."

Out of everything I told him, his first question was, "Who is Mama Jo?"

I gave a little laugh and started walking down the road again. "Mama Jo was my grandmother, also known as Joanne Morgan."

"Your mother is also Joanne."

"Yes," I answered through clenched teeth, "though she doesn't deserve it. It's a Southern thing, thankfully Shelby didn't believe in carrying on the tradition. I couldn't face being Brianna Shelby right now. Anyway, I always knew she ran away and got knocked up. But Daddy O said that when Shelby came back home, she was pregnant and spewing all this nonsense. She kept saying I was her ticket back and that she was going to take me to California and my dad would make us vampires."

Cameron walked beside me, his brow creased with concentration. "Considering you are not in California, what happened after you were born?"

"My grandparents had Shelby committed. But that doesn't mean she didn't get me to California."

We found ourselves at the end of the road which unfortunately meant we had to walk back up the steep hill. As though he understood, Cameron offered me his arm for the walk up.

"I can carry you if you would like," he said looking down at me. I shook my head and slowly started to climb the road back. "So when did you go to California?"

"When I was ten. The doctors said Shelby was cured and released her from the looney bin. She showed up here, had me pack my things, and took me away to California by way of Louisiana, Mississippi, Arkansas, and Arizona. We finally reached California when I was fourteen, but we only stayed a few days and then we moved back about a half hour away from here."

Taking a moment to enjoy the evening, I stopped and looked up at the sky to enjoy the beautiful star-filled night while Cameron stood behind me. In a tentative gesture, I leaned back into Cameron's chest, letting him support me as I fought fatigue and the slope of the mountain road. I felt the coolness of his fingers touch mine so gently as if asking permission, and I answered him silently by intertwining my fingers in his. We stood there, silent, enjoying our little private moment staring up at the stars.

Cameron finally broke the silence by saying, "It must have been nice to be close to your grandparents again."

"If I had been allowed to see them, yes, it would have been nice," I replied bitterly. "Shelby was always jealous of how much I loved them, so when we moved back, she never let me visit. That's when I started running away," I said as I pushed myself off of Cameron and started back up the hill. This whole topic was making me antsy.

"I am assuming you ran to Oliver and Joanne?"

"Sort of. The first time I ran away was the night I found out that Mama Jo had died three years earlier and Shelby never told me. If I didn't already hate my mother at the time, I despised her then. After that, I was always coming to check on Daddy O, but he would always bring me back kicking and screaming a few days later. Then when I was eighteen, a few months away from graduating, I met Sam at a party. I was so miserable with Shelby that Sam seemed like a knight in shining armor, and he totally preyed on that. I graduated, got pregnant, Shelby kicked me out, and Sam married me a week later. We moved to Connecticut right after and I lost the baby a few weeks later. The rest is history I guess."

We'd finally reached the house and not a moment too soon. I felt as though I might collapse. I stepped up onto the first step of the porch, still holding Cameron's hand which he tugged to turn me around and face him.

"That is right, Brianna," he said, "that is your history. Do not let it define your future. This is your chance to start over, and I have never met anyone who deserved it more. And although I have enjoyed our walk, I must insist that you get some rest."

From where I stood on the step, we were eye level with each other, and even with his request that I rest, neither of us moved to break away.

"Will you stay with me again?" I asked, unsure if I could take the rejection if he said no. I needed an anchor, something to hold me down from all the craziness that had entered my life in the past twenty-four hours. *He* was my anchor.

"If you wish it of me, I cannot refuse. However, I do need to take care of some business, but I will join you once I am done. If you need me, just call my name. I will hear you no matter how soft you say it."

"Really?"

Cameron simply smiled and shrugged as he said, "Vampire."

Chapter Sixteen

Cameron

I watched Brianna walk up the remaining porch steps and into the house, and with each step she took I had to plant my feet further into the ground to keep from running after her and kissing her. But I was waiting for her; she needed to take the lead. The timing could not have been worse; she just left her abusive husband, and I had no idea how much longer Victor would allow me to live.

When Brianna and I arrived at Oliver's home I called Victor right away to give him an update on the situation. Even before I called him, I knew that he would be furious at the fact that Brianna's arrival would be delayed for a few weeks, if she decided to come at all. Even though he would not admit it, I knew that Father was a little afraid of Eris's wrath if Brianna was not brought to San Francisco. Regardless, I had failed miserably with bringing Brianna in, and I defied him when I said I would be staying with Brianna until she was comfortable enough to go to the Facility. From here forward I would need to be diligent about watching for other vampires, anyone could have been sent to kill me on Victor's orders. My reign as favorite son was feigning.

Putting those thoughts aside, I had business I needed to take care. Brianna had mentioned earlier that Sam had cameras posted all over the house. That meant he could have me on tape assaulting him, using my vampire powers, and potentially exposing my race. That in itself was a death sentence.

I needed to call Jared, the world's greatest unknown hacker who could get into any and all systems undetected. Hopefully he could somehow get any video Sam may have gotten. I opened the door to the SUV, pulled myself up into the driver's seat, and dialed Jared's number.

"Hey, big bro, you okay?" Jared said sleepily since it was a few hours before his normal rousing time.

"I have definitely been better."

"Yeah, no shit. Dad is *pissed* at you. Now that's something I thought I'd never see."

"Well, you are young, little brother. I need your help with something right away."

"Ooh, you know that speedy service'll cost you extra." Jared charged everyone for his services, except for a select few including his brothers. But in case anyone ever overheard him, he always made it seem that he was bleeding us dry just like everyone else. "So I hear your mystery girl is Eris's daughter. Brittney something?"

"Brianna," I corrected.

"Is she hot?"

Ignoring him I said, "I need you to pull all hospital records and police reports for a Samuel A. Lewis in the state of Connecticut for the last twenty-four hours."

"'Kay, anything else?"

"Actually, there is. There is a possibility I was caught on tape."

"Caught on tape doin' what?"

"Trying to kill Brianna's abusive piece of shit husband."

"Dude! That's awesome."

"Jared, it could expose us, and if he files a police report they will have me on tape. Do you understand why this is not...awesome."

"Yeah, yeah, fine. So the husband is this Samuel Lewis guy?"

"Yes."

"Okay, so he has cameras in his house, but where are they transmitting to? Is it somewhere in the house?"

"I think it may be elsewhere, maybe his office, or his phone? What can be done?"

"I'll have to do some research first, bro. I gotta see where the feed is going, and what we're dealing with, but I'll figure it out."

"Jared, I never have any doubt in your abilities."

"Speaking of my righteous skills, I already have a hospital admittance record, but no police reports yet," Jared said with the sound of lightning fast typing in the background.

"Really? I thought for sure he would…" I said letting my thought die and a new question form. "Why would someone who was attacked by a stranger and who left with his wife, not report anything to the police?"

There was a brief silence before Jared answered, "So he could get revenge personally?"

Unfortunately, I was thinking the exact same thing. "Jared, put a credit card trace on him, and then let me know if he has any activity outside of Connecticut. And can you send me the hospital record, and continue to monitor the police records?"

"What am I, your servant boy?"

"Charge me double."

"Will do. But dude, is she worth all this? I mean seriously, Dad flipped a nut after he talked to you. You are in some serious trouble."

Without hesitation I answered, "She is absolutely worth it."

"Okay then. I'll let you know what I find. But one more thing, is she hot?"

I hung up on Jared, without responding. But yes, Brianna was hot and there was no doubt in my mind that she was worth any punishment from Victor. My short suffering was nothing compared to what she had been through, and before tonight I had only known the portion that I had seen. It took every ounce of control I had not to kill Brianna's mother today. The fact that the woman could claim to be her mother disgusted me. Even as I thought about her mother my hands began tearing a hole in the truck's upholstery. More evidence to the fact that the more time I spent with Brianna, the harder it was to stay objective. I was leading with my heart instead of my head, definitely something a Warrior such as myself should never do.

I kept thinking about my brother Alexander who had been married to Kyla for the last seventy-five years. Alexander was only one of a few Warriors who had taken a mate. Most Warriors found love a useless emotion that got in the way. When I was Turned, in order to survive the loss of my wife, I took on the same mindset. But everything had changed now, and I was no longer living on autopilot. The trouble was I did not know how to be a Warrior and a lover.

As I stepped out of the SUV a cool breeze swept across me and with it I heard the whisper of my name. Brianna! I dug my feet into the gravel and leapt up onto the porch. In milliseconds I was stepping through the French doors and looking wildly around the room. The only thing I saw was Brianna standing at the side of the bed with her back turned to me.

"Brianna," I said firmly.

She shrieked and jumped around to face me. She was wearing the button-down shirt I had given her last night, the first three buttons left open to reveal her chest and the outline of her bare breasts. I looked away quickly trying to find the floor more attractive than the milky soft skin of her chest and exposed legs.

"I did not mean to frighten you, but I heard you call my name. Are you all right?"

"Yes," she said tentatively, still shocked by my presence.

"Then why did you call?" I said, finally able to bring my gaze to hers.

She dropped her head and spoke to the floor. "I wanted to see if it worked?"

Walking over to her, I put my hands on her shoulders and bent my head down to get her to look at me. "If what worked?"

"I wanted to see if I whispered your name...you would hear it."

"It certainly did work. Feel better?"

She nodded and began to smile until she realized how exposed she was. She looked up at me, panic flooding her face. Proving to her that she could trust me, I reached for the ends of the open shirt, feeling Brianna tense slightly and look to her side to avoid my eyes. I buttoned the remaining three buttons and watched as Brianna slowly began to relax and her eyes return to mine. Her hair was damp and curling around her face, making her the sexiest thing I had ever seen.

"Is that lavender I smell?" I asked, trying to take my attention off her body which I so desperately wanted to touch.

"Yes," she replied as she backed away and got into her bed. "I finally took a shower. I apologize if I smelled, I kinda lost track of time."

"Brianna, trust me when I say you did not smell, but the lavender is quite nice."

"You think so? It's okay, but honeysuckle is still my favorite," she said as she pulled the covers over her and slid down into the bed. "I'm sorry for before. I know you had business to take care of. I interrupted you, didn't I?"

"No actually, I was just finishing up."

"Well then," Brianna said and patted the space next to her as she had done earlier, and for the second time today I willingly obliged and climbed up next to her. She curled up on her side and pushed her back against me, however, unlike before, I turned on my side and cradled her body in mine. She did not pull away when I began to gently caress her face and hair.

After several minutes, Brianna's eyes began to flutter with dreams, and I desperately hoped they were pleasant ones. I held Brianna in my arms while she slept, all the while thinking of how I would handle Sam if he came looking for her. I was conflicted as to whether or not I should tell Brianna if Jared discovered that Sam was searching for her. I did not want to lie to her, but I also did not want to add to her already fragile state of mind. As she shifted slightly in my arms, I turned my attention back to her and began thinking what my life would be like if I was able to hold her like this every night. Suddenly so many things no longer mattered.

Chapter Seventeen

Cameron

For the next week and a half, I turned into Oliver's workhorse by day and Brianna's bedmate by night. Neither of which I minded, although the night shift was obviously more pleasurable. In some ways I felt almost human again working hard in the daytime and sleeping at night. After the first morning of seeing me leave from Brianna's bedroom, Oliver had decided that I needed to *earn* my stay. Thereafter, I woke each morning to a list of items that needed to be repaired, moved, or even built, and I did them gladly. I was winning over Oliver a little every day and doing his chores reminded me of when I would help my own father on our farm. It was completely gratifying.

Evenings were always full of food and laughter, and once dinner was over I would either escort Brianna on a walk or sit with her and Oliver for a silent evening read. Every night I would accompany Brianna to bed where one of us would drape ourselves over the other. When everyone was soundly in bed, I would call Jared looking for updates about Sam Lewis, which there were none.

This morning started off like any other, although Brianna had decided to sleep for a little longer. She had been slightly under the weather the last few days, but considering the amount of stress she was under, it was understandable.

"Good morning, Mr. Morgan," I said, entering the kitchen to find Oliver drinking his morning coffee and reading his newspaper.

"Son, how many times do I need to tell ya to call me Ollie?"

"Probably many more, sir. It is my way of showing respect."

"Well, respect me by at least calling me Oliver, ya hear me?"

"Vampires hear quite well, actually," I replied, giving him a sideways glance while I looked over my list of duties for the day. "Oliver, does this say tree removal?"

"Now 'bout that, you strong enough to knock down some trees?"

"Yes sir," I laughed.

Oliver got up from his stool and pulled some bacon from his refrigerator. I had to admit, I had never met someone who loved pork as much as Oliver Morgan. As he began frying the bacon, I heard Brianna come through the living room and pad up beside me. I looked over at her and noticed she was extremely pale.

"I thought you were sleeping in."

"I couldn't get back to sleep," she said while looking over Oliver's list. "Are you tearing down trees today?" She tried to say it jokingly but what little color she had left in her face began to drain out of it.

I put my hand on her shoulder to ask her if she was feeling all right when Oliver turned from the stove and asked, "Mornin' 'Lil Bri, you gonna want some bacon?"

Suddenly Brianna's hand clamped down over her mouth as she turned to run out of the kitchen. Three steps out of the room Brianna froze and vomit splattered all over the floor. I rushed to her side and carried her to the bathroom. After placing her down in front of the toilet I stood behind her and swept her hair from her face.

She smacked my hand and yelled, "Get out!"

"Brianna let me..." but I did not finish before she was screaming at me again. Just then Oliver stepped into the room, grabbed my arm, and pulled me out before closing the door behind him.

"Son, it's been my experience that if a woman is pukin' and yellin' at ya to get out, it's best to do as she says. Come on now, let's give her some privacy," he said pulling me away from the bathroom door. "You grab some paper towels and I'll get the mop."

In a matter of minutes all evidence of Brianna's sickness was wiped away, and shortly after I heard her duck into her bedroom. I wanted to go to her, but Oliver's voice rang in my head telling me to give her some privacy. So instead, I walked back into the kitchen to discuss the day's activities with Oliver.

Twenty minutes later Oliver and I stood in the kitchen fixing a window that was loose in its track when Brianna came storming out of her room with a half-crazed look on her face.

"I need the keys to the SUV," she said holding out her hand. I stood frozen in the kitchen as I stared at a Brianna I had never seen before. "The keys, Cameron!"

I stumbled into the foyer and grabbed the keys from the small table by the door. "I should come with you..." I began but she took the keys out of my hand and ran out to the SUV in the driveway. I looked back to Oliver who simply shrugged. A second later Brianna ran back up the front porch steps and came stomping into the house.

"I forgot my friggin' purse," she said walking in the direction of her bedroom, but then turned quickly back around. "Christ, I don't have one. I don't even have any money! What am I going to do?"

Oliver and I stood in the archway between the kitchen and the foyer watching her pace back and forth. Dumbfounded and feeling completely useless, I pulled out my wallet and placed it in Brianna's hand. She looked at me for a moment, her eyes glazed with tears, but then rushed back out the door again and drove away. Oliver and I stood silent in the house for a few moments trying to make sense of what we had just witnessed, but after a while we concluded that some things were better left unexplained.

For the hour and a half that passed after Brianna's departure I fixed the window in the kitchen, replaced a few boards on the deck, and moved a large boulder from the backyard to the front. While Oliver and I were assessing what trees to remove in order to improve the view off the deck, I heard the SUV pull into the driveway. I turned to Oliver who gave me a disapproving look, but I fled to the house anyway.

Once inside, I heard Brianna moving around in the bathroom again, so I lightly rapped on the door. "Brianna?"

"Go away," she shouted, but then I heard her start to weep softly. "Please, Cam."

Her sad plea tore me apart, but I stepped away and slid down the wall next to the door. Through the wall I heard her puttering around, shower, brush her teeth, and then weep, again. I had never been affected by someone's tears as I was from Brianna's. It literally made me want to rip the door off its hinges.

Oliver came into the house a little while later and noticed me sitting on the floor. He laughed and stood over me with his arms crossed in front of his chest.

"Son, don't worry, she'll come out eventually. Hell, someone has to cook for us men," he said raising his eyebrows up and down.

"I heard that, you old coot," Brianna said as she opened the door and walked toward her bedroom. I quickly got up and followed her down the hall only to have the door shut in my face. For the first time since I had met her, I was angry with her, really angry with her. I was trying to care for her, and she slammed a door in my face. No one had ever slammed a door in my face and I could just as easily break it down and tell her to stop acting like a child.

"Oh okay, I know that look," Oliver said. "Ya know what the best cure for that is? Knockin' down trees."

Oliver pulled me away from the door and for the next four hours I cleared out three quarters of an acre of land. I pulled trees up by their roots, backfilled the holes, chopped all the trees into usable wood, stacked it on the side of the house, and burned the scraps. When I was done, I realized that Oliver was right, I was no longer angry. I was actually ashamed with myself. Brianna was obviously dealing with something that she wanted to handle on her own, and I needed to respect that. Even if it was against my nature.

When the last scraps of wood finally burned down to embers, I made my way back to the house. I looked down and noticed that my body and the work clothes Oliver had given me were caked with dirt and I smelled of smoke from the fire. I needed a shower. As I walked up the steep slope of the backyard, I noticed the sun going down behind the trees, illuminating the sky in bright oranges and pinks. It was a rare occasion where I actually took a moment and enjoyed such a beautiful sight.

I looked over at the house and noticed that the French doors to Brianna's room were open, which was a blessing since my bag was inside and I did not want to track all this dirt into the house. Bending my knees, I took an easy jump up to the balcony and knocked on the French door. "Brianna?"

She did not answer which meant she was either asleep or had left the room. I took off Oliver's old sneakers and shrugged out of the dirt encrusted shirt. Walking into the room I noticed my bag on the floor at the foot of the bed and knelt beside it to pull out clean clothes.

"Beautiful sunset, isn't it?" Brianna said quietly from the bed. She was curled up in a tight ball looking out at the majestic scene outside.

"You did not answer when I knocked, I thought you were asleep. I did not mean to bother you."

"You're not…um…is that a branch in your hair?"

I reached up and pulled a leafy twig from my hair, and thankfully we both laughed.

"Can I get you anything," I asked, not knowing what else to say. She shook her head no. "Will you join us for dinner?" She shook her head again and then began looking out the doors again so I took that as my cue to leave.

I showered and dressed into my favorite black designer jeans and V-neck shirt. I finally felt like myself again instead of some crazy vampire knocking down a forest. When I came out of the bathroom Brianna's door was still closed so I turned toward the living room. Oliver was busy in the kitchen making something that smelled utterly awful, unfortunately like most things he made.

"Dare I ask what you are making," I said as I entered the kitchen.

"Grilled bologna and cheese sandwiches, one a my favorites," he responded not turning away from his pan. "Since Bri's been ill today, I figured I'd cook tonight."

"Oliver, I am sorry to be the bearer of bad news, but Brianna will not be joining us tonight."

"Is she still feeling sickly?"

"I believe so. She is still in bed."

"Well then, we'll just have to make it a boys' night then. You play cards?" Oliver asked as he scooped up each sandwich and placed them on a plate.

"Yes sir, I do."

"Okay then, the cards are in the china cabinet drawer," he said as he put the plate of foul-smelling sandwiches down on the table and sat down. "I play gin, penny a point. Now don't you go usin' your Vamp psychic powers to cheat."

"You have nothing to fear, Oliver, I am not psychic," I replied and retrieved the playing cards.

"Well even better. Now I know you don't eat real food, but you have got to try one a these. Trust me, you'll never go back."

I gave him a quick laugh as I dealt the cards for our first game of gin.

"Speaking of," he began, "I've been meanin' to thank ya for the animal control." I gave him a slight nod, not truly wanting to admit to my hunting activities in his woods. "Ah, son, it's nothin' to be embarrassed about. I mean, we all gotta eat. You just like somethin' different, that's all."

And in that moment, I realized that Oliver Morgan had accepted me, somehow. And unfortunately for him I had made gin in three turns. Looking at my cards, and seeing the huge grin on his face, I could not help but let him win.

So I did, for seven hands. Finally, Oliver decided he had taken enough of my money and declared me the worst gin player ever, although I had gin for five out of seven hands. I reached back for my wallet and realized I had not retrieved it from Brianna.

Seeing me feel around my pockets Oliver said, "Don't worry about it, son, just buy somethin' nice for 'Lil Bri, like flowers, girls always like flowers."

"Yes sir, I will remember that. Speaking of your granddaughter, I am going to check on her."

"Why don't you take some a those crackers to her. I may even have some ginger ale in the pantry. That should help her stomach."

I looked around the pantry and located the ginger ale and the crackers and bid Oliver goodnight. Although depending on whether or not Brianna would let me sleep in her bed tonight, he may be seeing me on the couch shortly. I tapped lightly on the door and then let myself in. Brianna was nowhere to be found. Lifting my nose in the air I took a couple of whiffs and smelled Brianna's scent coming from outside. I placed the crackers and soda on the nightstand and walked out onto the balcony. I followed the balcony to the back of the house where it met the expansive back deck and found Brianna sitting with her knees to her chest, shivering while the moonlight reflected off her tear-stained face.

"Brianna, let me take you back inside," I said as I stood in front of her.

She looked up at me and stared for a moment before she said, "I'm sorry for yelling at you today."

Releasing a sigh through my smile I brushed her long bangs out of her face and said, "You are forgiven."

"I'm sorry I slammed the door in your face."

"Now I am afraid that will cost you," I teased.

"I guess I deserve that."

I knelt down in front of her and pulled her into my arms, rubbing her back to warm her. In her ear I whispered, "Please let me take you inside."

She nodded and in one movement I swept her up and carried her to her bedroom. I laid her on the bed and tucked the covers around her. Once I climbed up beside her, she rolled over and placed her head on my stomach and draped her arm across me. I could feel her tears soaking through my shirt as I squeezed her tightly and pleaded with her. "Please, Brianna, tell me what has you so upset. Whatever it is we can solve for it, I know we can."

She did not respond but merely cried harder. It had been a while since I had dealt with a crying woman, apparently I was severely out of practice. Finally, her sobs died down and she began to speak.

"Cam, I just don't know what to…"

When she broke down again, I began brushing her hair with my fingers to get her to relax enough to finish her statement.

She took a few more pain staking moments before she said, "I'm pregnant."

Admittedly, I had not been prepared for that, although now it made sense.

"Are you sure?" I asked.

"I took a test, it was positive. With everything that's happened I didn't even notice I'd missed my…," and then she fell silent for a brief moment before she continued, "It must have happened the night Sam…"

She did not finish her statement and once again broke down. But I knew what she had meant to say, the night that Sam had attacked her. The night I stood outside like a coward and watched it happen to her, and now I had to watch it happen to her again. For the remainder of the night, I comforted Brianna, but cursed myself since this was as much my fault as Sam's. But unlike Sam I would do whatever it took to get her through this, and if it meant ruining every one of my three hundred-dollar shirts, then so be it.

Chapter Eighteen

Brianna

Cameron's arms were around me tightly as we kissed each other passionately in the rain. We were both soaked through and his wet shirt clung to his well-defined abs. While he held me, I traced my fingers along the grooves in his chest and stomach wanting desperately to reach underneath his shirt. Cameron released my mouth and began giving me soft gentle kisses down my neck and shoulders. With a deep breath of pleasure, I tilted my head up to the sky, and began to get pelted with raindrops in my eyes and mouth.

Not quite as romantic as it seemed in movies.

Cameron took my wet face into his hands and began kissing me again as though a new fire had been lit within him.

"Bri Bri!" a man yelled behind me.

I quickly broke from Cameron and turned to see Sam standing on the front porch of my grandfather's house.

"Bri Bri, you stupid woman, get those babies into the house," Sam yelled as his face turned a scarlet red.

I was kissing another man, and all he cared about was getting the babies inside?

Wait, what babies?

I looked down at myself, unsure how I hadn't realized that I was extremely pregnant. I stood shivering in the rain looking from my stomach to Sam and then to Cameron, whose fangs were extended. Sam swept his leg over the porch railing and leapt to the ground. Before I knew it Cameron had Sam up against the porch and bit his neck viciously, blood spurting everywhere. Just then, Sam reached behind him and pulled out a silver knife and stabbed Cameron in the back. Cameron howled and hit Sam square across the face and then reached back to pull the silver knife out of his back, burning his hand in the process.

The rain began to pound harder against my face, making it difficult to keep my eyes open enough to see what was happening. I was able to make out Sam slowly pulling himself up to a kneeling position while Cameron walked slowly toward him. Cameron placed his hands on either side of Sam's head and easily snapped his neck...

With a gasp I opened my eyes, completely confused by my surroundings. I was lying down on my stomach at the foot of the bed and staring out my French doors as the rain from a heavy storm blew in and hit me in the face. Well that explained why the rain in my dream felt so real. It was a little after five o'clock which meant I had slept for almost three hours, but that was pretty normal this past week. Sleep, puke, sleep, puke, puke, sleep, puke, puke, puke. I had never had morning sickness this bad before, but considering how my life had been going lately, I really wasn't surprised.

Reluctantly I sat up and pulled my shirt over my head to wipe my face and neck dry, although my hair was still damp and sticking to my face. I stood slowly, steadying myself with one hand on the wall waiting for any nausea to appear, but thankfully none came. Opening my closet, I pulled out another one of the cheap T-shirts Cameron had purchased from the thrift store after I vomited on a couple of the nice ones he had bought me weeks before.

Ah, Cameron. The poor man, vampire, whatever he was, he was an angel. When he saw the color drain from my face he would rush me into the bathroom, or carry me back to the bedroom if I felt too weak to walk. Then I discovered that his cool skin was perfect to lay my cheek on to help the nausea pass. Again, an angel.

It was obvious to both of us that we had feelings for each other, although we never expressed them verbally, at least not yet. I was nervous to say anything, afraid that he would reject me or tell me that Gatherers and hybrids weren't allowed to be together. So instead of bringing my fears to light, I just ignored them, like any good Southern girl would do.

Before leaving the room, I put on a pair of soft socks and caught a look at myself in the full-length mirror on the bedroom door. I officially looked like crap, really frumpy crap, but then I didn't really care. All I really cared about at this moment was eating dinner *and* keeping it down, which I had only done once this week. Morning sickness, ha! All-day all-night sickness was more like it.

I opened the door and padded down the hallway, hearing the sounds of Daddy O and Cameron debating and laughing about something, though I didn't strain to hear what it was. They had really grown to like each other and I couldn't be happier. Daddy O deserved a good son-in-law and neither my mother nor I had ever provided one. So to make up for it, I gave him a vampire instead.

Cameron turned around on his stool as I walked into the kitchen.

"How was your nap?" he asked softly, placing the back of his cool hand on my cheek.

"Weird dreams again, but you can keep your hand there, that feels nice," I said, closing my eyes and breathing deeply through my mouth to keep my nausea at bay from the smells of whatever Daddy O was trying to cook.

"Well hey there, Pukey McGee," my grandfather said, flashing me a very bright smile.

"It wasn't funny when you called me that yesterday either, Daddy O. What are you making? It smells like, I don't know, warm paste," I said as I wrinkled my nose and turned my face away from the direction of the stove.

"It's just some Cream of Chicken soup."

He took the pot of creamy hot soup and began pouring it into a bowl located only a foot away from me. Even the sight made me ill.

"Good grief that looks like snot. I need to leave or else I'm gonna lose it all over the floor again."

I walked out of the kitchen and into the living room thinking if that was dinner then I was going to starve. I sat in Daddy O's recliner since it was in front of the open windows, enjoying the nice cool breeze on my face as it brought in the smell of fresh rain. A few minutes later Cameron came into the room with a roll wrapped in a napkin and a small glass of ginger ale.

"Thank you," I said, "I just can't watch him eat that stuff."

"Your color does look better than earlier today."

"Well considering I threw up everything including my toenails, you'd think there wasn't much left." I took a sip of the soda and turned the TV on to watch the news.

"Brianna, may I ask why your hair is wet?"

"Oh crap! I forgot to close my doors, there's water all over the floor," I stammered as I tried to get out of my chair, but then was hit by a sudden rush of blood to my head. Cameron caught my arm and lowered me back into the chair.

"Just rest, I will take care of it," he said as he turned and walked toward the bathroom for a towel.

"Angel," I whispered underneath my breath.

"Hardly," he replied, keeping his back turned to me.

"You're allowed to be wrong," I muttered and heard his laughter coming from the bathroom.

The rest of the evening went by torturously slow. Both Daddy O and Cameron read in the living room while I incessantly flipped through the channels. I came across a bad action film that I'd seen a dozen times and decided it was the best of the worst. I was only half paying attention when the title character was stabbed by the villain in the final fight of good versus evil, blah, blah, blah. Not sure why, but seeing the stabbing made me recall the story Daddy O had told me about when I was five. Not sure why I didn't think about it before, but a strange thought popped in my head. "Where did I get that knife from?"

Both men looked up at me confused, having no idea what I was talking about.

"When I killed that vampire, where did the knife come from?" I asked. "I couldn't have had time to go inside and get it. So where did it come from?"

Daddy O blinked at me several times while he tried to work through the answer himself. "I don't know, ya must a brought it out with ya earlier."

"But why? I knew better than to play with Mama Jo's silver, let alone a big knife. One of you would have seen me playing with it if I'd brought it out with me, right?" Daddy O didn't answer me, but Cameron looked at me with concern in his eyes. "Is that all you need to do to kill a vampire, stab him in the back?"

Cameron took a breath and explained, "First of all, his reaction was not to being stabbed, it was by being stabbed with silver. It is one of our only weaknesses, but it generally does not kill us unless you stab us through the heart or sever the head from the body. My guess is that he Projected away, but only once the knife was removed. A vampire cannot Project while silver is in the body."

"Okay, but how did I know? Of all the knives I could have grabbed from the kitchen, my five-year-old little self decided to sneak into the china cabinet, pull out the silverware case, and look for the biggest knife I could find, the only thing, by the way, that could hurt a vampire that might decide to come into my yard that day."

The three of us sat in silence as we pondered the coincidences, trying to make sense out of them. Daddy O finally broke the silence with, "What brought this on, sugar?"

"I...I don't know." The dream? The movie? I truly didn't know. "I'm going for a walk," I said as I got up slowly from the recliner and headed to the front door where my sneakers sat. While I knelt and laced my shoes, Cameron's came toe to toe with mine.

I stood up straight, coming eye to chest with him, boy he was tall. He took my hand and asked, "May I join you?"

"Duh," I replied, rolling my eyes and laughing as I pulled him out the door. The rain had stopped only minutes before, leaving the humid smell of wet asphalt behind. I stopped and took in a deep breath. No nausea. That was a good sign.

We walked in silence down the hill, although my mind was racing with half a dozen things. The evening was dark from the hovering storm clouds, but the road shimmered where the moon peeked through the clouds. It was a beautiful night, but there were too many things going through my head and it was hard to sort them out.

Once we got to the bottom of the hill, I turned around to start heading back up but was stopped when Cameron pulled my hand.

"Please tell me what is bothering you. I can see every thought pass over your face, yet you keep it within yourself. Just tell me what you are thinking about."

"Everything," I answered, dropping my head with a big sigh. Cameron lifted my chin and raised his eyebrows urging me to continue. "There's just so much going on that it's all running together. I'm worried that Sam is going to find me, which then makes me think about being pregnant, which just makes me cry, then I think of all the other times I've been pregnant and how they all ended in miscarriages, which then makes me wonder if it could be because I'm a hybrid, which means I'll never have a baby which tears me apart but then I think what if for some reason this baby lives, I couldn't raise it in the hybrid hotel or whatever you call it, which then makes me worry about not going to San Francisco since you've told me that other hybrids are being killed, so then I think I've made my decision to go and then I worry if I'll ever see you again, or my family, and then I get freaked out that I'm going to turn into some brainwashed pregnant hybrid thing who's locked away for her whole life, but then I think that I would at least be protected from Sam, and then the whole cycle starts over again." I finished and took a needed breath. "Now aren't you glad you asked?"

Cameron remained silent for a few moments while he recovered from my diarrhea of the mouth. Needing to keep moving, I started up the hill by myself but heard Cameron's soft footsteps behind me.

"Shall we take each item individually?"

I turned around to face him, but continued to walk backwards up the hill. "You got all that?" I asked skeptically.

"Item one, you are worried that Sam will find you. Answer, I have someone tracking him. So if he leaves Connecticut, we will know."

I opened my mouth, but was utterly speechless. He was tracking Sam? Taking my hand, Cameron led me up the hill and continued to break down each aspect of my rant.

"Item two, yes you are pregnant, and although the father of your child is, pardon me, a bastard, you are still holding a miracle inside of you. And know that I will do anything you need me to do in order to take care of you and your child. Item three," he lowered his voice slightly, "I am sorry that you have miscarried. Losing a child can be devastating for anyone, but I do not believe it is because you are a hybrid. Which brings me to item four, there are many hybrids that have children, with vampires and with humans. Although I will research to see if there is a higher rate of loss for hybrid-human pregnancies. Item five, if you do carry your child to term, we can make arrangements for you to be able to raise the child at the Facility."

By this time we were almost back to the house and I was still amazed at the fact that Cameron had somehow organized my off the wall ranting into complete thoughts and had come up with solutions at the same time. Once at the house, Cameron stopped and pulled me to stand in front of him while he continued, "Item six, you are worried about not going to San Francisco. Honestly, it is the safest place for you, as it is for most hybrids right now. You need to understand that hybrids like you are being found dead, and we have not been able to stop it yet, but we will.

"Item seven, you are worried about not seeing your family. I am sorry to say that your visits with your family will be limited, if at all, until we can control whoever is hunting the hybrids. And lastly, I assure you that you will not be brainwashed, but you could be living at the Facility for some time."

"What about you?"

"What about me?"

"Will I see you again once I'm in San Francisco?"

Cameron dropped his gaze. "I do not know."

I bit my lip to stop myself from crying, but it was difficult acknowledging my fear of losing him. Not knowing what else to say, I stood on my toes and reached around his neck, giving him a hug while breathing in his wonderful autumn-like scent. He returned the gesture and bowed his head on my shoulder while his arms completely surrounded me.

We stood in our embrace in silence, neither one of us wanting to let go. After several minutes Cameron raised his head and began searching my face with his dark black eyes. His left hand caressed my forehead and cheek as he leaned his face closer. I closed my eyes just as I felt his cool lips gently rest on mine. They were so soft and he was so gentle. Pulling his arm from around my waist he took my face between his hands and kissed me again, this time a little harder with his mouth slightly open.

"Well, well, what have we got here?" a woman's voice said from behind me. I felt Cameron tense and break away quickly as he pushed me behind him. Standing in front of us where the driveway met the road was a tall and very slender woman with straight black hair down to her waist dressed in an extremely tight and revealing black patent leather jumpsuit.

"Brianna, I would like to introduce you to my sister, Jazlyn," Cameron said through clenched teeth.

"So this is the Brianna everyone's talking about. This is who you lost the bet for?" she said with a disgusted look on her face while she eyed me up and down.

I so wanted to tell this bitch off, but then I realized I did look like crap. My hair was barely brushed and I was wearing pajama pants and a cheap T-shirt. But then what she said hit me.

"What bet?"

"Yes, speaking of Cameron, where's my car?" Jazlyn asked looking around the driveway.

Cameron began laughing hysterically and in one movement picked me up and ran me into the house. As the door closed behind us, I looked out to see Jazlyn stamping her feet around the driveway and screaming profanities at Cameron. They really were like brother and sister.

Chapter Nineteen

Brianna

While Jazlyn sulked outside, I ran to my bedroom, changed my clothes, brushed my hair, and even put on a little make-up while Cameron stifled his laughter and told me not to bother. Boys! Stupid, stupid boys! They just didn't understand. When you were about to be in the same room as an extremely beautiful, scantily-clad woman, you freshened yourself up. There was no way I could compete, but I wasn't about to lie down in front of her looking like a dead dog.

Once Jazlyn had calmed down, Cameron allowed her to come into the house, with Daddy O's permission of course. Standing next to each other, Cameron and Jazlyn truly could have been siblings with their jet-black hair, black eyes, and sheer height. Jazlyn's slender legs were almost as long as I was tall. Her voice was thick and sexy, but overall snotty. After general introductions, and after Daddy O could close his slack jaw, Cameron started right in.

"Jazlyn, how did you get here?"

"I drove," Jazlyn responded as she fell onto the couch and put her feet up on the armrest.

"Yes, I assumed so, but where is your car now?"

"Yeah, how'd ya get past the boys? They woulda called on the radio if they saw ya comin'," Daddy O said, suddenly worried that something had happened to his boys.

"Are you speaking of those hillbilly redneck swine who thought they could prevent me from turning on your street?"

"Yup, that'd probably be them."

"Jazlyn, what have you done?"

"Nothing!" she snapped like a spoiled child and sat up on the couch. "I'm offended by the accusation."

Jazlyn turned and put her feet down on the floor, crossed her arms, and actually pouted. Cameron changed his approach with her so naturally that it appeared he'd had to do this before, many times.

"Sister," Cameron said, "please forgive me. I know that you would only harm someone in self-defense. So I am merely asking if you needed to defend yourself when you met those men."

"Your boys," Jazlyn said, directing her statement to Daddy O, "stopped my car and began asking me where I was going. I simply Glamoured them into letting me pass and gave them my car as a bonus since I no longer needed it. That is until now," she finished and gave Cameron a murderous glare.

"But they're okay?" Daddy O asked.

"Yes, they're fine. Better even since they have a car that costs more than all of theirs put together, including the rusted-out ones in the yard. Since I have to get it back now, I guess I'll have to give them another visit. I need to eat anyway," Jazlyn said as she climbed over the back of the couch.

On her descent, Cameron thrust himself forward and launched her across the foyer causing her to slam against the corner of the kitchen's archway. Within seconds she was up and both vampires crouched into defensive postures, fangs exposed.

"You will NOT feed on any human in this area, do you understand," Cameron growled.

"I'm not sure who you think you are spouting orders to me, Brother. You don't have Father's power behind you since you took a pet," Jazlyn spat back, flinching her head in my direction. "I'm surprised he's spared your life for this long. If it had been anyone else, Devin would have been on your doorstep weeks ago."

Cameron moved in Jazlyn's direction as she crouched further in her stance, and then I did the stupidest thing a human could do, I stepped in between them.

"Stop! Stop," I said trying to get Cameron to look at me, but he wouldn't take his eyes off of Jazlyn. I pushed him hard in the chest and he shifted his attention from Jazlyn to me, but continued to glance back and forth between us. "Cameron, are you in some kind of trouble? Because of me?"

Cameron looked down at me with sad eyes unable to find the words he needed. But his gaze shifted quickly as Jazlyn began laughing mockingly behind us.

"You haven't told her," Jazlyn's sultry voice said through her laughter.

"Told me what?"

Jazlyn walked seductively to Daddy O and rested her elbow on his shoulder as she began playing with the thin gray hair on top of his head. I flailed my body in her direction, but Cameron caught both my arms and held me in place.

"Jazlyn," he said sternly, "you need to stop."

"Oh but Cameron, I have just begun," Jazlyn responded, flashing a brilliant white smile as her fangs retracted. "You see, Brianna, you were supposed to be in San Francisco over a month ago. Our father and your father demanded that Cameron be sent to gather you because they were under the impression that he was the best." Jazlyn let go of Daddy O and walked over to where Cameron and I were standing and pouted mockingly. "Sadly, they were mistaken. When Cameron couldn't produce you right away, our father became extremely angry. And when Victor becomes angry, people usually die. But that's where Cameron is lucky because Father has always shown him preference and leniency. Of course that was up until a few weeks ago."

"Jazlyn, enough," Cameron said as he pulled my arm to lead me away.

I planted my feet and slid my arm from his grasp. "What happened a few weeks ago?"

But Cameron didn't answer. Jazlyn came up behind me and placed her cold cheek up against mine as she whispered quietly, "You see, Cameron's very presence here is in violation of Victor's direct orders. His defiance of our father has sent ripples through our coven. Every day that Cameron remains here with you brings him closer to certain execution, and it's all because he can't bear to leave your precious, pitiful, breakable side."

As Jazlyn spoke, hot tears ran down my face. I was fearful of Jazlyn, angry at Cameron, and furious at myself for being selfish and foolish. Anger and panic grew from deep within my stomach, and I stormed down the hall to my bedroom. The room was stuffy and humid from having the French doors closed all evening, so I opened them to let the cool night air in. Seconds later Cameron walked into the room and closed the door behind him. I could feel his stare bearing down on me, but I didn't turn around.

"Why did you lie to me?"

"I did not lie."

Flabbergasted by his response, I spun around to face him. "But you didn't tell me the truth either. You let me assume everything was okay, and that I had all this time with you while I figured things out. All the while your father is planning on having you killed because of a choice I made. Why didn't you trust me? I would have understood. I would have stopped being selfish and done whatever you needed me to do. What must your family think of me?"

Cameron took a moment before he answered, crossing his arms in front of his chest. "First of all, I could care less what my family thinks. Your needs are none of their concern, and you are not being selfish."

"What about Victor?"

"Yes, my father is very angry with me. I was already delayed in getting you to the Facility, and he felt that my time may have been better spent gathering other hybrids while you recovered." Cameron's arms fell to his side as he stepped toward me. "I disagreed with him which is something he is not used to, and he is very angry and hurt at my defiance."

"So angry that he'll have you killed," I said as I sat on the corner of the bed and hugged my knees to my chest.

Cameron knelt in front of me and placed his hands around my ankles. "Victor is impulsive, and it is true that many vampires have been killed because they disobeyed him. But if my father wanted me killed, I would be dead already." Cameron took a pause before he continued, "When I first saw Jazlyn, I thought she was here to do exactly that, although I do not completely trust that she is only here to collect on our wager. But please, Brianna, let me worry about Victor and Jazlyn. I could not bear if you were to make yourself sick worrying."

I took Cameron's hand and pulled it up to my face, feeling the oncoming nausea. "She doesn't like me very much," I said, sinking my cheek into the coolness of his hand.

"Jazlyn does not like anyone, and most people do not like her," Cameron said with a sly smile.

"I can hear you, Cameron," Jazlyn yelled from the living room.

The two of us laughed lightly and I let my legs fall to the floor as I put my arms around Cameron's neck. "Please don't keep me in the dark like this again. I hate feeling like the only idiot in the room who doesn't know what's going on."

"I promise. Now I need to take Jazlyn hunting and make sure she behaves herself. Will you promise to get some rest?" I nodded. "That's my angel."

I smiled back at him since I'd always thought he was *my* angel. Holding my face with one hand he kissed me gently on the lips and then kissed my forehead as he rose and left the room. I got up from my bed, walked out my French doors, and sat on the floor of the balcony staring up at the stars as if they held the answers that I needed. Cameron told me not to worry, but how could I not? I was so conflicted with what I needed to do and what I wanted to do. I closed my eyes, enjoying the cool breeze that swept across the house, and tried to organize my thoughts. It was time to decide what the hell I was going to do.

Chapter Twenty

Cameron

If I could fly, I would have. I had kissed Brianna and it was...perfect. She did not pull away, more the opposite really. Sadly, Jazlyn's interruption and continued presence was not something I particularly enjoyed. Within the last hour Brianna and I had our first kiss, first meeting of a family member, first fight, and first make-up. The whole situation was a complete roller coaster making it difficult to stay focused. I needed to watch Jazlyn closely, not only because she might turn around and kill me, but because she might turn around and kill someone else.

When I reached the living room Jazlyn was lying on the couch again with her feet up on the armrest which I could see irritated Oliver, but he remained quietly seated in his recliner holding a silver tray across his chest. I raised my eyebrow at him, and he simply shrugged. I supposed he felt he needed some kind of armor while alone with Jazlyn, and honestly, I did not blame him.

"Jazlyn," I said firmly, "I will show you where to hunt."

Jazlyn shifted her feet to the floor and stood with a pout. "But I hate animal blood. Why do I have to suffer just because you've made up some stupid rule?"

"Either you hunt with me now, or I watch your every move and prevent you from hunting altogether," I said, looking her directly in the eye. She knew I was stronger, and rarely wished to test it. Jazlyn stamped her foot on the floor and stormed out of the house. I gave a quick nod to Oliver who waved back, still holding his protective tray in front of him. Unable to wipe the smile off my face at Oliver's makeshift armor, I stepped outside to Jazlyn's fury.

"What are you so happy about?" she asked as she followed me to the woods on the side of the house.

"Nothing I care to share with you," I replied breaking out in a run with her close behind me. It felt good to really stretch my legs, but with Brianna so sick lately I did not dare to go too far.

Within a few minutes Jazlyn and I had run about ten miles deep when we came across a herd of deer. Having each overtaken two, we were as satisfied as a vampire could be on animal blood and we began the journey back to the house, however at a slower pace.

"Jazlyn," I said, slowing down enough to where we could run side by side, "did Father send you for me."

An emotion crossed her face that I could not quite place, but then she answered, "No, he didn't."

"Has he sent anyone else?"

"Not that I know of, but you know Victor doesn't tell me much of anything."

"Yes, but that is probably because every conversation turns into an argument. You know you provoke him on purpose."

"Only because he deserves it," Jazlyn replied just as the house came back into view. "By the way, don't think I've forgotten about what you owe me. Just have Jared transfer the money into my account, but I need to think about what to do about the car. I cannot believe you traded the Vanquish for this piece of shit truck."

"It is not a piece of shit, besides, the car was ruined anyway. With the money you can buy yourself a brand new one."

"That is not the point! And what do you mean ruined?"

I did not get to answer her because as we came in front of the house, Oliver came running out the door. I closed the distance between us quickly seeing that he was breathing hard and I could smell the panic rolling off of him.

"Is Brianna all right?"

"Yes," he replied, trying to catch his breath. "I just got a call," he stopped to catch his breath again, "Sam, Sam is coming."

"Sam is coming here?" But how can that be? Jared was tracking his activity. He would have called if Sam's credit cards showed any movement outside of Connecticut. "Oliver, are you sure? How do you know he is coming here?"

"His name came across the caller ID, and all he said was 'just checking' and hung up. He's comin' to get her, I just know it. Son, you gotta stop him, he'll kill'er."

"Oliver, just calm down. He could be anywhere," I said, but at that moment the two-way radio crackled to life inside the house. I cursed under my breath as I heard someone come on the radio stating that a white SUV was blazing up the street and heading toward Oliver's hill. Oliver did not seem to hear the radio from his position outside, but Jazlyn had and came to stand next to me.

"Oliver, go back inside. Jazlyn, come with me, we need to make sure he does not get up to the house." I began to walk away but noticed that Oliver was still frozen in place. "Oliver," I said shaking him gently. "He will not get to Brianna, I promise you that. Now get inside."

Oliver suddenly grabbed my arm and looked at me with an intensity and anger I had never seen in him. "Son, just be careful. These roads up here are so steep and curvy that someone could just drive right off if you don't know 'em. And the rhododendron thickets are so dense people may never find ya. A course that's if the animals don't getcha first. Ya hear me?"

"Quite well," I replied, completely understanding his hidden message. I pushed him in the direction of the house and ran down the road with Jazlyn in tow.

"Cameron, what are we doing?"

"It's Brianna's husband."

"So?"

"So, he has either come to take her back home, or to kill her. Most likely the latter."

"Didn't Father tell you not to interfere?"

"Yes Jazlyn, Father told me a lot of things. If it means saving Brianna's life, then let Victor kill me for interfering." Suddenly the bright headlights of the white SUV came into view from around a tight turn more than a mile down the road. "Climb up onto the rocks, I will stay on the road and stop the truck. Then, you jump on the roof and make sure he does not escape."

Jazlyn nodded and began her climb up the steep mountain rock that the road had been carved into. A minute later, the large white SUV came barreling around the curve and slammed right into me, pushing me back a few feet as I held onto the front grill. The airbags deployed and hit the driver in the chest, blocking my view of his face. Jazlyn jumped down onto the roof of the truck as I walked around to the driver's side and ripped the door off. While the airbag deflated, the driver's face came into view. Even through the healed-over bruises I could tell it was Sam.

"So? Is it him?" Jazlyn asked peering into the cabin upside down.

"Yes it is."

"Are you just going to stand there and give him dirty looks, or are you actually going to do something. Otherwise, I'm going back to the house."

Taking her cue, I grabbed Sam's collar and pulled him out of the car throwing him down on the ground in front of the headlights that still illuminated the road. The impact from the ground woke Sam up from the dizzying state he was in, and as I walked toward him, he looked up at me with fear and recognition in his eyes.

"So you do remember me," I growled.

Sam began pushing himself away from me and clumsily pulled a small caliber handgun from within his waistband.

"Stay away from me," he said as the gun shook in his hand.

"Not a chance," I replied, taking another step toward him and causing him to pull the trigger. I moved slightly to my left to dodge the bullet, not daring to take my eyes off of him.

From behind me I heard Jazlyn gasp. "He did not just shoot me," she said jumping down from the roof of the car. "I just bought this outfit, and look, now there's a hole. Ok, now I'm pissed."

I looked back to see Jazlyn examining the hole in her jumpsuit.

"Are you going to live?" I asked condescendingly.

"Very funny. Of course I will, but he may not," she said turning her glare to Sam who continued to pull himself down the road.

"Sorry to tell you, Samuel Lewis, you have officially pissed off not one, but two, extremely lethal vampires."

Sam froze and I grabbed him by his leg and pulled him down the street, his screams of agony giving me great pleasure. I picked him up by his neck and slammed him up against the high rock ridge that lined the road. Sam's faced turned purple from the lack of oxygen so I softened my grip slightly since I did not want him to die so easily.

"From what I was told, you dragged Brianna down the driveway quite similar to that, did you not?" Sam did not answer, mostly likely because he could barely breathe, but his expression gave him away. "And from what I witnessed personally, you choked her like I am doing to you now, and then you punched her in the gut," I said and then jammed my fist into his stomach. Sam folded over and I let him fall to the ground. I picked him up and threw him into the side of the SUV, and before he could fall again, I picked him up by his throat and held him upright. "Then you violated her, you piece of shit, and for that you deserve every ounce of pain I give you. Jazlyn, would you like to show him what happens to rapists?"

Jazlyn stepped forward with her sinister smile, grabbed Sam's testicles, and squeezed while I clamped down on his mouth to muffle his screams.

"Do you want me to rip them off? It's no more than he deserves," Jazlyn asked as she held and twisted Sam's manhood in her hand.

I paused to think about what he deserved versus what would look like an accident. "Jazlyn, you can let go." Reluctantly she released her grip on him and I allowed him to slump to the ground. I knelt down and turned his face to see mine. "Did you come here to take Brianna, or to kill her?"

"Fuck you," Sam answered with labored breath.

I took Sam's chin in between my fingers and pulled him up to a kneeling position. "I will ask you again, did you come to take her, or kill her?"

"I should've killed the whore years ago," he said and then spit in my face. In one brief moment I twisted Sam's neck from one side to the other, breaking it cleanly. His lifeless body fell to my feet as I stood and wiped my face of his filth.

Though I was a vampire and a Warrior, I did not thrive on taking the lives of others, even when it was someone like Sam. I had let my anger for him and my love for Brianna cloud my judgment, but I was willing to accept the consequences of my actions if it meant Brianna would be safe from Sam for the rest of her life. Using that reasoning as my justification, I snapped into survival mode. There was cleanup that needed to be done, and I needed to get Brianna out of here before any authorities came looking for Sam.

"Jazlyn, you take the body, and I will throw the SUV over the ridge. Oliver said there are rhododendron thickets all over here so hide the truck and body within them. Make it look like an accident, but leave the body exposed for the animals. Then go visit those men at the bottom of the main hill, Glamour them to forget they ever saw the white SUV, get your car, and get out of here."

"I am not your errand girl, and I am not about to clean up your mess," Jazlyn shouted, not moving a muscle.

"Jazlyn, please, just once try and think of someone other than yourself. I need to get to Brianna. She cannot know about this." Jazlyn stayed in her position and began tapping her foot, waiting for me to give her a reason to help me. "Fine, I will buy myself the most expensive car I can find, fall in love with it, and then you can take it from me. How does that sound? I will even draw tears."

"Deal," she responded as she picked up Sam's body and threw it over the ridge. I pushed the SUV sideways to the edge of the ridge and then tipped it over, letting it roll down the mountainside. Jazlyn agreed to do the rest of the work and I made my way back up to the house.

As I walked up the front porch steps, I could see Oliver sitting on his usual stool in the kitchen, though he stood when he heard the screen door shut behind me.

"Did you find 'im?" Oliver asked gravely.

"Yes. He is no longer a threat." Oliver nodded slightly, not wanting to know any details. "Oliver, I will need to take Brianna out of here sometime tomorrow, though I am not sure how exactly I will accomplish that, but it must be done."

"Oh I expect you'll be leavin' a little sooner than that," he replied. I did not understand his meaning, and opened my mouth for him to explain, but he put his hands up to stop me. "Son, whenever it is you go, I just wancha to know that I will always be grateful for what you've done for my girl. Just take care a her, okay?" he said placing his hand on my shoulder and squeezing it.

"With my life, sir."

"Good, 'cause if you don't, I will hunt ya down. Ya hear?"

"Quite well, sir. Now Oliver, I hate to ask this of you, but if the authorities do begin to ask questions, I need you to be able to answer them with plausible deniability," I said as Oliver looked at me with confusion on his face. "I need to Glamour you. You cannot remember anything that has happened since you got that call from Sam. It puts all of us at risk. And I...I need you to be safe since I will not be here to help you."

"Son, do whatcha need to do, just don't make me come out a this crawlin' around like a dog or somethin'."

"Sir, I have the upmost respect for you, I would never do such a thing..."

"Cameron, I know," Oliver replied, squeezing my shoulder again. "I have the same kinda respect for you, son. Why do you think I call you that? It's not 'cause I'm some good ole boy. I call you that because I respect you and trust you. And if I coulda had a son myself, I'da been proud if he was half the man you are. Yur a good man, and I can tell you love my Bri somethin' fierce, otherwise you wouldn't be doin' all this for her. I trust you with my life, son, and if you need to do that Glamour thing then go on and do it."

Oliver's declaration left me speechless. He was the father that I missed, loving me for who I was, not my obedience. I extended my hand to him but he pulled me in, patting me on the back as he hugged me. When he pulled away, he told me he was ready, and I looked deeply into his eyes and pushed my will into his mind.

"Oliver Morgan, you did receive a call this evening from Sam Lewis, your granddaughter's estranged husband. However, you were left confused by his statement and hung up. He never arrived at your home, so you assumed he was playing some kind of trick. After the call you went to bed having been exhausted from seeing your granddaughter off earlier in the evening," I said, watching his eyes glaze over as his mind took in my Glamour. "You should go to bed now, Oliver."

With a distant gaze, he walked slowly to his bedroom, shutting the door behind him.

Now that Oliver was taken care of, I needed to figure out what to say to Brianna. She could never know about what I had done to Sam, but I needed to get her away from here without making her suspicious. I opened her bedroom door quietly and walked in to the sight of Brianna folding her clothes into a dark leather bag.

"Oh good, you're back. We need to go," she said as she turned into her closet and pulled a few more items.

"Brianna, why are you packing? Did something happen?"

"Well, you could say that, but there's no time to explain. Just trust me, okay?"

"Of course I trust you, but where are we going?"

"To San Francisco," she said and stopped to see my reaction.

"Are you sure?"

"Yes. I'm ready. I was going to pack your bag too, but you are so ridiculously neat that your stuff is ready to go. Seriously, it's a little freaky how tightly you can fold your shirts," Brianna said as she threw her leather bag over her shoulder and pushed her way to the bathroom. I grabbed my bag as well and followed, watching her throw her toiletries into her bag.

"Brianna, are you certain you want to leave right now? You should say goodbye to Oliver."

"I did already. Who do you think gave me the bag? Sorry, Cameron, we need to leave now," Brianna said pushing past me again and heading into the kitchen. She pulled out a plastic grocery bag from underneath the sink and began pulling crackers and other snacks from the pantry. "Do you have everything you need?" she said as she walked by me again, then stopped and turned to face me. "Did you roll around in the dirt or something?"

I looked down at myself for the first time since I had stepped into the house and noticed the dirt and dust covering my shirt and pants. "Sorry, big tussle in the woods."

"Huh, well I don't want to know. Hey, where's Jazlyn?"

"She had another hybrid case up in Virginia."

She nodded, turned, and then walked out the front door. I hurried after her, grabbed her bag from her shoulder, and placed it in the backseat with mine. Moments later we were backing out of the driveway.

"Take a right. I'm going to take you a back way out of here. We'll go a little further up the mountain and come down the west side to get us to the highway."

Not asking any questions I nodded and headed up the steep mountain road where the asphalt became thinner and the gravel thicker. Brianna directed me from one backwoods road to the next until we finally began winding down the backside of the mountain. I could tell from her body language that she was scared about something. When I asked her about it, she simply responded, "Later."

After twenty minutes of steep winding roads, I saw the state highway that would take us to the interstate we needed to head west. Once we turned off the mountain road, I glanced over to Brianna hoping she would finally tell me why we were apparently running away. But when I looked over, her head was tilted to the side, her eyes closed. The adrenaline she must have been running on finally caught up with her. That meant explanations would need to wait.

I looked down at the center console and found my phone where I had left it. I pressed the center button and told the phone to call Victor. After weeks of being angry with me, I was hoping that hearing the news that we were on our way would turn him around, although I knew there was only a slim chance at best.

After the fourth ring, the other side picked up, "Hello?"

"Devin?" I asked, not expecting to hear my brother's voice on Victor's phone. This could not be a good sign for me. Devin, my oldest and most lethal brother, was always sent to do Victor's dirty work, hence giving him the title Warrior Assassin. Although we were close as brothers, he would kill me if it were Victor's bidding.

"Yes, Brother."

"Is Father available?"

"Yes, but he sent me out to speak with you."

"That bad?"

"Yes, Brother."

"Tell Father we are leaving North Carolina now."

"It's about goddamn time. Let me know what flight number and I will have someone meet you at the airport."

"There is no flight, I have to drive her."

"Damn it, Brother, don't you understand the trouble you are in? You need to be here now! Not four days from now."

"I am fully aware of everything I have done, and almost as sure of what awaits me. But you need to trust me. You have known me for nearly three hundred years, have I ever done anything without reason? Whether it was to protect my family, or someone in need, I have always done what is right."

"Yes Brother, but...I just don't think you are thinking logically. You may be worried about this girl, but I am worried about you. Do not make me be the last face you ever see," Devin replied.

"I ask nothing of you but to tell Father I am bringing Brianna to San Francisco, and there are circumstances that are preventing her from flying. Whatever his decision is, so be it."

There was silence on the other line for several seconds while Devin contemplated the situation. "Just get here as fast as you can. I can only hold Father off for so long."

"Thank you, Brother," I said as I heard the other line click. Devin was angry, and rightfully so.

Another twenty minutes down the road and Brianna had not stirred from her position. She was sleeping so soundly that I did not dare touch her. The silence in the cabin was finally broken by the sound of my sister's ringtone.

"Yes Jazlyn?"

"Where the hell are you?" she replied. She was livid.

"We are on the road. I was not aware I needed to tell you."

"Yeah, it would have been nice. Where are you going?"

"Brianna has agreed to go to the Facility. She was actually waiting for me when I got back to the house, and insisted we leave right away."

"Oh for fuck sake, Cameron, you are a vampire. You couldn't convince her to wait until morning?"

"Jazlyn, why are you so angry that we left? This is good news. Besides, I told you to take off after you retrieved your car. It never occurred to me that you would want to come with us."

"Never mind. Everything else has been cleaned up. They'll never find him."

"Thank you, Jazlyn, I truly appreciate your help tonight."

"Screw you, you selfish prick." And for the second time in less than an hour I was hung up on.

Putting my phone down in the cup holder, I lifted the center arm rest and pulled the media cable out of the compartment and plugged my phone into the sound system. Scrolling through the gigabytes of music, I chose to listen to some classical music in order to relax and recover from the evening. Not two minutes into Beethoven's Pathetique in C minor, the music stopped to allow a call to come through. I was amazingly popular. I picked up the phone and was surprised that it was my brother Alexander.

"Alex?"

"Cameron, we've got trouble. Where are you?" my brother's deep voice rang in the phone.

"We just crossed into Tennessee, why?"

"We think Elaina is in North Carolina, and Jared just came across some reports of human attacks in Charlotte."

"Do you think Elaina is after Brianna?" I said looking over at the angel herself while she slept peacefully unaware of the mayhem we had just avoided.

"Cam, if Elaina is looking for her personally, you're both in real danger."

"What are you suggesting?"

"Activate the GPS in your phone, Jared will track you. We'll have the team flag any movement and sightings near or on your course."

"Make sure neither Devin nor Victor know that you are tracking me, otherwise this whole thing will blow up."

"You got it. Stay alert, Cam. The attacks are getting worse and more frequent. The teams can't even keep up."

"Will do. Is Jared with you?"

"Yes he is. I'll keep in touch," he said passing the phone to Jared.

"Hey bro," Jared's young voice said over the line, "what's up?"

"What happened with the track on Sam Lewis," I said quietly in the phone so that Brianna could not hear.

"What are you talking about? There's been no activity outside of Connecticut," Jared answered, his light-hearted tone changing into a defensive one.

"Considering he showed up at our door a couple of hours ago, I would say there is something wrong with your tracking system."

"Whoa whoa," he replied angrily, "it's called cash, bro. If he used cash, there's nothing I can do. He must have had it on him or buried in the backyard because he didn't even use his ATM card to withdrawal any money. If he had, I would have seen it."

Cash. In today's world where everyone used credit cards to make even a two dollar purchase it never occurred to me that Sam would have access to that much cash. But he was a banker, and if he needed to get a large sum of money, I am sure he would find a way. Plus, if he was planning on killing his wife, he would not want to leave a trail.

"Jared, I apologize. It has been an overwhelming evening. I never thought I would be glad to have Jazlyn around to help me."

"Jazlyn? What's she doing there?"

"Collecting on our wager supposedly."

"Huh, weird. But then again, she's a whack-job."

"I could not agree with you more, little brother."

"Oh, by the way. That whole camera thing, you're in luck. It was just a feed from the house to his office which means no tape, no vampire. So at least you're not in as deep shit as you thought."

Oh, but I was. "Thanks, Jared. Can you do me another favor?"

"Sure, I'll just put it on your tab."

"Trust me, by the end of this, I will be a homeless vampire having paid you so well," I said enjoying his laughter on the other line. "Brianna needs all new IDs – driver's license, social security card, credit cards, the works. And link the credit cards to my accounts."

"You got it, bro, I'll have them ready when you get here. You sure it's smart to give a chic access to that kind of money? She could do some damage."

"Jared…"

"Just warning you, bro. But don't worry, Alex and I will take care of you two. I promise."

"I know you will. Bye, Jared."

"Bye, big brother."

It was nice to end a conversation peacefully, although Alexander's message was not one I wanted to hear. Elaina could be on our trail as we speak. And if Elaina was looking for Brianna herself, she was desperate.

That only made my job of protecting her more difficult.

Brianna rolled over to her left side and began tilting the seat back. I was worried she had heard portions of my conversations, but her eyes were still closed seeming as though she was on unconscious autopilot. I took her hand gently and kissed the back of it. "Sleep, my angel."

Whether it was today or tomorrow, my deception would catch up to me, and she would be hurt. But all my intuitions were saying to keep Sam's death and Elaina's proximity secret from her at least for now. I would find a time to tell her. I had promised I would no longer keep her in the dark, but that was more difficult than I had imagined. I needed to concentrate on the long journey ahead of us. I turned my Beethoven back on, set the cruise control, and enjoyed the beautiful views around me as we cut our way through the Tennessee mountainside for what should be a smooth cross-country road trip. But as Brianna had told me before, I was allowed to be wrong.

Chapter Twenty-one

Brianna

I woke to the sound of rain hitting against the windshield with a soft but strong techno beat radiating throughout the truck. When I opened my eyes, I found Cameron bobbing his head to the beat, which made me laugh. When I had fallen asleep, he had been listening to classical music, and now it was techno. The man never ceased to amaze me. I uncurled myself in the seat and waited as the back of the chair rose into a straighter position. My entire body ached from sleeping in such a tangled position.

"Good morning," I said as I stretched my arms and back as much as I could. "Wow, is it really 7:00?"

"Yes it is. I am glad to see you were able to sleep as long as you did," Cameron said as he took my hand and kissed my fingers. "How are you feeling?"

"I just need to stretch my legs, and find a bathroom."

"We just passed a sign for a rest stop one mile ahead, will that suffice?"

"Anything will do at this point," I replied realizing I *really* needed to go to the bathroom. "Cameron, did that sign just say Memphis, twenty miles?"

"Yes, I believe so, why?"

"How fast were you driving?"

"You have been awake for two minutes, and you are already criticizing my driving?"

"I'm just saying that it won't help matters if we die in a car crash before we get to San Francisco."

"Brianna, I assure you that you are safe with me behind the wheel. You must remember that I have been driving since cars were invented," he said with his cute crooked smile. He did have a point.

"Okay, fine, but just don't drive that fast while I'm awake, and especially since it's raining."

"Of course, my love," he said as he pulled onto the off ramp for the rest stop.

Did he just call me his love? He did. He called me his love and I didn't know how to react to it. I felt so stupid, was I supposed to say something back? Sam had never used names of affection, and the ones I called him were always insincere. All of this was so new to me, and we were going a hundred miles an hour it seemed (literally in the car and figuratively in my heart). Pushing the thoughts out of my mind, I concentrated on the task at hand - getting to the bathroom without peeing my pants. Thankfully the rain let up slightly as I opened the door to the SUV and booked it to the bathroom before Cameron had even put the truck in park.

The rest stop was clean, but small, with only bathrooms and vending machines. I was starving, and if I didn't eat, I knew my morning sickness would be worse than usual. Once I'd finished my business, I stepped out of the stall only having to turn right back around and throw up. Thankfully no one else was in the bathroom to share in my humiliating moment. Once I was done, I sat back on the floor, propping myself up against the stall door. I knew it wasn't necessarily sanitary, but I really didn't care; I needed to calm myself down.

Why had I left Daddy O's? What made me think I could survive a cross-country trip? Idiot. If only I hadn't had that stupid dream with the beardless Jesus-looking guy. I'd dreamt about him before, and it was exactly like the last time. When Cameron had left to take Jazlyn hunting, I sat out on my balcony and closed my eyes for only a second, or so I thought when...

I was kneeling in Daddy O's front yard pruning the hydrangea bushes when I saw Cameron running up from the backyard yelling and pointing to something behind me, though I couldn't understand what he was saying. Following where he was pointing to, I turned around to see a vampire tearing at Daddy O's throat. I looked down at the ground and lying next to my feet was a long silver dagger with a curved handle that was intricately decorated with swirls of silver and pearl. Grabbing the dagger I threw it across the lawn, hitting the vampire square in the neck. He dropped Daddy

O's limp body on the ground as he fell backward writhing in pain while trying to pull the dagger out, but searing his hands on the silver handle instead.

I stepped over his body, grabbed the dagger out of his throat and cut his head clear off. I threw the head and the dagger on the ground and collapsed onto my grandfather's body sobbing uncontrollably into his blood-soaked shirt. Cameron's voice was in the distance calling my name and I looked up to see him struggling with five or six vampires while screaming at me to run. I turned to do what he asked but there stood what looked like fifty ragged, evil-looking vampires with drool and blood leaking from their mouths. Among them a woman with dark blonde hair twisted high on top of her head in a tight bun wearing an equally tight red leather vest and matching leather pants. The blonde woman began slowly walking toward me as Cameron's screams became louder. I grabbed the dagger from where I had thrown it on the ground and walked slowly toward her. As I drew my dagger back, the blonde took off in a run and as we collided the scene transitioned to the dark gray fluffy clouds I had seen in a past dream.

A black mist congealed in front of me creating the form of the familiar man with long brown hair, however this time in billowing black robes.

"You again?"

"Mia figlia, my Bri-an-na," the man said in his equally familiar thick Italian accent.

"Who are you? Why do you keep calling me that?"

"In good time, my darling, but I am here to tell you that danger is very close."

"Wha...what danger? Is someone after Cameron? Did Victor send someone to kill Cameron?"

"Not Cameron, my darling, you. Somehow our enemy has found you and they are coming, fast. You must leave now, or else the vision you saw will come to fruition."

"Vision, what do you mean vision? Are you talking about that crazy dream I just had? That was just nonsense."

"Bri-an-na, sometimes dreams are more than they seem, especially when you, mia figlia, are having them. Think of all you have dreamed about the last few months and look at all that has come true. You have a great gift that few have and will only be enhanced the longer you are around your own kind. But we must get you away safely."

"But if I leave, who's to say that still won't happen, and neither Cameron *nor I will be here to save my grandfather. Wouldn't it be better for us to stay and protect him?"*

"It has not been seen that way. If you stay, your grandfather will die. The only hope for you and your family is to leave."

"What do you mean, it has not been seen that way?" I yelled, but the gray smoke around me became thicker until both he and I were enveloped in it and I was forced to wake...

Even now as I sat on the floor of the restroom I was jolted by the sights and sounds of my memories. I had done what I was told to do by beardless Jesus, and I prayed that I had done the right thing. I would definitely be calling Daddy O as soon as I got back in the truck. He had refused to come with me and I couldn't even fathom losing Daddy O because of a choice I made based on a dream. Was beardless Jesus right though? Were my dreams more than just dreams? Only moments before I saw Cameron for the first time, I had dreamt about a vampire who looked just like him and then as the weeks went by his name came to me as well. And then just yesterday I dreamt that we kissed, and then we did. It was too much to be a coincidence, but also too farfetched to be real. Although I used to believe there were no such things as vampires, and look at how that worked out.

Just then another woman came into the restroom and tentatively knocked on my stall door. "Excuse me miss, are you Brianna?"

Getting up from the bathroom floor I slowly unlocked the stall door and opened it to see an elderly woman holding what looked like my leather bag.

"Yes ma'am, I am."

"Oh darlin', there is a worried young man out there waitin' for you. He asked me if I would bring this in to you, he thought you might want to freshen up."

I took the bag gratefully. "Thank you, ma'am. I'm fighting a little morning sickness today." Today? I laughed to myself.

"Well, we've all been there my dear. And may I say you've got a mighty fine-lookin' man out there. Your baby is sure to be just as blessed," the woman said as she stepped into another stall.

Awkward. Well, she was correct about one thing; Cameron was gorgeous. Only my baby would not be blessed with his good looks. I opened the leather bag and pulled out my toothbrush and toothpaste and began brushing as hard as I could to get the bile taste out of my mouth. While I brushed, I started thinking how different things would be if I were carrying Cameron's child instead of Sam's. Ha! Like that could ever happen.

I pulled out my hairbrush and began yanking it through the endless tangles in my hair. As I finished brushing, I nodded to the nice elderly woman as she left the restroom and minutes later, I left as well.

Cameron was pacing outside the bathroom entrance and had a look of relief when I stepped out. "Are you feeling better?"

"Yes, I'm fine, just the same old thing. Thanks for my bag."

"I was worried that something had happened when you did not come out."

"Sorry, I needed a few minutes to recover. By the way, I think I might have a little competition. I think that old lady has a crush on you."

"I did hear something about being 'mighty fine lookin',"" Cameron replied, trying his best at a Southern accent.

"Oh you heard that, did you? I see someone was eavesdropping while he was waiting."

"I was not," he replied, pretending to be offended. "I cannot help if my hearing is better than most."

I shook my head while he pulled me into his side and we ran into the storm to our SUV. Unfortunately, the rain had come back in force, and since there were people around, Cameron couldn't run the two of us at vampire speed. Therefore, we were soaked when we got into the truck causing us to laugh at one another while we tried to dry ourselves off with a few napkins that were stuffed in the glove box.

While I patted my forehead dry, I noticed that Cameron had become very quiet.

"Cameron? You okay?"

"Did her statement upset you?" Seeing that I wasn't sure what he was referring to he said, "When she inferred that the child was mine."

And in that moment, I saw a vulnerability that I had never seen in him.

"I was," I answered and Cameron's face fell slightly, "but only because I knew it wasn't true."

I reached up and touched Cameron's forehead lightly with my fingertips and then ran my fingers through his black wavy hair. His skin and hair were soft and smooth, though cool to the touch. I moved my fingers down his cheek and gently rubbed my finger along his soft lips where he kissed it gently. Leaning into him I combed my fingers into his hair again and kissed him. His lips felt and tasted like I remembered, his scent incredibly intoxicating. Cameron pressed into my lips a little harder and I opened my mouth to let his tongue inside. He placed one arm around my back while the other hand explored my face and neck, slightly tickling me at his gentle touch. Butterflies exploded in my stomach, along with my hormones, as our kiss became even more passionate. I started debating whether or not I could climb over the center console that was digging into my ribs, but then at that moment Cameron pulled away. Damn it.

Squeezing his eyes shut and breathing in deeply, I was glad to see I wasn't the only one who felt out of control.

"We should get back on the road," he said pulling my hands together and kissing the knuckles.

Reluctantly I nodded and settled back into my seat and buckled my seatbelt. As we made our way back onto the highway, I thought about all the things that my new mystery man had said in my dreams, debating whether or not I should believe him. But looking back at my dreams, not everything had come true. Cameron hadn't bit me on a terrace, Sam wasn't dead, and I wasn't pregnant with twins. Of course I couldn't be sure of the last one. Although, would that explain why I was so sick?

"Stop thinking, Brianna," I said, realizing too late that I had said it out loud. Cameron looked over at me. "Sorry, don't ask." So he didn't. Watching the trees and rain rush past me I couldn't get a thought out of my head. "Cam, what does *mia figlia* mean?"

Cameron looked oddly at me and then looked back at the road as he replied, "I believe it is Italian for, my daughter. Why do you ask?"

"Er, no reason," I replied, looking out the window to avoid his questioning eyes. You have got to be freaking kidding me.

Chapter Twenty-two

Brianna

"I'm sorry, I need a hotel," I said shifting in my seat for the one-hundredth-millionth time. We had been driving for almost eleven hours since we left the rest stop outside of Memphis. My back hurt, my knees hurt, and I could no longer feel my butt. I had even tried sleeping stretched out in the back seat, but I fell into the floor twice when I rolled over forgetting where I was. That was also when I learned that hitting a vampire for laughing at you actually hurt a great deal. Note to self.

"I was wondering how long you were going to last," Cameron said, giving me a charming smile.

We had passed through Amarillo a couple of hours ago, so the nicer hotels were long gone, but we were coming upon an exit that had a little mom and pop motel and I didn't want to be that picky but I at least wanted cable. As we pulled under the motel's vacancy sign and into the small driveway I whispered under my breath, "It's the Bates Motel."

"Nonsense. That was in Arizona," Cameron laughed as he stepped out of the SUV.

With the exception of the missing scary house on the hill, this was the Bates Motel's twin. I kept peering around seeing if Norman dressed in his mother's clothes would suddenly appear at my window. But instead, Cameron came out of the manager's office seemingly unscathed, and hopped back into the truck.

"Norman says hello," he said giving me his crooked smile and handing me two room keys. "He and Mother would like us to join them for dinner if we feel up to it."

"Ha ha very funny." Smartass. "Um, what's with the two keys?"

"I thought you might want your own room," he replied putting the truck in gear and slowly driving to the end of the block of rooms.

"First of all, no way am I sleeping here by myself. Second of all, you've slept in my bed for what, a month? Why on earth would you stop now?"

"Brianna, I only thought you might want some time alone. I can tell you are struggling with things you do not wish to discuss and I did not want to get in your way."

"Fine, do whatever you want," I snapped as I jumped out of the truck and slammed the door behind me.

I looked down at the first key and pushed my way into the corresponding room. Immediately I sat down on the bed, rubbing my temples as Cameron came into the room and placed my bag at my feet. He bent down, kissed the top of my head and started to leave, but I grabbed his hand and pulled him back toward me.

"I'm sorry," I said, looking into his eyes and seeking forgiveness. "I just need to collect myself. I didn't mean…it's the hormones I guess and I'm hungry, not a good mix."

"The owner told me there is a little diner down the road. I will get you something to eat and you can take a shower and relax. How does that sound?"

"Are you saying I smell?"

"Yes, but in a much more tactful way," he replied as he kissed the back of my hand. "What do you think you can stomach for dinner?"

"Order me a cheeseburger, well-done, with an order of fries and a ginger ale."

"Now Brianna, you should eat something a little healthier than that."

"Oh Cameron, you're right," I said in my upmost sickening sweet sarcastic tone, "please have them put on extra lettuce and tomatoes."

The two of us stood looking at each other like a shootout in the old west. Who would blink first? But in the end, he took a step back and yet again I won. Cameron closed the door behind him and I turned on the lights of my little bungalow. In all honesty, it wasn't bad. Clean and quaint, and thank goodness, there was cable. I grabbed the remote from the bedside table and turned on the TV to find something suitable to have on in the background while I took my bath. Thankfully there was a good trashy reality show on, the perfect mind-numbing show that I needed.

I walked into the bathroom and drew back the shower curtain only to find that the bathtub was made for someone half my size. So there wasn't going to be any kind of soaking tonight. Well, pooh. So instead, I pulled up the handle for the shower and began peeling off my clothes. Goodness I really did smell.

Steam started to wisp from over the top of the shower curtain so I jumped in and let the hot water sink into my skin and relax my aching muscles. After I had thoroughly scrubbed myself and washed my hair I sat down on the floor of the tub with my knees to my chest, allowing the stream of water to wash away all the thoughts I had been trying to keep at bay all day - Cameron, vampires, Sam, pregnant, Jazlyn, Victor, Daddy O, hybrids, beardless Jesus, Dad, scary blonde woman, evil vampires, over and over and over again. As my thoughts began to consume me, I hoped that Cameron would be able to break everything down into small precise compartments like he had before. There was simply too much to handle on my own, and honestly I trusted Cameron's council.

Looking down at my pruney skin I realized I had lost track of time so I reluctantly finished my shower. Going through my bag I found the pair of soft lavender jersey pajamas that Cameron had purchased for me. They were my new favorites (besides his shirt), and not just because he bought them, but because they were just so damn soft. Tonight, I needed comfy clothes and the comfort food I could smell coming from the other room.

When I opened the door and the whiff of my greasy cheeseburger didn't make me want to vomit, I took it as a good sign. Cameron was sitting stretched out on the bed, his arms crossed in front of his chest while he watched the trashy TV show I had left on. He looked up as I walked over to the bed and began setting up my space to enjoy my greasy feast. I stopped when I realized that he was still staring at me.

"Enjoying the view?" I asked.

"You just look very refreshed, almost glowing. It is hard not to look at you."

"Well, thank you. I didn't realize how long I'd been in the shower, it felt wonderful. I didn't know you were a fan," I said pointing to the TV.

"So, this is a show where they follow around a group of housewives while they fight and bicker and spend obscene amounts of money, and they consider it television?"

"Absolutely. And one of my favorites, actually," I said as I opened the food container. "Oh my god, Cameron, it's a miracle! My fries have been turned into a salad." Cameron said nothing, just sat and smiled at the TV. So much for being a complete pushover.

As unladylike as possible, I devoured my cheeseburger. I couldn't believe how hungry I was. I could have totally eaten the salad, but I wanted to make a point so I threw it away, watching in vain for a reaction from Cameron. When I returned to the bed I fumbled around in my bag and pulled out the deck of cards I had thrown in for occasions such as this.

"So Cameron, here's the deal," I began as I shuffled the cards like the pro that I was. "The reason I was so quiet today was because there is, yet again, ten million things running through my head, and I don't know how to deal with it all. So remember how yesterday you took everything I said and went through them one by one and gave me an answer?" He nodded. "Well, we're going to do that again. That is if that's okay with you?" I figured I should give him a choice. I had to remember my manners otherwise Mama Jo would haunt me from the grave.

"I am at your service, my lady," he said as he turned and sat cross legged across from me on the bed. "But may I ask, why the cards?"

"They help keep my mind on something else so that I don't just blurt everything out in one long cascading mind boggling thought. You play gin?" He nodded. "Good. I play a dollar a point."

"A dollar? Oliver only plays a penny a point."

"Yes, but that's because my grandfather has never seen the inside of your wallet, and I have. The cash alone could give someone a heart attack, but add that little black card and I should really charge you ten dollars a point."

He laughed as he said, "So you think I will be paying you money?"

"No doubt. And no cheating, no Vamp tricks, and no letting me win. I know you let Daddy O win, he's terrible at gin." I dealt out the cards and noticed the smirk on Cameron's face. This was going to be fun. "Okay, here we go. Worry one, I'm still pregnant."

"Yes you are, and I still can do nothing about that," he said as we began frantically drawing and discarding our cards.

"True, but I still wanted to put it out there. Next, I'm still afraid that Sam will come after me."

Cameron stopped for a second and looked at me, then continued with his draw. "I doubt that. He has no idea that you are heading to San Francisco, so in no way would he be on your trail. Next."

"How are things with Victor?"

"Fine."

"Bullshit…and gin," I said and laid down my winning hand, successfully wiping that cocky smirk off of Cameron's face. "So I ask again, how are things with Victor, and I want the truth, you promised."

He sighed before he continued with, "I have yet to speak with my father. He is still very angry with me. I did, however, speak with my brother Devin who I am convinced Victor has asked to kill me if I get too out of hand. But for now, he is supporting me the best he can." I stopped my shuffling and tried to hold back the tears. Cameron noticed my sudden change in demeanor and ran his finger down my face. "You told me to tell you the truth, love."

"I know, it's just…okay moving on." I couldn't dwell, so I dealt our next hand. "I'm worried about Daddy O. I just feel we've left him unprotected. I need to be able to check in with him on a regular basis."

"Then we will get you a cell phone tomorrow," Cameron replied very business-like.

"Really?" I said as I discarded and Cameron nodded. "Okay, next, did you ever sleep with Jazlyn?"

Cameron's head flinched up in shock. "Absolutely not! Why would you think that? I have never slept with anyone in my family."

"Yeah, but she's not really your family."

"To me she is, and the answer is still no."

"All right, I believe you. But she has something for you. And gin."

"What? When did you get a…Brianna, one would think you were counting cards."

"As are you, Cameron," I replied in my best imitation of him. "Now back to Jazlyn."

"Please do not dwell on Jazlyn. Trust me, she has nothing but contempt and jealousy towards me."

"No, there's something else there, I just don't know what it is yet. Don't worry, I'll figure it out. Shall we continue playing?"

Cameron nodded, but insisted on shuffling the cards this time.

"Have you ever met my fa…er…Eris?"

"Yes, but only the day that he and Victor asked me to find you. He tends to stay secluded."

"Picturing him in your mind would you say that he looks a lot like Jesus, but without a beard?"

"Jesus?"

"Yeah, you know, Jesus…Christ. High forehead, long wavy hair, robes."

"Well," he answered slowly, "when we met, he was wearing pants and his hair was tied back, but it was long I suppose and maybe wavy. Why do you ask?"

We had finally come upon a topic that made it difficult for me to concentrate on my cards. "I think I've been dreaming about him, and to me he looks like a beardless Jesus."

"And why do you think this is your father?" Cameron asked as he shuffled his hand.

"I don't know, a couple of things, I guess. He just seems familiar, I can't explain it. And then today I asked you what that thing meant, and you said it meant my daughter and that's what he calls me in my dreams. But that's the weird thing, they don't really seem like dreams. It's like we're having a real conversation."

"It certainly makes sense," Cameron said and took a card from the pile.

"What does?"

"Your father is a Dreamwalker."

"A what?"

"Gin."

"What!" Crap. I counted my negative score and threw my cards at Cameron. "So what the hell is a Dreamwalker?"

"Dreamwalkers are individuals who can penetrate other's dreams - control them, watch them, interact inside them," he replied as he dealt our next hand.

"Could that be why I knew about the knife that day when I was five? Could my father have known that would happen and tell me?"

"I am not aware that he can foresee the future, but if someone knew it was going to happen, then yes, I suppose he could have warned you in a dream."

"And because I am his daughter…"

"You could have some of his abilities," Cameron said, finishing my sentence while keeping his eyes on his cards. Realizing I was silent he continued, "Brianna, this is nothing to be scared about. All hybrids share their father's traits in some way. Your father is considered one of the most powerful vampires alive. There is no telling what powers you could possess once they are activated."

"Does Eris have any other children?"

"Not that I am aware of, however, no one knew you existed until a couple of months ago. Eris kept you very well hidden."

"You've said that before, why would he do that?" I said, finally looking down at my cards and getting my head back in the game.

"I assume he hid you to protect you. If other vampires knew you existed, they would want you for your blood, for its power."

"Do you want my blood?"

I could see that it was a difficult question for him to answer.

"Yes," he replied, keeping his eyes averted from mine, "but not for the same reasons."

"What are your reasons then?" He continued to look down at his cards when I drew the last card I needed. "Gin. Now seriously, do I need to worry that you're gonna bite me in the middle of the night?"

"Only if you wanted me to," he said with a seductive smile. "And for the record, I think you are cheating."

I laughed. "My shuffle, and I don't cheat. But seriously, are there times when you have trouble controlling the urge, so to speak."

Cameron scratched his head and shifted uncomfortably on the bed. This was definitely a conversation he wasn't prepared for. I dealt out the cards for another hand and while he sorted the cards in his hand he finally answered, "I do find that I have to…control my urges…more when we are…intimate."

Giggling like a little school girl I responded, "Oh Cameron, you're so cute." And then another worry came over me. "Do you have sex with everyone you drink blood from?"

"No," he answered adamantly. "Most times drinking blood is just for nourishment, nothing sexual. But biting during intercourse does heighten one's experience."

"I see. So you have had sex."

"Brianna, I am not dead…" he paused, "well, I am, but…you know what I mean, not sexually."

"Gin," I announced and laid down my cards. "Have you slept with other vampires?"

"Yes," he replied, throwing his cards down and rubbing his face with his hands.

"Hybrids?"

"Yes."

"How many?"

"Five."

"Were they just random hybrids, or were they your cases?"

"Cases."

"Did you love them?"

"No."

"Then why sleep with them?"

Our tit for tat stopped as he thought about his answer. "To feel…something, anything."

"Do you feel something with me?"

"Since the day I met you," he smiled.

"Hatred, frustration, irritation, I know, I know."

"What do they say? You hit the nail on the head?"

I threw my cards at him and he laughed with me as we tried to piece the deck back together. "Okay, one last game, before I bleed you dry."

"Not necessarily the best choice of words around a vampire."

"Oops," I laughed again as I pulled together my final hand. "Okay, last topic. You."

"Me?" Cameron asked as he fixed his hand as well.

"Yup. Where were you born?"

Cameron's voice dropped slightly, and the light-hearted feeling that was previously in the air became thick. "Outside of Boston."

"Really? You were born in New England?"

"Yes. My family had a farm a few hours ride outside of what used to be the city."

"Did you work on the farm?"

"Yes, until I moved to Boston proper."

"By yourself?"

"Yes." Cameron's movements became slow, his eyes avoiding mine.

"Were you married?"

"Yes. Brianna, it is getting late, I think it best you get some rest," he said abruptly as he turned away from me.

"Cameron, are you okay?"

"Yes. I just need you to get some sleep," Cameron fired back and rose from the bed.

"Did I upset you? I was just curious about your wife and…"

"I do not want to talk about it," he yelled. "They died hundreds of years ago, and I would rather not have to relive that. Please understand."

"I do," I said meekly as I wiped away the tear that had escaped down my face. "Maybe you're right, I should get some rest. Alone."

Cameron jammed his hands in his back pockets and lifted his face to the ceiling as he took in a deep breath. A second later he walked silently to the door and shut it behind him. I threw the cards onto the floor and climbed under the covers. Grabbing the remote from the nightstand I began flipping through the channels, barely able to see the TV through the tears.

Chapter Twenty-three

Cameron

When I woke, I was laying on my side with my hands bound behind me, my mouth gagged, and the back of my head pounding from the blow that caused my blackout. My eyes burned as I slowly opened them, trying to determine where I was. From the floorboards and the debris scattered on the floor it appeared I was still in my shop where I had been attacked, and I could hear footsteps creaking from my small residence above. Chloe!

Jolted into full consciousness, I tried moving but was greeted by agonizing pain from my legs. I screamed through the gag as I looked down at my battered and bloody legs, one of which appeared to be broken. My scream alerted my attackers that I was awake. The one assigned to stay with me yelled up to those on the second floor and several men came running down the stairs. One of them knelt down on the floor and slapped me across the face as he said, "Nice of you to join us. Your family has been waiting for you."

I began screaming at the man for fear of my family, but those screams were soon tied to the pain in my legs as the other two men pulled me upright and dragged me up the stairs, making sure that my broken leg hit each and every step. Once inside the small living quarters I was thrown across the room, landing on the floor and sending new shockwaves of pain throughout my body. Half in and out of consciousness I heard a man speaking to me, though I could barely hear him through my ringing ears.

"You see, Mr. Burke," the man began as he hovered over me, his breath smelling of stale whiskey, "when you shot my brother, you all but forced my hand. You should have just given us what we wanted, but you had to be the hero. So their lives are on your head."

After he finished his statement, he kicked me in the face with the heel of his boot causing blood from my mouth and nose to soak into my gag. With a second and third kick to my chest and stomach, he sent me rolling across the floor and into the legs of a chair. I rolled over onto my back and I was met by my wife, Chloe, staring down at me with glazed dead eyes. Her body was bound to the chair, arms behind her back, mouth gagged, throat cut. Blood had flowed down her white nightgown and pooled in places around her chair. Screaming and sobbing, I placed my forehead against her cold feet and noticed another chair next to hers, however, this one containing the body of my son. Christian, only five, was so small that his legs barely dangled over the edge of the seat that still dripped with his blood. They had killed my son, my sweet boy, and my Chloe, darling Chloe.

Despite the pain in my legs, I rolled over and tried to push myself upright. My attacker's laughter only made me push further through the pain, but my struggle was in vain as the brother of the man I killed stabbed his long knife deep into my gut, retracted, and then plunged it in again. After he retracted his knife for the last time, he pushed me back down to the floor while the other men kicked down the chairs that bound my murdered wife and son. Tears flooded my face as I watched the men leave and waited for my death to come. All of this pain and suffering had occurred simply because I refused to let them steal from me as they had so many others. The man was right; my family's deaths were on my head.

My breath was labored, and my shirt and coat were soaked with blood. I closed my eyes, waiting to take my last few breaths when I heard someone come slowly up the stairs and open the door to my home. The floorboards near me creaked causing me to open my eyes and see a man leaning over me. Carefully he removed the gag from my mouth allowing me to whisper, "My hands."

The stranger nodded and ripped the cloth that bound my hands. I reached painfully over to Chloe, placing my hand over her eyes to close them. The man ripped her bindings from the chair and moved her to lie next to me. I kissed Chloe's forehead, letting my tears drip onto her face. Behind me I heard the ripping of more cloth and I assumed the man was freeing Christian from his bindings as well.

"May I see him?" I groaned as I rolled onto my back again. The man carried Christian's small, limp body over to me and laid him in my arms. I *sobbed into my boy's precious head, holding him to me with what little strength I had left. I looked down at his angelic face, now free of the fear he must have felt before he died. Kissing his head one last time, I squeezed him to my chest and prepared myself to die.*

I had completely forgotten about the man in the room until he spoke.

"I cannot do anything for them," he said as he knelt down next to me. "But you, I can save you. I can give you a life that you could only dream of. Let me do this for you."

I looked up to notice the short, well-built, and well-dressed man whose clothes were now covered in blood.

"Please, let me die. Let me die with them."

The man bent over closer to me and took my forearm, holding it tightly in between his hands. His eyes were tightly closed as he tilted his head back and opened his mouth wide. When he looked back at me, long white fangs hung down from his mouth, his eyes wild with hunger.

"I am sorry, child," he said right before he bit into my wrist and drank the remainder of my life away...

The memory of the day I lost my family and my humanity remained a vivid one. Victor, who happened to be walking down the street on that fateful night, had followed the smell of blood in the air and found me bleeding out amongst my dead family. The leader of the Warrior coven had only ever chosen his Warrior children after careful research and proven skills made me a vampire out of sympathy and anger at what had been taken away from me. After draining me of most of my blood, he forced me to drink from him in order to live.

Even centuries later, I was brought to my knees with grief at the mere mention of my true family. So much so that I yelled at the defenseless and fragile woman I loved. And I did love her, though I could not bring myself to tell her. I had not loved another woman since Chloe, and I had fallen for Brianna hard and fast. Last night I left her lying in bed alone and crying because of how I had treated her. If I could flay myself for what I had done, I would. She had told me to leave, but I needed to apologize to her. Who she saw last night was not the real me. It was the pent-up anger that I could not release no matter how much time passed.

It was 6:00 a.m. and I had all but chained myself in my room to give

Brianna the space she asked for. I had spent 97,827 nights as a vampire without her, and now I did not know what to do with myself for one night. There would be no end to my brothers' ridicule if they could see me now. Angry and frustrated, I forced myself to stay focused on the task at hand. We needed to get back on the road and continue our journey to California, and I hoped Brianna would sleep most of the trip so that I could drive, as she put it, inhuman speeds. The more time it took us to get to the Facility, the more Brianna was exposed. And although she did not know the true depth of what that meant, I certainly did.

Not wanting to waste another minute, I changed my clothes and put on my last surviving cashmere sweater that had not been cried, snotted, or vomited on. Of course I had more at home, but I would definitely have to find something comparable today. While Brianna slept, I had found a mall that we would hit around noon where I could purchase her a cell phone and shop for any remaining items she would need for her stay at the Facility. I packed my remaining items into my duffle bag and placed it in the black SUV parked outside our rooms. I looked around and noticed no one around, so I closed my eyes and Projected myself into Brianna's room. She was curled up in her usual fetal position looking as angelic as ever with her hair tangled and messy across her face.

Her right arm was hanging over the side of the bed and was too enticing not to touch. I slid down to the floor and gently held her hand, kissing my way up her arm. Little moans and groans escaped Brianna's lips as she began to wake.

"But I don't want to go to school."

"No school today, love," I replied, sweeping her nest of hair out of her face. "But you must wake."

Brianna turned over and stretched upright, yawning widely as she did. As if the movement had taken every ounce of energy, she fell dramatically back down on the bed and opened her eyes to me.

"I'm sorry for last night, Cam. I didn't mean…"

But I did not let her finish. "Brianna, you have nothing to apologize for. It is I who should apologize. I cannot beg for enough forgiveness from you," I said holding her hand in mine and placing it over my heart. "My past is very difficult for me to talk about and I lost myself with you. Please forgive me."

She paused for a moment, taking the time to look apologetically into my eyes. "Cam, I am sorry though, I didn't mean to pry. But next time, you don't have to yell at me. If you don't want to talk, then just say so."

The way she called me Cam made me want to give in to anything.

"While you shower and get ready, I will pick you up some breakfast. What do you think you can handle today?"

"Just some toast and jelly," she said as she pulled the covers away and began her ritual of eating a cracker from the stack on the nightstand to let her stomach settle before getting up. "Oh, and some chocolate milk."

I raised my eyebrow at her although we both knew I would give in. She had made it apparent that she would eat what she wanted, even if I tried to force something healthier on her. I bent down and kissed her forehead, but she pulled on the collar of my sweater and lowered me down to her lips. I was officially forgiven.

Chapter Twenty-four

Brianna

After a quick shower, I changed and made myself look presentable since I would be in public for the first time in a long while. Cameron came back a short time later with toast and chocolate milk, which was a secret favorite of mine. After waiting a few minutes to make sure the toast and milk wouldn't come back up, we packed up the truck and were on our way.

Within minutes I was asleep, which I'm sure pleased Cameron since he could speed without me criticizing. When I woke up it was a little after 8:00 a.m. and we had crossed over into New Mexico.

"Cameron, I need to borrow your phone," I said and grabbed it before he could answer then dialed Renee's work number.

"Good morning, Advanced Financial, how may I direct your call," Renee answered in her usual miserable office receptionist voice. Renee was the most vibrant person I knew, but she hated her job and made everyone suffer along with her.

"Yes, could you please direct me to the snottiest receptionist on the face of the planet?"

"Bri! Ohmygod, where have you been? I called Daddy O and he said you'd left," she whispered harshly into the phone.

"We're on our way to California. We just crossed over into New Mexico. How are you? I miss you."

"I'm doing okay. Whoa, wait...California? When the hell were you going to tell me you were going to California?"

From out of the side of my eye I could see Cameron glancing over at me, which meant he could hear both sides of this conversation. "Um, now?"

"For goodness' sake, Brianna, California? What the hell is out there?"

"Well, uh, Cameron's family lives there and we figured it was a good place to hide from Sam."

"*Cameron's* family, oh I see," Renee said sounding like a teenager. I rolled my eyes as a wicked smile stretched across Cameron's face. "But I don't think you need to worry about Sam, that's why I called down to Daddy O's. Sam's missing."

"What do you mean he's missing?"

"I guess he didn't show up to work for a couple of days and his boss filed a missing person's report. The cops actually came to see me last night."

"And?"

"And nothing. They asked when I'd seen him last, and I told them it was at lunch the day he beat the crap out of his wife, my best friend. That would be you, by the way."

"Ask her if they asked how to get in contact with you," Cameron asked quietly.

I nodded. "Renee, did they ask you how to get in touch with me?"

"They did, but I told them you went underground with a woman's shelter. Wasn't that clever?"

I looked over at Cameron to see if her ruse set him at ease, and he nodded.

"Yeah, very clever, Re. How's Dr. John?"

"He's good."

"The two of you still going strong?"

"Yeah, stronger than ever. We're ah…moving in together."

"What!" I screamed, unfortunately so loud that Cameron swerved the truck into the next lane. "Ohmygod, ohmygod, ohmygod! Renee that's wonderful."

"I know, but I'm totally freaked out about it. I don't know the rules of living with someone. I mean honestly, do I need to get rid of my vibrator or am I allowed to keep it, and if I am, do I have to hide it?"

"Renee! People could hear you," I said meaning Cameron could hear her.

"Don't worry, there's no one here, and I wouldn't care anyway. But seriously, I need to know."

"I certainly wouldn't know. You guys will figure it out, I'm sure. Just don't blow it, okay?"

"O-kay, *Mom.*"

"Oh by the way, I'm getting a cell phone today so I'll give you my new number so you can call me anytime, 'kay?"

"You got it, babe. Crap, I gotta go, another call. Love ya!"

"Love you too," and with that we hung up.

There was a minute or two of silence before Cameron said, "It is nice to hear that John and Renee are moving in together."

"Yes, it is," I sniffled and looked out the window.

"I thought you would be happy."

"I am. Very happy," I replied, wiping away the tears that had leaked from my eyes.

"Then why are you crying?"

"Because I'm supposed to be there, okay?" I snapped at him. "She shouldn't be telling me that stuff on the phone. We should be sitting down at lunch or gossiping before church about this. I need to be there to keep her head on straight when she flips out the day he moves his stuff in."

Cameron took my hand and kissed it gently. "You will."

"Really? When?" I replied, turning daggers on him. He couldn't bring himself to lie to me. "See, you can't even say it. She's going to get married, and then have babies, and I'll be stuck in the hybrid hotel hell raising Sam's baby. And that's if the crazy blonde vampire doesn't kill me before that."

"What did you say?" Cameron said sternly.

I looked over at him and his face was fraught with concern. Was he reacting to Renee getting married, or the blonde vampire part? I'm guessing the second one. I had seen her in my dream and I had my suspicions that she was Elaina. His reaction pretty much confirmed it, but I couldn't admit to him why I knew her.

So my response to him was, "Nothing," and I looked back out the window.

Yep, I was real smooth.

Realizing I wasn't going to divulge anything, Cameron plugged his phone into the sound system of the SUV and handed it to me. "See if you can find some music."

"So where are we stopping to shop?" I asked as I began flipping through the albums on his phone.

"There is a mall in Flagstaff. We can get your cell phone there, and I need to buy a few shirts. I am getting low."

"You mean I've ruined the others."

"You said that, I did not."

"Yeah, but that's because you have manners."

"And because I am not a stupid man," he said, giving me my favorite crooked smile and then looking in the center console for something. Not finding what he was looking for, he said, "Can you see if my sunglasses are in my jacket?"

Looking behind me I saw his leather jacket laying across the backseat so I stretched backward and pulled it into my lap. While I looked in the various pockets of his jacket his signature autumn smell wafted around the cabin of the SUV making me take in a big whiff. Finally in the very last pocket I found his silver aviator sunglasses. I couldn't help but put them on and pull down the visor to check myself out in the mirror.

"Nope, I don't look as sexy in them as you do. As a matter of fact, I look downright stupid."

Cameron laughed as he pulled his sunglasses off my face and put them on. Damn he looked good.

"Put on the jacket and you look almost the way you did when we first met," I said as I tossed his jacket in the backseat. "You were such an ass."

"Yes, I was," he laughed. "I was angry and wanted to get it over with. Little did I know…"

"That you would fall madly in love with me," I joked.

"Precisely."

My smile fell. New subject, new subject, I needed a new subject. Did he mean it? Or was he joking too? I didn't want to embarrass myself, and I couldn't say I loved him because I didn't know. I didn't know how it would feel to love a man. New subject! I couldn't think of anything. Panic started to rise from my stomach and my heart began pounding.

Cameron took my hand again and kissed the tops of my fingers, a gesture I was definitely getting used to, and then said, "When we get to Flagstaff we will eat, more so, you will eat, and we will purchase your cell phone. Then we can do some shopping for clothes and other items you may need for the Facility."

My angel had changed the subject before the flop sweat started forming on my forehead. I sighed with relief and leaned over the center console, wrapping my arm around his and placing my head in the crook of his shoulder.

"There are no high-end stores, unfortunately," he continued, "but I cannot risk taking you through Phoenix."

"Why is that?" I asked curiously. Cameron was quiet at first, but if he didn't want me to question his statement, he shouldn't have mentioned it. So really it was his own fault.

"Alexander and Devin just returned from a mission where hybrids were found dead in that area. So it is a little too dangerous."

"And they know they were hybrids because of their eyes and their blood?"

Cameron tightened his lips. "Yes, because of their eyes. There was no blood."

"How's that?"

"Are you sure you want to know this?"

"Yes. I should know what's out there and what could happen. So spill it."

Cameron sighed, tapping his index finger on the steering wheel before he finally said, "Very well. Lately the hybrids they have found have all been drained. We believe Elaina's followers are collecting and drinking hybrid blood."

"What's the big deal about hybrid blood?"

"You see, when a human is Turned, their maker transfers some of their power into the new vampire. Hybrids, on the other hand, are born with their powers. But for some, it can take time to develop their powers, especially if they are not around vampires."

"But why drain the hybrids?"

Cameron sighed again. "When a vampire drinks a hybrid's blood, they will have the hybrid's abilities for a short time. The greater amount of hybrid blood a vampire drinks, the longer they will have those abilities. The more powerful the hybrid's father, the more potent the blood, and there are those among our race who are obsessed with having such power."

"And because this Eris guy is my father, Elaina may want my blood so she can have powers that I don't possess."

"You do not possess them, yet."

"Elaina can't be the only one drinking hybrid blood if you know all of this."

"True, but no one has tried to industrialize it as Elaina has. Previously her followers would keep the powerful hybrids alive to continually collect their blood, and then drain the weak ones once it was realized they did not have any real powers. But now we are finding that they have begun experimenting on them. Trying to find ways to combine powers, make them sustainable and reproducible."

"How do you know what she's doing if every hybrid you find is dead?"

Cameron didn't answer. "You found a hybrid alive?"

"One of the teams came across two hybrids who had escaped and they explained some of the experiments they had endured."

"Are they at the Facility now?"

"No," he replied quietly, "they were killed."

"By Elaina's cronies?"

"No, by Devin."

"Why would he kill them?"

"Many of the experiments had damaging effects, causing them to..." he struggled to find the words he needed, "...go crazy, I guess, much like rabid animals."

Not wanting to hear anymore, I turned the music up and tried to forget everything he had just told me. The center console was now officially digging into my side so I sat correctly in my seat and looked out at the flat highway in front of us.

"If you look in the backseat, Brianna, you will see a small cooler with chocolate milk inside."

I couldn't help but smile. It was exactly what I needed. Reaching behind my seat, I felt around for the cooler and pulled it over to where I could lift the lid. And there it was – a large bottle of extra thick chocolate milk sitting in a layer of ice.

"Where did you get the cooler?"

"From Magda."

"Magda? Magda who?"

"Magda, the owner of the motel. She was quite hospitable."

"Oh and I'm sure it had nothing to do with you charming her little socks off."

"I do what I must," he replied with a sly smile.

Not long after my chocolate milk had been devoured, I fell asleep and napped through New Mexico. Waking up in Arizona meant that food and shopping were close. I was definitely up for shopping and since it was just before noon I was starving. When we pulled into the shopping center a short time later, it had been left up to me whether I wanted food or phone first. I chose phone since I loved new toys. Thankfully there was a large electronics store associated with the shopping center so I had a good selection to choose from. But in the end, Cameron bought me the same high-end phone that he had instead of the cheap phone I was fine with.

"This way you can have music with you at the Facility," he said justifying the purchase to me. It was too much, but I couldn't stop him from buying it anyway.

Once the phone was purchased, we tried looking for some shirts for him, but nothing was good enough. He was quite a clothes snob. Either the material was crappy, or the stitching was shoddy. I mean seriously, what man looks at stitching? Apparently, Cameron Burke did.

"So is Burke your real last name?" I asked as we made our way to the food court.

"Yes, actually it is," he replied with a light laugh.

"What's your middle name?" I asked, enjoying the fact that he was actually sharing something about himself with me. It was usually the other way around.

"Jackson."

"Cameron Jackson Burke, that's certainly better than Bri Bri Marie."

Cameron laughed as he pulled me out of the way of a group of teenagers who refused to break up their large group in order to let us pass.

"Can I convince you to eat something healthy today?"

"If I get a salad, will you get off my back about it?"

"Yes, but you actually have to eat it."

"Details," I replied dismissively.

We walked down the food court trying to find a place where I could get a healthy lunch when Cameron's hand suddenly squeezed my arm and pulled me back in the direction we had just come from.

"Cam, what's up?" I whispered, trying to keep up with his long, fast stride.

"Could be nothing," he replied and pulled out his cell phone. As he began scrolling through his numbers, he stopped dead in his tracks causing me to run into him. In front of us were two men walking towards us relatively fast compared to the other shoppers. Cameron quickly pulled me in another direction and I noticed that the men's eyes were dangerously black.

vampires. I looked back towards the food court and saw another two vampires closing in on us.

Cameron let go of my arm and pulled me into his side as we started moving at a pace I couldn't keep up with. He put the cell phone to his ear and began speaking softly but amazingly fast.

"Alex, we have four Vamps on our tail. Wake up Jared, we need a diversion in order to get out of here." I couldn't hear what was being said on the other side of the phone but Cameron continued even more frantically, "I know what time it is, but we cannot get out of here without some help. We are in a mall, there has to be something Jared can do. Use the tracker in my phone, and make it quick." And then he hung up, jamming the phone in his back pocket.

"Cam, are we in trouble?" I whispered breathlessly since I hadn't worked out in, well forever.

"We are if Alexander does not wake up Jared within the next few minutes," he said, pulling me out of the main corridor and into one of the department stores.

"I thought Jared couldn't be out during the day."

"As long as he stays out of the sun, he is just weak in the daytime. Most of his computer equipment is in his room which does not have windows," he said and began winding us through the racks of women's clothes. He looked behind him and cursed as another vampire joined the ranks of the others who had separated to divide and conquer.

I was paying too much attention to the vampires who were following us than where I was running, and even though Cameron was holding me against him I still managed to catch my sneaker on the carpet and fall completely splayed out. Without missing a beat, Cameron picked me up off the floor and carried me upright against his hip so that it looked like I was walking even though my feet weren't touching the floor.

Behind us came a multitude of crashes as one of the vampires decided to knock over everything in front of him in order to clear a straight path. The disruption startled everyone in the vicinity causing them to run directly in front of us. Just when it looked like the vampire would catch up to us, we were suddenly showered with water. The sprinkler system for the entire mall had been activated causing everyone to come out of the woodwork to run toward an exit. A perfect diversion, I thought. And as the thought popped in my head, I heard Cameron say, "Thank you, Jared."

Cameron lifted me into his arms and ran with vampire speed to a side door that took us down a small flight of stairs and through a narrow hallway. I held onto Cameron for dear life, not only because I was scared, but because of the sheer speed he was running. When we came to the door at the end of the hallway Cameron kicked it open revealing a side loading alley that was completely empty. That was, however, until we had made our way halfway down. Suddenly a white van squealed into the alley with four vampires leaping out and blocking our way.

Cameron placed me down on the ground and pushed me behind him.

"Run as fast as you can, angel," he whispered, sneaking the keys into my hand.

Before I could protest, Cameron launched himself at the four vampires. I was frozen with fear watching Cameron knock down one vampire and then be thrown across the alley by another. Two of the vampires grabbed him by his arms while another ran towards him, but at the last second Cameron threw his legs up, kicking the third and then pulled in both arms causing his two captors to collide with each other. But at the same moment the fourth vampire rose from the ground and grabbed hold of Cameron from behind.

Cameron looked in my direction, noticing that I hadn't moved since he had left my side. "Run! Run!" he screamed as he pointed to something behind me.

But before I could find my feet, someone grabbed me and threw me up against the alley wall. It was one of the vampires from inside, the one who had plowed through the department store. He was enormous and full of muscles bulging from underneath his dripping wet clothes. He stretched me up against the wall by my throat causing my feet to dangle three feet off the ground. I kicked my legs as hard as I could, but all that I succeeded in doing was hurting my feet as they kicked what felt like rock. Vampire rock. Frantically grabbing at my throat and struggling for breath, I looked over to see that Cameron was struggling as three of the vampires held him so that another could beat him.

Only recently had I been choked by Sam, and here I was defenseless as it happened to me again. The vampire smiled and laughed at me while I writhed in his grip to get the smallest amount of air. A burning grew inside my stomach and began working its way up my chest and through my sore throat. I saw the vampires throw Cameron up against the wall again, this time leaving a hole in the brick where his body had hit.

NO, I screamed to myself just as the burning rose and exploded through the top of my head.

Just then, my attacker released me and we both fell to the ground, as did all the other vampires. All of them were cowering and grabbing their heads in pain. Unfortunately, Cameron was also one of them. Coughing and gasping for air, I clutched the keys in my hand and stumbled over to Cameron who was still dazed from whatever had happened to all of them. I grabbed him under the arm, pulled him upright, and we ran as fast as either of us could manage through the crowds of people who had evacuated the mall.

Thankfully we had parked pretty close to this side of the mall and by the time we got to the truck, Cameron had recovered. I tossed him the keys as we jumped in and he thrust the truck into gear just as two of the vampires came up to the rear of the truck. Cameron slammed on the gas causing us to barrel forward over the curb. As we swerved to avoid the emergency vehicles coming into the mall parking lot, we passed two of our attackers running after us, although there was a new vampire with them.

"That's her," I screamed.

"Who? Who did you see?" Cameron said in a panic and looking into his rearview mirror.

"The blonde, the blonde vampire. That's Elaina, isn't it," I said as my voice strained against the pain in my throat.

"How do you know that?" Cameron shouted at me, but I couldn't answer. I could barely breathe and the shock of everything that had happened was taking over. Thankfully Cameron's phone rang and he answered it, angrily. "Alex, get Jared and Devin now, and call me back when you are all together," he growled and then hung up.

Thirty seconds later Cameron's phone rang again and this time he placed the phone on speaker. "Alex, what the hell happened?"

"I don't know, Cam, you tell me," Alex responded, his voice sounding almost as deep as the Jolly Green Giant.

"We were just attacked by a pack of vampires in a public place, one of which was Elaina. Now tell me how something like that happens."

"Cameron, we haven't had any sightings since you left North Carolina, and that's the truth. We had no intel that she was in the area," Alex replied defensively.

"Well consider this your intel! They are in the area and almost killed us both. And thank you, Jared, for getting us soaking wet."

"Hey it worked, whadja expect with a second's notice," Jared said sleepily. Poor kid.

"How did they even know where we were? It must be the tracking program you put in my phone. They must have somehow tapped in."

"No way, bro, my network is secure," Jared replied in a raised voice.

"Apparently not that secure since they knew exactly where to hit us," Cameron snapped back.

"Brother, this would never have happened if you had not delayed so…"

"Devin, enough! You know the reasons we had to drive. Elaina saw our SUV so I need you to hook us up with someone to exchange it on the way. Damn it," Cameron shouted as he hit the steering wheel, jolting me in my seat. "We are going to need to go a different way to San Francisco. They will probably assume we will take the fastest route, which we were on."

Devin returned to the line, "How am I supposed to get you new transportation if you do not even know where you are going."

And then all hell broke loose. All four brothers began screaming at one another, blaming each other for actions that most likely couldn't have been prevented. The yelling was getting us nowhere and I couldn't take it anymore.

"Shut up, shut up, shut up! You stupid boys! Yelling at each other is not going to accomplish anything. So if you're done measuring, why don't you all put your dicks back into your pants and let's figure out what we're going to do from here," I yelled, barely recognizing my voice as it came out. It sounded more like something Renee would say than me. "Alex, you now have information that Elaina and some of her vampires might still be following us and most likely know we're heading to San Francisco. Do you have everything you need?"

"Yes," he replied in his deep voice. "I will get teams in the area."

"Good. Now Cameron, can you program the truck's GPS to take us a different route?"

"Yes," Cameron said softly, but irritated.

"Then do it. Devin, once we have a solid route, we'll text you. But from what I'm already seeing on the GPS screen it looks like we'll pass through Vegas. Do you have a contact for a new car there?"

"I am sure we do, but I will try and find someone closer on route," Devin said through what sounded like clenched teeth.

"Jared," I continued, "I'm sure your tracking thingy is fine, but they did find us. We're going to turn it off for the time being just in case. You should look to see if someone did hack in, and then get some sleep. I just feel terrible that you're awake in the daytime." As I finished there was a short, stunned silence.

"Dude, she is awesome," Jared finally said.

I could hear a couple of jeers from the other line, although Cameron wasn't amused. After everyone hung up, Cameron and I sat in silence until my wet clothes were too much for me to take. I unbuckled my seatbelt and climbed over the console into the backseat in what must have been a comical sight since my jeans wouldn't stretch. Grabbing my bag, I snuck down into the floor behind Cameron's seat to change. So much for looking nice today.

Leaving my wet clothes in the backseat, I climbed my way back to the front where my silent Cam awaited. His anger was palpable, and it was generally best to leave an angry man alone. Just as I fastened my seatbelt, Cam slammed on the brakes and pulled over to the side of the highway under an overpass. Too fast for me to even see, he put the truck in park, ran to the passenger side, and opened my door. He unbuckled my seatbelt and pulled me tightly into his chest. When he released me, he placed his hands on either side of my face and crushed his lips on mine. His kiss took my breath away, literally, because he was kissing me so passionately I couldn't come up for air. Feeling as though I was going to suffocate, I pushed him away slightly.

"Cam, I'm all right," I said seeing the panic in his eyes. Both of us were still breathing hard, although I knew he didn't actually need the oxygen. He kissed my forehead and hugged me to his chest once again.

"I thought I was going to fail," he whispered emotionally in my ear. "I was afraid I was going to lose you." Tears were building behind my eyes at the sound of his voice. I had never heard Cameron sound scared. Suddenly he broke out of our embrace and held me firmly by the shoulders as he said, "The next time I tell you to run, I need you to run. Do you understand me?"

I swallowed the lump that had formed in my throat and replied, "I couldn't leave you."

"I do not matter..."

"You matter to me," I interrupted. He wanted to argue, I could see it in his eyes, but instead he gave me a gentle kiss and helped me back up into the truck.

Once back on the road Cameron drove illegal speeds, but I didn't say anything. We needed to put as much distance between us and Elaina as possible. Devin texted back with a location where we could trade in our SUV since it was obviously known. While Cameron talked to the contact on the phone about what he wanted for the replacement car, I watched the scenery flash by. Tears came off and on for the next hour of our trip. Sometimes they were from reliving the events of the day, other times because I realized that another dream had come true.

Although I didn't kill the vampire today as I had in my dream, the similarities were frightening. It was as though my dreams were accurate to an extent, but the place and time hadn't been set. Had I avoided the attack in my dream, or just moved it to a different place because I had fled? Maybe my dream was showing me more of what was to come.

Reaching into the backseat, I pulled the bag of snacks I had taken from Daddy O's house and began to chow down. Crying and eating tended to go hand in hand. Cameron asked if I wanted to stop and get some real food, but I knew we needed to press on. Gleefully I ate the entire bag filled with junk food, which in the end meant I had still won. I never did eat that salad.

Chapter Twenty-five

Brianna

It was official. In the Warriors' eyes I had gone from a mere annoyance to a top security priority. Amazing how one incident could change people's entire perception. All you really had to do was almost die by a crazy vampire's hand, and suddenly you were important. Devin's network contact panned out, and we had been driving in our new sport coupe for five hours. Cameron had foregone the blend in factor for speed and better gas mileage. The car exchange had been a good idea since we received a call from Devin shortly after saying that a tracker had been found on the SUV, although it was unknown whether it had been put on that day or earlier. The tracker was removed and then sent to Jared for analysis. We were all hoping he would find something that would lead us to Elaina now that we knew she could get so close to me.

I waved to Las Vegas as we drove through and mentally added it to my list of places to visit before I died, which hopefully wasn't too soon. The new route had us going north through Nevada and then crossing over into California and then down to San Francisco. If today's incident hadn't happened, we would be almost to the Facility, but the new route would add an extra day. Only Devin, Alex, and Jared knew that we had taken an alternate route but didn't know the specifics per Cameron, though they probably had a good idea. Cameron admitted that Jared could still track us using cell phone towers, but was hoping that he would heed his warning not to. The attack had really thrown Cameron. During our entire ride he never let go of me - holding my hand, touching my leg, or running his fingers through my hair while I rested on his shoulder. Both of us had panicked about losing the other.

The only good thing that came out of what I was calling the Fiasco in Flagstaff was that my new phone had survived. It had been packed up in a box and placed in a plastic bag that had a pretty tight hold around my wrist. Through the water, the running, and the strangling, my phone was unscathed. It was a miracle phone. I texted Renee the new number and called Daddy O to tell him everything was fine, although he could tell it wasn't. Things in North Carolina were quiet. Even Shelby had come for a visit asking about how I was and saying how much she missed me. I wasn't about to accept the new Shelby, but who knows, people did change. Sometimes by force.

Only day two of our trip to San Francisco was coming to a close, but it felt like an eternity. Cameron could tell I was done for the day, so we stopped for the night in another nondescript little motel. Again, the place was small but clean, and thank the Lord it had a nice big bathtub. When I saw the tub, I dropped my bag inside the bathroom and closed the door behind me without saying a word to Cameron. I needed to soak and think and soak and think. And then maybe think a little more.

While the bathtub filled with steaming hot water I searched through my bag and pulled out the lavender body wash I had taken from Daddy O's and poured a large amount into the water and watched as bubbles started to form. Even before the bathtub was remotely full, I had ripped off my clothes, tied my hair back, and sat in the water watching it rise along with the bubbles up my body. There was nothing like a good hot bath and the smell of lavender to relax your muscles and take the stress away. Finally, the water had gotten to an acceptable therapeutic level, and the bubbles were almost overwhelming the tub.

"Cameron," I whispered softly after I turned off the water.

"Yes?" he answered at the door.

"Just checking," I said truthfully. "Cam," I whispered again.

"Yes?"

"Can you come in here?"

He paused. "Are you sure?"

"I wouldn't have asked if I wasn't. I just want to talk."

Although I was in the tub, he couldn't see anything through the absurd amount of bubbles. Slowly he turned the handle and peeked inside, obviously testing to see if it was truly okay for him to enter. Once he saw that I was covered in bubbles he relaxed and sat in the doorway with his back up against the door jam.

"Can I ask you something?" I said, closing my eyes to continue my relaxation.

"Of course. As long as it is not about today."

"Cam," I replied sternly, still keeping my eyes closed. But I knew he was joking by the sound of his soft laugh.

"Just kidding. Please ask me anything."

"Remember when that big creepy vampire was choking me?" I said as I gently rubbed my bruised throat. Cameron didn't answer, and I wasn't about to open my eyes and ruin the little amount of muscle release I had accomplished. "Cam, I can't see you. You have to use your words."

"Yes, I remember," he replied through clenched teeth.

"Remember how all of a sudden all of you went down? What happened?"

Cameron paused again before answering. "It is hard to explain, really. There was a very loud high-pitched scream, but it was so loud that it kept reverberating in my head. It felt as though my head was going to explode. At first, I thought it was you, but there is no way you could have screamed that loud and affected all of us like that."

"So what was it then?"

"Honestly, I do not know, love. I have never been affected like that, it was the strangest feeling. I was even pondering calling Father to see if he knew or had heard of anything happening like that. He is old enough to know, but that is if he would even talk to me. But I swear I heard…" he said cutting off his own thought and then giving up with a sigh.

"What? What do you swear you heard?" I said finally opening my eyes and turning my head to see him.

He turned his head to me as well as he reluctantly replied, "I swear I heard you. It was your voice in my head."

"And what did I say?" I said, almost worried what he would admit.

"I swear you were screaming 'no'. But you could not have screamed with him choking you the way he was," he said with resolve and turned his glance back to his feet that were now stretched up high on the doorframe.

I closed my eyes again and tried to relax since every muscle in my body had re-tensed at Cameron's response. I had yelled no, but only in my head. I remembered the burning sensation that rose from my stomach up through my head. Truthfully, I thought it had something to do with being strangled, but what if it was something else?

For the next twenty minutes I soaked silently while Cameron sat in the bathroom doorway. I glanced over at one point and noticed that his eyes were closed. I hated even thinking about waking him, but the water was starting to cool down. I said his name quietly in order not to startle him and he left willingly when I told him I needed to get out.

Once he had closed the door I stood up and rinsed the remaining bubbles away. My body felt better, as did my spirit. After drying off and wrapping a towel around me, I rummaged through my leather bag for clean pajamas. After finding pants I dug around for a top and a pair of underwear and came across Cameron's button up shirt. The sleeves were still rolled up from the last time I had worn it - the night that Cameron had scared the crap out of me when I tested his hearing. I remembered how he looked at me that night, like he wanted me, but in the end, he was always a gentleman. Well maybe tonight I didn't want a gentleman. Maybe it was time we kicked this thing into high gear, I had dreamt about it enough.

I dug around in my bag again and pulled out a pair of the sexier underwear he had bought for me and buttoned the shirt up except for the first two buttons. I brushed my hair upside down and did the famous volume flip up, and my hair did look nice and full for about three seconds. My stomach was fluttering with butterflies I was so nervous. I had never seduced a man, and I was worried about looking foolish. Cameron had feelings for me, this I knew. So I wasn't terribly worried about being rejected. I was attractive, except for the bruised neck, my legs were shaven, and I smelled good. So I needed to put my big girl panties on and get laid.

Okay, it would be more than sex with Cameron, which was probably why I was so nervous. I checked my appearance from all sides in the mirror, took a big breath, and opened the door. The lights were still off in the room, which was a godsend. Cameron had his back turned to me and appeared to be talking on the phone, though he was speaking so quietly it was hard to tell. I cleared my throat to get his attention.

"Cam?"

He turned around to see me trying to strike a sexy pose in the doorway with the bathroom light illuminating me from behind.

"I need to go," he said vacantly into the phone. From where I stood, I could hear the person on the other line yelling as he hung up the phone. I flipped the bathroom lights off before I walked to Cameron who met me halfway.

Rising up on the balls of my feet, I combed my fingers through his hair and brought his face to mine, kissing him gently at first. He wrapped his arms around me in response, pressing me tightly against his chest. I kissed him again, this time tickling his lips with my tongue. He opened his mouth and we began kissing each other with deep breaths. I lowered myself to my heels and gently prodded him to the bed, lowering him down to a seated position with me standing in front of him between his legs.

I ran both my hands through his hair as he nuzzled his face into my chest through the opening of my shirt. His fingers caressed the outside of my thighs as he moved them up under the bottom of the shirt where he began kneading his thumbs into my stomach. His kisses to my neck and collarbone became more intense as did he his grip when he moved his hands from my stomach around to my back. I could feel that my body was more than ready for him. As I tilted my head up to the ceiling, I pressed his face into my heaving breast. Then everything came to an abrupt halt.

I looked down at him quickly, afraid I had done something wrong, only to see that his head was hung low, hiding his face from me. I reached down and tilted his face up to mine. When he looked at me, I noticed his eyes were heavy as he opened his mouth, showing me his extended fangs. It's not like I didn't know that fangs and arousal were linked. Hell, I'd read enough vampire novels to know that. But when they're extended right in front of you, it can take your breath away. Knowing he needed my acceptance just as much as I needed his, I lowered myself down onto his lap, straddling him and placing my arms loosely around his neck.

"Just don't bite me, okay?"

Cameron looked at me seriously although his voice was very gentle as he said, "Never without your consent. You must promise to tell me if I hurt you or if you are uncomfortable."

Biting my lip, I nodded nervously. He leaned in and kissed my cheek softly, then my chin, and finally my lips. His gentle kiss set my nerves at ease causing me to crush my lips against his, thrusting my tongue into his mouth. Cameron responded with equal passion and then moved to the side of my neck, sucking it lightly and tickling my collarbone with his tongue. I grabbed the bottom of his shirt and began pulling it up his chest until he grabbed the ends from my hands and lifted it over his head. His chest was smooth and chiseled to perfection, the hard muscles of his stomach quivering slightly at my touch. It was good to know I was having some effect on him.

Taking a break from my neck, Cameron returned to my lips while he unbuttoned the remaining buttons of my shirt, flapping it wide open and exposing my breasts to him. With both arms he pulled me into him, crushing my breasts against his cool chest and making me gasp with pleasure at the sensation. Tentatively he caressed my breast with his hand, and the feeling drove me so insane that I grabbed his hand and squeezed it tightly showing him how hard I wanted him to touch me. He responded by flipping me onto my back and holding himself above me. The feeling of having him between my legs was amazing, but my nerves jumped into high gear. I could feel the bulge in his pants as his pelvis pressed against me and again it felt wonderful, but I was beginning to shake.

Cameron stretched himself down the length of my body, sucking my neck lightly as his hand moved from my breast down to my hips where he teasingly rubbed his thumb in tiny circles underneath my panties. The sensation made me moan with pleasure, but nerves and anxiety were beginning to overwhelm me. I could feel my breath getting faster at the anticipation of what was going to happen next, and my hands kept flexing with tension.

Cameron's weight shifted as he lifted his pelvis up and began unbuckling his belt with his free hand. I tried to help, but my hands were shaking so badly that I placed them on his chest instead. This was what I wanted. I wanted him. I wanted him on top of me. I wanted to feel him inside me, giving him all of me. But as I heard the sound of his pants unzipping, I lost it.

"Stop, stop, stop," I said pushing against his chest and trying to wriggle out from under him.

Cameron stopped immediately, his eyes wide as he leapt off the bed and watched as I curled up and wept, shaking uncontrollably. After putting himself back together, he knelt at the foot of the bed and began petting my head soothingly.

"Brianna, please talk to me. Did I hurt you? Brianna, please," he begged, pressing his forehead against mine. "Bri, I am sorry. Please tell me what I did."

"Nothing," I sobbed, "it's him. I hate him, I hate him."

"Who, my love," Cameron said gently as he wiped the tears from my cheek with the back of his hand.

"Who else! Sam!" I yelled. "That bastard made me this way. Even a thousand miles away that man still takes everything from me." I pushed myself up angrily and walked over to the nightstand and turned on the bedroom lamp. I buttoned up my shirt and went into the bathroom to grab the pajama bottoms I had pulled out earlier. After I had slipped them on, I walked back out to the bedroom where Cameron laid out on the bed with his arms outstretched. I ran into his arms, curling myself into him as he wrapped his arms around me.

"Cam, I'm so sorry."

"Shh, Brianna," he cooed, "you have nothing to be sorry about. I am sorry I took it so far."

"Cameron, no," I said pushing myself up so that I could see him, "I wanted this to happen, I really did. Sam, he…he really…every time…"

Cameron reached up and brushed my hair out of my face. "Bri, you do not need to explain."

"But I do. I know you know that he used to hit me, but…when he…" I couldn't help but stutter. I tried saying it differently since I couldn't actually say the word. "I can count on one hand the number of times I slept with him voluntarily, and even those times were at the beginning of our marriage. After that he forced me, all the time. As the years went by it just got rougher, and the rougher it was the more he liked it. Sometimes I would even try to pretend I liked it or that it didn't hurt, and that just made him mad so he would just make it hurt worse. He wanted to see the pain, that's how he got off." I pushed myself up to my knees, still facing Cameron and ringing my hands in my lap. "And now, when I'm not forced to do it, and I want it, I freeze. I'm sorry, Cam, I'm so sorry. I really wanted this, I'm so…embarrassed."

"Bri, please stop apologizing, you are breaking my heart," he said caressing my cheek. "What he did to you is unforgivable and only adds evidence to the fact that he is a monster. It has nothing to do with you. Making love is an expression of how two people feel about one another. You need to be comfortable with everything we do together." He paused as he brought himself up onto his knees, holding my face in between his hands and looking deeply into my eyes. "I love you, Brianna. I thought for sure I could never love anyone else, and truly I never wanted to again. But when it comes to you, I cannot help myself. After what happened today, I know I simply cannot be without you." He paused for a second before he continued, "I am scaring you."

"Now why did you have to go and say that," I wailed as I jumped off the bed and began pacing the floor.

"I know it is bad timing, but I needed to tell you. I could not lie to you or myself about it any longer."

"That's just it, Cam, I've been lying to you. This whole time, I've been lying to you," I sobbed hysterically.

"W-what about?"

"Lots of things," I replied and began pacing again. All the thoughts and fears and lies came out of my mouth all at once while Cameron looked on. "So today, when you swear you heard me scream? Well you did. I did scream, in my head. That huge vampire was choking me and I saw those others throw you up against the wall and I thought they were going to kill you. Then this horrible burning came up from my stomach and rose up through my head, and I screamed the word no, I did Cam, and it rang loud and clear in my head and then all of you went down. I didn't think anything of it until we started talking tonight, and then I got all freaked out again. Something happened, and I don't know how I did it."

Cameron took a second before responding, "Is that all?"

I laughed. "Hardly."

"Then keep going," he replied as he swung his legs over the edge of the bed and faced me directly.

"Okay, so remember last night when I asked you about Eris?" He nodded. "Well, it's true that he has been coming to me in my dreams. Actually, he's the reason we left North Carolina. I dreamt that Elaina and her Vamps were coming and then Eris came into the dream and told me we needed to leave."

"I do not understand."

"Of course you don't, because I'm talking like an idiot." I paused and took a breath. "I've been having dreams, Cameron, dreams that have been coming true. Not all of them, but a bunch of pieces. Take today, I had a dream about it, well sort of. I dreamt that you were being attacked by a bunch of vampires and you were screaming at me to run, and then you pointed to something behind me. When I turned around there was this big vampire, just like today. Then I saw Elaina, well I know now that it was Elaina, but that's where things get confusing. See in my dream the big vampire was really attacking Daddy O instead of me and I killed him. I killed him with this silver dagger that I can draw you a picture of it was so detailed, and after I killed him, I saw Elaina and she was standing in front of these vampires. That's when Eris came to me. He told me we needed to leave or else the scene would come true, but now I'm not so sure. Did we really avoid getting Daddy O killed, or did we just move the attack to the mall today? That's what has me so confused."

"Have other dreams come true?"

"Y-yes," I answered tentatively. "But they're all jumbled up with other things. Like when I first saw you, the day in front of the church, not fifteen minutes before I had a dream about you. Not just some vampire, you. So really I knew you were a vampire before you ever told me.

"And then over the next couple of weeks I kept dreaming about you, and kept using the name Cameron. So that night when you saved me from Sam and you told me your name, I almost shit my pants because seriously how could I have known your name. I even dreamt about our first kiss, and it was right in front of Daddy O's house where it actually happened, but I looked like I was nine months pregnant and then Sam appeared and you killed him, I mean you actually snapped his neck." Cameron sat in disbelief, and his silence was deafening. "See, I'm nuts! I don't know what to do with this, it freaks me out. I don't know what to trust and what not to since everything is jumbled up together, which is why I kept it to myself." Finally, I was finished, and it felt as though ten pounds had been lifted from my chest.

Cameron sat like a statue on the edge of the bed, and I was unable to determine what he was feeling. Just when his silence was to the point of being unbearable, he said, "In regards to the…mind projection we will call it for now, we need to do some research. I will limit it to people I trust, possibly some older vampires may have come across something like this. For now, we will keep the dreams between you and me. Eris seems to already have some idea about what is going on, but I fear telling others will expose you to even greater danger."

"So you're not freaked out?" The man just told me he loved me, and I answered by admitting to him I had some mutant dreaming power and could take down a group of vampires with one yell…from my head.

"Brianna, I am a vampire. I drink blood to survive. I have the strength and speed of a hundred men, and I interact with hybrids and other vampires whose powers exceed my own. So no, I am not freaked out, and I apologize for coming off as such. I am truly amazed by you." Cameron moved from his position on the bed to stand directly in front of me. "I will always listen if you wish to share your dreams, even if you feel they are unimportant. I will help you in any way you need me to. I meant what I said, Bri, I love you. And whether or not you ever love me back, I will be here, right here in front of you until you push me away. And even then, I will fight for you," he finished with a smile.

I smiled back up at him. "You called me Bri."

"You call me Cam."

"Yeah, but I never thought I'd get a nickname."

"I called you my angel," he said defensively.

"It's different. You don't even call your siblings by nicknames. Oh, well, except Alex I guess."

"Yes well, that is a story for another time," he said sheepishly. "You need to get to bed."

"Hey now, don't be thinking you can start telling me what to do."

Cameron looked down at me with a devilish smile on his face. In a matter of seconds, he lifted me up off the ground, flew across the room to the bed, put me under the covers, and tucked me in.

"Okay, now you're just playing dirty," I said as he reached over me and turned off the light on the nightstand. "You may have gotten me in this bed, but that doesn't mean I have to sleep."

"I have my ways," he said as he began brushing through my hair and gently caressing my forehead and cheeks with his cool fingers. "May I ask, will I ever get my shirt back?"

I laughed as I rolled into his side and nuzzled my face into his chest. "Nope. Not after that little stunt." After a few minutes I placed my hand on top of Cameron's. "Cam, about earlier…I don't know when I'll be able to…"

"Shh," he cooed into my hair and folded my hand back into my chest. "Sleep, my love, that is all you need to worry about tonight. Now you must get some rest."

Cameron was right, he had his ways because I was asleep in a matter of seconds. I was laying in the arms of a man who loved me, who wasn't afraid of my mutant powers, and lastly who had stopped when I asked him to. It may not have been the romantic night I had dreamt about, but it still had an amazing ending. I was loved; loved by a man, well vampire actually. Maybe that's where I had always gone wrong. I was looking for love from a human when I was supposed to be with a vampire all along. Nothing like a big, fat, juicy rationalization right before bed.

Chapter Twenty-six

Brianna

I was lying on a hard, cold, stone floor while Elaina stood over me. Nervously I looked around the room and realized that I was surrounded by a dozen of her vampires who all stood at attention in front of their mistress.

Elaina knelt down beside me, running the back of her hand down my cheek. "It is time, Brianna," she said in a sweet high-pitched voice, the sound of which totally took me by surprise.

I looked down at myself and saw that I was dressed in a thin, white, gossamer gown, my stomach extremely swollen with pregnancy. Even more frightening was that the gown was soaked with a mixture of fluid and blood. My water must have broken, I was bleeding, and surrounded by crazy vampires. I was in trouble.

Elaina caressed my face again as if to comfort me before she clapped her hands together, signaling for something. Just then another woman stepped forward and handed Elaina a large knife.

Elaina looked up at the woman as she said, "You will need to hold her down."

The woman left Elaina's side and came to kneel at my head, placing a firm grip on my shoulders. I struggled against her hold causing her to slam my shoulders down harder.

"Let me go! Please, please, let me go," I shouted through tears.

"The babies are ours!" Elaina yelled joyfully as she raised the knife above her head and plunged it into my stomach...

"Cameron!" I screamed as I flew upright in bed clenching my stomach.

Suddenly to my left the bathroom door exploded off its hinges and Cameron came barging through, fangs extended ready to fight. Seeing me in the bed, he flew to my side searching for injuries. "Brianna, are you all right? What happened?"

"I-I'm...I'm...sorry," I replied, trying to catch my breath. "It was just a bad dream. I'm sorry."

Cameron sat on the bed and his fangs retracted back up into his mouth as he rubbed the sides of my arms. "Do you want to talk about it?"

I shook my head. "What were you doing in the bathroom?"

"I needed to make a call and did not want to wake you."

"But why the bathroom? Whenever you talk to your brothers you speak so quietly I can't hear you even when I'm next to you."

"I needed to speak to a human," Cameron said as he stopped rubbing my arms and became very serious. "It has been a few days since I last fed, and especially after yesterday, I need blood. I will not be gone long, and while I am out, I will pick you up something to eat as well. You must be starving."

I looked at the clock on the nightstand. I had slept all day.

"Why didn't you wake me?"

"Because you obviously needed the rest."

I sighed and brushed my hair away from my face, suddenly feeling unbelievably guilty. "Yeah, food sounds good."

"Anything in particular?"

I shook my head no.

"Do you need your crackers?"

I shook my head again. "No, I'm good. Come to think of it, I didn't have any nausea yesterday either. Maybe I'm getting over the hump."

Cameron smiled and gave me a quick kiss on the forehead, and then a soft kiss on the lips. This was what I wanted; not sitting in a car, not running away from crazy vampires, just time together like we had at Daddy O's.

"I know this is a stupid question," I said as he rose from the bed, "but since it's so late already, do we really need to travel today? I'm exhausted and my back is killing me. After yesterday, I really just need a day of doing nothing. Is that in any way possible?"

Cameron pondered my proposal for a minute and then nodded his head.

"Fine, but it means we leave early tomorrow, all right?"

"Deal."

"I will be back as soon as I can," he said before giving me one last kiss.

"Um, Cam, what do we do about the door?"

Cameron smiled and began picking up the pieces of wood from the floor and piling them in the corner. "I will be sure to leave money to fix it. I have my phone, so call me if you need me."

I waved goodbye and took a good look at his ass as he left. I could have seen it last night, but no, Brianna Marie had to have a panic attack right before what could have been the most sexually pleasurable night of her entire life.

"Idiot," I groaned aloud and flipped on the small TV. There were only ten channels, none of which I particularly liked, but I was happy to find an older movie that would at least pass the time. I adjusted my position on the bed to take the pressure off my back, but I still needed to lie down. Yesterday's attack caused more damage than I thought. Having a day off from traveling was really what I needed.

After watching the old movie through the first few commercial breaks, I decided I needed to take a shower. Just as I lathered the sweet-smelling shampoo through my hair, I heard Cameron's cell phone ringing in the bedroom. That was weird since he told me he had it with him. Thinking nothing of it I continued to rinse my hair and let the call go to voicemail. Thirty seconds later, his phone rang again. It had better be important, or I was going to be pissed.

I threw a towel around me and ran out of the shower to answer the phone before it went to voicemail again. Just as the fourth ring was dying out, I pressed the call button, "Hello, hello?"

"Brianna?" Cameron said on the other end.

"Duh, are you okay?" I replied as I shivered from the cold water dripping down my back.

"Yes of course. Are you all right? The phone went to voicemail the first time I called. I was worried."

"I'm fine. I was in the shower and now I'm dripping all over the floor."

"Oh, well that explains it then. I was just calling to tell you that I grabbed your phone by mistake."

"Yeah, yeah, got it. Still dripping here."

"Yes, sorry. I should be back within the hour."

"Okay, bye."

I placed the phone back on the table and ran back to the shower. Just as I dropped the towel on the floor, the phone rang again. That Cameron Burke was going to get it. I grabbed a new towel since the old one was now soaking wet, ran back out to the bedroom, and answered the phone. "I am going to kill you!"

"I seriously doubt that," a raspy voice said on the other line. "As you are certainly not Cameron, am I to assume that I am speaking to Brianna Morgan Lewis?"

"M-morgan...just Morgan," I answered nervously. "Who is this?"

"My name is Victor. Perhaps you know me better as Cameron's father. I was hoping to speak to him, after all this is his number."

As Victor spoke, my knees began to shake so badly that I had to sit on the bed.

"He...he took my phone by mistake," I tried to say while my bottom lip trembled uncontrollably. "He n-needed to get blood. I can give you my number..."

"No, that will not be necessary. This actually gives us time to have a little chat."

"You...want to...talk...to me?

"You see, Brianna, I find you a nuisance. Yes, at first, I did feel for you because of your...situation. But now you have corrupted my child, caused him to recklessly disobey me, and put himself, our family, and our entire race in jeopardy, all for what? An emotional and stubborn hybrid that uses her charms to get what she wants."

His statements slapped me across the face. I was speechless. I knew that Victor was angry with Cameron, but I didn't know it was also directed at me. My silence urged him to continue.

"Because of who your father is, I supported his request to have Cameron personally take your case, but this has gone too far. Cameron's blatant disregard would be cause for execution if he was any other Warrior, but he is not. Cameron has always been loyal without question, until he met you. And you, my dear, will be his demise. I will have no alternative but to execute my favorite son unless he brings you to the Facility within the next twelve hours. You see, I have already shown Cameron such leniency and favoritism that others may believe I have softened. And I cannot have that, you understand, don't you?"

"Yes sir," I replied and wiped away the tears streaming down my face.

"Ah, good. I knew we could have an understanding. Now use those charms you have so successfully deployed on Cameron up until now and get him here within twelve hours, otherwise I will not be able to stop Devin from taking out his orders."

"Devin? But I thought he and Cam were…"

"Friends? Brothers? Ah, yes, they are that, but Devin does what I order him to do, unlike Cameron of late. It is part of being a member of the Warrior coven I'm afraid. Now, I would suggest that you not mention our little conversation to Cameron. I believe it would only hinder your efforts to get him home safely. Don't you agree?"

"Yes sir."

"Good then. Well, my dear, I cannot say it has been a pleasure. You have definitely been a thorn in my side. Hopefully Cameron will see his error in judgment, at least for your sake if not his own," Victor said before the line went dead.

I brought my knees to my chest, rested my head on them and sobbed. Seriously, could anything go right? Could there be one day where my life didn't suck? Even in the worst of times with Sam I didn't remember crying this much in such a short time period. I was surprised I even had tears left.

As I sat huddled in a little ball, I realized that crying wasn't going to do any good. Cameron's life was still in danger, and Victor had given me twelve hours to fix it. Even though Victor was an ass, he was right. If I told Cameron that getting to San Francisco tonight was a demand of Victor's, he totally wouldn't go. I know I wouldn't.

I jumped up from the bed and headed back into the bathroom to finish showering. Although I still felt like crap, I needed to pull it together enough to get packed and convince Cameron we needed to leave right away. I would need to use my "charms" as Victor put it. Damn he made me sound like a manipulative slut. For heaven's sake, enough of my personal baggage had been thrown at Cameron to bury him, but he still insisted on being with me. That was his choice, not mine.

Once out of the shower I threw on the sweats from yesterday. I hadn't worn them for very long, and I was running out of clean clothes. Grabbing the motel's hairdryer, I flipped my hair over and almost fell to the floor. My body was weaker than I expected. So, I finished blowing my hair dry standing upright and tried to ignore the pain in my back. The car ride wouldn't do it any good either, but it would be the last. The time had finally come. There were no more car rides and wonderful nights snuggling into Cam. That was all over. And at the thought of that, the tears came down again.

I splashed some cold water on my face to get rid of the redness and ran into the bedroom to finish packing. Just as I folded my last shirt, I heard Cameron unlocking the door. As he stepped inside, I took a deep cleansing breath to calm myself down. I still hadn't figured out what I was going to say to convince him we needed to leave after I had just begged him to let us stay for the night.

Cameron stood in the doorway with the small cooler we'd kept from Magda in one hand, and a paper bag in the other.

"Brianna, is everything all right?"

"Uh, well, no. We need to leave, right now, actually," I said turning to face him as I slung my leather bag over my shoulder.

"Why? What has happened?" I couldn't answer him; my mind went blank. "Did you have another dream?"

Dream? Yes!

"That's exactly what happened," I replied a little too eagerly. "I had a dream a few of Elaina's Vamps were near us. We need to get to San Francisco tonight. Preferably within the next twelve hours."

Cameron stared at me for a second, and then nodded. He placed the cooler and the paper bag on the little table and packed the few items that he had taken out of his duffle.

"Cam, what's with the cooler and the bag?"

"The paper bag is your dinner, and mine is in the cooler."

If I didn't feel bad before, I certainly felt sick now. "Well, just don't open the cooler, okay?"

Cameron laughed and we headed out the door and into the car. Once I had buckled my seatbelt, he handed me the paper bag that had a small bag of chips and a peanut butter and jelly sandwich.

"I am sorry, angel, there was really nothing to choose from. It was either that, or well, that."

"It's fine. I'm not all that hungry anymore," I said and put the bag in the floor.

Cameron gave me a questioning look, but then pulled out of our parking space and eased down the drive toward the motel office.

"Bri, are you sure you are well enough to travel? You look very pale."

"Yeah, just anxious to get going, that's all."

With one more concerned look, Cameron jumped out of the car and went into the office to check us out of the motel. By the time he returned, I was asleep. Or rather, pretending to be. If I forced myself to sleep, I wouldn't be tempted to blurt out the truth. San Francisco was roughly eight hours away which left us plenty of time to beat Victor's time demand, and Cameron would be safe. That's all that really mattered to me right now. Cameron loved me, and I needed him to be around long enough for me to truly love him back.

Chapter Twenty-seven

Cameron

Brianna was not well, though she would not admit it. Even more frustrating was the fact that I could not tell whether it was her pregnancy making her sick, or the stress from her dreams she only just admitted having. Certain aspects of her dreams were frightfully accurate. The fact that she dreamt I had killed Sam in the precise manner I had, terrified me. If her abilities as an un-activated hybrid were discovered, her life and freedom would be in jeopardy and not only by Elaina's followers.

We had been driving for five hours and Brianna slept for most of them, only waking to adjust her position. Although I did not want to delay our trip, her suggestion of taking a day off had really been a good idea for both of us. She needed rest, and I needed blood. But when I returned from the blood bank, she was insistent that we leave immediately because of a new dream. Unfortunately, because of the rush to get on the road I had not fed on the much needed blood that was still in the cooler.

Thankfully there was a rest stop up ahead. I was hoping to make it all the way to San Francisco before stopping, but the terrible burning in my throat made it necessary to stop right away before I was unable to control my bloodlust any longer. Seeing the off ramp for the rest stop, I pulled off the highway and was pleased to see there were no other cars around. I pulled the car in a spot close to the surrounding woods so that I could hide among the trees, but still keep an eye on Brianna. After turning the car off, I grabbed the cooler from the backseat and caressed Brianna's cheek, but she did not stir. I hated even leaving her, but my hunger was getting to an extreme level.

The moon was bright and full, causing the leaves to flash silver light as the wind blew through them. I found a tree with a large canopy of drooping limps where I could stay covered, but see the car. This meal was not going to be pleasant. The technician at the blood bank had given me plenty of ice packs to keep the blood fresh, but no vampire liked cold blood. However, when necessity called, you were forced to drink whatever you could get your hands on.

The first bag of blood was empty in a matter of seconds. Unfortunately, in no way did it quench the burning, but thankfully there were three more bags of disgusting, unappetizing, cold blood. After drinking the second bag, the anxious desire to feed subsided enough to where I could make the phone calls I needed to.

After listening to Devin's voicemail greeting, I left a cryptic message telling him we were about four hours away from the Facility. I was a little troubled by the fact he did not answer his phone. Hopefully he was not already hunting me, that was all this dreadful trip needed. Kneeling down to the ground I picked up another bag of blood and ripped it open with my teeth as I dialed Alexander.

"Cam!" Alexander's deep voice answered after the second ring.

"Hello Alex, are you busy?" I asked before emptying my third bag of blood.

"No, just sitting with Kyla. Are you all right?"

"For now. Just wanted to let you know we are about four hours away."

Alexander sighed heavily with relief. "You have no idea how relieved I am to hear you say that." As he spoke, I could hear Kyla having a similar response next to him.

"I know you are. Actually, I called Devin a minute ago but I got his voicemail. Has he left to find me?"

"Not that I know of. He and Father have been in conference for the last two days, no one has really seen either of them. "

"Plotting my demise, I am sure."

"Please don't joke about that, Cam. Do not underestimate Father's anger toward you."

"Trust me, in no way do I underestimate what Father will do to me. I am ready to accept my punishment for doing what I believe is right. Alex, can you hold for a moment?" I said, hearing the sound of a car door shutting and seeing Brianna walk toward the bathroom. I did not like that she was hunched and holding her back. I worried she was injured from the attack in

Flagstaff and was keeping it from me.

"Everything okay?" Alexander said, bringing me back to his attention.

"Yes, I heard Brianna getting out of the car and just wanted to check on her."

"Have I mentioned how bad you have it for her?"

"I love her, Alex."

Alexander was silent but Kyla cheered on the other end.

"Great, now I owe Kyla two hundred dollars."

"You bet on whether or not I would fall in love with her?" I said with a twinge of anger.

"No! Kyla bet me you were doing all of this *because* you were in love with her. I said there was no way and it was because you were seeing how far you could push Father."

"So sorry to disappoint you."

"Well, it certainly makes Kyla happy. I'm sure she is already planning the wedding," Alexander laughed.

"Tell her to wait. Brianna is technically still married, remember?"

"Not for too much longer I'm sure," he replied, unaware that she was already a widow. "Are you dropping her off and then coming home?"

"It depends on how Brianna is feeling. I am definitely worried about her transition."

"Understandable, but that's what the counselors are there for. You cannot be with her twenty-four hours a day. She needs to adapt too."

"I know," I admitted reluctantly. "It will be difficult to let her go."

"Cam, do not test Father any more than you already have. Drop her off at the Facility and get to the manor. Once you've diffused things with Father, then figure out what happens with you and Brianna. Regardless, you need to watch out for Devin, even if you are only four hours away."

"If Devin has been sent for me, there is no use hiding or pleading. Just as long as Brianna gets to the Facility safe, I do not care what happens to me."

"But Brianna may. How will she feel if you are killed because of what you did for her?"

His statement kicked me in the gut. Alexander may be intimidating to look at, but he had more heart and compassion than anyone I knew.

"Thank you, Alex."

"Get home."

"On my way. Give my love to Kyla," I said and hung up.

Before leaving the woods I quickly drank the last bag of blood before discarding the empty plastic bags into the garbage. Concerned that Brianna was still in the bathroom, I walked up to the small building to check on her. I still did not dare go into the ladies' restroom, so I merely called to her from outside the door.

"Bri?"

I heard her sniffle before she answered, "I'll be out in a minute."

"Do you need me?"

"No. I just need a minute."

Knowing something was wrong, but accepting she obviously needed space, I reluctantly answered, "I will be in the car, love."

Another ten minutes passed before she came out of the restroom. Her entire posture was defeated and her arms were crossed tightly around her stomach. All the color was gone from her face which was shiny with tears. She completely ignored me while I held her car door open and eased her down in her seat. Even after she buckled her seatbelt, she crossed her arms around her and waited for me to close the door.

What had I done now?

With a sigh I stepped back around to the driver's side of the car and a few moments later reversed out of the parking space. Just as I put the car in drive, I slammed on the brakes and turned to look in the backseat for where I had spilled blood on the floor, but found none.

Slowly I turned to Brianna. "Bri…I smell blood."

Brianna's stifled cries became an outpouring of emotion. "It's happening again," she cried, barely audible through her tears.

She was miscarrying. As if she had not been through enough, she was losing her child. Placing the car in park, not caring that I was in the middle of the road, I brought Brianna into my arms as much as I could with a console in between us. Stroking her hair I said to her softly, "We will find the first exit where we can get you what you need, and we will find a place for you to recover."

"No!" she screamed, jerking herself out of my arms. "We can't stop. Just find me a drug store and we'll keep going."

"Brianna, I understand you are worried about what you saw in your dream, but we need to get you…"

"We can't! We have to get to San Francisco tonight. We have to," she continued to scream at me. "You…you don't understand."

"Then help me to understand," I replied in a raised voice. "You are bleeding and in pain, and yet you will not let me help you. Forget San

Francisco, we will go there once you have healed. I refuse to take you there in this condition."

I slammed the car back in gear and sped down the ramp onto the highway.

"Cameron, please," Brianna cried hysterically, hugging my arm to her chest.

"Brianna, this is not up for discussion. We are spending the night in the closest hotel I can find and that is final."

Brianna curled herself up in the passenger seat holding her stomach. "But he'll kill you," she sobbed.

"Who?"

"D..Devin."

"Who told you Devin was going to kill me?" Brianna became silent, though still crying. "Bri, please."

Reluctantly and quietly, she replied, "Victor."

It was my turn to be silent. When had Victor spoken to her? It had to have been while our phones were switched earlier today.

"Did you really have a dream about Elaina's vampires coming for you?"

"No," she whimpered.

"Victor called looking for me, and got you instead?"

"Yes."

"And he told you Devin was coming for me?"

Brianna began gasping for air while her sobs became hysterical. "He said…I needed to…get you…home in twelve…hours…or else…he couldn't stop…Devin…from…killing…you…all…my…fault…can't…have…that… happen…"

Brianna was going to hyperventilate if she did not calm down. I wrapped my arm around her shoulder, leaned her into my side, and began helping her take deep breaths while I snaked around cars on the highway.

"Bri, I will fix this. Please do not worry about Devin. I will handle him and Victor. I need you to breathe with me, nice and slow. I will take care of everything, I promise," I said into her hair while keeping one eye on the road, looking for an exit with a commercial area.

A few minutes later Brianna's breathing was under control and we were pulling off an exit that had a twenty-four-hour grocery store. Once I pulled into a parking space, she gave me a list of items she needed, and I ran inside. In the store I began going down the list trying to find each of the items and feeling utterly lost in the feminine product aisle. Thankfully a young female sales associate noticed my complete helplessness and got me through the list.

Finally with all items in hand, the same sales associate rung me up and referred me to a motel one exit away. Once back in the car, I placed the bag of items into the backseat, and brought Brianna back into me as we drove to the motel. She continued to whimper that she was well enough to keep traveling, but I was staying firm for her sake. Even though on the outside I was calm with Brianna in my arms, on the inside I was furious. I had to loosen my grip on the steering wheel because I began to feel it bending underneath my hand. Victor could threaten me all day long, but not my Brianna. She was already ill this morning, but I was positive this did not help her condition. Damn him, damn my father, my maker, that son of a bitch.

The exit for the motel came up quickly, and several minutes later I was carrying Brianna into our room and into the bathroom where I turned on the hot water to start a bath.

"Do you need help undressing?" She closed her eyes and bit her bottom lip as she shook her head. "Alright then, I will bring in your bag."

Leaving the door open behind me, I ran back out to the car and grabbed our things. When I returned to the bathroom, Brianna was shrugging out of her shirt so I placed her bag inside and shut the door behind me to give her some privacy. Knowing this situation changed everything, I picked up my phone and dialed Alexander's number for the second time this evening.

"Don't tell me you are already here."

"Alex, I will not make it there tonight."

"Goddamn it, Cam."

"Alex, stop," I yelled back at him. "There is nothing I can do. Is Kyla still with you? I need to speak with her."

My brother's anger and annoyance were compounded by his silence as he passed the phone to his wife.

"Cameron, you are playing with fire," Kyla said in a worried voice.

"Kyla, I need your help in making them understand what is happening."

"One minute you're here in four hours and the next you're not. What is going on that you can't drive another few hours?"

"Brianna is miscarrying as we speak," I replied.

Kyla was silent for a moment before she said, "I don't think any of us were aware she was pregnant. It's not yours, is it?"

"She found out while we were in North Carolina, and no, it is not mine.

Now she is…in shock, I guess. Let Devin come and find me, but I will not leave her and I refuse to force her into a car in her condition. I need your help, Kyla, please. Please help them understand, they will assume I am making excuses."

"Cameron, you know how they are. What if they don't…"

"Kyla, please just try. That is all I am asking."

"I will do my best, it's not like I've ever…gone through this. I will try, though, for you."

"Thank you, Kyla," I said. My head fell into my hand as a small amount of relief came over me.

"Don't thank me yet. I'll call you after I've talked to Victor. Oh…oh poor dear. She must be so upset."

"I feel so helpless. There is nothing I can do for her. It has been so long since…" I stopped and cleared my throat of the emotions that were beginning to set in. "I will talk to you soon then."

As we said our goodbyes, I heard Brianna turn the bathwater off and fall back into the tub. I walked over to the door and knocked gently. "Love, do you need anything?"

"No," she said between sniffles.

"I am right by the door if you do."

She did not answer back, but I did not pry. Keeping to my word I sat with my back pressed up against the bathroom door listening intently for any movement or plea for help, but none came. After nearly a half hour of wanting to bang my head up against the wall, I heard the sound of Brianna stepping out of her bath. I stood as well and paced in front of the door waiting for her to come out.

After another ten minutes, she padded out of the bathroom and into my waiting arms. She was frighteningly pale and still slightly hunched from the pain in her abdomen. Holding her with one arm, I pulled down the blankets on the bed with the other and helped her underneath them where she immediately curled into herself. I walked around to the other side of the bed, taking my shoes off and slipping under the covers. With her rounded back facing me, I pulled her in snugly to my chest and held her while she cried uncontrollably for the next hour. It killed me each time she started weeping after she had calmed herself down for a few minutes. I knew she was not crying because of the pain, it was because of the endless cycle of losing one baby after another for the last fourteen years.

Her pain was my pain, and my unbearable helplessness caused me to say to her, "Let me help you."

"I'm sorry, I'll get myself under control."

"Shh, Bri please…it tears me apart to see you in pain like this when I can help you." Brianna remained silent and so I continued, "A vampire's bite can soothe you into a deep sleep. It will relax some of the physical pain, at least long enough for you to rest."

Brianna's crying subsided, but was replaced by nervousness as she asked, "Will it hurt?"

"Only for a second," I replied, brushing her hair with my fingers and feeling her body jerk.

Brianna turned painfully around to face me and I could see her eyes were extremely swollen. Holding her face in my hand, I leaned in and kissed both of her eyelids knowing my cold lips would soothe them.

Brianna reached up and touched my cheek with her hand and then rested her lips on mine. When she pulled away, her bottom lip was trembling as she said, "Just hold me while you do it."

"I will not let go until you are deeply asleep."

She nodded and moved the hair away from her neck and let me cradle her in my arms.

"I love you, angel," I said while her body shook in my arms. "I promise you will only feel it for a second, just stay still. I do not want your skin to tear," and before she could react, I extended my fangs and bit into the soft skin between her neck and chest. Her body flinched at first but within seconds she completely relaxed. Her warm blood filled my mouth and I had to force myself to stop drinking from her even after it quenched the burning that the earlier cold blood had not. The desire for more was difficult to fight since her blood was so sweet and flowing with extreme power. Carefully I pulled my fangs from her neck and licked the wounds to seal them.

Not fully trusting myself, I slowly crept out from under the blankets and stepped outside. My fangs retracted once the fresh air entered my nostrils and my bloodlust subsided. Having tasted Brianna's blood for a second time, it was even more evident that she would be in extreme danger if Elaina ever got her hands on her. And that could very well happen if I was no longer around to protect Brianna because I had provoked Victor to the point of my execution. I needed more time. Not just to be with her, but more time to allow Bri to heal without feeling any pressure from my family. She should be allowed at least that in her current condition. Knowing there was only one person who could help me, I went back into the bedroom and called Jared.

He answered before the first ring had even finished. "Not a good time."

"Jared, I need you to find a number for me."

"Seriously dude, not a good time," he whispered. I could hear angry voices in the background; no doubt having to do with me.

"Then text me the number as soon as you can."

Jared sighed. "Okay, who do you need to find?"

"Eris."

Chapter Twenty-eight

Brianna

The sun shown above me in beautiful bright rays as it refracted through the thin, white clouds stretched across the Carolina blue sky. The mist-covered mountains reached high above the trees surrounding my grandfather's mountain home. Daddy O sat asleep on the wraparound porch in his rocking chair with the day's newspaper strewn across his chest. I was sitting on a large boulder located in the front yard and watched as a young boy, no more than four, in tiny overall shorts with black curly hair came running up the side yard toward me. About halfway up the slope of the yard he stopped and turned around, yelling something back at Cameron who was now coming up the hill and carrying a young girl with equally dark hair and long soft curls. Cameron put the little girl down on the ground and straightened her pink frilly skirt. The little girl ran to the boy, who was obviously her brother, grabbed his hand and the two ran the rest of the way up the yard and into my arms.

"I wuv you, Mama," the little girl said as she kissed my cheek.

"I wuv you more, Mama," the little boy said.

"No, you don't," the girl shouted, and the two of them began to squabble.

"You're both wrong, I love you both more," I said, calming them down and kissing the tops of their curly heads. "Now go play."

The children ran back to Cameron who grabbed both of them at the same time and threw them in the air, catching them a second later while they exploded with bubbly laughter. The scene was as beautiful as it was heart wrenching. While I watched them, I saw a flash of billowing red out of the corner of my eye, bringing my attention around to see Eris walking toward me with long flowing red robes, his hair loose and long.

"I know who you are, you might as well drop the charade," I said, turning back around to watch the children laugh and play together.

With a burst of light, Eris's attire changed from red billowing robes to modern loose slacks and a white linen shirt, his dark hair pulled back in a leather tie. He went from looking like my beardless Jesus, to a wealthy man on vacation.

"Is this better?" he asked.

"Is this what you really look like?"

"In this decade, yes," he replied as he sat next to me on the boulder and observed the children running around the yard while Cameron chased them.

"So why the gray clouds and big robes?"

"I thought it was more ominous. If I had come to you dressed liked this, you would not have listened to me or heeded my warnings. I know how you love the fantasy novels, so I figured I would give you something that you would connect with."

He was right. If the vampire next to me had come dressed like he was now, I would have dismissed him.

"You look younger with your hair back."

"Well, thank you, although I am quite old," he replied with a slight smile.

"So I have been told. You certainly don't look like you could have a daughter my age."

"Ah, so you know. I believe that is a good thing. We can be more open with each other now, my Bri-an-na."

"I wouldn't go that far. I don't even know what to call you."

"You can call me Father, or Daddy, like any other child."

A little bit of anger rose inside of me, he had hit a nerve. "Do you see that man in the rocking chair?" I said standing and pointing to Daddy O. "He is my father. He raised me and fixed up my skinned knees and tucked me into bed at night. You, sir, are only a sperm donor, and don't you dare think otherwise."

I started to walk away only to have the scene around me refresh and I was sitting back on the rock with Eris.

"This isn't me dreaming, is it," I said as I watched the two little children scurry around the yard, then stop and wave at me before they leapt on

Cameron. "*Are you showing me all of this?*"

"*Yes I am,*" Eris responded while he laughed at the scene in front of us.

The sight of Cameron playing with the two children who looked exactly like him brought tears to my eyes.

"*Why would you show me this, especially after what just happened. Why are you showing me something I will never have?*" I cried as my head fell onto my knees.

Eris began rubbing my back, reminding me of something Daddy O would have done. Oddly enough, I didn't stop him.

"*The Warrior told me what happened. I have to admit I do not have much experience in these situations and I wanted to help you. I am giving you the only thing I can. I thought showing you what is to be would help your spirit.*"

Abruptly I sat up and looked at him, tears still stuck in my eyes. "*What?*"

"*Bri-an-na, I cannot comfort you in person, and the Warrior stated how distraught you were. I thought this would give you the hope you need. You will have a family, mia figlia, it has already been seen.*"

"*But how do you know?*"

"*I have a source.*"

"*Oh well that helps.*"

"*Bri-an-na, I cannot give away all my secrets just yet,*" he said as he rose from the boulder. "*Now if you will excuse me, I am going to play with my grandchildren.*"

"*Are they twins?*"

"*They certainly appear to be,*" he replied and continued to walk toward the children who smiled and ran to him. "*Now is probably a good time for you to wake, figlia. But believe me when I say, you are to be a mother someday. Our very existence depends on it.*"

The scene around me began to fade in color which caused me to stand in a panic. "*Wait, not yet. What do you mean our existence?*"

"*Another time, mia figlia,*" and with a snap of his fingers the mountain scene swirled away...

My eyes flutter opened and the familiar motel room came into view. On the nightstand next to me was a small spray of wildflowers sitting in one of the glasses from the bathroom. The sight of the flowers made me smile and as I stretched to touch them, I felt Cameron's cool arm curl around me. I took his hand and squeezed it before slipping out of bed and walking to the bathroom.

The problem with motel bathrooms was that you couldn't avoid looking at yourself in the mirror since it covered an entire wall. My eyes were puffy and dark, my skin pallid and sickly. I undressed and stepped into the shower to clean myself up from a night of sweating and bleeding. After I lathered and rinsed myself of soap, I sat down on the floor of the tub, letting the hot water hit me all over. My back ached, my stomach was cramping, and I just wanted to live in a hot shower for the next week.

Last night was a nightmare. Devin was probably on his way to kill Cameron, and there was nothing I could do. Victor was right; I was Cameron's demise, even when circumstances were beyond my control. I started thinking about if I had only pushed myself to ride for longer periods of time, or if I hadn't slept all day yesterday, then all of this mess would have happened at the Facility, and Cameron would be safe. I would have been alone most likely, but you had to make sacrifices for those you cared about. Now Cameron's life hung in the balance, and I could barely keep myself together.

The shower wasn't helping as much as I had hoped, so I turned the water off and flung the shower curtain open to step out. By the sink sat a pair of pajamas and underwear that Cameron must have snuck in while I was showering, and I felt my heart beam. While I put on the pajamas, the steam on the mirror began to evaporate showing me once again just how scary I looked. I began to brush my teeth when my eyes zeroed in on two little holes at the base of my neck. I leaned into the mirror to get a better look and saw that the two puncture wounds were red but nearly healed. Another dream had come true, and even Cam's statements as he prepared me for the bite were dead on.

While I continued brushing my teeth, I tried to remember the moment itself, but could only remember the initial prick. Everything after that was forgotten, and maybe that was for the best. I spit out the remaining toothpaste, rinsed my mouth, and then popped some ibuprofens for the pain. After brushing the rat's nest out of my hair, I padded back into the bedroom where Cameron laid expectantly on the bed. Once under the covers I turned into Cam and brought my knees into my chest.

"Are you all right?" he breathed into my hair and began rubbing my back gently.

"I will be," I replied, relaxing into him with each stroke of his hand. "I never wanted you to see me like this. I'm such a mess."

"You are perfectly well considering the circumstances."

"Always the gentleman."

He laughed lightly. "Not always."

"Can I ask you something really embarrassing?"

"You can ask me anything."

"Does it bother you to be this close to me while I'm bleeding?"

Cameron paused his stroking for a moment before he answered. "It is definitely an exercise in control."

I tilted my head to look at him directly. "I'll understand if you need to leave."

"Not a chance," he replied and then kissed the tip of my nose which made me smile, and then I kissed him back on his soft lips. "Now can I talk to you about something?"

"I suppose it's only fair."

"I believe there is a side effect to drinking your blood."

I raised my eyebrows at him. "So you're going to tell me there is something *else* wrong with me?"

"No," Cameron answered with a frustrated sigh. "Remember how I told you that when a vampire drinks a hybrid's blood, they take on some of the hybrid's powers?" I nodded, but he struggled with how to phrase what he wanted to say. "Were you dreaming about being at Oliver's?"

Stunned by his words, I nodded slowly.

"And about Eris?"

I nodded again.

"Children?"

I bit my lip and swallowed. "You saw all of that?"

"No, not everything, it was more like flashes. It terrified me at first because I had no idea what was happening. It was as though I was watching a movie and seeing myself through someone else's eyes."

"Cam, that wasn't me. Eris was showing me those things," I said defensively.

"Brianna, I did not bring this up to make you upset."

"I just...I don't even know what to say. H-how can you see my dreams?" I asked and tucked my head under Cameron's chin.

"I do not know, love. I am figuring this out just as you are. It could be a combination of your dreaming and projection abilities."

As if my frustration with Eris entering my dreams wasn't enough, now I couldn't even keep them to myself? Not wanting to dwell on yet another new found ability, I went back to my anger toward Eris.

"I know Eris was trying to help, I guess, but how is seeing a dream like that going to help me right now? I obviously can't have children. Yeah, way to go, *Dad*, I feel so much better."

"How do you know what he created is not true?"

"Oh for crying out loud," I said and flipped the covers off me and got out of the bed. Cameron scooped me up in his arms a millisecond later and placed me back into bed. "Cut that out! If I want to get out of bed because you are being ridiculous, then I will." I grabbed the covers to flip them off of me again, but Cameron clamped his arm down and shook his head.

"I will tie you down to this bed if I have to."

"Cameron, you don't honestly believe what you saw is really going to happen, do you?"

"I know that your dreams come true, and Eris seemed certain that what he was showing you was going to be your future. It is hard not to think that it has merit. I thought you would be happy to know that in the years to come you will have children. That is what you want, a family of your own?"

"Look at me, Cam," I said, pushing his arm away and sitting up to face him directly, although my body wasn't pleased. "I cannot have children. I have demonstrated that too many times over the last fourteen years. If you want to have a happy little family of four, you have got the wrong girl, because I can't help you." Flustered and angry, I flopped back down and rolled away from Cameron. "For goodness' sake, we still barely know each other, and now you're convinced we're going to have kids and a happy fairytale life? Well, it's not going to happen, because that kind of stuff never happens for me. Never has, never will. So go find someone else to play house with."

I'll admit I was being bitchy. I was having a bad day, bad month, bad life, but it was no excuse. My anger wasn't directed toward him, he just happened to be there. As I wiped my tears away with the sheet, Cameron curled up behind me, spooning me and wrapping his hand over mine as his head rested just above me. The anger began to subside as my breathing calmed down to match the slow rhythm of his, and I knew very well that he was only pretending to breathe for my sake.

"My name is Cameron Jackson Burke, born December 13, 1709 on my father Thomas's farm in Massachusetts. He married my mother Catherine at the age of nineteen, and he often told me it was love at first sight, though my mother did not agree. She said he was quite arrogant when they first met, and that she rejected him several times before finally agreeing to let him call on her. But in the end, they loved each other deeply and were blessed with two children, me and my older sister Elizabeth, or Eliza as we all called her.

"When I got older, I realized that I did not want to make my living on a farm. To the disappointment of my father, I left home and moved to Boston, and that is where I met my wife, Chloe."

As her name came across his lips, I felt his body tense.

"Cam, you don't need to do this…"

"Chloe Patterson," he continued, "was the daughter of a local clothier, and did most of the sewing for her father after her mother died. I began working for him in his store, and eventually ran most of the day-to-day activities. That is where I got my fondness for fine clothes."

"Clothes snob. That's what you are."

Cameron laughed lightly. "When you have seen clothes go from intricate layers of detailed craftsmanship to mass produced garbage, then yes, one becomes a snob. As I was saying, after working for him for three years, Chloe's father offered to transition the store to me, as long as I married his daughter. To me, it was the deal of the century, for I had developed a fondness for Chloe. It was only her shyness that prevented me from pursuing her. Though my mother and father were upset that I would not be returning to the farm, they were very happy to see that I had made my way and was getting married. But being the only son, I would still visit the farm and help out during planting and harvest times.

"Chloe and I were married and then a year later we had a son, Christian, who was…" he paused. I squeezed his hand and tucked it into my chest by my heart. "My son was a delightful boy. He was extremely small for his age, but he did not let that stop him from doing what boys twice his age did. He was such an affectionate child and had so much love to give that everyone he met fell in love with him."

"Like father, like son," I said quietly.

"Hardly. He was very much like his mother in that respect, but he did not have her shyness. Chloe rarely left our home, but everyone knew her because of her sewing talent. Even Boston's most elite would come to her to improve the fashions they had ordered from Paris. Everyone loved my wife and son which made their deaths even more shocking."

We continued to lay in silence, Cameron's arm draped around me and his legs tucked in behind mine. After several minutes Cameron turned over to lie on his back. I stayed on my side trying to give him some space.

Just as my eyes were starting to feel heavy, I felt Cameron caress my middle back gently with the tips of his fingers.

"Bri," he said softly but with effort, "I am willing to tell you about how my family died and how I became a vampire, but I must warn you that it may be difficult for you to hear."

Achingly I turned to my other side to face him. "Cameron, I will listen to whatever you want to tell me. I want to know, but if it's too hard to talk about, I understand. *Believe me*, I understand."

Cameron rubbed his eyes with his hands and then opened his arm for me to lie on his chest, which I obliged. He wrapped his arms around me, giving me a little squeeze before he said, "Our home was located right above our shop and one evening while we were asleep, Christian woke me saying he heard noises downstairs. I grabbed my rifle and pistol and was halfway down the stairs when one of the men raiding the shop turned to come upstairs. I reacted quickly and ended up shooting him in the chest. Two of the men ran out, but the other two came over to the stairs. One of them, I later found out, was the dead man's brother and we both drew our pistols on each other. When we finally started hearing shouts of others on the street, the men grabbed the dead man and left.

"I thought it was over. I had heard reports from others in the area about a gang of men who were robbing homes and shops in the area. So when I shot one of them, I was the hero. Everyone in our neighborhood was grateful and even helped us put the store back in order. After three weeks there were no further reports of the gang so I thought it was safe enough to go up to my father's farm to help him with planting for the season. I did not return home until very late the next evening and when I rode up to the front of the shop, I noticed that the door had been kicked in. When I went inside, someone hit me over the head, and to make a long story short, when I woke, I found my legs broken and my family murdered by the men who had raided our store weeks before."

"Even little Christian?" I asked, feeling my nose tingle.

Cameron nodded as he raked his hand forcibly through his hair. "I was bound and gagged so no one heard me screaming, even when I was stabbed in the stomach. They left me bleeding out on the floor, and that is how Victor found me and for whatever reason made me a vampire."

"I'm so sorry, Cam," I said giving him a light kiss on his chest. "Did they ever catch those men?"

"No. Victor made it appear I had been abducted, and then once I had recovered, we fled. I could not even bury my family. My parents and sister were left to grieve without any explanation. It was why I was so angry for many, many years. Devin was actually the one who helped me assimilate."

"Devin? Really?"

"It was actually how we became so close. Every other Warrior was scouted by Victor and given the choice to join the coven, except me. Devin trained me in combat and showed me how to be a vampire. That is why I consider him a brother."

"Not much of a brother if he's willing to kill you just because Victor tells him to."

Cameron sighed. "I cannot judge him for doing his job, love. I know it would not be easy for him."

"Does that make it better?"

"A little," he replied and shifted his hold on me so that he could see me better. He brushed my face with his fingers. "Although many people in my coven know what happened to my family, none of them learned about it from me. You are the first person I have ever told."

"How do you feel?"

"Relieved, I suppose. But I always find it difficult to deal with the images of my last moments with them, especially Christian. It was why I was so short with you the other night."

Still lying sideways against Cameron, I began drawing little circles with my fingers on his chest and stomach. It always appeared he liked when I touched him like this and I wondered if it was as soothing to him as it was for me when he stroked my hair. Cameron took my hand that was caressing him and brought it up to his lips and kissed each finger. It was a gesture from another era, which would make sense, and it was truly romantic. After he kissed my pinky, he placed my hand over his silent heart and flattened his palm over mine.

"No more talk of me. How are you feeling, my love," he asked as his eyes searched my face.

Now I felt plain guilty for being bitchy. I had forgotten that this all started because of a stupid dream my father put in my head.

"Just tired and sore. Thank you for the flowers by the way, they're beautiful."

Cameron smiled as he touched my cheek. "You deserve better, but it was all I could find around here."

"Well, thank you anyway," I replied and then resumed my finger circles on his stomach, this time reaching under his shirt. His skin was cool to the touch, though the cold didn't run through my body. In the past, I was always a little cold, always needing a blanket or socks. But being close to Cameron, who was always several degrees cooler than me, never made me chilled. It was probably another weird hybrid/vampire thing that I did not wish to explore.

"Cam, do you have my cell phone? I need to call Renee and Daddy O and let them know about...um, the baby."

"Are you sure you are up to that?" I nodded reluctantly. "All right," he said. "Just so you are aware, Renee already knows."

Blinking my eyes hard I asked, "How's that?"

"While you were sleeping, I called her to obtain a number for Dr. Ryan. I wanted to make sure that you had everything you needed in order to heal, and I knew you would eventually tell Renee so I took a risk."

"Did John tell you anything different than I had?"

"No," he said with a big sigh, "he confirmed that you had everything and that I was just as helpless as I felt when it came to this."

I smiled at him, took his hand, and mimicked his own romantic gesture by kissing his hand and placing it over my heart.

"Just keep doing what you're doing for me and I will be fine. Without you, I would be a basket case right now. So who didn't you talk to last night?" I said and Cameron gave me a quizzical look. "Renee, Dr. John, Eris..."

"How did you know I talked to your father?"

"My dream. He said that you had told him I lost the baby. Why would you call him? It's not like he really cares."

"Despite your beliefs, he cares a great deal about you. I contacted him last night in order to call off Victor and Devin so that you could rest and heal without the worry of either of us being hunted."

"But why would he do it? More importantly, why would Victor listen?"

Cameron lowered his eyes slightly. "I may have given Eris the impression that Victor threatened you and the stress caused you to lose your baby." His eyes met mine again when he said, "It is not far from the truth. All I care about is your well-being, and I will call whomever I need to in order to make you safe and well." Cameron paused and leaned down to kiss me. "Because I love you."

I love you too. I love you. I love you. I love you. But the words wouldn't come out of my mouth. They would in time, just not yet apparently. I stretched my hand up and put my fingers through his hair, scratching his scalp a little as I did. His eyes closed slightly as he took in a deep breath.

"Finally," I said with an exasperated smile.

"What?"

I ignored him and put my nails through his scalp again, this time pulling his hair a little when I reached the back of his scalp. Cameron sighed again with pleasure, but with a soft whine he pulled my hand from his hair and rolled on his side, hovering over me.

"Love, you test me more than you realize," he said as he grazed my cheek. He stayed there for several moments, gazing into my eyes before his devilish, crooked smile stretched up his cheek.

"What's that smile for?"

He shrugged and his smile deepened. "I was thinking about what you said earlier, asking me why I thought the dream Eris showed you would come true."

"Well then enlighten me, Mr. Burke," I replied smugly.

"Because those children had your beautiful eyes," Cameron said before lowering his lips down onto mine. When he pulled away a moment later, his crooked smile returned as he said, "And I am definitely their father."

Chapter Twenty-nine

Cameron

Last night had been one of revelations for me and Brianna. I realized that in order to gain freedom from my past and move on whole heartedly with Brianna, I needed to admit what had happened to my family. Brianna absolutely deserved to know as much about me as I did her, and as I should have known, she opened her heart to me.

Brianna continued to discover abilities I had never seen or even heard about. Though I thought of her abilities as amazing gifts, she was frightened of them. Her gifts definitely seemed raw in their current form, but with training and activation from Eris, I was positive that she would be an extremely powerful hybrid. That alone could be why Elaina was after her, though I did not know to what extent she knew about Brianna's abilities, if at all.

Brianna slept for almost eighteen hours, waking only for trips to the bathroom and watching an occasional reality TV show. Her spirit was better, and her bleeding had almost dissipated. Though I did not have the heart to tell her at the time, being with her while she bled was definitely more than an exercise in control. There was more than one occasion where I needed to step outside for fresh air. The situation made me think about how we would handle her monthly bleeding. Yet another item we would need to discuss. Of course that was if she still wanted to be with me. With all our time together we had not discussed what would happen once Brianna got to the Facility. I believe we were both scared at what the answers would be.

With her now in the shower I decided to change my clothes, if anything to revitalize my mood since the clothes were not dirty. I pulled on another pair of pants and pulled off my old shirt when my phone rang. When I picked up the phone, I saw Eris's name flash on the screen.

"This is Cameron," I answered with the speakerphone so that I could continue to dress.

"Warrior, I am glad I caught you. I was hoping to get an update on Bri-an-na. How is she feeling?"

"She is doing better today, sir," I said with a smile as I heard her singing softly in the shower. It was something she had not done before, at least within my earshot, and it was absolutely adorable.

"That is certainly good to hear. Is she resting? I do not wish to disturb her."

"No sir, she is actually in the shower."

"Well then I guess we can talk business," he said, changing his tone abruptly.

I threw my shirt on the table where the phone sat and listened intently. "Certainly, sir, I am all ears."

"Per your request I did speak with Victor, and needless to say he is furious. I did convey that in no way was he to hinder you from delivering Bri-an-na to the Facility personally, and in her own time. Unfortunately, there is not much I can do for you in terms…"

"Can I ever take a shower where I remember everything? Where is that freakin' razor…oh sorry!" Brianna interrupted as she bolted out of the bathroom with only a towel wrapped around her. Her exit from the bathroom took me completely by surprise, as apparently it did her when she saw me standing shirtless in the room and hearing Eris's voice coming through the speakerphone.

"Bri-an-na, is that you, mia figlia? How are you today, my darling?" Eris said changing his voice from a businesslike tone to one of affection.

Brianna's tone, on the other hand, was less so. "None of your business. What are you guys talking about?"

Eris spoke before I could. "I was just telling the Warrior that you are safe to take as much time as you need before coming to San Francisco. No one will interfere…

"What happens to Cameron after he takes me to the Facility?" she asked as she took my hand in hers and squeezed tightly.

"Mia figlia, there is nothing I can do to stop Victor from punishing his children how he sees fit. I am sorry, Warrior, but I have done all that I can."

"And I am grateful. In no way would I expect you to interfere with Victor on my behalf. Thank you for all you have done for Brianna. I will have her contact you once she is at the Facility."

"Thank you as well for ensuring her safety. Goodbye my Bri-an-na, I am very eager to meet you in person. We have so much to discuss," Eris concluded and hung up.

Brianna remained silent and still as she stared at the phone. I pulled her hand and brought her into my chest. Her chilled, wet body was covered in goose bumps. As I kissed the top of her head, she pushed away from me and walked silently back into the bathroom without glancing back at me when I called her name. It felt as though whatever amount her heart had opened to me was now slammed shut.

Pulling my shirt on quickly, I walked to the bathroom door and knocked.

"Brianna, talk to me," I said, but there was no answer. "Please, Bri." Again, there was no answer, only the sound of the shower running. I remembered the last time she had shut a door between us and Oliver had told me the best thing to do was leave her alone, but I could not bring myself to do that. My time with her was limited. "Bri," I said as I stepped into the steamy bathroom, "do not shut me out. Please tell me why you are upset."

"Please just let me deal with this alone," she said weakly.

"Brianna, any other day I would certainly give you your space, but I can smell the fear coming off your body. You are afraid and we are going to stay here and talk through it." Brianna remained silent on the other side of the shower curtain. "Angel, I am not leaving until you tell me what is upsetting you."

"I'm afraid they're going to kill you," she shouted suddenly and sounding as though it was through tears. "Because of me, they're going to kill you because of me."

"No, love. Any punishment I receive is solely based on the decisions I have made these last couple of months. At any point in time, I could have said no to you, or taken you to San Francisco by force. Instead, I chose a path that has repercussions and I must accept the punishment that comes with them."

"Dammit, Cam, you make it sound like Victor is going to ground you and send you to your room," she said as she cut the shower off violently. Her thin arm stretched out of the shower searching for a towel and I placed one in her hand.

"I do think that Victor will be a little more creative than that," I replied.

"Cameron, stop," Brianna said as she flung the shower curtain open. "Don't do that. You're not even taking this seriously."

"Yes, Brianna, I am."

"No, Cameron, you're not."

"Yes I am!" I shouted. Brianna flinched, making me want to hurt myself for scaring her. "I apologize," I said quickly, bringing my voice down to a calmer tone. "I am very aware that Victor may take my life as payment for my disobedience, and yet I cannot let my fear of dying cloud my judgment when it comes to getting you to safety. You are my priority, and I have no control over what happens to me. I do not want to spoil what time we have left together pining over what is beyond either of us."

Brianna still stood in the shower, biting her lip as she looked up to the ceiling, seemingly trying to keep tears from running down her face. I took the two steps towards her that separated us and took both her hands in mine and kissed them.

"Finish getting ready and I will get you an early dinner. I want to sit, relax, and truly enjoy our time together. I will even let you cheat at cards again," I said trying to get her to smile, which she did. "I love you, angel," I said, giving her one last kiss and then pulling myself away from her wet, towel-covered body. It was certainly a test of strength.

As I left the hotel room, the grief of how few times I had left to say those words to her took over. Anger and despair raged within me as I started the car and sped out of the parking lot. Before getting Brianna food I needed to blow off some steam. I was no good in public or to her if I returned in this state. Just because I handled my fate gracefully in front of her, did not mean I had to once alone. Speeding down the street, I began looking for anything I could destroy – a car, a building, it did not matter. And if I found someone along the way from which to feed on, I would not have control to stop myself. The true vampire was being released and I neither had the strength nor the desire to restrain him.

Chapter Thirty

Brianna

It had been two days since I sat in this car watching the trees streak by, and I certainly didn't miss it. After an hour I was already uncomfortable, although it was probably more because where we were driving *to* versus in. When Cameron returned with dinner last night, his shirt dirty and bits of rock in his hair, we sat and had an honest conversation about when to finish this harrowing trip to San Francisco. Therefore, we agreed that once my bleeding had stopped completely, we would leave. No excuses. Had I known that meant today, I might have padded the caveat a little. Without tears or words, we packed our things, loaded them into the car, stopped for chocolate milk, and were on our way.

"Why was there rock in your hair last night?" I asked.

Cameron self-consciously put a hand through his hair. "Sorry, I thought I got it all out."

"You didn't answer my question."

"I found a quarry," he said looking at me from the side of his eye. "I needed to blow off some steam."

His statement made me laugh a little which felt good. I hadn't laughed much in the last two days, and probably wouldn't tonight. Any time I would think about being alone at the Facility I would shake with nerves.

"Are you cold, love?"

"No, I'm fine. Just nervous."

"So am I, angel," he said, taking my hand and kissing it. This familiar act caused my nose to tingle. "We are about an hour away from the Facility. Do you want to eat now or wait and eat there? I have heard that the food there is quite good."

An hour?! Where had the time gone?

"I'm not hungry."

The last hour of the trip was driven in complete silence. I didn't speak because I was afraid that tears would come instead. It was tougher to get a reading on Cameron. Although he held my hand and would squeeze it any time, I would start shaking with nerves again, his face remained stoic. I wish I could hear his thoughts; just once get into that head of his.

Although I was apprehensive about the whole hybrid hotel thing, I was excited about seeing San Francisco. It was a city I had only ever seen in movies. Needless to say, I was a little disappointed when we didn't go over the Golden Gate Bridge. Who knew there was more than one bridge into San Francisco. I felt like such a tourist, a geographically-challenged tourist.

I couldn't tell you where exactly we were in San Francisco, but we started rising above the crowded streets to a more vegetative mountain area. As we curved upward, we turned off onto a road that no one would have seen unless you knew it existed and began our assent toward the Facility. The long narrow driveway widened as we pulled up to a large electrified gate complete with armed guards. A squat vampire with fangs extended stopped us and asked us to roll down the window while his co-workers surrounded the car. Cameron handed over an ID of some sort and moments later the gate opened.

The wide driveway continued to curve upward and cut through thick trees that eventually cleared and revealed an expansive contemporary-looking glass and steel compound. It didn't look like a prison as I had often pictured it, but it wasn't a hotel either. It was more like a modern corporate building you would see in an architectural magazine. The driveway curved around to the front of the building with walls of glass that stood fifty feet tall. The building was stunning. Cameron slowed as he pulled into the first available parking space, which seemed almost a half mile away.

"How many people live here?" I asked, squinting through the windshield trying to get a better look at the massive building.

"Definitely over one hundred hybrids, then you have the staff, guards, and some solitary vampires who are traveling through the area."

Cameron turned off the car and was opening my door from the outside in the blink of an eye. Reluctantly I stepped out of the car and reached into the backseat to grab my leather bag, and a wave of depression came over me as I realized that after Cameron left me tonight, I would have nothing but a bag of dirty clothes and a handful of toiletries.

Still looking down at my pitiful bag, Cameron turned me around and tilted my chin up to face him. I didn't try to hide the tears and allowed them to streak down my cheeks. Cameron wrapped his arms around my waist, lifted me off the ground, and kissed me. I wrapped my arms around his neck, grabbing handfuls of his hair with my fingers. His kiss was hard and passionate, as though one of us would cease to breathe if he stopped. My heart was pounding so hard in my chest that it felt as though my ribs would crack.

Placing me gently down on the ground, Cameron bent his head down and kissed my beating heart, and then kissed me gently on the lips one last time.

"I love you, Brianna Marie Morgan, never forget that," he said as he took my hand and placed it over his heart.

I couldn't reply. Instead, I fell into his chest and sobbed. I would miss his smell, the safety of his arms, his soft whispers in my ear. My world with Cam was crumbling around me, and I was ruining yet another one of his shirts. Cameron was calm and patient, simply holding me and stroking my hair until I was done. When I lifted my head, he wiped away my tears and kissed each cheek. After a deep sigh, I sucked up my pain and then grudgingly made my way toward the magnificent glass doors of the Facility.

Cameron's posture immediately changed as we walked up the steps of the compound. The loving, caring Cameron had been replaced by the vampire I met that first day; distant, all business, chest high with power and confidence. The glass doors parted ways as we approached, leading us to a lobby filled with warm leather couches and chairs. In front of us was a wide mahogany reception desk where a small gray-haired woman sat with narrow glasses hanging down on her nose. She turned to us as the doors whispered to a close behind us.

As we stepped up to the desk, the receptionist looked down her nose at Cameron. "Mr. Burke," she said with a tight smile, "how nice to see you again. It has been some time since you visited us."

"Good evening, Maddy," he replied, his charm at maximum level, "you are looking as beautiful as ever, and keeping this place running smoothly no doubt."

"They couldn't run it without me, and you know it," she said and gave a wink. "And who are you checking in today?"

"Madelyn Forebush, meet Brianna Morgan. Brianna this is Maddy, the eyes and ears of the Facility."

Maddy gave me a quick nod and began tapping away on the computer in front of her. "Sorry, no Morgan, but I have a Brianna Lewis."

My hands flinched at the sound of my former name, but Cameron remained stoic as he replied, "That is her. When I made the initial reservation, I did not know she had returned to her maiden name."

"Yes, but that was weeks ago. A little off your game, are we, Mr. Burke?" she asked giving Cameron a look that would cut any man's confidence down to size. I loved her. "Unfortunately, we gave her room away, but let me see what I can do." With that, Maddy began feverishly tapping away on the computer again. I felt as though I was at the airport, and having missed my flight was now at the mercy of the ticket agent and her endless speedy typing. "Sadly, with all the attacks lately, we haven't been releasing many people. So we've started doubling up until the new wing is finished," she said as she tapped, tapped, tapped. "But since I'll do just about anything for you, Mr. Burke, I am willing to move a few people around."

"I don't want to take anyone's room away," I said, feeling guilty at the prospect.

"Oh don't worry, dear," Maddy said over her glasses, still tapping away. "There's a Vamp I've wanted to kick out for weeks."

Maddy finished her typing and pushed away from the computer, grabbing a shiny blue folder and the paperwork she had sent to the printer next to her. Leaning over the desk, she presented the blue folder to me as she said, "Now here is your orientation packet. This gives you the schedule of meal times, your seminars for the next couple of days, and a map of the building. I've circled your room in the east wing, and if you give me just a second, I will have someone take you there with your belongings," she said as she punched in a number on her desk phone.

"Maddy, that will not be necessary. I will escort her there myself."

Maddy hung up the phone and raised an eyebrow at Cameron. "Well, I'm sure you remember the way."

"Yes ma'am. May I ask another favor of you?" Cameron said, showing her my favorite crooked smile and making me suddenly jealous of a little old lady. "I need you to put a different name on her room, and make sure that any reference to her in the computer is changed to that name. Are you able to do that for me?"

Maddy quirked her lips and finally replied, "Promise to send over that little brother of yours to visit me and we'll call it a deal."

Cameron laughed and nodded. "I will see that Jared visits you immediately."

Maddy clapped her hands softly and then closed my folder and handed it to me as she said, "Now listen, dear, if you need something, you come see me first, understand?"

I nodded gratefully as Cameron pulled me down the length of the desk toward the main corridor and gave Maddy a quick wave goodbye.

"So she has the hots for Jared?" I said looking sideways at Cameron.

"Jared reminds her of her grandson who was killed in a hybrid attack several years ago," he replied softly.

"Is she a hybrid?"

"No, just her grandson. He was one of the first to go missing and she really put our feet to the fire to do something to protect other hybrids. And she is right, if you need anything, she will certainly take care of you."

I nodded as we continued down the brightly lit corridor that opened up to a tall multi-level indoor atrium with a glass ceiling. The number of stars shining through the ceiling reminded me of the night sky in North Carolina. In awe by my surroundings, I didn't even notice that I had stopped walking and let Cameron get three paces ahead before he turned around.

"Brianna," he said looking back and extending his hand, "this way."

Cameron pulled me to another large corridor on the right that led to a bank of elevators. We took the first available elevator up to the second floor where the doors opened to a long hotel-like hallway with room doors on either side.

As we exited the elevator I said to Cameron, "If Madelyn kicked someone out of a room for me just a few minutes ago, shouldn't we wait until they move out before we just barge in?"

Cameron laughed. "Knowing Maddy, she had his things packed, the room cleaned, sheets changed, and even the mattress flipped before we got in the elevator. Things have to move quickly around here."

Cameron and I continued down the hallway and rounded the corner to the next set of rooms when a group of three women, roughly in their mid-twenty's bumped right into us. As I backed out of the collision, I heard one of them squeal with delight as she threw her arms around Cameron and kissed him right on the mouth. I flinched forward to knock her down on her ass but Cameron quickly removed the woman's arms and stepped back from her. Now that I could see her in her entirety, I could tell she was a slut. Her skin tight jeans barely came up above her pubic bone and her boobs were practically popping out of her shirt.

"Melanie, you seem well," Cameron said in a very nonchalant way. I slowly began turning my face to him and must have had a crazy look on my face since the two other girls in the group took a step back. However, slutty Melanie couldn't keep her stupid slutty eyes off Cameron. My Cameron, bitch.

"Oh Cameron, I am much better now that you're back. It has been forever! When you're done dropping off the newbie why don't you come up to room 402 and we can, well…reminisce," slutty Melanie said, walking her fingers up Cameron's arm.

I wanted to punch her in the mouth, but goodness knows where it had been.

"Melanie, I apologize, I will not be staying. But maybe you could show Brianna around the next few days," Cameron said gesturing to me. Now I wanted to punch him in the mouth, and I could, I knew where it had been.

Not able to take slutty Melanie a second later, I brushed past her and her little gang just in time to hear her say seductively to Cameron, "Well maybe you can come back tomorrow…"

I was furious. This was the last thing I needed. Of all the people that could have come around the corner it had to be one of Cameron's ex-lovers. At least she better be an ex, or I was going to be the first hybrid in history to remove a vampire's testicles. I was walking eight or nine paces ahead of Cameron and had no intention of stopping. I wanted him to know I was mad. He just stood there and let her kiss him; let her say those things to him. Boys, stupid boys!

"Crap," I yelled and stopped in my tracks.

Cameron caught up to me and handed me my room key. "It is room 239, just up ahead."

I grabbed the key from his hand and continued down the hall until I found room 239. After sliding the little card into the lock, I opened the door and the smell of air freshener and disinfectant wafted into my face. Maddy was a miracle worker. You would have never known that someone else had stayed in the room only moments before. The room was a typical hotel layout – bathroom immediately to the right, closet to the left, king size bed in the middle of the room, and a sitting area with a small couch and desk. My new home.

Cameron took my bag from my hand, tossed it on the bed, and then placed his hands on my shoulders. Being as mad as I was, I stood in front of him with my arms crossed in front of my chest. "Anything you'd like to say?"

Cameron looked down at me, annoyance plastered on his face. "Brianna, I would rather not spend what little time we have left talking about Melanie."

"Sorry, Cam, I would really like to talk about her. Was she one of your cases?"

"Yes."

"Was she one that you slept with?"

"Yes."

"Multiple times?"

"Why would it matter?" My eye squinted into an evil glare making Cameron put his hand through his hair and sigh. "It was a moment of weakness to say the least and she became a little obsessed."

"Well you certainly didn't mind her attention."

"I pushed her away as gently as I could. I was not about to fling her up against the wall because she made an inappropriate gesture in front of you. Are you really mad about that, or something else?"

"Like what," I said nastily.

"Possibly you are upset that I must leave soon."

"Maybe what I'm upset about is the fact that as soon as we walked in the door I became your case, not your girlfriend...or whatever I am."

Cameron stood still as he clenched and unclenched his fists. "Bri, I have never done this before."

"Done what?!"

"This! Us," he said gesturing between us. "I have never been around anyone, not even my coven, with someone that I loved on my arm. And it is taking all my energy to put one foot in front of the other to keep you here and not run away with you. So yes, maybe out there I needed to think of you as a case in order to bring you through the door. Even though it rips me apart to leave you, I must and unfortunately soon. Please do not let my behavior get in the way of what time we have left."

My arms were still crossed in front of my chest, however, now they were holding me together versus showing that I was angry. My stomach was flipping around, making me feel nauseous and light headed. Cameron took me in his arms and kissed me deeply with his fully open mouth, his hands pressing firmly into my back.

Unable to breath, I pushed him away. "I can't do this, Cam. Just go, okay? I thought I could, but I can't. It'll just be easier if you go."

Cameron stood in front of me in shock. He stepped toward me again trying to bring his arms around me but I took another step back, putting my hand on his chest to keep him away.

"Bri please, let me leave you on better terms than this."

Unable to speak I shook my head, holding my free hand up to my mouth to contain the sickness I feared would come out.

Just then a knock came from the door. Neither of us moved hoping they would go away, but the person behind the door was persistent and knocked several more times. I walked up to the door and flung it open to find a tall, olive-skinned, muscular man dressed all in black standing in front of me.

"Can I help you?" I asked rudely.

"I am here for Cameron," he said.

"And you are?"

From behind me I heard Cameron say, "Devin."

The blood ran from my face as I looked upon the Warrior Assassin himself, and my knees buckled. Thankfully Cameron was quick enough to catch me and bring me back inside the room. Unfortunately, Devin came in as well.

Cameron sat me down on the edge of the bed, and my head fell between my knees while he rubbed my back.

"Dare I ask what you are doing here, Brother?" Cameron asked.

"Father has sent me to escort you to the manor immediately," Devin replied.

"I just need a little time to settle Brianna in and then I will go."

"Brother, you have run out of time and Father's patience. Please do not make me have to take you by force in front of Brianna. I am here in peace, but will resort to violence if I have to."

"If you must, then so be it," Cameron said angrily and standing from the bed. "I refuse to leave her like this. Let me go to the manor when I am ready, otherwise, kill me now."

"No!" I screamed looking up at him as both he and Devin extended their fangs.

"Brother, you are a Warrior, someone who does not shirk their responsibilities and steps up to their punishment with dignity. Do not grovel for more time with the hybrid that created this mess in the first place."

Cameron crouched down as did Devin, growling fiercely at each other, and for the second time in my life I stepped in between dueling vampires.

"Stop! Stop it, both of you," I shouted, putting my hands up on either side. "He's being punished because of me?" I said to Devin. "It was my fault we were delayed in coming here. I refused to go unless he let me stay with my family in North Carolina. He shouldn't be punished for something I made him do." Even as I spoke to Devin, he was looking right through me to see Cameron.

"He is not being punished for the time delay," Devin answered, finally turning his gaze to me. "He is being punished for murdering a human."

I lowered my arms and looked at Cameron. "Cam? What is he talking about?" Cameron, however, didn't answer. Instead, he looked over my head and glared at his brother. "Cameron, what have you done?"

The truth had to be bad because Cameron still wasn't making eye contact with me. Devin, however, seemed more than willing to bring the truth out in the open.

"Jazlyn came home yesterday, Brother. She told us everything."

"Jazlyn?" I said. "This happened…in…North Carolina?"

Cameron opened his mouth to speak, but it was Devin who continued the story. "According to Jazlyn, Cameron pressured her into helping him cover up the murder of your husband."

"My hus…S-sam? You…you killed Sam?"

My breath became ragged and I was barely able to get the words out of my mouth. In the pit of my stomach a familiar burning started to flutter.

"Bri, please understand, he was coming for you. He was never going to stop until he found you," Cameron said stepping toward me, but stopped when I put my hand up in front of him.

"That's why he's missing? He's dead? And you forced Jazlyn to help you cover it up?"

"I did not force her," he replied and then looked to Devin, "and you very well know that no one can force Jazlyn to do anything. Brianna, I did not plan on killing him…"

"But you did, Cameron, you did! And then you lied about it. You lied to me, again. And if this happened the night Jazlyn was there, it was the same night that you promised never to keep things from me. So you honored that for what, five minutes?"

The anger within me rose and the gentle burning in my stomach started to grow.

"Brianna, please just listen to what I have to say," Cameron pleaded.

"Why should I? What gave you the right to take someone's life? That's why I stopped you that night at the house when you tried to kill him. I didn't want you to be a monster like him," I yelled. My knees started to crumble under me as the burning from my stomach rose into my chest making it hard to breath.

"Me the monster?" Cameron said angrily. "After all he did to you, you are upset that he is dead? He was planning on killing you, Brianna."

"Then how are you any different than him? He didn't succeed, you did."

Silence fell between us while Cameron tried to control himself, and I tried to get my breathing under control.

"Brother, there was another incident?" Devin asked. "Father said you left the man alive after her first attack, so what is Brianna referring to?"

My head jerked up to Cameron whose lips were drawn tight, fists clenched.

"First attack?" I said to him, but he didn't answer. "Dammit, Cameron," I screamed at him as I rose from the bed and pushed him slightly. "You better tell me what the fuck you all know that I don't. What first attack? When?"

Cameron lowered his head, his eyes concentrating on the ground. "The first day you saw me, that day at the church."

It was difficult to concentrate with the fire burning in my chest, but searching my memory back to that day, I quickly realized what he was referring to. The day I first saw him was the day that Sam beat and raped me in my home. The day when I imagined seeing Cameron's dark eyes appear in the window helping me concentrate on something other than the horrible acts that were happening to me.

"You were really there?"

Cameron closed his eyes tightly as he nodded ever so slightly.

"You...watched as Sam...and you did nothing?"

"Brianna, my hands were tied, I was ordered not to..."

"Nothing! You let him...do that...to me...So when I bared my heart to you about what he used to do...you already knew..." I stuttered as the burning in my chest became unbearable and heavy tears streamed down my face. "He did that to me because I was caught talking to you! Think of all…the pain…you would have stopped…"

This time, Devin tried to come to Cameron's defense. "Brianna, you must understand that Cameron was under orders not to interfere."

"Under orders? How can you honestly justify having someone watch another person be…torn apart…from the inside out…and then hide behind orders. You people are sick, just get out of here."

Cameron stepped closer to me and tried to take my hand. "Brianna…"

"Don't touch me," I screamed at him, swatting his hand away.

"Angel, let me explain."

"I don't want to hear it! I can't even look at you. If it weren't for you…"

"If it were not for me, you would still be sitting in that house waiting for Sam to hurt you again," Cameron shouted at me, and then caught himself and lowered his voice. "Bri, I did not mean…"

"Yes you did," I replied softly, feeling my throat closing as the burning from my chest rose again. "Get out."

"Love, please," Cameron begged.

The burning in my throat rose up through my head as I screamed 'Get out!', though only the two vampires heard me as they both fell to the ground with their hands over their ears. The pounding in my head caused me to collapse to the floor, my stomach folded over my knees while I wept uncontrollably. The two vampires moaned softly as they picked themselves up from the floor, steadying themselves against the wall.

"Brother," Devin said, "what was that?"

But Cameron ignored him and bent down across my back and nuzzled into my ear. "Brianna, I hate myself for what I did, please give me a chance to explain. I love you so much, Bri, please," he whispered into my hair but I was inconsolable.

When I didn't answer him, Devin took the opportunity to take Cameron by his leg and drag him off of me while he continued to plead for my forgiveness. A moment later, Devin opened the door and dragged Cameron out into the hallway. As the door shut behind them, I caught one last glance of Cameron's dark eyes; the eyes that had once given me hope now represented nothing but lies and pain.

I had lost everything - my friends, my family, my baby, and now my heart. It felt as though the burning that had risen from my stomach had burned everything in its path, leaving only the raw nerves that could *feel* everything. Unable to move from the floor, I tugged on the edges of the comforter and draped it around me hoping that it would absorb my agonizing screams as I waited to finally pass out from exhaustion, and a broken heart.

Chapter Thirty-one

Cameron

"Brother, it is happening again," Devin said as he released my leg and was forced to stabilize himself up against the wall. "We need to call security right away," he said pulling his cell phone from his pocket.

"It is Brianna. She is doing this to us," I replied, grabbing the phone from his hand while Brianna's wails echoed in my head.

"Brianna can take two vampires down by screaming?" Devin said skeptically.

"Last time it was five vampires."

Before Devin could say anything else, Brianna began screaming again, taking both of us down to the floor.

"Why is she screaming," Devin yelled, trying to overcome the volume of Brianna inside our heads.

"Why do you think!? I killed her, Devin," I yelled as I pressed him up against the opposite wall. "She was already dying inside and you had to help me deliver the final blow."

"How was I supposed to know you had kept those things from her," Devin said and pushed me down the hallway.

There was no point in resisting. Devin had a mission to bring me to the manor, and although he considered me a brother, he would bring me there in pieces if it was necessary. With the pride and strength a Warrior should have, I straightened my posture and made my way down the hallway with Devin directly at my side.

As we rounded the corner I finally said, "I thought I was protecting her."

"Lying to her does not protect her, Brother," Devin said as we reached the bank of elevators.

Sadly, Devin was right. As we walked further away from her room the intensity of Brianna's wails waned, making me want to turn around just so I could feel her in my head and share in her agony. My arms ached to be around her, holding her while she cried and cursed me.

Then as if the evening could not be any worse, the doors to the elevator opened to reveal Melanie.

"There you are, you naughty boy. I was beginning to think you had forgotten about me," Melanie said as she stepped out of the elevator and began winding her arms around me.

"Melanie," I began, pulling her hands out from under my shirt and holding them firmly, "I apologize if I have led you on in some way. There is simply nothing between us. I am with someone now and..."

"Is it that skinny, brown-haired, bitch newbie you were bringing in," Melanie yelled, wringing her hands free from mine. "What can she possibly be doing to you that I'm not better at."

"Melanie, I said enough," I growled as I stopped her hand from going down the front of my pants.

"But Cameron, come on..." she said just before Devin grabbed her around the waist and held her against the wall.

"What do you not understand," Devin spat at Melanie, his face only inches away from her with his fangs extended. "My brother may have the manners and patience of a saint, but I do not." Melanie tried to squirm under Devin's grip which simply made him push into her harder. "You may not listen to him, but you *will* listen to me. Stay away from my brother or else you and I will have another visit where I do not show this much restraint. Do you understand me?"

Melanie answered by slowly nodding her head, fear very present in her eyes. Devin released her, causing her to slide limply to the floor. At that point we chose to take the stairs rather than wait for another elevator. Most vampires steered clear of us as we walked through the main atrium, though it was truly Devin they were scared of. Devin was the Warrior Assassin and his face was not one you wanted coming toward you. It generally meant you only had a few moments left of your life.

As we approached the lobby Madelyn stepped to my side.

"Mr. Burke," she whispered, "you know I had to let him through."

"Maddy, you could not have stopped him if you tried," I whispered in reply, seeing the worry in her eyes. "It may be a while before I can return," I paused, "if at all."

"I'll keep my eye on her, Mr. Burke."

"Thank you, Maddy," I responded and kissed the back of her hand.

Devin grabbed my arm and led me out of the building to the parking lot.

"I need to get a few things from the car."

"I will send someone to gather your things, Brother. You need to get into the truck," Devin said and pulled me to the black SUV that was sitting idle in front of us.

"This is unnecessary."

"You do not have the authority to tell me what is necessary and what is not. Do you have any idea what I have been asked to do to you over the last month? I have defended you and your actions countless times even though I do not understand nor agree with anything that you have done."

"I am sorry, Brother."

"Do not apologize to me!" Devin yelled. "Explain to me how you can throw away your life and your family for some hybrid you just met. This is not you, Brother."

"Devin, before tonight were you aware of the extent of Brianna's abuse by her husband?" Devin shook his head as he released a frustrated sigh. "Did you know that what happened to her that night was a regular occurrence?" Devin shook his head again. "Did you know that she became pregnant, and between then and three days ago she lost that baby?"

"Kyla informed us about the pregnancy and the…the loss of it."

"I did what I thought was right, Brother, and I would do it again if I had to. I could not stand by and…and…" but I could not bring the thought to light as the anger began to swell within me.

"Cameron, you are a Warrior, and we do not let our emotions get in the way of our duty."

"I could not let it happen again," I said through clinched teeth as the anger from the last three centuries began raging inside of me.

"What are you talking about?" Devin yelled back at me.

The horror of the last night with my human family began flashing in front of my eyes. I could see Chloe's lifeless eyes staring down at me and Christian's tiny body tied to the chair. Then I saw Brianna lying on the couch, her face bloody and streaked with tears while Sam pounded himself inside her. The pictures of both incidents began melding into each other causing my anger to reach a fever pitch.

Unable to control myself, I pushed Devin to the side, placed my hands underneath his SUV, and threw it across the parking lot causing it to land on top of another car over 200 feet away. Keeping my eyes tightly closed I said, "I refused to fail Brianna as I failed my wife and son."

Devin remained silent for a few moments as the sound of several car alarms cut through the quiet night. Devin squeezed my shoulder which caused me to open my eyes to look at him. The way he looked back at me made me feel like he may not have completely understood my actions, but now he understood enough.

"You will pay for the damage to my car. Now can you Project to the manor from here?" he finally said to me, and I nodded. "If you are not there within ten seconds, I will not hesitate to hunt you down and bring Father your heart."

I closed my eyes, took a deep breath, and Projected to the driveway of Victor's Warrior manor. As the black mist around me began to dissipate, the massive dark gray stone manor formed in front of me. There, standing in front of the double oak doors were Alexander and Jared along with several other of my Warrior brethren. While black mist swirled next to me creating the form of Devin, both Alexander and Jared gave me a cursory nod before flanking me.

"Only seven to escort me?" I asked as we approached the other four Warriors waiting at the front door. "That is a bit underwhelming."

Alexander tilted his head toward me as he said, "Don't be disappointed, Cam. Father has pulled out all the stops for you."

"How many have come?"

"Almost everyone," he responded. "Julian is practically chomping at the bit."

A laugh escaped my lips at the sound of my Warrior nemesis' name. Julian and I hated each other, and Victor knew it. Father was going to make an example of me, and he wanted everyone present to see it. He needed to prove that he was not showing favoritism.

My entourage escorted me to the south wing of the manor which held only the Council Hall and the dungeons. The Council Hall was built to replicate the Roman council and senate halls of Victor's past. The hall itself was oval, with Victor's throne located at the center's back edge. Stone rows circled around where Warriors and guests would sit to observe the trial of a condemned vampire or where the Elite Warrior Council would strategize and debate over the latest issues. Up until now I had been a member of the

Elite Warrior Council, and had observed many a trial. However, I was intimidated by my current view while I was looked down upon by almost all of my sixty-two siblings.

Victor sat on his throne in white Roman robes with Julian standing just in front of him. Once my entourage had escorted me to the center of the room they parted and took positions along the front row of the stone steps. I bowed deeply, showing everyone that I was ready to proceed with my trial. Victor did not look at me as I did so, instead he nodded to Julian to begin the formal proceedings.

Julian stepped forward with a sly grin. "Cameron Burke, you have been brought before this assembly of Warriors to be tried for insubordination, reckless exposure of our race, breaking of the Gatherer's code, and the unauthorized murder of a human. How do you defend yourself?"

As I heard the charges against me, I realized that I was absolutely guilty on all counts. Avoiding Julian's glare, I looked directly at Victor and said, "I feel defending my actions would be pointless as I fear my punishment has already been decided."

My statement caused Victor to shift his gaze from Julian to me.

"Very well then," Julian cut in, "we will go directly to sentencing."

"Hold, Julian," Victor interrupted. "Cameron, your actions have wreaked havoc in our family. I will not let you simply be sentenced without an explanation. I demand to know why you have brought shame to our coven."

As I looked into my father's eyes, I could see the extreme hurt in them, however, it did not faze me as much as it would have two months ago. My father's actions against Brianna had negated any sympathy I had for him.

"Father, I in no way purposely brought shame to our coven. As a Warrior, I was unable to stand by and watch as a despicable human reveled in beating and attempting to kill a helpless woman."

"A woman you claim to be in love with," Julian interrupted smugly. "Isn't it true that your feelings for this hybrid caused your judgment to be tainted?"

"My feelings for Brianna Morgan only strengthened my need to protect her, which all in all is the duty of a Gatherer as well as a Warrior."

"Yes, but disobeying a direct order from your master is not," Julian replied.

"Brianna refused to come to the Facility unless she had time to contemplate her future. The powers she displayed as an un-activated hybrid pushed me to allow her to take the time she needed to make her decision, versus losing her all together. I did what I needed to do in order to get her here. Unfortunately, along the way events occurred beyond my control which delayed our arrival even further."

Julian's nostrils flared as he said, "Regardless of your intentions, you killed a human you were specifically told to stay away from. That in itself is punishable by death."

"Yes, Julian, I am aware, and I am more than willing to accept my punishment. However, knowing at that time the powers which Brianna Morgan possessed, and my sworn duty to protect her, I felt the threat to her life was a bigger priority than the threat to mine." I turned my gaze to Victor. "Father, you can make a million more children like me, but you will never find another hybrid as unique and powerful as Brianna. We need her on our side."

Victor stayed silent, although his gaze upon me was fierce. I was taking a significant risk telling him what his priorities should be. Also, if he were to ever know that I was lying to him, I would certainly be put to death since at the time I had no idea about Brianna's powers when I killed Sam.

After several minutes Victor stood from his throne and said in his raspy voice, "Is there anyone here who will defend their Warrior brother on these charges?"

To my right I saw both Alexander and Jared step forward, only to be stopped by Devin. At first, I thought he was preventing them from helping me, but when he stepped to my side, I realized he was willing to take any repercussions himself for defending me.

"Father," he said as gasps echoed throughout the hall, "although Cameron's actions are certainly punishable, his intentions were honorable. I myself have experienced a taste of Ms. Morgan's powers and I agree that she will be a great asset to us."

Victor sat back down on his throne. "What powers has she displayed?"

"I do not believe there are words to explain, Father. I have never experienced such a power. Needless to say, this evening she was able to bring me and Cameron down without touching either of us. And Cameron informed me she was able to do this during the incident in Flagstaff where she saved both of them by taking down five enemy vampires."

Admittedly I had not been prepared to explain Brianna's unique gifts. However, I was more than willing for them to know about the mind projection than the dreams. Victor again went silent as hushed murmurs scattered around the room.

Obvious to everyone, Julian became agitated at the direction my trial was now going when he yelled, "Father, he murdered a human! You have killed other vampires for less."

Victor nodded at Julian and stood from his throne again. "Although you have presented additional evidence that defends your actions, our ways must be upheld otherwise there is chaos. Therefore, I sentence you to board and chains for a term of my discretion effectively immediately."

"But Father," Julian interrupted like a spoiled child.

"That is my final word. You and Liam shall bind him alongside Jazlyn. We are adjourned," Victor stated as he walked out of the Council Hall without acknowledging me in any way.

My life had been spared. It meant I had a lifetime with Brianna, so I did not care that I would be in excruciating pain for who knew how long. In the end, I would be with her, and perhaps her dream about our future family would come true. While Julian and Liam led me down to the dungeons beneath the manor, all I pictured in my head was the sight of my daughter and son running around me while my Brianna sat in the distance admiring our precious family. Somehow the prospect did not seem so farfetched. I had convinced my father, ultimate and unforgiving head of the Warrior coven, to forgive me. Now all I needed to do was have Brianna, possessor of my heart, forgive me as well. Thankfully as a vampire I had time on my hands, I had a feeling I would need it.

Chapter Thirty-two

Brianna

Cameron held me close while the rain pelted my face. His lips were cool as was his tongue as it explored the inside of my mouth. When he pulled away and looked deeply into my eyes, he placed his hands on my very pregnant belly. He kissed me gently on the lips when I heard Sam's voice behind me screaming for me to get inside.

I pushed Cameron away and screamed, "Brianna, wake up!"

Sam held me by the throat up against the tall cabinet in our kitchen. As he squeezed the air out of me, he reached back and then jabbed his fist into my stomach causing me to slump over his shoulder. He carried me to the couch where he threw me down on my back. With a quick motion he ripped my pants open and climbed on top of me. I frantically looked up at the window above the couch to see a pair of black eyes staring down at me.

"Cameron, help me," I screamed as I placed my bloody hand on the glass, but his eyes simply faded away.

I was lying on the floor in a white gossamer gown encircled by Elaina's vampires. Elaina herself was kneeling down next to me while another female vampire held me down on the floor, her dark hair covering my face.

"Let's get this over with," the dark-haired vampire said just before Elaina stabbed my pregnant stomach with a large knife.

"Wake up!" I screamed.

Cameron sat on the edge of the bed while I stood between his legs. He bent his head down, giving me gentle kisses up my chest through the opening in my shirt. His fingers grazed up the outside of my thighs and underneath my shirt. Cameron moved his mouth to my neck, sucking slightly at my skin. With a quick motion he grabbed me around the waist and laid me down on the bed, moving to position himself between my legs.

"I am begging you, Brianna, please wake up," I whimpered.

The Carolina-blue sky was bright and clear while Cameron and the twins ran around the side yard of Daddy O's mountain home. To my right I could feel Eris's presence next to me on the large boulder located in front of the house.

"Bri-an-na," he said gently, "it pains me to see you like this. It has been two days."

This was not how I remembered the dream going.

"Are you in my head, Eris?"

"Mia figlia, you do not answer your phone. You refuse to eat or leave your room. This is the only way I can connect with you."

As he spoke, the familiar scenery dissolved into grayish smoke sweeping both Eris and I away to a sun-filled bedroom with wide opened doors displaying a brilliant ocean view. The room itself was completely white except for the bright turquoise bedspread that was draped over me that matched the beautiful ocean outside. Eris sat on the edge of the bed dressed in loose white cotton pajamas and his hair pulled back.

"Eris, what is this?" I said impatiently.

"You are in my home, mia figlia. At least your mind is."

"I was perfectly fine in my self-induced suffering," I replied.

"I know you are hurting, but I can no longer allow you to keep doing this to yourself. You need to pull yourself together, and that cannot happen with these dreams you have been having. Therefore, I will control your dreams so that you can sleep soundly and get out of this depression you have gotten yourself into."

"No, Eris. I have been controlled for the last fourteen years, and it all stops now. I am allowed to be upset and depressed if I want to be. So get out of my head, and leave me alone," I said as I pulled my knees into my chest and rested my head on them. Eris shifted closer to me on the bed and pulled my head onto his shoulder, hugging me tenderly. The tears began to stream down my face onto his shirt as he began rubbing my back gently. "Sometimes I can't breathe it hurts so bad."

"Mia figlia, I need you to be strong now. This is a critical time for you, one where if you do not have your wits about you, you could be killed. And believe me when I tell you that our future depends on you staying alive."

I raised myself from his shoulder and wiped the lingering tears from my cheeks. "How could anything be dependent on me? I can't even stop crying for more than an hour."

Eris squeezed my shoulders tightly as he said, "In time, my dear, you will understand. But now you must concentrate on releasing your sadness and anger at the Warrior, it only hinders you. If you do not want me to control you, then pull yourself together on your own terms, and I mean now."

"I am not like you, Eris, or any vampire for that matter. You can't expect me to jump out of bed and be happy just because you told me to. You can't...you just can't expect that, okay?"

"But I do, Bri-an-na. I expect that of my daughter, and I will settle for nothing less."

"Then get used to disappointment."

Eris threw his arms up in the air and stood from the bed. "Lives are at stake, and you lie here and cry. How many more need to die before you start realizing this isn't just about you, mia figlia?"

"Are we done here?"

Eris sighed and snapped his fingers...

Lying on my side, I opened my eyes slowly seeing it was pitch black in my room. My stomach growled and cramped so hard that I brought my legs up into me. I hadn't eaten in two days, and I was so hungry that I was imagining the smell of burgers and fries. The aroma was so real that I tilted my head upwards to the nightstand and sitting on top of the table was a brown paper bag with small oily spots of grease that had soaked through from the obvious deliciousness inside. But how did it get here?

As my brain started to wake up, I heard the clicky-click-click of what sounded like someone typing softly on a laptop computer. Without turning around, afraid of what I might see, I said softly, "Cameron?"

"Ha! Not even close," a young man's voice answered.

The sound of the unfamiliar voice scared me to death and caused me to jump up on top of the bed screaming bloody murder when I saw the slim figure of a man sitting stretched out on the little couch in my room. I grabbed the alarm clock from the nightstand and threw it at him, and missed. Then, still screaming, I grabbed the lamp and threw it, this time hitting the man in the shoulder as he walked slowly toward me with his hands up shouting, "Brianna, I'm Jared! Cameron's brother, Jared!"

I froze with my hand in the air holding the phone prepared to throw it at him. "Ohmygod! Jared, I'm so sorry, I didn't know."

"Damn woman, what is wrong with you," Jared said, picking up the broken lamp off the floor. As he stood back up, I hit him square in the chest with the phone causing it to shatter into a thousand pieces. "What the hell was that for?"

"That's for calling me woman," I responded, suddenly feeling light-headed and lowering myself back down on the bed. Jared laughed while he picked up all the pieces of the phone in a blur of activity. As he threw the pieces into the garbage, I crawled over to the other side of the bed and turned on the remaining table lamp on the other nightstand.

Jared came to the side of the bed and held out his hand as he said "Jared Ranger, it's good to finally meet you. You're even more fun in person."

Cameron had told me that Jared was a baby vampire, but he looked like a baby in general. Looking at his face it was hard to believe he was older than sixteen with his buzzed strawberry blonde hair and splattering of freckles. Unlike Cameron and Devin who both dressed as though they were going to a funeral, this Warrior brother was wearing a pair of khaki cargo pants and a bright red concert T-shirt from a band I had never heard of.

Jared walked over to the other side of the bed, picked up the greasy paper bag and handed it to me.

"Mads said I needed to get you to eat, and I remember that when I was human it was impossible to pass up a good greasy burger and fries."

If my stomach could have jumped out of my body and grabbed the bag it would have, but instead it growled so loud that Jared laughed which made me jerk the bag out of his hand. Immediately I grabbed a handful of fries and stuffed them all into my mouth. Mama Jo would have been appalled at my behavior in front of company, but honestly my stomach didn't care about manners right now. Jared returned to the couch and pulled his laptop back onto his lap and began typing again.

Taking a slight break from stuffing my face I asked, "Who's Mads?"

Jared didn't look up from his computer as he answered, "Madelyn. The woman at the front desk. Some people call her Maddy, I call her Mads."

"Oh, right," I said, shoving the last ten fries into my mouth. As I worked to swallow, I reached into the bag and pulled out the biggest burger I had ever seen. I could barely get my mouth to open wide enough to get a full bite. I practically unhinged my jaw, and it was totally worth it. It was the juiciest, greasiest, most delicious burger I had ever had.

"Whawarwooroowinweer?"

"What?!" Jared laughed as he saw me trying to chew.

"Sorry," I replied after swallowing. "I'm so hungry I can't stop myself. I said, what are you doing here?"

"Orders," he replied and then continued typing.

Orders. Was that all vampires did, order other vampires around?

"Well, Jared, Cameron's not really in a position to be ordering people to look after me..."

Jared looked up from his incessant typing. "They're not Cameron's orders."

"Eris?" I said taking another large bite out of my burger.

Jared shook his head. "Devin."

At the sound of Devin's name, I took in a shocked breath which caused the burger to get lodged in my throat. My hands flew to my throat and Jared leapt from his position on the couch. Quickly he pushed his fists into my stomach causing the burger to fly across the room and hit the wall.

Jared began laughing hysterically. "Dammit, I didn't even get that on camera. I would have loved to see the look on Devin's face when he saw your reaction. That was classic."

"Not…funny…Jared," I coughed and gasped for air.

"You're right, that was hysterical!" He cleared his throat when I gave him the dirtiest look I had in my repertoire. "You okay?"

I nodded and handed him the bag with the remaining half of the burger. Suddenly I had lost my appetite.

"Why did Devin order you here? He hates me, blames me for everything that's happened with Cameron. Why on earth would he send you here?"

Jared threw the bag of food into the garbage as he replied, "Oh it's not just me. I can only come at night because I'm still sun sensitive, so he has Alex staying with you during the day."

"Wait, how's that possible? I know I was barely awake, but I don't remember seeing anyone here during the day."

"You didn't see Alex because he chooses to stay outside your door," Jared said lazily as he sat back down on the couch and began typing on his computer. "I did that last night, no way was I going to do that again."

"Why's that?"

"Brianna, you have to understand that I have a certain reputation to uphold. I can't have the ladies thinking I'm tied down to the hybrid on the other side of the door. So I decided like it or not you have a roommate tonight."

"Oh no," I shouted at him. "No way are you staying in here."

"Brianna, come on," Jared whined. "Don't make me go back out there. I'll be quiet, you won't know that I'm here. Please?" Jared's big, black, puppy dog eyes were so drastically different than the rest of his fair features that they were even more pronounced, making them hard to resist.

"Fine," I replied with a frustrated sigh.

"Great. Now let's talk about maybe brushing your hair? Teeth? No offense, but your breath is nasty and you look like shit."

I glared at him, although I knew he was right. When I stepped into the bathroom I was appalled by my appearance. My eyes were dark and puffy, my hair matted on one side of my head. After brushing my teeth, I worked on detangling my hair and asked, "Why does Devin care what happens to me?"

"He's doing it for Cameron," Jared responded from the bedroom. "We're all doing this for him."

Hearing Jared say Cameron's name brought a rush of blood to my head, making me rub my temples with my fingers. I suddenly regretted stuffing my face as my stomach started flipping upside down. Anxiety started to take over, making me feel extremely antsy. With my hair looking decent, I stepped out of the bathroom and walked over to the dresser where my leather bag sat on top. Placing the bag on the bed, I rummaged through it to find my deck of cards.

"Do you play gin?"

"Isn't that like an old person's game?"

"Don't make me smack you."

"Oh I'd like to see you try," Jared laughed under his breath.

"I took Devin down, didn't I? I'm sure I could do the same to you," I said, even though it was a lie. I had absolutely no control over my weird mind power. Regardless, Jared did look a little less cocky after I'd said it. "So what do you play then?"

"I know how to play rummy and poker," he replied.

"Okay, rummy it is."

Jared straightened the comforter before he sat down, only to mess it up again when he jumped back over to the couch where he reached into a black computer bag.

"I almost forgot, I brought you something," he said as he pulled out a silver laptop. "It's not new, only a year old, but you'll be able to get to the internet and send emails and stuff. I've created an email account for you too. It's secure and untraceable, so you can email your family. Also, I downloaded like a million songs and videos, so you can transfer them to your phone."

"Wow, thank you," I said as I took the laptop from him. Finally, something I could call my own. "You'll have to transfer the music for me. I have no idea how to do that."

Jared rolled his eyes as he sat back down on the bed. "Do I need to show you how to turn the computer on, too?" Squeezing my eyes shut, I put my fingers up to my temples like I had seen psychic superheroes do. "Okay, okay! Just don't do whatever it is you do."

I removed my fingers from my temples, gave him a sly smile, and began dealing the cards. "So how old are you, Jared?"

"Technically I'm twenty-six, but I tell everyone I'm twenty-one since that's how old I was when I was Turned," Jared said putting down his first play.

I picked up his discarded four of hearts and said, "Good lord, you are a baby."

"Well if Dad had had his way, he would have Turned me at twenty." Jared picked up another card and quickly discarded it, showing all his frustration on his face.

"Dad?" I said as I picked up his discarded six of hearts.

"Victor. Everyone else calls him Father, but that just sounds stupid to me. Plus, he's the only real dad I've ever had, so..."

A smile came across his face as he finally picked up a card that he could use.

"So, what about the rest of your family? What did you tell them when Victor Turned you?"

"Don't have any family," Jared replied matter-of-factly.

"I...I'm sorry," I said as I picked up his last discard, completing my hand.

"Don't be. From what I've found out, my mom was a drug addict who left me at the hospital, no father listed on the birth certificate. But hey, I have a family now. It just took twenty-one years to find them."

"Rummy," I said, placing all my cards down and feeling guilty that I had won. Jared tossed me his cards. "How did you find them, by the way?"

"The Warriors?"

I nodded as I dealt the cards out again and we started our second game.

"Well, because I was a drug-addicted baby no one wanted me. So I basically became a delinquent ward of the state. There really wasn't much choice of where I could go when I turned eighteen. It was either the military or wind up in jail, and seeing that I could at least do cool computer things in the military that's where I went. And why do you keep picking up everything I put down?" Jared said as I picked up his second discard.

"Sorry," I replied, giving him a little pout. "So you were in the...Army?"

"Yup, scored off the charts, of course," he answered smugly. "Did a stint in Iraq and then Afghanistan, and when I finally got home, I was totally bored and started getting into computer hacking again. That's when I came across this piss poor network where there were all these emails going back and forth about blood and money and blood and property and of course blood. So I start snooping around and…" Jared mumbled something else, but I couldn't understand him as I put my cards down again.

"Rummy. What did you say?"

"Crap! How do you do that?"

"Magic. What did you say?" I said and tossed my cards at him.

"I uploaded a virus to their network."

"You did what?! Did you have a death wish?" Jared began laughing so loud that it made my ears hurt. "Okay, bad choice of words, stop laughing at me."

He didn't stop laughing until he finished dealing the cards for our third hand.

"Basically, yes, I had a death wish. Victor found me, told me that I could be Turned or killed. I chose to be Turned, but not until I was twenty-one. And now I handle all the networks and IT security stuff."

Looking at my cards I knew that he was going to be upset since I already had one set, and the beginnings of two others. Jared was horrible at shuffling.

"Why the hang up on twenty-one?"

"Legal drinking age," he replied. "I couldn't be frozen at twenty forever. At least at twenty-one I can do whatever I want and no one would question me when I got carded."

"I thought you could only drink blood?"

"That's not the point," he replied, concentrating hard on the cards in front of him and then discarding the exact card I needed to win.

I picked up the card and threw down my hand. "Rummy."

"What…how…you cheat."

"That's what Cameron says," and just as his name came across my lips, I bit the inside of my cheek in order to stop the tears from coming. After three hands of avoiding the subject, I knew I needed to get it over with. "Is he alive?"

"Yeah, he's alive, though he probably wishes he wasn't."

"What does that mean?"

"Dad let him off with a stint on board and chains. Problem is he's right next to Jazlyn. That alone is worse than death," Jared said with a light laugh, and then clamped his mouth shut when he saw the horror on my face.

"Board and chains?"

"It's totally old school vampire tort…ah…punishment," he said though I knew he was totally going to say torture. "So they put you on this long wooden board and strap you down all over with these big silver chains. Then they hoist you up in this room with a glass ceiling and they leave you there. The pain is excruciating, and if you're young like me you don't last an hour once the sun hits you. But Cameron will be fine. He's old enough where the sun won't burn him that bad, but the silver will hurt like a bitch!"

While Jared explained Cameron's torture, I couldn't keep my lower lip from trembling. My Cam, stretched out on a board, bleeding and burning in the baking sun. All because of me. Me, me, me. Fucking me. I couldn't keep them back anymore and the tears began to flow. Then the ragged breathing started and snot began to fill my nose.

"No, no, no, Brianna don't cry. I don't know what to do when a chick cries," Jared whined as he stood from the bed in a panic. "Do you...where...tissues woman...where are your tissues?"

But I couldn't answer and continued to picture Cameron with thick silver chains burning into his skin. That's when I noticed Jared rummaging through my leather bag and then throw me something to wipe my eyes. When I realized it was Cameron's shirt another wave of uncontrollable sobbing came over me.

As I buried my face into the pillows, I heard Jared speaking into his cell phone, "Mads, help me! I need help...I know it's late...but ...but she's crying...Brianna's crying...I don't know what to...hey I didn't do anything. She asked about Cameron and I told her...but she asked...Mads don't...but...but...ah come on. Dammit!" Jared tossed the phone over to the couch. "Okay, I can handle this," Jared said to himself. "Ice cream. Chicks like ice cream when they're upset, right?"

Rising from the pillows, my face covered in tears and snot I yelled, "I am not five years old, Jared!"

With that, Jared Projected out of the room. Within five minutes he was back with a bottle of some kind of rum, diet sodas, and ice.

"This is all I could find on short notice around here."

Jared went into the bathroom and grabbed the glass from the sink, scooped some ice in it, and poured in a bunch of alcohol then only a dribble of soda. I took the glass gratefully as I said, "Okay, start from the beginning. I want to know everything that happened."

Chapter Thirty-three

Cameron

"Jazlyn, your screaming is not going to get you down any sooner," I said to her wishing my arms were not bound so that I could strangle her. It had been two days of torture, not just because I was racked to a board by silver chains that were eating away at my skin layer by layer, but because I had to listen to Jazlyn's insolent complaining, whining, screaming, and ranting.

"Shut the fuck up, Cameron," she screamed, leaning against the chains causing them to dig deeper into her. "This is your fault. Just couldn't keep your dick in your pants, and then you had to drag me into your mess."

"I am afraid I do not remember flaunting my genitalia outside of my clothing or dragging you by your hair kicking and screaming to help me. Neither of us would be suffering like this if you had not felt the need to confess our sins without even the slightest bit of context."

"I should have known that even after all you did, Victor would still punish me," she said in a breathless tone. "I hate you."

The feeling was mutual.

"Jazlyn, Father punished you because your reasons for turning me in were for personal gain rather than being an honorable Warrior."

"Honorable my ass. This whole family is corrupt and hiding behind their so-called honor," Jazlyn replied angrily and then screamed as the chains settled deeper into her skin.

"Jazlyn, I have found that if you stay calm and keep your movements to a minimum, the silver does not burn as badly. Save your strength, the sun will be up in a couple of hours."

"Fuck you."

"You first."

The sun itself did not burn either of us to ash as it would younger vampires. It did, however, drain your energy and make the silver hot, creating an entirely new wave of pain. Jazlyn could have the silver burn right through her for all I cared.

Just then the heavy wooden door opened, backlighting Alexander's large frame in the doorway. No one was allowed to visit prisoners except for Julian and the guards, however, if you were the size of Alexander few ever stopped you. While I was being prepped for my punishment, Devin had promised that he would coordinate extra security for Brianna at the Facility. Alexander and Jared had volunteered for alternate shifts, and thankfully so since they were really the only people I trusted with Brianna's life.

"How is she?" I asked before he could shut the door behind him.

"Good news is she woke up, ate, and managed to hit Jared with a phone," he said, his deep guttural voice echoing against the stone walls.

"Bad news?" I asked.

"Who cares!" Jazlyn shouted, and then screamed in pain once again.

Alexander paused and glared at her.

"Bad news is, Jared got her so drunk that she became extremely sick and then passed out."

It was my turn to scream in agonizing pain as I tried to rip the chains from my board.

"You know, Cameron," Jazlyn began condescendingly, "I've heard that if you stay calm and keep your movements to a minimum the silver does not burn as badly."

"Cam, calm down," Alexander pleaded. "Brianna asked about you and of course Jared didn't spare any details about your sentence. She became upset and Jared didn't quite know when to stop pouring. Apparently crying women make him nervous."

"Tell him I am going to kill him when I get down from here," I said, letting my head fall into my chest from exhaustion and pain.

"I will," he laughed. "I'm going to relieve him now. Lanashell said she wanted to meet with Brianna today. Do you trust her enough to know everything, or should I tell Brianna to limit it?"

"Lanashell is trustworthy. It is hard to keep anything from her anyway."

"I'll try and drop by tonight too and give you an update."

"Can you tell Brianna I am sorry and that I love her."

"I am going to be sick," Jazlyn moaned.

"Shut up, Jazlyn," I growled at her. "Alex, please tell her that I love her and…that I will still be waiting. Make sure you tell her that…that I will wait."

Alexander nodded and left the room, once again leaving me with Jazlyn.

"After everything she made you do, you still want to be with her?" Jazlyn asked.

"Everything I am being punished for I did of my own volition. I do not expect you to understand anything that has to do with loving someone."

"I don't even know who you are anymore. The old Cameron would never have put a woman between his family and his work. You're just pathetic."

"I would rather be pathetic than be alone for all eternity. Like you," I said with as much hatred as I could muster.

A little while later the sun began peeking over the horizon, meaning the real torture would begin. Just then the wooden door opened again, however, it was not my brother who walked through the door.

"Good morning my criminal siblings," Julian announced as he shut the door behind him. The only thing that Jazlyn and I had in common was our hatred for Julian. "Nothing? No good morning, Julian? Very well then. Jazlyn, good news, you are to be released today."

"Thank you, Father," I laughed.

"Oh, I am sorry, Cameron, you're still sentenced to hang there like the criminal you are. The release is only for Jazlyn," Julian said smugly.

"I know, Julian. It is the best gift Father could ever give me."

The smug look on Julian's face fell quickly and was replaced by a snarl. Jazlyn began screaming profanities at me, but I could have cared less. Even though my pain would become increasingly unbearable, I would finally be able to suffer in silence without Jazlyn's insufferable tirades. As the sun began to shine on my face and chest, I closed my eyes and imagined my life with Bri - countless nights of her curling into my side, endless kisses upon her warm lips, days where she laughed more than cried, which was something that had been rare since we met. I only hoped that once my punishment was over that my Bri wanted me to be her Cam.

Chapter Thirty-four

Brianna

I don't drink. A glass or two of wine here and there, but never to get drunk. After the second glass of rum with a dash of soda I should have stopped Jared from making more drinks, but I was too far gone. But I think he learned his lesson when I puked all over the bathroom floor and his shoes. If I thought last night was a nightmare, I had no idea how to explain how I felt this morning. Seriously, when had a freight train come into my room and run over me? Twice.

At 8:00 a.m. my cell phone alarm rang. I was in hell and being punished for my over indulgence of alcohol. Maddy had scheduled a 9:30 meeting with some woman I couldn't remember the name of, only that it was weird, and that a hybrid named Hannah would be coming to my room around nine to show me around.

After taking a long shower, I took out every piece of clothing I had and determined which outfit smelled the freshest since everything I owned was dirty. I settled for a pair of jeans and a blouse that was thin enough where I could wear the black sweater coat over it to cover up the food stain near the collar. The first thing I needed to find out about was where the laundry room was.

After dressing and brushing my teeth and hair, I sat on the bed and waited for this Hannah person. On the dresser I saw the shiny blue folder which had all the info on the Facility and next to it was the computer bag that Jared had brought with him last night. That's when I remembered I had a computer. I unzipped the main compartment and pulled out the slim silver laptop and placed it on the small dining table in the corner. When I opened it up, there was a large sticky note with cramped chicken scratch writing:

Brianna,
The big grey button turns the computer on. You press it.
Login name (type this in): Jared_rulz
Password (type this in too): Jaredisbuff
Email address; coolchick@JRinc.com
Music is under "Music"
Movies are under "Movies"
Be back tonight. No booze this time.
    –Jer

Jared really was the cutest asshole I knew, and it was hard to be mad at him. After all, he did clean the gallons of vomit up off the floor, although he complained the whole time about his ruined sneakers. Just as I turned the computer on, there was a knock at the door. Miss Hannah was right on time.

"Coming," I said as I took a deep breath and opened the door to meet my tour guide. Instead, I came eye to stomach with the biggest vampire I had ever seen. He must have been almost seven feet tall and extremely broad and muscular. Although his size made him terrifying, he looked down at me with gentle eyes.

"Alex?" I asked tentatively.

"Good morning, Brianna," Alex responded slightly pleased. Now that he was right in front of me, he really did sound like the Jolly Green Giant and his size solidified the comparison. "This is Hannah Berkshire. She will be escorting you to breakfast and then to your meeting with Lanashell."

That was the weird name I heard Jared say! So it wasn't just because I was drunk, it really was a weird name. As Alex introduced Hannah, he opened himself up to reveal a tiny young woman who looked younger than Jared and was the size of a peanut next to Alex.

"Hi, Hannah, I'm Brianna," I said extending my hand to her.

"Nice to meet you," she replied, unable to take her eyes off of Alex while she shook my hand. "Maddy asked me to show you around."

"That sounds great," I said as Alex stepped back allowing me to exit my room. "You will have to show me where everything is. I have been sick since I got here and can't remember anything about this building." My excuse was certainly plausible.

Hannah let a little laugh escape before she said, "I've been here for three months and besides the cafeteria, the gym, and the laundry room, I really don't know where anything else is."

Relieved to know there was a laundry room, I started down the hall with Hannah until Alex cleared his throat causing me to turn back around.

"Brianna, a moment?"

"I'll meet you at the elevators," little Hannah said as she continued down the hall.

I looked back at Alex whose expression turned from gentle to serious in a matter of seconds. "Brianna, Jared and I are here to provide you with extra protection while you are at the Facility, but I want you to have your space and privacy as well."

"And I appreciate that," I replied, imagining how I would walk around this building with Alex at my side. Would he even fit in the elevator?

Just then Alex pulled out a small box from his pocket and handed it to me. I flipped the lid of the box open to reveal a beautiful steel watch with a pale pink pearl face and tiny diamond dial markers.

"Thank you, Alex, but I actually already have a watch."

"It's more of a tracker and panic device."

"Oh."

"Wear it at all times so that I know where you are in the building. If you need me, just press the side button and I'll come running. Kyla picked out the watch, but she said that if it isn't your style, you can pick something else out and we'll retrofit it."

"Tell Kyla it's perfect. Thank you," I said, taking the watch out of the box and replacing my old worn out one. The watch was beautiful, and served dual purposes: privacy and safety. Oh, and it told time, so really three.

"I will be able to get to you within seconds no matter where you are. Jared rigged it so that it has a transmission distance of ten miles, but I won't let you get that far anyway," he said with a wink.

"Nine miles max, got it," I said giving him a little salute and making him laugh. "Oh, poor Hannah is still waiting at the elevators."

"I will be keeping an eye on you," Alex said, taking the empty box and my old watch out of my hands. "Good luck on your first day."

"Thanks. Now one last thing, where are the elevators?"

Breakfast at the hybrid hotel looked amazing, and they were all about being healthy. There were massive displays of fruit and low-fat muffins, yogurt, and plenty of fiber products to help the hybrids stay regular. Unfortunately, the minute the smell of food hit me, I felt like I was going to be sick. So today I stuck with a diet soda and a piece of whole wheat toast. The cafeteria was the typical big open room with various sized tables spaced throughout, however, I am sure few had two full walls of windows with a stunning view of San Francisco. Of course the day when my head felt as though a construction worker was pounding on it with a sledge hammer, the sun was filtering in through the windows at full strength.

While I sat nibbling on my toast, Hannah gave me the lowdown on the place itself and who you needed to go to, to get things. With few exceptions that person was always Maddy, but if you were on her bad side, she certainly would close up shop. We gabbed about ourselves a little and I found out that Hannah had just turned nineteen, and like Jared she was an orphan. However, unlike Jared, she knew her family very well, and they had been killed by vampires working for Elaina who were trying to get to her. Though I truly wanted the scoop on how she escaped and made her way here, I didn't want to pry. I certainly wasn't about to tell her my wonderful story.

Little Hannah, as I called her in my head, was just that, little. She looked like she barely stood 5'0", and there wasn't an ounce of fat on her teeny little body. Her petite frame and angelic face surrounded by her long wavy brown hair made her look nine instead of nineteen. She was also a delightful, well-mannered young lady, and it made me sad that her parents were no longer around to see her develop into a woman.

During breakfast we talked about boys, well she talked about boys, and I listened about who she liked, one of them being Jared who apparently visited the Facility quite often. I tried to break it to her gently that Jared was pretty much a male slut, even though I had only spent a few hours with him, a woman could tell. While we ate, one thing we both noticed was that I had attracted the attention of slutty Melanie and her gang. They chose to sit at the table next to ours and stare us down. Thankfully my hangover made me appear aloof and unaffected; at least it was good for something.

Glancing at my new fabulous watch I noticed it was only a few minutes before my 9:30 appointment with Lamadell, Lanabell, whatever her name was. Hannah noticed the time as well so we both exited the cafeteria and made our way through the large open atrium toward the front of the building.

But before we reached the offices Hannah pulled me aside and said, "Just a piece of advice. Lanashell will seem like a very nice person, but if you want to keep something secret, don't tell her, don't even think about it. Try and keep your mind on other things while you're in there, okay?"

"Oooh-kay?" I answered tentatively. "Is there anything else I should know?"

"No, that's it. I'll look for you afterwards so we can maybe grab some lunch?"

"Absolutely," I said, giving her a quick hug, "and thank you so much for taking the time to show me the ropes. You are definitely my go-to girl."

Hannah's face glowed three shades brighter, making my heart feel extremely warm.

Just as Hannah turned away, I heard a familiar voice behind me. "Good morning, my dear," Maddie said. It is so nice to see you around and about, although I wish you had more color."

Maddy's doting made me blush.

"I'm getting there, I promise."

"Well, you better. I can't have you going back to Mr. Burke looking so pale," she said, patting me gently on the cheek, although the mention of Cameron made me nauseous. "Lanashell has asked that the two of you meet in the conference room versus her office, so I will escort you there. Unfortunately, she is running a little late, I hope you don't mind waiting."

I shook my head as Maddy took me gently by the arm and pulled me down a narrow hallway where the administrative offices sat side by side. At the end of the hallway was a large room with a conference table that filled the space. Maddy left shortly after ensuring I was comfortable and I began my agonizing wait alone. It was hard not to look at my watch and stare as thirty minutes slowly ticked by. Finally, after I had successfully counted the holes in each of the ceiling tiles, an impeccably dressed, strikingly beautiful woman with severe angular-cut blonde hair, ruby lips, and large vampire eyes walked into the room and extended her hand across the table.

"Brianna Morgan, it is a pleasure to finally meet you. I apologize for my lateness, my name is Lanashell, but you can call me Lana. We have long awaited your arrival, and may I say it is an honor to have a child of Eris in our midst. We have high expectations of you."

"Well, I hope I don't disappoint."

"I do not think there is a chance of that. I have heard some very interesting things about you already, so let's get started." Lana sat down in one of the conference chairs on the opposite side of the table, although it was hard to see how she could sit in the black pencil skirt suit that hugged her legs together. Once seated, Lana pulled out a manila folder from within her black leather portfolio. "So Brianna, I am going to ask you some basic questions so that we can get a good solid history on you," she said looking through the various forms. "As soon as our interview is done, I will test for your abilities, and then our medical staff will do a complete physical. Nothing to worry about, all very standard stuff. Okay first, just some standard family history questions. First name, Brianna, Middle name?"

"Marie."

"Ah, how nice. Maiden name, Morgan, married name?"

"No," I responded quickly. Lana met my eyes with a smile that made me think she knew exactly what my situation was when she asked the question.

"Okay. Father's name is Eris," she said filling in the space on her own. "Mother's name?"

"Shelby Joann Morgan."

"Shelby? Really?"

I nodded at her question.

"Well that is certainly…interesting."

Interesting? Ooh, there was some gossip to be learned here. How in the hell did this vampire know my crazy ass mother?

"Have you had any interactions with vampires other than your Gatherer? And if yes, please explain the incidences as best you can."

When I didn't answer at first, Lanashell looked up from her stack of papers and stared at me intently, narrowing her eyes slightly. Suddenly images of everything and everyone I had seen over the last few weeks began flashing before my eyes. I wondered if this was what Hannah had alluded to

- if I didn't want Lana to know something I shouldn't even think about it. But what if she was pushing me to think about it, Hannah didn't warn me about that. Thinking that the flickering images would stop if I gave her what she wanted, I tightened my sweater around me, crossed my arms in front of me and began thinking about the Fiasco in Flagstaff.

"Now seeing that a vampire had you by the throat, and your Gatherer was being taken over by four others, how was it that you were able to get away?"

"My head thing," I responded and pointed to my head. I could tell from Lanashell's face that she wasn't quite sure how to take my revelation.

"Okay, we will get into your abilities in a moment. Besides that incident, were there any other encounters?"

"Not one that I can really describe, but my grandfather told me that when I was five, a vampire came to our house and attacked him and my grandmother. Apparently, I stabbed him with a knife and he disappeared."

"I am skeptical," she said in a snarky tone, "that you were able to stab a vampire with anything."

"It was a knife from my grandmother's silver."

That certainly got her attention.

"How did you know that silver would hurt a vampire?"

"Well that is certainly a question for the ages. We haven't quite figured that out yet," I said as I rubbed my arms to get the blood flowing into them again. Why was it so freakin' cold in here?

"And prior to that, you had never been educated about vampires?"

"Or after. I didn't know vampires existed until Ca...my Gatherer told me." Cameron's face flashed in my head and I quickly pushed it away and began thinking about all the foods that started with the letter A: apple, artichoke, asparagus, aardvark. Crap I was bad at this.

I could see that Lanashell suddenly became frustrated and shuffled a few more papers around until she found the one she wanted. "Let's talk about your abilities. You mentioned a 'head thing,' is there anything else you have discovered besides that?"

"Nope." Anchovies. Arugula. Almonds.

"I would think that a daughter of Eris would have some kind of Dreamwalking ability. Have you noticed anything unusual about what you see in your dreams, or those of others?"

"I don't see much besides what Eris wants me to see," I lied.

"Well that does sound like Eris," she said into her papers. I wanted to tell her that she sounded like a jilted lover, but I had a feeling I would win no points with her. "So let us discover a little more about this head thing, can you describe what it is in as much detail as possible. And please understand that I am only asking these questions in order to fully understand your powers as they stand now so that we can find the appropriate resources needed to harness and train that power. Keeping things from me, Ms. Morgan, only deters your progress." Lanashell's caring tone turned cold. Somehow she knew I was holding back, and she was a little perturbed.

"To say the least it is difficult to explain and I can't control it in any way. It just sort of happens," I said, feeling like a child. I looked down and started worrying my watch's face in tiny circles with my index finger. "It only happens when I'm scared or angry, and this burning starts in my stomach and explodes through my head."

Lana wrote feverishly in the allotted lines on the form and then asked, "What exactly explodes from your head?"

I laughed. "I'm sorry, Lana, I am totally failing at this."

"Brianna, it is always difficult for us to explain things we do not understand ourselves. And I have never heard of this kind of ability, therefore I am unable to prod you along. So truly, you are doing fine. Just explain as best you can, and we will figure it out," she responded, the caring returning to her voice. I wondered what her reaction would have been if I pictured a bottle of mood stabilizers.

"This burning…it comes up through the top of my head, and whatever I'm trying to say just comes out of my head. Only thing is, no one can hear it but vampires." That certainly got her attention.

"Well, I assume it is because of vampire's superior hearing."

"It could be, but when it happens, I'm not really having a conversation. Vampires tend to be taken down, almost knocked unconscious. That's how I got away from those vampires in Flagstaff. All of them fell to the ground. The same thing happened with Devin and Cameron the other night." Well, I'd finally said it. All the emotions and images of that night when Cameron admitted killing Sam, and Devin took him away, began flooding into my head, although this time Lana wasn't looking at me. All of these images were my doing.

"This was the night you came here?"

"Yes," I answered quietly, still unable to forget the feeling of abandonment and betrayal from that night.

"Interesting. We received several reports that night from vampires about a strange…um…" but she couldn't find the words.

"See, I told you. Really hard to explain."

"Agreed. I think we need to do some tests in order to get a full view of this emerging ability." Lana got up from her seat and opened a door located at the back of the conference room and whispered something unintelligible to someone on the other side.

"Lana, I…I told you that I have no way of controlling it."

"Yes I understand, but there are ways," she said as she walked back to her seat and gestured toward the door she had just left. "Ms. Morgan, I would like to introduce you to Harrison, however, I believe you have met."

As she introduced Harrison, a tall vampire bulging with muscles stepped into the room, his black eyes full of hatred. It was him, the vampire from Flagstaff. He was standing in the doorway; this whole thing was a trap. After everything I went through to get here, it was a trap, and this vampire was going to kill me after all.

I jumped from my chair and ran toward the door only to be grabbed from behind by the evil vampire and thrown up against the wall by my throat. He looked at me and gave a haunting laugh as he began squeezing my throat. The burning in my stomach came quickly this time while I tried ripping his hand away. Within seconds the burning had traveled up my throat and out of my head as I screamed, *not again.*

As it happened with the others, both the evil vampire and Lanashell were on the floor clutching their heads in their hands while I fell to the ground gasping for air. I pressed the panic button on my watch and climbed over my attacker. As I reached the door it was suddenly flung open and the doorframe was filled by Alexander. I could see the confusion on his face when he saw the other vampires on the floor.

"Wait! Brianna it was just a test. Alexander, please wait, I swear it was just a test, it wasn't real."

Alex hesitated at Lana's plea, but I screamed back at him. "Don't listen to her, she knows the vampire who attacked us in Flagstaff! It was a trick Alex, they're in it together."

"Brianna, please hear me out," Lana said as she walked around the table and came over to Harrison's side. "Harrison, please look at Brianna." The vampire did as he was told and looked right at me, still dazed. "Is this the vampire who truly attacked you in Flagstaff?"

I looked at the vampire again, but all of his features were completely different. His hair color wasn't even the same, and his muscles no longer bulged from underneath his clothing. How could I have made such a mistake?

"I'm so sorry," I gasped, completely embarrassed. "I could have sworn you were…"

Lanashell cut me off. "That is my fault, Brianna. I needed to understand your ability, and the only way I could do that was to frighten you, make you relive the moment when it first happened," she said as she placed a stabilizing arm on the table and massaged her temples.

"But he looked just like the vampire who attacked me, how did you know?"

"Your father can control the dreaming mind, I can control the conscious one. You pictured your attacker and I was able to see that. I made your mind see your attacker instead of Harrison."

Listening to her explanation only made me angry. No matter if I was awake or asleep, a vampire could control me. Hannah's warning made perfect sense now. Don't think about what you don't want seen, otherwise it'll be used against you.

"Are we done?" I asked flatly.

Lanashell nodded and closed the folder containing my personal history and endless notes. "Alexander, if you could take her to the medical wing, we need her to complete the standard physical."

Alex nodded and escorted me out of the room and into the narrow hallway, but quickly pulled me to the side. "Brianna, are you okay?"

"I'm fine, my head always hurts afterwards," I said and rubbed my forehead.

"If you're not feeling up to it, I will have your physical rescheduled for tomorrow."

"No, it's not that. I just hate being manipulated, and that's all that seems to be happening to me lately. Let's just get the rest of this nightmarish day over with." With a sigh I pushed forward toward the atrium. "By the way, you were pretty quick with the panic button thing."

Alex's deep laugh echoed loudly in the open courtyard. "Thank you, I do try."

An hour or so later, after I had officially been poked, prodded, and gave what seemed like gallons of blood, I was released, but not before the doctor guaranteed me that the blood was for medical tests only, not for vampire consumption. Well that's good to know.

Once I walked out of the medical wing, little Hannah was standing in the atrium waiting for me, looking so small and meek in such an open space.

"So, how did it go with Lana?" she said with a slight irritation.

"Does she do that with everyone? Take your worst fears and display them in front of you to see your abilities? Or was it just me?"

"Yep, she does that with everyone. And if she can't really figure out your power, she just keeps doing it again and again and again. Every time I see that woman I cringe. It took weeks to figure out what my ability was, and even then, I think she just made it up so that she wouldn't have to see me anymore."

"Well, she won't be coming after me anytime soon. I scared the crap out of her."

"You did!" Hannah cheered with wide eyes. "Serves her right."

"I couldn't agree more. Now how in the heck do we get to the cafeteria from here? This place is like a freakin' maze."

Hannah laughed and grabbed my hand, pulling me through the bright atrium and down one of the many wide hallways. Stepping into the cafeteria it was clear that the healthy eating regime continued at lunch with one of the largest salad bars I had ever seen. If you wanted more than salad there were chicken breasts, fish, and various roasted and steamed vegetables.

With trays in hand, Hannah and I chose a small table that was surrounded by other occupied tables since slutty Melanie and her gang had entered the cafeteria as we came out of line. We didn't want to give them the opportunity to stare us down, and frankly I wasn't really up for any more high-school antics.

"What exactly did you do to Melanie?" Hannah asked as she began cutting her chicken into tiny pieces.

I stole her imaginary boyfriend, I wanted to say, but instead replied, "She and I had the same Gatherer. I guess she thought they had some kind of relationship, but they didn't. And when he brought me in, she got really jealous," I said as I cut through my salad which looked a lot more appetizing when I was creating it than it did now.

"Oh yeah, I hear her talk about him all the time. She's always going off on how once he's done with the Gatherers, he's going to take her away and they'll live happily ever after or some shit like that."

"Well, she's on crack then because Cameron really isn't into sluts." My comment made the two of us laugh and start biting into our food. "May I ask you a personal question?"

Hannah's face suddenly became worried. "I guess so."

"What *is* your power?"

Hannah looked down at her half-eaten chicken breast and began moving it across the plate with her fork. "They tell me I'm fast. That's it, fast. Which really means, I don't possess any real powers."

I felt bad for Hannah, being so young and without parents to encourage her.

"I'm sure you possess incredible speed. And when you're activated it'll only get better, won't it?" I asked, not really knowing what the heck I was talking about.

"That's just it," Hannah answered, frustration and sadness coming out of every pore. "They really only want you to be activated by your father. My father is dead, and even though he was the best father ever, people here call him a disgrace because he wasn't a very strong vampire. He fought those guys that came after me...he tried, he really tried and he...gave his life for me." Hannah grabbed her napkin and dabbed away the small tears that were collecting at the corners of her eyes.

"Hannah," I said, squeezing her hand in mine, "who cares what they think. To me, being a great father is a heck of a lot more honorable than being a powerful vampire. Everyone tells me how my vampire father is one of the most revered, yet he has never been a father to me. And when he tries to be, we end up arguing. You keep those memories of your dad close to your heart, and never let anyone make you feel ashamed him."

I let go of her hand and dabbed my eyes with my napkin. Then we both laughed at each other for being weepy girls. I stretched out my arms and gave Hannah a big hug, patting her back as I imagined her mother had. But our little moment was interrupted by the sound of catty girls making comments next to us. I released Hannah to find slutty Melanie standing in front of our table with a tray of food while her three drones stood a few steps behind her whispering to one another.

"You know, for a while there I really thought I had some competition with you," Melanie said in an annoying bitchy voice, "but I guess I can tell Cameron you've gone over to the other side." She laughed at her own comment causing her mindless drones behind her to laugh as well. "But I have to say your choice in women is sad. I mean really, Hannah? The weakest, loserest hybrid in the whole building. Cameron will be so disappointed."

The sound of his name coming out of her slutty lips was like nails on a chalkboard. Plus, the girl was an idiot. Loserest? She probably thought it was a real word.

"Look, Melanie," I began, trying to control every word that came out of my mouth, "I don't know why you're so upset with me, but I really just want to enjoy my lunch and go about my day. There is really no reason for this."

"You just think you're all that, don't you?" Melanie snapped back at me.

"And a bag of chips," I replied, channeling Renee.

"Well read my lips, Cameron's mine so back off," she yelled as she took a step closer and proceeded to dump her entire tray of food on me which consisted of salad with tons of dressing and what seemed like a pound of tuna pasta salad.

The entire cafeteria went silent as they watched the drama enfold before their eyes, though no one stepped in. With my head held high, and the poise of a true Southern woman, I stood up from my seat letting the bulk of the food fall from my lap to the floor.

I came eye to eye with Melanie then leaned into her ear and whispered, "The only reason Cameron slept with you was because he was desperate and lonely. In no way does he love you, or would ever come back for you because if he is anything he is a gentleman. And gentleman don't love skanky whores like you." I stood back and straightened my posture, shocked at my choice of words and stared directly into her eyes. "Now I suggest that *you* back off."

I stepped past Melanie so that I could get out of this horrible situation and go to my room and cry like a little girl. I took only two steps away when I heard Hannah shout from behind me, "Brianna look out!"

I turned around just in time to see Melanie swing her tray at me like a baseball bat, but the second before it hit me, Hannah pushed me to the ground and took the hit in the head instead. Hannah fell to the floor, the plastic tray clanging loudly next to her, but Melanie still came after me. Backing up across the floor like a crab, I looked around at the other stunned hybrids who instead of helping me, just stared and watched. Melanie grabbed the collar of my sweater coat with one hand as she crossed the other hand in front of her preparing to backhand me. Looking at the table next to me, I grabbed a knife that lay on the edge just as Melanie let go to slap me and swiped the knife across her arm causing her to drop me hard on the floor.

Screaming as she clutched her arm she lunged for me again, but I quickly ducked out of the way, swiping the knife again and getting a good slash across her cheek. It wasn't anything gory, I was holding a butter knife for goodness' sake, but you would think I was committing bloody murder from the way Melanie screamed. Her screaming in turn caused other vampires and staff to come running into the room. Afraid Melanie wouldn't stop attacking me I pressed my panic button for the second time that day. Within seconds Alex was pushing through the staff members that had converged on me and Melanie - one of them being Lanashell with Maddy right over her shoulder.

Lana looked between me holding a knife, to Melanie clutching her bleeding arm, to Hannah lying unconscious on the floor. "Someone better explain what is going on here."

Melanie started yelling gibberish so I cut in acting calm and coherent. "Melanie was trying to provoke me with some derogatory remarks and when that didn't work, she hit Hannah with a tray," I said kneeling down to Hannah's side. "Then she attacked me, and I merely defended myself."

"She's lying, Lana," Melanie screamed. "Look what she did to me," she said holding up her bloody arm causing many of the vampires to flee the room.

Lana's jaw flexed several times before she spoke, "Harrison, take Hannah to the medical wing for treatment." Harrison nodded and lifted Hannah into his arms, causing me to step in front of Alex. "Ms. Morgan, I assume there are no other problems here?"

"None," I said with a sly smile. "Right, Melanie?" Alex stepped up right behind me casting a shadow over me and onto Melanie who became terrified as she looked up at him. Lana didn't wait for an answer and dragged her out of the cafeteria.

"Brianna are..." Alex started.

"Just get me out of here," I interrupted as I felt my knees starting to buckle. Alex lifted me up with one arm and ran me out of the cafeteria and up two flights of stairs to my room. After depositing me at my door, I went through my pockets looking for the key card and trying to hide the fact that I was starting to cry. As I pulled the card out of my back pocket my hand began to shake uncontrollably, making it impossible for me to get it into the slot. Alex took the card from my hand, unlocked the door, and pushed it open for me.

"It's just the adrenaline, Brianna. It'll pass," Alex said kindly, but I ignored him and stepped inside. As soon as the door was shut, I slid to the floor. With my knees in my chest, I let out all the fear and anger from the entire day, not just the episode with Melanie, but also my time with Lana.

Alex knocked on the door gently.

"Alex, I'm fine. Just a little freaked out."

"I understand. I'll be right out here if you need anything," he replied softly.

"Could you find out where the laundry room is? That bitch ruined the last thing I had clean."

I could hear Alex's grumbling laugh through the door. "I will. Also, I've been meaning to tell you, I spoke with Cameron this morning."

The thought of him talking to Cameron made me jump up off the floor and open the door.

"How is he?"

Alex looked up at me and then stood, towering over me. "He is doing as well as is expected in this situation. It is certainly easier to cope with Jazlyn having been removed. He wanted me to give you a message, but I know things were difficult the last time you saw him..."

"No, no, tell me please, whatever it is," I interrupted, sounding as desperate as I felt.

"He said to tell you that he loves you, and that he'll continue to wait?" Alex said questioningly, not understanding its meaning, but to me, it meant everything. "I can give him a message from you if you wish."

I looked up at Alex not sure what to say. After a few moments I finally replied, "Tell him...tell him I still want him to wait...and that...uh...no, I guess that's it."

I shut the door on Alex again, this time choosing to collapse on the bed, then remembering I had tuna pasta salad all over me. I grabbed my bag of clothes and changed into a pair of pajama pants and Cameron's shirt, neither were that dirty but terribly mismatched. I grabbed the small laundry basket located in the closet and filled it with all my clothes, pasta salad and all. Before I left, I packed up my computer and my cell phone so that I could finally contact Renee and Daddy O.

Alex was already facing me when I opened the door and said, "So do I need to bang these clothes against a rock, or is there a washer around here?"

Chapter Thirty-five

Brianna

For the rest of the day, life seemed pretty normal, as normal as life could be in a vampire hybrid training facility. But it certainly felt normal to fold and put away clothes and watch a little daytime TV. Around 5:30 p.m. Alex knocked on the door to see if I was going to dinner and I told him I would pass. There was no way I could show my face in the cafeteria after what happened today. Fifteen minutes later there was another knock at the door, this time it was Maddy with a covered tray of food.

"Maddy, what are you doing?" I asked, putting my hand through my hair and feeling completely guilty.

"A little birdie told me you weren't going to eat. So I'm bringing the food to you," Maddy said and pushed her way into the room. I glared past her at Alex who smiled and turned his back to me in the doorway.

"Maddy, you really shouldn't have," I said, taking the tray from her and putting it on the little dining table in the corner.

When I turned back around to face her, she was looking down her nose at me while she said, "Well I certainly wasn't going to let Jared bring you that greasy junk food again."

"Thank you, Maddy," I said, giving her a hug. She gave me a light pat on the back and then quickly exited the room, no doubt to continue to save the world.

Dinner smelled wonderful, and I quickly discovered I was hungrier than I thought. Lifting the lid of the tray I revealed a beautifully blackened piece of fish with steamed vegetables and rice. Within minutes the entire dish was devoured, making me wonder if I could face my peers in the cafeteria and get a second plate. But before I could truly consider it, a cloud of black smoke formed in the middle of the room that soon took the shape of my fair-haired night guard.

"Hey there, good to see you survived last night," Jared said as he dumped a heavy bag onto my bed.

"No thanks to you," I replied with a glare. "By the way, no more Projecting into my room without asking. You need to use the door like everyone else."

"Ahh cumon, Bri Bri," Jared whined.

"And *don't* call me Bri Bri," I snapped back.

"Okay, okay. So get dressed, you can't go where we're going in your pajamas," Jared said as he plopped down on my bed, grabbed the remote, and started flipping through the channels.

"Um…wanna tell me where we're going?"

"We're going to the shooting range downstairs," Jared answered without taking his eyes off the TV.

"And why in the world would I go to a shooting range?"

Jared threw the remote over his shoulder and stood to face me in his camo pants and grey T-shirt.

"Well, you're going to start your defense classes tomorrow and eventually you'll need to pick something for specialty weapons training, so I thought we could get started early," he said as he tapped the heavy bag on the bed. "Besides, I really want to go to the shooting range, and considering I cleaned up your endless supply of spew last night, I think you owe me."

Reluctantly I grabbed some clothes and retreated into the bathroom to change. When I came out minutes later, Jared was standing with his bag that I assumed was filled with guns (which terrified me) and just as I was about to open the door, someone knocked. Jared dropped the bag, pushed me behind him, and looked out the peephole to see who it was.

"It's some girl."

"Oh that helps," I groaned, pushing his arm away to look out the peephole myself and quickly flung the door open to find little Hannah.

"Thank goodness, Hannah, are you all right?" I said as I gave her a big bear hug and brought her inside my room. "I kept calling down to the medical center to check on you, but they just kept saying you were in with the doctor. How's your head?"

"It's fine," Hannah replied, reflexively putting her hand back to where she had been hit. "Just a little bump. They just kept me to make sure I didn't have a concussion. I heard you stabbed…" Hannah suddenly stopped and I noticed that her eyes went to something behind my shoulder. I looked behind me to see what she was looking at and noticed Jared right in her view.

"Whoa, Bri Bri stabbed someone?"

"Jared, don't call me that," I said between clenched teeth. "And I didn't stab her, I just grazed her arm…and her cheek."

"Awesome," I heard in stereo from both Hannah and Jared. It was kismet, and I would have to endure a session at the firing range in order to play matchmaker.

"Jared, this is Hannah, she saved my life today with her unbelievable speed."

"Hi Hannah, thanks for…uh…saving my sister-in-law," Jared said taking Hannah's hand and kissing it gently, no doubt stealing one of Cameron's classic moves.

Hannah blushed as Jared smiled at her. "I didn't really do anything, just jumped in the way," she said unable to keep Jared's eye contact and looking at me instead. "Brianna, I didn't know you were married."

Well if that wasn't the most loaded question ever. "I'm not," I mumbled. "Jared shouldn't have called me that."

He shrugged off my glare as he said, "It's just a matter of time. So are we going or not?"

"Hannah, Jared is insisting on having me make a fool of myself at the shooting range, would you care to join us?"

"Sure. Let me just run to my room, I have my own gun."

The fact that little Hannah had a gun shocked me, although it excited Jared. "I'm sure I have something that you can use," he said in an arrogant tone as he slung his weapons bag over his shoulder.

Hannah twisted her lips and responded, "No that's okay, my standard issue is just fine. I'll meet you at the elevators."

Hannah left and the sparks that were flying between the two of them traveled through the door.

I turned on my heel and pointed my finger right in Jared's face as I said to him sternly, "If you hurt her in any way, I will find a way to rip your balls off, do you understand me?"

Jared shrugged and laughed at me as he pushed by me to open the door. "Shall we?" Jared said gesturing toward the hallway.

"I hope you don't have any high hopes that I'll be good at this,"

"None whatsoever, Bri Bri." Jared laughed as he closed the door behind him and stopped short when he saw me glaring at him again. "What?"

"Listen, Jared, I know you think it's cute calling me a name that you know I don't like. But my…ex…husband, used to always call me that and I would rather not be reminded of him and everything he…" I cleared my throat "…used…to do to me. Call me anything else you like, just not that. Okay?"

Jared shifted his weight uncomfortably and sighed before he spoke. "Brianna, it'll never happen again."

"Jared, it's okay, I just…"

"No, I mean no one in my family will ever let anything like that happen to you again." His stance was firm in front of me as his statement shocked me to the floor.

"But you don't even know me."

Jared shrugged and smiled as he rubbed the back of his neck. "Doesn't matter. Cameron's willing to risk everything for you, so when he's…uh…missing in action, we're here to do what he can't. Oh shit, please don't cry again," he said as he noticed the tears gathering at the edges of my eyes.

I laughed, which caused two tears to escape down my cheeks. "Come on, Hannah's waiting."

Wiping away the tears with one hand, and grabbing his shirt sleeve with the other I pulled him down the hall toward the elevators.

"So, sis, I'll need to think of another nickname to call you."

"Brianna is fine, and I'm not your sis either."

"Not yet."

"Jared, stop."

"Whatever you say, B-na."

"B-na?"

"Na-na?"

"No."

"Briannakins?"

"No."

"Bibi it is."

Knowing I wasn't going to win, I threw up my hands, "Fine."

Chapter Thirty-six

Brianna

My first day of classes made me feel every one of my thirty-one years. From 9:30 a.m.-10:30 a.m., physical training, which was me basically huffing and puffing like an old lady on the treadmill while Hannah reminisced about our evening with Jared. From 10:30 a.m.-12:00 p.m., self-defense class, and 12:00 p.m.-1:00 p.m. was lunch where I successfully ate without incident. From 1:00 p.m.-3:00 p.m. was Hybrid 101, at least that's what I called it, and though it was a two-hour seminar I was thoroughly entrenched in taking studious and copious notes because I was afraid I would have to write a paper for homework.

Hybrid basics :

1. Hybrids can only be created by a human mother and vampire father

2. A hybrid's powers are dependent on the strength of his /her father's (weaker the Vamp, weaker the hybrid)

3. Powers/abilities are semi-dormant until in the presence of other vampires and hybrids (reasons unknown)

4. A hybrid is fully activated when they drink the blood of his/her vampire father.

- Blood received directly from the hybrid's father is more potent, and powers are more heightened and defined
- By drinking the father's blood, the amount of human blood in the body is reduced, vampire traits become more dominant
- Hybrids can be activated by other vampires if the father is unknown or dead, though not ideal

5. Drinking the blood of a vampire or hybrid allows you to take on the powers of that vampire/hybrid for several hours
6. Hybrid blood can provide vampires protection from the sun

Dangers for hybrids:
1. Drinking from multiple vampire partners consecutively will overload the hybrid's body with powers (causing death)
2. Drinking excessive amounts of vampire can cause an improper Turning, the human body decays (causing death)
3. Powerful hybrid blood can be addicting to vampires (potential death)

There is nothing like a good lecture on the many different ways you could die as a hybrid, and all because your father couldn't resist getting in the sack with your mother. There were so many do's and don'ts I wanted to laminate my notes so that I could study them each night. I couldn't really see myself drinking excess amounts of various vampires' blood, but I supposed there were hybrid sluts (i.e., slutty Melanie).

After the lecture I was exhausted. Between having Jared ask me questions about Hannah until the wee hours, and then burning a trillion calories during morning training sessions, I seriously could have fallen asleep in the elevator on the way up to my room. As I rounded the corner, I didn't see Alex, who had been a permanent fixture in front of my door during the day, and I got a little worried. I pulled the key card out of my pocket and opened the door only a couple of inches when I heard the voices of two women inside.

"Brianna? Is that you?"

It was Hannah, but I couldn't understand why she was in my room or who she was talking to. I opened the door slowly, staying in the doorway when I saw Hannah sitting on the narrow couch with a female vampire I had never seen before.

"Hey, Hannah," I said tentatively.

"I hope you don't mind," Hannah said as she stood up from the couch and walked toward the door, "they gave me a roommate today and I was trying to give her some space to unpack so I came by to see you. Kyla answered and we just got to talking."

The stylish vampire who I assumed was Kyla stood from the couch letting her orangey red hair fall down the entire length of her back. By the mask of freckles that covered her face you knew that when she was human, she must have had the most gorgeous emerald green eyes.

I tentatively stepped inside my room and extended my hand. "Kyla, Alex's wife, right?"

Kyla took my hand and pulled me in for a hug instead. "Oh Brianna, it's so nice to finally meet you," Kyla said and then pulled me down onto the couch. "How are you feeling? I have been so worried about you this past week."

"Fine, I guess," I said confused, "why wouldn't I be?"

Kyla looked at me with concern in her eyes as she said, "Cameron told me about the miscarriage, and then you were suddenly here a couple days later, and then those two stupid heathens had to get into a fight in front of you in your delicate condition, and then you were down for the count again. So I have just worried to death about you and of course I can't get any real answers from Alex or Jared since they are, well men, and so I told Alex I was just going to come here and see how you were doing. I hope you don't have plans for the rest of the day because I've looked through your drawers and your wardrobe is abysmal. So I was thinking we could do a little shopping since Jared gave me your new ATM and credit cards. So get freshened up, Alex is pulling the car around since he'll be playing chauffeur. Oh this is going to be fun!"

I opened my mouth to protest but then was quickly interrupted by Kyla again, "You don't have to worry about the money. Cameron had Jared connect all the cards to his accounts. And trust me, you could buy the mall a hundred times over and still barely make a dent into that man's money. Besides, you don't honestly want to keep dressing like that, do you?" Kyla gestured to my oversized T-shirt and sweatpants.

I had four hours of training this morning. Did she expect me to dress in couture and heels? Although I was a little perturbed, I stood from the couch and began pulling together an outfit I hoped Kyla would approve of.

Hannah gave me a quick wave, seeing that I obviously had no choice but to go with Kyla. "Have fun, Brianna, I'll come by later tonight then."

As I headed to the shower, I gave Hannah a quick hug and whispered in her ear, "If I'm not back by tonight, send the search teams. I may have been taken hostage by the fashion police."

Hannah smiled and laughed as she walked out the door, though when I looked at Kyla before stepping into the bathroom she was not as jovial. My late afternoon shower felt wonderful as I scrubbed the film of sweat off every inch of my body. Once out of the shower, I dressed in jeans and a sleeveless V-neck blouse, trying not to look like a total slob while out with a fashionista like Kyla. When I opened the door to the bathroom to let the steam out, I was greeted by Kyla's freckled face in the doorway.

"You do know that I can hear you even when you're whispering, right?" Kyla said raising her orangey red eyebrow at me.

"Really?" I replied sarcastically. "That must be covered in my vampire 101 class tomorrow. I'll have to remember that next time."

"Brianna, I'm sorry, I know I come on a little strong," Kyla said, twirling her hair between her fingertips. "It's just that the only other girls I ever have contact with are Warriors, and you can't really consider them girls since all they care about is being like one of the guys. So I apologize if I got a little over excited about the prospect of having one of those, girls' days, I think you call them."

I had to bite my lip in order not to laugh and possibly hurt Kyla's feelings. Picking through my makeshift makeup bag I replied, "Yes, Kyla, it's called a girls day. But you're a Warrior too, how come you're not like the other Warrior women, like Jazlyn?"

Kyla rolled her eyes at the sound of Jazlyn's name. "Please, she'd probably sell her soul for a penis if it meant Victor would pay more attention to her. But technically I am only a Warrior by marriage. One of only seven other Warrior wives, and unfortunately the only one that lives in the manor, so needless to say I have never had a girls' day. Come to think of it, the only other person I've actually shopped with on a regular basis is Cameron. That sounds really odd, I know, but the man loves clothes and has quite a good eye."

"Yes, he is quite the metro-sexual snob when it comes to fashion, don't you think?" I said smiling at Kyla through the mirror while I tried to put on a little lip gloss. But then my thoughts got the better of me as I thought about him still being tortured, and my smile faded away.

"Brianna, he's..."

"So Jared was telling me last night that all of the Warriors have special talents," I interrupted as I stepped out of the bathroom wanting to avoid the topic of Cameron all together.

"Yes," Kyla responded understandingly, "every Warrior was chosen by Victor for a reason. Jared was originally chosen because of his technology knowledge, but he's also an excellent marksman."

"I certainly got a display of that last night at the shooting range. Of course I think he was really showing off for Hannah, but still he was certainly impressive. So why was Alex chosen?"

"Brawn, pure brawn. Seriously, have you seen my man?"

"I think most of San Francisco can see him up here. So do you have any special powers?"

Kyla grabbed her purse from the couch and then gave me a strong pageant pose. "I used to think it was my fabulous fashion sense," Kyla said making me laugh as I laced up my sneakers. "But actually, I do have a little self-defense mechanism."

"Really, what is it?"

"I can see a few seconds ahead in time."

"You see the future?"

"No, not really. I can only see my own path, and only about five or six seconds, which is why I knew you were going to turn me down on the shopping since you didn't think you had money. But you do, voila!" Kyla pulled three cards out of her purse and handed them to me. One ATM card, one black credit card (lord help me), and a driver's license all in the name of B.M. Morgan.

It was certainly nice to have an ID again, but I handed the cards back over to Kyla. "You'll have to hold them for me. I don't have anything to put them in."

"You don't even have a wallet?" Kyla asked sadly. "Okay, first order of business, a new purse, then a wallet, and then shoes. Deal?"

I nodded. "Deal."

"I mean as long as that's what you're supposed to do on a girls' day. I want to do this right," Kyla said with a very serious tone.

"Absolutely. Usually more time is spent in the shoe department than anywhere else."

"Ooh, shoes are my favorite."

"You would love my friend Renee."

I could honestly say after officially seeing a little more of San Francisco, I loved it. Although I was still seeing most of it through the window of Alex's ginormous SUV, there were so many wonderful sights to take in. Kyla had decided that our girls' day would take place in an area where there was both outside and inside shopping in the vicinity "depending on our fancy", and had many of her favorite designer shops. After finding a spot in the garage that the SUV could actually fit in, Kyla and I walked through the main square arm in arm, with Alex only a few steps behind looking like our personal body guard, shades and all.

Kyla was a master shopper, and within the first twenty minutes of our shopping excursion I had a purse over my shoulder with a wallet inside that carried my license and two cards. Although Kyla pushed me to go for one of the designer purses, I just couldn't justify spending that much money, especially when it wasn't mine. After we had conquered shoes, we began shopping for clothes, which I'll admit I needed, but with every purchase I felt guiltier and guiltier since I was having a wonderful time with Kyla while

Cameron was suffering. That's when I started looking for things that Cameron might like, and since he had been Kyla's previous shopping buddy, she knew him best.

Quickly Alex became our mule as we continued to pile the bags on him, but he didn't complain. It was actually quite sweet how Alex and Kyla interacted with each other. Alex may be as big as a grizzly bear, but he was as sweet as a lamb when it came to Kyla and they were very affectionate with each other. Little kisses here and there, somehow touching at all times. I even caught a butt pinch from Kyla when she thought no one was looking. Even with the difference in size, when they hugged you could see both of them melting into each other. The love between them was electric, making me miss my Cam even more. Just as the feeling of foreboding began to take over, my stomach growled painfully loud.

"Goodness, Brianna, we need to get you something to eat," Kyla said taking my newest purchase from me and hanging it on Alex's outstretched arm.

"I'm fine, really. I'm surprised I'm hungry it's only," I looked down at my watch, "wow, it's 7:00. Okay I am hungry, but I can make it back to the Facility."

Kyla stamped her foot down and crossed her arms in front of her. "Brianna, this is girls' day, and we're supposed to have lunch, but since we started so late, we're supposed to have dinner. That's what they do. I've seen it on TV."

"But Kyla," I whispered, "you don't eat."

"Details. It's not like we haven't had to fake it before. Plus, it completes the experience."

Kyla grabbed my arm and pulled me toward one of the many bistros that had outdoor seating. The battle was over. She wasn't going to let a silly thing like not being able to digest any food get in the way of the perfect ending to her girls' day. Alex excused himself and took the bags back to the SUV since there wasn't going to be a place to sit at the small bistro table.

A few minutes later, after the waiter had taken my order of a turkey club sandwich and the left side of the menu for Kyla, Alex returned with everyone's eyes following him as he sat down at our table. It didn't seem to faze him or Kyla that people stared. Although I didn't know how old Alex was, I was sure he had had many years to get over caring that people couldn't stop themselves from looking at him. As the waiter began bringing out item after item that Kyla had ordered, Alex just laughed and simply loved the smile on his wife's face as she enjoyed getting her food and gossiping about the other Warriors who lived in the manor. The waiter checked in with us several times, worried that there was something wrong with Kyla's dishes since she hadn't touched any of them, but each time Kyla simply smiled and told him that everything was perfect.

After inhaling my sandwich, I felt brave enough to talk to Alex a little about Cameron.

"Alex, has Victor given any clue as to when Cameron will be released?"

Alex paused for a second, giving Kyla a quick glance before he answered. "No. Father keeps those things to himself."

"Yes, honey," Kyla chimed in, patting his hand, "but you were just saying this morning you didn't think it would be much longer, right?" I could tell that Kyla was kicking Alex under the table.

Alex cleared his throat. "Oh, yeah. I can't see it being more than a few more days."

"Do you think…do you think we'll be able to see each other after he's released?"

"Why wouldn't you?" Alex asked matter-of-factly.

"I don't know," I replied, shrugging my shoulders high. "I thought maybe the Gatherers would send him right back out." Alex and Kyla became quiet. "What?"

"Cameron is no longer a Gatherer, honey," Kyla responded.

"Because of me?"

"No," Alex answered, shaking his head, "because he chose to disobey orders and broke their code."

"Because of me."

"Fine, it was because of you. He realized that he loved you more than anything else in the world, no matter what the cost. Now he is realizing the consequences of his actions. That's how we work, Brianna." Alex's deep voice felt like thunder in my chest causing me to stop breathing. Kyla touched Alex's arm gently, signaling him to stop. He wasn't yelling at me by any means, but the truth was certainly heavy.

"I'm going to run to the bathroom. Then can we leave?" I asked, and Alex nodded as I got up from my seat.

While I walked through the bistro to the back where the bathrooms were, my purse began to sing. I pulled out my cell phone and noticed that it was Jared calling, but since I was walking into the bathroom, I pushed the call to voicemail. I ducked into the first stall, grabbed some toilet paper, and dabbed my eyes. As I stood crying in the stall, another woman walked into the bathroom and came to stand right in front of my stall.

"Kyla?"

But there was no answer. Just then, the woman on the other side of the stall door grabbed the handle and tried to open it.

"I'll be out in a minute," I said angrily.

In a flash, the metal door flew off of its hinges causing me to fall back onto the toilet, holding the door up with my legs as the woman on the other side began growling at me, her arms flailing around the door to get to me. With all the strength that I could muster I pushed the door with my legs, causing my attacker and the door to fly up against the opposite wall.

Afraid I had only seconds before my attacker got back up again, I pressed the panic button on my watch just as my phone started ringing again. I looked down where my phone and purse had fallen and noticed it was Jared again. As I picked both items up off the floor, my attacker began to move underneath the door. There was only one way out, and that was over the stall door. Taking a leap of faith, I jumped out of the stall just as Alex came barreling through the door. Just as I took another step towards him, my attacker grabbed my ankle causing me to fall and hit my head hard on the tile floor. Alex grabbed my arm and pulled me towards him just as the female crawled out from underneath the door, ripping and clawing at my legs and ankles, drawing blood. She looked like a caged animal as she hissed and crawled toward us. Alex kicked the crazy woman in the face and ran me out of the bathroom, catching everyone's attention. Kyla was holding the front door of the bistro open for us and talking quickly into her cell phone.

Cradled in Alex's arms, I noticed that a few people were getting up out of their chairs and running in our direction. "Alex," I whispered shakily, "there are more."

"I know," he said as he met Kyla at the door and we raced across the square.

Kyla was ahead of us as we ran up the stairs to the third level of the garage. Just as we bolted through the door Kyla screamed, "Alex, throw her!"

As if part of a dance, Alex threw me up and across the driveway where Kyla caught me a second later just as a large truck came squealing around the corner. Alex planted his feet and lowered his shoulder just before the truck hit him dead on, causing the engine to spilt down the middle. It was as though the truck was made out of butter, and Alex was simply a knife cutting through it. The two individuals who had been sitting in the front seats flew through the windshield, landing on either side of Alex, dying on impact. Alex pushed the truck away from him while Kyla carried me to the SUV that was located just a few feet away. As she helped me into the backseat, I saw through the window that Alex was being attacked by two more crazy-looking vampires that seemed to have magically appeared.

"Shouldn't we help him," I said frantically to Kyla as she closed my door and Projected into the driver's seat.

"Brianna, there would need to be ten more in order to give him a real challenge," Kyla said with a hint of pride as she roared the SUV to life and punched the gas coming just inches away from Alex as he snapped the neck of his last attacker. Within seconds Alex Projected into the driver's seat as Kyla Projected into the passenger seat next to him, filling the front seat with black smoke. I found myself in awe at how in sync they were with each other.

Once both of them had fully formed, Alex slammed on the gas and threw some cash at the garage attendant before breaking through the gate. Kyla was texting feverishly on her cell phone as we headed back to the Facility at lightening speeds.

"The cleanup crews are on their way, I told them about the garage too." Kyla grabbed a few napkins from within her purse and then quickly crawled into the backseat with me. "Brianna, let me look at those scratches," she said as she dabbed the cuts around my ankles with the napkin.

"I've never seen vampires like that before," I said as I sucked in a pained breath. "Were those Elaina's?"

"They were Elaina's, but they weren't vampires," Kyla replied, not looking up from her examination of my ankles.

"If they weren't vampires, then what were they?" Kyla didn't answer as she picked out what looked like a fingernail from one of the cuts, causing me to suck in another breath. "Kyla!" I shouted at her, demanding an answer.

Kyla looked up at me, worry contorting her freckled face. "Those were hybrids, Brianna. Elaina's hybrids."

I didn't respond, which prompted her to continue to clean up my bloody legs, although now her lips were tightly clamped together. Cameron had told me about Elaina's experiments with hybrids, and I realized now that if I was ever to be captured by Elaina, I might end up a crazed animal just like them.

Alex remained silent as he swerved through traffic, checking the rearview mirror for anyone who might be following us. Once the cuts on my legs and ankles started to clot, Kyla gave me some clean napkins to keep applying pressure and moved back into the passenger seat where she and Alex began debating what the next steps were.

At one point Kyla asked, "Why would Elaina send hybrids? They're so unpredictable, and so much weaker than vampires. I just don't get it."

Alex shrugged, his Warrior mind working a million miles a second, reminding me of how Cameron would often do the same thing.

Suddenly a thought came out of nowhere. "Because of me, I think." Kyla turned in her seat, a questioning look on her face. "The last time Elaina sent vampires, I was able to take them all down with my gift...my...uh...head thing. I wonder if she was testing to see if I was able to do the same thing with hybrids."

Kyla looked over at Alex who in turn replied, "It's possible."

Fifteen minutes later Alex pulled into the turnaround driveway in front of the Facility, a place I never thought I would be so happy to see. Alex stepped out of the truck first, surveying if it was safe, and then opened the door for me, helping me slide down to the ground.

"Let Kyla help you in, I'll get the bags."

Kyla was next to me in seconds wanting to carry me, but I insisted on walking on my own two incredibly painful legs. As we walked into the Facility's lobby we were greeted by Lana and a frantic Maddy who hugged me and fussed with me about getting into a wheelchair. I assured her I was fine and just wanted to get to my room. She reluctantly let me go, but not before insisting that Kyla come back down and retrieve a salve from the medical wing that would help heal my wounds.

While we walked through the atrium, hybrids and vampires alike parted ways as they stared at the three of us, wondering and fearing what had happened. Once in the elevators, I let the majority of my weight fall onto Kyla, who easily carried it all the way to my room. I handed my key card to Kyla knowing I wouldn't be able to get it into the slot. As the door opened, the smell of my room was so inviting that I practically ran inside and turned on the lights.

"Ohmygod!" I yelled, almost stumbling to the floor when I saw Jared and Hannah in various states of undress on top of my bed. The two of them jumped up and began putting themselves together, all the while frantically saying various apologies.

"Jared, what the hell?" I yelled, throwing one of his shoes at his head.

"I kept calling you and you didn't answer," Jared said as he zipped up his pants and pulled his shirt down.

"That's because I was being attacked by crazy hybrids, you jerk," I screamed in reply, throwing his other shoe at him. "How dare you do that on my bed."

"Brianna, I'm sorry," Hannah said, holding her shirt in front of her, completely embarrassed by the situation. "I came to see you, and Jared was here, and it just got out of hand." Unable to say anything more, Hannah pushed past Kyla and Alex and bolted out the door. I felt bad for her, but I was also pissed off.

"So, crazy hybrids, huh?" Jared said as if nothing happened.

"Out, everyone out! You too, Casanova, you're staying outside tonight like the dog that you are," I yelled, shooing him out of the bedroom and toward the door. Alex dropped all the shopping bags in the corner near the door and opened it so everyone could leave.

"But Bibi, come on, you know I don't like…"

"I could give a shit what you don't like. You almost had sex with a girl barely old enough to vote, and on my bed. Now get out!"

I shut the door in Jared's face just as he was about to say something. As I turned around to face the bedroom, the space in front of me filled with black smoke – that little shit was trying to Project himself into my room. Hoping I could do it, I closed my eyes and could feel the burning in my stomach coming on strong. I concentrated on the burning, pulled it up through my head, and imagined I was grabbing hold of that black smoke and sending it right back out the door. My eyes flew open at the sound of a loud thud, but there was nothing in front of me. I opened the door to find Jared splayed out against the opposite wall with Kyla and Alex standing on either side looking down at him and then looking back at me. I had done it. By some freak act of nature, I had pushed Jared while he was still Projecting.

I straightened up, trying to look like I had confidence in what I had done, and pointed my finger at Jared as I said, "And don't even think about Projecting yourself in here again or you'll find your precious computer drowned in the tub. Now stay out!"

After slamming the door again, I ran into the bathroom to splash cool water on my face in order to calm my nerves. The adrenaline that was coursing through my body was making me shake all over. Just then there was a knock at my door which completely pissed me off. Didn't Jared understand that I wanted to be left alone? I went to the door and opened it dramatically only to find Kyla standing with a small jar in her hand.

"Maddy wanted me to give you this salve, remember?" she said tentatively.

"That's right," I replied, completely lowering my defenses. "I'm sorry, come in."

Kyla stepped into my room, revealing Jared behind her who was still sitting up against the opposite wall and giving me his big vampire puppy-dog eyes which made me stick my tongue out at him before closing the door.

When I turned around, I was caught in a tight hug by Kyla. "I'm so sorry, so, so, sorry."

I pushed away from her gently. "Why are you sorry?"

"This was all my fault. Alex warned me about taking you in public, but I insisted. I told him that as long as you were with me, I would see anything coming," she said frantically, almost so fast that I couldn't understand her.

"And you did, Kyla, you saw that the truck was going to hit us."

"No, before that," she said as watery red tears escaped down her cheeks. I was taken aback a little by the sight. I had never seen a vampire cry. "I should have been with you in the bathroom, but I knew you were upset. If I had gone with you, I would have seen that hybrid coming. This is all my fault."

I wiped Kyla's tears away and grabbed her by the shoulders. "Kyla, not your fault. This was Elaina's fault, no one else's. I'll be fine. I won't be going to a mall anytime soon," I laughed, trying to get her to understand that I wasn't upset. She smiled weakly in return and I gave her a forgiving hug. "But there is a way you could make it up to me."

"Anything," she responded and wiped away a few more red tears.

I walked over to the desk and pulled out an envelope with a letter I had written the day before. "It's a letter to Cameron," I said as I handed the envelope to her. "If there's a way to get it to him, I would be…grateful."

"I'll get it to him, I promise," Kyla replied as she gave me one more hug, handed me my jar of salve, and left.

Now that I was finally alone, I headed into the bathroom. After today, I certainly deserved a good soak, and I would keep filling the tub with hot water all night until my muscles stopped shaking. I didn't feel safe, not even with Jared outside my door. There was only one person I felt safe with and I was stupid to have pushed him away. My body ached so badly I wasn't sure if it was still from the adrenaline or my need to feel safe in Cameron's arms. Stupid girl, that's what I was, just a scared, stupid girl in a tub.

Chapter Thirty-seven

Cameron

"Psst! Cameron," someone whispered, jarring me back to consciousness. "Cameron, wake up."

I opened my eyes slightly and squinted to see Kyla crouched in the corner by the large wooden door. As I woke, my body seared with pain deep within its depths. "Kyla, leave," I whispered, unable to take in a full breath in order to say much more.

"But I have something for you," she whispered.

"You will get caught."

The guards ignored Alexander, but they would not be sympathetic to Kyla.

"Don't worry. I'll be able to see if anyone is coming. I need to tell you about what happened with Brianna today," she said as she peered out from the corner, just enough to where the moonlight illuminated her face and bright orange hair.

"What happened," I said, jerking fully awake and then clenching my jaw as the silver burned deeper into my skin.

"Cameron, I'll tell you, but you have to stay calm so that you don't hurt yourself even more, okay? You look just awful."

"Please tell me she is all right."

"She's...okay. She's safe at the Facility, Jared's with her. Although I'm not sure if Jared is safe from Brianna. Her gifts are really coming out, Cameron. She was able to stop Jared in the middle of a Projection and slam him up against a wall while she was in another room. Brianna's lucky to be as powerful as she is."

I could not help but smile at the fact that Brianna had been able to focus her power to inflict pain upon my youngest brother. It felt only right since it was something I had been unable to do to him for getting her drunk a few nights before. But I had a sinking feeling that was not all that had happened today.

"What else?"

Kyla let out a sigh before she continued, "Don't blame Alex, I didn't give him a choice but to let me take Brianna out today." She paused allowing me to react.

"Elaina found her," I said painfully.

"Elaina wasn't there, but she sent a bunch of her hybrids. One of them clawed up Brianna's legs pretty badly, but we were able to get her out before they could do any real harm. She was already starting to heal when I left her." Kyla paused again and I could see the moonlight shining off the reddish tears sliding down her cheeks. "I'm sorry, Cameron, I'll never let her leave my side again, I promise. Alex is upstairs debriefing the council, and he has teams everywhere looking for any clues that may lead us to Elaina since she's obviously somewhere in the area."

"But Brianna is safe."

"Yes, just a little shaken. Lanashell was calling in extra guards for the Facility when we left, and Victor sent another detail for added protection overnight. So Brianna is definitely safe." Kyla wiped away the remaining tears from her face before she said, "I do have a couple of good things to share with you though."

"You have brought bolt cutters?"

"They didn't really go with my outfit, but they may go with some of the things Brianna bought you today. I could tell she was feeling guilty about shopping with your money, but I will admit that the girl has good taste. Cameron, she really is wonderful. I am so happy for you. I can't wait until she's at the manor, I'll finally have another girl in the house."

"Kyla."

"I know, I know, I'm getting ahead of myself. But I can dream, can't I?"

"You and me both, darling sister."

The thought of having Brianna here in the manor seemed to make the pain dull slightly. Even though Kyla was still talking to me, I was concentrating on the images in my head of Brianna and I reading by the fire, walking together in the gardens, and lying with her in my bed. All things I had thought about every conscious moment I had during my punishment.

"Cameron, did you hear me?" Kyla asked, realizing I was not listening. "I said I have a letter for you from Brianna. I didn't know what you wanted me to do with it."

"Would you mind reading it to me? Who knows how long I will be up here." It had been torture not being able to talk to Brianna herself, but I could not pass up a chance to hear her words to me. Even if they were words of anger, they would still be hers.

"Good, I was hoping you'd say that," Kyla said excitedly as she tore into the envelope and examined the pages. "It's not very long," she said with a pout.

"Kyla, please. Before I lose consciousness again."

"All right, all right. Okay here we go. Dear Cam," she began and then looked up at me. "You let her call you Cam, oh that's wonderful. And you didn't even have to battle her like you did Alex."

"Kyla."

"Okay, okay. No more interruptions."

Kyla sat down on the floor in front of the door in a pool of light where I could still see her as she read my letter.

Dear Cam,

I keep thinking about that saying that old married couples always say to newlyweds, "never go to bed angry." Since the night you left I keep thinking that in our case it should be "never leave each other angry when one of you may never come back." I think it is safe to say that we both said regrettable things, and I am sorry for pushing you away. I was angry at you for what you had done, and I can't lie, I still am. After you left with Devin I felt as though I would die from grief. At first I thought I was crying because I had lost my possessions, my friends and family, and my baby. But eventually I realized that I wasn't grieving for any of that, I was grieving over losing you.

You were absolutely right when you said that if you hadn't stepped into my life I would still be in my house waiting for Sam to attack me. I had become complacent with my life and accepting of my choice so many years ago. I never left because I was too afraid of what he would do if he found me, and because I never thought I was worth saving. Though I'm still not totally convinced that I am worth the risks you took for me, I do feel that my life is worth more now and that is because of you. I was never truly alive until I met you.

We have had some wonderful moments together that still give me butterflies when I think about them. I remember the first time you held my hand walking down Daddy O's hill and how I loved feeling your cool fingers around mine. I still laugh when I think about the time you burst through the bathroom door at the motel. And when I think I may never see you again, I think about our first kiss and every one thereafter, trying to remember what it felt like to have your arms around me. It's only been a few days since you left, and I miss you so much it takes my breath away. I miss curling into you when I go to sleep and knowing you'll still be there when I wake. I miss looking into your eyes and seeing the intense love that you have for me, though there are times I don't feel I deserve it.

I wouldn't be alive today if it weren't for you, and although it still hurts knowing that you could have stopped Sam that first night, I am slowly beginning to understand the pressures and loyalties that bound you. I realize now that it was you who cleaned up after the attack that night. It was you who kept covering me with blankets in the middle of the night, and I have a feeling there is more I don't know about.

Since we've been together you have done nothing but take care of me and put yourself at risk. You trusted me enough to confide in me about the loss of your family, and yet I still can't seem to find the strength to tell you what is in my heart.

"You told her about Chloe?" Kyla asked as she looked up from the letter.

"No interruptions?"

"You really do love her."

"Yes," I replied, but I struggled to say aloud what I had realized only days before, "more than I ever loved Chloe."

My response stunned Kyla into silence, her face once again streaked with reddish tears. Suddenly she stood as she said, "Victor's coming. I'll come back, I promise."

Within seconds Kyla disappeared into smoke just as the big wooden door opened and my maker stepped into the stone dungeon. Victor stood in silence for several minutes, still dressed in his council robes and looking up at me intently.

"Child, it pains me to see you like this," he said, finally giving in to the uncomfortable silence.

"I am sorry to hear about your pain, Father," I said, having no control over my tone.

"Is there anything else you are sorry for?"

"No, Father. Nothing."

Victor let out a furious wail that reverberated off the thick stone walls of the room. "Cameron, why do you do this to me," he shouted as he slammed his hand against the large pulley that controlled the ropes of my elevated board causing me to slam face down on the ground. The thick silver chains still bound me to the board and the force of the fall caused them to cut further into my already deep wounds. Only seconds after I hit the floor, Victor grabbed the board and flipped it over causing the chains to cut into me again at different angles. The burning was so excruciating that my body started to convulse. Victor knelt next to me on the floor, staying clear of the silver as he placed his hand on my shaking chest. I could see the pain in his eyes as he looked over my revolting, bloody body.

"Father," I said with great effort while trying to control my shaking, "it was not...my intent to hurt you. I did...what I thought...was right."

"Child, we have rules for a reason," Victor responded, removing his hand from my chest and wiping the blood off on his robe.

"They are wrong, Father. You always tell us...be better than the monsters...we are believed...to be. Brianna was raped...because of your rules. How is that right?"

"If you had interfered you would have exposed us. We cannot interfere with the affairs of humans."

"Even when humans are the monsters?"

Victor did not respond to my question, but instead changed the subject. "This will certainly make it harder for you to lead the Warriors now."

"Father, I do not wish to lead."

Victor stood quickly and angrily. "No, Cameron. I will not let you throw this away. It is your destiny to lead the Warrior coven."

"No, Father."

"This is because of *her*," Victor said with disdain.

"Father," I said trying to stay calm and prevent the chains from moving now that my body was beginning to calm. "I only said I would in order to please you."

"But child..."

"I think of nothing but a future with *her*. Have Devin lead, he wants it. He can lead without emotion, that is what you want is it not?"

Victor began to pace next to me. "Is that what you think of me? That I am without emotion? I created you, did I not? Look at your other siblings, all chosen for a specific strategic or military reason, except you. Even though your betrayal runs deep within me, you are still my most beloved child." Victor paused and knelt next to me again, placing the back of his hand on my forehead. "You amazed me at how much love and grief you had for your family, something that I had never felt in the centuries I had lived. I was envious of you, Turned you so that I could learn how to feel that, and yet I managed to make you like me instead. I do not want the Warriors to be an emotionless coven of assassins. I just do not know of any other way."

"Father," I started to say but he stood and dismissed me.

"I must go. Kyla," he shouted upward, "you can come back and finish reading that letter." Within seconds Kyla appeared in front of the door, both she and I shocked that Victor knew what we had been doing. "I may be old, but I am not deaf. Besides, I do know *all* that goes on here."

As he approached Kyla at the door, she lowered her head. "Are you angry with me?"

Victor put his finger under her chin and lifted her head to meet his gaze. "No, my dear. Finish his letter, and then back to your quarters. Understood?"

Kyla nodded and stepped to the side to let Victor exit the room. As he opened the door he paused and turned back around to say, "I will inform Julian to release you tomorrow morning."

"Thank you, Father," I said sighing with relief.

"Do not thank me yet. Removing the chains can be even more painful. Have strength, child. We will talk again once you have healed."

Victor left and shut the door firmly, leaving behind him a sense of hope I had not felt in days.

"There's only a little left of her letter, and then I can let you...get some rest?" Kyla said and walked slowly over to me, careful not to touch me in any way.

I tried to laugh, but the pain was too great. There was no way I could rest in this state. However, knowing that I only had one more night of this torture would get me through the next several hours.

"Okay, here's the last part. I think you'll really like it," she said, inferring that she had already read it. "So, the last part I read was...yet I still can't seem to find the strength to tell you what is in my heart...

You told Alex to tell me that you loved me, and that you would still be waiting, but there is no need. I love you,

Cameron. I am not afraid to say it now because I know deep down that I love you as I have never loved anyone before which in many ways is why I have been so scared. My heart is completely yours, and in some way I feel that it has been searching for you all these years. I love you, Cameron Jackson Burke, and I cannot wait to tell you in person. My heart and love are waiting, no matter how long it takes for you to return to me.

Lovingly and eternally yours,
Bri

"She loves me," I said, feeling as though every cell in my body was glowing with energy.

"I told you you'd like it," Kyla said as she folded the letter back into its envelope. "I am going to put this in your room and I'll be sure to tell Alex that Victor said you were to be released tomorrow morning. He'll make sure that Julian doesn't conveniently forget."

"She loves me."

"Yes, Cameron, she does. Now don't screw it up," she said and then turned on her heels, leaving me alone to gaze upon the full moon directly above me, repeating Brianna's words over and over again in my head: lovingly and eternally yours.

"*The* Brianna Morgan loves me," I laughed lightly to myself.

Chapter Thirty-eight

Brianna

I walked down a short staircase which led down to a long breezeway with evenly spaced archways cut into the right side revealing a large open courtyard surrounded by a tall stone wall and well-manicured landscaping. As I walked past each archway the bright sun burned my eyes, causing me to bring my hand up to my face to cover them. Bright, dark, bright, dark, bright, dark was the light behind my eyes as I walked the length of the breezeway.

I reached for the door in front of me but it was suddenly pulled open revealing Jazlyn's tall, slender figure in the doorway. Her face lit up as she quickly put her arms around me, hugging the breath out of me. As I pushed against her, she released me, hurt etched into her face.

"I'm sorry, Jazlyn," I said. "You were hurting me."

But she didn't answer. Instead, she reached into her back pocket and presented me with a small black velvet box. When I didn't take the box, she took my hand roughly and placed the box in the middle of my palm.

"It is a gift, Brianna."

Reluctantly I opened the box to reveal a circular black onyx ring encircled with tiny diamonds. It was beautiful, but I debated whether or not to accept it.

"Put it on. Cameron gave it to me years ago. I thought you would want it," Jazlyn said, her smile stretching from ear to ear.

Taking the ring out of the box, I placed it on my left hand, mesmerized by its beauty and perfect fit. But as I stared down at the ring, a searing, stinging pain began pulsing in my hand. I fell to my knees, clasping my hand in agony as the onyx ring burned through my skin.

Screaming all the while, I pulled the ring off my finger and threw it into the courtyard. Suddenly the courtyard was filled with hundreds of vampires viciously ripping each other apart. Someone crashed into the archway next to me causing pieces of stone to crumble to the ground. From the blanket of bright orange hair, I instantly recognized the injured vampire as Kyla. Looking around the courtyard I could now distinguish Devin and Alex taking on several vampires at once, while Cameron was entangled with an enormous vampire one on one.

Jazlyn began cackling wickedly behind me, amused by the scene of her siblings being taken over. In a moment of panic, I pushed myself up from the stone floor and started running back down the breezeway, the sun once again hitting my eyes through the archways - bright, dark, bright, dark, bright, dark. Just as I reached the small set of stairs I was pulled down to the ground from behind, cold arms locking themselves around my neck. The vampire took one hand and forcibly titled my head to the side. Before I knew it the vampire's fangs were tearing at my throat, my warm blood dripping down the length of my chest. I reached around my back where I felt the cold swirling silver and pearl handle of my dagger. Quickly I pulled it from its holster and cut across my attacker's forearm until I was dropped to the ground. I rolled over and looked up to see Elaina standing over me, clutching her arm in pain while I put my hand up to my neck to slow the blood that was still draining out of my torn throat.

Elaina hissed viciously at me as she leaned down to finish her kill. Just as her nose touched mine, she was suddenly thrown down the length of the breezeway, crashing into the door at its end. I looked up to see Jared as he fell down beside me, the smell of burning flesh filling my nostrils as smoke rose from his body. The sun was hitting Jared at full force, causing his skin to sizzle and reveal deeper layers of muscle and bone. His agonizing screams jolted me to a standing position and pulled Jared's smoldering body out of the sun. I knelt down beside him, his charred body refusing to heal.

"I don't want to die like this," he said with tremendous effort.

"Just tell me what you want me to do," I cried.

"Help me up," he groaned as he put his arm around my neck. Just as I helped him to stand, Jared gave me an apologetic look, took a step back, and then threw himself into the bright sun-filled courtyard. Within seconds

Jared's body exploded into a cloud of ash...

"Jared, no!" I screamed, bolting upright in bed.

Just then my room's door was kicked opened and Jared came bursting in with guns drawn looking for intruders. Of course there were none, just crazy old Brianna having one of her dreams again. I would never have a working door if I continued to wake up screaming in the middle of the night.

"Bibi, you okay?" Jared asked, lowering one gun on the bed and reaching his arm out to me, but still looking intently around the room.

I jumped out from underneath the covers and grabbed his extended hand with my left. "It's fine, there's no one here," I said frantically.

Jared put his other gun down on the dresser and turned back to face me, seeing that my entire body was shaking uncontrollably. Reaching behind me he pulled the comforter around me and held my hands tightly. "What happened? I heard you scream and..."

"Sorry, just a really bad dream," I interrupted and then bit my lip to keep it from quivering.

"It's okay," Jared said softly as he rubbed my arms trying to calm me down. "It was just a dream, nothing to be scared of. Just a dream."

"Yeah, but mine tend to come..." I stopped myself short remembering that Cameron had said no one should know about that particular gift. Jared looked at me curiously, knowing I was keeping something from him. Taking a deep breath, I looked him in the eye and said, "Will you promise me something?"

"I'll try."

"No, you have to promise. Promise me that if there is ever a time when I am in trouble and it's daylight, that you will *not* help me. Promise me please, Jared."

My shaking got worse as I spoke and my grip on Jared's hands tighter.

"Bibi, you're upset. Let's just calm down."

"No, I'm serious Jared!" I screamed. "Even if I'm bleeding out from my throat, promise me you won't come out into the sun to help me. You can't, you just can't do it, okay!"

With my last statement I completely broke down, feeling all the emotion of my dream come to the forefront. Jared sat next to me on the bed, putting his arm around me and letting me cry into his shoulder. Thankfully he didn't freak out this time, and merely waited for me to get myself under control.

After several minutes my emotions died down, although I was still scared to sleep. Jared propped the door shut with one of the chairs from the dining table and then turned on the TV. A moment later he was stretching out on top of the comforter, and I climbed over to be only inches away.

While Jared surfed through the channels, he began laughing to himself.

"Are you laughing at me?" I asked softly out of embarrassment.

"Oh…no, not about that."

"Then what?"

A sly grin stretched across his face. "I don't have to stay outside after all."

He was such a little shit.

Through the thick cloud of sleep, I heard the familiar sound of my cell phone alarm telling me it was time to start another exciting day in Brianna Morgan's life. Today I really hated the fact that I was Brianna Morgan, but then again, I could still be Brianna Lewis so at least some things had changed for the better. As I rolled over to turn off the alarm, I felt the crinkle of paper on my cheek.

I peeled a thin sticky note off my face and saw one line written in Jared's cramped handwriting: Sorry, can't promise anything.

I crumpled up the small piece of paper and threw it on the floor. I could never live with myself if he burned to oblivion trying to save me. The little shit was already pissing me off and I had been awake for less than a minute.

Before I got too comfortable in my bed and fell back asleep, I threw off the comforter and began picking through the bags of new workout clothes that I had bought the day before. After everything that happened last night, I didn't have the energy to put anything away. So instead, the bags lined the wall next to my bed making it even easier to get ready this morning. My legs were still sore from the attack, but the deep claw marks were now only light red streaks; a combination of my increasing healing abilities and Maddy's miracle salve.

After showering and vigorously washing my hair, I felt revitalized and ready for anything that the day could throw at me, unless of course it was another truckload of crazy hybrids intent on killing me. Anything else I could handle.

Just as I was packing up a towel and water bottle for my class, there was a light knock at my door. The peephole was cracked from Jared's assault last night, so I reluctantly pulled away the chair that was propping it closed and opened the door only to slam it shut in a panic and lean up against it trying to figure out what to do.

"Brianna?" Devin said from the other side of the door as he knocked gently again. "Brianna, we are here to escort you today."

The last time I had seen Devin he had come to either take Cameron away or kill him. I knew he was a big-time assassin for the Warrior clan and I was afraid that he was here for me, especially since he was being accompanied by Jazlyn.

"Look for the signs, look for the signs," I whispered to myself.

"Signs, Brianna? Is everything all right?" Devin asked as he lightly pushed on the unlatched door.

"Where's Alex?"

"Due to yesterday's incident, Alex is working on finding Elaina."

It made sense. And if he truly wanted to kill me, he could have several times by now. I turned and slowly opened the door to find Devin and Jazlyn standing in the exact positions they were in prior to me slamming the door in their faces.

"Brianna, I understand my appearance at your door could be jarring for you after my last visit," Devin began in a very emotionless tone. "But Alex asked me to be his replacement for the day, and Jazlyn said she could not wait to see you."

"Brianna, it is so good to see you again," Jazlyn said as she pushed Devin aside and hugged me so hard that it knocked the breath out of me. Signs! Signs! I wriggled out of her arms to see if she pulled anything from behind her back, but she didn't. "How's that adorable little Oliver doing? I left without saying goodbye, it was so rude of me."

"He's...uh...fine, I guess. I haven't actually talked to him in a couple of days."

"Brianna, shall we escort you to breakfast?" Devin asked, stepping back and gesturing down the hallway.

"Alex usually stays here while I'm gone for the day. I have a panic button if…"

"Yes, but after yesterday's events we cannot risk having you out of our sight," Devin interrupted firmly. "I am also teaching your self-defense class today, so this will give me a better idea of your skills."

My skills? What skills? I sighed at the realization that he would see I had none. Grabbing my bag from where I had dropped it on the floor, I stepped out into the hallway and turned to ask Devin how we were going to keep the door shut when I saw Jazlyn duck inside, close the door, and then Project herself back into the hallway. As we started toward the elevators, Hannah stepped around the corner. She stopped as Devin took a quick step to intercept any contact between us, but I put my arm up to stop him.

"No, she's okay. Hannah and I go to breakfast together every morning," I said with a forgiving smile.

Hannah ran the few steps to where I stood and threw her arms around me. "I'm sorry, Brianna," she said releasing me, tiny tears collecting in her eyes. "Last night everything happened so fast. I mean one minute Jared and I are just talking and then…"

"That's okay, Hannah," I said cutting her off. I didn't want to get Jared in trouble, or have Hannah be mortified when she found out that Devin and Jazlyn were Jared's siblings. "Um, Hannah this is Devin and Jazlyn, they're filling in for Alex today."

Hannah nodded in acknowledgement and I led her down the rest of the hallway to the elevators. The ride down to the main floor was silent, most likely because as we got into the elevator three vampires that were already in there chose to exit the car rather than ride with us. When we crossed the atrium toward the cafeteria, I couldn't help but notice that vampires and even a few hybrids were avoiding us, some even turning around in their tracks to steer clear of our little group.

"Why is everyone acting so funny?" Hannah asked.

Devin didn't falter in his stride as he answered, "I believe it is on account of me."

Hannah looked back at Devin but continued walking as she asked, "Why?"

"Because I am the Warrior Assassin."

Hannah stopped short causing me to run into her.

"Do not fret," Devin continued, "I am only a protector and teacher today."

I think that Devin may have been kept away from the human world too long. You couldn't just tell someone that you were an assassin and then wave your arms and say *oh but today I'm a good guy*. I placed my arm around Hannah's shoulder and pulled her to the cafeteria while giving Devin an annoyed look.

"Come on, Hannah, let's get something to eat," I said trying to get her mind off of Devin's admission. As we stepped into the food line, I was happy to see that there were carbs on the menu today. I had a feeling that self-defense class with Devin was going to be a workout, so I placed several croissants on my plate along with a pile of fresh fruit (balancing the bad with the good).

Hannah made a similar looking plate while she nudged me and asked, "Brianna, you totally don't have to answer, and I've always been nervous to ask, but how come you always have vampires guarding you?"

"Well, uh," I started very confidently, "there's this...er...you know that hybrids are being kidnapped, right?" She nodded. "Apparently they want me pretty badly, and the good guys feel that it would be bad if they did." Dear lord I sounded so stupid. "Or I guess you could say, my father has pull and he got me some protection since everywhere I go people are trying to kill me."

"Is that what happened last night? Why your legs were bleeding?" she asked as we made our way to the tables.

"Unfortunately, yes. But they're almost healed. See," I said glancing down at my right leg and sticking it out so that she could look at it. "Where do you want to sit?" I said before glancing out at the open space where the tables were scattered around the room. At a table in the middle of the cafeteria sat Jazlyn and Devin, where all the surrounding tables were empty except for one, and the hybrids who sat there looked terrified. "Sorry," I sighed. "I don't think I have a choice. You don't have to sit with me."

Hannah shook her head and walked over to the center table where the two vampires sat extremely upright, no food in front of them, of course, and looking very out of place, especially Devin who had an odd smile on his face.

"So this is what it is like to eat in a cafeteria," he said, surveying his surroundings.

"You've never been in a cafeteria?" Hannah asked sweetly.

Devin shook his head as he said, "I do not interact with humans very often, or their gathering places."

That's because he was usually going around killing naughty vampires, I thought as I pushed a piece of melon into my mouth so that the thought couldn't accidently slip out. The rest of breakfast was pretty quiet, leaving most of the conversation to me and Hannah. Jazlyn didn't say a word the entire time, she seemed quite annoyed actually. Though I might be annoyed too if every male in the room was ogling me. One guy actually tripped over himself as he walked by. But honestly, I couldn't blame them since she was wearing her usual skintight patent leather jumpsuit.

While I picked at my last buttery croissant, I noticed that Hannah kept peering down at my legs. After the third time I finally caught her gaze and she immediately looked away embarrassed.

"Sorry," she said softly.

"It's okay, sweetie," I said reassuringly as I popped the last bit of croissant into my mouth.

"Is that what I have to look forward to?"

"Nah," I lied, "once you take Devin's self-defense class, they'll never be able to touch you. Right, Devin?"

Devin didn't answer but instead swiftly got up from his chair.

"Speaking of, I must prepare for the session. Jazlyn will escort you there. Ladies," he said and then left.

"He's teaching our class today?" Hannah said watching Devin walk out of the room, the river of people parting as he exited. "Is he going to teach us how to kill people?"

Jazlyn rolled her eyes as she crossed her arms in front of her chest. "Devin is a master martial artist," Jazlyn said with annoyance.

"Oh," Hannah said, finding her empty plate suddenly very interesting.

"What is he a master in?" I asked curiously.

"Everything," she answered back with eyes that could kill.

That was certainly my cue to shut up, and thankfully it was only fifteen minutes before our class. Hannah and I decided that we needed time to stretch, which really meant we needed to find a way to get away from Jazlyn. We threw away our plates and then headed across the brightly lit atrium with Jazlyn following close behind us.

Once outside the training room, Hannah ducked in quickly and I began to follow, but then noticed that Jazlyn wasn't behind me. "You're not coming in?" I asked.

"No, you'll be fine with Devin in there," Jazlyn replied, looking around the hallway.

"Should I wait for Devin after the class, or will you be here to…"

Jazlyn sighed heavily. "I'll come back before the class is over, okay?"

I lowered my eyes and nodded my head as I entered the training room. God she made me feel like shit, but I couldn't let it get me upset. I had a feeling I would need all my wits about me to get through Devin's class. Hannah had parked herself in one of the corners of the room, stretching out her calves as she waved me over.

"So Kyla seems nice," she said as I sat down next to her and began stretching.

"She is," I replied with a smile. "A little forward, but she's a lot like my friend Renee. I guess I'm used to it."

Hannah leaned forward and whispered, "So Cameron isn't just your Gatherer, is he?"

I shook my head. "No. He's much more than that."

"I'm sorry about your baby. That must have been hard for both of you."

"It wasn't his," I sighed. "And Kyla shouldn't have said all of that."

"Wow," Hannah teased, "you have a bit of a past."

I laughed. "Only for the last few months. Before that, a book about me would have put you to sleep."

The room was packed even though it was still too early for the class to start and I wondered if it was because everyone wanted to get a few tips from the Warrior Assassin. There were definitely people in the room who weren't supposed to be here. Devin was certainly a draw, and as he entered the room it fell silent. His previous outfit had been shed and replaced by a pair of wide legged martial arts pants, high-waisted belt, and no shirt. As he stepped to the front of the room, everyone filed into neat staggered lines, the anticipation growing thick throughout the room.

"As a hybrid, it is unlikely you will ever be faster or stronger than a vampire," Devin began. I wouldn't recommend that he go into motivational speaking. "However, if you are disciplined, committed, and master various sequences of movements, you will at least be able to give yourself opportunities to escape from potential threats." Devin held his hands behind him as he paced the front of the room. The mood in the training room went from pent up excitement to doom and gloom within seconds, and even Devin noticed. "I tell you this because you need to be aware of the dangers that face each and every one of you when you are outside these walls. If you want to be coddled and made to believe that your life is not in danger, then leave now. Otherwise, it is time to get to work."

And work we did. After Devin performed a dazzling display of his skills against several other vampires, we began our intensive training. I wasn't as bad as I thought I would be. Actually, I picked up things pretty quickly, although I certainly needed to gain some strength.

When only ten minutes remained of our three-hour training session, Devin pulled us back into our neat rows for one final demonstration. Just as he began to show us our practice assignment, dust from the ceiling shimmered down on our heads as the walls shuddered around us. A few individuals located in the back of the room ran to the doors where screams echoed down the hall just as the walls began to shake again with the sound of loud boom. This time everyone in the training room rushed for the doors, engulfing me and pushing me out into the flood of panic outside.

I kept looking behind me trying to see Devin, but instead I saw Hannah's small head bobbing up and down. Fighting backwards through the crowd I was able to grab her hand and together we ran across the dust-filled atrium. Thankfully I saw Jazlyn towering over everyone and I instantly screamed her name.

"Brianna, get up to your room," Jazlyn yelled as she came toward us. "There's been an explosion in the medical wing. Your room is the safest place you could be right now. I'm going to find Devin." I hesitated, wanting to ask her why she wasn't coming with me but when I didn't start running, she became furious and screamed, "Run, Brianna, now!"

Startled, Hannah and I ran through the atrium past the bank of elevators just as another explosion shook the building. Hannah screamed as dozens of hybrids fell to the ground screaming in pain as they were showered by shards of glass and metal from the atrium's massive ceiling. I grabbed Hannah and pulled her down to the floor as debris flew in our direction.

"Hannah, listen to me," I yelled to her, trying to focus her attention, "you need to run. Run as fast as you can, go to my room. I'll catch up with you there, okay?"

Hannah shook her head frantically. "I can't. I won't leave you alone."

"Hannah, you're faster than me, you know you are. I need you to be safe. Now run, please run. I'll be right behind you," I said pushing her up in the direction of the stairs.

Hannah hesitated for a second, then dug her feet into the ground and launched herself toward the stairs. I did the same, but was again caught in the tide of everyone else trying to make their way into the stairwell.

Thankfully I only had two flights of stairs to run up, but it was slow going with the number of people. As I rounded the first landing, I could see Hannah disappear through the door to the second floor. I was breathing hard because of the adrenaline pumping through my veins, but was relieved that she was at least going to get to safety first. But then panic erupted within me as I remembered that the door was propped shut from the inside by a chair.

When I finally made it to the second-floor door, I reached up with my left hand to hold the door open and noticed my watch. The tracker! Alex must have given it to Devin or Jazlyn, right? I pressed the panic button on my watch while running down the hall and in less than five seconds black smoke appeared about twenty feet in front of me and quickly took the shape of a shirtless Devin.

"Where have you been," he yelled at me, taking my arm as I approached and dragging me the opposite direction of my room.

"Jazlyn told me to run to my room because it would be safer," I replied while struggling against him.

"Idiot," he growled between his teeth.

"Hey!" I said planting my feet into the ground.

"Not you. Jazlyn," Devin responded angrily. "That's exactly the opposite of where you should be. That's the first place they would look for you." Devin's grip relaxed just enough for me to slip out of it and run back toward my room, but of course Devin quickly stopped me.

I struggled against him screaming, "I have to get Hannah! She was going to my room. We have to get her!"

Devin let out a breath of frustration, but quickly gave in. "All right, but stay behind me no matter what."

Devin ran down the hall at my pace so that I would still be near him. Just as we rounded the corner, we heard a woman screaming which caused Devin to push me up against the closest doorway. A moment later several vampires exited my room and headed the opposite way toward the emergency exit. One of them was carrying a struggling Hannah, his hand across her mouth to muffle her screams. Sneaking around Devin's outstretched arms, I ran two steps before he wrestled me to the ground, his hand coming across my mouth just as I was about to scream Hannah's name. He was letting them get away. He was letting them take her. They were taking little Hannah, and the thought of them torturing her made me blind with fury.

Devin was lying on top of me, pushing my face into the ground while I continued to struggle against his strength. In my ear he whispered, "Let her go. They think she's you. Now stop struggling and let her go."

Hearing Devin's words only made me angrier. In no way did I want Hannah to be a sacrifice. She was young, and had so much life ahead of her. She shouldn't have to die just because she was my friend. I had told her to go to my room, this was my fault. If she died, it would be on my head. As the anger rose within me, the burning in my stomach began to tingle and I breathed deeply into it, letting it rise to the top of my head and thinking the words, *get off me!*

Just as the thought pushed through my head, Devin threw himself off of me like someone had grabbed him from behind and thrown him up against the wall. Seizing the opportunity, I pushed myself off the floor and began running as fast as I could toward the fleeing vampires as they disappeared through the emergency exit door. Just as I passed my room, the door exploded, the impact of which tossed me up against the opposite wall and caused me to crash down on the floor just in time to see the door fly off its hinges towards me. Reflexively putting my arms up in front of me, I suddenly felt Devin's cold body surrounding me a second before the door crashed and splintered against him.

Allowing a few moments for the dust to settle, Devin slowly rose from his protective position and surveyed the damage around us. He looked down at me and extended his hand to help me up, but I was shaking so hard that I couldn't even hold out my hand to him. Devin nodded silently and lifted me into his arms.

"We need to get you out of here. Just hold on to me," he said as he began running down the hall toward the same emergency exit that the other vampires ran through. "And if I tell you to do something, you better do it." Devin squeezed me slightly to get his point across, and I nodded against his chest.

We flew down the stairs to the basement level, checking of course for any enemy Vamps, which there were thankfully none. Just as Devin leapt off the last step, we both noticed Jazlyn leaving through the emergency exit door.

"Jazlyn!" Devin growled, startling his sibling into turning around and facing us.

"Devin," she said holding the door open, "I have been looking for you everywhere. I was leaving to see if you had fled to the car."

Even through my shock I could see the exasperation on Devin's face. He ignored Jazlyn's comment and pushed past her to the parking lot. Both Devin and Jazlyn were on the defensive, ducking behind cars and checking if anyone was around before moving to the next aisle. Finally, we reached a large SUV, and Devin helped me into the backseat while Jazlyn circled around to the front passenger side.

Devin sped out of the parking lot and drove down the long winding driveway passing through the once extremely secure gates that were now in pieces with guards lying dead on the ground. It had been an ambush. No one saw them coming until it was too late, and now they believed they had what they had come for. Me. Unbeknownst to them, they had Hannah, little Hannah, and the thought made me start crying hysterically.

"Will you shut up," Jazlyn yelled at me. "Crying will solve nothing."

I was no longer in the mood for Jazlyn's rotten attitude.

"Screw you," I yelled back at her. "They took Hannah. She's just a kid!"

Feeling the burning in my stomach start again, I crossed my arms around me and folded myself over my knees. The last thing I needed was to have Devin crash the SUV because I was screaming in my head. But the burning didn't stop, and instead it turned into something else. "Devin, pull over."

"Brianna, we cannot risk it," Devin replied firmly.

"Devin, I'm going to be sick. Pull over!"

Immediately he slammed on the brakes and I jumped out of the SUV and threw up everything I had in my stomach onto the pavement. Even after my stomach had emptied itself it continued to retch until I couldn't breathe, feeling the agony of what had happened to Hannah coming out with each heaving movement.

When I was finally able to pull myself together, I made my way back to the SUV. Unfortunately, I had to listen while Devin and Jazlyn argued back and forth over Jazlyn's flawed exit strategy. Once I buckled my seatbelt, they stopped their arguing and Devin stepped on the gas, continuing down the winding hill toward...well honestly, I had no idea. The silence in the SUV was broken by the sound of a cell phone which Devin pulled out of the middle console.

"Alex, I suppose you have heard," Devin said into the phone. "Yes, we have Brianna. We are on our way to the manor. We are coming in hot, have cars sent to escort us in, and have extra guards posted at the gates."

Devin said a few more things but they were too quiet to hear. Kyla had mentioned the manor once before, so I assumed it was where the Warriors were based, and I hoped Cameron was there. Just the thought of seeing him after what just happened caused me to sit upright, trying to shake the shock out of me. As I sat up, Jazlyn looked back at me, anger and annoyance displayed firmly on her face, though I didn't understand why and I was too tired to worry about it.

Thirty minutes later we were heading up another winding road and several additional black SUVs had filed both in front and in back of us along the way. We continued up to a tall, black iron gate that was surrounded by individuals in combat attire. As they waved us through the gate the backup SUVs parted ways and Devin drove straight up to a large castle-like structure. The expansive manor was made of dark gray stone mimicking the architecture of the large Victorian homes in Europe. As we pulled around to the massive arched front door, I noticed Kyla standing on the steps next to Alex and a few other vampires I didn't recognize.

Once Devin turned off the SUV, I opened my door only to be helped out by Kyla who tucked me under her arm and helped me inside. While Kyla led me down a long hallway, I couldn't help but feel as though I was on a tour of a historic home. Even the tapestries and artwork looked authentic and then it hit me that they could be originals. I was suddenly overwhelmed by my surroundings, and the stress of the day made my knees buckle. Kyla caught me under my torso and pulled me the rest of the way down one stone corridor after another until we came to a sitting room decorated with several plush couches and chaises, perfect for passing out in.

Kyla pulled me to one of the couches and removed my shoes just before I collapsed into the fluffy pillows.

"I'm going to call a doctor," she said looking me over.

"I just need to sleep for a little while," I said, barely able to keep my eyes open.

Kyla draped a blanket over me and I snuggled deeper into the couch. "I'll stay with you as long as I can. Alex may want me to go back to the Facility with his team, but someone will be here with you. Brianna? Brianna, did you hear me?"

I stretched my heavy lids open as far as I could. "Yes. Someone here with me. Got it. Not Jazlyn, okay?"

As I drifted off to sleep, I could hear Kyla laughing in the background as she said, "No, definitely not Jazlyn."

The light behind my eyes turned a deep orange, meaning the afternoon sun was beginning to set as it filtered brightly through the windows in the sitting room. As consciousness returned to me, I heard the tap tap tapping of a computer somewhere in the room. My eyes fluttered open, though I still felt groggy and weak. Tucked in the furthest corner of the room was Jared endlessly typing away on his laptop, but then reality hit me as a cloud passed over the bright afternoon sun.

"Jared!" I screamed, throwing the blanket off of me. Jared looked at me startled, but didn't move from his seated position in the corner. "What are you doing here? The sun is still out," I said panicked, remembering my dream from last night.

"Bibi, relax," he responded calmly. "I know when and where the sun hits in every corner of this place. I couldn't take down an army of Vamps right now, but I can at least babysit you, Sleeping Beauty."

Checking the room for where the sun hit, I realized he probably knew better what he could handle. The cushy pillows started calling my name and I fell back into them, pulling the blanket back over me.

"What is it you're always typing into that computer?"

Jared snickered but kept his eyes focused on his screen. "Unlike my wealthy siblings who have had centuries to fill their bank accounts, I actually have to work in order to pay my bills."

"What do you do? Besides drive me crazy."

"Ah, little this little that."

"Well that certainly helps."

"I help keep the network running secure and sometimes I have to do a little hacking which I charge mega bucks for. But most times I'm doing research for the Gatherers, you know social security numbers, police records, bank records, the usual."

The usual, like everyone else in the world did that on a daily basis.

"Did you hear about what happened today?" I asked quietly. Jared nodded. "Did you hear they took Hannah?" Jared nodded again. "Don't you care?"

Jared stopped his typing, moving the laptop to the floor and placing his elbows on his knees to talk to me. "Look, I feel bad that Hannah was taken, but…she's a nice girl and all, but I can't let feelings for some hybrid…"

"Was that all it was? You were just trying to get into her pants!"

"That's not it. I…yes, I'm worried about her, but I can't let it cloud my judgment. I have work to do in order to find who did this, and if all goes well, we'll find her quickly. And yes, that would make me happy. Is that what you want to hear?"

I didn't answer him since he was obviously upset, although I wasn't sure if he was upset about Hannah or admitting that he had feelings for someone. Since he was obviously a little touchy, I dropped the subject and laid in silence, watching the sun inch slowly across the room, as did Jared.

"So how many Warriors live here? This place is huge."

"Well, everyone on the Elite Warrior Council has to live here, so that's fifteen, another twenty Warriors here off and on, and then maybe twenty or thirty humans. So we're usually pretty full, but we always have plenty of room for when the family needs to come into town."

"Hold it, there are humans living in a castle full of vampires?" I asked loudly, throwing the blanket off of me again and putting my feet on the floor.

Jared rolled his eyes at me. "We have to eat," he said, and then laughed at my mortified expression.

"So there are humans who actually just live here to give you blood?"

"Uh…yeah. We call them donors."

"That's just wrong."

"Bibi, you gotta understand that some humans would give just about anything to be a part of our world. So we let them help us, and we in turn take care of them. That is until they get too greedy, or clingy in some cases." I scoffed at his comment. "Hey, don't judge. You'll be thanking that human once Cameron fully heals."

"Whoa, whoa, Cameron's free?" I asked, leaping over to Jared.

"Yeah," he replied casually. "He was released late this morning."

"So the whole time I've been here he's been free somewhere in this place sucking on a human and you never bothered to tell me!"

"Hey, don't yell at me. Cameron said he didn't want you to see him until he was completely healed and that could be awhile."

"Where is he?"

"Probably in his room, why? Wait," he said as he chased after me through the door. "Bibi, where are you going?"

"To find Cameron," I replied and began running down the stone hallway crying out his name.

"Brianna, stop. Cameron will kill me," Jared said, grabbing my arm as he pressed himself tightly up against the wall to avoid the sun shining brightly through a window at the end of the hallway.

"Jared, you either tell me where Cameron's room is, or I'll...mind throw you through that window."

"Upstairs, fifth door on the left."

Chapter Thirty-nine

Cameron

"I think it is best that you leave," I said as I wiped away a lingering drop of blood from my lips. While I still held the donor's arm, I licked the puncture wounds closed and showed her the way out through the sitting room just off of my sleeping quarters. I could hear Brianna yelling for me from downstairs, so I knew I did not have that much time before she came bursting through my door.

This morning, just after Julian had finished ripping the silver chains from my body, Alexander had come in to tell me that the Facility had been attacked and that Devin and Jazlyn were bringing Brianna to the manor. In no way did I want Brianna to see me until I had fully healed. With the extent of my injuries, I needed a significant amount of blood, meaning I needed to feed from several humans that resided in the manor. Alexander promised me that he would make it perfectly clear to everyone that Brianna and I were to remain apart until I could control myself around her. Jared, however, caved quickly.

"Cameron Jackson Burke, you better *not* be sucking on some girl," I heard Brianna yell, now only feet away from my door. I eased my way back over to the edge of my large bed, leaning on one of the wide posters just as my love burst through the door, her chest heaving from running up the stairs and down the hall. She was even more beautiful than I remembered, although I could see a few new bruises, a scrape on her face, and she looked like she had lost ten pounds in the few days we had been apart.

"Cam," she said softly, still frozen in the doorway. I walked slowly toward her and she matched my steps. Her tears started quickly and ran down her cheeks. I wiped them away with my fingers, causing her face to melt into my palm. I ached for the warmth of her skin but I could feel my fangs extending while my throat began to burn with my growing bloodlust.

Brianna's tears continued to flow as she traced the thick red slashes across my chest and stomach. If I had been at full strength, I would have had time to cover myself with a shirt, but unfortunately, I stood in front of her in only a pair of pajama pants with my scars blazingly red and raw. The feeling of her warm fingers on my healing skin made me take a step back in order to put some distance between us. Brianna matched my step again and pressed her lips gently against mine. Unable to control myself, I slid my arms around her as she wrapped hers tightly around my neck just as she slipped her warm tongue into my mouth. The searing pain in the back of my throat made me grab Brianna by the shoulders and push her away from me.

"Bri, I am sorry," I said as the hurt in her eyes tore me apart. "It is difficult to control myself right now."

"You need blood," she said as she led me to the bed and lowered me down. "Do you want it from the wrist or the neck?"

I sat looking up at her as she stood offering herself to me, and it took all my strength not to sink my teeth into her milky white skin.

"Angel, please do not make such an offer. I may not be able to stop myself."

"Cam, I know you need it," she said as she extended her wrist to me.

Gently I took her wrist into my hand as I stood and towered over her. "After what you have been through today, you need every ounce of your strength. I will not take your blood from you." Seeing the hurt set in her eyes again, I placed my hands on either side of her face. "Oh my angel, please do not be upset. You worry me with how pale you are, and you are so thin."

"I just want to help you," she said, her dark eyes melting my heart.

I kissed her forehead and wrapped my arms around her, bringing her cheek to rest in the crook of my shoulder. Her brown hair was unbelievably soft as I petted her head, feeling the warmth of her skin and the pulse of her body radiating against mine. Feeling my self-control falter again, I stepped away from her and sat down on the bed, a wave of exhaustion hitting me suddenly.

"Do you need me to leave?"

I took both her wrists in my hand and kissed the back of each of her hands. "If you left me now, I would surely die. I could not bear being away from you again."

The tears in Brianna's eyes flowed over her lids again as she flipped her hands over and examined the scars on my wrists and arms. "Oh, Cam, they look so bad."

"But I am healing, love. Please do not worry."

"There has to be something I can do for you?"

I leaned into her and rested my forehead against her abdomen, her thin shirt smelling heavily of smoke and sweat.

"You could change your clothes," I said playfully. "Your outfit smells."

Brianna stepped back and crossed her arms in front of her chest with her lips tightly pursed. "If I had clothes to change into I would, but unfortunately this is the only thing I own now since my room was blown up. So you better start liking it since it's the only thing I have to my name. How come I keep ending up with nothing?" Brianna's tone quickly turned from playful to angry in seconds.

"I thought only the medical wing was bombed."

"Yup, the medical wing and my room, just after they took Hannah thinking it was me. It has been a stellar day."

"I did not know, love. I apologize for my thoughtlessness," I said as I stood again and hugged Brianna tightly against my chest.

Brianna stretched her arms around my back, making our embrace complete. As we stood holding each other, letting the energies of our bodies meld between us, I heard the rustling of bags and the clicking of high heels followed by two pairs of heavy combat boots.

"I think Kyla may have been able to salvage some of your things." Brianna looked up at me, her brow furrowed with confusion. "Turn around. She will be coming through that door in three, two, one."

"Cameron, the only reason that works is because I'm the only woman in this house who wears stilettos," Kyla said as she opened the door and entered my quarters with Alexander and Devin close behind her. "Brianna, it's not much, but a few things survived. You at least have enough clothes for tomorrow and the next day if you're not picky. We can go online and get some items shipped overnight since you don't have a good track record with malls."

Alexander and Devin were shocked at Kyla's forward remark, but Brianna and I laughed knowing it was the truth. Kyla handed Brianna the small bag of clothes and personal items along with a plastic bag from a local pharmacy filled with toiletries. I loved Kyla for so many reasons, one of them being her innate gift of knowing what others needed without asking.

"And surprisingly your phone made it through the blast. It had fallen in between your bed and nightstand. The only reason we found it was because it started ringing while we were in your room."

Brianna took her phone from Kyla's extended hand and quickly pressed the button to see who the missed call was from. "It's Daddy O. I need to call him."

I nodded to her and pointed toward the sitting room. "Go right through that archway and you will be able to have some privacy." Brianna looked at me, worry written across her face. "I will be right here, love." She nodded and I watched her walk away dialing Oliver's number as she disappeared into the sitting room. Turning quickly to my siblings I said, "Tell me everything."

Devin stepped forward, putting his hands up as he said, "Brother, maybe you should rest before we get into this."

"No," I snapped at him and then regretted it. I walked over to my eldest brother who I had not talked to since the day of my sentencing and placed my hand on his shoulder. "I apologize, Brother. Thank you for your concern and for bringing Brianna to me, but I need to know what happened today."

"Fine, but I will insist that you sit down," Devin said, gesturing to the chaise lounge that was located in front of the fireplace. As I laid out on the chaise, Devin and Kyla chose to sit on the couch located next to me while Alexander stood in front of the mantle to begin the debrief.

"What we have been able to ascertain is that after they blew through the gates, they were able to penetrate the building through the back of the medical wing."

"How was internal security not prepared once the gates were blown?"

"We don't know yet," Alexander sighed. "The security video could have been tampered with. We will be helping Lana to investigate if someone within her staff is working for Elaina."

"That's comforting," Kyla grumbled.

"And then what?" I asked.

"They used explosives to blow a hole through the building's wall where they killed several of the medical staff, and absconded with blood samples and medical records. There was a second blast to close off the medical wing so that security couldn't stop them from taking everything they needed.

"It appears that while one team was charged with gathering the records, another team was charged with kidnapping Brianna. The bomb that was ignited in her room was a small one, really only meant to give them time to escape. From what Devin has told us, they took a hybrid named Hannah Berkshire, most likely thinking that she was Brianna. Elaina's vampires knew exactly where to hit and where Brianna's room was located. Yet another reason why we suspect there is someone within the Facility having contact with Elaina's people."

"Did they get my blood?"

As startled as everyone else, I turned my head to see Brianna standing in the archway between my bedroom and the sitting room. I wondered how long she had been standing there listening to Alexander's debrief.

Alexander looked at me for approval whether to tell Brianna the truth, and I nodded to him. She had every right to know.

"Yes, they have your blood and Lanashell's records."

Brianna looked down at the floor as she obviously processed this information. Painfully I got up from my chaise and walked to her. I could tell she was nervous from the way her hands were shaking and how quickly she started talking.

"Well if you're looking for someone inside the Facility with a vendetta, then I would talk to Melanie. She would certainly love to see me gone. And if they have my blood, they'll know what I can do, right? I mean the records only say I have the mind projection, I didn't tell Lana anything about the dreams," she said but then sucked in her breath as she realized she had said the last part in front of my siblings. She looked at me panic stricken, but I responded by kissing her gently on the forehead.

I turned around to see that both Kyla and Devin had risen from their seated position and Alexander was now in line with them, all of them wondering what Brianna was referring to.

"Brianna, are you a Dreamwalker?" Devin asked, his eyes hopeful with possibilities.

"No, she is a prophetess," I answered.

Brianna smacked me lightly on the arm. "No I'm not."

"Bri, you have certainly demonstrated some prophetic skills."

"Father will want to know about this, Brother," Devin said moving toward the door.

"Devin, wait," I shouted at him as Brianna's hand squeezed my arm tightly. "We cannot tell Father."

Devin stopped just in front of the door. "Wait? Why? Brother, in times like these having a prophetess among our ranks will only help us. If we had only known of Brianna's gift sooner, we may have been able to prevent the events that transpired today."

"That's just it, Devin," Brianna said as she walked to stand in front of my brother. "I didn't see today coming. Well, not really, I actually saw another battle completely, in a different place, with all of you guys fighting, and that obviously didn't happen today. My dreams aren't always cut and dry. Sometimes they're multiple events pushed into one dream, and I only realize it's coming true after it's already happened. So you see I am not a prophetess. I am a…an after-tess."

Both Kyla and I could not help but laugh at Brianna's made-up word. To me it only made her more charming, but it seemed to annoy Devin.

"But you dreamt of a battle that involved all of us? That is something we need to discuss right away," Devin said taking a step toward Brianna, causing her to take one back.

"Devin, I don't want to be labeled a prophetess, that is just way too much pressure, and I'm not truly confident about interpreting what I see. So please, don't tell Victor, or anyone else for that matter. Especially Jared, he can't keep a secret to save his life."

"That's not true!" Jared shouted from somewhere in the room, though none of us could see him.

"You eavesdropping little shit, where are you," Brianna yelled, looking around the room trying to figure out where the voice had come from.

"In the closet where there are no windows you can throw me out of."

"Jared, you get your little buns out here right now!" Brianna commanded. Seconds later Jared stepped out of the archway that led to my wardrobe room. Brianna stomped over to Jared who actually took a step back as she approached him. "What's your middle name?"

"Huh?" Jared asked completely confused, as were most of us.

"What is your middle name?"

"Michael," he responded to her, lowering his eyes as he said it.

Brianna pointed her finger at Jared as she said, "Jared Michael Ranger, if you so much as whisper to anyone about anything you just heard I will rent a billboard that has your picture on it and says in big letters 'Jared Ranger has genital warts.' Got it?"

"You are so mean sometimes," Jared said as he scrunched up his face and put his hands in his pockets, though I knew his feelings were not truly hurt.

Brianna turned her back to Jared and I could see the exhaustion taking over her body, and I felt the same way. As she walked back over to me, I put my arm around her shoulders and steered her to sit on the bed where she instinctively melted into my side, her head resting once again within the crook of my shoulder.

"So what happens now?" she asked weakly.

Alexander stepped around the couch as he spoke. "Security teams have been sent to the Facility while they rebuild the medical center, and everyone has been put on lockdown for the time being until we have completed our investigation. We are also keeping close tabs on the hybrids whose blood and files were taken. Beyond that, we have several Warrior teams continuing to search for Elaina's base of operations."

"So when are you taking me back to the Facility?" Brianna asked sadly from my chest.

"Brianna, you cannot go back there," Alexander replied firmly. "Once they discover that they kidnapped the wrong hybrid, they will be looking for you in force. The Facility could be hit again."

"Then where will I go?" she asked as she lifted her head.

"You will stay here," I reassured her as I brushed her hair out of her eyes. I heard Devin take a step forward ready to challenge my statement, but I simply put my hand up in his direction as I said, "I will request permission from Father as soon as he will see me."

"In that case, Brother, if your intent is to have Brianna stay here, I will offer my services to train her personally. I think it is imperative that she learn how to defend herself." I nodded to Devin in agreement, though when I looked back at Brianna, I could tell she was intimidated by the prospect of Devin as her personal trainer. "It is settled then, we will start in the morning."

Brianna collapsed her head into my chest with a dramatic sigh, making me laugh as I hugged her tightly and gave her a light kiss on the top of her head. At the same moment her stomach released a ravenous growl.

"And on that note, let's give these two some time to rest," Kyla said as she began shooing Alexander and Devin toward the door. "That means you too, Jared. No more hiding in Cameron's closet." Jared rolled his eyes as he waved to us and then Projected out of the room. "Brianna," Kyla continued, "I will send up some food, and Cameron I will have some drawn blood warmed for you."

As Alexander shut the door behind them, I could hear Devin say, "Kyla, in Cameron's condition he should really drink directly from a donor."

"Yes Devin, I'm sure that's exactly how Brianna pictured her first day back with Cameron, the two of them lying in bed with a human between them. It's no wonder you don't have a mate."

I laughed to myself as their conversation continued to echo off the walls of the manor, but I tuned out when Brianna shifted under my arm. "Did you speak with Oliver?"

"No," Brianna said flustered. "I called the house and Shelby answered. I got so nervous that I hung up the phone. I just... I couldn't..."

I could see her frustration getting the better of her. "What is it, love?"

"Nothing," she said as she stood from the bed. "I need to change out of these clothes."

"Go right through that archway and there is a changing area and the bathroom if you want to freshen up."

She nodded as she picked up the bags from Kyla and started to walk away, but then she turned back around and kissed me gently on the lips. Slowly she pulled away and looked at me tearfully as she said, "I love you."

A relieved smile stretched across my face as I took her hand and flattened it against my quiet heart. "Three words have never sounded so beautiful, my love. Now go enjoy a nice hot shower and then let me hear you say that to me a hundred more times."

She smiled and squeezed my hand before she disappeared through the archway and into the bathroom where I heard the shower turn on shortly after.

This day had exhausted me. My throat was burning with thirst even with all the blood that I had ingested. The areas where the chains were stretched across were particularly sensitive and stung as the late afternoon sun from the windows hit my healing skin. Julian took great pride in ripping the silver chains out of me today, taking with them large sections of skin and muscle. The removal of the silver was more of a punishment than anything else I had endured.

I was thankful for Kyla offering to send up blood since I did not have the energy to get it myself. Feeling as though I could not sit up for another minute, I pushed myself to the opposite side of the bed and propped myself up on several pillows. It was then that a shiver went through my body at the realization that Brianna would be in my bed for the first time. With a nervous energy I began fluffing the remaining pillows, straightening the sheets and comforter, all in all needing to make everything perfect.

"Cam," Brianna called from the bathroom, "we have a problem."

"And what is that, my angel?" I replied, relieved that she had not caught me futzing with the bed.

"I have no pajamas," she said flustered as she stepped out of the bathroom with only a towel wrapped around her.

"I am not sure I see the problem."

"Well you're the one who said you couldn't control yourself."

I hated to admit that she was right. "Look in the third dresser to your right, and help yourself to whatever is in there."

I could hear her muttering to herself about how she could not believe one man could have so many clothes.

A minute later there was a knock at the door, and Christine from the kitchen staff entered with a large tray.

"Good evening, Cameron," she said cheerily. "Kyla asked that I bring up some dinner. I hope your guest doesn't mind garlic. Kyla kept adding clove after clove while I sautéed the chicken."

As Christine placed the tray on the bed, the smell of garlic coming from the large bowl of pasta and chicken was overpowering. Yet another example of Kyla going above and beyond. She understood that controlling my bloodlust around Brianna could be difficult. Having Brianna eat a significant amount of garlic would certainly keep my desires at bay. Garlic itself did not hold any mystical powers over vampires, it was simply that its odor was so potent to a vampire's heightened sense of smell, and the taste could be detected in the skin.

Christine walked around to my side of the bed and handed me a warm bottle of blood and a glass. "If you need more, just ring down to the kitchen. I'll make sure someone brings some up right away."

"Thank you, Christine, this should be fine for now."

She smiled and looked toward the wardrobe room as Brianna starting singing from inside. "Also let me know if there is anything else I can do for your guest."

"I will, Christine. Everything looks perfect," I said as I poured myself a large glass of blood and began to drink it quickly.

Christine nodded with a wide smile and let herself out.

"Please tell me that smell is my dinner."

"Yes it is. I hope you are hungry, the bowl itself is almost as big as you are," I said and then filled my glass with more blood.

"Cam, we need to talk," Brianna said as she padded out through the archway wearing a white cotton camisole and clutching the waist of a pair of my pajama pants in her hand.

"Yes, Bri, we certainly do."

Brianna stood on the opposite side of the bed, her facial expression very serious as she said, "Honestly, how many pairs of satin pajamas do you own?"

Taken off guard by her comment, all I could say was, "I only ever wear the bottoms."

"Speaking of, they don't fit. So you're going to have to control yourself," she said letting go of the pants and causing them to slide down her slim thighs to the floor. Brianna did not need lingerie to look sexy. Seeing her standing there in nothing but a camisole and colorful underwear made me have to clamp down every masculine urge that I possessed. She quickly got into bed and pulled the large bowl of pasta onto her lap. "I'm going to apologize now. There will be nothing ladylike about me as I eat this entire bowl of pasta."

I could not help but smile as she plunged her fork into the mound of pasta and chicken, twirled it around, and came up with a large serving that she forced into her mouth. I gulped another large amount of blood from my glass to keep from laughing as she tried to chew. After several minutes she was finally able to swallow and she quickly plunged her fork back into the bowl.

"Angel, we do need to talk," I said reluctantly.

"I know we do," she replied softly, dropping her fork back into her bowl. "But…can we wait? I just want one night with you where I'm not crying my eyes out. It's not even seven o'clock and I'm ready to fall asleep. I really just want to eat, kiss you goodnight, and curl into you as much as you'll allow me to. Would that be okay? After everything that happened today, I just can't process anything else right now."

Brianna's dark eyes were wide and slightly glassy with the threat of tears. I cupped her face with my hand as she pressed into it, closing her eyes when I rubbed her cheek with my thumb.

"Eat, my love. Then I will kiss you goodnight and hold you until you fall asleep. Everything else can wait until tomorrow. But we will talk…about everything."

Brianna smiled sleepily and then began eating her garlicky pasta. All I could think about now was how much I wanted her to finish. Even with the smell of garlic on her breath, I wanted to kiss her so badly and feel her body draped over mine while she slept as she had so many other nights. As I emptied the bottle of blood into my glass, I remembered that Brianna had never been with me while I fed.

"Would you be more comfortable if I drank this in the other room?"

"No," Brianna replied, shaking her head but not looking up from her bowl. "I need to get used to it. We can't eat separately for the rest of our lives now, can we? I'll just think of it as a really thick merlot. But no way am I going to be the third wheel at your blood sucking party."

As the words came out of her mouth, blood spurted out of mine, thankfully only landing on my chest. Brianna laughed as I wiped the blood away. Although she thought her comment was humorous it did make me think that I should refrain from drinking from anyone directly. Since bloodletting was pleasurable for the human, it could be looked at as cheating. But as Devin had alluded to earlier, drinking blood directly from a human certainly had advantages that drawn blood did not. It was something that certainly needed to go on the list of topics to discuss tomorrow.

Shortly after I swallowed the last bit of blood, Brianna placed her empty bowl on the tray along with my empty bottle and carried the tray to the table next to the door giving me a view most men dreamed about. As she returned to the bed, I noticed her stomach was swollen from her meal, the rest of her body fraught with exhaustion as more bruises made their appearance known on her legs and arms. As she tucked her feet back into bed, I noticed the red streaks near her ankles and I could not help but touch them. My guilt must have been displayed on my face since Brianna gently took my hand away and looked into my eyes as if saying it was another topic for tomorrow. I reached behind me and pulled the blankets back from my side of the bed and slid in next to her. Quickly she wrapped her warm legs around me and snuggled into my chest. My body started to relax as I held her in my arms and it felt as though the heat from her body was healing what was left of my wounds. Knowing full well it was the blood at work, I could not help but think that it was partially her as well. She had mended my irreparably broken heart, what was to say she could not heal the rest of me?

I reached over to my nightstand and held down the switch that drew the thick sun-blocking window shades, though there was little left. As I wrapped my arm back over Brianna, she tilted her head up to me and I kissed her gently.

"I love you, Cam," she whispered.

"Always, my love. Now I only need to hear it ninety-nine more times."

She giggled into my chest. "I love you, Cameron."

"Ninety-eight."

"I…love…you," she said between yawns.

"Rest, my love," I said, giving her one last kiss. "You can start where you left off tomorrow."

"It's a really good thing I love you," she mumbled sleepily.

"Yes, angel, it certainly is."

"That's ninety-six, by the way. I want to make sure I get credit."

"Oh Bri, how I missed you."

Chapter Forty

Cameron

I awoke to the sound of someone clearing his throat at the end of my bed. Discretely I inhaled the visitor's scent and immediately opened my eyes.

"Hello, Father."

"Oh good, you are awake," Victor said, knowing full well I had been asleep. "I take it this is Brianna Morgan," he said gesturing to Brianna who at some point had turned away from me and curled herself into a tiny ball. In the past I had rarely been underneath the blankets with her, and if I was, I was always fully dressed. Tonight, neither of us had much of anything on and Brianna looked frozen. I heard my father clear his throat again and I realized I had not answered his question.

"Yes, Father, this is Brianna. Can we talk in the other room?" I asked gesturing toward the sitting room behind him. He nodded and made his way through the archway as I rose from the bed and folded the extra blankets onto my sleeping angel.

When I entered the sitting room Victor had started the gas fireplace and taken a seat in one of the two high-back chairs located in front of the fire. Of all the rooms in the manor, the ones that got the most use were the Council Hall, the training area, and my sitting room. Fellow Warriors and I spent many a night at the table behind me debating and strategizing resolutions for the latest conflicts. Victor and I had sat in these very chairs and discussed endless topics, vampire and human events alike.

Sitting next to him I found myself nervous at the request I was about to ask of him. "Father, I am sure Alexander and Devin have debriefed you on the attack at the Facility today." Victor raised his eyebrows slightly and nodded, so I continued. "It is obvious that Brianna is no longer safe there and I would like to request that she be allowed to stay at the manor."

Victor took a dramatic deep breath in and exhaled slowly as he pondered the request.

"You know, child, when I first realized that you had feelings for her, I will admit I was a little upset, jealous even. Having had you at my side for so long I feared that she would somehow take you away from me, and like a spoiled child I lashed out." Victor paused as he stood from his chair and stepped closer to the fire. "I see now how much you are willing to sacrifice for her, and I could not bear it if you were to leave because of my refusal of her. Therefore, I accept Brianna Morgan into my home with open arms and I promise I will try to be on my best behavior around her."

I knew Victor well enough to know he would never give in so easily. "Eris called you."

"He might have," Victor replied with a sheepish grin. "But my fears of losing you are true. If accepting her is what I need to do in order to keep you, then I will do my best. Please, child, you must know this is difficult for me."

Although Victor was very small in stature, his presence could overwhelm you. Times like these where he would show an ounce of humility were rare and I had to appreciate that.

"I do, Father, thank you," I replied truthfully. "But I do wish that one day you will come to respect and accept Brianna for who she is and not because of pressure from Eris."

"Time will tell," he replied as he returned to the chair next to me. "I assume she will be staying in your quarters?"

"If she chooses. After all of today's events we have not had time to discuss it."

"If she requires separate quarters, please let me know."

Victor and I sat for several minutes in silence as we watched the fire flicker in front of us when I heard Brianna stir and mutter something in the next room. Quietly I rose from my chair and peeked into the bedroom only to notice her turn over and drift back off to sleep. When I returned to my chair, I noticed Victor examining the remnants of my scars.

"You are healing nicely," he said as he looked back at the fire.

"Yes, Father. I should be fully healed by tomorrow."

"Cameron, you have to know it was not easy for me to punish you, but it had to be done. I cannot show favoritism to you or anyone else. If I did, our family, our authoritative structure would fall and there would be no order amongst our race. I had to do it, child."

"Father, I am not angry at you. I knew what I was doing and accepted the consequences of my actions. However, changes need to be made. We have sat complacent too long, times are changing."

"Yes, child, I know. Another night though. I wish to enjoy your company without arguing for a little while longer." I laughed lightly in agreement. "So what are your intentions with Ms. Morgan?"

"Intentions, Father?"

"Do you intend on marrying her?"

"I am not sure. It is a complicated situation. She is still married."

"Yes, but to a dead man."

"And no one knows that but us. Brianna and I are still figuring things out."

"Well, I would suggest the two of you do it quickly seeing that I spoke with Eris earlier this evening and he will be here in a few days. He is quite interested to know what kind of future you are planning with his daughter."

"Why is he coming?" I asked, knowing that Eris rarely made an appearance in vampire circles.

"Child, when a vampire like Eris tells me he is coming to my home, I do not ask him why. I merely open the door. I assume it is to see his daughter and forge some kind of relationship with her. I assume they have not met."

"No, they have not."

"Well then, I would prepare Brianna for his visit. Now, I think I will take my leave and let you get back to her, and to your healing." Victor stood from his chair, placing his hand on my shoulder and squeezing it before he walked to the door at the back of the room. "I am happy for you, child. It has been a long time since you have loved someone. Maybe Eris is right, this woman may just change everything."

While Victor exited the room I thought about his last comment and wondered what he meant. Did Eris and Victor know more about Brianna than they were letting on? How could Brianna change everything? That was certainly a pressure-filled statement I did not want to explore at the moment. There were bigger issues for me and Brianna to work through.

Looking at the fire as it flickered and licked at the fake logs, I thought about the different ways I could tell her that she would be meeting her father for the first time, and none of them seemed like they would go over well.

Finally giving up, I stood from my chair, turned off the gas fireplace and walked back into my living quarters just as Brianna roused.

"Cam?" she said sleepily, feeling around the bed for me.

"Right here, love," I said as I snuck back under the covers. Brianna pulled herself back over to my side of the bed and curled into my side. She muttered something unintelligible and quickly drifted back off to sleep. I had missed this. I never wanted to have a night without her curled into me, and then I thought about Eris wanting to know my true intentions.

There was no doubt I loved Brianna, but marriage? Brianna Burke had an amazing sound to it. However, I knew Brianna would most likely not entertain the idea any time soon. She was only just able to say that she loved me. I certainly could not discuss marriage with her and I only hoped Eris did not mention it. The topic would not be welcomed coming from him.

Brianna began muttering in her sleep again and I was able to hear her say, "He told me so."

Curious, I asked, "Who told you so?"

"Cameron," she said sleepily.

"What did he say?"

"He loves me."

Brushing my fingers over her eyebrows to ease her deeper into sleep I said, "He does love you, very much."

"She doesn't believe me."

"Who?"

"Shelby."

Continuing to soothe her back to sleep I whispered, "Tell her that no one in this world loves anyone as much as Cameron loves you. She is merely jealous that she will never know such love. Tell her, Bri. You tell her just that."

Chapter Forty-one

Brianna

The first morning in the manor I woke up to cool, gentle kisses all over my face and the smell of scrambled eggs. When I opened my eyes, I saw my Cam standing just above me with a breakfast tray. It was a wonderful way to wake up. The eggs were deliciously hot in contrast to the cool kisses Cameron gave me while I ate.

As promised, Devin trained me all day and just when I was ready to collapse, Cameron rescued me for dinner. Unfortunately, dinner wasn't quite the romantic event I had imagined. My day may have been full of physical pain, but my evening was fraught with emotional turmoil as Cameron and I discussed everything that we had avoided the night before. We started with the easiest items first, such as me living in the manor with him, though we would need to put a good amount of his clothes in storage in order to give me some closet space. I could tell he wasn't too happy about it, but he took it in stride. Then we moved our way into extreme emotional territory; my rape, Sam's murder, and meeting Eris. We yelled, I cried, he apologized, we yelled, I cried, I apologized, I cried, he made promises of change, and lastly, I yelled and cried again over having to meet my father.

So my first full day in the manor sucked, and my night was restless from the loud voices in the sitting room just off of the bedroom. Apparently, Cameron's room was where the Warriors came to strategize before presenting plans to the Elite Warrior Council. Now that Cameron was back in Victor's good graces, he was a major player in these strategy sessions which soon started going all night and all day.

On day two I woke up alone, thankfully no Warriors in the next room, but no Cameron either. At first it was hard to keep my loneliness in check, but just as I stepped from the changing area, Cameron walked through the door with a pastry and coffee. It certainly wasn't breakfast and kisses in bed, but I knew what he was doing was for me and every other hybrid out there, so breakfast and kisses in the hallway while he escorted me to my training session with Devin would have to do.

Devin worked me hard and didn't care that every muscle in my body screamed in agony while we practiced routine after routine of strategic self-defense moves. There were only two ways to kill a vampire – decapitation, or a stab through the heart. And the only two things able to penetrate a vampire's skin were silver or another vampire. So since I wasn't a vampire, I would have to use a silver weapon. There certainly wasn't an expectation that I would be able to decapitate anyone, but hopefully be able to injure a vampire enough to have time to get away.

After a tiring morning of martial arts, my afternoon was filled with Devin trying to get me to use what he called my "mind trick". And sadly, I still couldn't do it at will, and Devin didn't have Lanashell's talent of showing my fears in front of me. There were tingles here and there, but nothing like either of us knew I could produce.

My frustrating afternoon was followed by a five-minute sighting of Cameron at dinner before he retired to the sitting room with his brothers and several others for another all-night session. At first, the strategy session was tame and voices were soft per Cameron's warning, however, as the night drew on, tempers raged and egos collided. After the third eruption woke me around 3:00 a.m., I got out of bed, waved to Cameron through the archway, and left for Kyla's room hoping I could sleep there since Alex was in with Cameron.

So knowing that I had fallen asleep on Kyla's couch, I was surprised to wake up in Cameron's bed to my cell phone alarm. At some point Cameron must have carried me back, leaving behind a vase of flowers and a note. As I smelled the beautiful bouquet of plump, white roses and fragrant lilacs, I opened the note realizing it was the first time I had ever seen Cameron's handwriting. Honestly, I shouldn't have been surprised that his handwriting was just as amazingly perfect as he was.

Dearest Brianna,

It saddens me that I will not be able to be with you when you wake, but I will be detained most of the day. I know our time together has been limited. Please forgive me for my absence and know that I think of you every minute we are apart. You are mine for dinner this evening and I have planned a wonderful surprise for you.

Eris is expected this afternoon, stay calm and be the strong Brianna I know you are. I love you, angel.

Always,
Cam

P.s – A door to the sitting room will be installed today.

I smiled as I read the postscript, kissed the note, and placed it in the nightstand drawer next to me. Even with the promise of dinner and a surprise, I had to chew the inside of my cheek in order not to cry. If I started now, I wasn't sure I would get out of the bed. Today would be hard enough if Eris actually graced me with his presence. So, as I had done so many times in the past, I pushed my feelings down deep and walked through my morning preparations like a zombie. Shower: check, though I didn't really see the point since I was only going to drown myself in sweat. Deodorant: check, not that it worked against Devin's workouts. Hair secured: check. Tight spandexy outfit: check. Feeling ridiculously lonely and pathetic: check, check, check.

After leaving my room and cursing every step I had to walk down, I stopped by the kitchen to grab a quick breakfast before proceeding with the day's torture. When I finally entered the training room, Devin had started without me, performing moves so difficult yet poetic it made me want to turn around and curl back up under the covers. I was watching a brilliant martial artist twist and turn in the air, and once I joined him on the mats, I would look like a three-year-old in her first karate class. My thoughts were only making my depression worse, so much so that even Devin noticed, which was saying something.

"Good morning, Brianna. How are we today?" he said, surprisingly chipper.

"Fine." I grumbled.

"Really? You seem…glum."

"If I were to tell you that every muscle in my body hurts so bad that I can't even sit down, and that I gave up using a fork this morning and began eating a bowl of fruit like a pig from a trough because my hands were numb, actually numb, and that I miss Cameron so much I want to crawl into a hole and weep, and I have to meet my father in person and I am so nervous that I want to puke. If after telling you all of that, would you let me out of training today?"

Devin blinked several times before speaking. "No?"

"Right, you wouldn't. So why bother bringing it up. Can we start?" I said, sounding like a disgruntled teenager as I stepped onto the mats.

After our usual warm ups, Devin started in hard, probably to keep me from breaking down again. With each hit, block, and kick, my body screamed with pain, but it kept me from thinking about Cam or Eris. After a couple of hours of hard cardio, Devin decided to work on my mind trick, and yet again it only resulted in me having a headache and needing a nap, which I took instead of eating lunch. It wasn't the best idea, but I needed the sleep more and it would help pass the headache too.

By the time 1:00 p.m. came around I was rested and even a little revitalized, though still sore. When I returned to the training room, I was shocked by an elaborate display of weapons that Devin had brought out onto a long line of tables.

"What's all this?" I asked him as I eyed the dazzling death instruments.

"It is time you chose your weapon," Devin said proudly. "Every hybrid is asked to choose a weapon to specialize in. Take your time, and feel free to pick up anything you like. It's important that you choose what feels right."

"Is this why you've been so happy today?"

He nodded with a guilty smile. "This is a very exciting and important day, Brianna. Years from now when you look back, you'll remember the day you found your weapon. I am very curious to see what you will decide on."

"Well at least one of us is," I replied sarcastically. Slowly I began walking down the table, letting my hand graze over each weapon. "What, no guns?"

Devin looked sheepishly to the floor as he said, "Ah, no. Jared told me about your session in the shooting range. He might have suggested that you never touch a gun again."

I rolled my eyes as I walked down the long tables and finally came across various lengths of knives and daggers. Although the dagger I had dreamt of wasn't here, there were others that were similar in size. I picked one up, felt the weight, and put it back down because it was too heavy in my hand. I tried several others and found a length and weight that I could stand. As I picked up its twin, I felt a sudden urge to fight. I looked up to see Devin pick up similar daggers and return to the mats.

"Now, Brianna, what are the two things that can hurt a vampire?" Devin asked, as he did every day.

"Silver, or another vampire."

"Correct. For training purposes your weapon is not made of silver. So for now, you can hit me, stab me, try to filet me, and it will do nothing. Do not be afraid to hurt me. Got it?"

I nodded my head vigorously with excitement. My dagger training started slow of course, but even after an hour Devin and I were practicing routine moves that incorporated much of the martial arts training. It was amazing how much easier everything seemed with the daggers in my hands, and it was oddly fun. Devin was certainly enjoying the fact that I was more eager to learn.

After another hour, Devin was able to show me more difficult offensive moves, and again I caught on pretty quickly. The volleys between us began getting faster, and the movements more fluid. During one particular routine Devin picked up the pace significantly, trying to test if I could keep up, and surprisingly I did. The daggers felt like extensions of my arms, and at one point I was actually able to get a long swipe at Devin's arm causing small sparks to fly from his skin. I stepped back, shocked and apologetic, but Devin's glare reminded me that I couldn't be afraid to hurt him. Biting my lip, I let out a small laugh, as did Devin who gave me a well-deserved high five.

From behind us I heard the sound of someone applauding.

"Brava, brava, mia bella figlia."

The sound of my father's thick Italian accent made me freeze with my back still to him, both daggers clanging to the floor. Swallowing hard, I turned around slowly to see Eris in a light-colored linen outfit, escorting a blonde, middle-aged woman into the training room. As they stepped closer, I stepped back until I was up against Devin who decided to push me forward with his weight. Jerk.

As Eris approached, I could see the joy in his eyes, and I wondered if he noticed that it wasn't reciprocated in mine.

"Bri-an-na, mia figlia, you are more beautiful in person," he said as he took my face between his hands and kissed me on both cheeks. He turned back to his escort and presented me to her. "Bri-an-na, this is my Sera-phin-a, my wife. Sera, this is my daughter, my little Bri-an-na Mari-len-a."

Seraphina and I nodded to each other in acknowledgement, but then I looked to Eris as I said, "Marie."

Eris looked at me puzzled. "What is Marie?"

"My middle name. My name is Brianna Marie."

Eris flinched, almost as though he had been smacked in the face. I wasn't trying to be rude, honestly, I wasn't, but my middle name wasn't Mariala, Marenala, or whatever he had said. Seraphina placed her hand onto Eris's shoulder causing him to turn to face her, and whatever upset he had felt seemed to melt away at the sight of her. At first glance, the pairing was odd, and to a human's eye Seraphina was robbing the cradle based on their visual difference in age. But it didn't seem to matter to either of them. They obviously had a tremendous amount of love between them.

"I see that you are handling daggers," Eris said as he turned back around. He picked up both daggers from the floor and walked over to the long table of weapons.

"Yes, sir," Devin answered, "she chose the daggers just today and showed remarkable…"

"You are the assassin, are you not?" Eris said with his back to us.

"Yes, sir," Devin replied. "I have been the Warrior Assassin for…"

"And you allowed my daughter to select daggers?"

Devin paused a moment before he finally answered, "Yes, sir."

"That will certainly need to change," Eris said as he threw the daggers down onto the table. "I am a master of swords, and therefore my daughter must be a master of swords. So continue any additional training you may think necessary, but I will be taking over Bri-an-na's weapon training effective immediately."

I took a step away from Devin, about to lash out uncontrollably with an inappropriate mouth, but Devin grabbed my arm at the last minute and shook his head slightly with warning in his eyes. I looked back at him in utter confusion since it didn't make sense that *the* Warrior Assassin was afraid of my old man.

As Eris turned around and walked toward me holding four swords, Seraphina glided to one of the benches that surrounded the room. Eris handed me two of the swords, and right away they felt wrong. They were too heavy, too long, too wide, too heavy, too heavy, too heavy. It was hard to hold one, let alone two, but apparently, I had no choice, which I couldn't stand. I gave Devin a pleading look, but he simply walked off the mat. Even he knew this was a battle he couldn't win.

Eris started simple at first, showing me proper stance and grip, which I got, but I failed miserably when he started showing the various kinds of cuts. I would come down vertically, he'd hit my swords from underneath and out of my hands. I would come in from the side, he'd knock my swords out from the other side. After a while he seemed to give up on the offensive tactics and went for the defensive. This only ended up with me continuing to move backwards until I tripped over my own feet and fell on my now boney ass. He would yell to guard high, I would guard low. He would scream to guard back, and I would thrust forward. I'm sure he assumed I was stupid. The whole ordeal was absolutely ridiculous, and to compound the situation I was irritated by Devin's refusal to stop the madness and Seraphina's constant adoring smile.

The training session continued for another hour and the frustration escalated to tremendous levels. Personally, I was shutting down, but Eris was getting angry with disappointment. My wrists and forearms ached from the hits that Eris would get in. Fatigue was starting to set in, and my body was slowly giving up with each step. From the corner of my eye, I saw Devin leave the training room causing me to curse him up one side and down the other, in my head of course.

"Again, Brianna. Again!" Eris shouted, his accent no longer drawing out the syllables in my name.

I was barely able to close my fingers around the grip of the swords, but shakily took my stance in front of him as my muscles trembled with fatigue. Eris lunged at me quickly, bringing both swords down hard on top of mine causing one to fall instantly to the floor. Eris lunged at me again, and I blocked his hit by grabbing my remaining sword with both hands, though it didn't do much good. His hits came quick and fast and from all sides as he continued to push me across the mat. From my peripheral I could see the tables of weapons coming up behind me and I was desperate not to crash into them. Honestly that would have been my luck. After surviving three attacks by Elaina's followers, I trip over my own feet and die.

When the tables were only inches away, I ducked under Eris's arm just as he cut in from the side. When he turned around to face me there was a frightening burning in his eyes. His attack on me intensified and I tried defending myself, blocking him up, down, up, right side, left side, down, up, but then tripped and fell flat out onto the floor. Eris seized the opportunity and threw himself on top of me, his sword only inches from my face being held up only by my own sword. My arms screamed and burned while Eris pressed hard against me, causing my blade to shake under the pressure.

"Enough," I heard Cameron shout from somewhere in the room. I looked past Eris as he leapt off of me and noticed both Cameron and Devin standing just inside the doorway. Rage and panic radiated from Cameron as he looked between me and Eris, and I could see Devin's hand lightly holding the back of Cameron's arm. "Enough," Cameron said again, however, much softer and almost apologetic.

Eris stood rigid at my feet, refusing to take his eyes off of Cameron. I looked to my side and saw Seraphina slowly rising from her seat.

"Are you going to dictate how I train my own daughter, Warrior?"

"Not at all, sir. Brianna is still weak, and I am only concerned about her well-being and…"

Eris let out a sharp growl as he snapped his jaw, cutting Cameron's statement off.

"She *is* weak," Eris said, curling his upper lip and taking steps in Cameron's direction. "That is why I need to instruct her. Weakness is not an option in her case, and I will do what I must in order to ensure her safety."

"As will I," Cameron shouted back as he shrugged out of Devin's clamped hand. "I am only suggesting that…"

But Cameron was cut off yet again when Eris leapt the thirty-foot distance between them. Cameron tried to jump back to avoid his trajectory, but instead Eris caught him in midair causing both of them to crash against the far wall, but they didn't fall. Eris held Cameron by the throat with one hand, and holding them both up against the wall ten feet off the ground with the other. "You suggest nothing to me, Warrior."

Exhausted, but panicked by the site of my love being strangled by my father caused the burning in my stomach to come quickly. With the little strength I had, I let all my fear and anger push the burning through the top of my head, though not able to focus on anyone in particular, it was my turn to scream, e*nough!*

Eris and Cameron came crashing down to the floor while Devin fell to his knees covering his head with his hands. Only Seraphina and I were left unaffected by my mind projection. She was frozen with fear, unable to comprehend what had just happened and looked to me for an explanation. I avoided her gaze and rushed over to help Cameron who was already pulling himself back up the wall. I mouthed a silent apology to him, but he just shook his head and rubbed his temples.

Eris stood slowly as well, his eyes wide with shock and uncertainty.

"Was that the...the," he stuttered.

"Don't ever attack Cameron like that again," I said, standing in front of Eris with my chest up and shoulders back. "I don't care how old or scary you are. I don't even care that you're my father. You will not treat either of us this way. I'm done. You will never train me again, do you understand me?" I said and threw my arms up as I walked toward Devin and the door. "Sorry, Devin, I'm done for the day, I'll see *you* tomorrow."

I stomped out of the training room with Cameron close behind me. Just as I walked halfway down the corridor, I turned around and walked back into the training room, ignoring the confused faces of Cameron and Devin as I double backed.

"And how dare you," I yelled as I walked to stand a few feet away from my father who was confused by my accusatory statement. "How dare you come into my life after thirty-one years and expect me to...to what? To love you? Welcome you into my life with open arms after being abandoned by you and left with..." But I shook the thoughts of Shelby out of my head, not wanting to lose my train of thought. "And then you come in here and decide that a great father-daughter bonding experience would be to scream at me and try to impale me for two hours? Oh yeah, great idea, *Dad*. Maybe next time we could get a couple of revolvers and play a nice family game of Russian roulette. How does that sound? Stay out of my dreams, and stay out of my life. I don't want you in either."

Eris stood in front of me expressionless. I could have been telling him that I was switching to decaf coffee for all the emotion he showed. I looked away first, shaking my head as I walked back out of the door, this time leaning into Cameron while he led me down the hall away from the training room. When we got to the stairs, I groaned in complaint causing Cameron to whisk me off my feet and run to our room in a matter of seconds.

Once inside, he placed me down on the ground and shut the door.

"Bri? Are you all right?" he asked softly as he came up behind me, putting his arms around me and resting his chin gently on top of my head.

I nodded and turned in his arms to look up into his beautiful, dark eyes. "Are you?"

Smiling his signature crooked smile, he let out a stifled laugh. "Yes, love. Your scream hurt me more than Eris did." My face dropped knowing that I had hurt him, and he could see the tears forming in the corners of my eyes. "I...I did not mean it like that, Brianna," he said, fumbling his words and caressing my cheek with the back of his hand.

The coolness of his hand on my face made my entire body melt and then fill with butterflies and desire. Looking into his dark eyes I placed my hands on either side of his face and brought his lips down on mine gently. He kissed me back with the same gentleness, and then again with added passion that almost took my breath away. I opened my mouth and let him explore every inch of it as we kissed each other feverishly. Without removing his lips from mine, he bent down and pulled my legs up around his waist. I squeezed my thighs tightly around him as he wrapped his arms around me, pressing me tightly up against his chest. He moved to the small table at the side of the door and placed me on top of it. As our bodies parted for a brief moment, Cameron looked down at me with such desire it made my heart beat painfully fast, which only caused him to smile crookedly at me from its sound.

He kissed me again and my hands went right to his shirt, un-tucking it from his pants and sliding it up his chest where he took over and shrugged it over his head. I was staring at a masterpiece. He was so unbelievably beautiful. My fingers couldn't help but trace the lines of his sculpted abdomen while he bent his head down and kissed me tenderly on the lips, lingering there for a moment. Crossing my arms, I grabbed my tight workout shirt and lifted it over my head causing me to get a whiff of myself.

"Oh, I smell," I said completely embarrassed.

"I do not care," he replied dismissively as we wrapped our arms tightly around one another. His kisses went from my lips slowly down my neck while his hands unhooked my bra, tenderly removing the straps from my shoulders and then pressing me tightly against his chest. The feel of his cool skin against my breasts sent ripples through my body, but then I lost all sense of self when his firm hands crushed my pelvis against his. His hands remained there, pressing me against him while we found a mutual rhythm that caused waves of pleasure I had never felt down in that area.

Cameron's fingers started to pull at the elastic waistband of my pants, just a little, as though he was testing the waters. Could I? Could I do this?

My head was racing, so was the pulse between my legs, the two key players fighting against each other in my body. As our pelvic rhythm started to quicken and breathing with Cameron's lips crushed against mine became almost impossible, there was a knock at the door. Holding me to him with one hand, Cameron thrust his other hand up against the wall as he stopped abruptly.

"Yes?" he growled impatiently with his eyes closed tightly.

"Cam, they're looking for you," Alex's deep voice sounded through the door.

With his eyes still closed, Cam answered, "Two minutes."

I didn't hear Alex walk down the hall, but he didn't answer so I assumed he was no longer on the other side of the door. Cameron removed his hand from the wall and gently caressed my back with his fingers. I unwrapped my legs and kissed him softly causing him to open his eyes, showing nothing but guilt. I shook my head letting him know that I wasn't upset, and kissed him again as I lowered myself off of the table.

Cameron placed his finger under my chin and tilted my head up to his. "You are mine for dinner, remember?"

"Not literally, I hope."

He laughed and kissed my forehead. "Come down to the main corridor at six, I will meet you there."

I nodded, rose up onto my toes to kiss him once more, and then stepped around him toward the bathroom for a much needed cold shower. Hearing our room's door close I couldn't help but picture Cameron's guilt-ridden eyes. We had finally stolen a few unplanned minutes together only to have them taken away. Though in a way I was happy where it stopped. Another few minutes of rocking on the table and it would have been me giving him guilty eyes.

With a deep sigh, I walked into the shower and turned the dial onto the colder side in order to regulate my body. Honestly, I had never been so aroused, not even with my imagination and certainly never with Sam. My body was on fire with sensation, and my emotions were raw from the entire day. As the freezing cold water washed over me, all my injuries rushed to the surface. Round welts were forming on the backs and sides of my hands and arms, while purplish bruises were starting to come through on my knees and shins. My poor body, some things never changed. Suddenly I was miserable in the cold water and quickly turned it over scalding hot to try and relax my muscles.

I had no idea how long I had actually been sitting on the shower floor when Kyla knocked on the bathroom door.

"Brianna? You in there?"

When I looked down at my hands, my fingers were shriveled like prunes, meaning my shower time was officially over. Reaching up to the shower's control nozzle, I pulled myself up and shut the water off. I opened the door to the shower, grabbed the towel on the hook next to it and said, "Yeah Kyla, I'm here."

"Oh good," she replied enthusiastically. "Come out here when you're ready, I have some things to show you."

Through the door I could tell that she was about to burst with excitement. I wrapped myself in the towel since I had neglected to bring any clean clothes into the bathroom with me, but I could sneak into the changing room slash biggest closet I had ever seen and slip something on before seeing what Kyla needed.

But surprisingly, when I opened the bathroom door Kyla was standing there with a sly grin on her face.

"You may need these," she said as she handed me the shirt and bra that I had left on the floor in the bedroom. "It's good to see that you and Cameron can find time to…ah…play."

I rolled my eyes and took my discarded clothing out of her hands and stepped into the changing room. "Yes well, it would have been better if *your* husband had let us finish…ah…playing."

Kyla came around the corner, guilt filling her eyes now. "I'm sorry, Brianna. We know you two haven't had any time together. But when there is so much going on…"

"Will it always be like this?" I interrupted.

"No. It's never been like this. Things are just really bad out there. Cameron and the others are working so hard to get a handle on this whole Elaina issue, but they always seem to be a step behind. It really started taking a toll on Alex which is why I think Victor has been looking to Cameron the last few days. I promise it'll get better. But in the meantime, look at what I have for you."

Kyla grabbed me by the wrist and pulled me into the bedroom where boxes upon boxes were stacked on top of each other by the bed.

"Kyla, what is all this?"

"I thought you would still be with Devin, so I had planned to surprise you by unpacking everything before you got here, but of course you had to go and ruin it with…playtime," she said provocatively as she waggled eyebrows with insinuation.

Kyla opened box after box and pulled out shirts, pants, dresses, skirts, shoes, lingerie, you name it, she pulled it out of a box.

"Kyla, where are you planning on putting all of this stuff? So far Cameron has only been able to clear out one drawer for me. There is no way all of this is going to fit in my clothes whore's closet."

"Let me take care of that. He can get mad at me for clearing out his things instead of you. What we need to do now is get you ready for dinner and your surprise."

"You know about my surprise?"

"Of course I do."

"How come you get to know and I don't? You know girlfriends tell each other *everything*," I said knowing I was pulling at her heartstrings.

Kyla blinked and bit her lip, her face wrought with conflict. "They do? But Cameron really, *really* wanted to surprise you. He feels so guilty about leaving you alone so much that he wanted to make it up to you. He made me swear I wouldn't tell you."

I smiled back at her and placed my hand on her shoulder. "Ky, I'm kidding. It's fine."

Kyla let out a huge sigh of relief, and I felt a little guilty over what I had tried to pull. That was until she started pulling together an outfit she thought I should wear tonight.

"These are the pants I think you should wear to dinner, and I just need to find that blouse," she said, handing me a pair of skinny jeans that looked too small for a nine-year-old, let alone me.

"Kyla, the legs of these pants would barely fit over my arms."

She turned around quickly, placing a hand on her hip. "Well then that's a good thing since your legs are almost as skinny as your arms. Have you looked at yourself lately? Bibi, you are wasting away."

"Oh not you, too," I moaned.

"Why? You call me Ky."

"Then call me Bri. Bibi is just weird. I don't even understand where Jared got it."

"Oh I do," Kyla answered, telling me with her face that she wasn't about to tell me that little secret.

I threw the jeans at her. "Okay, let's get this over with. You push, I'll pull."

Chapter Forty-two

Brianna

After fifteen minutes of successfully lying on the bed and sucking in everything possible, Kyla and I were finally able to pull on the torture devices called matchstick jeans. Although they made my butt look good, I kept imagining sitting down at dinner and having them explode open right in front of Cameron. That would be a great way to celebrate our first romantic dinner together; at least it would be memorable. Panicked thoughts aside, my butt was lifted, hair coiffed, I smelled of honeysuckle, and was clicking down the stone hallways in the four-inch heels Kyla had picked out that were just as feminine and frilly as the ruffles on my printed chiffon shirt. I'll admit it, I felt great. I couldn't breathe, but that didn't stop me from strutting down the hall.

Cameron's instructions were simply to meet in the main corridor at six, but not anywhere in particular. As the end of the corridor drew near, an archway opened up on my left which revealed my incredibly good-looking boyfriend running up from a small staircase. Cameron's anxious look was quickly replaced by a relieved smile as he scooped me up off the floor and pressed his cool lips against mine. A few seconds later he put me back down on the ground, though not quite prepared for my elevated height.

"Are you wearing heels?"

I smiled and stepped back, giving him a quick turn so that he could admire my sexy outfit. Seeing his eyes flare made the tight jeans completely worth it. It was the first time I had ever looked more than below average in front of him. Cameron looked me up and down, and anyone within ten miles could have seen that he wanted me. He took my hands in his and pulled my arms behind my back, causing me to tilt my head up for him to kiss me again, however, this kiss was so soft and lingering it felt as if a part of my soul escaped into his mouth.

"Come, before I cannot control myself any longer," he said as he pulled me down the remainder of the hallway, but not before I saw him lick his lip and bite it with a mischievous smile.

"What's down there?" I asked, pointing down the corridor he had just come from.

"That leads to the courtyard and the Council Hall where the Elite Warrior Council is currently meeting. Why do you ask?"

"No reason," I shrugged, but still took a long look.

There was only ten feet left of the main corridor and at the end of it was a wide, arched door, similar to the hundreds of other doors in the manor. Cameron pushed the door open and guided me inside where I was surrounded by books, hundreds of books with dark leather bindings on shelves stretching from the floor to the extremely high ceiling. The smell of old paper and ink was as amazing and comforting as the general atmosphere. The room itself was four times the size of my study in Connecticut with various sized couches and chairs scattered throughout, along with four wooden desks in each of the corners. Even with the many thick cushioned reading chairs, I knew the only place I would be reading was on the window seat of the large bay window that was now flooding the library with red and yellow hues of the setting sun.

"It's wonderful, Cam."

"I am sorry to say that you will only find one or two vampire novels in here, although I believe Kyla keeps a secret stash of her own if you feel the need for one."

Taking his jab at my reading preferences in stride, I simply smiled and answered, "Why do I need a vampire book when I have the real thing?"

Cameron's cocky, crooked smile spread across his face.

"This is only the first part of your surprise, the second is over here," he said as he escorted me over to a small, round table for two in front of the fireplace. The table was simply set with two candles and a covered entrée dish I assumed was for me. As we neared the table, Cameron pulled out my chair and stole a kiss from my cheek as he placed the cloth napkin over my lap.

"Now this next part you will have to forgive me for," he said as he placed his hand over the cover of the entrée in front of me. "I had been meaning to speak with Christine all day on what to make for you, and each time I was sidetracked. Jared came down earlier and I told him to tell her to make you something for our dinner together. So unfortunately, we are stuck with what Jared believes is romantic."

Cameron lifted the cover to reveal a thick burger covered in cheese and bacon with a large side of homemade fries. I couldn't help but laugh, although I could tell that Cameron was annoyed by his little brother's choice so I put his worries at ease.

"Cam, it's fine. Don't be so hard on him. He's only seen me eat a burger, so that's probably why," I said, squeezing his hand and bringing him down to me for a kiss.

"There are so many things I need to teach him," he replied as he rose from my lips and walked to his chair across from me.

While I dug into my juicy burger, Cameron opened the dark bottle that was in front of him and poured himself a large glass of blood. Cameron caught me looking at him and raised his eyebrow causing me to look away. He laughed to himself as he put his bottle down, and began pouring me a glass of red wine which I noticed was a merlot, obviously on purpose.

"Um...you said," I began before I was done chewing and had to wipe my mouth with my napkin, "Jared came down? But it's still daylight."

Cameron nodded and gave a slight smirk. "It is all hands-on deck at the moment. When Father needs you, being sun-sensitive is not an excuse."

"Speaking of Victor, how long do I have you?" I said taking a big gulp of my wine.

Cameron tightened his lips and furrowed his brow slightly.

"I do not know, love," he answered honestly. "Alexander is covering for me, though he does not know why."

"How come?"

"I barely got out of there as it was which was why I was a little late. I told Alexander that I needed a break to clear my head. If I told him I was really having dinner with you he would tell Devin exactly that if he was asked. You may have noticed that my eldest brother does not have patience for such things." A snort escaped from my nose at his comment. "Only Kyla knows we are here. She will come for me when Alexander cannot stall any longer, but that could be an hour it could be ten minutes."

Cameron sat back in his chair, taking a long drink from his glass and allowing his thoughts to torture him in silence. Taking the napkin from my lap, I wiped my mouth and placed it on the table causing Cameron to look up at me in confusion.

"Not that this set up isn't beautiful and romantic, because it is. But knowing that I may only have you for a little while longer, could we just sit in the window over there? We could finish our meals, talk, read, whatever, but at least I could curl up with you. Something I have a feeling that I won't be able to do tonight. Would that upset you?" Almost before I could get my last word out, Cam was carrying me over to the large cushion in the window seat and then coming back with my dinner and wine. "Cam, you know you don't have to impress me with how fast you are."

Cameron walked away from the window toward one of the book shelves as he said, "I was not trying to impress you, my love. You simply had a wonderful idea."

As he looked through the various shelves of books, I took the last few bites of my burger and decided to forego the fries and stay with the wine. While Cameron's back was turned, I snuck over to the table and poured myself another glass of merlot.

Just as I sat back down in the window, thinking that I hadn't been caught, Cameron said, "With your weight as it is, it will not take much more to make you intoxicated. We do not want a repeat of what happened that night with Jared."

I froze in embarrassment, unaware that he knew about that. But my response was merely to take a nice long sip of my wine.

Cameron finally chose a book and then perched himself long ways against the window and pulled me up against him so that I could lay with my back against his chest. The wine and cushions and his smell were making every muscle in my body begin to relax, but unfortunately my enormous burger was causing my stomach to distend and press tightly against my jeans. Sucking in my stomach as much as I could, I took the book that Cameron offered me and noticed it was one of my all-time favorites.

"*To Kill a Mockingbird*! Oh Cam, I love this book. Mama Jo read it to me when I was younger, and then I must have read it, goodness, another twelve times. What made you pick this one?"

"I remember seeing the tattered copy in your room at Oliver's, and I had a feeling that after everything that happened today you might want a little feeling of home."

The dust jacket was one I had never seen, and felt so delicate under my fingers. As I opened the book I looked up at Cameron.

"It's a first edition?"

"Most are in here. Although, that one is only from 1960, there are some from my time and before. There are also some historic journals, and there is even a vault that contains ancient scrolls and documents from before Father's time."

"Shouldn't those be in a museum?"

He laughed. "Only if we wanted the world to know about vampires. Most of them, especially those recounting wars and battles, reference the use of vampires in the armies. Not quite something you want modern historians to discover. Father especially likes to leave humankind in the dark."

Cameron took another large sip from his glass while I carefully turned to the first page of my book. Immediately I could hear Scout's comforting Southern accent coming through the pages and bringing me into her world. But just as I started reading, I changed my mind and closed the book, leaving it on my lap.

"How bad is it really?" I asked. When he didn't answer I sat up and turned to face him. "I have a right to know. How bad is it?"

Cameron shifted his weight before answering, "It is getting worse. Elaina is basically smearing it in our faces that we cannot catch her. We get a lead, and it never pans out. They are always a step ahead of us."

"Have you found anymore dead hybrids?" I asked, worrying about Hannah who still hadn't been found since Elaina's Vamps took her.

"Actually, we have not. It appears that they are now surviving Elaina's experiments. From the accounts of Alexander and Kyla from the attack at the shopping center, they are showing greater strength and organization. It is painfully obvious that she is in the area, and yet we cannot find her. Now I see why Alexander was so eager to guard you at the Facility, he needed a break from the frustration. Our family has never experienced anything like this. The entire vampire race is looking to us to fix this, and we have nothing, absolutely nothing."

Cameron finished and I could see the weight lift from his shoulders as he admitted what had been going on behind closed doors. I put my fingers through his thick, wavy hair, grabbing a handful of it and pulling it slightly, causing his eyes to close as he relaxed.

"You don't think Alex came to the Facility because of my amazing good looks?"

"There is no doubt, angel. What was I thinking?" he laughed, keeping his eyes closed and prompting me to run my fingers through his hair again. "Speaking of Alexander, do you still have the watch he gave you?"

"Yes," I replied as I held up my wrist to show him.

"Good. I want you to always wear it. No matter if you are training, sleeping, eating, all the time. Understand?" I scrunched my face not understanding the need, but he quickly explained. "I am away from you so often I want to make sure that if anything happens to you, we can find you. Please, love, just do this one thing for me."

I gazed into his worried eyes and couldn't help but nod in agreement. I leaned into him, wanting another one of our passionate kisses, but was cut short when he pulled away, his face strained.

"I have to go," he said as he swung his legs over the edge of the window seat. "I can hear Kyla coming down the hall."

"You can hear that?"

Cameron shrugged as he stood. "Vampire."

Within seconds Kyla came through the door, shutting it behind her quickly.

"Cameron, I'm sorry. Alex tried to stall, but Victor is looking for you specifically. There's been another attack."

There was panic in Kyla's voice, something I was not used to hearing from her. Cameron looked back at me regretfully.

"Go, go," I said quickly, trying to ease his guilt. He bent down and kissed me gently before walking past Kyla through the door.

Kyla looked at me apologetically. "I'm sorry, Bri. I know this was supposed to be a nice night for you two."

"It's okay," I lied. "Did you want to join me instead?"

"Oh honey, I'm sorry. Victor is asking me to sit in as well. I'm really, really sorry."

"Ky, it's fine. Wait, give this to Cam," I said, walking over to the table and grabbing the bottle of blood. "He didn't finish, and I don't know the last time he fed. Now go, before Victor thinks I've corrupted you, too."

Kyla took the bottle and gave me one last apologetic glance before she left. Rather than sulk in my room, I decided staying in the library was definitely the better option. I grabbed my book and my glass of wine and stretched out in the window right where Cameron had been only moments ago. Trying to get comfortable was definitely a feat since my stomach was bulging over my jeans. Only because I knew I was alone, I unzipped my pants, and my stomach thanked me as it spilled out.

Now I was able to relax enough to let the words of my book take me away from all the stress of the day. After only reading a few pages, the door handle of the library lifted. I quickly pulled down my blouse to cover my exposed stomach and then took a sip of my wine to look casual. Unfortunately, my casual demeanor didn't last long since it was my father who walked through the door. Just as he made eye contact with me, I quickly looked back down in my book. Smooth, real smooth.

"Ah, figlia, I was hoping I would find you," Eris said as he crossed the room in my direction.

"Really, why's that? Want another go at almost killing me?" I said, my mood already declining and my uncontrollable sarcasm taking over.

"Bri-an-na, I am sorry about today. May I sit with you?"

No, no, no, I said stubbornly in my head, but I gestured for him to sit on the window seat.

"Mia figlia, I am sorry for the way I behaved today," he said as he sat across from me, keeping his feet on the floor where his eyes continued to focus. "I have lived a very long time, and in all that time I have never learned how to be around a child. Until you, there was never an occasion or desire. After you were born, I kept my distance, thinking it was safer if the vampire race knew nothing of your existence." Eris lifted his head to look at me in the eyes. "I now know that was a mistake, and I am doing everything I can to protect you. I have never been a father to you, so I do not know how to *be* with you. Most parents tend to raise their children how they were raised, and unfortunately this is all I know."

"Your father tried to kill you, too?"

"Yes, but he succeeded," he replied as he pushed himself back up against the window and stretched his legs out towards me. "My father made me a vampire, Bri-an-na."

So he won. I was the ungrateful, thinking-she-had-it-worse, shitty daughter. Now wanting to know the full story, I shut my book and placed it gently on the floor while I stretched my legs out on the other side of him. We looked like male and female bookends. Seeing him this close and showing no threat, he could pass as my brother. Our legs were almost the same length, same dark eyes and hair, though his was wavy and mine was painfully straight. Even as he spoke there were certain mannerisms that were similar to my own.

After taking a big gulp of my wine I asked, "Why would your father make you a vampire? Was that what you wanted?"

Eris shook his head. "No, it was not what I wanted, but I did not have much choice in the matter. You see, my father was a very powerful man, second only to the Pharaoh, but he always craved more power. And whether he got it through me or my sisters, he did not care. He would never even allow us to look at someone of the opposite sex unless they were individuals who would get us or him greater standing. But even then, no one ever seemed good enough. It was quite lonely, for my sisters' as well. Both my sisters had many, I guess you would call them suitors, and every time my father always found a way to dispose of them."

"So you never fell in love with anyone?"

Eris gave a sad smile. "Actually, I had fallen in love with a lovely young woman. We kept our relationship a secret because I knew my father would never approve of her. I remember we were lying underneath a blanket of stars when I asked her to be my wife. She understood that our engagement meant we would have to leave our families and be left with nothing. But she was willing to make the sacrifice, and I loved her for it.

"What I did not know was that around the same time my father had come across a curious creature which he witnessed having incredible strength and would vanish in an instant. For several nights he stalked this creature that feed on the blood of men. My father was entranced by this creature and felt that if he had this kind of power, he could overthrow the Pharaoh and take the kingdom for himself. So one night, he went to the area that he often saw this powerful man and slit his own wrist to draw the creature out. Within seconds the creature was on him, feeding from him. My father begged the man to give him some of his powers, offering to pay anything to be what he was.

"My father was turned into a vampire that very night for the price of half my father's fortune and my youngest sister, Anoi. When I returned that evening from proposing to my love, I found my father weak and pale, and Anoi missing. My older sister, Eliah, had no recollection of what happened, as if it had been erased from her mind. The two of us pleaded with my father to tell us what happened to Anoi, but he simply kept saying it was a sacrifice for the family.

"When his heart stopped, we thought dark forces were at play since he was still conscious. When the sun rose in the morning, we had to rush him to where the sun did not touch his skin because it was burning so badly. Out of exhaustion, both Eliah and I fell asleep late in the day, and I woke up when my father bit into my neck and drained my life away. He told me the only way I would stay alive was to drink from him, but I refused. I cried out to Eliah, only to see her body lying lifeless on the floor. My father's bloodlust had not allowed him to stop from draining all of her. A mistake he was trying to remedy with me, and my refusal only made him furious. He bit his wrist and forced me to drink his blood. My father gave away his life and those of his family for personal gain, and my anger towards him was indescribable."

"Did you ever find out what happened to Anoi?" I asked trying to take in my father's horrific family history.

"Yes," he replied. "Two days later her body was found drained and floating down the river. My father showed no remorse for what he had done, or even sadness over losing his daughters. The night after Anoi's body was found, my anguish over losing my sisters and the hatred I felt for my father overwhelmed me. Just as the sun was setting, I rose before my father in order to search for my daggers, avoiding the sun as best I could.

"Little did I know that silver would burn me since I had no idea what I truly was. So when I grabbed the silver handle of my dagger it burned right through my skin, but it did not stop me. Nothing was going to stop me from avenging my family. I wrapped a thick piece of cloth around my hand and I slashed my father's throat just as his eyes opened. I wanted him to see me before he died, to make sure he knew it was me who had taken his life. I packed what little I could and I fled, learning how to be a vampire as I went.

"But no matter how long I lived, my anger was always with me. That is why I have the reputation that I do. Everything they say about me is true. I have killed more than I would ever care to admit. But, mia figlia, my Bri-an-na, I am telling you that I am trying to change. I no longer wish to be defined by my violent past. I wish to be a father to you, but you need to be patient with me. It is hard to change after three thousand years."

My eyes bulged out of their sockets at my father's age. I blinked them back in, cleared my throat, and finally said, "Having lived for so long, what possessed you to finally have a child? Why now?"

Eris smiled as he answered, "Your mother."

I felt my face drop. "You have got to be kidding me."

"You see, Bri-an-na, even the oldest of vampires cannot turn away a woman who fate brought back into his life."

"I don't understand," I admitted as I took the last sip of my wine, and desperately wanted more.

"Figlia, my life has always been about violence and indulgence. As more vampires came to fear me, less challenged me, leaving me with endless temptations. My last home was here in California where I had endless women at my feet, and one evening a young girl was brought to me as an offering from another vampire. I thought I had finally died, for in front of me stood the woman I loved and left behind when my father Turned me. Your mother was the spitting image of my betrothed, and I could not stop myself from wanting the life that I had left behind."

"Well, then it must have been a rude awakening when you realized Shelby was a lunatic," I said as I pushed myself from the window to grab my bottle of wine. If we were going to talk about Shelby, I needed to drink.

"Your mother was troubled, yes, but she seemed to flourish around me, at least at first. I was too enthralled with her to notice that she was becoming dependent on me, and my blood."

"She drank your blood?"

"Of course," Eris replied, giving me a peculiar look. "Many human consorts and lovers do, it is pretty custom, but only small amounts of course. It was only when she became pregnant with you that I realized how dependent she had become."

"Is that why you abandoned her on my grandparent's doorstep?" My tone was nasty and I knew it.

Eris took a moment to gather himself before he answered, "When your mother became pregnant, I was overjoyed. For the first time in my long life, I cared about someone other than myself. But I quickly realized your mother did not feel the same way. She continued to ask to drink from me, but when I refused her, she would go on these endless tirades demanding that I Turn her." Eris stopped for a moment and took my hand, squeezing it softly. "I refused because I wanted my child. After several months she started hurting herself. She was trying to lose you so that I would Turn her."

"That's nice. Even before I was born Shelby didn't want me."

Eris squeezed my hand again. "But I did, Bri-an-na. That is what I need you to understand. I wanted you so desperately that..."

"So what did you do? I'm obviously here," I interrupted, my nasty tone uncontrollable.

Eris sighed before saying, "It became necessary to Glamour her to keep her from inflicting harm upon herself, but remarkably my Glamours never lasted long. There were times I pushed so hard I thought her mind would detach itself, but each time the Glamour would wear off several days later. One night I left so I could feed, thinking that I had Glamoured her enough, but when I returned, she was standing in the doorway, blood flowing from her forearms where she had cut them deeply. I stopped her just before she jabbed the knife into her stomach. Into you."

"Shelby doesn't have scars on her arms."

"That is because I gave her my blood. If I hadn't, she would have died and taken you with her. I had no choice. I healed her wounds and let her ingest a small amount of blood. From then on, she knew my weakness was you. After that night I knew the only way for you to survive was to get her away from me. I figured if she was surrounded by your loving family that you would have a chance."

"A chance? A chance!" I screamed at him and stood from the window seat. "You said it yourself she didn't want me, and yet you left me with her?"

"I left your mother with her parents. I knew they would care for you even if your mother could not," Eris replied defensively.

"But why now? Why abandon me and then decide to take an interest after thirty years?"

"I did not *abandon* you, Bri-an-na. I have always loved you. I will never forget the day you were born. I could feel your spirit as you came into this world, and it took all of my willpower not to sink myself into your every sleeping moment."

"Is that supposed to make me feel better?"

"A few days after you were born my Sera came to me," Eris said, ignoring my snide comment.

"Well, I'm glad your new wife helped you get over your guilt so quickly."

"Figlia, stop it!" Eris screamed as he moved to stand in front of me. "You have every right to be upset about the choices I made, but do not behave like a spoiled child. Seraphin-na has saved your life so many times and you do not even know it."

"What are you talking about? How has Seraphina saved my life when I just met her today?"

Eris waited a beat and then gestured for me to sit back down. I waited another beat to make him sweat a little before I finally gave in.

"My Sera has many gifts, including psychic abilities," he began as he sat down next to me, rubbing his palms on his knees nervously. "She came to me because she had had a vision about the future of our race, one that you play a significant role in. She had seen the vision many times, but the night you were born the vision changed."

"Why would the vision change when I was born?"

"It changed because our enemy found the source of the prophecy. They started to hunt for you that very night."

"By our enemy you mean Elaina?"

"Yes, I am speaking of Elaina and her followers."

"How did they know I had been born?"

Eris paused a moment, looking down at his shoes. "Sera told them."

I turned my head quickly in shock, but Eris refused to meet my eyes.

"She told them!"

"It is not what it seems," he replied with his hands up defensively. "Sera was young and frightened and unaware that she was a hybrid. She was terrified by these visions that she would have since they involved monsters she believed were only myths. Elaina came upon her one day and took her in, realizing the importance of these visions. Elaina manipulated her, pushed her to give details of the visions. Sera was so naïve, and did not see the manipulation until it was too late. It wasn't until the night you were born when she overheard Elaina give the orders to kidnap you that she fled."

"And that's when she came to you?"

He nodded. "She still cannot fully explain how she found me, but late one night she came to my home and explained how your life was in danger, as was the future of our race. Vampires were hunting you, and I knew that Elaina would eventually come for Sera. At the time I could not explain why I was so drawn to her, willing to do whatever I could to protect her, but I did. Ever since then she has always seen when a vampire threatens to harm you, allowing me to help you in any way I could."

"I don't understand. How did you help me?"

"Depending on the situation, sometimes I would keep you asleep until the threat passed, or put ideas in your grandparent's heads the night before to get you out of the house. And once when you were little, I told you in a dream to hide a silver knife under your favorite tree."

"That's how…" I began, the mystery of the silver knife had been solved, but then I thought, "If you knew these things were going to happen, why didn't you just come for me? Stay with me to protect me. Actually *be* my father rather than just stand on the sidelines hoping I would live long enough."

"I always knew you would live. I could not risk exposing you or Sera. I wanted you to have as much of a normal life for as long as possible."

"But I didn't!" I yelled. "Shelby hated me. She treated me like shit. She still does! From her I went to Sam, who made Shelby look like Mother Theresa. You said that Seraphina would see when I was in trouble and that you would help. Why didn't you save me from Sam?" Eris looked at the floor. "Answer me! Sam inflicted ten times more pain. Why didn't you stop him? Why didn't you stop him from…"

But I couldn't finish my thought as images of all the slaps and kicks and hits I had endured flashed in my head. My knees buckled, but Eris caught me and together we sank into the floor. My head found his shoulder and my tears began soaking through his linen shirt. His cool fingers caressed my cheek, which only made me weep more.

"I did not know, my darling. I only found out the night the Warrior contacted me. If I had known, I would have found a way to help you."

I lifted my head to see him. "But you said Sera could see…"

"I know. But the prophecy was still intact. Elaina's coven hadn't found you, which is why Sera did not see anything. Perhaps if you had come close to death, she would have seen something. Only a few months ago did Sera see that you were in trouble. Sera had a vision which showed her that Elaina would find out your location in Connecticut. Immediately I sought out Victor and the Gatherers to bring you to safety." Eris pulled a white handkerchief from his pocket and dabbed my eyes and face gently. "I am so sorry for your pain. If Cameron had not already killed your husband, I would have, and not as humanely as the Warrior did."

No longer having the strength to kneel, I sat on the floor with my back propped up against the window seat as I continued to process the enormous amount of information that Eris had given me. I closed my eyes in order to reach deep into the back of my head to find those questions that I had always wanted answers to.

"You said you lived in California, right?"

"Yes, up until you were fourteen."

"Um…when I was fourteen Shelby brought me to California. D-did she bring me to see you?"

"I am afraid not," he answered sadly, dabbing away a tear that had streaked down my neck. "She had come to beg me to Turn her, even offering to hand you over to me. She desperately wanted back into our world."

"Figures," I huffed.

"Knowing that a Glamour would not work on her, I had her escorted out of my home and under threat of death. I told her that if she ever sought me out again or ever searched for another vampire to Turn her that I would have her killed. I was not having my daughter be without a mother. After that night Sera and I fled to an island that is now our home."

"We'll have to agree to disagree about your decision not to Turn her. I would have been better off without a mother."

"I have definitely seen the error of my ways, mia figlia," he said, causing us both to laugh a little, lightening the mood slightly.

"Okay, here's something I've been curious about. With a couple of exceptions, I haven't really seen why everyone is so terrified of you. I say your name and vampires want to hide."

Eris grinned, letting another laugh escape.

"Like I said before, when my father Turned me into a vampire I was filled with anger and hatred at all I had lost. I let that anger control me, and I did kill many of my own kind that got in my way. When I met your mother things did change, but I still only knew how to live in hatred, and unfortunately your mother perpetuated that. It was not until Sera came to me that I was able to live a life without anger. Well, most times. She has taught me peace. Where your mother looked like my long, lost betrothed, Sera has her spirit. She is able to calm me when I think I will be taken over with rage."

"But she also has that hand thing," I said, remembering how calm Eris became at Seraphina's touch.

"Yes, one of her many gifts. Sera is also an Empath. By touching someone, she can take over their emotions, it is only when she lets go do they rush back. It took years for me to be able to control myself when she would let go, and even now I still struggle at times. Let people think of me what they wish, I only care that you and Sera do not see me as a monster. I will do whatever it takes to get you to trust me when I say I only have your best interests at heart, and that I do love you very much."

Eris's words kept echoing in my head. My father, the man I had longed to see for over thirty years, loved me. He loved me very much, my brain kept saying. And then I realized something and slowly turned my head to look at my father.

"What is that look?" he asked.

I scratched my head as I put my thoughts together and said, "Do you realize that you've been talking without your accent?" Eris bit his bottom lip nervously, but didn't answer. So I continued, "When you were talking about your family you said that your father was just under the pharaoh or something, right?"

"That is correct," he replied slowly.

"To me that means you were born in Egypt." Eris smiled and nodded. "So why do you speak Italian and have a thick Italian accent?"

Eris smiled sheepishly as he picked a speck of something from his shirt.

"I think it makes me a bit more exotic, don't you?" he said.

"So you're a fraud."

He shrugged, looking for some forgiveness. "I have been speaking like that for so long that it just comes naturally. I have always had a weakness for Italy. Of all the countries I have lived in, I have returned to Italy more than any other."

"I like you without the accent," I replied honestly.

Eris laughed, but gave no response. In fact, neither of us said anything for a few moments, letting the dust continue to settle. Finally, I asked, "Why were you surprised that my middle name was Marie?"

Eris sighed. "Your mother and I had agreed that your name was to be Bri-an-na Mari-le-na," he said, his Italian accent back in fully swing. "I had always thought that was your name. Today I was quite embarrassed to find out that it wasn't. It was yet another stab in the heart by Shelby."

"Well, get used to that. I certainly have, though it never gets easier. Mari...what again?"

Eris laughed lightly. "Lena. Marilena. Bri-an-na Mari-le-na. It flows so beautifully, unlike Marie."

"I'll try not to be offended by that, although I have to agree with you a little," I replied with a slim smile. "So where do we go from here?"

Eris stood and hovered over me as he said, "I know that today did not go as well as I had hoped, but I would like to continue to train you. I am sure the Assassin is very capable, but I only trust my daughter's future in my hands." I opened my mouth about to cut him off, but he interrupted first. "It will be a way for the two of us to bond, and truly become father and daughter. Please give me this opportunity to make up for everything I have done in the past."

Biting my lip, I thought hard and fast about Eris training me. It was a bad idea, and I knew it. He could say he was at peace all he wanted, but I had seen the anger flair in his eyes. He still didn't have full control of himself, and that scared me. But then there was a part of me that wanted to give him a chance. I finally had the opportunity to have a relationship with my father, something I had always wanted. I couldn't pass it up. I knew I would regret it if I did.

"Fine, but the minute I feel threatened I'm pulling the plug. Got it?"

Eris clasped his hands together with joy. "Oh mia figlia, you make my still heart beat. This will only be the beginning. Soon enough you will be activated and everything will be complete," he said and turned to leave the room.

"Whoa, wait. What do you mean, soon I'll be activated?"

Eris turned back to me, unsure why I was questioning his statement.

"Figlia, you are a hybrid. You must be activated by your father in order to reach your true powers. We must make preparations immediately."

"No," I replied firmly.

"Pardon?"

"No, Eris. I do not wish to be activated, at least not yet. I'm not ready."

"We will discuss this later. You must get some rest," he said as he walked across the room. Just as he reached the door he paused and turned back around. "If you were to allow me to activate you…"

"Won't happen."

"*If* you let me activate you, when we are together, I will speak without my accent."

I narrowed my eyes at him. Eris didn't know me well enough to know how stubborn I could be. His offer wasn't enticing enough to make me give in so quickly.

"Goodnight, Eris."

"Goodnight, mia bella Bri-an-na."

And with that, my pain in the ass father left the library. In less than an hour I had gone from hating my father to giving him a second chance and allowing him to train me. I was letting my daddy issues take over. Just another day in the life of Brianna Marilena Morgan. Hmm…it did have a ring to it.

Chapter Forty-three

Cameron

"The best course of action is to fight back with everything we have. The time has come for us to act aggressively," Julian said emphatically, trying to convince the other Warriors to come to his side of the debate.

Alexander stood to the left of him in the center of the Council Hall touting a much different strategy. "And who do you suppose we fight? We cannot fight what we cannot see, Julian. Our goal should be what it has always been - find Elaina's bases of operations, and *then* attack."

"And just how are you doing on achieving that goal?" Julian asked snidely.

Although I should have been concentrating on the issue at hand, I could not help but think of the various ways I could take Julian down. Since he and I were always so at odds with each other, it was natural that he continued to debate our current strategy because it was *my* strategy. The fact that I was once again in favorable standing with Victor only fueled the animosity he felt toward me.

Shortly after Victor had forgiven my indiscretions he added two chairs just behind his grand throne – one for Devin and one for me. Even with my protestations of leading the Warriors I could not refuse a seat of honor behind my maker and next to my brother. If I had, it would have been another slap in Victor's face, and that was something I could not afford. The Council Hall looked completely different from this view. The long, multi-leveled cement landings that stretched across the hall's distinct oval shape allowed me to see my Warrior siblings who had been convened to discuss the latest hybrid attack.

A few hours ago, calls came in from Warriors across the country stating that hybrids were found dead at their homes. Each hybrid had been drained of blood, showed significant electrical burns all over their bodies, and all had the same message carved into their skin: *I'm not Brianna*. Fighting Julian would not only have given me great personal pleasure, it would also take my mind off of the anxiety and anger that was brewing in the pit of my stomach. Elaina was toying with us, and we knew it. Also, based on the fact that she was able to deploy her followers to Warriors' homes made many of us believe that there was a traitor in our coven. The only thing worse was how personal Elaina was hitting.

The sound of Victor's voice broke me from my reverie, as I had tuned out the bickering between Alexander and Julian.

"Warriors, thank you both for your convincing arguments, but I will have to agree with Alex. We must concentrate our efforts on finding Elaina's operations. Several covens have given us their support and volunteered their resources. Cameron, I suggest that you and Alex convene with the heads of those covens to create a broader, more intense plan of action," Victor said, turning to his left to see me directly.

"Yes, Father. We will," I replied, nodding to Alexander who dipped his head slightly in acknowledgment.

"Good," Victor continued, "now onto another matter. It is obvious by the messages carved into the hybrids found today that Elaina has realized the attempt to kidnap Brianna failed, and she is none too happy about it. Ms. Morgan continues to be a major target. What is being done to prepare her for this threat against her?"

I stood from my chair and said, "Father, permit me to speak?" Victor nodded and gestured that the floor was mine. I stepped down and turned to face him and Devin. "Brianna has been successfully training with Devin for the last several days, and based on his assessments has improved significantly and shows potential with daggers."

"Which is only natural since Eris has always been a master swordsman," Victor said lightly, not knowing what had happened between Brianna and her father this afternoon.

"Speaking of Eris, he has made it clear that he wishes to take over Brianna's training. I understand that he has all the best intentions, however, there was an incident today that gives evidence that he is unable to completely control himself around his hybrid daughter. I would like your support on suggesting that Eris not be allowed to train Brianna for the time being."

Devin gave me a slight nod in agreement. Devin was almost immune to violence, and even he did not agree with Eris's methods.

Victor glared at me for a few moments, tapping his fingers on the arm of his throne as he always did when he considered one's request. Finally, he said, "Child, although I understand your protective feelings towards Ms. Morgan, I cannot stop Eris from instructing his own daughter the way he sees fit. He is her father, and therefore I have no authority on the matter."

"I completely agree," Eris said from behind me as he pushed his way through the thick Council Hall door. The hall was suddenly filled with the sound of hushed whispers by my fellow Warriors who were now in awe of seeing the great Eris. "So here is where everyone has gathered."

"Eris," Victor began and sat up straighter, "it is a pleasure to have you in my home. My children and staff will provide you and your wife with anything that you may require, you need only to ask. Right, Cameron?" Victor said sternly, making sure I took in every ounce of his meaning.

"Of course, Father," I answered, keeping my gaze on him rather than Eris.

"Ah yes, Cameron," Eris said to the side of my face. "My outburst earlier today was inexcusable. Please allow me to apologize." He extended his hand to me, and from the glare I received from Victor I shook Eris's hand. "You see I could not be more ecstatic as I am right now because my daughter has also accepted my apology and will now allow me to train her."

"When did this happen?" I asked as I ripped my hand from his grip.

"Only moments ago, my dear Warrior. We had a lovely talk, one of many I hope," Eris said with a peculiar smile. "Victor, I would like to ask a favor of you."

"Of course, Eris, if it is within my power."

"Now that it is known that Bri-an-na is my daughter, I would like to have a formal claiming ceremony. Since we are all here, I was hoping that you would allow me to have the celebration here in your beautiful home."

Behind me I could hear a soft, shallow gasp of breath, and I did not need to turn around to know it was Kyla. The prospect of a party in the manor would elate her for weeks on end. My father also had a peculiar reaction to Eris's request, he smiled.

"Eris, we would be honored to host a claiming ceremony for you and your daughter, and she will be well protected. We certainly need something to celebrate during this dark time. My staff is at your disposal."

"Thank you, Victor. Actually, I will need Cameron's help as well," Eris said looking back to me. After being pinned up against a wall earlier today, I felt it difficult to be obligatory towards him. "You see, Warrior, my Bri-an-na is somewhat nervous about the activation process and wishes to delay it. I need you to convince her to think otherwise. It is in her best interest to be activated, we all know this."

"Yes, but it is her choice," I replied firmly.

"She will no longer have the choice if she is dead," he said coldly. "I only ask that you try. Well then, my business here is done. Good evening, Victor. Good evening, Warriors."

Eris walked swiftly out of the Council Hall while the Warriors stood and gave him an honorary salute by hitting their chests hard with their fists. I, however, did not salute him, which was noticed by Victor and Devin. I needed to concentrate on calming myself down after Eris's attempt to have me manipulate Brianna on his behalf.

Once I returned to my chair, Victor called the meeting back to order.

"Before we adjourn, I would like to say this to all of you in hopes that it will circulate to those not in attendance. We are a family, not merely a coven, something I take great pride in. With a family as large as ours, we are bound to have our disagreements. I do not expect everyone to like each other, but I do require that you respect one another. A betrayal against one is a betrayal against all, something I do not believe anyone here could forgive, most of all me. Tonight's attacks have hit too close to home, and for many of your siblings that is a literal reference.

"Elaina is a new and different kind of enemy for us. Unfortunately, it is apparent we are not as prepared as we should be and that causes other vampires to lose confidence in us. We are the protectors of our race and therefore cannot afford any kind of treachery or deceit within our coven. If I find that one of my children has betrayed us, the last face you will see is Devin's the moment before he removes you from this earth. Now with that said, stay vigilant, my children, and unleash the full fury of the Warrior inside you when our enemy is upon us. We are adjourned."

His message was lost on no one, and everyone knew Devin had no qualms about killing a fellow Warrior since he had done it before. Victor stood from his throne and Projected away.

I stepped down from my chair but Devin grabbed me firmly by the shoulder as he said, "Brother, you need to control yourself around Eris. Say

342 ~ C.R. Quinn

what you like to us about him, but do not provoke him to his face. I would hate to see another episode like this afternoon."

I shrugged out of Devin's grip. "I know, Brother, but I will not let him manipulate Brianna into anything she does not want to do."

"Cam, we all agree with you," Alexander said with Kyla nodding her head next to him, "just be careful with Eris. You openly provoking him will only hurt Brianna in the long run."

"Hey, are we meeting tonight or what?" Jared asked annoyed. "I'd really rather get it over with. I need to feed like it was my job."

"Yes, Jared, we are meeting tonight. Feed now and we will meet in my sitting room in an hour," I replied. "Alex, please tell everyone else the plan and we will begin contacting the other coven leaders. See you all in an hour. I am going to check on Brianna."

Just then the door to the Council Hall opened and several perimeter guards came rushing through.

"Sir," the supervising guard yelled to Devin as he pushed through the parting sea of Warriors. "We just found a hybrid on the grounds."

"Where?" Devin replied as the room became silent.

"The front gate, sir."

"Is he alive?" I asked.

"No, *she* is not alive. We found her hanging on the gate."

"And no one saw anything?" Devin asked angrily.

"No, sir," the guard replied nervously. "No one saw anything. We have had constant patrols since the other hybrids were found. She just suddenly appeared."

"Was the message the same?" I asked.

"No, this time it's different," he replied. "It was hard to tell at first, but we think it says 'I am Hannah.'"

Chapter Forty-four

Cameron

The manor was a flurry of activity since the body of Hannah Berkshire was found at the front gate. Her face and body were burned so badly there was hardly any skin left except for where someone had carved the words "I am Hannah" into her abdomen. It was a message to Brianna, a message to us all. Not only did they know where Brianna was, they knew how to get to every Warrior outside the manor. For the first in many of our long lives, none of us felt completely safe.

It was 1:00 a.m. by the time the scene at the gate had been cleaned up and the deep investigation had begun. Cameras located at the gate caught nothing, at least at first glance, but the footage was being analyzed. The guard had been right, initially it seemed like Hannah had just suddenly appeared.

I was walking to my bedroom where my Bri hopefully slept soundly, unaware that her friend had been slain. I struggled with how and when to tell her, but I knew that she would hear about it eventually and I would rather she hear it from me than one of my unemotional siblings. As I approached the door, I decided to Project myself into the room to avoid waking her, hoping I could prolong telling her the bad news until the morning.

The inside of the bedroom came into focus as did the enchanting sight of Brianna sprawled out on the bed, her hair splayed messily across her face while she held her book firmly in her hand. I stepped to the nightstand next to her and turned off the light that she had left on when she finally gave in to her exhaustion. Taking the book out of her hand gently, I removed the thick strands of hair from her face and gazed down at my beautiful angel. There was never enough time to be with her, and now as I looked down at her, the images of Hannah's mutilated face and body kept flashing over Brianna's.

I stepped away from Brianna's side as anxiety and fear filled every inch of my body. Having to protect someone was one thing, having an emotional tie to that person only created a frenzy of panic. I walked around to the opposite side of the bed and sat quietly on the edge, unable to stop my head from falling into my hands. I felt almost human sitting on the bed, massaging my temples while trying to figure out what the next steps should be after tonight's startling events. But no thoughts came. So engulfed by my own frustration, I did not hear Brianna stir until her warm arms snaked around my neck, remnants of the honeysuckle perfume still radiating from her skin.

"Rough night?" she asked as she ran her fingers through my hair.

"I did not mean to wake you," I said as I lifted my head and looked behind me to see Brianna staring back at me with a worried smile.

"I tried to stay awake. I didn't even realize I had fallen asleep."

Brianna settled herself into my side as she stretched her arms across my chest and back, finally placing her head on my shoulder. We were silent for a few moments while I absentmindedly brushed her forearm with my fingers. Feeling the rolled-up cuff of the shirt she was wearing I turned my head to her and said, "I see you have taken ownership of yet another one of my shirts."

She smiled and shrugged. "It only took a week to find them," she chided. "Besides, the old one didn't survive. But if you'd rather I didn't…"

"No," I replied, taking her hand from my shoulder and kissing it lightly, "I love seeing you in my shirts. My entire wardrobe is at your disposal."

"As mine is for you. But you have to tell me first so that I can get a camera."

My laugh escaped loudly without thinking, but quickly died as the weight of the evening dropped back down on my shoulders. Brianna noticed the sudden change and quietly put her arms back around me, allowing me to caress her forearm again.

"I hear you have decided to give your father another chance."

"Are you upset?"

"Why would I be upset?"

Brianna shrugged. "I don't know, maybe because of what happened today."

"This is your choice, love. If you want your father to train you, then I will support your decision. I only worry about his methods."

She nuzzled her head back into the crook of my shoulder as she said, "I told him if there was a repeat of today it would be over. It was hard to say no to him tonight. We...we talked about a lot of things, actually. I'm not saying I'm nominating him for father of the year anytime soon, but I got a lot of questions answered."

I wrapped my arms around her, pulling her in tight and rubbing her back gently. It was amazing feeling the warm contours of her smooth back through the fabric of my shirt. I wished that somehow she and I could stay in this position and forget everything that happened this evening. But after another few moments of silence, Brianna pulled out of our embrace as she said, "Are you going to tell me about the attack?"

I was certainly hoping that I would have more time, but Brianna being the pointed person she was, I should have known better.

"Tonight was a bad night."

"How bad?" she asked tentatively.

"Fifty hybrids were found tonight," I replied.

"W-where?"

"Unfortunately at the homes of fellow Warriors."

Brianna swallowed hard and began biting her lip. "All dead?"

"Yes."

"Were you able to identify them all?"

"Yes." I could see her mind racing, trying to find the courage to ask the next question, but not wanting to hear the answer. I held her hand tightly, preparing for her reaction. "Love, we found Hannah."

Brianna's reaction was small and quiet at first while she processed the fact that Hannah was dead, but soon she began to shake from underneath my arms as the tears and grief came out from deep within her. I felt helpless, unable to take away her guilt from Hannah being mistaken for her. Her crying started and stopped several times, each time mixed with statements of fault. As her tears died down for the last time, I wiped the wetness from her face, unable to escape from the pain that was etched into it.

Taking her face firmly in both hands, I looked intensely into her eyes and said, "Brianna, none of this was your fault. You have to know that I will do anything to protect you, my family as well. We are all here to protect you at all costs. *Nothing* will happen to you, I swear it on my life."

In a sudden movement Brianna removed my hands from her face and leapt off the bed.

"That's just it, Cam. I don't want anyone else to die for me. I could give a damn about *myself*. Just let Elaina have me and let it be done with. I'm not worth all of this," she yelled and fell to her knees just as I caught her in my arms. She rested her forehead on my shoulder while she took deep, heaving breaths through her tears.

I held her as tightly as she would allow, trying to soothe her as best I could. Holding her and rocking her gently, I whispered in her ear, "You *are* worth it. You are everything to me, Bri. Elaina must not have you." I pulled her face up to meet mine. "Please promise me you will not be a martyr. Do not give up on me. You must promise me, Brianna."

As I looked into her tearful eyes, I was overwhelmed by the prospect that she would surrender herself to Elaina in order to stop what she deemed unwarranted. Brianna nodded slightly, causing her hot tears to crest over her eyelids and stream onto my hands. With my thumbs I wiped the remaining tears from her face and kissed her gently on the lips. Her pain was tearing me apart.

She curled herself back into my chest as I pulled her legs across my lap and held my weeping love as she continued to release her sorrow; it was all I could do. After several minutes she calmed down enough to ask, "Does Jared know?"

"Yes he does."

"How is he? Was he upset?"

"He was there when they identified her, he seemed fine."

Brianna stiffened under my arms, and I bit the inside of my lip as I realized my mistake.

"Cameron, where did they find Hannah?" Brianna demanded. My avoidance of the question only made her push harder. "Cam! Where did they find her?"

Knowing there was no point in hiding the truth from her now, I gave in.

"She was found here."

Brianna's muscles tensed, ready to spring, but this time I caught her before she could flee from my arms again.

"Cameron Jackson Burke, you let go of me this instant."

"Brianna, I will give in to almost anything, but I will not let you see her."

"Why not? It's my fault she's dead. I should see what I'm responsible for."

Brianna continued to writhe in my arms, causing me to tighten my grip more than I wanted to.

"You are not responsible, Bri," I yelled too gruffly at her, causing her to stop abruptly. "Trust me when I say you do not want to see her."

Brianna's muscles relaxed as she gave up her fight, and melted once again into a tearful fit. We sat silently on the floor of our bedroom for almost ten minutes, allowing the remaining emotions to flow out. Just when calm was finally beginning to set in, I heard the sound of heavy boots coming down the hall. I closed my eyes, praying that they would pass by my door, but it was to no avail. Moments later Devin burst through my door, startling Brianna.

"Devin," I said firmly, still seated in the floor, "you need to knock before you come in."

Devin flinched with offense. "Brother, I have never needed to announce myself before."

"It is different now, Brother," I replied as Brianna shifted out of my arms and rose to grab a few tissues out of the box that sat on the nightstand.

"How is it different?" Devin asked defensively.

"Devin," Brianna interrupted before I could respond, "he means because I'm here. It has nothing to do with you." Thinking that Brianna was wrong at his reasons for protesting, I was completely taken off guard when I saw my brother's posture relax at her comment. "Just knock, okay? Otherwise, you'll catch me like this," Brianna said gesturing to my shirt that just covered her.

Devin waited until Brianna ducked into the bathroom before he spoke. "Brother, I did not mean to interrupt. I am just not used to…"

"I know," I replied as I rose from the floor and patted him on the shoulder. "This is new for both of us."

Devin nodded curtly and then got down to business. "Father is reconvening the Council."

"I assumed as much."

"He wants a full report from everyone, not that there is much to report."

"Is Jared still looking at the video footage?" I asked just as I heard Brianna come out of the bathroom and step into the closet.

"Yes, I just left his room. He'll join us once he has something."

"I think I should stay with Brianna. She has had quite a shock tonight. I do not feel right leaving her."

Devin's expression was blank. "Brother, although I understand your need to be with her at this moment," Devin started, but stopped when I gave him a skeptical brow. "Okay, not really. You are still a part of the Elite Council, a big part. Your duty is as much with us as it is with her. I will send Kyla up if you do not want her to be alone, but you are coming with me."

"Cam, you need to go," Brianna said from behind me.

I turned to see her stepping out of the changing room still wearing my shirt, but now with a pair of pajama shorts underneath.

"Bri…" I started

"Devin, does Cameron need to go?" Brianna asked as she walked over to the two of us.

"Absolutely," Devin answer firmly.

"Then you have to go. I'll be fine," she said and headed toward the door.

I grabbed her wrist lightly, pulling her back to me. "Where are you going?"

"I'm going to see Jared."

"I would rather you stayed here."

"I would rather you stayed here, too. So it looks like neither of us is getting what they want tonight."

Knowing there was no way I was going to win this battle, I just shook my head and said, "Do you have your watch?"

Brianna rolled her eyes and held up her wrist to show me the steel watch that held her tracker inside.

"I'm just going to see Jared, it's not like I need it when I'm with him."

"It's not him I'm worried about," I said as the flashes of Hannah came to the forefront of my mind.

"I'll just stay for a few minutes. I want to make sure he's okay," she said looking up at me with her dark eyes. "Love me?"

"Always," I answered quickly, never wanting her to think otherwise.

She stretched up on her toes as I leaned down and gave her a gentle kiss on her warm lips. Once she stepped away, my longing for her deepened; I missed her. Watching her walk out of our bedroom, the panic and worry that I had felt earlier had now turned into anger, vengefulness, and rage. How dare Elaina threaten my Brianna. How dare Elaina make my love crumble into a million pieces. How dare she make Brianna feel like a burden and want to give herself up. Elaina was trying to take Brianna away from me, and that stirred the rage of the Warrior within me. No one was going to take her from me, not now, not ever.

"Brother?" Devin asked curiously, trying to understand why I was looking murderously at the door.

"You know, Devin, I am going to have to concede to Julian," I said as I rushed into my closet to change my shirt since mine was now covered in tears and mucus.

"On what point exactly?"

As I pulled a sweater over my head and walked back into the bedroom I answered, "We need to fight hard and fast. Pull everyone in, we need to smoke this coven out and kill them all." Devin looked shocked as I narrowed my eyes and concluded, "And when we find Elaina, I am going to rip her head off myself."

Chapter Forty-five

Brianna

Cameron could hold me down all day and tell me that Hannah's death wasn't my fault, but I knew he was wrong. If only she hadn't come to my door that day at the Facility, if only we hadn't bonded over our dislike of Lana, if only she hadn't listened to me the day of the attack, if only she had never met me, she would still be alive. If only, if only. As I walked down the cold stone stairs to Jared's room, I couldn't help but cry, which caused some strange looks from the vampires I passed along the way. Although it could have been the fact that I was walking around the manor in the wee hours of the morning wearing a men's button-down shirt and a pair of PJ shorts. Cameron had said that Jared seemed okay, but I wanted to see for myself. Jared would certainly be more willing to admit his sadness about Hannah's death to me versus his brother.

Wiping away the tears that had streaked down my face, I pulled myself together and knocked lightly on Jared's door. At least I was pretty sure it was Jared's. I had only been to his room one other time during my first week here, and honestly every door and hallway in this place looked the same. When he didn't answer I worried that I had the wrong room. I knocked again hoping that I hadn't disturbed an unsympathetic Warrior, but just as I was about to step away, I heard Jared's voice coming from inside.

"Are you fucking deaf? I said come in like twelve times," Jared said angrily as he swung the door open, and then froze once he realized it was me. "Sorry, I wasn't expecting a human."

The Jared that I knew was not the Jared that stood in front of me. This one looked cold and angry, and I could see the slight hint of red staining the corners of his eyes. Hannah's death had affected him, and only I knew it. Jared stood impatiently staring at me while I struggled to find the words I wanted to say to him.

"Did you need something, Brianna?" he asked annoyed.

His tone was harsh, and the fact that he called me Brianna versus one of the many nicknames he had for me convinced me that his anger ran deep.

"I just wanted to see how you were doing."

"I'm fine," he snapped.

"Can I come in?"

Jared turned and walked back into his room, leaving the door open.

"You need to be quick, I have a lot of work to do," he said as he sat down at his long desk that was covered in computers and other technological equipment that I couldn't even begin to tell you what they were used for.

Jared's room was about the size of Cameron's sitting room, only without windows for obvious reasons. It was only big enough to fit his bed and his desk of equipment with a narrow archway that led into the small closet and bathroom. He sat at his desk staring intently at one of the many monitors, but the frustration on his face was hard to ignore.

"Jer, I know you're busy, but like I said I just wanted to check on you. Devin said you were looking at some kind of footage."

Jared kept his eyes on the monitor as he said, "I told you I'm fine, just irritable because I haven't fed and I'm frustrated that I can't get a better image of who left her here."

"Maybe I could help?"

Jared's reaction to my offer was anything but gracious. His narrowed eyes were so full of hatred that they made me want to cry.

"What makes you think that your pathetic human eyes would see something that I couldn't?"

"Look, Jer, I'm hurting too. Hannah was my friend and..."

"Yeah, some friend,"

"What is that supposed to mean?"

"Are you fucking joking?" he laughed as he came around the desk towards me, suddenly making me feel like a trapped animal. "You let them take her."

"I tried to stop them," I said and took a step back.

"You told me yourself you watched them take her. You sure did a lot to stop them."

"Jared, I did try. Devin held me down. You want to be mad at someone, be mad at him."

Jared's anger overcame him as he swept his desk clear of all the equipment that sat on top of it, causing everything to crash loudly to the floor.

"You could have taken all of those vampires down, but you chose not to, you coward," he yelled, stepping way too close to me.

"That's not what happened!" I replied, trying to step around him, but he stepped in my way.

"You were happy when they took her instead, weren't you?"

"No!" I screamed, trying to step around him on the other side as tears of both fear and guilt started to rush down my face. "Jared, please let me go."

"Why, so you don't have to face the truth?" he growled at me, hovering his face only inches from mine.

"I know the truth, Jer. I did what I could, it wasn't enough. You don't think I feel guilty? I loved that girl."

"Liar!" he screamed as he took me by the shoulders and slammed me up against the stone wall, knocking the breath out of me.

Stars flashed in front of my eyes as my head bounced off the wall. Jared's face came back into focus and fear shook my body when I noticed that his fangs were fully extended. His grip on my shoulders was so tight I thought for sure the bones would break. My bottom lip wouldn't stop trembling as I whimpered, "Please let me go."

Jared pressed me against the wall and said, "I bet Hannah said the same thing."

Before I could say anything more, Jared sank his fangs into the base of my neck. My skin was tearing underneath his mouth and without having to concentrate, the burning within me rose to the top of my head as I pushed Jared off of me with my mind causing him to rip two gashes down my neck. Usually when I hit a Vamp they were writhing on the floor, allowing me a few seconds to escape, but Jared quickly leapt for me again. Putting pressure against my bleeding throat, I hit him with my mind again, but it didn't stop him and he leapt for me once more with crazed and uncontrollable anger. I hit him again, but I could tell that my energy was waning. Suddenly remembering that I had my watch, I pressed the panic button and hoped to God that I had enough strength to keep pushing Jared away until someone came.

After hitting him for the fourth time, feeling barely a sliver of the burning sensation, I saw a large cloud of black smoke appear behind Jared. Just as Jared leapt for me again, Alex's large muscular arms came around his chest and wrestled him to the ground. Cameron and Devin appeared out of nowhere, black mist still coming off their backs as they ran to me. Cameron's eyes were wide with terror as he saw the blood dripping through my fingers.

"Kyla," Devin yelled behind him, "help Cameron."

As Cameron lifted me from the floor, I noticed Kyla running into the room. Devin ran to aid Alex while Jared screamed profanities and writhed under Alex's grip. Cameron sat me down on the floor of Jared's bathroom and removed my hand so that he could see the extent of my injuries. Kyla grabbed a washcloth and ran it under water before handing it to Cameron who gently cleaned the gashes on my neck and collar bone. While he wiped the blood away, I could see the rage flaring behind his eyes.

"He bit you," he said through his clenched teeth.

"It doesn't matter," I said fearfully, afraid that another vampire would lose control at the smell of my blood. "Please Cam, just make it heal."

Cameron squeezed my hands in his as he licked my wounds closed. I knew it had to be difficult for him not to drink from me, which was obvious by how tightly he was squeezing my hands. But after a minute or so he raised his head and began wiping away the remaining blood that had dripped down my chest. As I looked down, I noticed that the front of my shirt was stained with blood.

"You're never going to let me wear your shirts again, are you?"

Cameron didn't smile at my joke, his anger was too great. He opened his mouth to say something, but then tightened his lips and shook his head. Kyla stepped to his side, realizing how upset Cameron was.

"Let's just get her out of here, Cameron," she said pulling on his arm.

He nodded and then helped me to a standing position. Besides the pounding in my head and being a little weak in the knees, I was okay, shaken, but okay. Cameron bent down to carry me but I shrugged him off. Kyla opened the door slowly, but the sound of Jared's continued profanity was too much for Cam and he bolted into the bedroom. Kyla grabbed me when I tried to run after him, putting herself between me and the awful scene in the bedroom.

Alex was now holding Jared in a standing position while he screamed unspeakable things to Cameron who was being held back by Devin. It was devastating to see them this way, but every time I would think about moving around Kyla to intervene, her grip would tighten around my arm.

Just then, a sudden roar filled the room as two men entered. One was a tall, average looking Warrior, but the other was short and stocky, unlike any of the other Warriors I had seen. His stature, however, did not match the power he exuded when he yelled for the fighting to stop. Seeing as everyone in the room suddenly froze, I assumed that the short man was Victor. Everything about him was the complete opposite of how I had pictured him. Seriously, he was short. It was hard not to hear the name Victor and think of all the fierce, intimidating vampires from movies and books.

Jared suddenly broke the silence, unable to keep his anger in check. It frightened me to see Jared this way, but I was terrified when Victor slapped him across the face causing bits of his cheek to fly across the room.

"Get a hold of yourself, child," Victor roared, but Jared was unable to stop.

Victor reared his hand back, ready to strike Jared again.

"Stop, please!" I yelled a spilt second before Kyla pulled me back to her side.

Cameron turned quickly around and came to stand in front of me.

"Brianna, it is best you stay out of this," he said sternly which pissed me off to no end.

"I don't need you to help me, you bitch!" Jared screamed.

Cameron's entire body contorted in rage as he leapt for Jared, only to be stopped by Devin. Victor let out another loud wail, commanding that everyone in the room be silent, but the silence was quickly broken by the sound of a woman's voice just outside the door.

"So here iz everyone," Seraphina said in a thick French accent as she glided into the room. We were all shocked by the randomness of seeing Eris's wife walk into the room. I also realized that when I met her earlier today, she never said anything, so hearing her French accent made me wonder if it was real since I now knew my father's wasn't. "Dez hallways all look zhe same, I went to ze wrong ruum," she said smiling.

All the vampires in the room looked at one another not understanding why Seraphina had come. Victor was the only one who seemed willing to say, "Seraphina, it is good to see you as always, but this is a family matter. I do not understand why you are here."

Seraphina simply smiled and knelt down beside Jared who was still jerking and flailing in Alex's arms.

"I am here for him," she said as she placed Jared's hand in hers.

Everyone in the room took a solid step toward her, but I quickly interrupted. "It's okay, she's helping him."

Jared's shouting immediately stopped as his emotions were taken away from him and sent into Seraphina. You could almost see them leaving his body in waves. Everyone in the room was stunned, unable to fathom what was really going on.

"Zat's right, young one. Let everyzing flow into me," Seraphina continued as she stroked Jared's hand gently.

"Thank you for your help, Seraphina, but as I said before, this is a family matter. I will happily have someone escort you back to your room," Victor said gesturing to the door.

"She can't," I said quickly, causing everyone to look in my direction. "She's keeping his emotions under control. If she let's go, he'll go crazy again."

"Ah, my secret iz out," Seraphina said calmly, giving me a little wink. "He iz calm now, ready to answer your questions."

Flustered at not fully knowing what was happening, Victor stepped forward to stand in front of Jared as he asked, "I want an explanation as to why in the middle of a crucial council meeting, three of your brothers Projected themselves out because of a distress call coming from your room only to find *you* behaving like an animal and a hybrid bleeding. What do you have to say for yourself," Victor yelled as he reached for Jared's throat.

"It was an accident," I yelled, causing the entire room of vampires to turn their heads in my direction yet again.

"Brianna?" Cameron said quietly with a mix of anger and confusion.

The unknown vampire in the room took a step in our direction, a snide smile across his face. "By the look of things this was no *accident*. The evidence is still wet on your shirt."

Boy he was a dick.

"And you are?" I asked, trying to mimic his cocky tone.

"Brianna," Cameron started, "this is Julian, who is for all intents and purposes the Warrior's warden."

"Well, I hate to burst your bubble, Julian, but this was an accident," I reiterated without looking at Cameron who was more than slightly irritated at the fact that I was defending Jared. "Yes, Jared and I had an argument and he even gave me fair warning that he hadn't fed, but I kept trying to push him to talk to me about Hannah, the hybrid who was found dead tonight. Jared got upset with me, and yes he lost his temper and threw all of that in the floor," I said as I stepped from Cameron's side and gestured to the broken computer equipment scattered on the floor. "I got scared, and being the klutz that I am, I tripped over the mess and ended up cutting myself. Jared couldn't help himself when he smelled the blood. It was an accident, I assure you."

Alex, Devin, and even Jared in his altered state, looked at me with shock plastered on their faces.

"A story fraught with lies," Julian replied with a look of disgust on his face. "You don't want to see your lover's brother punished, so you make up this story to defend him. But it is my job to discover the truth and punish those who deserve it. Now I want to see those wounds you call an accident."

Julian stepped towards me, his hand lifted to open my shirt collar only to be stopped by Cameron's outstretched arm.

"Look, it's my word against Jared's, and I'm the victim here. If I say it's an accident, then it's an accident. Now I suggest you back away because the only person in this room who is going to get close enough to examine me is Cameron. If you have a problem with that, I suggest you take it up with him or my father. I'm sure Eris would love to go toe to toe with a vampire who dared to touch his daughter without her consent."

Victor walked over to Julian and pulled him away from me as he said, "Julian, Ms. Morgan is right. She is the victim. If she claims this was an unfortunate accident then we must view it as such, even if we believe there is more to this story."

"But Father, it is obviously a lie," Julian whined, making him even more pitiful in my eyes.

"Julian, send one of your men to stay with Jared, he will be on restriction in this room until I deem he is able to control himself. Be sure he is brought blood on a regular basis. Force him to drink it if you have to. I do not want another episode like this happening in my own home." Julian stepped around Victor and Projected out of the room like a spoiled child. "Kyla, I assume you can escort Seraphina and Ms. Morgan to their rooms?" Kyla nodded. "I will expect the rest of you back in the council meeting after you have composed yourselves.

"Seraphina, Ms. Morgan, let me convey my dearest apologies for this unfortunate event. I do not wish for Eris to doubt his daughter's safety in the Warrior manor. I can assure this will never happen again."

Victor bowed his head curtly and exited the room in seconds.

Everyone released a sigh of relief once Victor left, especially me. My relief, however, was short lived since Cameron turned me around to face him, a multitude of emotions crossing his face at once.

"Why did you do that, Brianna? Why would you defend Jared after what he did to you?"

The answer was simple. "Because it's Jared," I said matter-of-factly, but then the gravity of the incident flooded over me. My hands flew to my face as the tears came down and I could feel Cameron's arms wrap around me. The room was silent except for my blubbering and I tried as hard as I could to stop, but it took a couple of minutes. Finally composed, I pushed myself out of Cameron's embrace. "You need to go," I said and wiped my eyes and face.

"You need me," Cameron said plainly.

"They need you more."

Cameron leaned down, worry and fear still on his face as he kissed me hard on the lips, showing me just how scared he had been. After releasing my lips, he gave me one more kiss on the forehead.

"I will try not to wake you."

"No, wake me," I said, shaking my head. "If you're there, I want to be awake."

Cameron hesitated in front of me, not wanting to leave, but Devin pulled gently on his shoulder.

"Brianna," Devin said, "what you did for our brother tonight was very brave. We are all grateful for the sacrifice you made, it will not be forgotten."

I nodded and managed a slight smile even though on the inside I was about to fall apart. Just as Devin and Cameron reached the door, Julian's guard came to replace Alex as Jared's keeper, though he was barely moving underneath Seraphina's spell. As the guard took Jared's arms, I ran to Alex and gave him the biggest hug I could manage.

"Thank you," I said as I mushed my face into his chest.

"I would have been here a second sooner, but I couldn't believe you'd be in trouble in here. Next time I will not hesitate. I promise you that."

"Let's hope there won't be a next time."

Alex sighed in agreement and let go of me to give Kyla a quick kiss before he too left to return to the council meeting.

"Brianna, I would suggest zhat you leave zhe ruum before I let go of zhis young one. His emotions are very strong," Seraphina said as she gently caressed Jared's placid face.

Kyla gently guided me out of the room and a minute later Seraphina closed the door behind her, sounds of Jared's heart wrenching wails of apology coming through the walls.

"Seraphina, how did you know?" I asked softly.

"I have my ways," the sweet French lady answered, squeezing my hand again. "But zhis iz our secret. If your fazer knew what happened tonight I know he would try and take you from here. I could not let him take you away from your true love."

Though I barely knew the woman, I hugged her tightly, thanking her for all the times she had saved my life not only from dangerous vampires, but from my father as well. When I released her, she looked back at me with a mother's caring eyes while she wiped away a tear that had escaped down my cheek.

"Seraphina, I will escort you to your room once I take Brianna to hers," Kyla said, pulling me back into her supportive arms.

"No need. Bon soir," Seraphina replied as she turned and headed down the hallway, disappearing as mysteriously as she had arrived.

"Can we please get out of here," I said to Kyla, unable to take Jared's cries any longer.

Kyla reacted quickly and squeezed me snuggly into her side as she walked me to my bedroom.

"You really stuck it to Julian."

I laughed lightly underneath her arm. "He's a real piece of work, isn't he?"

"You have no idea," Kyla replied as she opened my bedroom door. I ran immediately to the bed, sinking into the many plush pillows as she said, "I'll stay with you until Cameron comes back."

I shook my head. "Thanks, Ky, but I really just need to be alone."

Kyla scrunched her eyebrows together, but realized I wasn't going to change my mind.

"Well, then call me if you need anything."

I nodded and with a sigh Kyla reluctantly left. Feeling the stickiness on my chest I sat up from the bed and ran to the bathroom. I ripped Cameron's blood-stained shirt open and threw it in the garbage. In the mirror I could see the scars from Jared's fangs at the base of my neck. It was devastating to see that scared woman who used to stare back at me so many nights after Sam had beaten me. Dark circles and sunken cheeks aside, my emotions were carved into the lines of my face. I needed to find that strength I exuded in front of Julian tonight, it was the only way I was going to survive the hand I had been dealt. I needed to say goodbye to the scared thirty-one-year-old woman who was a victim no more.

I left the bathroom and grabbed a soft T-shirt from my dresser, pulling it on as I stepped back out into the bedroom. My cell phone was still on the nightstand where I had left it and I quickly dialed as I sank to the floor, tears already coming down my face as the phone rang on the other end.

"Someone better be dead," Renee answered sleepily and irritated.

"Bad choice of words," I cried.

"Bri, ohmygod, are you okay?"

"No, Re, I'm not. I'm not okay."

"What's the matter, did someone die?"

I could hear her rustling covers as she pulled the phone away and said something to someone near her.

"Oh Renee, I'm sorry. I didn't even think about John being there. I'll call back another time."

"Bri, it's fine, I'm going into the living room. What's going on, you're scaring the crap out of me."

"Are you sitting down?"

"Yeah, but what are you telling me that I need to sit down for?"

I swallowed hard and sighed before I answered, "The truth."

Chapter Forty-six

Brianna

Cameron held me gently at the waist as he led me around the spacious ballroom full of beautiful couples spinning on the dance floor to the fast waltz. The light from the tall candelabras and chandeliers cast a warm yellow glow and caused the women's jewels to sparkle like stars. Even the wide, scrolling silver and diamond bracelet clasped over my opera length glove kept catching my eye while Cameron held my arm out while we danced.

"Shall we go out onto the terrace, love?" Cameron whispered in my ear just before taking a step back and extending his hand, allowing me to take him all in. You would have thought that he was born in the tuxedo tails he was wearing, only enhancing his perfect physique.

"I would love to," I replied and then allowed him to escort me through the wall of doors opening up to the expanding terrace outside. As we passed through the doors, I caught my reflection in the glass. My dark hair was piled high on top of my head, held together with sparkling pins while the neckline of my dress was scooped low with cream chiffon billowing down to the floor.

Cameron led me to a secluded corner of the terrace that overlooked the beautiful gardens of the estate. Standing behind me, he began softly kissing my neck and shoulder and then brushed his opposite hand across my breasts. As I tilted my neck, exposing the pulsing artery beneath, Cameron moaned softly in response as he began to nip slightly at my pale skin with his fangs. I wanted to see the pleasure my blood gave him as he took it from me, but when I turned around, he was gone, and in his place stood Jared. His eyes were full of hatred and hunger while he leaned toward me.

"Please let me go," I said breathlessly, looking for a way around him as the ledge of the terrace pushed against my back.

"I bet that's what she said," he said and bit into my neck...

My hand flew to my throat as I bolted upright in bed gasping for air. Cameron was at my side in seconds, taking my hand away and assuring me that I was safe. It was the third morning in a row where I had woken up screaming. Unfortunately, Jared's attack had combined with the Cameron biting dream that I had dreamt months before. With everything going on, I couldn't bear to tell Cameron his involvement in the dream, merely that Jared kept coming after me.

"The same dream?" Cameron said, raking his worried eyes across my face as he sat opposite me on the bed. "Was he biting you again?"

"When are you going to forgive him?"

"Once you stop having nightmares."

Knowing there was little I could do to make light of the situation, I threw my arms around Cameron's neck, tucking my head in my favorite spot just under his chin.

"If I can forgive him, you can too. You can't tell me that you never had an accident when you were a younger vampire."

"We are not talking about me right now, and no, I never let my bloodlust get to a point where I lost control and bit my brother's significant other."

"Maybe not your brother's significant other, but someone," I said playfully.

Jared was still a young vampire and there were extenuating circumstances that I unfortunately walked right into and poked with a big stick. Although the whole incident had shaken me, I had forgiven Jared when I heard him wailing and crying to me through the walls. I hadn't seen him since Victor restricted him to his room three days ago and I wondered if we would still have that fun, easy going relationship once his punishment was lifted.

"Come, angel, Eris will be expecting you in twenty minutes. I will get you breakfast while you change," Cameron said as he kissed me on the head and eased out of my arms.

A second later he disappeared in a cloud of black smoke and I fell back into bed, curling the covers tightly around me. Twenty minutes was a lifetime when all I had to do was throw my hair into a ponytail and slip on some workout clothes. I had started taking showers at night since it didn't make sense to do it before my training sessions with my father. By the end of the day, I looked like a drowned rat from the amount of sweat that poured down my body.

I had agreed to let Eris train me in an effort to get to know one another as well as teach me the skills he felt I needed in order to survive. By the end of day one I was already regretting my decision as Eris's forceful badgering and impatience grew worse by the hour. I had told him that I would put an end to it all if he became too violent, and I feared that day was coming soon.

As I snuggled deeper into my pillow, I heard someone clear his throat behind me. I rolled over onto my side and saw Cameron holding a tray full of carb and protein packed foods, all of which he expected me to eat. Whining as I stretched my arms above my head I said, "Doesn't my father know it's Saturday?"

Cameron didn't answer, but continued to stand next to the bed tapping his fingers lightly on the tray, waiting for me to get my tired butt up. Throwing the covers off of me in dramatic fashion, I heard Cameron laugh quietly to himself while I stomped (yes, literally stomped) into the closet to change into my workout clothes.

"Have you spoken with Renee lately?" Cameron asked from the bedroom.

His question made me freeze.

"Um...yeah, just the other day," I replied, leaving out the part about telling her that Cameron and his family were vampires and that other evil Vamps were trying to kill me.

"How is she doing?"

"She's good. She moved in with Dr. John last weekend and she hasn't killed him yet, so that's a good sign."

Renee was still in shock when we got off the phone, and since then had left me endless messages with questions that I didn't have the time to answer. It was hard finding time that I wasn't training, eating, sleeping, or being hounded about this stupid claiming ceremony that Eris was insisting on. Thankfully Seraphina and Kyla were taking the lead on the party with the manor staff, but it was endless questions about colors, fabrics, food, music, blah blah blah blah blah. The statement I made to them about just having a bar-b-que in the backyard didn't go over well, and therefore I was thrust into the passenger seat of my own party. I hadn't even been allowed to pick out my dress, oddly enough that had been done by Cameron.

Shaking myself back to the task at hand, I pulled on a black two-piece outfit and caught a glimpse of myself in the tall mirror at the far end of the changing area. Even with the amount of stress and working out, my body hadn't forgotten it was getting close to that time of the month. Everyone would be so please that I looked like I had gained ten pounds, but it also meant that Cam and I had to broach yet another awkward subject that would most likely result in being apart. It was way too much to think about this early in the morning, and if I didn't think about it, it didn't exist, at least for another day or so. Right now, I needed to change my shirt, no bare mid-drift today, which was so odd to say since I had never been thin enough to show it before. So, I pulled on another shirt that covered me, but still showed my figure. I wouldn't see Cameron all day and I needed to send him off looking semi-attractive.

I stepped back out into the bedroom to find the bed perfectly made and breakfast laid out on the table in front of the fireplace where the two of us could sit and enjoy each other's company while I ate. Since Jared attacked me, Cam and I had breakfast like this every morning and I fell asleep in his arms every night. According to Kyla, after the council meeting adjourned that night, Cameron had an explosive argument with Victor and Devin where he stated that twice a day he would be unavailable to anyone except me. I had become quite a scandalous topic among the Warriors since then, and certainly not making any points with Victor.

As I walked over to the couch, Cameron's eyes flared slightly at the sight of me, and of course it felt amazing. Quickly he cleared his throat as if locking away any feelings of desire.

"Is there something you want to tell me?" he asked with raised eyebrows.

I swallowed hard, quickly stopping the sexy walk I was trying to pull off. "I love you?"

"And I love you. Try again."

"Can you give me a hint?" I asked and sat next to him.

With a smile he pulled his cell phone from his back pocket and began scrolling through various text messages.

"You should really call Renee, my love. She is worried about you."

"How do you know?"

Cameron turned his cell phone around. "Because her text says, 'Hey

Vampy, where's Bri? I'm worried. Tell the bitch to call me.' So I ask again, is there something you would like to tell me?"

The lump in my throat wouldn't go down no matter how hard I tried to swallow.

"Are you angry with me?"

"No, I am not angry. I just wish we had discussed that you wanted to tell her what I was before doing so. There are always risks with telling humans about us and Renee is not the most," he cleared his throat, "discreet person you know."

"Cam, it wasn't something I planned. The other night when everything happened with Jared, I was upset and alone and didn't want to dump any more on you."

"Bri, that is what I…"

"Let me finish," I said gently, placing a finger up to his lips. "You have so much on your plate and that night you were so angry and guilty and…well I just couldn't put any more on you. I needed to vent to my friend who I knew would just listen to me and keep my confidence. Not to say I don't love Kyla, I do, but she tells you everything."

"I thought we were not keeping secrets from each other."

"I'm not keeping secrets, Cam. But there are times when I want to talk about something and not burden you while you have the world on your shoulders. Besides it was ripping me apart that I was always lying to her. I just couldn't do it anymore. Is Victor going to have me killed now?"

Thankfully he laughed lightly, handing me my bagel with a pound of cream cheese spread on top.

"Just make sure Renee understands that she cannot tell anyone. I would hate to be forced to have someone Glamour her, and then in turn have you keep lying."

"So I'm forgiven?"

"As long as you can convince her not to call me 'Vampy.'"

I laughed and bit into my bagel, knowing that it would be hard to convince Renee of doing much of anything.

"Angel, there is something else I want to discuss with you," he said as I stuffed another large bite into my mouth. "The night Eris came to the manor he asked me to persuade you to be activated, and of course I told him that it was solely your choice. However, now I think you should seriously consider it," he said putting his hands up to me so that he could finish his statement while I tried to argue with half a bagel in my mouth. "Only for the fact that it will solidify and strengthen your powers, and after the other night I need you to be as strong as you possibly can be."

"You're that worried about me?"

"I would put you in one of Devin's suits of armor if I could."

"He has more than one?"

"He has armor like Kyla has shoes."

"Or like you have clothes?"

"We are not discussing me right now," he replied flatly. "Will you please consider your father's offer?"

I sighed, then pouted, then sighed once again before finally saying, "Fine, I'll think about it, but no promises."

"It will only help you, love."

"How do you know?" I said angrily. "Have you *met* my father? Oh yes, that's right you have. Remember when he held you six feet in the air by your throat? You want more of that man's blood in my body? I'm his only child, so we have no idea what his blood will do to me. What if his blood is too strong for me to handle? What if it turns me crazy violent like he is? You would rather have me strong and psychotic than slightly vulnerable and the person you fell in love with? Enough has changed already, why throw another log on the fire."

Cameron stayed silent for a moment, processing everything I said like he always did when one of my verbal fits came over me. The back of his hand caressed my cheek as he said, "Hybrids are activated all the time, and it is always safest with the father's blood. Eris's blood cannot change who you are, love. So what is this really about?"

"This," I said, holding his hand up in mine.

"My hand?"

"It's not as cold as it used to be and since you can't get any warmer it means I'm getting colder. You have to have noticed."

Cameron furrowed his brow. "Bri, you are a hybrid surrounded by vampires. When this occurs, the vampire blood inside of you becomes more dominant. Of course your temperature dropped slightly, for the same reasons your powers became more prominent after you spent time with me. It is nothing to be upset about. We are still the same two people who fell in love with each other."

"That's just it, Cam," I said as I stood from the couch, unable to control the anxiety inside me. "Since we met, our relationship has been nothing but running for our lives and other endless drama. We keep saying that when this is all over, we'll finally have time together. But what if when that day comes, we look at each other and don't know why we're together. I don't even know your favorite color and we sleep in the same bed for crying out loud."

Flustered, I grabbed a pillow from the couch and threw it on the floor as I walked toward the door only to be met by Cam's caring face.

"Angel," he said, folding me into his arms, "you are right. We did not meet under usual circumstances and since then we have had our share of drama, as you say." Cameron crooked his finger under my chin and tilted my head up so that he could look into my eyes. "But I still fell hopelessly in love with you despite it all. You may not know my favorite color, but you know when I am hiding something from you. When I am overwhelmed, you know exactly what to do to calm me down. You know things about me, about my past, that I have never told anyone.

"Trust me when I tell you that I regret all that we have had to endure in such a short time, but at least we had each other to overcome it. People spend years with each other without a care in the world and fall apart the minute a crisis comes along. I do not worry about our future because after everything you and I have been through I know that we will be at each other's side in bad times and just enjoy each other during the good ones.

"Now we may be doing some things a little out of order, but it does not change my love for you. Brianna, do not doubt what we have together, or how completely devoted I am to you."

"I don't, Cam," I replied quickly and threw my arms around his neck, almost on the verge of tears. "I love you, more than I ever thought possible. I just miss you, and I'm totally PMS-ing," I said as I lowered myself back to the ground.

"Oh…um…pre-menstrual?" he stuttered and I nodded. "I see. Well…then should we discuss…"

"Bri-an-na Mari-lena," Eris shouted as he burst through the bedroom door, "I have been waiting for you downstairs for almost five minutes. You must take this training seriously. Have I interrupted something?"

"Yes, as a matter…" I started.

"No sir," Cameron said over me. He brushed my cheek with the back of his fingers. "We can discuss the…thing, later. Be strong today, my love."

Cameron took my hand and kissed the back of it and then gave me another quick kiss on the lips before he walked out the door, leaving me alone with Eris.

"Daughter, I am sorry for interrupting," Eris began, but it was obvious he was in a bad mood.

"Don't start lying now, Eris, it's only 8:00 a.m.," I replied and walked toward the door.

"When are you going to start calling me Father, or Dad, or something?"

"When are you going to start talking without that ridiculous accent?"

"I told you, when you are activated."

Heaving a long sigh as we walked down the hallway I admitted to him, "Well, we may both get what we want sooner than you think."

If I thought for a second that letting Eris know I was considering the idea of being activated would lessen the torture he put me through during training I was sadly mistaken. He was in a foul mood and seemed down right angry about something which he in turn took out on me. If I blocked high, it was too high. If I thrust forward, it wasn't forceful enough. My wrists were still weak to truly work the long, curved swords my father forced me to use. Often times he was able to twist or knock them out of my hands, which in turn made him even angrier. Seraphina was always in the background during my training sessions, but today on more than one occasion she had to step in to take Eris's anger away. Unfortunately, it always came back. If Devin hadn't come in at 1:00, Eris probably would have worked me all day without a break.

Although Devin wasn't officially training me anymore, Eris allowed him to come in the afternoons and work with me for a short period of time, mainly at my insistence. I never thought I would be so happy to see Devin of all people, and each day he came in was a blessing. His presence meant a break from the swords as well as my father. However, today my time with Devin was spent eating since Eris had refused to stop earlier, even at the behest of Seraphina. Like I said, f-o-u-l mood.

After an hour of eating, and making Devin hold bags of ice on my sore wrists and arms, I reluctantly picked up my swords and began a full afternoon of swordplay with my erratic father. Even Devin was concerned about my father's agitated state. He had already seen one display of Eris's temper and didn't want me being alone if there was another one.

The afternoon session with Eris declined quickly as my muscles began to fatigue. I was exhausted, drenched in sweat, and frustrated at myself for not doing better, although it didn't help that Eris screamed at me in multiple languages. When 5:00 finally came along, my time with my father was up and Cameron came walking into the training room. My knight in black cashmere was here to save me.

I was just out of Cameron's reach when my father suddenly scooped me up and brought me back out to the middle of the training floor.

"Come, Bri-an-na, we are not done for today. Do not let the Warrior be a distraction to you," Eris growled.

I looked back to see Cameron standing next to Devin as the two of them whispered intensely to one another. Their conversation, however, quickly halted when Eris brought both of his swords down on mine. His blows sent shockwaves through my body and I didn't have time to recover before he began pushing me to the edge of the mats. Just as my footing began to slip on the slick surface of the hardwood floor, I was able to turn quickly and arch my back, just missing Eris's blade. Unfortunately, in the process I lost the sword in my left hand as he twisted his blade around mine, taking advantage of my weak wrists.

Even with only one sword, my muscles burned and shook in protest at the physical exertion I was placing on them. Eris's speed was quickening as he hit me from all sides, pushing me across the floor all the while. I was never in control of this fight. At several points I tried to lunge forceful enough to get him to take a step back, but he merely absorbed my impact and then pushed me away. With every hit, my arms screamed in pain. My thrusts were so weak they barely made contact. Using the last of my strength, I grabbed my sword tightly with both hands and lunged forward, unfortunately so did Eris. My father's sword skidded off the edge of my blade and sliced the top of my right hand and forearm cleanly open. My sword fell to the floor and I sank to my knees, cradling my bleeding arm to my chest.

"Get up! You will not be weak. Get up and fight," Eris screamed and lunged at me again only to be stopped by Devin clamping his arms down at his side. "Do you think our enemy will stop? I am barely using my true strength and look at you!"

In a flash Cameron was kneeling down in front of me, covering my arm with a towel and applying pressure, although my blood soaked through its fibers within seconds. I couldn't help but notice Cameron's fangs were extended and all I kept thinking was that I was in the same situation as the other night – bleeding, and surrounded by vampires.

"Release me," Eris growled, but Devin only responded by clamping his arms down harder. I noticed Seraphina slowly walking forward, almost too afraid to approach her husband in his current state. "I know who you are, Assassin, but trust me when I tell you that I have been killing much longer than you have. Release me or I swear I will tear you apart," Eris roared and continued to flail under Devin's firm grip.

I had made a promise to myself the other night never to be the victim again, and here I was letting Cameron take control of me while Devin fought to control my father, and I couldn't have it anymore. Using my good arm, I pushed myself up to a standing position, but was happy to feel Cameron's supportive arm around my waist.

"Devin, you should let him go," I said to everyone's surprise.

"That's right, Assassin, heed my daughter's warning," Eris said snidely.

"It wasn't a warning. I'd bet on Devin any day of the week," I replied just as snidely, causing him to jerk in surprise. Devin released his grip on my father, but stayed close behind him. "Eris, I told you that if you ever got violent again, we were through. And this more than proves to me that you will never change. You said to me you wanted to be a father. Well, a father doesn't do *this* to his daughter," I yelled, raising my arm wrapped in the blood-soaked towel.

"Bri-an-na, we cannot stop. You are still too weak. These vampires are much stronger than you…"

"And they always will be!"

"No," he snapped back. "You are my daughter. You have my blood, my strong blood inside of you."

"But I am still human, Eris!" I screamed, flinching my arm in frustration and then sucking in a deep breath from the pain. Cameron squeezed me into his side and guided me in the direction of the door.

"Figlia, I am doing this to protect you," Eris said as I passed.

I whipped around out of Cameron's arm. "This does not protect me. *This* causes me to bleed in a house full of vampires. *This* makes me wonder why I ever wanted to have a relationship with you. *This* makes me ashamed to admit that you're my father."

"Figlia, please, I was trying to provoke you to use your mind power,"

Eris said in a much lighter tone.

"But I told you that I can't control it," I replied, leaning back into Cameron's supportive side.

"Which is why you must strengthen it. It only appears when you are in danger and I have been pushing you..."

"So you thought that by stabbing me..."

"That your power would come out."

"I don't know how! I can't do it."

"You must learn how to! You will die if you do not."

"Then I will die!" I yelled, causing total silence.

Knowing there was no more to say, I turned back toward the door and let Cameron lead me out with Devin close behind. I heard the mutterings of Eris and Seraphina as we left, but I didn't dare turn around. I could yell all I wanted at Eris, but Seraphina was always so gentle and caring that she could probably convince me to do just about anything. But at this moment, I needed to make a stand against my father.

Once we were halfway down the corridor, Cameron stopped and sat me down on a wooden bench to take a look at my arm. While he opened the bloody towel, Devin knelt in front of me and gently took my arm from Cameron hands.

"You're going to need stitches, Brianna," Devin said as he examined the cut while it continued to bleed into the towel.

I looked up at Cameron, noticing that his mouth was clamped shut, the muscles in his jaw flexing tightly.

"Cam, can't you just heal it?"

"The cut is too deep, Brianna," Devin answered instead. "Vampire blood would heal it pretty quickly, but since you haven't been activated you really shouldn't have another vampire's blood before you have your father's. I can stitch the deepest layers, and then we can seal the rest," he said as he stood from the floor and then looked down at Cameron. "Brother, why don't you stay here for a few minutes while I escort Brianna to my quarters. You can join us once she is cleaned up."

Cameron nodded tensely, giving me an apologetic look. Before I could say anything, Devin lifted me from the bench, carried me down a side hallway and then up a flight of stairs I had never seen before.

"Is Cameron okay?"

"He hasn't fed in a few days, and I could sense the pull your blood was having on him. I thought it best to get a little distance between the two of you. No worries about me though, I fed this morning."

"Good to know," I replied, although I was still panicked about having a vampire stitch me up. "Where are we, by the way?"

"This is the back way to the living areas. I could not very well parade you down the main hallway as you are."

"True," I laughed. "You'd be beating Warriors off with a stick."

"I'm not beneath killing a sibling if needed."

Ah, Devin. I hoped more than believed that he was kidding.

We continued to his room, which I realized I had never been to. It was the same size as Cameron's, but extremely sparse. Based on the conversation that Cam and I had this morning, I was expecting a room full of weapons and armor from the different eras of Devin's life. Surprisingly enough, the only pieces of furniture in the expansive room was a thin mattress on top of a wooden slat bedframe and a small table with two chairs up against the wall.

Devin pulled out one of the chairs and helped me sit down before he disappeared through an archway at the side of the room. Moments later he returned with an old-fashioned medical bag and placed it on the table. With quick hands he placed various instruments, bottles, and gauze on the table's surface and then placed the bag on the floor.

Devin worked so fast that I barely felt the needle of numbing solution he stuck in my arm after he'd wiped the long gash clean of blood. Although my wrist and arm were mostly numb, I could feel my skin being pulled from deep within while Devin sutured me back together, something I definitely couldn't watch him do. Scrunching my eyes tightly closed, I turned my head and rested it up against the wall, all the while seeing flashes of Eris's sword coming at me.

"Brianna, keep still," Devin said softly, pressing down on my arm.

I hadn't even realized that I was flinching, but the sight of my father's monstrous glare more than terrified me. Now that the adrenaline was no longer pumping through me, everything began to hit me all at once. It didn't matter that I was thirty-one years old, the hope never died that I would have those special moments with my real father. When I was living with Shelby, I would pray that my father would find me and take me away. But in the end, one parent was just as bad as the other. My mother would have rather killed herself than have me, and my father had no qualms inflicting pain upon me when it suited him. I missed Daddy O, and I was suddenly feeling homesick. I needed his comfort, and his love. I just needed my Daddy O.

With my eyes still tightly closed, I let the tears trickle down my cheeks. I didn't care about crying in front of Devin. I figured he would just ignore me, which was why I was surprised to feel cool fingers lightly wiping the tears away. My eyes flew open and caught the beautiful sight of Cameron's dark eyes looking down at me.

"Are you in pain, angel," he asked and knelt down beside me.

"No," I answered, shaking my head slightly, careful not to disturb my arm while Devin finished his sutures. "Not on the outside at least."

Cameron understood my meaning and gently kissed me several times on the cheek.

"Brother, are you in control?" Devin asked without looking up as he cut the last of the thin suture wire.

"Yes, I am in full control," Cameron replied, but then put his lips up against the lobe of my ear. "I apologize for before."

"What can I say, I'm just too irresistible."

Cameron's breath tickled my neck as he laughed.

Devin cleared his throat, reminding us that we were not alone. "Brianna, your stitches are complete. Now if Cameron is in full control he can seal the wound, otherwise I can lick you myself."

Pulling my arm slowly out of Devin's hands and giving him a coy look, I said, "Devin, you have to wait until Cameron is out of the room before you make such a pass at me."

Devin stood abruptly, looking offended. "Brianna, this is not a sexual act, it is purely for your benefit. You are with my brother, I would never…"

"Brother, it was a joke," Cameron interrupted calmly, unable to control his smirk.

Devin sighed in relief and I suddenly felt guilty at trying to tease him. But when the two brothers laughed at each other, I joined in trying to let the stress of the day dissolve away. Cameron knelt next to me again, taking my arm gently in his hands and slowly gliding his cool tongue up the open wound. When he reached the end, he looked up at me and I could see the desire in his eyes, though I couldn't be sure if it was for my blood or my body; neither one I was particularly comfortable with giving away at the moment.

Once Cameron released my arm, Devin wrapped it quickly with a roll of gauze, tying it in a neat knot at the top.

"The outside of the wound should close within an hour or so, but the inside of your arm will probably be sore until tomorrow. You can take the dressing off once the cut seals itself, but you'll most likely have a scar tonight."

Tonight! Eris's stupid claiming ceremony, the one where *he* claimed *me* as his daughter. It should definitely be the other way around - the hybrid should choose whether or not she accepts her father in her life. And right now, I didn't.

"No big deal, I'm not going tonight."

Cameron and Devin looked at each other and then back to me with looks of distress on their faces.

"Brianna, you have to go tonight," Cameron said in an almost forceful tone that he seldom used with me, frankly because it really didn't work.

"Cam," I said and stood from my chair, "I don't *have* to do anything. The man just sliced my arm open, and now you want me to parade around with him in front of everyone pretending that I'm happy he's my father? No way."

I turned toward the door only to see Cameron suddenly in front of me.

"It is not just about him, love," he said, gently caressing my shoulders, obviously trying to win me over. "Tonight is a chance to celebrate you, probably the only thing your father has done that I agree with. It is also a chance for you to meet our family, all of whom want to meet the Brianna Morgan they have heard so much about."

I took Cameron's hands off my shoulders and held them down in front of me. "Cam, I know you're trying to help, but you're just adding a lot more pressure to the situation."

Cameron shook his head realizing that he hadn't chosen the best words, but lifted my hands and rested them on his heart.

"Then let us have just one evening where there is no talk of attacks or deaths and we all have a little bit of fun for once. Brianna, let me celebrate you. I want everyone to see just how amazing you are."

Looking at those big, beautiful, dark eyes it was impossible to say no to him.

"Fine, but I'm only going because I want to see you in a tux," I said with a coy smile.

"Speaking of, we need to go," Cameron said, guiding me toward the door. I tried to wave to Devin as we left, but Cameron scooped me up and ran down the hallway and up a flight of stairs to our room. "Kyla said she would meet you in our room a half hour ago to start getting you ready. She will be furious with me that you are late."

"Well, then she can be mad at Eris. But seriously, do I need three hours to get ready? I'm not that ugly."

Cameron laughed as he opened the door to our room revealing an annoyed Kyla tapping her foot like an impatient mother.

"Where have you been?" she shouted at the two of us.

"Kyla be gentle, Brianna has had a difficult afternoon," Cameron said as he carefully set me down on the floor and gestured to my bandaged arm.

"What happened," she exclaimed, rushing to my side.

"Don't ask," I replied. "But according to Devin, I'll still have a scar on my arm tonight."

"We'll figure out something," Kyla said flustered as she took me by my good arm and led me to the bathroom. "Cameron, your services are no longer needed, so get out."

"Ky, he needs to get ready too," I said as she threw a towel in my direction.

"He can't see you until the big reveal. I let him choose your dress, that's as far as I'm willing to go here. Now shower, and then we'll do your hair and makeup." I stood frozen in the bathroom having never seen Kyla so keyed up. "Brianna, now! Go! We don't have all day."

Afraid of the hurricane named Kyla, I stripped down trying to avoid hitting my arm which seemed to groan as the numbing solution began to wear off. Just as I shut the shower door behind me, I heard the door to the bathroom creak open and could see a flash of bright orange hair.

"Bri, sorry about being so crazy. I'm just excited about tonight."

"I know, Kyla, don't worry about it."

"Sorry about your arm. Do you want to talk about it?"

"Nope," I answered as I tried massaging shampoo into my hair with one hand.

"Oh okay," she said. I could hear the surprise in her voice, but she didn't press. "I'll bring your dress up in a little while. The hairdresser will be here in a few minutes, I'll bring her in once you're done. 'Kay?"

"Sounds good, my friend."

Even through the sound of the shower I could hear Kyla giggle as she replied, "Okay then, *my friend.*"

And with that I was finally alone to sink into the vastness of my shower, letting it pelt me with hot, steamy streams of water to wash away all the pent-up stress and sorrow from the day. I had to be careful not to let myself get depressed, it would be so easy to do. But after only a few minutes of being clean and just sitting in the shower, Kyla knocked and yelled at me to get out. I was putting her behind schedule, and she really didn't like it.

The hairdresser was pleasant, human, and I had no idea if she knew about what kind of house she had walked into, but I wasn't about to ask either. My hair was blown dry and put into tight curlers per Kyla's instructions. While the curlers cooled, Kyla applied my makeup making me feel as though I was a movie star, though I didn't want to get used to it. The poor hairdresser had to redo my hair three times because nothing seemed to be accurate to Kyla's vision. After starting the second attempt I ended up falling asleep while Kyla held my head up. Every inch of my body was exhausted and I felt I deserved a nap after everything I went through today.

When my hair had finally been pulled up to Kyla's liking I was left to change. I stepped out of the bathroom and into the bedroom to find a beautiful cream cocktail dress laid out on the bed. It was a piece of art with its modern ruching and draping across the left side. As I lifted it up in my hands, I noticed it was almost completely backless. Although the dress was absolutely gorgeous, I couldn't help but be more excited about the midnight blue satin sling back peep-toe platform shoes. They had to be at least four-inch heels with an inch platform at the ball of the foot. I would certainly suffer through whatever pain I needed to in order to keep them on as long as possible.

Taking the dress into the changing area, I slipped into it quickly, and zipped what little of a zipper there was in the back. The dress felt as though it had been made for me as it cinched and hugged what little curves I had left. But I gasped when I saw myself in the full-length mirror. I was standing in a cream-colored dress with my hair piled high on my head with sparkling beads looking similar as I had in my dream. The dress wasn't exact, but the combination of the dress and hair was too much to be ignored. Tonight was supposed to be a magical night, not one where I'm held against my will and bitten again. It wasn't before Jared had attacked me that I was scared of being bitten, I had offered myself to Cameron the first day in the manor. But now it felt too soon. Just as Sam had ruined me with sex, Jared had placed a damper on being bitten.

Still staring at myself in the mirror, a fury began to wage inside of me. Quickly I pulled out all the pins from my hair, flipped over and began to run my fingers through it, trying anything to make myself look different from the dream. When I flipped my hair back up, I was relieved to see that most of the curl held and with a few quick brushes and spurts of hairspray it would be fine. Different.

Just as I was finishing my hair in the bathroom, I heard Cameron calling me from inside the bedroom. Taking a deep breath and one last look in the mirror I opened the bathroom door as I said, "Cam, I think there's something wrong with…the…dress."

Cameron stood impeccably dressed in a jet-black tuxedo, white shirt, and thin black tie. I knew my man was gorgeous, but oh my god.

"Wow," I accidently said out loud.

"What is wrong with the dress?" Cameron said in a panic as he stepped over to me and inspected the dress up and down.

It was adorable to see him like this. Of all things that he could be concerned about, his clothing obsessive disorder was taking over and I couldn't help but prey on it.

"Well, the entire back of the dress seems to be missing. You should really give the designer hell. I mean this is really shoddy work if you ask me."

The dead eyes that Cameron gave me in response to my snide comment made me think he wasn't amused.

"You are teasing me."

"Yes. Yes I am, but you deserve it by picking out a dress that's this revealing."

"I think you look stunning," he said lovingly.

"Well I hope so since I have to stand next to you all night," I said and walked to the bed to slip into my new shoes. "Seriously, Cam, you should definitely think about wearing a suit every day."

"There was a time when that was the fashion. I have to say sometimes I miss those days."

"Why should you miss them? I'm sure you have every suit you ever wore in the closet. You could start a new trend."

I had to admit I was on fire, although I wasn't sure where this added sarcasm was coming from. It could have been the nerves, or it could have been the fact that I was feeling completely inadequate in Cameron's presence. When I looked over my shoulder to see how much trouble I was in for my last comment, I was surprised to find Cameron giving me a raised brow and my favorite crooked smile. Melt my heart.

"Love, it is natural to be nervous," he said, knowing me better than I thought. Then he reached into his jacket pocket and pulled out a set of surgical scissors. "Now for a few final touches."

I offered him my injured arm and he carefully cut away the gauze. Gently he turned my wrist over to examine what was left of my wound. The scar on the back of my hand had all but disappeared, but the deepest part of the cut on my forearm was still raised and red and very visible. Cameron kissed the scar softly causing goose bumps to rise all over my body, which of course he noticed and smiled at his achievement.

As was often the case, just as Cameron and I were having a romantic moment, Kyla came energetically through the door with Alex and Devin in tow. The boys were also dressed in tuxedos whereas Kyla was in a revealing violet silk dress that only made her fiery hair glow brighter as it cascaded down the length of her back in perfect ringlets.

"Cameron, I thought I told you that you couldn't see Brianna until…my god, Brianna, what have you done to your hair," Kyla shouted.

"It fell?"

All the fire from before had been doused. I couldn't even come up with a good lie, let alone be brave enough to tell her the truth.

Kyla let out an exasperated sigh, "Let me see if I can catch the hairdresser. We don't have much time…"

"Kyla," Cameron said calmly, taking her arm in one hand to stop her from leaving the room, "just because the woman in the picture had her hair up, does not mean that Brianna has to look exactly the same."

Kyla opened and closed her mouth trying to find something to say, but in the end just shook her head in acquiescence. "Fine. Let's do gifts then?"

"Gifts?" I asked, suddenly worried.

"Of course," Kyla replied. "It's tradition. The newly claimed hybrid always gets gifts. The first one is from Victor."

Slowly I took the velvet box from Kyla's outstretched hand, completely surprised and skeptical that Victor would have bought something for me. When I opened the box, I gasped at two large sapphire earrings intricately surrounded and hung by diamonds.

"This is from Victor?"

Kyla scrunched her eyebrows together and tilted her head as she said, "I picked them out, but they are from him. Why do you look so surprised?"

"Brianna is under the impression that Father does not care for her," Cameron answered before I could open my mouth.

Kyla shook her head. "That's absolutely not true. Victor just doesn't show it. Actually, he can be worse than Devin if you can imagine."

Devin didn't react to Kyla's dig. In all honesty he looked quite bored sitting on the back edge of the couch. Cameron held the velvet box while I put the earrings in my ears one at a time. They were extremely heavy, and the throbbing coming from my earlobes reminded me how long it had been since I had worn earrings.

"So since you've decided to wear your hair down, at least keep it back, otherwise we won't see them," Kyla said slightly irritated, but she continued her gift giving and held out her hands to Alex who gave her two items from within his inside pockets. "I brought you some gloves in case we needed to cover the scar on your arm," Kyla said as she extended me a pair of cream opera length gloves.

"No," I said too quickly, and unfortunately too loud. "No gloves."

I tried to smile, but the damage had been done. Everyone in the room looked at me like I was insane.

"O-okay then, this is from me and Alex," Kyla said as she offered me another velvet box. This one, however, was larger and more rectangular than Victor's. She was practically vibrating with excitement, and when I opened the large box, I stopped breathing for a moment.

"Kyla, this is way too much," I said looking down at the wide, white gold bracelet with scrolling sparkling diamonds creating the look of flowers and vines. My hands became numb as I realized that it was the same bracelet from my dream. Cameron noticed the blood draining from my cheeks and stabilized me with an arm at my waist and the other hand under the elaborate bracelet's box. Suddenly everyone in the room was on the defensive, and I hated myself for causing that reaction. "I'm sorry, it's just too…overwhelming. Kyla, it's beautiful. I don't know what to say."

Kyla bounced for joy, clapping her hands lightly as she said, "Don't say anything. Let's just hope it covers that scar."

Kyla swiftly took the bracelet from the box and fastened the three clasps around my wrist, masking most of the red scar underneath. Even with the low light in the room, the bracelet sparkled like the fourth of July. I hugged Kyla tightly and thanked her again, it was certainly more than I deserved.

When I released her, I noticed everyone in the room straighten up and look to Cameron whose cheerful demeanor suddenly stiffened.

Kyla shook her head at Cameron as she said, "Well? Are you going to let him in or not?"

"Let who in?"

"Jared's outside," Kyla said softly and looked around me to see if Cameron was going to explain, but when he didn't speak, she rolled her eyes and said, "Victor released Jared this afternoon. He's standing right outside asking Cameron permission to come in, but he's talking soft enough so only we can hear him. He doesn't want to upset you, he just wants to talk."

"Let him in, Alex," I said over Kyla's shoulder noticing that Cameron's head shot up in surprise.

Alex nodded in my direction, but kept his eyes on Cameron for any major opposition, which he received none. Alex opened the door slowly to reveal a demurer version of the Jared I was used to seeing. He stood nervously in the doorway holding a large wrapped package and looking from Alex to Devin to Kyla and then to Cameron who refused to look in his direction. When Alex stepped aside and waved him in, Jared finally rested his eyes on me and kept them there as he stepped cautiously into the room. Like his brothers, he was dressed in a tux, however, his shirt collar was open and his bowtie hung untied around his neck. I smiled and went to take a step toward him when Cameron stretched his arm across me.

Jared abruptly stopped his progression, his hurt expression burning a hole in the floor. I pushed Cameron's arm down gently, and threw my arms around Jared. The package he held in his hands dropped to the floor making a loud thud as he put his arms around me. The sound made me laugh through the few tears I couldn't hold back.

"That's probably not good," I said, trying as always to lighten a tense situation.

"I'm sorry, Bibi. I'm so sorry," Jared whispered without acknowledging my attempt at humor and then released me. "I didn't mean what I said. I'm...I'm such an asshole. And if you never forgive me, or never want to see me again, I totally understand. I just didn't know how to...I'd never had anyone..." Jared's nostrils flared as his breathing quickened, and anyone else might have thought it was anger, but I knew he was trying to keep himself from getting upset in front of his brothers.

"I miss her too, Jared. I'm sorry I kept pushing you to talk about it. I was already feeling guilty enough..."

"Bibi, what I said to you was so...horrible. You took the brunt because you were there. I'm sorry. You're like my big sis, and...and I love ya."

I shook my head unable to speak through the tears that were threatening to come again and hugged Jared one more time.

"Okay," Kyla interrupted, "not that I want to stop this little family moment, but Bri, you have to stop crying. We don't have time to do your makeup again." Jared and I broke from our embrace and laughed along with

Alex. "What?" Kyla asked defensively, looking between the three of us.

Jared knelt down and picked up the package that had fallen on the floor.

"Here, it's for you. It took me like two hours to wrap it," he said as he handed me the package wrapped in newspaper. I ripped the paper off to reveal a brand new laptop computer and I shook my head. "Don't even think about giving it back. I know you don't have one anymore, so just take it. And if you try to sell it, I'll know," he said giving me the Jared smile that I missed.

"Yes, it's very nice, Jared, but we have to go downstairs. Brianna has to greet her guests," Kyla nagged and began shooing Alex and Devin out of the room.

"Wait," Devin interjected, handing me his present. "You don't have to open it now, they're just wrist weights."

"Did you seriously buy her wrist weights," Kyla groaned as she pulled Devin out by his elbow leaving only me, Jared, and Cameron in the bedroom.

Jared took a step in Cameron's direction, but kept his head down as he addressed his brother in an apprehensive tone. "Cameron, I don't know what to say. I…" he paused, trying to gather himself. "I let you down and I hurt the one person that means everything to you and…she means a lot to me too and I will never forget what I did. I don't know how, but that night after…what I did…I kept seeing flashes of me coming at her, actually seeing me with my fangs out and…" Jared paused again and looked between me and Cameron as we both realized that Jared must have seen my dreams that night, a side effect of having my blood in him. "I hate myself for what I did. And…if you want me to stay away I will, but just so you know you've always been like a real big brother to me, and it will totally suck if you kick me out of your life, but it's what I deserve. You're the last person I would ever want to hate me."

Cameron stood silent while Jared poured out his heart, and it was evident that he was crushed when Cameron didn't respond in any way. With his head hung low, he took a step back towards the door.

"Jared, wait," Cameron said finally, "at least button up your shirt and tie."

"Dude, Kyla keeps giving me these bowties that you actually have to tie. I don't know how to do that shit," Jared responded with a big smile as the unsaid man to man apology was accepted while Cameron tied his younger brother's bowtie.

"Next time you are going to learn how to do it yourself, little brother. A gentleman always knows how to tie a bowtie."

"Or a gentleman always has an older brother who can do it for him."

The two of them laughed lightly as they gave each other a forgiving hug before Jared left the room. Finally having a moment to ourselves, I gave Cameron a gentle kiss on the lips, trying not to ruin my lipstick at the threat of death by Kyla.

"Thank you," I whispered to him.

"Like you said, if you can forgive him, I can. Shall we?" Cameron said as he extended his arm, allowing me to wrap my hand around his elbow. "I have to say it is difficult to get used to you at this height."

"I like it. I don't have to get up on my tiptoes to kiss you."

Cameron stopped just before we exited the room and searched my face so intensely it was hard to breathe.

"You are exquisite, Brianna Morgan, both inside and out. You make me a better man and I cannot tell you how honored I am to be on your arm. No one will shine as brightly as you tonight, my love."

"I only shine because of you," I replied truthfully. His feelings for me made me stronger and I felt his love radiating in every cell of my body.

In that moment I realized I truly had everything I needed. I had a man who adored me, a grandfather who loved me like a daughter, a girlfriend who accepted me for who I was no matter how bizarre the situation, and three new brothers and a sister who welcomed me as one of their own. I didn't need my father's affection to make me happy; I had all the family I needed.

Knowing that Kyla would be shouting up the stairs any minute, Cameron kissed me gently on the forehead before leading me down the hallway.

"Tell me three things I don't know about you," I said as Cameron lifted me into his arms and carried me down the stairs. There was no way I was walking down three flights of stairs in these heels.

Cameron thought for a moment and then began, "Since you were so worried about my favorite color this morning, I will admit that it has changed over the years. Even though you might assume it was black, it is actually the color of your earrings and shoes, a very rich, dark blue."

I reached up and touched one of the large sapphires that dangled from my ear thinking that Kyla probably knew that when she picked them out. Cameron smiled as he saw the realization on my face.

"Let me think, what else?" he continued. "Well, you make me weak in the knees when you put your fingers through my hair. And now that I have been home for more than a day at a time, I realize that I am happiest when my siblings and I are all together." Cameron set me down when we reached the bottom of the stairs, then took my hand and kissed each one of my fingers gently. "Now your turn," he said and pulled my arm through the crook of his elbow and escorted me down the main corridor to the ballroom.

"Er...well...my favorite color is green, you make me weak in the knees all the time, and I am so nervous I think I'm going to puke," I said, taking in a deep breath as the tall ballroom doors came into view.

"Please, just not on the tux, my love," he laughed.

"You're going to be with me the whole time, right?"

"Angel, it will be hard getting rid of me with you looking like this," he replied, smiling affectionately as he softly touched my cheek with the back of his fingers. "I love you."

"You better," I replied.

I took in another deep breath just before we stepped into the grand ballroom of the Warrior manor where tonight an elusive but recently famous hybrid was being claimed by her infamous vampire father in an evening that was sure never to be forgotten. I only hoped it was for the right reasons.

Chapter Forty-seven

Brianna

Gabriel, Tao, Lev and Isla, Maxim, Connor, Skylar, Stavros and Ellen, Sabine, no Sable, no Sybil, crap! The female Warrior just walked away and I've already forgotten her name, but after the last hour of a steady stream of people coming through the traditional receiving line, I was lucky to remember my own name at this point. Cameron had told me that all sixty-two Warriors would be at the party this evening. Essentially, I was meeting the extended family. I wasn't surprised to see that the majority of Warriors were men, or that most of them had come alone. Not to say they were all like Devin, there were definitely degrees, but even some of the female Warriors made Jazlyn look like Holly Homemaker.

The ballroom was beautiful and exuded royalty. Chandeliers hung from above, and candelabras seven feet tall flickered soft light around the room. An orchestra was tuning in the far corner while another gentleman played soft music from a DJ's station next to them. Being my first vampire party, I half expected fountains of blood everywhere, but none were to be found. Waiters carried trays of gourmet appetizers for the humans while all bloodletting was to be done behind closed doors. Though the room was gorgeous, it was also a terrifying replica of the room I had seen in my dream - right down to the wall of open doors leading out to a terrace. My heart nearly stopped when Cameron escorted me in, and since then he had been keeping a particularly close eye on me.

"Brianna, you remember Julian," Cameron said next to me in his upmost pleasant tone, even though we both knew it was all for show. Julian was a jerk, and neither Cam nor I liked him, though the feeling seemed mutual as he shook my hand tersely and moved on.

"Always a pleasure," I said to his back with a wide, condescending smile which quickly dropped when I turned back to see Cameron raising his brow at me. "Maddy!" I shouted as I looked past Cameron's scolding look.

"You know, Miss Morgan, I don't bother coming to many of these things, but I have to say you are the most stunning hybrid I have ever seen. Just look at you," Maddy said as I bent down to hug her since she was about seven inches shorter than me in these heels. When I released her, she looked over at Cameron and pointed her finger at him. "A little too skinny though, and I'm holding you responsible, Mr. Burke."

Cameron gave Maddy his most charming smile before taking her hand and kissing it gently.

"Madelyn, as always, you take me to task. I assure you that Brianna is in perfect health, but I will see to it that she gains weight to your satisfaction."

Maddy twisted her lips together in a smug smile. "I'm holding you to that, Mr. Burke, and you stop that Madelyn nonsense right now."

"Forgive me, Maddy, I apologize most sincerely," Cameron replied and bowed deeply.

"Mads!" Jared shouted as he pushed his way through the crowd toward the receiving line. "I've been waiting for you all night," he said to Maddy who merely smiled and blushed as she took his hand. And though he didn't have to, Jared went out of his way to make Maddy happy, knowing who he reminded her of. Just another reason why he was so endearing.

As I watched Jared part the crowd to allow Maddy to pass, I felt cool hands take mine which startled me to look back and see Lanashell standing in front of me.

"It always seems quite pointless to enter a room after Madelyn," she said, giving me a warm smile.

"She is quite a lady," I replied.

"As are you. I have been hearing some good things about your progress," Lana said as she handed me a little blue box tied up with a pretty white ribbon (yes *that* kind of little blue box).

"I guess that depends on who you ask. Eris would definitely say otherwise."

"I don't think anyone could ever live up to your father's expectations. He sets the bar pretty high."

"Well, I'm certainly going to try and knock it right off his head," I replied, feeling as though she was telling me I would never be good enough. Cam, feeling my tension, put his strong arm around me and kissed me gently on my temple. Lana nodded awkwardly, causing her short, angled hair to fall in front of her face as she walked away to join the other guests.

"So this is the famous Brianna Morgan," a sandy blonde-haired vampire said to me as he kissed my hand. "Damn, Cameron, I heard she was pretty, but aren't you a lucky son of a bitch."

Cameron laughed as the unknown vampire shook his hand and patted him on the back with the other.

"Brianna, this very inappropriate gentleman is Aidan Pierce. Aidan, this is Brianna, and yes she makes me quite a lucky son of a bitch."

I raised my eyebrows at Cameron since he rarely swore, at least in front of me. This Aidan character seemed to bring out a side of Cam I hadn't seen before.

He and Cameron were similar in height and build, though Aidan was hardly as charming, which was obvious when he said, "Damn, Brianna, you look good enough to drink, but I guess that's Cameron's job, huh?"

"Wow, you really are inappropriate," I said, feeling the blood rushing to my cheeks. "I'm hoping you aren't a Warrior, because I'd really hate to have to ask Cameron to punch one of his own siblings."

Both Cameron and Aidan burst into laughter.

"A Warrior? Please. No way Victor could control this handsome specimen," Aidan said as he took a step back and smoothed the front of his tux.

"It is good to see you are still modest," Cameron said, shaking his head. "Brianna, Aidan is a Gatherer."

"Former Gatherer," Aidan corrected. "Consulting money was just too good to pass up."

"He is also a Tracker, one of the best. Just ask him."

"One of? Try *the* best Tracker."

"Sure, Aidan, just keep telling yourself that."

"Good to see you again, Cameron," Aidan said, giving Cameron a punch in the arm. "Oh, and the package has been delivered. Sorry it's late."

Aidan walked away, disappearing into a crowd of women who seemed to flock around him. He was handsome, not as chiseled as Cameron, but good looking. But there was something that bothered me about him. Maybe it was his cockiness. I was a little surprised that Cam liked him so much. Then again, I had only known Cam for a couple of months; I couldn't even begin to judge his friends.

"What package, Cam?"

Cameron didn't reply, merely gave me his crooked smile. Before I could press him, Kyla stormed over and took Cameron by his arm, pulling him over to a circle that included Devin, Alex, the orchestra leader, and a couple of others I didn't recognize. Something was wrong since Kyla didn't even say boo to me. Realizing I still had Lana's gift in my hand, I placed it on the table behind me that was embarrassingly overflowing, shook the hand of one last vampire (Peter, Pace, Percy, who knows), and stepped over to the circle of vampires who were bickering softly.

"Okay, what the heck is going on?" I said as I pushed my way into their little gathering. Kyla didn't even glance my way. Instead, she looked like she was going to kill the short orchestra conductor standing opposite her holding his baton protectively against his chest. "Ky, what's going on?"

Kyla didn't take her eyes off her prey, so Cameron answered instead as he searched the space between us, finally curling his fingers gently around mine.

"Bri," he said softly, "it is tradition that a female's claiming ceremony be opened with a dance between father and daughter. Apparently, Eris insisted that this happen."

"But he's not even here," I said, trying to keep my other thoughts about that to myself.

"Precisely," Kyla shouted, throwing her arms up. "It's been over an hour, we need to start without him. People are asking when we're going to start the ceremony. Now just go and start waving your wand, little man, or I'll wave it for you."

The conductor shook his head causing Kyla to take a step toward him, but Alex's arm encircled her from above.

"He's afraid of Eris, isn't he," I whispered in Cameron's ear who nodded. "Excuse me, sir," I said to the conductor, "I'm Eris's daughter, and honestly I don't want to dance with my father anyway, so I could care less what he asked you to do. Now go play something before my girlfriend breaks that baton in two. It's really for your own good."

But the conductor stood his ground, shaking his head once again and causing groans from everyone in the circle.

"May I be of some assistance?"

I turned to my right to see Victor standing next to me, only coming up to my shoulder.

"Father," Cameron began, "Eris has not yet arrived and the Maestro will not play until he does."

Victor nodded as he stepped in front of the conductor. "Maestro, you have been paid for your service, have you not?" The conductor nodded slowly, unable to keep eye contact with the Warrior leader. "Then I suggest you play." The conductor opened his mouth to speak, but Victor interrupted, "I will handle any fallout from Eris. I assure you he will know that you had to start at the threat of death."

The conductor nodded nervously as he backed away and crossed the room. Miraculously the orchestra was playing within thirty seconds and everyone cleared the floor to make room for the traditional father-daughter dance, although there wasn't a *father* to speak of.

"Don't just stand there, do something," Kyla whispered angrily to Cameron, pushing him from behind.

Cam took my hand to lead me onto the dance floor, but Victor interceded. "Child, I must object. The tradition is for a father and daughter to open the ceremony, and since I am technically the only father in this little congregation, I will be having the honor of dancing with Ms. Morgan."

Everyone, including Devin, smiled as Victor escorted me to the center of the dance floor. Cameron nodded encouragingly to me when he saw the sheer panic behind my eyes. The first time Victor and I spoke he had threatened me. The second, I had lied to him about what Jared had done to me, and I'm sure he knew it. Now I was expected to dance with him in front of everyone and pretend to be happy about it. I hated my life right now.

Victor stretched out my right hand, placed his other around my waist, and began shuffling me around the floor. I'll admit it was a little awkward having him be almost eye level to my breasts as we danced.

"Brianna," Victor said with a relaxed smile, "I believe we got off on the wrong foot and that was totally my doing." My breath caught in my throat at his admission. "I can see that I was wrong to judge you, and I hope that you can forgive my actions. Brianna, I love all my children dearly, but Cameron has always been...special to me...and..."

"And you were afraid of losing him," I interrupted. "Victor, I love Cameron. I didn't think it was possible, but I love him. And I know what you mean, he is so special and I thank God and *you* for sending him to me."

"You should really thank your father for that. He insisted on Cameron being sent."

"For my sake, let's just say you sent him. I'd rather not have to be grateful to my father for anything right now." Victor laughed as he spun me around, causing the murmurs around us to grow louder. I had a feeling that it was a rare sight to see Victor spinning a woman around on a dance floor. "All kidding aside, I know how much Cameron respects you and loves his brothers and Kyla, and I love them, too. They have all thrown themselves in harm's way to protect me, and I just want you to know that I would do the same. I'd give my life for any one of them if I needed to."

"I have a feeling Cameron would be opposed to that."

I laughed. "He made me promise never to be a martyr, but if it's a choice between my life and his, I'm always going to choose his. I know no one wants to talk about this, but that's why this whole Elaina nonsense really has me aggravated. Everyone says I have to survive, I can't be taken by Elaina, yadda, yadda, yadda. But honestly if I came toe to toe with her and I could save any of you by surrendering to her, I would. I am no more important than anyone else in this room."

Victor smiled as he turned me under his arm. The height difference definitely made it difficult. Once I was facing him again, he stepped back and bowed deeply in front of me. When he stood back up, he removed a gold circular pin from within his pocket causing another round of soft murmurs and gasps from the crowd. I looked back to where Cameron and the others were standing, and from the sight of Kyla jumping up and down, and the congratulatory pats that Cameron was receiving, I assumed the pin meant something. Of course, I was clueless.

Victor extended his fangs and pricked his index finger. He dipped the stem of the pin into the tiny bubble of blood that had formed and then fastened the pin to the strap of my dress. I was a little upset that my new dress now had blood on it, but I clamped my mouth shut. With another bow, Victor backed away from me revealing an elated Cameron behind him. After shaking hands with his father, Cameron took me into his arms, his cool hand resting on my exposed back as he began gliding me across the floor.

"What does the pin mean?" I asked quietly.

"Victor has officially made you a member of our coven. Love, you are a Warrior now, the first ever hybrid Warrior," he said beaming.

As he twirled me around the floor, I saw that he too had a small circular pin on his lapel that I hadn't noticed there before. But then I saw it everywhere - glimmering from Alex's tie while he turned Kyla under his arm, flashing from Jared's collar while awkwardly trying to dance with

Maddy. All around us were little gold pins telling me that I was now one of them.

"But why?" I asked, feeling my self-consciousness closing in.

Cameron squeezed my hand gently and shrugged. "That I could not tell you, my love. He must have had his reasons. Something you said perhaps?"

Something I said. Hmm, well, it could be that I proved to him I was not some money-grubbing slut looking to take his favorite son away. That in fact, I loved Cameron so much I would lay down my life for him, or his siblings. Cameron let go of my hand and completely encircled me with his arms while others whisked by. It was a little moment of our own, one where no one else existed. I could feel his energy radiating through me as he pressed his hands firmly into my bare back while he kissed me in the middle of the dance floor.

When he pulled away, I noticed the light sparkle off my wide diamond bracelet and suddenly images of my dream flashed before me, causing my knees to buckle. Thankfully Cameron caught me, his smile changing quickly as he said, "Angel, are you alright?"

Not wanting to bring him into my crazy Brianna world, or ruin the joy of the evening, I lied.

"Yes, I-I'm fine."

Although he wasn't fully convinced, his eyes focused on something over my shoulder. "Good, because now it is time for my gift to you."

"Cam, no," I whined, feeling embarrassed enough about the gifts I had already received.

"Well, if you want to tell him to go home, then by all means," Cameron said as he pointed to someone behind me.

I turned around to see Daddy O's little gray head bobbing through the crowd in our direction, pulling and tugging at his tuxedo shirt and tie.

"Dang, Lil Bri, ya know I don't like a wearin' a monkey suit," he said, but the rest of his complaints were muffled into my shoulder as I threw my arms around him. "Now, now, don't go wrinklin' the dang thing," he laughed. "Well good grief, since when ya been six feet tall?" I smiled and quickly took off my beautiful blue shoes and handed them to Cameron. "Now you're my Lil Bri again. Lookin' good, sugar, little skinny though," he said and then leaned over to Cam. "Son, I'm holdin' ya responsible."

Cameron sighed, but then smiled as he extended his hand. "Oliver, always good to see you."

"Now, son, I think we're past handshakes," Daddy O said and pulled

Cameron in for a hug.

"I see you survived the plane ride. I was getting worried after you missed your connection," Cam said, still holding Daddy O by the shoulder.

"Good-ness. The first plane was late, then we missed the second, thank goodness that Aidan fella can do that thing you guys do or we woulda never gotten here."

"Aidan?" I said, looking at Cameron with eyes wide. "Is Daddy O the package?"

Cam shrugged and smiled sheepishly. "I could not send a Warrior, so I needed someone I could trust. Aidan was available so I called in a favor."

My nose started to tingle from the threatening tears as I nuzzled my head underneath his chin.

"Thank you for always knowing what I need. Give everything else away."

"Including these?" he asked, swinging my sling backs on his index finger.

"Okay, maybe keep those."

Cameron smiled and turned me back to my grandfather who was waiting patiently for my attention.

"Oliver, she is all yours."

Daddy O picked up my hands and started slowly moving me around the floor, reminding me of how we used to dance when I was a little girl in stocking feet.

"Sugar, why ya cryin'?"

"I just missed you," I replied as I wiped my tears away. "I'm just happy that after all these years we're finally getting a father-daughter dance together."

"Bri honey, this ain't a weddin', is it?"

"No!" I said too loudly, causing the couples around us to stare. "I just meant that we've never gotten to do this."

"That's 'cuz ya'll decided to elope and not tell anyone you were gettin' married in the first place." Touché Daddy O. "Speakin' of," he whispered into me, "what's goin' on with that?"

"It's over. Sam won't be bothering me ever again."

"Well that's good to hear. You gotta good man now, even though he's a vampire of all things, but even a vampire is better than Sam. I mean look at this place, this is some fancy shindig."

I laughed, but then had a twinge of guilt. "Daddy O, did Cameron explain what tonight is about?"

Daddy O twisted his lips around and nodded his head. "Somethin' about your vampire daddy sayin' you're his daughter. Dat right? Cameron sorta explained it, but I had to have that Aidan fella explain it to me again. I just didn't understand why he has to claim ya. I mean yur his kid, what's there to claim?"

"I know, right? I said to Cameron that it should be the other way around, especially after today."

"You two not gettin' along?"

"No, we're not."

"Why's that?"

"Because he's an asshole."

"Language, little girl," Daddy O scolded.

Not wanting to have Daddy O feel any sympathy for Eris, I pulled my bracelet up to expose what was left of my scar.

"He did this to me today. I have half a mind to leave when he gets here. Try and let him claim me then."

"How'd ya get that?"

"He cut me with a sword."

"What in tar nation were ya doin' playin' around with a sword?"

"It's part of my training...I have to...see he...it's a long story."

"Why haven't ya told me any a this?"

"I keep trying to call, but you're never home. Where have you been? You've never been out of the house this much."

Daddy O sighed deeply, making his lips buzz together as the air came out of his mouth.

"Don't be askin' questions you don't wanna know the answers to."

"Do you have a girlfriend or something?"

"A course not."

"Then what?"

"I've been spendin' time with yur mamma."

"Why?"

"Lil Bri, don't forget she was my daughter before you were." I scoffed at his remark, flabbergasted that he was right. "Now I knew you'd be mad which was why I didn't tell ya. But she's different ever since Cameron did that thing on her."

"It's called a Glamour, and it doesn't work on her very well. So whatever she's feeding you is an act."

"She asks about you."

"She wants something."

"Yes, she wants to know how her daughter is."

"Bullshit," I said and then regretting it right after. "Sorry. What have you told her?"

"Nothin'. She asks if I've spoken to ya, and I say no because I haven't. She asks if I know where you are, and I tell her that a young woman like you isn't gonna tell an old man like me what yur doin' all the time."

"She wants something," I repeated.

Daddy O and I agreed to disagree as the music from the orchestra was replaced by a fade in of R&B coming from the DJ's station.

"Well, I think that's my cue to leave the dance floor," Daddy O said, taking a step back from me.

"No wait, I'll come with you."

"Sugar, I'm gonna be here all night, now go have fun. Besides, it looks like your friend there wants to dance with ya."

I looked behind me to see Jared dancing toward me, waving for me to meet him.

"But Dad…"

"Now go, I need ta sit down anyway. There's food, right? Real food?"

"Yes, there's food all over. I'll come find you."

Daddy O waved me away just as Jared took my arm and pulled me over to his place on the dance floor.

"Bibi, I requested this song specifically for you," he said as the beat to the song shook the chandeliers above us.

Jared and the other younger vampires and humans looked like cool young people dancing the latest moves, whereas I looked like the awkward country white girl trying to find the beat. I looked over to see Aidan laughing at me while Cameron looked sympathetic as Jared kept trying to get me to move around. Finally giving up, I retreated back to the safety of Cameron's arms, relieving him of his shoe sitting duties.

The music transitioned between the orchestra and the DJ for the rest of the night so that vampires of all eras could enjoy the dancing festivities. It had been three hours since the party started, and still no sign of my father. A part of me was hoping he wouldn't show, but there was a worry in the back of my mind. However, no one let me dwell on his absence. In fact, I danced to almost every song, and was constantly eating since both Daddy O and Maddy kept sending waiters with trays of food my way.

But now the orchestra had taken over and I was back in the arms of my Cam, however, my feet were screaming at me. My shoes were beautiful, but with great beauty came great pain. After three hours on my feet, I was ready to go barefoot. Sensing my hesitation as he tried to move me around on the floor, Cameron stopped slowly, brushed my hair out of my eyes, and kissed me. His cool fingers trailed down my back, sending shivers up my spine and causing him to smile on top of my lips.

"Shall we go out to the terrace, love?" he asked, taking my hand.

My eyes flew open as the words that came out of his mouth rang familiar. Not waiting for me to respond, he led me out the doors where I caught a glimpse of myself in the glass, however, looking terrified rather than the elegant creature from my dream. Once outside I noticed the expansive gardens surrounding the wide terrace and my heart sank. Change it, you can change it.

"Bri?" Cameron said, wondering why I had stopped just outside the door.

"Hmmm?"

"Come with me, love," he said, gesturing toward the far end of the terrace where my nightmare would begin.

"No," I replied loudly, startling Cameron.

"What is it, Bri?"

"N-nothing," I stuttered as I looked around. "Let's go down by that fountain instead. I can sit down and get these deathtraps off my feet."

Cameron didn't buy it, but nodded and led me down the wide stone steps to the enormous fountain that showered water over floating lotus blossoms in its pool. I was hot and sticky from dancing and the mist from the fountain felt refreshing on my face, as did Cameron's cool hands on my feet as he massaged them. A girl could get used to this, I thought as the fears I had moments before began to fade.

"The gardens are so beautiful," I said, resting back on my hands. "I can't believe I haven't been out here."

"That is because my brother and your father are slave drivers that torture you day in and day out, and I am so neglectful towards you that I have not brought you out here."

"Stop that right now, Cameron Jackson, you are not neglectful."

"We will have differing opinions on that," he replied with a smiled, but I knew he wasn't kidding. "It has been a while since I have been in the gardens. I forgot how beautiful they are."

"It's ironic that the leader of the ferocious Warriors has such a woman's garden. I have never seen so many flowers except in an arboretum."

"This area here is actually part of the midnight garden."

"What is that?"

"Victor may be a soldier at heart, but he understands that newer vampires may miss some of the things you saw during the day, as he did when he was Turned. So wherever he lives, he creates a garden where the flowers bloom at night so that everyone can enjoy a little beauty. Actually, they remind me of you."

"How's that?"

He shrugged as he replied, "They may bloom late, but they are amazing and beautiful when the conditions are right. Just like you."

"I feel like you're about to talk to me about going through puberty."

"*Brianna,*" Cameron groaned playfully. "Look at how far you have come. A few months ago, you would never have had the courage to pick up a sword, or stand up to your father, really stand up to anyone for that matter. You just needed the right conditions."

"And the right man," I replied.

Cameron stopped massaging my feet and leaned over to kiss me the way I wished he kissed me every time. His cool lips pushed against mine while his tongue slipped in and out of my mouth, teasing the desire within me. I felt his fingers slowly trail up my leg as his lips moved down my neck causing a wave of sudden panic to come over me. Not knowing what to do, I opened my mouth and let the first words I could think of come out.

"That tickles."

His body tensed as he lifted his eyes to mine and I was guilt ridden at the sight of the sadness in them.

"I have made you uncomfortable."

"No, no, of course not, honey. You really were tickling me," I lied and hoped he believed me.

"Honey?" he said as he sat upright, resuming his massaging of my feet. "That is something I certainly have never been called."

"Would you rather I call you Pooky?"

"Absolutely not," he answered, squeezing my feet harder than necessary. "So you have not told me how you like your celebration. Is it to your satisfaction?"

"Of course it is. A little too much like a wedding, though."

"How so?"

"I'm in a white dress, you're in a tux, food, dancing, receiving line, gifts, aching feet."

Cameron nodded, but was silent for a few moments before he said, "Would you ever consider getting married again?" I actually stopped breathing, and Cameron absolutely noticed. "Bri, it is just a question and not one that you need to answer. I was just curious."

"Do you?"

"Why, are you proposing to me?" he said, looking at me through the sides of eyes with a crooked smile.

"I just can't, Cameron. Marriage is...pain and...and...for crying out loud I'm still married."

I jerked my feet out of Cameron's grasp and put them on the ground as my head fell into my hands. I felt a whoosh of air as Cameron knelt down in front of me, stroking my hair.

"Brianna, my love, I am very aware you are still legally married, and that marriage has bad connotations for you." I lifted my head from my hands to see Cameron's loving eyes staring right into mine. "It was insensitive of me to ask. I really was just curious. Since the first day I met you, I never wanted to be without you. I am just uncertain as to how you feel about that."

Not knowing what to say, I crushed my lips against his as new worries came over me. I wanted to be with him, forever even, but how would that happen? Like Eris and Seraphina? After a while Cameron would look like my grandson rather than my lover, and then what would I do. Hot tears trickled from the sides of my eyes only to be wiped away by Cameron's cool fingers.

"What is it, love? Please tell me."

"Sorry," I sniffled and wiped away the remaining tears. "Just a weepy woman tonight."

Cameron opened his mouth to say something, but quickly shut it and stood to face Jazlyn who was propped up on one elbow on the terrace ledge.

"Ah, young love. How disgusting," she said in her deep, sensual voice.

"Good evening, Sister, I had almost given up hope that you were coming."

"You would have liked that, I'm sure. Father is looking for you."

Cameron sighed and I waved him away. "I need a few more minutes."

He nodded and bent down to kiss me, holding my hand to his heart. "Love me?"

"Always," I relied as I pulled his hand to rest on my heart.

After one last kiss he was a blur of black and white as he ran up the stairs while Jazlyn made her way down. Jazlyn's outfit made my jaw drop. She was wearing a skintight black dress with a plunging neckline down to her navel and a skirt so short I marveled at how she was walking down the stairs without flashing her fine china.

I had told Cameron I needed a few minutes, but with the last visions I had of Jazlyn I didn't want to spend them with her. Casually I put my shoes back on, grinding my teeth as I tried to stand in them.

"Brianna, wait," Jazlyn said as she came to my side and pulled my arm to sit me back down. From a place that was a mystery to me, she pulled out a small black velvet box and presented it to me. When I didn't take it at first, she took my hand roughly and placed the box in the middle of my palm. "It is a gift, Brianna."

But I knew exactly what it was. It was a ring that would melt my hand as it had in my dream. Goddamn it, all my dreams were running together into one night of hell. When I didn't open the box, Jazlyn reached over and lifted the lid to reveal the exact circular onyx ring encircled with diamonds.

"Cameron gave it to me years ago so I thought you would want it. I certainly never wear it. So are you going to put it on or just stare at it?"

I froze. I simply looked at Jazlyn with terror on my face, and she looked back at me as though I had lost my mind. Which I was pretty sure I had.

"Brianna, we need you."

Startled, I looked up at the terrace to see Cameron standing at the top of the steps looking down at us. Jazlyn rolled her eyes at me and then ran to her brother's side.

"Your girlfriend's weird," she said and then walked back into the party.

Cameron joined me as I stood, still holding the open ring box in my hand.

"I remember that ring. I gave it to Jazlyn for her birthday. Good to see she liked it," he said as he took the ring from the box.

"Cam, no!" I shouted and batted the ring out of his hand, but he quickly caught it in the air with the other.

"Brianna, what is wrong? You have been on edge ever since you came out here. Please tell me why," he said as he secured the ring on his little finger.

It didn't burn him, his hand didn't melt. Nothing happened, nothing! It only demonstrated that my dreams were once again sketchy and I looked crazy.

"I'm sorry, Cam. I had a weird dream about that ring, but it was obviously wrong."

"Do you want to tell me…"

"No. I just want to forget about it."

I could tell he was frustrated by the way he rested his hands on his hips and looked down at the ground. Knowing he wasn't going to get any further with that conversation he changed topics. "Your father has arrived and would like to start the ceremony."

"Is Sera with him?"

"Sadly no, and he has not said why. He is, however, insisting we start the ceremony immediately. So on that note, may I escort you back inside?"

"I'm sorry about before."

"Sorry for the weeping or hitting a family heirloom out of my hand?"

"Ohmygod, is it really a family heirloom?"

"Hardly," he teased. "Although it is extremely old, I think heirlooms have to have some kind of sentimental value, and Jazlyn certainly does not have that for this ring," he said, taking the ring off of his finger and examining it closely. "It looks like she changed the setting a little. Perhaps it had worn down. Shall we see if it fits?" Cautiously I extended my right hand and Cam slid the ring on my fourth finger. Unfortunately, it only got down as far as my knuckle before it was too tight. "Left hand maybe?" I gasped softly as Cameron stifled his laugh and took my left hand. "I promise there will be no kneeling, no popping of questions," he said as the onyx ring slid perfectly onto my left hand's ring finger. "That did feel nice, though."

Raising an eyebrow, I said, "Let's just cool the marriage talk for a while, okay?"

"You have my word, angel," he replied with a crooked smile as he snaked my arm through the crook of his elbow and led me up the stairs.

When we entered the ballroom, the music had stopped and everyone had gathered to the front of the room where Victor now stood with Eris on the platform in front of the orchestra. Cameron moved me through the crowd where I found Daddy O and pulled him along with us to the front of the ballroom. Standing with Cameron on one side of me and Daddy O on the other, I felt safe, and both of them were squeezing my hand in silent encouragement.

With a loud clap of his hands, Victor called the ceremony to order.

"Welcome, welcome," he announced with a commanding voice. "It is always wonderful to see friends both human and vampire alike, but I am particularly overjoyed to see all my children gathered together for celebration rather than war. And yes, we are here to celebrate. Tonight is about a father claiming a daughter and welcoming her amongst our kind. But not only is she being claimed by her father, but also by our proud Warrior coven. Please welcome her as I present to you our newest Warrior, Brianna Marilena Morgan."

The room burst into thunderous applause and thumping of chests (though I didn't quite get that one). I looked over to Daddy O who was the only one in the room not applauding and I was fearful he was upset by the announcement.

"Daddy O, are you okay?" I whispered as I looked at the wrinkles on his face deepen as he furrowed his brows together.

"Sugar, does that man know he got yur name wrong?"

"I'll explain later," I replied and Daddy O nodded, though he wasn't too pleased about being in the dark, but didn't argue as Victor continued.

"It is now time for me to turn it over to a vampire who needs introduction by face only since his name and history is known by us all. I present to you, Eris."

The room erupted again into applause and chest thumping (which I still didn't get), but it was my turn not to applaud.

Daddy O nudged me as he pointed to the stage and said, "That's yur daddy? He looks more like your brother."

"Tell me something I don't know."

For the first time since we had met in person, my father had his hair down, once again making me think he looked like a beardless Jesus. He was wearing a tux, although without a tie, his collar left open, still giving him that relaxed vibe. Victor bowed slightly as he stepped back to allow Eris full control of the stage and he took one look at me before he spoke.

"Thank you, Victor, as always you and your Warriors are the epitome of honorable vampires," Eris said with his Italian accent dripping from each word. "We are a prideful race, one full of traditions. However, this evening I am stepping away from such traditions." Eris's announcement caused Victor to look at Cameron who merely shrugged while the others around us muttered back and forth to one another. "Being a vampire does not prepare one to be a father. For many of us elders, I believe our age impairs our ability to remember what it was like to be a loving human."

Thankfully Cameron was a vampire, otherwise I would have broken his hand from squeezing it so hard.

"All of you here cheered for my daughter for being inducted as a

Warrior, and I am extremely proud of her accomplishment, too. My Bri-an-na is a beautiful, intelligent, and strong woman, and I am sad to say that it is by no means because of me. What may not be known to many of you, I have been absent from my daughter's life since before her birth. Although I am extremely proud of the person she has become, I must thank the man standing next to her, the man who has been a true father to her, Oliver Morgan. Please, let us show our appreciation for the man who could do what no other vampire could, and that is handle my daughter for thirty-one years."

The crowd applauded as I threw my arms around my grandfather. I wasn't even mad that Eris had told everyone in the room my age. Daddy O truly was a saint.

"Like I said before, this evening I am breaking away from tradition. As is customary with this ceremony, the father claims the child, and I absolutely claim my daughter as my own in front of all of you this evening. But in my case, I have failed to show her the true love and respect she deserves. Therefore, I am asking my Bri-an-na, mia figlia, to instead claim me as her father. To give me yet one more chance to show her I can be the father she wants me to be."

My eyes were bulging out of my head. I had said if I had the choice I wouldn't do it, I wouldn't claim him as my father. But now faced with the choice, I was frozen. I didn't want to be judged by those around me if I refused him, but I also didn't want to be pressured into making the decision either.

I looked at my grandfather, the man who always stood by me whether he liked my decisions or not. "What should I do?"

Daddy O patted my hand gently. "Lil Bri, he's your daddy."

"No, you are. You always have been."

"Nah, sugar. You were always on loan, I knew that," he said, catching a tear from his eye with his finger. "There's nothin' sayin' you can't love the both of us. Now get up there, the man's waitin'."

Almost as if someone else had taken over my body, I stepped onto the stage to join my father, in turn accepting him as such. Was I seriously doing this? Like I said, it was an out of body experience.

Eris threw his arms around me while the crowd applauded and cheered at my acceptance. While he hugged me, he put his lips close to my ear and whispered, "You will never have a reason to be ashamed of me again."

His statement was sincere, and with his true voice rather than the accent that supported his façade. But as soon as he released me, he was the Eris that everyone else thought they knew.

"Mia bella figlia has made me the happiest of men. The one tradition I would like to keep this evening is the presentation of a gift." Eris gestured to Victor who stepped forward with a thin, rectangular wooden box and placed it into Eris's arms. "Bri-an-na, please accept this gift and may they give you the protection they did me so many millennia ago."

Eris opened the wooden box to display two silver daggers set firmly in green velvet. The handles were rounded and slanted down with patterns of swirling silver and pearl on the faces. They were the daggers I had seen several times in my dreams and not one detail was different. As Victor gestured for the music to begin again, I picked up one of the daggers and it felt as though the silver was melting and forming to my hand. It felt natural to be holding it, another perfect fit. I looked up at my father's expectant gaze.

"You knew, didn't you?"

Eris pressed his lips firmly together and sighed. "When I saw them in your dreams, I did not want to think it was true. There was a reason I was pushing you to use swords instead of daggers. But you continued to say to me that it never felt right and that's because you were destined to have these. Let us hope I do not have the same fate as my father."

Eris smiled at me, though it was a sad, shameful one. He had killed his father with one of the daggers he was now presenting to me. Suddenly the fact that I had seen myself holding these very daggers in my dreams and all the while they were my father's was just way too freaky. I placed the dagger back into its velvet form and closed the box to shut out all the thoughts that were racing through my head.

"Where's Seraphina?" I asked, changing the subject.

"Yes well, I was hoping I could speak to you and the Warrior about that," he replied as he transferred the wooden box into my arms and escorted me off the stage.

Once on the floor I caught Cameron's attention and waved him over. As he approached, he extended his hand to my father, which surprised me at first, but then on second thought Cameron was always a gentleman.

"Congratulations, sir."

Eris shook Cameron's hand firmly and smiled as he said, "And to you for having convinced Victor to make Bri-an-na a Warrior."

My face fell, but Cameron shook his head and interrupted quickly. "No sir, that was all Brianna. You know as well as I do that no one can ask Victor to do something like that."

"Even more evidence to how wonderful mia figlia is."

"What about Sera? Why isn't she here?" I prodded.

"Oh yes. Warrior, is there a place we can speak privately?"

Cameron nodded and escorted me and my father outside of the ballroom and into an office just down the hall.

"This is Father's private study, no one will bother us here," Cameron said as he closed the door behind him.

"Warrior, there is at least one member of Elaina's coven here tonight. I do not know who, Seraphina could not see, but that is why she is not down here. She all but threw me out of the room to come to the ceremony, and I must get back to her immediately to ensure she is safe. But know that someone in there is working against you."

Cameron stood still as a statue, and neither of us was breathing, although he didn't have to and I did. Tension grew behind his eyes as he analyzed everyone who was in that room. Sadly the majority of guests were Warriors. The odds were pretty high a Warrior had gone rogue, and Cameron knew it.

"And you say Seraphina does not know who," he said flatly.

"No, just that someone is here. If my Seraphi-na is seen, they will come after her. That much she knows."

"Then I must get Brianna out of here."

"Patience, Warrior, you do not catch the traitor by running. It is best to keep your ear to the ground. Sera will know when the threat has left and we can determine suspects from there. No, now you must return Brianna to the party and not leave her side. You cannot make it appear you are on alert."

"So I'm a sitting duck?" I said flustered.

"Brianna, no one will touch you in there," Cameron replied firmly. "Seraphina has not seen any threat from my brothers or Kyla so we know you are safe with them. We will go back in, say goodnight, and then we will retire. You are half human so it would be natural for you to leave this late in the evening. Eris, I will need to share this information with my brothers and Victor, but I can assure you it will not go beyond them. When Seraphina feels that the threat is gone, I can have Jared survey the footage and hopefully narrow the pool."

"With that said, I shall bid you goodnight," Eris said as he walked to the door. "Daughter, please know that Seraphi-na was devastated not to see you tonight."

"Wait," I said to him as he opened the door but then stopped and turned back to me. "Why did you do it?"

"Do what, Bri-an-na?"

"You know what. In there, why did you give me the choice?"

Eris shoved his hands in his pockets as he looked down at his feet.

"It was difficult for me not to watch your dreams while you slept this afternoon. In your dream you were screaming at a little pig with brown hair that was tied back like mine often is. I could not help but make the connection. Also, your stepmother was quite angry with me today and when Seraphi-na gets angry even I am afraid. You deserved the choice, and I am happy at the one you made. I meant what I said, Bri-an-na, I will never again give you a reason to be ashamed of me. Whether you believe it or not, I do love you very much. I have only ever cared about your safety and preparing you for what I fear is to come. However, it is obvious I am not equipped to train you as I had hoped. Thankfully you now have a family of Warriors to guide you in ways I could not. I am happy for you, figlia, truly happy. Now I must get back to Seraphi-na, she will want to know all the details of your claiming. Goodnight, Warrior. Goodnight, Bri-an-na."

Without another word Eris left quickly through the door. I was still so shocked I must have stared at that door for nearly two minutes before Cameron brought me back to reality.

"Bri, we should really get back to the party."

I sighed loudly and nodded.

"Game face, love," he said as he pulled my hand through the crook of his arm.

"Honey, if my Southern upbringing taught me anything, it is how to pretend everything is perfectly fine even when it isn't," I replied as we exited the room.

"I do not prefer 'honey' as a term of endearment."

"Fine, dear."

"No."

"Snookums."

"Absolutely not." I opened my mouth to tease him again, but he interrupted me quickly as we entered the ballroom. "Perfect, Oliver is with Madelyn. Stay with them while I speak with Devin. Then we will leave together."

"Yes, darling."

Cameron paused, but chose to walk away, shaking his head as he went to find Devin in the crowd.

I walked over to where Daddy O was speaking with Maddy and announced that I was leaving, but as were they. Maddy was leaving with Lana, but Daddy O was actually staying in the manor overnight until Aidan escorted him back home tomorrow morning. It was sad not to have more time with him, but I was also relieved he was getting further away from the danger I seem to have attracted.

Cameron was back in minutes with Kyla in tow.

"Impressive, Cam, you actually pried Kyla away from Alex," I said as Kyla bound toward me.

"What can I say, we're still in our honeymoon period," she retaliated before she turned her attention to Daddy O. "I don't think we've met, I'm Kyla Hunter."

"Ollie Morgan, Lil Bri's granddaddy."

"Lil Bri! I love it! That's just the cutest thing I've ever heard."

"So Miss Kyla, yur a newlywed?"

"Oh yes, for seventy-six years now."

Daddy O's eyes grew large as he said, "You got married when I's born. Now that's sumthin."

"Kyla, we really should be going," Cameron interrupted.

"Oh yes, right. Come on, Lil Bri."

I rolled my eyes. "First, don't call me that. Second, why are you coming with us?"

"We haven't spent any time together tonight, and I want to *see* you to your room," Kyla replied as she led me out of the ballroom with Cameron and Daddy O following close behind.

I looked back at Cameron over my shoulder. "You're pretty smart sometimes," I said, realizing that he brought Kyla along so that she could see anyone coming to harm me on the way back to our room.

Cameron just winked at me and smiled as we continued our way down the hall toward the stairs where once again I was carried up the three flights of stairs like the spoiled princess I was. When we reached our room, Cameron went inside to inspect it while the rest of us stayed in the hallway waiting for his all clear.

"Do ya have to do this every time ya wanna get in yur own bedroom?" Daddy O asked.

"No, Ollie, tonight is a first," Kyla replied in her usual bubbly voice. Daddy O nodded, but still didn't understand and I didn't want to tell him the truth. "Oh Bri, just so you know, I left you something in your closet," she whispered to me, waggling her eyebrows up and down.

But before I could press her, Cameron came back through the door. "All clear, my love. Oliver, always a pleasure."

Daddy O pushed Cameron's outstretched aside and went for the hug, something Cam was still not used to.

"Take care a my girl, son."

"I will, sir."

Daddy O turned back to me, wrapping his arms around me and squeezing me tightly.

"Love ya, sugar. You take care a him, too. Now don't go cryin' again."

I shook my head and wiped away the tears from under my eyes. "Sorry, I can't help it. I always hate saying goodbye to you. We're still doing breakfast tomorrow before you go, right?"

"That's right, sugar. I'll see ya in the mornin'."

Daddy O started down the hall with Kyla close at his side and I watched them go around the corner before I retreated into the bedroom. Cameron stood by the bed while he undid his tie and top collar button. How was it possible for him to be even sexier? He smiled when he caught me staring, which of course made me blush. I placed my new daggers on the nightstand and hurried my way into the closet.

The heavy earrings came off first, and then the shoes. Though my shoes were beautiful, it felt as though my feet would be perpetually shaped into a high arch. When I reached back to unzip what little of a zipper there was, my fingers were met with Cameron's. Startled, I looked up to the long mirror and saw Cameron standing behind me.

"I didn't hear you come in."

He shrugged with his crooked smile. "Vampire."

"Yes, as I am often reminded."

"May I?" he said as he slowly unzipped my dress, causing the straps to loosen around my shoulders. My eyes closed at the feeling of his fingers trailing down my neck, moving my hair to one side. His lips touched my tender earlobe, sending sparks all through my body while butterflies fluttered in my stomach. My head felt heavy as he began kissing my neck gently at first and then applying more pressure as his hand brushed the tops of my breasts. I opened my eyes just in time to see our reflection in the mirror and panicked as Cameron began nipping at the side of my neck.

"Cam, don't!" I shouted at him, one hand reflexively flying to my throat as the other pushed him away.

At first, he was shocked, and then his face changed to something similar to betrayal.

"Bri, I would never…I was not going to…" he sighed in frustration and rested his hands on his hips. "Brianna, something is wrong and you are keeping it from me. All night you have been having these moments of panic but you will not tell me why. I cannot understand why you choose to keep me out. I promised never to keep things from you. *You* made me promise that. I just wish you would do the same."

In the blink of an eye Cameron turned and disappeared into the bedroom, and I felt like shit. I fell onto the sitting bench and let my head fall in between my knees. Stupid, stupid, stupid dreams. They had ruined this evening for me. How long had I wanted a night with him, and this is what happens? Cam's pissed off out there and I'm sitting here crying in the closet. Was I really that scared of being bitten? The thought of being bitten scared me, yes, but moments ago it might have happened on its own. I wasn't scared until I opened my damn eyes and saw what looked like everything I had been trying to change about this evening. That was the problem.

I could change my hair and my dress, or where Cam and I sat outside, but in the end, fate was fate, no matter how hard I tried to run. So, it came down to staying in the closet crying or just letting fate do what it was going to do anyway.

Sitting up, I wiped away the smears of mascara from underneath my eyes and suddenly noticed a box wrapped with a wide blue ribbon sitting on the dresser in front of me. Kyla. She said she had left something for me, and there it was laughing at me and telling me how stupidly childish I was being. I removed the ribbon and opened the box to reveal an elegant cream-colored negligee. As I lifted it from the box, the chiffon underlay fell from the satin empire bodice. Biting my lip so hard I could taste blood, I realized I held the shorter replica of the dress from my dream. I took in a deep breath and slowly exhaled as I glared at myself in the mirror. With another deep exhalation I let my dress fall to the floor and slipped into the negligee along with the satin panties that came with it. Suddenly I felt something I had rarely experienced, I felt sexy.

I walked right up to my reflection in the mirror and whispered, "You will get a grip on yourself, you crazy lady who talks to herself in the mirror. Now go out there and tell Cam the truth and make out with your boyfriend like a grown woman."

I was an idiot. Hopefully only my reflection knew that. I took one big breath and marched out of the closet. Just past the archway I could see Cameron sitting upright in our bed, his bare chest exposed from above the thick comforter. When he saw me, his eyes grew wide with surprise and desire, but he stayed frozen in the bed. Sexily I walked toward the bed, picking seductively at the hem of one of the layers of chiffon. Cameron swallowed hard as I approached the bed, and unable to stay in his position any longer he slid under the covers closer to me.

As I made my final approach to the bed, I stubbed my toe on the nightstand, tripped forward, and fell face first onto the bed.

"Not a word," I threatened as I noticed him clenching his jaw, trying not to laugh at me. "Ohmygod this is a nightmare."

Cameron couldn't hold his laughter any longer, but as he laughed at my expense, he pulled me into the bed next to him and kissed me several times on the cheek.

"Forgive me, love, are you all right?"

"Besides realizing I can't do sexy?"

With his crooked smile inching up the left side of his cheek he replied, "Bri, trust me when I say you do sexy very well."

Slowly I slid out of his arms and sat up on my heels as I said, "Cam, I don't mean to keep things from you. I never see you, and the little time we have together I don't want to take up with explaining some stupid dream that may or may not come true. So yes, tonight I was a little crazed because two separate dreams were coming together, and they were wrong and right at the same time." Cam stayed silent while I tried to find a better way of explaining my nonsense. "Okay, for example, this ring," I said holding up my left hand. "I had a dream about this very ring. Jazlyn gave it to me, and she even told me that you gave it to her, just like she did tonight. Only in the dream it was poisoned which was why I was so scared to put it on tonight. I don't know what the dream meant, or why the ring is perfectly fine on my finger."

Cameron took my left hand and kissed my ringed finger.

"Alright, that explains the incident with the ring, but I know there is more."

I sighed. "Okay, you see there are some dreams that I never remember, like what Eris was saying about me screaming at a pig. I don't remember that one at all, but there are others that I have had a couple of times that are so real it scares me.

"Now remember the first night at Daddy O's, the night I woke up screaming?" He nodded as he began gently rubbing his thumb in soothing circles on the top of my hand. "I had a dream where you and I were dancing in a beautiful ballroom and then we went out onto a terrace where you...you told me to hold still so that my skin wouldn't tear and...and then you held me down and bit me."

Cameron looked mortified. "I would never," he said through clenched teeth.

"I know," I replied as I cupped his cheek. "But then the night at the motel when you fed from me, you said those exact words to me, 'so the skin does not tear.' At the time I thought that was the end of it because the dream had sort of come true. But then the last few days the dream came back. So to bring this full circle, when we stepped into the ballroom tonight, I was a little freaked out and then when we went out onto the terrace..."

"You asked to go to the fountain instead because you were afraid that..."

"I didn't know what to think," I interrupted, trying to calm the anger that was bubbling inside him. "I just wanted to try and change it. And then when we were in the closet, it was the dream all over again just in a different place. So basically, I really can't change anything, no matter how hard I try."

"But you did change it, you have not been bitten."

"Well...not yet," I replied, inching closer to him and placing my hands on his sculpted chest, feeling the cool, smooth muscles under my fingertips. I kissed his lips but he did not kiss me back which prompted me to begin kissing his cheek and then his jaw.

Suddenly his hands were on my shoulders pushing me back.

"No," he insisted, "no."

"Cam, it's going to happen. No matter how hard we try to resist, it's going to happen one way or the other so you might as well enjoy it."

I kissed his lips again, and only after a second kiss did he respond. His arms snaked around me, pulling me down underneath the blankets and intertwining his legs with mine. We were separated only by his snug boxer briefs that were struggling to secure what was waking underneath.

Cameron pressed and massaged his hands into various parts of my body. The thin straps of my negligee didn't stand a chance and were easily ripped from their seams as he pulled the bodice down to cup my breast in his hand. I felt like I was on fire, even with his cool skin pressing against mine. I couldn't get enough of him. His smell filled my senses and the feeling of his tongue flicking against my neck made my toes tingle. In one quick move he rolled me over onto my other side, ripped my negligee completely off, and threw it on the floor. He pressed his chest tightly against my back while his fingers slid down my stomach and brushed the skin just under the top of my satin panties. I turned my head to kiss him and saw that his fangs were extended, but they did not frighten me. He kissed me softly on the lips while his fingers slid tentatively down another inch.

Nervously I grabbed his wrist, my eyes flying open while my breath caught in my throat. Cameron's kind eyes stared back at me while he gently brushed his lips over mine. There was no disappointment or frustration in those eyes, only love and understanding. He began to retract his hand, but I stopped him once again. He knitted his brows together slightly before I crushed my lips against his and guided his hand back down between my legs until his fingers plunged deeply inside of me. The feeling made me gasp and have to turn my head away from him in order to breathe while his fingers continued to explore areas inside and out that I never knew could feel anything but pain.

My heartbeat quickened as Cameron's lips traveled down my neck, the tips of his fangs grazing across my skin. I gasped again when they sank into the side of my throat but I was not afraid when he began drawing my blood. A blanket of relaxation and pleasure sank deeply into every muscle, causing my eyelids to feel extremely heavy. All I could do was whisper to him that I loved him, although I wished I had enough energy to tell him more. I loved him, and more importantly, I trusted him.

After Cameron's fangs retracted from my neck, I felt his tongue lick my wounds close. My head sank into my pillow, unable to keep my eyes open for a second longer. As the darkness began to consume me, I could feel Cameron nuzzle his face into the back of my neck. It was barely audible, and I was barely conscious, but I swear I heard him say, "I am so sorry, Chloe."

Chapter Forty-eight

Cameron

Brianna looked so peaceful as she slept. Her new negligee laid in creamy white pieces on the floor causing images of the exact moment when I ripped it off her body to flash before me. I had never lost control like that in all my three hundred years, but I was consumed with desire for her. She had not stopped me when the need to caress her more intimate areas had become overwhelming. The fact she let me touch her like that at all was an enormous step for her and for us. My feelings for Brianna were unlike anything I had had for anyone, and that unfortunately included my late wife. I had loved Chloe dearly, but my passion for Brianna surpassed anything I had ever felt before which made me feel unbelievably guilty. Although I had not been celibate since becoming a vampire, it had never meant anything. Being able to be intimate with Brianna meant everything to me, but again it came with a feeling of guilt and betrayal.

"Beautiful, beautiful Bri," I whispered in my love's ear as I stroked her bare arm softly. Her skin was still on fire even with the amount of blood I took from her, and I loved the way it felt pressed into my chest and torso. From her hot skin and blood, I felt as though I was human with real blood pumping through my veins. There were so many instances in the brief number of months we had been together where she made me feel this way, and each time I was reminded of how long it had been since I had cared this deeply for someone. Although I hated to admit it, Eris was correct when he said that we vampires easily forget what it was like to be human.

Most times I was able to address the fears that Brianna felt so often, but her vulnerability against an unknown hunter in my own home terrified me. She needed to be stronger, that was plainly evident. The easiest solution she had refused and I had been unable to quell her fears over drinking her father's blood. I would not force her as so many others had in her life, but the danger around her was growing. Her one true defense against our kind was raw and inconsistent. Her power needed to be honed, but I honestly had no idea how that was to be done.

Reluctant to leave her, but having a sudden need to find answers, I gently slid my arm out from under her neck and turned to grab my cell phone from the nightstand to call Devin.

"Yes," he answered with the sounds of the party still going on in the background.

"Are all the guards in place?" I asked softly as I walked into my wardrobe area.

"Yes. Two at your door and two at each staircase."

"Suspicious activity?"

"None so far, but being monitored."

"Make sure no one comes down this corridor for the next thirty minutes, including me."

"Understood."

Having been at each other's side for several centuries, Devin understood that I was leaving Brianna for a period of time, and if someone who appeared to look like me was seen, that person was an enemy.

"Thank you, Brother."

"Yep," he replied before he hung up the phone.

After I zipped up the black jeans I had pulled from my armoire, I shrugged on a gray T-shirt I rarely wore except underneath another shirt. No one would see me and this was hardly the time for my compulsion to rear its ugly head. Once dressed, I gave Brianna one last kiss on the cheek. Thankfully she did not stir so hopefully she would not wake while I was gone. Standing at the corner of the bed, I took a deep cleansing breath, imagined the sight of the library surrounding me, and pushed my spirit and body to the back corner.

A low gas flame burned in the fireplace, although the room appeared to be empty which meant I would be able to search the library in peace. I had read every book in this room and many that were in the vault, and I did not recall reading anything that described powers such as Brianna's, though I was not looking for it either. Scanning the bindings around me I thought the best place to start would be any information on telekinesis, or diaries of vampires with known mind controlling abilities. Neither of which was a match for what Brianna was able to do, but it was a start. I pulled one book down from the shelf, remembering it had some accounts of individuals with telekinetic abilities, and tucked it underneath my arm. Though it was originally written as fiction, most fiction was based on unexplained truth; at least it was when vampires or other mythic creatures were involved.

Knowing the acquired diaries were located in the second level stacks, I crossed the room to the narrow, winding staircase.

"Ah bonjour, Cameron."

The woman's voice startled me, but my posture relaxed when I saw Seraphina sitting curled up in the high-back chair next to me.

"Bonjour, Seraphina. Ça va?"

"Ça va bien. You speak French?"

"Yes, as a matter of fact, although I do not get to speak it often," I replied to her in perfect French. "Are you sure it is safe for you in here?"

"Oh yes, at least for a short while," she answered, continuing our conversation in her native language. "I was unable to sleep, and did not want to disturb Eris while he worked."

"Eris is working?"

"It is usually how he passes the time while I sleep, but tonight he is watching as many of the humans as he can. He is looking for anything from their dreams that would help find who is working with Elaina. I was devastated to miss Brianna's party. I hope she is not upset with me."

"Absolutely not," I answered and sat in the chair next to her. "On the contrary, she was quite worried about you."

"As I worry for her. But I know she is safe when she is with you, and so happy. From the looks of it, you are as well," she said with a coy smile as she made a circular motion with her index finger around my face.

"I am not sure I understand what you are implying."

Seraphina laughed sweetly as she closed the book she had in her hands.

"Cameron, you cannot hide those pink cheeks from me. I have seen them many times on my husband after he drinks from me. There is no disguising when you have new blood flowing through you. I am assuming it is my stepdaughter's. That is unless there is someone else who…"

"It is hers," I interrupted, running a hand through my hair to hide my embarrassment.

"Good, you will need it in order to help her."

"How is that?"

She rose from her chair and sat on the ottoman that was positioned between us. As she took both my hands in hers, she said, "A battle is coming, Cameron. It is coming for her."

"When?"

"Soon. I have seen it. Eris says she has seen it as well."

I could feel the anxiety mixed with anger rising within me, but it was quickly taken away, feeling as though my breath was being sucked out of me. I now realized Seraphina had taken my hands in order to control my emotions.

"You are certain it is a battle? A full-fledged battle?" Seraphina nodded. "Why has she not told me? A battle is not the same as a few hybrids attacking her at a mall. A battle is…" but again, as though my breath was taken from my lungs, I could not continue speaking while my emotions flowed into Seraphina.

"Her dreams are still new to her, and she is frightened by them. She may not always remember them, or she chooses not to. But you have a way to help her for you can see what she is dreaming, can you not?"

"Yes, I saw them once before."

"Then you can see what she sees, help her to remember, recognize places she does not."

"Even if I can see the battle she dreams of, that is not going to help her defend herself. How do we develop her power? It is her only way to survive against the vampires that are after her. How do we teach her to use a power no one understands? If she is unable to use her power effectively, she could very well hurt those that are trying to help her."

Seraphina was silent for several minutes, taking in deep breaths while all my panic and worry and frustration flowed into her. I moved my hands from under hers, feeling guilty at the amount of what she was relieving me of, but she quickly took them back into hers.

"Not yet," she said, taking in a deep breath. "I can feel your guilt, Cameron, do not be. If I can handle the emotions of my husband, I can certainly take in yours. You are correct, Brianna's power brings with it certain complexities. Think about those who have the ability to control and alter other's minds. How does Eris find those that are dreaming? How does Lanashell only look into the minds of those she wants to?"

"I do not know."

"Then ask," she replied simply and then paused. "Do you know all you need to do?"

I nodded, ashamed that I did not see some of the answers that were right in front of me. "I must get back to her."

"Of course. I must get back as well." Squeezing my hands gently she said, "When I let go, just breathe and remember all you must do. Let that be your focus."

Slowly she removed her hands from mine, and all my emotions began flooding back into me at once. Remembering her words about my focus, I blew my anxiety and anger out with my breath.

"Thank you, Seraphina. Do you need me to escort you back to your room?"

"No, no, now hurry. You never know what you could be missing," she said, shooing me away. Then she quickly rose from her chair and kissed me on both cheeks before she left the library.

Knowing what I needed to do, I flew to the closest desk and withdrew several pencils and all the paper from its drawer. Standing in front of the desk, I closed my eyes and Projected myself intensely back into my bedroom. The impact of Projecting myself so violently left me slightly unbalanced, but the thrust of Brianna's visions knocked me completely over.

Grabbing a piece of the paper and one of the scattered pencils, I tried concentrating on what I was seeing before drawing it. Although I was expecting, or at least hoping, for a glimpse of a battle, I was presented with the sight of Brianna yelling at a little pig. Disappointing, yes, but humorous. As the image faded, I gathered my materials that had fallen on the floor and took position next to Brianna on the bed. When another image began to hit me, I put my pencil to paper, hoping this time her dream would reveal what I assumed was the beginning of our great war.

Chapter Forty-nine

Brianna

"Shut up, Shelby, just shut up!" I screamed at my mother who stood in front of me.

"Do not call me Shelby, Bri Bri, I am your mother."

"Could have fooled me," I snapped back and turned to walk into the living room of my grandfather's home. Shelby's hand gripped the back of my arm and spun me around to face her. I pried her hand off and looked down at my tiny mother ready to unleash on her, but as was often the case when I tried to confront her, I lost my voice.

"Bri Bri, you listen to me. That man is a vampire, and one thing I know about vampires is that they don't love anyone but themselves."

"Cameron loves me."

"He loves this," she said, picking up my arm and slapping the veins on my wrist. "They only care about where their blood is coming from. That's all you are to him, Bri Bri, a blood bag."

"No, he loves me, and nothing you say will make me think otherwise."

"It doesn't mean anything, don't you understand? He's taken what he wanted. Now he's going to leave you just like your father left me. Like mother like daughter."

"Oh, no. Eris loved you. You screwed yourself on that one. I am nothing like you."

"Then where is he?" Shelby shouted. "Where is your precious Cameron? You don't know, do you? Trust me, Bri Bri, you're going to end up alone with a baby you don't want, just like me."

"That is enough," Eris growled from behind me. When I turned my head to look at my father the tears that were being held by my eyelids overflowed down my face. My father's face was kind as he extended his hand to me. "You don't need to see this now."

When I turned my head back to look at Shelby, the scene around us began to dissolve. I took my father's hand and watched as my surroundings faded from the foyer of Daddy O's home to a bright, sprawling ocean view where the sun's rays flashed against the tips of the waving water.

A long chaise enveloped me from underneath, supporting my head and legs while an expansive balcony formed in front of me. I looked to my right and noticed my father sitting in a similar chair and holding a tropical drink with a little umbrella.

"See, my darling, isn't this better?"

"Of course it is," I replied, looking down to see that I was laid out in a white swimsuit with a sheer white cover-up, the brim of a big floppy hat dipping down in front of my eyes. "I thought I told you to stay out of my head."

"I try not to pry, but something was telling me to take a peek tonight and then I found it difficult not to step in," he said in a conflicted tone. "Figlia, if I had known she would...dislike you so, I would have figured something out. It pains me to think that you have had to hear similar things from your mother's mouth. Just more things I need to make up to you."

"This is your house, right?" He nodded. "Just bring me here from time to time and we'll call it even," I replied with a smile from underneath my floppy hat. Eris smiled back at me and we sat in the sun and listened to the waves crashing below us. It was peaceful and easy, two words I had never been able to use when with my father. "Why can't we be like this in real life?"

Eris laughed lightly. "Because I can't control you in real life."

"That's certainly true. How much are you controlling now?"

"I am only controlling your surroundings. So far," he said with a sly smile.

"What all can you do?"

"Obviously I can see into your dreams, alter them, or keep you from having them at all. I can put you to sleep, and keep you asleep if I choose."

"It sounds like you're talking about putting a dog down," I said nervously and took a long sip of my drink. "So what's your plan from here?"

"I have discussed it with Sera, and we are going to stay until I feel you are able to defend yourself. I may not be able to train you, but who better to test your readiness than me."

"I don't understand. What do you mean by testing my readiness?"

"Figlia, at the end of each week I will challenge you to a duel, or a battle I believe the Warriors call it. When you defeat me, I will leave and not a moment before."

I stood quickly from my chair, dropping my drink and causing it to shatter on the ground.

"Eris that is ridiculous. You can't expect me..."

"I expect you to survive, Bri-an-na," he said flatly. *"I will not budge on this. If you can defend yourself successfully against me, you can survive against anyone. There is too much at stake if you were to be killed,"* he said as he stood from his chair and walked over to me.

"I hate when you say things like that."

"I know," he said and then gave me a quick kiss on the cheek. *"One week, daughter."*

"I still think it's ridiculous...Daaad," I slurred.

Eris smiled widely. *"Now that wasn't so hard, was it?"*

"More than you think. I can't promise I'll always call you that, but after what you did last night, I'm...trying."

"I can ask for nothing more."

With one more kiss on the cheek the ocean view dissolved and I nudged myself awake...

As my eyes fluttered open, I heard the sound of something being lightly scratched against a hard surface. I turned to Cameron's side of the bed to find him sitting up and vigorously scribbling on a piece of paper.

"At least that dream ended better than it began," he said without looking up from his drawing.

"How much did you see?" I asked, remembering that he could see flashes of my dreams when he drank my blood.

"Have a look for yourself," he replied, gesturing to the end of the bed with his chin.

I propped myself up on my elbows to see the entire bottom half of our bed covered in sketches of various scenes. I looked over at the sketch that

Cam was still working on and noticed that it was a drawing of Eris kissing my cheek with the ocean view from the balcony behind him.

"You never told me you could draw like that."

He shrugged. "I certainly would not call myself an artist."

"Cam, if I had drawn that you would have seen two stick figures and a big round sun in the corner."

He laughed as he put his pencil down and leaned over to kiss me gently on the lips.

"How are you feeling?" he asked, searching my face.

"Fine."

"Truly? You were not…uncomfortable with anything I did last night?"

"No," I answered, blushing and securing the sheet around my bare chest.

Cameron nuzzled his head against mine, kissing me on my cheek and ear.

"I will go down and get you some breakfast."

"Breakfast!" I shouted, bolting straight up in the bed. "What time is it? I was supposed to meet Daddy O for breakfast."

"He came by an hour and a half ago."

"Why didn't you wake me?"

"He said, and I quote, 'you'll sooner find a stake in your chest before I let you wake her up just to see me.' I am sorry, love, I will go up against you before Oliver any day."

"Did he leave yet?"

"He is in the sitting room with Kyla and Alexander. Aidan will be coming to escort him home in about thirty minutes. Change and freshen up, I will bring you up some breakfast while you visit with him," he said, tilting my chin up with his index finger and kissing me before I could object any further.

I grabbed his shirt as he rose from the bed and pulled him back in close to me and said, "I really am okay with what we did last night. I know it's just a start, and you've been so patient with me…"

"Love," he cooed and petted my hair softly, "we have all the time in the world…"

"Not true."

"*Brianna*," he said firmly, "if we never go further than we did last night I will be a happy man. You are…" he lowered his head and cleared his throat, "…you are the most beautiful thing I have ever held in my arms and if we keep talking about last night, I will be unable to walk."

I giggled and traced my finger along the sharp edge of his jaw.

"Maybe we can do a little more tonight, see where it leads."

"I may not be able to wait that long," he replied teasingly and then kissed the tip of my nose. "Now go and shower, angel. Oliver is waiting."

With a deep sigh I got out of bed and within minutes I was showered and changed into a pair of lose fitting sweatpants and T-shirt. While I crossed the room I glanced down and noticed scenes of the battle I had dreamt of before sketched on numerous pages scattered all over the bed and floor. The one that grabbed my immediate attention was one of me holding a badly burned Jared in my arms. Taking the sketch in both hands, I ripped the page in two and folded the pieces in my hands to rip them again.

"Brianna, what are you doing?" Cameron asked as he came through the sitting room door and closed it quickly behind him.

"Is this what you saw last night?" I said, waving the ripped pages in my hand.

"Yes. You do not remember?"

"No. I only remember the last one I had."

"But you have seen it before."

I nodded. "The night before the attack at the Facility. You're planning on showing these, aren't you?"

"Only to my brothers."

"Jared can't see this," I said, fanning through the sketches in a panic to see if there were more of these images.

"Brianna, stop," Cameron said as he pulled my hands together. "Is it not better for him to see the signs?"

"No, it's not. Not this. No one should see how they die." Cameron furrowed his brow in confusion. "You didn't see what happened after this?" He shook his head. I paused, unable to tell him the full story. "Don't show him. Please," I said, handing him the ripped pages and walking toward the sitting room.

Opening the door, I caught both Kyla and Alex laughing at something that Daddy O had said.

"Oh hey, sugar, you're awake," Daddy O said with his charming wrinkled smile.

"No thanks to you," I replied, whacking him lightly in the arm as I sat down at the small circular table in the middle of the room and began eating the hot scrambled eggs Cameron had brought for me.

"Don't be usin' that tone a voice with me, Lil Bri."

"Lil Bri," Kyla chuckled, "it really is the cutest name ever."

"Yes, Ky, you've said that," I replied embarrassed. "Could you guys give us a few minutes?"

"Of course, Lil Bri," Kyla teased as she and Alex rose from their chairs. "Aidan will be here in about twenty minutes to take you to the airport. It's been such a pleasure, Ollie, I hope we get to see you again soon."

"The pleasure is mine, Miss Kyla," Daddy O replied, accepting her hug and then shaking hands with Alex before they left the room. Once the door was closed, Daddy O looked back at me and whispered, "That is the biggest man I have ever seen."

I smiled. "He's a teddy bear most of the time."

Daddy O gave me a skeptical look as he sat back down next to me.

"It's been good seein' ya, sugar. You seem to be doin' really well out here."

"Why are you leaving so soon? Why can't you stay for a few more days?"

"Lil Bri, you know I don't like sleepin' anywhere but my own bed."

"Well, I've been thinking, what if you came to live out here?"

His eyes were kind and pleaded for understanding.

"Sugar, you know I'd love to come out here and be whicha, but I can't leave my home. Your grandmother and I built that house. You and yur mamma grew up there. Most of my memories of Jo are in that house, I just can't leave it. I'm sorry, sugar, but you come on out and see me when you can. Now what'd I say about cryin'?"

"I'm sorry," I wailed as I threw my arms around his neck and the tears came streaming down my face and onto the collar of his shirt.

Daddy O patted me gently on the back, trying to calm me. I didn't even hear the outside sitting room door open.

"Sorry, Oliver, we need to get going," a man said behind me.

I turned to see Aidan standing just inside the door, his jeans and baseball cap a drastic difference from the tux he was wearing last night.

"Already? It hasn't been near twenty minutes," I said, wiping my eyes.

"Traffic's a bitch at this time of day. I don't want us to miss our flight," Aidan said as he crossed the room, taking Daddy O's small overnight bag and placing it on his shoulder. The arrogance he had so deliberately displayed last night seemed to have faded, making me wonder if the whole thing was an act to somehow impress the mighty Warriors. "Ollie, I'll be right outside."

"Wait," I said, leaping over the chair to catch him before he left the room. My attempt and failure at trying to be graceful made him produce a cocky smile. "He's important, okay."

He squinted at me, trying to understand. "Ooh-kay."

"I mean it. He's *really* important. You can't let anything happen to him."

"I promise you, nothing will happen to him," he replied seriously and then took a step out into the hallway. "Make sure the Warriors don't let anything happen to you either. You're pretty important, too."

Before I could process any further meaning in his statement, Daddy O grabbed me from behind and gave me one last kiss and hug.

"Love ya, sugar."

"I love you too."

"Maybe think about talkin' to yur mamma."

"Won't happen."

He sighed and pressed his lips firmly together, finally admitting defeat and allowing Aidan to guide him down the long hallway.

No matter how old I was, it was always hard saying goodbye to him. Seriously, how many more times would I get the chance? The thought made another sudden wave of emotion come over me, causing me to run into the solace of my bedroom. If I had hoped for a minute or two to myself, I was sorely mistaken. In the short time I had been with my grandfather, Cameron had convened Devin, Alex, and Kyla to view the battle sketches strewn on the floor.

Kyla looked over at me as I entered the room, noticing the tears leaking from my eyes.

"Bri?"

"I'm fine, really," I replied, walking to the nightstand for a tissue to wipe my snotty nose. Cameron looked at me concerned and took one step toward me, but I quickly waved him away knowing that I would only cry more if he were to comfort me.

Taking the cue, he turned back to his siblings to bring their attention back to the sketches.

"Do you recognize the location?" he asked.

"It's the courtyard," Alex announced first.

"Courtyard? Where?" I asked, walking over to the group.

"Here," Alex answered tentatively.

I looked up at Alex and felt the blood rush out of my face. I stepped back, feeling a little queasy, and felt Cameron's arm come firmly underneath my back.

"Love, this is good news."

"Good news?"

"Yes, good news. We know where we are going to be hit. This is a win for us."

"Brother, we need to share these with Father," Devin said, collecting a few of the pictures in his hands.

"No, Devin. As I said before, this stays between us," Cameron replied in an angry tone I rarely heard from him.

Alex took a step back from the two of them while Kyla took me from Cameron's hold and sat me on the bed20. just behind us. I went along with it, but wasn't exactly sure why they were retreating until Cam and Devin began shouting at one another.

"If we are to win this battle, we need everyone up to speed. This is a blueprint of the future. We can use this to our advantage," Devin started in.

"Brother, I will not expose Brianna like this. Father may have the best of intentions at first, but he will exploit her. I refuse to let that happen."

"This is for the good of the coven, Brother. You hinder us by keeping everyone in the dark."

"The Warriors have been fighting wars for the last seven hundred years, and you have been there for most of them. You of all people know we have never needed something like this in order to win a battle. We will say we have received intelligence from an outside source, but this does not leave this room."

"That is not your decision to make, Brother."

"Like hell it is," Cameron spat in his brother's face.

"Stop it, both of you," Kyla screamed, quickly leaving my side. "We need to get out of here. Now!"

"Kyla, what..." Cameron started, but quickly stopped as all four vampires turned in my direction.

"Oh shit," I groaned as I felt the wetness between my legs.

Cameron pushed everyone out of the room while I ran to the bathroom. I had known this was coming for days now, however, having to actually deal with the situation was another story entirely.

"Brianna," Cameron said, tapping lightly on the bathroom door.

"Cam, now would be a good time to talk about...the thing."

Chapter Fifty

Brianna

Having your period in a house full of vampires meant isolation. It was that way for the other humans that lived in the manor, so I couldn't really complain. Although isolation meant time away from Cam, it was nice in the sense that I could get things done. It allowed me to unwrap all my gifts from the claiming ceremony and set up the new laptop that Jared had given me. I was even able to check my email, and had a happy surprise waiting for me from Jared. Apparently during the party he had taken several pictures and sent them to me. One in particular of Cameron and I dancing together and looking lovingly into each other's eyes was enough to make you sick, and I wanted the biggest copy I could get. It was the first and only picture I had of us together, and frankly it was beautiful.

After only a few hours of lying around like a big house cat and thinking about how lucky I was not to have to do any physical training for a few days, a knock came at my bedroom door.

"Brianna, it's Lana."

Crap, crap, crap. What the hell was she doing here?

"Uh, sorry Lana. I'm in…uh…isolation." And I don't want to see you. Crap, don't think it, don't think it.

"Yes, Brianna, I know. Cameron sent me to work with you."

Flipping the comforter off of me, I walked up to the door and opened it just enough to poke my head out to see Lana. She was standing very straight with her arms crossed in front of her tailored and very expensive suit jacket. She couldn't even loosen up on a Sunday?

"Cameron sent you to work with me…how?" And how could I punish him the next time I saw him.

"Don't be cross with him. He thought you might be more apt to work with me regarding your mind projection. I know I am not your favorite person…"

"It's not you as a person, Lana. I just don't necessarily agree with your methods."

Lana sighed as she tucked a thick section of her angled hair behind her ear.

"Brianna, it was necessary for me to show you what you feared…"

"Not just with me," I interrupted, giving her an evil eye.

"You're referring to Hannah Berkshire," she replied. The sound of Hannah's name hit me sharply in the heart. "No one regrets her death more than I do."

"I seriously doubt that," I said harshly while purposely thinking of the nights I cried myself to sleep over her death. I couldn't quite picture Lanashell doing the same thing in her expensive suit.

Lana's lips became thin as she pressed them tightly together for several moments before replying, "She was my failure, Brianna, and I often lost patience with her. Something I deeply regret."

"She wasn't a failure," I shouted, and then instantly regretted my childish tone. "I don't feel like training today and besides you can't come in here anyway."

"Yes, I know you are menstruating, but being the head of a facility full of hybrids, the majority being women, there is nothing you need to worry about. Cameron inferred that time was of the essence, may I come in?"

"No." Okay, it was rude, and I was hormonal. "Fine, come in."

Wednesday, hump day, crappiest day ever…day. The only good thing about Wednesday was that I was no longer a walking bloody threat and could actually leave the prison of my room, but Lanashell and Cameron had different ideas. Since Sunday, Lana had tried working with me on strengthening my mind power and speaking to me in terms I didn't understand. She would tell me to search and feel for a person's essence, their lifeline. After three days of fatigue and headaches, I didn't feel shit.

Yesterday Lana had resorted back to showing me images of things that would provoke me, and every now and then I would push her a little, but nothing like what the two of us knew was possible. We were on the verge of giving up since neither of us could explain why I couldn't use my power on command. Secretly I had decided that my power was just as stubborn as I was and it would manifest when it damn well pleased.

Since it was safe for me to have visitors, Cameron had asked Devin to assist Lana in an effort to combine my mind powers with self-defense since it would be the only way for me to defend myself against any vampire, especially my father whose challenge was only days away. It was almost five o'clock, and the three of us were at wits end. Like Lana, I had been able to push Devin a little here and there, but nothing that would help me defend myself. My head was pounding, nerves raw, muscles aching, and still nothing to show for it.

"Let's try it again," Lana said in a snippy tone that had worsened as the day continued. "Take a breath, close your eyes, and reach out with your mind searching for Devin's..."

"Please don't say essence," I groaned. I was so sick of that friggin' word. "How many times do I have to say it, I don't *feel* anything. We all know this isn't working. Let's just cut our losses and hope that Eris will scare me enough to make it work. My head is pounding, I'm done for today."

"Brianna," Devin began, placing his hand lightly on my shoulder in a rare display of affection, "you must push through this. Eris will not show you any leniency on Sunday. We must continue to try and provoke..."

"Devin, I'm done. It's my ass out there on Sunday, not yours. I am well aware of what my father will do to me, but I'm telling you now that you're not getting any more out of me today." Devin turned away from me and exchanged a look with Lana as he walked out the door. "Lana, that means you, too. Please," I added, still unable to be a complete bitch to her. She nodded without saying a word and took two steps toward the door.

I turned into the archway toward the closet, and suddenly behind me the bedroom door burst open. Quickly I turned around, half falling into the archway just as Samuel A. Lewis leapt toward me from the doorway. He was supposed to be dead, but his broad shoulders and short salt and pepper hair were too real to ignore. The fire in my stomach burned and quickly rose through my pounding head as I screamed and pushed him away with all my strength back through the doorway, shattering a narrow table in the hallway.

Lana was crouched in the floor, her hands over her ears, while Devin slowly rose from amongst the pieces of the shattered table where Sam had been lying only moments before. They had tricked me, both of them, in cahoots together. Lana had tried other images to provoke me, but never an image of Sam. I was furious and still shaking with fear and adrenaline on the floor when Cameron's tall, thin frame cast a shadow above me.

Slowly he knelt down, brushing my hair out of my eyes and kissing me gently on my cheekbone.

"Brianna? Love, can you tell me what happened?" he asked, but I was unable to speak. "Thank you, Lanashell, I believe Brianna is done for today."

Lana still looked a little shaken as she left the room, closing the door on the sight of Devin removing bits of wood from his clothes.

Cam still knelt beside me as I looked into his comforting eyes.

"I'm tired of being weak, Cam."

"Tell me what I can do," he said, squeezing my hand tightly against his chest.

I waited a moment and sighed at the resignation of what I needed to do. Finally, I looked back up at him and said, "Don't let go. Whatever you do, just don't let go."

Cameron knitted his brows together as I stood from my pathetic position on the floor and silently led him out of our bedroom. Once I turned down the long hallway and headed one floor up, he knew exactly where I was going and squeezed my hand tightly.

At first, I knocked on the door quietly, but when no one answered I pounded harder, afraid my resolve would leave me at any moment. I banged on the door once more, but this time I was unable to stay silent.

"Eri...Da...dammit it's your daughter, open the door I know you're in there."

The door to my father's room quickly opened to reveal Eris in his usual linen pants and loose shirt, his hair hanging loose around his shoulders.

"Bri-an-na, what a truly wonderful surprise. I apologize for not answering. Honestly, Warrior, your brethren have been knocking day and night. We have become accustom to ignoring anyone who comes to our door."

"Eris, sir, I sincerely apologize. I will make sure no one bothers you from now on."

"Thank you. Now, come, come, before someone else tries to sneak in," Eris said with a relaxed smile as he waved us in.

Their room was only slightly smaller than ours, the bed sitting two steps up with the bathroom directly next to it, while two small loveseats faced each other in front of a large fireplace on our left. Just as we entered the room, Seraphina stepped out of the bathroom and came down the two narrow steps towards me with her arms outstretched. Refusing to let go of Cameron's hand, I wrapped my free arm around her as she hugged me around the neck.

"Ma petite chute, I have been waiting all day," the lovely French lady said as she cupped my cheek in her hand. "It has taken all my strength to keep zhis from your fazer."

Eris took a step from around Cameron, raising his left eyebrow at his wife. "And what would that be, my darling wife?"

"Zhe reason she is here."

"How do you know why I'm here?"

"Because I have seen it, ma petite chute."

"I don't know what that last part means," I whispered to Cameron.

"I will tell you later," he whispered back. "Why not tell your father why you are here."

Eris was biting his bottom lip, trying to contain his hidden anticipation at the reason for my unexpected visit. Cameron squeezed my hand and nodded his head, basically giving me the nudge I needed.

"I need you to activate me. Please, D-dad."

Eris clapped his hands together in excitement and led us into the small sitting area.

"It might be easiest if we sat on the floor," Eris said, gesturing to the thick carpet between the two loveseats.

Initially Cameron sat next to me, but my nerves were getting the best of me so I quickly moved to sit in between his legs with my back pressed against his chest, wrapping his arms around my waist.

"So how do we do this?"

"I will puncture my wrist, and you will drink. But you must begin to drink quickly, or else the wound will close. Are you ready, mia figlia?"

But before I could say no, my father bit into his wrist and thick droplets of blood began to leak from the two puncture holes. As he brought his arm toward my lips, I squirmed further into Cameron's chest and turned my head away. Eris dropped his wrist and the two holes closed, leaving behind only a small smear of blood on his forearm. Without saying a word, Sera wiped the blood away and placed her finger in her mouth to lick it away. Seeing as though she didn't react violently to my father's blood, my body relaxed slightly, but only slightly.

"Okay, let's try again," I said, squeezing Cameron's arms tighter around me. "On second thought, cover my eyes. That way I don't see it coming."

Cameron obliged, though with a soft laugh, and placed his cool hands over my eyes. Before I could change my mind, my father's wrist was placed to my mouth, but I was still resistant to drink.

"Bri-an-na, you must drink or it will close again."

"Just let it in, love, I am here. I am not letting go, remember," Cameron said softly, obviously seeing my bottom lip quiver.

Feeling his strength and support behind me, I pressed my lips against Eris's bleeding wrist and drew a small amount of blood into my mouth. It was thick and cool and surprisingly sweet. So sweet, that I sucked in another small amount into my mouth, and then another, and another. Cameron's hold on me loosened as I began steadily drinking my father's blood to the soothing and encouraging words of everyone in the room. When I released his wrist to draw a deep breath, my father quietly announced that I had had enough. My activation was complete.

Cameron removed his hands from my eyes and wrapped his arms tightly around me while releasing a loud sigh of relief. Peering through his arms, I watched Sera press her forehead against my father's while he whispered something softly that was meant only for the two of them. Cameron had told me once that many hybrids were activated at their claiming ceremonies. Sitting here now, wrapped in Cameron's arms and watching my father wipe away a thin red tear, I realized I wouldn't have wanted to do this any other way. It was an intimate family moment, one that brought a tear to my own eye.

"So that's it?" I asked, feeling foolish at how scared I had been.

"Yes, that is it. Now you must rest, Brianna," he said, raising his brows to me as he spoke without his Italian accent.

"You remembered," I said, smiling broadly and feeling Cameron's eyes on me for some kind of explanation.

"And only in your presence, and those in this room," Eris replied and rose from the floor. "You have no idea the relief I feel now that you are fully activated. I cannot wait to see how you will perform on Sunday. It should be an epic battle now that you have more of my blood inside of you."

"Let's not get ahead of ourselves," I groaned while Cameron helped me to my feet.

After each of them had given me the once over, I was allowed to give my goodbyes. Eris nearly squeezed the breath out of me, and Sera called me a name in French I didn't understand. Eris was right about one thing, I needed rest. After we stepped out into the hallway, Cameron tucked me firmly into his side and guided me back to our bedroom.

"So your father is not Italian?" he asked curiously.

"No. He is a convincing Italian from Egypt. He is amazingly fake."

Cameron and I laughed the rest of the way back to our room, but quickly stopped when we found our door open and Devin sitting in the chair next to the couch.

"Brother? Is everything all right?" Cameron asked anxiously as he shut the door behind us.

"I came to apologize to Brianna," he said as he stood from his chair.

"To Brianna? For what?"

"I had agreed with Lanashell that if we were unable to bring out Brianna's powers that further provocation was needed. But Brianna, I assure you I did not know who she would make you see. If I had, I would not have done it."

Cameron looked down to me. "Who did you see?"

"Sam," I sighed.

Cameron's jaw flexed tightly as his nostrils flared and he clenched his fists.

"Brother," Devin said, holding his hands out defensively, "she was struggling. We thought it would help."

"Help?" Cameron shouted. "You thought that it would help her to see her dead, abusive husband coming to attack her?"

"Lana did not tell me who it was until I confronted her afterwards. I thought it was going to be one of Elaina's Vamps that attacked you in Flagstaff, but when I saw your reaction, I knew something was wrong. Brianna, Brother, you must believe me when I say I didn't know."

"Dev, it's fine," I said to Cameron's surprise. "If they hadn't done it, I wouldn't have pushed myself to get activated. I will never work with Lana again, but it had the right outcome. You know I'm right."

Cameron sighed, unable to argue the point, but not liking the fact that he

A MIDNIGHT BLOOM ~ 429

had to concede.

"You are an active hybrid?" Devin asked. "Do you feel any different? Stronger?"

"Just a little tired," I replied and then realized my body felt as though I had just finished an extensive workout. I looked back up to Cameron and said, "I'll freshen up and then can we have a little time together before you have to go again?"

Cameron nodded and kissed me gently before I left his side and walked into the bathroom. I could hear the two of them arguing in hushed tones as I closed the bathroom door, but I couldn't concentrate on their fight because I suddenly needed to lean back against the door for support. I was having trouble catching my breath, and now my head was extremely heavy. My legs felt like lead as I tried to cross the room to the sink, only to watch myself in the mirror falling down in slow motion. My skin felt like it was on fire while my veins were circulating ice cold fluid throughout my body causing me to shiver violently on the floor. I was in such shock I couldn't speak, or even whimper.

My heart started beating so violently I thought it would break through my ribs. My lungs were burning from breathing so hard, but I was finally able to call for help, though it came out no louder than a whisper. Never had I been so thankful that Cameron was a vampire than when the door to the bathroom flew open and he was kneeling in front of me.

"Devin, find Eris and Lanashell, now," Cameron shouted and Devin disappeared instantly into black mist. Cameron stepped over me to grab a hand towel from the sink and began wiping away the sweat that was forming in large beads all over my face and neck. Suddenly my body was racked with searing pain. It felt as though I was being burned from the inside out. Cameron placed one arm under my back and the other under my legs and carefully lifted my shaking body from the floor. His hands felt like shards of ice on my skin as he carried me into the bedroom and laid me on the bed.

Bombs were going off inside my head making the voices of others in the room sound garbled and unintelligible. I closed my eyes and tried to concentrate on taking a solid breath when two more shards of ice were placed on either side of my face. I opened my eyes to see my father hovering over me, his hands flinching away at the sounds of my screams.

"Dammit, Lana, what is happening to her?" Eris yelled over his shoulder.

"I don't know, Eris! I've never seen anything like this," Lana yelled back.

"Cam?" I said breathlessly.

I felt Cameron's cool fingers move the sweat soaked hair from my face and tuck it behind my ear.

"I am right here, angel," he said leaning over me from the edge of the bed. "She's burning up. We should get a doctor."

"And tell them what, Warrior?"

"Then we will take her to the Facility."

"It is too far away," Eris snapped.

"Then what do you suggest," Cameron shouted.

But their arguing stopped when another wave of pain came on so strong it made my back arch unnaturally. My throat burned raw as the screams passed through my lips and echoed off the stone walls.

Eris once again squeezed my face tightly between his ice cold hands.

"Tell me what to do!"

"Make it stop," I begged. "Put me under."

Red tears streaked down Eris's face and he nodded with understanding.

"Eris, what are you doing?" Cameron said in a panic, pushing Eris out of his way and taking my face into his own hands. "Brianna, no, stay with me."

My head was swimming as I looked into Cameron's fearful eyes. Just over his shoulder I saw my father give me one final nod before closing his eyes. I could feel the darkness begin to surround me and the weight of my eyelids overwhelming me. "He's taking it away, Cam. He's just..."

Chapter Fifty-one

Cameron

"Bri? Brianna!" I screamed at her lifeless face in my hands. I shifted my arms and pulled her body closer, relieved to feel her breath brush against my face and hearing the continued beating of her heart. "Bri angel, open your eyes. Come back to me," I said frantically, brushing the hair out of her face and tapping her cheeks to get her to wake up. Even with all my attempts, her body still lay limp in my arms.

What had happened? Her decline was so rapid, and it was torturous to see her in so much pain. No one in the room knew what was happening to her, or why, which made the entire ordeal even more frustrating.

I felt someone's hand squeeze my shoulder. When I turned my head, I found Eris looking back at me.

"She cannot hear you, Warrior. Let her rest," he said softly and urged me to lay Brianna back down on the bed.

Reluctantly I obliged and laid her down on her pillow, carefully tucking the blankets around her. Once her calming force had left my arms, the monster inside me began to rage. Unable to keep it tame, I took a step away from Brianna's bedside and leapt at Eris, launching us twenty feet back and breaking the couch that sat in front of the fireplace in half.

"What have you done to her," I screamed like a wild animal while pressing my forearm firmly against his throat. My fangs had extended quickly, as had his, although he was not resisting me in any way which seemed to make me angrier.

From behind me I heard Devin yell for assistance and within seconds both Devin and Alexander were prying my hands from Eris's body. Alexander clamped his arms down around me, pulling me into his chest while Devin mediated the space between me and Eris. Kyla, who had come into the room at some point, began to weep loudly while she leaned over Brianna's still form.

"Wh...what's the matter with her?" she asked between sobs, shaking Brianna's body.

"Ask him," I shouted, directing all my anger at Eris.

"You must calm yourself, Warrior," Eris said with intense control while he adjusted his shirt and smoothed back his hair. "I have induced her sleep, which if you recall she asked me to do. I can keep her under until whatever is happening to her passes. If I didn't know that your anger towards me was out of love for her, I would have killed you with no regard for your family here. Do not test me again, Warrior, I do not wish to break my daughter's heart. Do we have an understanding?"

When I did not answer, Devin turned around with his eyes blazing at me.

"Answer him, Brother."

"I understand," I grumbled and reluctantly continued with, "I am...sorry. Sir." Eris nodded curtly and walked back to Brianna's side. "Alex, you can let go. I am in control now."

Alexander laughed low in his chest, but he did not let go.

"Now Eris," Devin began calmly, "could this have been a reaction to your blood?"

"Humans have tasted my blood for thousands of years, Sera for the last thirty, and Shelby before her. No one has ever reacted like this. Lana, have you ever seen a hybrid react so violently at receiving their father's blood?"

I looked in the direction Eris was facing, and saw Lanashell standing in the far corner of the room. In the midst of the chaos, I had completely forgotten she was still here.

"No I haven't," she replied softly. "Fatigue, chills, more like flu symptoms, but nothing like this. But Eris, we need to consider that you are one of only a few Ancients and the only one I know of who has created a human child in this century, let alone activated her. It could be that your blood is simply too pure and powerful for her. Is she having any visions?"

Eris closed his eyes for a moment and then shook his head.

"Wake her," I said firmly. "You were able to put her to sleep, so you have the power to wake her. I...we must know what is happening to her." Eris opened his mouth to challenge me, but I continued, "If she is still in pain, then put her back under. Please, Eris, no one in this room knows what to do. We need her to help us."

Eris turned slowly back to Brianna and closed his eyes. The room was eerily quiet while we waited for Brianna to awaken. But after a few agonizing moments, Eris opened his eyes and they were full of fear.

"I cannot wake her. Why can't I wake her?"

"Because la petite chute needs her sleep of course, mon amore," Seraphina said as she padded into the room.

"Sera," Eris said, rushing to her side, "why won't she wake?"

"She will wake whin she iz ready. We must wait for her. She will find her way." Seraphina looked past her husband, catching my attention. "I promise, Cameron. She will find her way."

We all remained silent for several minutes, merely looking at one another trying to think of what to do next. Lanashell left once Seraphina and Eris decided to stay to help monitor Brianna's progress. Alexander finally released me so that he could dispose of the broken couch and pull another one from storage. Kyla left for only a few minutes and then returned to stay curled at Brianna's feet reading from a stack of novels she had retrieved from her room. Since it was obvious to Devin that I was not leaving Brianna's side, he excused himself to handle pending matters in my absence and inform Victor of the situation. Then when the sun was low enough, even Jared sat vigil at Brianna's side, though covered in laptops and headphones.

Brianna had not moved a muscle since Eris put her under, and I was certainly looking for it. Every time I touched or kissed her, I hoped she would magically wake up as in the fairytales. Sadly, I had to admit my growing desperation to hear her voice again tell me that she loved me. Until recently, I had not heard those words said to me in three hundred years, and now the thought of never hearing them again made me feel as though my existence was pointless. It was pointless without her.

The sun rose, bringing with it a new day, another stack of books for Kyla, a second knitting project for Seraphina, and another day of agony for me and Eris. Everyone could see the guilt he felt. His blood had done this to her, but I was just as guilty for pushing her to do it. I assured her that being activated was nothing to be scared about, that nothing would happen to her. And yet, her screams still echoed in my ears. Every so often I would look over to Eris, searching for any sign that Brianna was somehow conscious, but each time he met me with sad, desperate eyes and shook his head.

Once evening came again, Jared returned, taking the same position as the night before. Our room was filled with those who loved Brianna, even though she was only known to them for a short while. But their sadness and longing were nothing compared to what I felt. What if she never woke up? What if she died? The possible realities were overwhelming, and I wanted her to myself. I needed time alone with her, or more so, time to express my grief without the presence of others.

"Well, that's my last book," Kyla announced dramatically, closing the back cover of her book and throwing it in the pile on the floor. She glanced at me and gave me a quick wink. "I think we should leave Brianna in Cameron's care this evening."

Jared pulled his headphones down around his neck and said, "But I just got situated."

"Then it's a good thing you didn't get comfortable. Now move," Kyla commanded and began stacking her books in her arms.

I thought for sure I would hear an objection from Eris, however, when I looked in his direction Seraphina had already taken his hand to keep him calm as she walked with him to Brianna's bedside. He kissed her gently on the forehead, and then surprisingly patted me on the shoulder.

"You will tell me if she wakes," he said stiffly under Seraphina's control.

"Of course. And you will tell me if you…see anything?"

Eris nodded and stepped away from his daughter's side. Our somber moods were in complete contrast to Seraphina's, whose spritely demeanor seemed out of place as she kissed everyone's cheeks and led Eris out of the room. But knowing her, she knew something that the rest of us did not.

Kyla was the last to leave, literally pushing Jared and Alex out the door ahead of her. But before she closed the door behind her she turned back around and said, "She is going to be okay, right?"

"Kyla, since I met Brianna, I have been uncertain of so many things. I only wish whether she was going to live was not one of them."

"Well, she just has to be, and that's final. I am not going to lose the only other girl in this house. So pray, sacrifice all the lambs you can find, sell your soul, whatever, just…just fix her, okay?"

"I will do my best," I replied, squeezing my temples tightly between my fingers. I only heard her shut the door, unable to look at the worry in her eyes any longer.

With everyone out of the room I was overtaken with grief. At first, I watched my Bri, caressed her face and hands, trying to convince myself that she was merely sleeping. But then I yelled at her, shook her, bargained with her, anything to get a response. At one point late in the evening, I even draped her across my body. With the exception of feeling her heart pulse against my chest, her body was limp and lifeless. It was as if Chloe was lying dead on me all over again. The feeling was so real and raw that I placed Brianna back to her original position.

Nights like this I despised being a vampire. Fatigue would never really come, and I could feel every second of every minute slowly pass by. Not long after midnight I found myself wiping away watery red stains from Brianna's face when I finally released my pain from within. There were moments when I would look at my angel and remember her dancing in her beautiful white dress; kissing her for the first time in front of Oliver's home; playing cards and unable to figure out how she cheated; watching her as she tripped and fell into the bed while trying to seduce me. I replayed every moment we had together in my head, each bringing with it a stab of pain at the thought of not being able to add more.

It was just after 4:00 a.m., my shirt was damp and ruined, and Brianna's face was stained with my tears. Hating the feeling of the wetness on my chest, I left Brianna's side and stepped into the closet. I shrugged out of my shirt and threw it in the garbage. Instinctively I reached in my dresser for yet another black sweater, but changed direction when the sight of my blue and white pinstriped shirt that Brianna had worn just the other night caught my eye. The shirt still had her smell woven into the fabric, again reminding me how beautiful and seductive she looked in my shirts and how much I would miss seeing her in them.

Shaking the negative thoughts out of my head, I stepped into the bathroom and wetted a washcloth to clean Brianna's face with. When I walked back into the bedroom, I was startled to find my father standing at the foot of the bed. He must have Projected in or else I was truly void of all my senses in my current depressive state.

"Still no progress?" Victor asked.

"None as of yet," I answered. "I have stained her face."

Victor stayed silent for a few moments, watching me wash away the signs of my grief.

"She will pull through, child. I know this," he said with great confidence.

"*How* do you know this?"

"Look at all she has endured in her life, and yet she still survives. Abuse at the hand of her husband, vampire attack, hybrid attack, *father* attack. She truly is a Warrior, Cameron. She will pull through this and surprise us all as she has done before."

"Why did you do it?"

"Do what, child?"

"Make her a Warrior?"

Victor paused for a moment, and sat on the corner of the bed. "That is an interesting story. I had pondered making her a member of our family merely because she was a daughter of Eris, or more so to keep you within these walls. But that has never been my way. A Warrior is a Warrior, a title that is earned and deserved, not something given arbitrarily. But I knew she had shown powers we had never seen, and I felt that if she could hone that power, it would be an asset for us. Then, on the night of her claiming, in the few moments I spent with her I realized I had completely misjudged her. She proved to me that she has many of the same qualities as my other children. Though she is not the strongest or fastest, she is loyal, assertive, and willing to sacrifice herself for others in our family. That is why I made her a Warrior. She is not my sire, I did not create her, but there is a force about her that would sadden me if she were not with us. I cannot say that about many people."

I clamped my jaw tight, trying to keep my emotions under control, but failing miserably as my fears poured out in front of my maker.

"I cannot lose her, Father. I cannot lose her as I did Chloe. My life will be worthless without her."

"Child, I am going to assume that is your grief speaking because your life has never been worthless nor will it ever be. She will come out of this, child, you must have faith in that and stop this nonsense about losing her. Now, I must insist that you refrain from staining her face. It is too beautiful to be streaked with your tears."

"Yes sir," I answered, feeling embarrassed.

As Victor stood to leave, Devin came through my bedroom door with a look of panic, something I had rarely seen on his face.

"We have a situation."

"What is it, child," Victor asked as he sat back down on the bed.

"Tao has gone missing," he announced. Tao, a Warrior of thirty years, had been a valuable asset in tracking activities related to Elaina's coven. "He filed a report two days ago stating he believed he had found a laboratory connected to Elaina, and no one has heard from him since."

"Brother, he might have gone dark for reconnaissance."

"I disagree," Devin snapped. "We should have heard from him by now.

We need to gather the team," he said, turning toward the door.

"Devin, wait, I am not leaving Brianna."

Devin turned slowly around to face me. "Brother, I understand your concern over her. I care for Brianna as well, but we are talking about a brother Warrior who needs our help. We must gather and form an action plan for his rescue."

"But we do not know if he needs rescuing, Brother. We know nothing. Although it seems a little premature, gather the team yourself and formulate a plan if you feel you must, but it will be without me. I am not leaving her."

Devin's chest rose and fell quickly several times, actions I had seen many times over the centuries we had been together. It meant he was beginning to lose control. I loved my brother, but we argued and clashed liked stubborn mules at times.

"Brother, you need to get your priorities straight. Your loyalty should be to your family."

"*Brother*," I replied through clenched teeth, "my priorities *are* my family. That includes Brianna, and right now my loyalty lies with her."

"As it always does," Devin lashed back. "It is so easy for you to turn your back on us when it suits you."

Unable to contain myself any longer I launched myself off the bed and into Devin's face. "And you would no sooner kill any one of us if it suited you or Father."

"Tao is not some human in trouble, he is a Warrior," Devin screamed, pushing me back with his chest.

"As is she," Victor interrupted, separating us and pushing us away from each other. "Devin, you must remember that Brianna is a member of our coven now, and is as much of a priority as anyone else. Cameron is right that he should stay with her until she recovers." I smiled smugly and noticed Devin clinch his fists. "Cameron, you must also remember that you are a leader in this family and cannot completely devote all of your attention to one person, others need you as well. Therefore, Devin will gather the team and we will meet here to form a course of action regarding Tao." It was Devin's turn to gloat. "Devin, how much time do you need?"

"A couple of hours, maybe more."

"I will give you until 6:00 a.m. then," Victor replied, and Devin left without another word. "Why must these things always happen close to daylight hours? I despise being awake during the daytime."

"Father, I would hardly call it daytime. The sun is several hours away from rising."

"Yes, but I can feel it. You do not criticize Jared on his aversion to the sun."

"Father, Jared is only five. The sun will burn him to ashes. You have no such aversion."

Victor grunted in defeat. "Old habits die hard I suppose. Speaking of, I know there is no hatred between you and Devin, but the two of you must learn how to...debate more peacefully."

"Debate?" I replied, smirking at Victor's choice of words.

"You cannot always rely on me to settle your differing opinions. You have to learn to listen to each other and compromise without intervention. I am putting this in your hands since I know your brother will have more difficulties with this than you. I am counting on you, child."

"Yes, Father."

"Very well then, I will return in a couple of hours. Now remember, no more staining Brianna's face."

"Yes, Father. I will not cry again," I replied softly.

"Child, you can certainly show emotions. Just not on her face," Victor said with a sympathetic smile.

Alexander stood at the foot of my bed presenting the findings of Tao's investigation regarding a laboratory found fifty plus miles outside of Phoenix. Around the room were other Warriors - members of the team Alexander and I had compiled to find Elaina's coven. Victor sat in one of the high-back chairs, listening intently to Alexander's debrief like I should have been. However, at the moment I was unable to keep from glancing at Devin sitting upright in my bed on the other side of Brianna. Several minutes earlier he had stormed into the room before everyone else, came to Brianna's bedside, took her hand while he apologized, and then turned her over and took her place on the bed. She was officially the middle of a vampire sandwich. Everyone in the room, including Victor, stole glances at the two of us sitting in bed with Brianna sleeping soundly between us. But how could you blame them, it was truly bizarre. Devin's behavior about this entire ordeal was completely out of character.

"Tao had been very confident about this particular site," Alexander's deep voice broke through my thoughts. "His report filings over the last week all had to do with this warehouse he believed Elaina was using as one of her laboratories. He was taking extra precautions not to alert them of his presence. However, he might have gotten too close after all."

"How long since last contact?" I asked

"Thirty-five hours."

"With whom?"

Devin cleared his throat. "With me. He stated he was going to break into the laboratory that evening. No one has heard from him since."

"Alex," Victor began, "could Tao simply have gone dark in order to keep from being discovered?"

"I thought that might be the case, Father, but we received confirmation that his hotel room has been ransacked and materials stolen."

Victor took in a deep breath while he pondered everything that had been presented. Finally, "With this additional information I think we are all in agreement that something may have happened to Tao. Where do we go from here?"

"Go and get him of course," I heard from below me. I looked down to see Brianna yawning wide, her eyes opening sleepily. The room went completely silent as Brianna rolled over onto her elbows and then was startled when she saw Devin in the bed next to her. "I feel like I've missed something."

I laughed and pulled her tightly into my chest, kissing her incessantly on her face.

Victor rose from his chair, prompting everyone in the room to leave as he said, "Alex, please inform Eris that his daughter is awake."

Alexander nodded and Projected immediately out of the room. Devin rose from the bed and began pacing the area in front of the fireplace.

Holding Brianna's face in my hands, I asked, "How do you feel?"

Without pause she replied, "Fine."

I looked past Brianna at Victor and Devin who were just as shocked as I was, but before I could ask her anything else a cloud of black mist formed at the foot of my bed quickly taking the shape of Eris.

"Figlia!" he shouted once he was completely formed.

Brianna removed the comforter from around her and placed her feet down on the floor. I leapt in front of her to offer my supportive arms, but she did not need them. She stood on her own and hugged her father as he wrapped his arms around her.

"Bri-an-na, mia figlia, I thought I had lost you. How do you feel?"

Again, without pause, she answered, "Fine."

"Fine?" When she nodded, he looked to each of us in the search for an explanation, but there was none. "Do you remember anything about what happened?"

Brianna released her father and turned to me.

"Yes, I remember the pain, but I don't feel anything now. Really, I feel fine." She looked up at me, staring straight into my eyes as she said, "I do. I feel really, really good. How long was I out?"

"Nearly thirty-six hours. It is Friday, love," I said, unable to keep my fingers from sliding down her cheek when I saw her realization of losing so much time.

"Well then," she sighed and stepped toward the closet, "I better get going."

I tugged on her arm lightly. "Wait, where are you going? You should see a doctor, just in case."

"If it's Friday that means I only have two more days until my challenge, right Dad?"

I whipped my head in Eris's direction who stuttered, "Yes...daughter...that is correct."

I felt Brianna begin to pull out of my grip, but I pulled her back. "Bri, you cannot be serious."

My eyes were wild with frustration, confusion, even anger, and she saw it.

"Cam, I'm okay. They need you right now, and I *really* need to use the bathroom."

I shook my head, feeling guilty for not realizing she would have human needs. She rose onto her toes and kissed me, but when she lowered herself, she had an odd expression on her face. Before I could ask her what was troubling her, she escaped into the bathroom, and I could hear Devin behind me trying to get my attention.

"Now that Brianna has recovered, can we please concentrate on finding Tao?" he said curtly.

"Yes, Devin," Victor replied. "Now that Brianna appears well enough..."

"Hold on now, we know nothing about her recovery..."

"*Cameron*, you will lead the team to search for Tao."

"But Father..."

"*And*," he continued, "you will further search Tao's hotel room for any additional information that his captors might have missed. Then you will take the team to the laboratory and hopefully find him and Elaina's coven. Devin, you will stay here."

"W-why!" he growled.

Victor moved slowly toward Devin, his arms stretched out in a defensive stance.

"Child, oddly enough I have to say that you are too emotional about this. You will be of no use to Cameron, possibly even a hindrance. Since Brianna seems willing, I want you to prepare her for her battle on Sunday."

"I will not," Devin yelled. "I will not stay behind to...to babysit a human. I am your assassin, Father, let me kill them. I refuse to stay here while everyone else goes and does what you have trained me to do."

"Victor, he doesn't really need to stay," Brianna said from behind me.

"Brianna, I beg pardon, but *yes he does*," Victor corrected and gave a challenging look to Devin.

"Father, may I interject?" I asked softly. When he nodded, I continued, "In these situations we count on Devin being there from a combat perspective. Losing Devin leaves me at a significant disadvantage."

"Cameron, I understand your apprehension, but I have made my decision. Devin stays."

"Then I will go," Eris said from his seated position on the bed.

"Eris," Victor replied, "thank you for your offer, but this is more of a family matter that I do not wish to burden you with."

"Yes, Victor, but your family is making sacrifices for mine," Eris said, gesturing back to Brianna. "Besides, I have not battled in decades. The thought of it is quite thrilling. Cameron, I will gather my things. Oh, and we can use my jet."

"You have a jet?" Brianna asked.

Eris smiled slyly. "Figlia, I have everything."

Without waiting for an answer, Eris left the room, strangely happy at the prospect of killing some vampires.

"Then we are settled," Victor said, giving one more intense look to Devin before leaving.

Devin's jaw was taught with rare emotions still crossing his face.

"Brother, I tried."

Ignoring me, he said, "Brianna, be quick. I will be waiting outside."

Devin slammed the door so hard that Brianna jumped and gasped.

"Doesn't look like he'll be going easy on me today," she said, trying to deflect as usual.

I turned quickly, scooped her up in my arms and kissed her hard on the lips. When she finally needed breath, I squeezed her tightly and placed her gently back on the ground.

"Do not ever, ever, *ever*, do that to me again," I said kissing her on the head after each word.

"What happened?" she said, looking up at me with curious eyes.

"We were hoping you could tell us."

She shook her head, pulling my hands into hers. "Like I said, I remember the pain and...and then...nothing. The next thing I know, I'm hearing that there's a Warrior missing and find Devin lying next to me in our bed. What did my father see? What was I dreaming about?"

"Nothing, love. If your heart had not been beating, we would have thought you were dead."

Brianna's eyes grew wide and squeezed my hands tightly.

"Cam, I'm so sorry. I didn't mean to scare you."

I brought her back into my chest, wrapping my arms around her and resting my cheek on her soft dark hair.

"I cannot lose you like that again."

"You won't," she said reassuringly. "I promise never to drink my father's blood again."

She unraveled herself from my arms, only to wrap her arms around my neck and pull me down to her lips again. My kiss to her was passionate. Two days of agony released onto her lips and into her mouth. If she would have allowed it, I would have made love to her right here. But before we were unable to control ourselves, Brianna pulled away, once again having an odd look on her face.

"I'm colder, aren't I?"

"Is that what you are worried about?" She nodded. "Yes, love, you are a few degrees cooler, but you are not cold and dead like I am."

"You almost feel...normal."

"Is that bad?"

"Oh no," she replied defensively, shaking her head vigorously from side to side. "Not for me. Is it for you?"

I scooped her up once again, allowing her feet to dangle a foot off the floor and kissing her again. I could feel her body relaxing, letting my love and affection shower over her. After another dozen soft kisses, I set her back down on the floor.

"I should get ready. Devin is waiting," she said reluctantly.

"Why are you insisting on doing this now? You should be resting."

"I believe I've been doing that for almost two days," she laughed.

"*Brianna*," I groaned warningly. "Thirty-six hours ago, you were convulsing on the floor and screaming unlike anything I have ever heard. Do not stand there and lie to me and tell me that you feel one hundred percent."

"I don't, Cam," she answered and I was about to lay into her when she continued, "I feel better than that."

I shook my head in frustration. "W-what? How?"

She shrugged. "I don't know, I just do. My muscles don't hurt, my joints don't ache. I feel great."

"Then just take a day for yourself to make sure you have fully recovered."

She cupped my cheek with her hand, her eyes telling me I was not going to get my way.

"I am doing this for myself," she replied. "I need to prove I can do this. Besides, you're going to be on a mission. I need something to take my mind off of that."

I sighed and pulled her hand up to my heart. "Why is it that I get you back only to be ripped apart from you again?"

"Makes the heart grow fonder?"

"My heart is already very fond of you."

"I love you, Cam."

My head suddenly felt heavy, as though all my strength had been needed to hold it up until I heard those wonderful words.

"Not as much as I love you, angel. Now brace yourself," I whispered to her as I heard the sound of Kyla's heels clicking quickly down the hallway toward our room.

A second later our bedroom door flew open with Kyla whipping through it. Within seconds Kyla's arms were surrounding the two of us.

"Ky, you're suffocating me," Brianna said with her face mushed into my chest.

"Sorry!" Kyla screeched, but only loosened her hold. "I have been worried sick about you. Don't ever, ever, ever, ever, do that to me again."

"I feel like I've heard that before," Brianna said, giving me her own devilish smile.

Kyla laughed along with us, but then quickly dropped her jovial mood and said, "Seriously, Bri, never again."

"Suffice it to say, Kyla, I assume the two of you can keep each other company while Alexander and I are away?"

"Kind of a given, Cameron," Kyla replied and then took Brianna's hands firmly into hers as she said, "Oh Bri, we're going to have so much fun. I have one word…no two words for you. Slumber. Party."

"Oh holy hell," Brianna muttered under her breath.

Chapter Fifty-two

Brianna

I felt fine, much to everyone's surprise. I could feel their frustration at not having an explanation for what had happened to me, or why I was suddenly cured. While we dressed, Cameron kept throwing out different theories – Eris's blood was too powerful, I was too strong of a hybrid, maybe Eris wasn't my father after all. One theory I had was that my father's blood was burning away all the scars I had accumulated from Sam. It was probably nonsense, which was why I kept it to myself, but it was hard to deny how good I felt. I'd been ready to take on the world until I saw Cameron in his full Warrior gear. All the wind had been taken out of my sails once I realized he would be going on a mission. This was a first for us, and we were both a bit awkward when saying goodbye. Frankly I was just trying not to cry in front of him, he was having a hard enough time letting go of me as it was.

After Cameron left, Devin kept banging on the door every thirty seconds which prevented me from sulking. When I was finally ready, I took a deep breath and opened the bedroom door to find Devin scowling back at me.

"Do not waste my time today," Devin growled. "If you are not willing to work then I might as well leave."

"No, Dev, I'm ready."

"Grab your new daggers."

I ran back into the room and grabbed the thin wooden box that held my father's silver daggers. There was a bit of excitement building inside of me at the prospect of using them. When I stepped back out into the hallway

Devin had already started down the corridor. I could tell it was going to be a long day, especially if Devin was going to be in a miserable mood. I ran the few steps down the hall to catch up with him.

"I'm sorry you have to babysit me today, Dev."

"I have no choice when it is Father's bidding."

"Were you and Tao close?"

"Yes," he said quickly and then regretting it. "No. Why ask such a thing?"

"Well…" I began and pulled him to a stop, "I know that when things happen to me, Cameron gets irritable and defensive, so I just wondered if you were close to Tao."

Devin's lips were pursed tight, his nostrils flaring while his chest rose and fell dramatically. The sight was similar to a bull ready to charge. I didn't know whether to run or throw my arms around him. Knowing that he could outrun me, I gambled on the latter and hugged him gently although he did not reciprocate.

When I released him, he looked uncomfortably around us and then pulled me back into my bedroom by my elbow. Once the door was shut, he began to stutter, "You cannot…c-cannot tell anyone. T-Tao was…I…Brianna, I am…*different*." I could see the shame he felt in his admission, and my heart went out to him. "I do not expect you to understand, but…"

"No, Dev, I think I do. I have a good friend who is…different," I said using his term rather than throw out a term such as gay in his face which was obviously frightening for him. "So Tao is…"

"A friend," he interrupted, but then sighed and leaned up against the door with his head hanging low. "No, he was more than that. That's why I was so angry with Cameron when he didn't seem the least bit concerned at the fact that Tao had disappeared."

"Maybe if Cam had known what Tao was to you, he would have been more sympathetic."

Devin's head shot up, his stance straight and rigid. "No one can know, Brianna. I am the Warrior Assassin. If people were to find out that I was…" but he could not bring himself to say the word. "If people knew who I truly was, I would lose the respect I have built over the last five hundred years."

"Is it respect or fear, Devin?" He didn't answer me, but he knew what the true answer was. "Look, I know your brothers love you. I'm not saying go and put up fliers all over the manor, but you may want to think about telling those closest to you. How can they help you if they don't know why you're being such an ass?" Devin raised his eyebrow at me. "With good reason of course," I said quickly. "They'll find him, Dev."

"No, they won't. Not alive at least."

"Do you know something the rest of us don't?"

He let out a frustrated laugh, allowing the corners of his lips to curl in a sad smile. "I know death too intimately to ignore the signs. I can always feel when someone's death is upon them. It is hard to admit, but I fear that he is already dead."

I stood silent for several moments, letting Devin process through whatever emotions he needed to in the comfort of his own head. Finally he sighed, opened my bedroom door, and gestured to the hallway. I patted him on the shoulder as I passed.

"No one can know my secret, Brianna," Devin whispered as we made our way toward the stairs. "I need to know I can trust you with this."

"Of course you can," I replied to his relief. "But for curiosity's sake, what would you do if I accidently leaked it?"

"I would kill you. Literally," he answered fiercely, sending a shiver down my spine.

"So...uh...five hundred years, huh?" I asked nervously and headed down the stairs.

"Yes, I am Victor's oldest living child."

"Living?"

"Technically I am his tenth sire, but the others were killed."

"Really, how?"

"I killed them," he replied flatly. "At Father's request of course."

"Oh yes, of course."

"They deserved it."

"I should hope so. Hopefully you don't go killing your siblings for fun."

Devin was quiet while we made our way down the main corridor. But instead of turning down the usual hallway for the training room, Devin pulled me along in the direction of the library. Just as we approached the library door we veered to the left and down a few steps that led into another corridor. From what I remembered, Cameron had said this one led to the Council Hall.

"Dev, where are we going?"

"I thought we should have a change of scenery," he said as he pulled me along a breezeway with consecutive archways that revealed a wide-open courtyard. When the sunlight from the second archway hit my face, I frantically backed away until I hit the wall and slid down to the floor. I looked to the end of the breezeway to see the door I recognized from my dream, and it was just as exact as the sprawling courtyard in front of me. This was where the battle would happen, I was dead sure.

Devin knelt in front of me, his eyes surprisingly kind.

"I did not mean for this to startle you. I only wanted to confirm that this was the site of the battle you saw in your dream without Cameron's interference. Is this it?"

I nodded slowly as my breath began to slow to a reasonable rate. "Just...just not today."

"That is certainly good to hear," Devin said, helping me from the ground. "Cameron and I may disagree about telling Father about your gift, but I firmly believe we should at least get you prepared in case it does happen. Shall we get the lay of the land?"

Devin led me across the courtyard, passing other Warriors who were also training in the hazy morning sun. Sitting on a large blanket near the far corner were Kyla and Seraphina looking as though they were having an early morning picnic. Both waved as we approached, but Kyla held something strappy in her hands.

"I made a couple of new holes to make it smaller for her," she said as she handed a leather strappy contraption to Devin.

Devin took it from her and then held it out to me as he said, "When Eris gave you the daggers, I thought you could use something to hold them in. I asked Kyla to alter one of my older holsters until you find another one that you like."

Devin stretched out the leather straps in both hands and helped me lace them over my shoulders and across my waist, tightening them into the right settings. In the middle of my back were two thin compartments which held my daggers perfectly. One compartment opened just below my left shoulder, where the other opened downward by my right kidney. The fit was perfect, and my daggers clicked snuggly into place.

After thanking Devin for his gift, I stepped over to my stepmother and kissed her on both cheeks and said, "Sera, what are you doing out here?"

"Your fazer told me you were awake, so I wanted to see you. Only Kyla told me you were going to train, so I thought I would watch you. Zhat is okay, ma petite chute?"

"Uh...yeah, I guess," I answered nervously as I stood and turned back to Devin.

Devin smirked as he led me a few steps away from our guests. "You know she calls you a cabbage, right?" I looked at him confused. "My French is pretty rusty, but I believe chute means cabbage."

I stopped and turned to Seraphina who was smiling delightfully at me, and I couldn't be mad at yet another horrible nickname.

"Why does it have to be a smelly vegetable?"

Devin laughed, but then we got to work. First order of business was how to get the daggers out quickly. Depending on the attack, I had a choice of reaching over my shoulder, or down at my back. I preferred the one at my back since I was faster with my right hand, which was why Devin insisted we continue to use the left. For two hours we practiced whipping my daggers out in various scenarios – being attacked from the front, the back, surprise hit from the side. I even jumped up and down like a cheerleader when I nicked Devin in the hand. He had insisted we use my silver daggers, so it was his own damn fault if he got hurt.

The second order of business was to evaluate what (if anything) had been enhanced by my activation. Even though we didn't stop for a break for the first four hours, my muscles weren't burning which made me want to push harder and get into the real stuff to see if my father's blood was really worth the pain. I had been so used to sword training with Eris that my daggers felt like feathers in my hands. They flew around in defense of my body like extensions of my arms. The intricate silver and pearl swirls on the faces of the curved handles seemed to melt into my hands as the day continued.

After hours of work, Seraphina insisted on a brief lunch, even though my muscles weren't screaming with fatigue. Unfortunately, the break made my head swim with worry. I knew Devin was holding back, which didn't help me against a vampire in real life. I needed to be pressed. The clock in my head was ticking down, and growing louder. The moment of truth was approaching and I could no longer be afraid of it or even making a fool out of myself.

"Dev, I'm ready to do this for real."

Devin's brows rose. "Then you need to use your mind trick. Your power is the only way you're ever going to beat me, or Eris, or any other vampire."

"I know. I just have trouble getting started."

Seraphina took my hand gently. "Cloz your eyes, Brianna," she whispered. "Now just relax, breathe, and use what Lana taught you."

The sound of Lana's name made me flinch, but I knew that Sera was trying to help. With my eyes closed, I took a deep breath and cleared my head. Then, as Lana had taught, thinking as if my mind had tentacles, I reached out into my surroundings looking to find the essences of those around me. Ready to give up right away and open my eyes in defeat, I suddenly saw a tiny light in the vicinity where Devin was standing. I concentrated on the ball of light and then noticed another near him begin to glow where I remembered Kyla sitting. Pushing my mind out further, my eyes flew open when I realized I could see the essences of the others scattered around the courtyard. The small lights glowed like halos around each of the vampire's head even in the bright midday sun. I could even feel the pulsating energy coming from each ball of light pushing slightly at my own mind.

"Brianna?" Devin asked softly, offering me his hand. I didn't take it, but instead closed my eyes, feeling a tingling in my abdomen, and with a deep breath I pushed it through the top of my head and directed my energy towards Devin's light. When I opened my eyes, Devin was finding his balance after having staggered back a few steps and then quickly looked at me and said, "Again."

I took in another deep breath, filling my lungs and back with air and feeling the tingling in my abdomen grow and expand through my body. With a jolt of energy, I thrust my hands out in front of me as I pushed Devin's light away and watched as he flew fifty feet backwards, hitting the stone wall behind him. You could have heard a pin drop in that courtyard.

Only taking a moment to brush off, Devin raced towards me with his own daggers drawn. I shot up from my position next to Sera, drawing both my daggers from my harness and began defending myself against Devin. His thrusts were faster, but he was still holding back. As his daggers flew at my face, pushing me back across the lawn, I focused on his light and pushed him back with three quick pulses at the same rhythm of the hits from my daggers. Devin's face was confused and surprised as my mind hit him over and over again. He stopped his attack, looking very human as he caught his breath.

"Damn that hurts."

"Really?!" I replied with a little too much excitement.

"Thank you for your concern."

"You're not training me to be concerned."

He laughed. "You are correct, I'm not. I think we've found the right combination. Let's try it again."

Although I did trip over my feet a few times, I didn't fall from being overpowered. To me, that was a win. When Devin was starting to get the better of me, I would hit him with my mind trick – into the wall, into the ground, screaming in his head until he fell to his knees, whatever I could do to give my body a break. As the day went on, both Devin and I needed to take breaks from each other to catch our breath, which made me happier than a pig in shit that it wasn't just me. Throughout the rest of the day, humans and vampires alike came to watch as Devin and I battled each other. None of them, however, were as much of a welcomed sight as Jared running down the long lawn when the sun had finally set.

"Bibi, you are kicking his ass!"

"Jared, I would hardly call it that," I said, trying not to make Devin mad.

"Dude," Jared said over my shoulder at Devin, "I've been watching all afternoon. You're totally getting your ass kicked by a girl."

"Maybe you should have a go with her then," Devin growled.

"Hell no. I've felt what she can do. Not only am I here to watch you humiliate my brother, but you are missing one thing," he said pulling the strap of a bag from across his chest over his head, and letting it fall to the ground. "You need some music. We need to find your fighting groove."

Quickly Jared unpacked equipment from inside the bag and within seconds loud pump-you-up music was blasting throughout the courtyard. I had to admit it got me pumped up. As each new song came on, I felt as though I was fighting in a movie with a great soundtrack. Devin, however, continually yelled at Jared to "shut that racket off", but of course he didn't since he was enjoying toying with Devin just as much as I was.

When nine o'clock finally rolled around, I was starving and tired, but my muscles still had a little fight left in them. My father's blood had definitely made some significant changes, and I had to admit it was almost worth the pain it caused me. Devin had asked for one more round before wrapping up, and I agreed even though my head was achy from using it to push Devin around for the last eight hours.

Devin started by coming at me from above, causing me to pull his light forward as I turned around, getting a hit on his back while he was dazed. He spun around whipping his daggers left and right, and with great effort I kept up with his speed, pushing him as I could through my fatigue. Devin continued to come at me, wanting to see how far he could press me before I gave up. He lunged forward, both daggers coming at my abdomen before I pushed his light backwards several feet resulting in both of us hitting the ground. Before I could completely get up, Devin flew into me, knocking me back down. His daggers were crossed against mine, my strength alone unable to hold him up, but a combination of weakly pushing his light back. Devin's eyes were blazing into mine, growling at me not to give up even though my arms were shaking under his weight.

"Push through it, Brianna. Come on now, do not let me do this to you."

"I c…can't," I whimpered while my arms burned and shook with fatigue, allowing Devin's daggers to come scarily close to my face.

But Devin didn't let up. Suddenly he threw his daggers on the ground and pinned my arms down above my head. We were nose to nose, his fangs extended as he growled again in a low voice, "You'll never be strong enough, Bri Bri. You'll always be the pathetic weakling you've always been. You have no business being in the Warrior coven."

"Devin, that's enough," Kyla yelled as she rushed forward, only to be stopped by Jared's firm grip around her waist.

Even with Kyla's protests, Devin continued pressing into my arms and then locked down my pelvis with his as I began to squirm under his weight.

"Give up, Bri Bri, just lie there and take it like a good girl, like you've always done, *Bri Bri*."

As the sound of that name came across Devin's lips, horrible memories came flooding into my head - nights of Sam holding me down while he violated me over and over again, the feel of his open palm as he slapped me across the face, struggling to breathe while his hands closed around my throat. I wasn't a victim anymore. I had made that promise to myself, but bound by Devin's grip it was hard to think otherwise.

Devin lifted up slightly, changing his grip to hold both my wrists in one hand while his other reached back. Just as Devin's fist started to come down, a sudden bolt of energy raged through me. With a loud scream and every ounce of energy I had, I pushed Devin with both my body and mind causing him to fly back into the courtyard wall. Scrambling to my feet I gripped my daggers firmly as Devin began to fade into a black mist. Remembering that at one time I had somehow pushed Jared when had Projected, I concentrated on Devin's fading form, seeing his light dimming while another began to appear in front of me. Mentally I grabbed both lights and pulled them both together roughly to the ground. Devin lay fully developed and disoriented as I leapt on top of him, plunging my silver daggers into his shoulders and pinning him to the ground beneath.

I sat on top of Devin, exhausted and out of breath as the forgotten crowd applauded and cheered around me. Jared whipped me off of Devin and spun me around so fast I thought I was going to puke. Begging him to put me down, I was suddenly being crushed by not only Jared, but Kyla, Seraphina, and even a few others I didn't know. I had beaten Devin, the mighty Warrior Assassin. *I* had beaten him.

Speaking of, I pushed everyone aside and found Devin still lying on the ground with my daggers in his shoulders burning his skin inside and out. He was in pain, but speaking only slightly tense to the surrounding vampires looking down upon him. The Warriors backed away when I approached Devin and knelt beside him.

"Nice job," he said, rolling his head over in my direction. Overcome with emotion, my head fell to his chest as tears of joy, fear, and resolution came pouring out. "Brianna," Devin said softly, touching me with as much of his hand as he could move, "you know I didn't mean what I said. It was only…"

"I know, Dev," I replied, lifting up and embarrassingly wiping my face free of tears.

"Are you angry with me?"

"No, of course not…"

"Then do you think you could remove your daggers?"

"Ohmygod," I yelped, grabbing the silver hilts that stuck up through his shoulders and slowly began retracting them while Devin groaned in pain. When he was finally free, he stood from the ground, patted me on the shoulder, and began to walk away.

"Come, Jared, we should check on the team's progress in Phoenix," he said. Jared whined but reluctantly walked alongside Devin as he made his way back to the manor, the holes in his shoulders finally beginning to close as he approached the breezeway.

Although the crowd still milled about, all I wanted was to be back in my room. I was exhausted, a little achy, and more importantly missing Cameron. His was the face I wanted to see in the crowd more than anyone's, and he was hundreds of miles away.

"Okay, show's over," Kyla said from behind me, handing me a towel to clean my daggers with before placing them back in their case. With me in tow, Kyla shooed people aside as she pulled me through the crowd. "Seriously Bri, I can't watch that again. Jared was literally wrestling me to the ground."

"Sera! Where is she?" I said, whipping around only to find my stepmother gliding across the courtyard towards us.

"Right here," she said, hugging me gently and then cupping both her hands around my face. "Your fazer would be so proud. He will have his work cut out for him."

"I couldn't have done it without you."

Sera smiled and patted my cheek. "You did all zhe work, ma petite chute."

"Cabbage, Sera? Really? I remind you of cabbage?"

"It is a term of endearment where I'm from, I promise. Je t'aime, ma petite chute."

Before I could reply, Sera bid us goodnight and glided back into the manor. Kyla took my elbow and within minutes we were in the kitchen for food supplies for the slumber party. Although I was the only one eating, we had enough food for an army.

Once in my bedroom I feared that Kyla's vision of an all-night slumber party would be cut short since my bed looked unbelievably comforting, and then suddenly empty without Cameron.

"Hey Ky," I called to her as she fumbled around in my closet looking for who knows what, "does Alex ever call you when he's out on these missions?"

"Forbidden," Kyla answered as she stepped out and leaned against the archway. "One of Victor's rules. No distractions when on a mission. Are you worried about Cameron?"

"Aren't you worried about Alex?"

"Bri, if I worried myself to death every time Alex was on a mission, then I'd be dead…er. Okay, bad analogy. It's always hard when he leaves, which is probably why I have a new wardrobe by the time he gets home. Not only am I really good at shopping, but it distracts me while he's gone."

"Aren't you scared that he'll get hurt, or…die," I said with great difficulty as I sat down on the bed.

"Sometimes. But then I remind myself that he is extremely strong, even for a vampire, and he has a team of Warriors around him all handpicked and trained to be the most ferocious fighters in existence. And then, I buy a new pair of shoes." Kyla stepped out of the archway and squeezed my shoulder. "Cameron will be fine, Bri, I promise. Now, no more talk of the boys, we have a slumber party to get underway. You start eating the ice cream right from the container and I'll take these downstairs."

"Er, Kyla, why do you have my underwear in your hands?" I asked, seeing several pairs dangling from her fingers.

"They have to go in the freezer, of course. Haven't you done this before?" she huffed. "Jeez, and I'm the vampire."

Chapter Fifty-three

Brianna

"Put it on, Brianna," Jazlyn said as she gestured to the onyx ring in the velvet box. "Cameron gave it to me years ago. I thought you would want it."

Taking the ring out of the box, I placed it on my left hand, mesmerized by its beauty and perfect fit. But as I stared down at the dark oval of onyx on my finger, a searing pain pulsed through my hand and up my arm causing me to fall to my knees, clasping my hand in agony. I looked up to see Elaina coming towards me, her thick blonde hair twisted tightly on the back of her head. I tried to crawl toward the courtyard, but Elaina grabbed me from behind, thrusting me up against the stone wall and holding me by the throat. Her fangs were extended and her eyes were hungry as she brought her face right up against mine.

"Wake up, angel," she said as she kissed the tip of my nose.

What the?

She was still squeezing my throat as she kissed both my cheeks and began to move down my neck...

My eyes flew open to see Cameron hovering over me and gently kissing my face.

"Oh thank god," I said relieved.

"Why is your face sticky?" he asked, licking at his lips.

"That is your sister-in-law's doing. She ran out of shaving cream on

Friday night, so last night I kept waking up to whipped cream on my face and just started eating it rather than keep getting out of bed. You should see how many pairs of underwear I had to rescue from the freezer downstairs. I love her, but she's killing me."

Cameron's lips curled up one side, showing me my favorite smile. "I will never understand the rules of a girl's slumber party."

"Trust me, I don't either. Who knows what book she read or movie she watched. I don't have lipstick all over my face, do I?"

Cameron laughed and shook his head. "No, angel, but it is time to wake."

"Who says I'm getting out of bed?"

"Devin," he replied, taking both my hands in his and kissing them softly. "He is expecting you in half an hour."

"But you just got back," I whined, wrapping my arms around his neck and taking in as much of his rustic smell as I could.

"I know, love, but it is a big day. Come, Devin is waiting," he said as he untangled himself from my arms and stood from the bed.

"I learned a new trick while you were away."

"And what is that, love?"

Quickly I opened my mind to find his essence and in a sudden movement I pulled his light down on the bed next to me, threw myself on top of him, and held his arms down above his head.

"Now you're going to lay there and let me kiss you, and you're going to like it."

I lowered my lips onto his, relaxing my grip and allowing him to encircle me with his arms. His kisses were gentle and somewhat restrained as I pressed my lips harder and harder against his. I pressed myself up so that I could see him better, and for the first time I noticed the appearance of purplish circles under his eyes. He looked exhausted in an almost human way.

"Cam, what's wrong?"

Cameron tilted his head slightly while his fingers grazed the side of my cheek.

"Nothing is wrong, Bri. I have simply let myself go too long without feeding." Before Cameron could say another word, I shifted my hair to one side and pulled my shirt collar down across my shoulder. "Absolutely not," he said loudly and pulled my shirt back into place. "You need all your strength for tonight."

"But if you really need it, why go and get it when you can drink from the cow that's sitting on your lap?" Cameron knitted his brows together. "I guess that really didn't work. Okay, just take it if you need it."

"No," he answered firmly. "I am fine. It is only a combination of not feeding for several days before I left and then having to deal with your father for two days."

"And?" I said, raising my eyebrow at him.

Cameron rolled over so that he was now on top of me, and I completely loved the feeling of him between my legs.

"I thought missing you was a given," he said, twining my hair between his fingers. Almost as if it was too much for him to restrain himself any longer, he kissed me even harder than I had before. His tongue slipped into my mouth finding mine eager to play. After only a few seconds, I felt a small prick on my bottom lip as Cameron's fangs extended and nicked my skin. Quickly he licked away the small droplet of blood that had formed and then looked up at me with conflicted eyes. He pushed himself off of me, swung his legs to the floor, and stared intently at the opposite wall.

"So my father was a little hard to take?"

Cameron released a stifled laugh and squeezed my hand, silently thanking me for doing what I did best.

"Your father has a rather disturbing past."

"That doesn't really surprise me."

"Honestly, Brianna, let us hope you never have to hear the gruesome things your father has done. There were things he described that made even Alexander uncomfortable. On the flight over he was so eager to battle that he was completely dejected on the way home because we did not have to defend ourselves against anything. Then we had to hear about how it seemed that the Warriors were getting soft due to the lack of opportunities to truly use our skills in battle. Needless to say, he will be itching for a good fight tonight, which of course terrifies me since he is battling you, and I have no idea how I am going to be able to stand there and watch as he attacks you."

He took a quick breath and opened his mouth to continue, but I nudged my way up against his left side, placing my arms around his neck and resting my forehead against his cheek.

"You're beginning to sound like me with all that panicked talk."

"I apologize. I do not wish to burden you…"

"And I don't burden you?" I interrupted. "How many times have I had diarrhea of the mouth in front of you and you just sit there and listen?"

"You never burden me, love."

"You're being kind," I laughed and received a slight smile in return, but it quickly fell. "Did you find Tao?"

"Yes."

"Alive?"

"No."

"Does Devin know?"

"Yes, we relayed everything to him early this morning."

"Was he okay?"

"I suppose. Why do you ask?"

"Just wondered," I lied and from the way his eyes narrowed he knew it. "Where did you find him?"

"At the laboratory facility, displayed for all to see. They knew we were coming. Father is now even more convinced we have a traitor among us."

"Did you find anything else?"

"The laboratory was empty. They must have cleared out once they captured Tao. We only found a few bodies and some equipment that was left behind."

"Could you tell what they were doing to the hybrids?"

Cameron turned his body to face me, his brows knitted together while he described how the bodies had electrical burns, similar to what they had recently seen on others. Reasons why they were electrocuting hybrids, of course, were short. One theory was that they were trying to somehow over-activate the vampire blood in the hybrids, but even that seemed farfetched. They couldn't even test the blood of the dead hybrids since there wasn't a drop of it left.

I looked at the clock behind me and noticed that I was already late for my session with Devin.

"Ohmygod, I've got to go," I said in a panic, rising from the bed and heading through the archway to our closet. "Your brother is going to kill me for being late, and then kill you for making me late." I heard Cameron laugh to himself as I began ruffling through my drawers to find a clean outfit. "You know it's sad that could actually happen."

"Welcome to my world, love," he replied behind me.

Slightly startled I turned around to face him, seeing more than ever the exhaustion in his body. I stepped over to him, gently tracing the purplish circle underneath his eye with my thumb.

"Please go and drink something, or someone, or whatever it is you need to do."

Cameron nodded in relief. "I only need an hour or so to recharge. May I come and watch you afterwards?"

"Yes," I answered eagerly, causing him to smile. "Sorry. I just missed you and completely hate the part where I can't talk to you when you're on a mission. Pardon my language, but that's bullshit."

"I know, my love," he said and pulled me into his chest. "I now realize why Alexander gets sullen after a few days on a mission."

"And why Kyla has a new wardrobe by the time he gets home."

"I see that you do not have a new wardrobe."

"That's because I was too busy kickin' Devin's ass and surviving Kyla's antics. I missed you Cameron Jackson, and don't you begin to think otherwise."

"As I missed you, Brianna Marie," he said, kissing me gently on the lips.

"Marilena," I corrected him.

The strategy was to keep Eris off guard as much as possible. So I couldn't come in hard with the mind trick at first, more so let him think I was still unable to control it and then, bam! Devin had also decided since Eris would assume I would come at him with my newly acquired daggers that I should start out with a sword, just one thank goodness, but still something else to keep Eris guessing. It certainly took Cameron by surprise when he joined us. He was my only audience today since Seraphina was with Eris, and Kyla with Alex. I was a little jealous that they could spend time welcoming their loved ones home while I was stuck out here trying to keep from looking over at mine.

Once early afternoon had arrived, Devin declared that our session was over in order to provide me with enough time to rest and recharge for tonight.

"Brianna, it is important that you eat now and not right before the battle. We will stretch out beforehand, but I want complete rest until tonight, understood?" I nodded and he looked over my shoulder to Cameron who was standing close behind me. "Brother, that means complete rest. There should be no intercourse of any kind."

"Oh. My. God, Devin," I said, feeling my cheeks become flush.

"Understood, Brother. No intercourse, or coitus, or any other word that will make Brianna blush," he laughed as he placed his arm around my shoulders and started pulling me down the courtyard.

"Cam, wait, I need to ask Devin something. I'll meet you at the library?"

Cameron nodded, though I could tell he was confused by my urging him to leave. I ducked under his arm and headed back to Devin who was sheathing the remaining swords and daggers.

"Dev, I wanted to make sure you were okay."

"Yes, why wouldn't I be?"

"You know exactly why," I said softly. "You don't need to handle Tao's death alone."

"Yes, Brianna, I do," he replied flatly.

Knowing I wasn't going to get any further, I gave him a hug which again he did not reciprocate. When I stepped past him to leave, he grabbed my elbow and said, "But...thank you."

"If you change your mind..."

"I won't," he replied and turned his back on me to gather up the weapons.

With a sigh, I turned and made my way across the courtyard. When I joined Cameron at the library door his arms were stacked high with books.

"Are you planning to haul up for the winter or something?"

Cameron laughed as we started toward the main corridor of the manor.

"These will aid me in complying with Devin's demands."

"All of those are for you?"

"One is for you."

"Oh, thank you for thinking of me," I answered sarcastically.

"That is the problem, love, I cannot help but think of you."

You and me both, I thought as we headed up the stairs to our bedroom where there was a large cushy bed with plenty of room to roll around on top of each other with nothing separating us, just the feeling of our skin melding into one another.

"Oh for goodness' sake," I unfortunately said out loud. Cameron looked at me out of the corner of his eye, but didn't say a word. I grabbed the first book on Cameron's stack and said, "Is this one mine?"

"It is if you want to read about the battles of ancient Rome."

"Sounds perfect."

Chapter Fifty-four

Brianna

"So, were you in a coma or something that prevented you from calling or texting or emailing your very best friend?" Renee said loudly through the phone.

"Um, well, you could kind of say that," I responded, feeling Cameron tense slightly underneath me as I lay on top of his chest.

"No excuse. I miss you, when are you coming home?"

"I don't know, it could be a while. A lot's going on. How's Dr. John?"

Renee paused, and I wasn't sure if it was reluctance to answer or the fact that I heard the TV on in the background. "He's good."

"That's all I get?"

"I haven't killed him yet."

"Not killing him is a start, and the fact that he hasn't killed you is also a good sign. So you're surviving cohabitation?"

"Oh yes, I *love* picking up his dirty socks off the floor, never having any toilet paper because he used the last sheet and chose not to replace the roll, and the best part is that *he's always there*. In the kitchen, in the bathroom, watching TV, everywhere! He wants to cuddle, he wants to hold my hand, he wants the remote. For crying out loud he never gets tired of me."

"Re, he's an ER doctor. I doubt he is there all the time."

"Yeah, well, that's what happens when he is here."

"And what happens when he's not?"

There was another pause. "I miss him."

"Right. See, he misses you too. It can't always be on your schedule."

"Stop being right. I hate that."

"I know, but that's why I'm your best friend."

"So, how's your Mr. Dreamy?"

"Cam's fine, he's right here, actually," I said, tapping his arm that was wrapped around my waist while his other was stretched out with a book.

"So have you slept with him yet?"

"Re!"

"Come on, you gotta tell me if you've done the deed."

"Ohmygod Renee, stop. I don't ask about you and John."

"Yeah, that's because it's pretty much a given. Besides I'd tell you."

"But I don't want to know."

"That's your choice. *I* want to know. Seriously, is it like getting screwed by a popsicle?"

"Renee!" I screamed in the phone, my cheeks hot with humiliation. "He's right here. He can hear you!"

"Ohmygod, why didn't you tell me?!"

"He's a stinking vampire, Re, it was kind of assumed."

"Hey, I'm new at this."

"Goodbye, Renee."

"No, don't Bri, I'm sorry. Don't go," she begged.

"Sorry, you're so done. Goodbye, Re." I was completely embarrassed, and my stomach churned knowing I needed to say something to the vampire lying beneath me. "Cam, I'm so sorry. She's…impaired."

Thankfully Cameron laughed, and I rolled over to see him face to face. He actually seemed slightly amused by the whole thing.

"Brianna, it is not like the question has not been asked before, maybe not in such a way, but I assure you it is not a…*popsicle*."

"Well, there is only one way to find out," I said seductively as I tried pushing my hand down his pants.

Cameron quickly grabbed my wrist. "Brianna, no."

"Why not?"

"Devin's orders."

"Since when do you follow your brother's orders," I said, pushing my hand down once again.

"*Brianna*…" he groaned, struggling to remove my hand from his pants without hurting my wrist, "…you have less than an hour before your battle." Carefully he rolled me back over so that my back was once again on his chest with his inside arm wrapped tightly around my waist. "And when we are together for the first time it should be done right and not rushed. When the time comes, I want to make love to you long and slow and perfect," he whispered in my ear and then gave my earlobe a tiny kiss. "Are you able to live with that?"

"Yes," I answered shyly. "Long and slow and perfect?"

"Would you rather quick and fast and disappointing?"

"I'll settle for anything that doesn't hurt," I grumbled before I could stop myself.

Cameron's arm tightened around me, but he didn't respond. I could only imagine the thoughts that were going through his head. Unable to take the silence, I picked up my book that I had thrown at my feet when Renee called and tried to get interested in it again. But only after reading three pages I tossed the book on the floor.

"Why is this thing scheduled so late?"

"Father moved the time so that Jared could see you," he answered in a calm tone, keeping his eyes on the book he held out in his right hand.

"It's not fair that I have to suffer."

"Would you rather Jared did?" he asked, turning the page of his book slowly, still ignoring my nervousness. I turned my head up to face him and stuck my tongue out. In response he kissed my nose, always the gentleman. "Bri, this is a big occasion in our coven. I am sure people are excited to see someone battle besides Devin."

"Other people are coming?"

"I am sure it will be only a few people, nothing to be nervous about."

I laughed. "Easy for you to say. Why does Devin keep challenging people to battles?"

"Other way around, love," he said into his book.

"Sorry, new Warrior here. Why would they ever want to go up against Devin?"

"When you want to make a name for yourself, you always want to go up against the best. Devin is one of the best."

"Has he ever lost?"

"No."

"Have you ever battled?"

Cameron closed his book and dropped it on the floor, realizing that my questions were probably not going to end any time soon.

"Yes, I have battled on four occasions."

"Did you win them all?"

"All but one."

"Who did you lose to?"

"Alexander."

"What possessed you to go up against Alex? He's twice your size."

"That he is, and speaking of, I believe I hear him and Kyla coming down the hall," he said, obviously avoiding the topic. Note to self, find out about their battle.

Kyla and Alex came through the door a moment later with Devin right behind them, and Kyla immediately came over to the couch and placed two bags onto the table in front of us.

"Okay, no more lying around, we have work to do," she said as she pulled items out of the bags.

"Kyla, I have forty-five minutes until the battle starts. I have plenty of time. Let me spend it with Cam. I let you enjoy your time with Alex."

"And boy did I," she said looking seductively over at her husband, "again, and again, and again."

Alex was just plain embarrassed as he said, "Kyla, I'd appreciate it if you would keep our private activities, *private*."

"Why bother," Jared said as he pushed open the door and entered the room. "The whole dang house can hear when you two are going at it. Dad needs to seriously invest in sound proofing."

Everyone in the room laughed except for Alex.

"Jared, if you're up already, why do I need to wait until seven? Let's go right now," I said and stood from the couch.

"Er, you can't just up and change the time when there's like fifty people coming."

"What?!" I screamed and turned to Cameron. "You said it would just be a few people."

Cameron stood up from the couch, hands in front of him defensively. "Bri, this is the first I am hearing about this."

I rounded on Jared. "What. Did. You. Do."

"I take the fifth, I will not incriminate myself," he said quickly, but Alex grabbed him up by his collar. "Okay, okay, an email may have been sent out, but that's all you're getting outta me."

Alex dropped Jared on the floor like a ton of bricks while I sat on the arm of the couch. Placing my head in between my knees I tried not to hyperventilate at the prospect of being humiliated in front of so many people. Cameron stood next to me, rubbing my back and yelling at his youngest brother in my defense.

"Everyone just needs to calm down," Kyla interrupted. "What's done is done, and since there are so many people coming, Bri, you need to look your best."

"Oh, Kyla, don't start," I begged.

"*Oh, Brianna*, don't argue," she whipped back at me, actually causing me to sit up and look at her. "Now, I have two outfits for you to choose from," she said, lifting both of them in the air. "So which one, the purple," she said shaking a strappy, purple spandex outfit. "Or the leather," she continued, looking to her other side at a skimpy, black leather jumper.

Of course I said purple the same time Alex, Jared, and Cameron said leather. Devin respectfully declined. I looked at the three guys who voted for the leather and said, "Are you guys insane? Who do you think I am? Jazlyn?"

Everyone in the room laughed at my comment, but it still didn't change their vote. I grabbed the hanger holding the purple outfit and headed into the closet to change. I wasn't sure what I thought I would wear tonight, but suddenly I was self-conscious about wearing anything this tight and revealing in front of so many people. So many people, so many people, oh good grief I felt like I was going to puke. That would certainly be a memorable battle for everyone as they talked to one another in the years to come, *"Oh hey, do you remember when that crazy dark-haired hybrid puked all over the floor in the middle of her battle? I wonder whatever happened to her."* She crawled into a dark hole and died is what happened to her.

Looking at myself in the full-length mirror, the purple looked good against my pale skin and the straps that crisscrossed over my stomach definitely made me look a little sexy. I had come a long way in the past couple of months from only wearing boring blouses and slacks and reading books all day to fighting a dual wearing purple spandex. It was not a typical jump that a woman my age made. Today was important. If I won against my father, it was a big leap in the new direction my life was taking. I no longer wanted to be thought of as weak little Bri Bri, but strong Brianna Morgan, daughter of Eris, who successfully kicked his butt today.

I grabbed my dagger harness from the top of my dresser and began slipping into it as I stepped through the archway, only I didn't get too far. Kyla stood in front of me with a hairbrush, a teasing comb, a bottle of hairspray, and a huge smile on her face.

I put my hand up and said, "Ky, I let you dress me in this purple contraption, but that's as far as I go. My hair is going into a ponytail, and I'm not even going to put on lipstick."

Kyla twisted her lips and stalked back into the bathroom, muttering something I couldn't make out. Cameron smiled crookedly, definitely liking what he saw as he walked toward me with my wooden box that contained my daggers. Seeing the box caused me to take a deep breath and admit to myself that this was really happening. This was what I had trained so hard for, and why I was so nervous about failing. Once Cam opened the box, I took each dagger from its green velvet holding and placed it into its sheath on my back. As each dagger clicked into place, the butterflies in my stomach started to flutter more violently.

Kyla stepped to my side and held out a hair elastic with a full-on grumpy pout on her face. I laughed to myself while I pulled my hair back into a ponytail and turned to face my new family who gathered in support of this important day. Cameron took my hand and kissed the top of each finger before kissing me once more on the lips.

"Ready, love?"

I nodded and then looked past him to the others in the room.

"You guys go on ahead, we'll be right behind you."

Devin stepped forward and said, "Brianna, we all go together. It is tradition that the closest family members escort each challenger to the battle."

I was honored that they all wanted to escort me, but couldn't I have one moment with Cameron alone before this whole fiasco? That question was answered right away when Devin gestured to the door and we all filtered out of the room. Walking down the main corridor surrounded by my vampire family, I could hear the pumping beat of loud music coming from the hallway that led to the training room. This seemed more like a main event in Las Vegas than a training dual between father and daughter.

When we entered the training room, the music was quickly drowned out by the sound of *more than fifty* people shouting and cheering. The room was electric with energy, but it only succeeded in enhancing my nerves. Shortly after my big entrance, Eris entered the training room followed by Seraphina and Victor to the sound of more thunderous applause and members of the crowd pointing in awe at the sight of my father.

Eris didn't dress any different for the occasion. He was in his usual pale linen pants and loose button-down shirt with his hair tied back in a black sling. I watched Eris prepare his weapons on a table on the opposite side of the room which made Devin snap me back to attention.

It was five minutes until seven and I was stretched, warmed-up, and ready to vomit. Cameron could see (and probably smell) how nervous I was and hugged me tightly, kissing me several times on the top of my head. "Eris will not show restraint so do not show him any. And remember the trick Devin showed you today in order to keep your daggers from being knocked out. And your mind projection is key," he instructed, his voice quickening with his own nervousness.

Alex stepped up next to Cameron and said, "Just stand your ground, Brianna. Remember, anything goes in here, just keep your head about you."

"And don't forget to stay low, and quick feet, always quick feet," Jared added doing his best imitation of Muhammad Ali.

I knew they were all trying to help, but they were overwhelming me instead. Devin took my arm and thankfully pulled me away from his brothers.

"Do you remember the strategy?" he asked calmly, though looking sternly at me.

"Yes. Ease into the mind trick, start with the sword and then move to the daggers when it feels right. Keep him guessing and don't give up."

"Right, do not give up," he said, placing both hands on my shoulders. "But if you have done your best there is no shame in yielding if you need to. We'll simply come back and try again."

"No, I'm not doing this again next week. I'm winning this sucker," I said with a sudden urge of confidence.

Devin smiled devilishly at me. "Damn straight you are. Is he looking over at you?"

I looked past Devin's shoulder noticing that Eris had removed his shirt and was now unsheathing two wide swords that curved like an hourglass near the hilt. He caught my eye and gave me a quick wink before whipping his swords around in a display of what was to come.

"Yep, he's looking." Looking pret-ty scary.

"Now grab your sword and make sure he sees it."

I stepped over to the table and took up my own sword, throwing its sheath off dramatically to get Eris's attention. Devin was right, Eris was certainly surprised at seeing a sword in my hand, or perhaps it was pride, it was difficult to tell.

"Brianna," Devin said curtly, jolting my attention back to him, "you need to remove your jewelry." Devin held out his hand expectantly and I placed my watch in his hand, but paused when I reached for the black onyx ring. "I will keep it safe, Bri, I swear."

"Has anyone ever puked at one of these things?" I asked before ripping the ring off my finger and placing it in his hand.

"No," he laughed lightly, "but only because vampires cannot vomit. But as your instructor, I forbid you to do so. You have Eris's genes and my training. You are too good for anything like that. Put all thoughts of biological functions out of your head."

"Great pep talk, coach."

The crowd noise in the room began to die down as Victor, dressed in white Roman-like robes, made his way to the center of the room. I looked back nervously at Cameron who placed his fist over his heart and mouthed the words that he loved me. I gave him a wink and mouthed that I loved him too.

Devin turned my chin to look him dead in the eye. "I need you to concentrate, Brianna. Now, take a deep breath and close your eyes," he whispered and I obeyed. "Open your mind and search for your father's essence."

After exhaling, I reached out with my mind and my head was suddenly filled with the lights of all the vampires in the room. There was no way I would be able to pinpoint Eris, so I opened my eyes and was almost blinded by the number of haloes glowing. But amongst all of them, Eris's light was brighter than the others in the room and I wondered if it had to do with his power and age. Because it was so bright, I focused intently on his essence and closed my eyes once again, working hard to clear my mind of all others. When I opened my eyes again, only his light shone in the room, and I did not take my eyes off of it.

With sword in hand and daggers on my back, Devin directed me to the edge of the mat where I stood and waited for the battle with my father to begin. My hands were shaking to the same rhythm of the music that began to die down once my father took his place on the other side of the mat clear across the room. Victor raised his hands and the entire room went silent in anticipation.

"Today is both a sad and exciting day," Victor announced in a booming voice that was so much bigger than his stature. "Today you lost a brother, and I a son, to our enemy of late. Tao was a soldier, the fiercest of fighters, and a respected Warrior. His death is a blow to us all, and a hard reminder that even though we are vampires, we can still suffer a true death. Tao died defending those we have sworn to protect."

As Victor continued on about Tao, I stole a glance at Devin who stood at my shoulder. He was stoic, unemotional, the typical Devin, but I wondered what was going on inside of him while his father praised his secret lover and was unable to show any sign of caring for him.

"But let us celebrate our fallen brother by continuing on with a tradition that we Warriors have participated in for centuries. Tonight, we have a battle," Victor yelled victoriously to the erupting crowd, many of them beating their chests as they had the night of my claiming ceremony. It was some kind of Warrior thing, and I still hadn't been given the handbook.

Victor continued on, his voice still able to be heard over the roar of the chanting crowd. "Tonight is a battle of many things. A battle between vampire and hybrid. A battle between father and daughter. A battle of pride and establishment. And finally, a battle of acceptance and freedom," he said gesturing to our two corners on each point. "There is only one rule, there will be no help from others." Victor turned to the corner where my family stood together. "Alex, I suggest you hold down your brother and your wife."

The room erupted once again, but this time with laughter as Alex put his arms jokingly around both Cameron's and Kyla's necks.

Victor smiled as he bowed slightly to me and then to Eris, and then finally stepped off the mat as he shouted, "Begin!"

The room was suddenly flooded with my favorite pump-me-up song. I looked quickly over at Jared who gave me two thumbs up, knowing he had put that song on specifically for me. As I smiled back to him, from my peripheral I could see Eris coming in my direction. Staying with the strategy of keeping my father off guard, I continued to look at Jared until Eris was only inches away and tightened my grip on my sword. Quickly I swung it in his direction, successfully hitting the side of his arm before I ducked away.

The battle had begun. Eris was taken aback only for a second while he looked down to see the cut on his arm close. Giving me a sly smile, he came at me with both of his swords swinging gracefully like windmills while I deflected his blows. He was faster and hitting harder than he ever did when he trained me. Though my arms and wrists were absorbing the impact, I needed to start slowly using my mind trick. So I started singing.

Eris jumped back, shaking his head and looking around the room for the source of the noise in his head. When his eyes met mine, I raised my eyebrows at him and said, "Everything okay, Dad?"

My father smiled wickedly as he narrowed his eyes and began another volley of wildly flailing swords. My singing in his head became louder and I could see the flinching in his eyes and face from time to time. He began pushing me across the mat until I was at the edge where the crowd of people stood. Just as I stepped on the foot of a vampire I didn't know, I took a deep breath and pushed Eris's light back with soft bursts as I swung my sword at him at the same time. I moved Eris back across the mat, his head jutting back each time I hit his light.

With sudden frustration, he roared at me, bringing both his swords down hard from above his head. I fell to the ground, rolling away as his swords hit the mat, leaving rips in the fabric. He turned around just as I leapt to my feet, and in a move he had done so many times before, he thrust his sword at mine and twisted it around in order to relieve me of my weapon. Planting my foot, I twisted my sword along with his and then plunged it into his arm. Effectively, my father lost his sword and now had a cut similar to the one he had given me. Unfortunately, the tip of his other sword nicked me on the chin. Thankfully the blood that escaped was minimal, but I looked over to see Cameron's face tense with anger while Alex's arm covered his chest.

"Do you yield, Brianna?" I heard Victor say from behind me.

With my index finger I wiped away the blood from my chin and placed my finger in my mouth, licking it away and effectively causing quite a stir in the crowd.

"I'm not yielding until he does," I replied to Victor, causing the crowd to cheer and Eris to smile in a devilish and prideful way.

Eris stayed with the one sword and tossed it into his right hand while I threw mine down dramatically on the ground. My arms fanned out and grabbed the daggers from either end of my harness while Eris ran towards me whipping his sword around wildly. My daggers hit his sword on all sides as he hit me from above and changing the tilt from left to right. Left, right, left, right, left, up, down. Left, right, left, right, left, up, down. He was methodical and repetitive, like drills with Devin. Finding his rhythm, I pushed his essence to the weak side each time he came at me. After bouncing back up a second time, he lunged forward and caused me to spin the opposite direction. But as I turned away, he Projected behind me, causing me to run right into him. With little effort he kicked my legs out from under me and leapt on top of me as I held his sword up using all my strength and power.

Even though his eyes were wild with pain as he resisted my attempt to push him away with my mind, he wasn't giving up. My arms were shaking under his weight and I knew I couldn't endure much more of this. With a loud scream, I felt the nagging burning in my body explode as I threw my father's essence across the room and into the crowd of vampires. He didn't give me a second to rest before he Projected himself toward me. This time I concentrated on watching his light form in front of me, and with all my strength I thrust my arms out at him and pushed his misty ass away.

The room went silent. The blaring background music was abruptly shut off. Eris had disappeared. I closed my eyes tightly, trying to concentrate on where I felt his essence. Just as I found his light, the paneled wall behind the crowd exploded, exposing my father's form as the dust settled.

Without his sword, he took two large strides and then leapt in the air towards me. Having only enough energy left for one more push, I clamped my mind down on his and threw him up against the wall as I flung my daggers. The crowd leapt out of the way as Eris hit the wall and one dagger pinned his arm and the other sunk in just above his heart.

"Eris, do you yield?" Victor asked from somewhere in the crowd.

But Eris didn't answer. Thick, dark blood dripped from his wounds while his skin burned from where it touched the silver of my blade. I stepped in front of him and wrapped my hand around the handle of the dagger sticking out from his chest. Slowly I pulled the dagger out, watching as my father's fangs extended from the pain. Just as the tip of my dagger was free from his skin, I heard someone shout behind me as Eris's left arm flexed to grab me. Quickly I pressed the side of my blade into my father's throat, breaking through a couple of layers of his skin and continuing to cut in deeper until Eris growled, "Good girl."

I had won. By some miracle I had won. Eris wouldn't stop until he made me realize that I could take someone's life if I needed to, even if that meant my own father, as he had done. I removed the dagger from his throat and pulled the other out from his arm, dropping both of them on the floor before my father wrapped me in his arms and lifted me off the ground in his embrace. The training room exploded with cheers. The sound was deafening, yet I could hear my father telling me how proud he was. Just hearing the words made me breakdown, even when we were engulfed by the crowd. Suddenly Eris and I were pulled apart and vampires were congratulating me from all sides. But there was only one person I wanted to see, and he was having just as hard of a time pushing through the crowd as I was. I practically slapped a Warrior's hand away when Cameron was only a foot away and I was able to leap into his expectant arms. He only gave me a quick kiss before tossing and holding me up near his shoulder. The crowd around us went wild and for the first time in my life I held my head high in victory.

Even after the battle had been over for nearly twenty minutes the excitement still hung in the air. My little family was huddled in a circle in the center of the room with Cameron holding me securely against his chest.

"BiBi, you! Were! Awesome!" Jared shouted. "OMG Beebs, you just kicked the ass of the wickedest Vamp ever. I'm so glad you're part of our family. You guys are going to the reception, right?"

"I think we will pass," Cameron replied before I could ask Jared what he was talking about.

"Come on man, you won't believe the chicks Dad brought in. They are on fi-ya," he said, causing Kyla and I to glare at him at the same time. "Uh, I mean for me and Devin, duh. More women for us, right Dev?" Jared said and punched Devin in the shoulder.

"I'm going to pass as well," Devin answered and punched his youngest brother back in the shoulder hard enough to knock him to the floor.

While we all laughed, Devin stepped out of our circle and walked toward the door. I broke away from Cameron and caught up to Devin, hugging him tightly and not allowing him to move any further.

"Thank you, Dev," I whispered through my tingly nose and throat. "I couldn't have done this without you."

Surprisingly, Devin hugged me back and said, "You did well, Brianna. You didn't give up." As he released me, he patted me on the shoulder and turned his back to me as he said, "But we do have some things to fix. Your footwork was a bit sloppy."

I rolled my eyes and turned back to my family, noticing that my father had joined them. Eris went around the circle, shaking everyone's hand and saying goodnight, leaving Cameron for last.

"I am entrusting my daughter's safety to you, Warrior. Do not disappoint me," Eris said with his thick Italian accent. He had to perform for the masses, I guess.

"Brianna is safe with me. I will see that no harm comes to her," Cameron replied sincerely.

"Be sure to find those leaks," Eris whispered and then turned to me, placing his hands on either side of my face and kissing each cheek. "Mia figlia, there is no father prouder than I at this moment. But as promised, I shall take my leave sometime tomorrow. I must say I will be very happy to see my home for real instead of only in your dreams." My father hugged me tightly, whispering to me in his unaltered voice, "I love you, Brianna Marilena."

"I love you too, Dad," I replied, surprised at how natural it came out. I could feel my tears trying desperately to escape while I said my final goodbyes to him and Seraphina, feeling a little lonelier when they walked away from us. They entered this very room as strangers and were now leaving as my parents. The notion took my breath away.

Shortly after, everyone else left the training room for the reception, leaving Cameron and I alone. With everyone gone, my aches and pains began to make themselves known. My head was pounding at the same rhythm as my heart, which only worsened when Cameron put his arms around my waist and leaned down to kiss me. When he rose, his eyes searched my face for any signs that I would suddenly crumble in his arms.

"I'm not sure if you're aware," I began, twisting one of his dark curls with my fingers, "but your girlfriend is a pretty awesome fighter."

"Is that right? My girlfriend, you say?" Cameron laughed as he tossed my legs up into the crook of his arm and carried me out of the training room.

"You know I heard she almost cut off her father's head," I said, pressing my forehead against his cool neck.

"Really?" he answered cheerily, playing along with my little game. "She must be pretty vicious to do that to her own father."

"Mmm-hmm," I answered sleepily while my body drained itself of the adrenaline that was coursing through it earlier. "You better watch out. When that time of the month comes, you never know what could happen. She could just fly off the handle."

"How is that different than any other day?"

I lifted my head, giving Cam a dirty look, but it quickly dissolved at the sight of his crooked smile.

"Oh, by the way, did you get in trouble?"

Cameron knitted his brow. "In trouble for what, love?"

"For warning me during the battle. That's against rules, isn't it? I thought Victor would be mad at you or something."

"That was not me, angel. It was actually Devin who shouted out."

"Devin? Mr. I-Don't-Break-The-Rules-For-Anything, Devin?"

"I am not the only one who worries about you."

I tucked my head back under Cameron's chin, continuing to press my forehead against his neck to soothe my aching head. "I love your family."

"They are as much your family now as mine."

"Then I love our family."

"And they love you. Does your head ache?"

"Mmm-hmm, but nothing a pill can't get rid of."

Cameron turned the corner to the stairwell and carefully walked up each step to avoid jostling me.

"Cam?"

"Yes, my love."

"Were you proud of me tonight?" I asked childishly.

"Yes, very much so."

"Would you say I was becoming a good Warrior?"

"Yes."

"Able to defend myself?"

"Yes," he replied, though his tone was questioning.

"Does that mean I can leave the manor now?"

Cameron paused and then sighed, "No."

"But Cam," I whined as he opened the door to our bedroom and closed it behind him with his foot.

"Brianna, possessor of my heart, must we argue about this tonight? It is the first evening we will be able to spend together uninterrupted for weeks, and I would rather not have it occupied by that conversation. I will gladly fight and argue with you about it tomorrow, but tonight can we celebrate your enormous victory? Please, angel."

I twisted my lips in a pout and avoided his gaze, but the sound of my stomach growling loudly was enough to kill my attempt at making him feel guilty.

"Hungry?" he asked, gently lowering me to the ground. I nodded as my stomach growled and cramped at its lack of food. "Go in for a shower and I will bring you something to eat."

"Why can't we go back downstairs, eat, and I'll shower later?"

"Or, you could shower now and by the time you get out, I will have dinner for you."

"Are you inferring that I smell?"

Cameron smiled, digging his hands into his pockets. "Only slightly. But I am sure you want to wash…the…ah…blood off," he said gesturing to my chest.

I looked down to see that my chest was smeared with dried blood and I could suddenly feel the stickiness of it on my neck. How did I not notice it before? It must be Eris's from when he hugged me after the battle, but seriously, how oblivious was I?

"I've been like this the whole time and no one bothered to tell me?"

"I believe they were trying to save you the embarrassment."

"Handing me a towel would have done that," I said snidely. "Fine, I'll shower, but it'll be a quick one." Cameron raised a skeptical brow. "It could happen."

"After today, I am a believer that anything could happen."

I smiled and rose to my toes to give him a quick kiss before I turned to walk to the bathroom. With my back to him, I said, "So what's at this reception thing that you don't want me to see?" Cameron was silent behind me. "Oh yeah, don't think I didn't notice. I know you too well, Mr. Burke."

Chapter Fifty-five

Cameron

As I watched Brianna duck into the bathroom with her mischievous smile there were four things I knew. One, no one knew me like she did. Two, there was no way I was going to take her to the traditional after-battle reception which was basically a large blood orgy, even if it was in her honor. Three, Brianna never remembered to take everything she needed with her into the bathroom, and she would be shivering from the shower looking for something to wear. Four, I desperately wanted to make love to her tonight.

My love and desire had peaked when watching her battle. She had grown in so many ways since we first met, however, being completely intimate with each other was still a hurdle. She was aware that I loved her, but I needed her to trust that I would not hurt her. In her entire life she most likely had never made love, and honestly the last time I was with someone I loved, I was human. Making love and having sex were two completely different things in my mind. One was a beautiful act, the other a nagging necessity when the first was missing.

The shower turned on, startling me out of my thoughts. If I was going to try and make love to Brianna, I needed to create a relaxed and romantic environment for her, and I did not have a lot of time to do it. First, she needed clothes for when she exited her shower. I darted into the wardrobe room to her dresser and was torn between a revealing black negligee that Kyla must have bought for her, or her usual camisole and jersey shorts. It was a battle of what I wanted to see her in and what was the least pressure-filled. Camisole and shorts it was. However, I did choose sexier underwear.

I was still a man.

Quietly I pushed the bathroom door open and placed the garments on the sink's counter where she would easily find them. It was hard not to glance at her muted silhouette through the glass shower door as I left. Before she could turn and find me staring, I pushed myself out of the room and closed the door behind me. If I had stayed a second longer, all my attempts to ease her into this would have been forfeit.

I looked out at our bedroom, cold and dark and in no way exuding romance. Romance? What did I know about romance? Thinking hard, I flipped through all the books I had read during my long lifetime, pulling inspiration where I could. My brain was scattered with images both exciting and frustrating. Romantic dinners were done by the fire. I had a fireplace! Candles. Romantic scenes always had candles. Where on Earth was I going to find candles? What Warrior was romantic enough to use them? Kyla! Kyla would have them, and hopefully she and Alexander were still at the reception. Not wanting to waste any time, I Projected outside their door and knocked. When no response came, I walked right in, and thankfully saw dozens of candles in all shapes and sizes, most likely from their activities earlier today which Kyla so graciously informed us about. Grabbing as many as I could, I Projected myself back into the bedroom to the whispered sound of the shower still going.

With vampire speed I placed and lit the candles in the small living area and flipped on the fireplace. The room was glowing in warm amber, but the setting was still missing something. Looking at the bed, I whipped the large overstuffed comforter off and folded it in front of the fireplace, placing as many pillows as we had all around. It was better, and acceptable for completing in less than five minutes.

Food. That was the next task and hopefully it would be quick so that I would be back before she was done showering. I walked to the door, catching a glimpse of myself in the mirror and adjusting my hair and shirt. It was not a favorite of mine, but if I changed clothes would that signify something? Yes, it could, I guess. I was nervous.

After one last hair adjustment, I Projected into the kitchen where I found the head of our kitchen staff, Christine, wiping down the countertops.

"Have I missed all opportunity for dinner?" I asked as I stepped into view.

"Oh good evening, Cameron, for heaven's sake no. This is the earliest I've ever been able to clean up in a long time. It's because of that reception tonight. No one wants to eat what I make, just each other I suppose."

I smiled, slightly embarrassed, and found the floor suddenly interesting. "Yes well, I was hoping I could bring something special up to Brianna."

"Well, food I can make, special could be hard. You're at the mercy of what I have already. I heard she did very well today," Christine responded as she threw her sponge into the sink and stepped over to the industrial refrigerator marked Human Food Only.

"Brianna did very well, and has not eaten since this afternoon."

"That girl needs more meat on her bones."

"So I have heard," I replied, laughing to myself at the voices of Madelyn and Oliver telling me the same thing.

"How about some chicken?" Christine asked as she moved around items on the refrigerator shelves, delving for any hidden treasures.

"Chicken is fine, only no garlic please."

"One of those nights, huh?"

I did not answer her, though she smiled devilishly as she turned to her enormous stove and began working her magic. With the sound of banging pans, I almost missed my father entering the room.

"Here you are, child," he said, having shed his formal robes from the battle and changed into more casual modern attire. "You are not attending the reception tonight?"

"It is not something I want to introduce Brianna to just yet."

Victor cocked his eyebrow at me. "She is aware you are a vampire, is she not?"

"Yes, Father, very much so. That does not mean I want to share her blood with anyone else."

"And why is that?"

"Because they would drain her dry at the taste of Eris's power."

It was partially true. I also did not want anyone to see her dreams. More to the point, I did not want anyone else having any kind of access to her but me. Yes, I was being possessive.

"She has surprised us all, including her father. I am very impressed by my newest Warrior."

"You should tell her that. I am sure she would be honored to hear that from you. She believes you dislike her."

Victor stood straighter, tightening the corners of his mouth before he said, "But I made her a part of our coven. I wouldn't have done that if I disliked her."

"Yes, but that is all you have done. You do not treat Brianna as you do your other children. She is an intelligent woman, Father, she notices the difference." My father opened his mouth to protest, but I continued quickly, "It is not a criticism, merely an observation."

"Any update on our *problem*," he said, changing the topic and referring to the traitor within our coven.

"Jared compiled a list of those who left the manor after Eris notified us the threat had disappeared."

"Any front runners?"

"It is a mishmash of people, including Tao, who we well know was not with the enemy. Brianna's grandfather is on there as well and it goes without saying he is not associated with Elaina."

"It cuts me deeply to think that one of my own has betrayed us."

"I know, Father."

"Find him, child, and have Devin kill him," Victor said with his eyes narrowed at me. His expression lightened as Christine turned from her stove, placing her masterfully cooked chicken onto a plate in front of her. "Goodnight, Christine," Victor said cheerfully and left.

Christine nodded to Victor and then looked down at the plate in front of her. "Why couldn't you give me more time? Chicken and vegetables. So below my usual culinary standards."

I took the plate from her, placing it on a tray with napkins and utensils.

"Christine, it is fine. I apologize for the short notice."

"Wait, I have a salad I could give her."

"No need, she would not eat it anyway," I laughed. "Thank you, Christine, have a nice night."

"You too," she replied and waggled her eyebrows with insinuation.

I smiled as I left the kitchen and made my way back to our bedroom. I stared at the door for nearly thirty seconds, my nerves settling back in from wherever they had disappeared to. After taking a deep breath I finally entered the room and noticed that the shower was no longer running, but Brianna was nowhere in sight. The room was silent, but I could smell the scents of soap and shampoo in the air. Quickly I stepped over to the couch to set the tray down, only to find my angel curled up and asleep on the comforter I had placed down on the floor. Her hair was damp and strewn across the pillow next to her. The fragrant smell of honeysuckle filled the area around her. It was her favorite scent, and subsequently mine too. Sweet but strong, just like my new Brianna.

My romantic gestures and desires would have to wait another night. There would always be another night. Brianna did not flinch when I lifted her from the floor and laid her down on our bed, bringing the comforter back over and tucking her in. I doused all but one candle, leaving it lit on the side table next to the chaise I chose to sit on and delve back into the stack of books I had gathered earlier in the day.

I was feeling a bit nostalgic reading by fire and candlelight. In order to pass the night, I decided to read at human speed in order to savor each word and make the rest of the evening bearable. Besides finding someone to feed on or taking a cold shower, there was little else I could do to dampen the feelings of lust that were raging inside of me. The first I refused to do since it would not be for sustenance. The other was a silly human remedy. I was a vampire; the most vicious predator alive. I should be able to handle my own hormones for one evening.

Even the oldest of vampires can feel refreshed after a nice cold shower, and that had been its purpose. At least that was what I was telling myself. I felt like a teenage boy, unable to control what lied beneath his pants. It was shameful, and Jared-like. But now I was more than refreshed. I had changed into a pair of silk pajama bottoms and continued reading while watching Brianna's animated sleepwalking. Several times she stood from the bed and walked into the wardrobe room, each time exiting with various articles of clothing draped around her. I had always heard never to wake a person sleepwalking, but when she continued layering herself in T-shirts and several pairs of my underwear, I tried removing them. As a result, I got my hand slapped and she yelled at me in some made up language.

So Brianna was now lying in bed, most likely sweating from the number of layers she had on, but that was how she wanted it. She tossed and flailed around in her sleep, making me wish that I had a little of her blood in me so I could see what she was dreaming about.

Just as I turned the delicate page of my tattered book, Brianna sat upright in bed. I was not sure if she was truly awake, so I simply stared at her until her eyes focused enough to recognize me.

"Cam?" she whispered in an uncertain tone.

"Yes, love?"

She looked down at the bed, still making sense of where she was. With sudden realization she threw the comforter off of her and rose from the bed, her hands cupped around her nose and mouth.

"Ohmygod, Cam. The candles, the fireplace, I ruined it. I'm so sorry." Just then she looked down at herself. "What the hell am I wearing?"

I bit my lip, trying not to laugh at the sight of Brianna trying to untangle herself from the clothes stretched oddly around her neck and arms. I waved her over to me and she sighed in defeat before sitting lightly on my lap.

"Cam, I'm sorry," she muffled as I pulled off the first T-shirt whose neck was stretched across her arm and chest.

"No need to be sorry, my love."

"Yes there is. It was so beautiful and cozy that I couldn't stop myself from lying down. I didn't even realize I went to sleep. I ruined everything."

"You did no such thing," I replied as I removed two pairs of my boxer briefs from around her neck. "It was only dinner. You had more than enough reason to fall asleep."

"Please tell me that you at least did this to me as retribution," she said while I pulled the last T-shirt over her head.

"Sorry, love, this was all you," I laughed lightly, giving her a quick kiss on the tip of her nose. She placed her hands under my jaw, pulling me to her lips and pressing them against mine. I loved her lips. They were warm and sultry and the softest thing I had ever kissed besides the skin on her neck.

When she pulled away, her eyes were still closed as she said nervously, "You forgot one."

Though I was not certain she could see my confusion, before I could ask, she placed my hands on the bottom edges of her camisole and helped me pull the thin shirt over her head. She repositioned herself to straddle me, the fire casting small shadows of her supple breasts down her curved waist. She was the most beautiful person I had ever seen, and she was trembling.

I wrapped my hand around her neck, pulling her to me and kissing her gently as I reached for her discarded camisole.

"No," she breathed into my mouth, taking her camisole and tossing it on the floor.

She crushed her lips against mine and then plunged her tongue into my mouth. I could still feel her muscles trembling underneath my hands at her waist, making me too afraid to move them. Brianna pulled away from my lips, slightly breathless as she dipped her head down, kissing and tracing the lines of my chest with her tongue and then moving my hands up to her breasts. My touch was gentle at first, but at the sound of her soft moan I was unable to stop myself from squeezing them harder which resulted in another intoxicating and sultry sigh.

I pulled her flat against me as I took my time searching the skin of her neck, feeling my fangs extend slowly at the prospect of having her sweet, warm blood flow into my mouth. I felt Brianna's hands shake as they traveled down the length of my abdomen, clumsily trying to untie the drawstring of my pants. I was torn between my desire and her nervousness. With gentle hands I pulled her face up to mine and looked deeply into her dark eyes.

"Are you sure, love?"

She nodded tensely and stretched my waistband as loose as it would go. Unable to control myself any longer, I picked her up from the chaise, wrapping her soft thighs around my waist as my pants slid to the ground. There could not have been a more perfectly timed moment in history.

Brianna's arms were tight around my neck while she kneaded her lips feverishly against mine. Her thighs felt like fire around my waist, pulsing with blood and desire. But when I laid her on the bed her eyes were tightly closed and her bottom lip was trembling in fear.

"Bri," I whispered gently, "look at me." Slowly she stretched her eyes open, looking as though she would cry at any moment. "Am I your angel?" I asked, shifting my weight to the side of her and slowly moving my fingers down her stomach.

"Yes," she answered with staggered breath, her stomach quivering underneath my fingertips.

"Do you know that my love for you surpasses all the greatest love stories of the ages?"

"It does?" she asked weakly, tears still threatening in her eyes.

"Without a doubt," I replied and pressed my palm flat on her lower abdomen. "And do you believe that one day, right here under my hand, you will carry my children? Conceived in every ounce of love I have for you."

The tears breached her lids and trailed in thin lines down her face as she answered, "I'm not sure how, but I do believe it, Cam, I really do."

"Then also believe that I will never hurt you. You will always be safe with me."

"I know," she whispered. "Just…just…"

"We do not need to do this, love."

But instead of replying she pulled my face back to hers and lowered my hand to the edge of the pajama shorts she was still wearing. She pulled the edge of the elastic waistband down, and I did the rest, pulling them down her legs and freeing them by her ankles. With ease she pulled me on top of her, opening her legs to me and once again feeling the fire between them. She did not take her eyes off mine as I entered her, feeling the scarring inside her and seeing her past stretched across her face.

Although her moans and her hot skin were driving me crazy, I took my time pushing myself inside of her. I laced my fingers with hers, squeezing them tightly and feeling her finally start to relax. Her breath quickened as our rhythm became faster and suddenly Brianna's eyes shot me a questioning look as the pulsating muscles inside her began to quicken at my insistent pushing.

"Cam?"

I wrapped my arm around her back, pulling her up quickly while I rose up to my knees and held her pelvis firmly against mine.

"Just hold onto me, love. I promise this is a good thing."

Chapter Fifty-six

Brianna

"I had an orgasm. I had an orgasm. I had an orgasm. Iiiiiiii had an orgasm," I sang in my head to the tune of the "The Lone Ranger" while I danced around the bathroom naked. Oh! My! God! If I had only known this was how it could be with a man. I'll admit, at first, I was terrified. I knew Cameron would never hit me, but I kept waiting for his fist and the nauseating pain between my legs. Of course it never came, and he was as gentle as I needed him to be, until I didn't.

I took my hairbrush from the counter and began brushing through the mats in the back of my head in order to make myself presentable for a hopeful round two. This was completely new for me. I never wanted to have sex with Sam a first time let alone a second. Cameron had peaked with me, making the moment even more satisfying. However, he didn't bite me. He had told me that a vampire's experience was heightened when he or she bit his or her partner during sex, and it was confirmed by Kyla during one of our slumber party chats. So I felt, not guilty, but maybe more obligated to make his experience as amazing as mine.

Once primped, I opened the bathroom door and padded out into the bedroom, slightly self-conscious by my nakedness. The bedroom was now absent of its previous warm yellow candlelight, and was now only illuminated by a sliver of moonlight coming through the window. Cameron lay on his side, inviting me back into the bed as he lifted the blankets and tucked them around me while I curled into him. We melted into each other as if we had been chiseled from a single piece of marble, a perfect fit. No talk was needed as we lay in our bed holding one another and feeling the love pulsate between us.

"Oh, I almost forgot," Cameron said softly as he rolled over to his nightstand. "Devin returned your ring while you were sleeping."

"Thank goodness. I feel so naked without it…well more than I am now," I said holding my left hand out and allowing him to slide the ring onto its proper place. The weight of it around my finger made me feel oddly complete.

Cameron tilted my chin up to his face. "What if I were to buy you a different ring?"

"What's wrong with this one?"

"N-nothing, I guess," he replied in surprise.

I knew exactly what kind of ring he was talking about, but the subject would cause my defenses to go up and that was the last thing I wanted. I ran my fingers through his hair, knowing it would soften him up.

"I love you, Cam."

His eyes were slightly furrowed as he said, "Bri, I will always love you. I just want to make sure you know…"

"I don't need a ring to know that, and right now I don't want one. Earlier tonight you asked that we hold our talk about me leaving the house, I'm asking the same on this. What was it you said? I'll fight and argue with you about it tomorrow?"

"That sounds somewhat familiar."

"Good, because right now," I began, leaning into the crook of his neck and moving up to his ear and cheek with tiny kisses, "it's my turn to give you what you want."

Cameron tilted his head back, pushing me away slightly with a curious smile.

"What is it you think I want?"

"I want you to have fun, too."

"Were we not just in the same bed? I believe the entire wing of the house knew we were having fun."

"I know," I replied, feeling my stomach flip while remembering the moment when he reached his climax releasing a guttural sound that you almost couldn't hear over my own high-pitched moans. "But I thought having my blood made it better for you."

Cameron laughed lightly as he released his hold on me and leaned back against his pillow.

"Honestly, Bri, I am not sure how anything could be better than what we just did. I do not need your blood in order to enjoy making love to you."

"But I want to give it to you," I whined as I traced the lines of his stomach with my fingertips, and then re-traced the same patch with my tongue.

"Bri, you do not need to do this."

"Sorry, Cam," I replied, looking up at him seductively as I positioned myself just below his waist. "I'm suddenly in the mood for a popsicle."

Elaina's arm was clamped down on my chest, forcing me to watch the carnage in the manor's courtyard. The beautifully landscaped grounds were a sea of vampires ripping each other apart, but the hardest thing was seeing my family suffering. Jared was burning and screaming in agony in the sun while Cam, Devin, and Alex were covered with Elaina's minions like locusts.

"You can stop this, Brianna," Elaina growled in my ear. "You have all the power to stop this. Or do you value your own life more than theirs?"

"What do you want me to do?" I said without hesitation.

"Just come with me, Brianna," Elaina replied. "Come with me, and all their suffering will be over."

In that moment Jared's screams were unbearable as black smoke rose from his body. For the first time I noticed Kyla slumped over near one of the archways that was crumbling around her. If I could help everyone with one choice, then it was a simple one.

"I'm sorry, Cam," I whimpered, knowing I was breaking my promise to him.

Elaina's hold on me loosened and she pulled me up a short set of stairs and the entire scene around me changed.

I was no longer in the manor. The room was Victorian-looking and surrounded by tall windows with cascading red and yellow embroidered draperies. The thick, red carpet beneath my bare feet was similar in color to the blood that ran down the front of my white gossamer gown. My stomach was now distended to the point where I couldn't see my feet, but I could feel that I was standing in a puddle of water. My babies were coming and I was encircled by viscous looking Vamps.

Elaina stood in the center with me, smiling as she said, "You have made the right choice. It is time to bring these babies into the world."

The vampires yelled and cheered around me while Elaina took me by the shoulder, forcibly lowering me to the ground. She snapped her fingers and a tall, slender figure stepped from the circle and knelt beside me, handing Elaina a large ceremonial knife. As Elaina took the knife, she began raising the white gown over my large stomach causing me to flinch and kick my legs.

"Hold her down," Elaina commanded. "This will hurt."

The female vampire held my wrists above my head, pressing them painfully into the hardwood floor. Elaina began teasing my skin with the edge of the blade causing me to scream and writhe in my captor's grip.

"Let's get this over with," the woman said in a low but harsh voice as she pressed harder into my wrists, her dark hair covering me like a blanket.

Just then, Elaina plunged her knife into my abdomen. The pain was blinding and I was unable to move from my captor's iron hold. Elaina began slowly cutting across my stomach and pulling away the skin. The taste of copper filled my mouth as blood began to rise in my throat. I was dying. My babies were being ripped from my body, and I was dying.

I fought to push my dream away, but I was stuck in this nightmare without a way out. The pain was so real, so agonizingly real. Elaina's knife was still inside me as she drew the blade upwards, slicing the skin up and over my belly. The burning pain caused me to scream with new found strength, able to break free from my captor's hands as I sat upright in front of Elaina. Suddenly seeing her halo of light, I pushed her away as hard as I could.

Elaina's hands released the knife, but held my face tightly on either side.

"Wake...up...please...wake," Cameron's voice somehow came out of Elaina's mouth.

I continued to push her light away from me but she refused to let go. Elaina wailed in pain as I pushed her harder and harder with my mind, although the timbre of her voice was completely male. Finally, her hands left my face...

...and I was thrust back into my bedroom watching Cameron fly backwards beyond the edge of the bed and down to the floor.

"Cam!" I screamed as I weakly rushed to the end of the bed seeing Cameron curled up naked on the floor and covering his head with his arms. "Cameron?" I whispered, reaching down with my fingers and touching his arm gently. My hands were shaking as he reached up with one hand and entwined his fingers with mine.

"Just a little dazed, love," he said weakly.

The tips of his fingers were warm and rough as they touched my skin.

"Cam, your fingers are burned."

Cameron pulled his hand from mine and examined his fingers just as they began to heal.

"So they are. Let us add this to the list, do not try to hold onto Brianna Morgan when she is mind projecting you."

"But I was sleeping."

"It appears not to matter."

"I wasn't...I wasn't trying to push you."

"I know," he replied, slowly sitting up from the floor. "I was trying to help you. I could not get you to wake, and you were in so much pain."

My hand flew to my stomach, remembering the pain that had been afflicted on me in my dream. Cameron, seeing my sudden panic, stood up as I revealed a light red line swelling up on my abdomen. His face was strained as he stared at me rubbing the scar. It was tender, like a new scratch, and scarily similar to the path Elaina's knife had made. But before I could begin to stress about it, the room was flooded with the sound of a high-pitched alarm.

Cam looked quickly to the door, and then back to me with a hard look. Taking the sheet in his hand he wrapped it around me, carried me into the closet, and finally set me down on the narrow bench inside.

"What's going on?"

"It is the house alarm. I need to..." but his thought broke off as his ears perked up toward the bedroom. "Stay in here. Devin and the others are coming."

Cameron kissed me quickly and then spun on his heel to leave.

"Cam! Pants!"

Cameron turned startled, standing in front of me in all his masculine nakedness, and gave me a thankful smile before he dove into the armoire in front of him and pulled out a pair of black jeans.

"Brother! Brianna?" Devin shouted from inside the bedroom.

Cameron slipped on the jeans and dashed out into the bedroom. I couldn't hear anything from the bedroom which meant they were speaking in soft secret vampire tones which generally meant bad news.

My head was aching, my stomach scratched and burning, and parts below were tender from the night's activities. This was not how I pictured the morning after Cameron and I had made love for the first time. And as usual, it had everything to do with me. While I laid wallowing in my own self-pity, I noticed in the opposite corner a gathering of black mist that began to take the shape of my favorite, though intrusive, strawberry blonde vampire.

"Jer?"

"Oh shit!" Jared said startled as he fell back into the wall. "Seriously, Beebs, what the hell are you doing in the closet? Is this some kinky thing between you and Cameron? You guys didn't do anything over here did you? Shit, am I standing in it?" he asked while lifting his feet and checking the soles of his shoes.

"No! And even if we did, it would serve you right."

"At least someone got lucky last night," he said waggling his eyebrows up and down and gesturing to the sheet that was wrapped around me.

"You mean none of the 'hot chicks' were desperate enough?"

"They were all *too* desperate, if you know what I mean."

"What's going on out there? Can you hear them?"

"Of course I can hear them," he scoffed, rolling his eyes at me. "Cameron told them everything was all right, and Devin just left to tell security to turn off the alarm."

"Why did it go off in the first place?"

"Bibi, whadja expect to happen? You hit the whole dang house!"

I felt the blood rush from my face. "Wh-what are you talking about?"

The alarm finally went silent as Jared answered in a whispered tone, "The alarm was pulled because the vampires in the house were all suddenly seeing themselves being cut open by Elaina. But what I found really scary was that I was seeing myself pregnant. I mean seriously, this really isn't a good time for me to have a baby, ya know? I'm just not ready for that kind of responsibility. And the loss of my figure…"

"Stop it, Jared! Just stop…" I whimpered at the realization that everyone in the manor had shared my agony.

"Why are you always crying around me? Is it something you hold in until you see me? You know I don't do well with this."

"Wouldn't you be upset if everyone you knew suddenly saw your private dreams?"

"It would depend on what it was. If it were me and a gorgeous Swedish model, now that would…"

"Get out, Jared," I cried and used the sheet to wipe my face.

Jared knelt in front of me, his joking mood stripped from him altogether and pulling my head down onto his shoulder.

"Sorry, Beebs, I was…just trying to make you laugh."

"It's not funny," I sniffled, letting my tears stain one of his many concert T-shirts. "What else did you see?"

"Nothin' much. Mostly just being held down and then seeing Elaina. Why, was there more?"

I lifted my head from his shoulder, looking at his sweet, kind eyes while tears crested my lower lids.

"Remember back in the Facility, I asked you to promise me that no matter what, you would never try and help me during the day?"

"And I remember leaving a note on your face telling you I couldn't."

"I'm serious, Jer. You have to promise me, don't do it. I'm not worth it, please just promise me."

Jared scrunched his brows together as he said, "You had a dream about me, didn't you?"

"There's a battle in the courtyard and you come down to try and help. You start to burn, and I can't help you and then…I can't lose someone else because…" I sobbed. "Hannah has been hard enough. I can't lose you, Jer, or anyone else in our family."

"Bibi, I'm a Warrior, and before that an Army Ranger. It's my job to help people, and maybe die doing it. I could never just sit in my room safe and sound while you and others are struggling for your lives. I just can't do it, Beebs, that's not who I am. I know you don't want me to call you Sis, but you really are to me. Since that first night we got to know each other, and ruined my shoes by the way, we had a connection. Don't ask me why, but we do. So no matter what, I am going to do whatever I need to do in order to save you. You're my sister." His arms tightened around me and I buried my face into his shoulder, feeling that yes indeed he was my brother. "Er…yep, my sister who is very naked underneath this sheet. Kind of awkward."

I laughed. "There's a white robe in the bathroom, can you grab it for me?

I don't think the sun hits the door."

Jared nodded and within seconds returned with my white fluffy robe in his hands. I shoved my arms into it and wrapped it around me, shaking the sheet off underneath while Jared listened intently to what was happening in the bedroom.

"So what's going on now?" I asked, walking over to him and finally looking out into the bedroom.

"The usual. Devin wants to tell Dad about your dreams, Cameron says no, they argue, blah blah blah. Kyla tells them to stop, Alex tries to calm Ky, you know the drill. But Dev does have a point. Dad's gonna wanna know what the hell happened."

Cameron stood in the center of the room, his pale bare back facing us while his arms flailed at Devin who was doing the same. I stepped over to *one* of Cameron's armoires and pulled out one of his many black shirts and took a step out of the closet.

"Hey, where're you going?" Jared asked, pulling my arm slightly.

"Going in there to get Cameron mad at me."

"Awesome," he laughed.

As I stepped closer, I could hear the muffled tones of Cameron and Devin yelling at one another on my behalf. They had had the argument several times in front of me, goodness knows how many times out of my sight.

"Father will want an explanation, as does everyone."

"We do not know enough about this for it to be shared."

Coming up next to him, I tucked the shirt in the crook of Cameron's arm and he took it absentmindedly, but then reacted when he saw me standing there. He smiled as he took the shirt from his arm and then kissed me gently on the forehead.

"Well since she's here, I think it should be up to Brianna. It is her gift after all," Devin said gesturing toward me.

After pulling the shirt on, Cameron shook his head and opened his mouth to speak, but I spoke up first and said, "Cam, I think I should tell Victor." Cameron froze. "I'm sorry, babe, but Devin's right. Victor is going to want to know what happened to everyone. Wouldn't you?"

Cameron kissed my hand and squeezed it gently. "It is your choice, my love. I am only afraid that…"

But suddenly Cameron was interrupted by the sound of the manor alarm going off again. Everyone looked to me.

"Whoa, I'm just standing here," I said defensively.

"I will go check it out," Devin said before Projecting out of the room.

Before the black mist completely faded away, Eris burst through the bedroom door.

"Warrior, you test my faith in you," he shouted and pointed his finger directly in Cameron's face. "I trusted you with the safety of my child against Elaina's coven, and yet you continue to have members of the enemy coming into your home! I have to get Sera out of here immediately, and I am taking my daughter with me."

"Dad, wait, what happened?" I said as Cameron spoke at the same time.

"Eris, sir, I do not understand what you are referring to."

"You assured me you would catch the traitor in your ranks and have not, and now the enemy is coming right through your door. I cannot allow my daughter to continually be placed into danger."

"Dad! Wait," I yelled over the sound of the alarm ringing in my ears. "Elaina's coven is here?"

"Yes. Well, at least one member of the coven is here within these walls."

"Eris is right," Devin announced as he walked into the bedroom just as the alarm went silent. "Jazlyn's just returned with a prisoner. She's saying he is a member of Elaina's coven."

"Ha! You see," Eris shouted. "Sera is quite distraught. I need to get her out of here without being seen. Bri-an-na, I believe you will be safer if you come with me."

"No, Dad. I...can't go. This is where I live, it's my home," I replied and squeezed Cameron's hand that was fidgeting in mine.

"Father is requesting that the Elite Council convene immediately," Devin announced.

Cameron's face was apologetic and guilt stricken as he hugged me into his chest and kissed my cheek.

"I will return as soon as I can. This was not quite how I pictured our morning together."

I smiled up at him. "I know. I was thinking exactly the same thing."

His face was still riddled with guilt as he lowered his head into the crook of my neck, squeezing me tightly against him and making me well aware that he didn't want to leave me.

"Babe? Was that what you called me?"

"Trying something new until I get it right."

"I love you, angel," he whispered and then kissed me on my lips before he pulled away.

"Love you too, babe," I said winking at him as he left through the door with his brothers, leaving me alone with Kyla and Eris.

"Eris, sir," Kyla said softly behind me, "once the council convenes, the doors will be shut and the prisoner will be brought out. You should be perfectly safe to leave with Sera at that time. We can have someone escort the two of you if you like."

"I can take care of my wife," he snapped, but then apologized under his breath. "Bri-an-na, I worry about you here. Please come with me."

"Is it because of the dream today?"

Eris looked down, disappointment across his face. "I only saw what you somehow projected to everyone. Isn't that enough?"

"You're the one who told me I couldn't run from my fate."

"Foolish words said by a foolish father."

"You aren't foolish, Dad, just scared. Now get Sera out of here, I'll be fine."

I pushed the lump down that had formed in my throat as my father looked lovingly at me, torn between what he wanted and needed to do.

"If you need me for anything whatsoever, call me or say my name in your dreams. I can always find you," he said and hugged me tightly before he retreated reluctantly out of the room.

A few seconds later Kyla placed her arm around me and my head fell onto her shoulder.

"Is Jared still in the closet?"

"No," she replied softly, "he left when the others did."

"Oh Kyla," I wailed, throwing my arms around her and relieving myself of all the grief I had been hoarding inside. "I don't...want...to lose...my babies!"

"I know, Bri, I know. It was so awful," she cried into my hair.

"I've lost so many," I sobbed. "It isn't fair that they'll be taken away, too. I can't do it, Kyla, I can't let her take them. They're Cameron's, I just know it. Is that how I die? Elaina rips them out of my body? I don't want to die like that, alone and ripped to shreds and leave...my...babies without...a mother..."

"We won't let it happen, Bri. We'll protect you, all of us," she said, holding me tightly against her shoulder. "Come on, let's see what we can do to make you feel better."

Kyla guided me to the bed and pulled the comforter over me. She reached for the phone and dialed quickly.

"Christine? It's Kyla. Can you send up whatever chocolate you have? Oh and maybe some ice cream if you have it, it's an emergency."

After hanging up, Kyla sat next to me on the bed and I laid my head in her lap continuing to let the tears flow out of me. I didn't want Cameron to see me this way. This was girlfriend territory, and Kyla was my Renee in abstentia. She petted my hair and handed me tissues, and like a true friend she made me feel that my sorrow was her own. More importantly, she let me know that I wasn't alone.

Chapter Fifty-seven

Cameron

"Cam, how is this possible?" Alexander said gruffly while we walked along the main corridor, making our way to the Council Hall. "We have been hunting Elaina for two years. *Two years.* How does Jazlyn of all people suddenly capture a member of Elaina's coven? I mean, really, Jazlyn?"

Feeling the eyes of the other council members around me, I said in my most politically correct way, "Alex, Jazlyn has been a Warrior longer than either of us. She is just as capable at capturing a member of Elaina's coven as any one of us."

"But how?"

"We will know soon enough," I replied, patting his shoulder as we stepped through the Council Hall doors. Others around us were taking their seats when Jazlyn entered from the prison door at the far end of the room. Some congratulated her, while others like Alexander simply glared.

"This is bullshit," he said under his breath and sat down.

"It certainly is," I replied before walking up to the front of the hall and taking my place behind Victor's throne.

Seconds later, Devin entered with Victor from the prisoner rooms with Julian and several of his guards escorting a shackled vampire into the center of the oval shaped room. The hushed murmurs among the council members stopped when Victor stood in front of his throne and gestured for Julian to begin the interrogation.

"Please announce your name," Julian said, turning to face the prisoner.

"Up yours," the prisoner replied snidely.

Julian gave a curt nod to one of the guards who quickly thrust his fist into the back of the prisoner's knee causing it to break and hang at an odd angle while his screams echoed throughout the room.

"Well, 'Up Yours', you've just met Liam, and I can assure you he will keep breaking your leg until you begin to cooperate. So let's try this again. Please announce your name."

"Dylan. Dylan Bray," he screamed as the bones in his leg knitted themselves together.

"So, Dylan Bray, how long have you been a member of Elaina's coven?"

"A year and a half."

"Father, at this time I would like Jazlyn to present her information."

"So granted," Victor answered, waving his fingers for Jazlyn to stand in the center of the room along with Dylan.

"Jazlyn," Julian continued, "please elaborate on how you came across the prisoner."

"Being the attentive Gatherer that I am," she said in a cocky tone and raising an eyebrow in my direction, "I personally escorted my latest hybrid to the Facility early this morning. After I left the Facility, I noticed someone ducking into the surrounding woods when I turned onto the main road. Having been present at the last Facility attack I went on the defensive and began tracking him through the woods on foot. I captured him right before he started to cross the Facility's grounds. After a short tussle, I was able to get him to confess to me that he was a member of Elaina's coven and I brought him straight here."

"Well done, child," Victor acknowledged.

"Yes, Jazlyn, well done. You have succeeded where other Warriors have failed," Julian said snidely. "And is it true the prisoner confessed to you his purpose for being at the Facility?"

"It is. He said he was on a final reconnaissance mission."

"Dylan Bray, in exchange for leniency, are you willing to divulge the details of your mission?" The prisoner nodded nervously when Liam reached back with his fist. "Why were you surveying the hybrid facility?"

"I was sent to check out the changes in the construction of the building since the last time we attacked it."

"Why?" Julian pushed.

"I don't know."

"Liar. Tell us why."

"I said, I don't know."

Dylan's first mistake was continuing to lie to Julian. His second was exposing his fangs. In a spilt second Julian gave the order with a blink of his eye and Liam's fist came down on Dylan's knee once again.

"Ooookaay," he screamed. "Elaina's going to attack it again."

"When is this attack to occur?"

"Two days from now."

"Why attack the Facility a second time?" Julian prodded, ignoring the murmurs of the council members in the room.

Dylan looked past Julian, meeting my gaze with an evil smirk as he replied, "To capture Brianna Morgan of course."

"Liar," I said without realizing it.

Both Julian and Devin turned to look at me, but it was Victor who said, "Cameron, do you have something to add?"

"This man is lying, Father."

Julian sneered at me. "I believe it is my job to determine whether a prisoner is lying or not."

"Then do your job, Julian," I growled and then Father warned both of us on our tone. "Forgive me, Father, but Elaina knew very well where Brianna was being held once she realized her men had mistakenly kidnapped Hannah Berkshire. The message was left right on our front gate. Elaina knows Brianna Morgan is not at the Facility, so why attack it again? Who is to say that this prisoner was not sent to deliberately throw us off guard?"

"Father," Julian cut in, "no man would endure such pain for a lie."

"Cameron, do you have a rebuttal?" Victor asked.

"Perhaps what he says is the only truth he knows. Perhaps his information is meant to draw us out of the manor. For all we know Dylan Bray was a plant waiting for anyone to drive by."

"That's not true!" Jazlyn yelled as she lunged forward, only to be caught by Julian and writhe in his grip. "Just because *you* didn't capture him doesn't mean you need to shit on the rest of us."

"Sister, I swear that is not what I am doing. I am merely suggesting that..."

"Like hell you are. Julian, let go of me!" Julian released his grip on Jazlyn only when Liam took her arm and pulled her back down to the center of the room. "Father, you believe the prisoner, don't you? This is what we have been waiting for, a chance to stop Elaina. Isn't that what we've all been working so hard for?"

Victor sat silent for a moment, looking between Jazlyn and the prisoner while he tapped the arm of his chair.

"Cameron," he said, "why do you feel so strongly that this is a ruse?"

"Father, you have instilled in us your power of strategy. Why would anyone attack a location they know does not hold what they wish to possess? Would it not make more sense for Elaina to attack the manor where she knows full well Brianna Morgan is located? Or even better, send us a martyr who is willing to endure great pain to support his cause and put us on the wrong course. No Father, I feel that if Elaina is to attack it will be here."

"Yes, child, but your logic only makes sense if Elaina is as strategic as we are. That is, unless you have some kind of proof to dispute the prisoner's account?"

Devin's eyes were burning into the side of my face, urging me to tell the truth. But instead, I responded, "No, Father, just a gut feeling."

Victor was skeptical; I could see it in his eyes as he stared me down. When I didn't budge, he flinched his head in Liam's direction and Dylan Bray's knee was quickly broken in half. Over the prisoner's screams Victor asked, "Where is your base of operations?"

"Out...outside...the city. A couple of hours from here," Dylan stammered while his leg hung crookedly underneath him. "Th..there's a warehouse. We had to mmmove after...you found us in Arizona."

Victor paused, wringing his hands together and waiting for Dylan to quiet down before deciding what actions to take.

"I find this a difficult situation. I agree with Cameron in the fact that Elaina's strategy is not necessarily sound, however, the evidence provided by the prisoner under pain prompts me to believe that there is some merit to his claims. Therefore, if Elaina plans on attacking the Facility in two days, we will attack her in one and at her base of operations.

"Devin, I want you and Cameron to coordinate our forces. We will use the majority of those in the manor rather than draw in Warriors from outside the city and call attention to ourselves. We will keep a select few here to protect Brianna Morgan and put Lanashell on alert at the Facility. This operation relies on the element of surprise. If Elaina's coven is in anyway alerted to the fact that we know of their plan, we lose our window of opportunity.

"I want the battle plans by this afternoon and all teams prepared by this evening. That means full restriction beginning at midnight. I want every Warrior at full strength for our attack tomorrow night." Victor stood from his throne. "My Warriors, be vigilant, be strong. And Julian, be sure our prisoner lives to see our victory, but for now, get this piece of filth out of my sight."

Everyone stood and Victor walked swiftly out of the hall, saluting him with their fists against their chests as he passed. I caught Devin's glance as I stepped down from my chair and walked quickly toward the Council Hall doors.

"Brother, wait," Devin said, grabbing my arm and pulling me out into the courtyard. "Why did you say nothing of Brianna's vision? You know this feels wrong."

"Yes, this is totally wrong. Nothing about this feels right."

"Then why stay silent?"

"I could ask you the same thing, Brother. You could have just as easily exposed Brianna's gift, but you did not because deep down you know her vision could be a battle today, tomorrow, or three years from now."

"Cam's right, Dev," Alexander said as he joined us from behind. "We need to prepare for what we've been given and hope to hell that piece of shit wasn't lying."

"He is lying, Alex."

"I know, Cam. Just trying to make you feel better."

I sighed. "I need to tell Brianna what is happening and then we can all meet in a half an hour."

Devin nodded and walked back into the Council Hall while Alexander followed me to my room where we suspected that both Brianna and Kyla had remained. The entire walk up the stairs I dreaded telling Brianna that I would be going to battle, one that looked nothing like what she had seen.

Another day ruined. When I should be lying next to her, stroking and kissing her bare shoulder, begging her to let me make love to her again, I would be in the next room strategizing against a blind enemy and hoping I would come home to her again. It was not the situation I wanted to walk into, especially after the grief she went through this morning.

When we approached my bedroom door, I took a deep breath before I opened it and stepped inside. On the bed was Brianna, still in her white terrycloth robe, curled tightly in a ball and lying in Kyla's lap with tissues strewn all over the bed. The TV was on, but neither of them was watching the program on the screen. Instead, both were wiping away their tears, Brianna's eyes swollen and puffy, and Kyla's face stained red.

Alexander looked down at me and said, "This does not look good."

"Just wait," I whispered, knowing the storm we were both heading into.

Every Warrior prepared for battle differently. Some drank a rare blood type, others cleaned and primed their weapons. And in my tightknit vampire family it was tradition to play poker before every major battle. There were Warriors who criticized us for not considering the levity of the situation, but our response was always it was more important to have a little fun with each other in case it was our last.

Right now, I had a pair of twos. That was all, a pair of twos. I was not losing, but I was not winning by any means either. I decided to fold when Devin raised his bet by one hundred dollars just as my angel walked through the sitting room door. Bri and I had argued a great deal after I told her we were going to battle, and that battle was not in the courtyard as she had seen several times before. She was angry and confused, and did not know quite how to handle the situation. This was new to both of us, and when she was scared, she cried and yelled. At least that was what she did now. Before I met her, she would have simply locked herself away in her library and avoided the situation. Unfortunately, neither of us could afford to ignore the fact that I was going to battle in twenty-four hours.

Brianna crossed the room and wrapped her arms around the back of my neck and whispered in my ear, "Forgive me?"

I kissed the tip of her nose and patted her hand as I said, "There is nothing you need forgiving for."

"Still love me?"

"Always, angel," I replied and kissed her on the lips, forgetting everyone around us.

"Gross, get a room," Jared said rolling his eyes as he folded his cards.

Brianna pulled herself away from my lips as she stood and said, "Oh, you're playing cards?"

"Do not try and be coy, my love," I said, raising a skeptical brow at her. "Your chips are there. And even though Jared and I told them you cheat, Alex and Devin insisted that you be allowed to play if you decided to join us."

"I do not cheat," Brianna said sweetly as she sat down next to me.

"Like hell you do," Jared grumbled, throwing his cards at Devin.

"Shut up, Jared," she rebutted. "Ky, you're not playing?"

Kyla leaned over the arm of the high-back chair positioned in front of the fireplace and held up her latest novel.

"Oh no," Alexander replied, "my darling wife would rather read a sappy romantic novel that defaces our entire race rather than spend time with her family."

"Ooo, which one?" Brianna asked and Kyla showed her the cover of her book. "Oh yeah, I read that one last winter. It's fantastic. And Alex, it's about werewolves, not vampires, so there."

"Thank you, my friend," Kyla cheered.

"You're welcome, my friend," Brianna replied, exchanging smiles with Kyla.

They had really grown close, and I was thankful they had each other in times like these. If something were to ever happen to me or Alexander, at least they would be able to comfort each other.

I sighed and reached for my new cards, shaking away the thoughts of leaving Brianna behind, and concentrated on the bad hand that Devin had dealt me yet again.

"Sera says hello," Brianna said as she shuffled the cards in her hand.

"I assume she and Eris made it home?" I asked.

"Mmm hmm, earlier this afternoon," she replied lazily as she placed her first bet. "She totally agrees with me that you guys are totally barking up the wrong tree with the battle tomorrow night. But of course, what do we know."

My brothers each took a pause and looked to me at how to react to Brianna's statement. Unfortunately, I had heard it several times already and simply raised her bet.

Brianna removed two cards from her hand and traded them in for new ones as she said, "So Alex, I've been meaning to ask you, what's the story behind the battle you had with Cameron?"

Alexander met my gaze while Jared laughed next to me. I had to admit that Brianna's distraction tactic was quite good.

"Tell her if you must, Alex," I sighed.

Brianna smiled energetically to Alexander, but it was Jared who relayed the story.

"So ya know how Cameron's this totally formal guy, like 'My name is Cameron and I speak like a robot because I am better than you.'"

"I do not sound like that," I said defensively.

Jared tilted his head. "Seriously dude, say the word can't. Won't. Call me Jer, call Devin, Dev." I did not concede. "See! You can't do it, ya fuckin' snob."

Brianna knitted her brows together and then looked to Alexander who explained, "I challenged Cam to a battle because he always called me Alexander. I hate being called Alexander, my name is Alex. So we placed a wager that if I won, he would call me Alex and *I* would be allowed to call him Cam. It's pretty stupid when you say it out loud, but hey, it was his bet to lose. So you see, Brianna, you're the only other one who ever calls him Cam, although I seriously doubt you had to toss him up against a wall."

Brianna smiled and replied, "Just so you know, he only calls you Alex to your face. When you're not around he calls you Alexander."

"You little snitch," I said and pinched her side where I knew she was ticklish. The room bounded with laughter as Brianna squealed at my touch.

"Jeez, Bibi, vampires in the room. You're totally piercing my ears here," Jared whined as he placed his bet.

"For cryin' out loud, Jared, where did you come up with that awful name?"

"I can't believe you haven't figured it out yet, B…B…"

I cleared my throat in hopes he would stop. Everyone in the room knew what his nickname meant except Brianna, and I knew she would be uncomfortable at the revelation.

"Two pair," I announced, trying to get everyone's attention back on the game. Alexander folded as did Jared while Devin displayed a flush.

"Ha! Full house, aces high," Brianna cheered as she took all the chips in the pot. "Sorry, Jer, I don't get it."

"Beebs, it's your initials, duh!"

"Jared, stop," I threatened quietly.

"Seriously, Jer, are you impaired? My initials are unfortunately B.M., like bowel movement."

"Well eventually they'll be B.B., like Brianna Burke."

The room went quiet and I could see from the corner of my eye that Kyla had turned in her chair to see Brianna's reaction. The tiny lines around her eyes tensed, I was waiting for the tears, but surprisingly none came.

"I'm still mar…I'm not Brianna Burke," she muttered under her breath while she threw her cards over to Devin.

"Yeah, no shit, but it's only a matter of time," Jared said proudly, unfazed by Brianna's sudden change in mood.

I squeezed her hand lightly, bringing her eyes up to mine. "Are you upset?"

"No," she replied, shaking her head, although I knew it did bother her. I could see it on her face that she was saying to herself she was still technically Brianna Lewis, not even Brianna Morgan, let alone Brianna Burke. I kissed the back of her hand and she gave me a tight smile as she began shuffling her new cards. "All of you have such cool names and I'm stuck with Bibi? Seriously, the name Jared Ranger should be in a book."

Alexander and I laughed lightly behind our cards.

"Okay, what am I missing?" Brianna asked, looking at each of us.

Alexander placed his bet and said, "Brianna, you're not the only one who wishes they had a different name. Jer, would you care to tell Brianna what's so funny?"

Jared kept his cards in front of his face while he threw in his chips.

"You see, Brianna, Jeremy Smith is truly sitting at our table right now pretending he doesn't hear us."

Brianna's eyes grew wide as she placed her bet. "Jared! You're really Jerry Smith? Where the heck did Jared Ranger come from?"

My youngest brother, fraught with embarrassment as his true identity was revealed, refrained from speaking. It was my eldest brother who interceded.

"Brianna, Jeremy Smith was an Army *Ranger*. Little brother, where did Jared came from? Did Father make you change it?"

"I don't need to take this abuse," Jared said, rising from the table.

"Jerry, come on now," Brianna said quickly, causing another round of laughter. "Sit back down so that I can take more of your money."

"As if!" Jared shouted and put four of a kind down on the table.

The rest of us folded when Brianna revealed a royal flush.

"Fuckin ain't right!" Jared shouted. "You cheated."

Brianna smiled as she raked in another full pot.

"Jerry, you're just mad because everyone in the room has a better name than you. But trust me, Jer, you're not the only vampire I know who wants to be something they're not."

The game became quiet while everyone studied their hand. As we shuffled around our cards and went around the table placing bets, it was Devin's turn to raise or call, but he was silent.

"Brother, it is your bet," I prodded.

Devin looked down at his chips as he said, "I am a homosexual. Tao was my lover for the last three years and I was devastated when he was killed."

The only sound in the room was that of Brianna's heartbeat. Everyone was frozen in silence and staring at Devin. As his admission sank into my head, I realized it should not have been that much of a shock. He never seemed to be attracted to women, though I had always assumed it was because he did not need love from anyone. But how absurd was my assumption. We all needed affection in some capacity. I just never saw Devin needing anything. Memories of Devin's reaction the day Tao disappeared seemed so natural now.

"Dude, where the hell did that come from?" Jared said, lifting the awkward veil of silence.

Devin threw his cards down on the table as he replied, "Brianna's right, I've been trying to be something I'm not."

"Dev, I didn't mean…" Brianna began, but Devin put his hand up to stop her.

"I know you all think that I am callous and unfeeling, but all of you are the most precious things in my life. Tomorrow night I stand with my brothers in battle, willing to lay down my life for each of you and yet I am a coward when it comes to telling you the truth about who I really am. I expect nothing less than absolute truth from all of you which makes me the biggest hypocrite. However, now that it is out in the open, I would understand if you chose not to stand with me any longer. I…I just wanted you all to know."

The room was silent again; each of us wondering who was going to break the silence. Again, it was Jared.

"Seriously dude, it took you five hundred years to come out of the closet? That's gotta be a record or something. I don't wanna speak for the rest of us, but just as long as you don't try and suck my dick while I'm trying to take down Elaina tomorrow, we'll be fine."

"Jared!" I yelled, but Devin held his hand up once again.

"Trust me, Jerry, I will never be interested in that pitiful thing you call a penis."

Everyone at the table roared with laughter and afterwards assured Devin that his admission would stay within these walls. None of us would want anyone other than him at our sides. I could see a weight lift from my eldest brother's shoulders, one that I had never noticed was there. I did, however, notice Brianna mouth to him *"I told you so"* meaning she knew about this before us all. Whether she figured it out or he told her, I cared little. It was yet another example of how my Bri loved my family and vice versa.

After another hour of poker, Alexander finally announced, "You're right, Cam, she cheats."

Brianna stretched, stuck her tongue out at Alexander, and looked at her watch.

"What time does that restriction thing start?" she asked.

"Midnight. No exceptions, and Father checks," Devin said firmly, glancing directly at Alexander and then at Kyla who ducked quickly back around in her chair.

"All right then, I'm going to bed," Brianna said as she yawned and rose from the table. "Jared, I think I have enough for my *own* bank account now," she said before giving me a lingering kiss and then exiting through the sitting room door into our bedroom.

"She can never play cards with us again," Devin growled as he collected the cards.

"I tried to warn you," I laughed.

As I watched Devin shuffle the cards for another game I heard Brianna's voice in my head, and I knew she was projecting the message just to me.

Your choice, Cam, black negligee or nothing at all. Offer lasts for thirty seconds.

Immediately I stood from the table.

"Goodnight, everyone."

Chapter Fifty-eight

Brianna

The vampires in the manor were on complete restriction meaning beginning at midnight they had to sleep and feed and nothing else until "wheels up" as Devin said. That meant I didn't have any physical training today and I could sleep in and lay next to Cameron all day and all night. However, my body had other ideas. Beginning at 6:00 a.m., I woke up every fifteen minutes convinced I had missed my non-existent alarm. I felt bad jerking awake for nearly two hours knowing that Cameron woke up each time as well. It wasn't fair to him, and there was no way I was going to be able to go back to sleep without a little help. Pills weren't the answer, so I quietly, and begrudgingly, changed into my workout clothes and strapped on my dagger harness. Cameron asked me to stay, but instead I kissed him and headed to the training room so that he could recharge in peace. I needed him to have every ounce of strength when he attacked Elaina tonight.

It was a battle that he and I had fought about. We both knew it wasn't the battle I had seen in my dreams. He had refused to tell Victor about them even though I had said we should, but to his point, I had no way of knowing when that battle would occur. Nothing about the attack felt right, but as he said to me many times yesterday, he didn't have a choice. Orders were orders and he had to ensure that the mission was accomplished and everyone made it home. That was the hardest part to handle - would Cameron come home? I had even suggested that I come along with them, but the thought was barely out of my mouth before Cameron was shutting me down.

Either way, we more than made up before Victor's restriction went into effect. What can I say, I inferred that Cam had a choice of sexy lingerie or nothing, and he chose nothing. He got to me so fast that I was still in the closet and then we never made it out. If I thought my insides hurt yesterday, I could barely walk today without wincing. It made working out a little more painful, but my racing thoughts were the real problem. The whole time I was working with my daggers I kept thinking, why me? What did Elaina truly want with me? Or with my children – which I have none…yet. Why would she want to kidnap me when I'm not even pregnant? Or is the father of the children I see in my dreams not Cameron, but one of the members of Elaina's coven? The thoughts sent shivers up my spine and only made me want to know the answers even more.

And then it hit me, one of Elaina's own was in this very house. I didn't know the rules about talking to a prisoner, but I needed to see him. He was the closest I'd get to knowing Elaina's real plans for me. Maybe he'd be more willing to talk to me than the Warriors. It was a long shot, but I was willing to take it if it meant understanding even the tiniest bit about why I was being hunted.

It was settled. I secured my daggers in their holders, wiped myself down with a towel, and shrugged the T-shirt I'd stolen from Cameron on over my harness. However, the real challenge was going to be how to find where the prisoner was. Based on what I had pieced together from conversations here and there, the prison cells were beneath the Council Hall. I knew where that was, well just the door, beyond that I had no idea where the hell I was going.

I made my way down the long main corridor and just before I hit the door to the library I turned to my left and stepped down the few stairs to the breezeway of the courtyard. The weather was beautiful - a bright, crisp San Francisco morning that probably wouldn't last that long. Once I stepped off the last stair, I had to raise my hand up in front of my eyes to shield them from the sunlight flooding into the breezeway. The door to the Council Hall stood fifty feet ahead of me, and the butterflies in my stomach felt like they were trying to jump up and out of my throat. But something pushed my feet forward, walking through the striped floor of sun and shade as the light came through the archways. Bright then dark then bright again…Oh. My. God.

My feet were suddenly heavy as I dropped my hand slowly from my eyes just in time to see Jazlyn slipping through the Council Hall's door, closing it quietly behind her.

"Shit," escaped under my breath causing Jazlyn to turn quickly to face me. I could see her shock through the thick strand of black hair caught on her face. As she whipped her hair away, her expression changed in a quick and manic way.

"Brianna, you scared me," she said, smiling widely and wrapping her arms tightly around me.

I pushed her away and she looked upset by the gesture.

"I'm sorry, Jazlyn. You were hurting me." Shit, shit, shit, that was way too familiar. Shit, shit. What came next, a velvet box? But I already got that. Then what? Think! Think you nit wit!

"I have something for you," she said and reached behind her back.

"No!" I screamed and ran down the breezeway. Someone pushed me from behind, causing me to fall and hit my head on the stone walkway. When my eyes began to focus, I saw a slim vampire standing in front of me in a tight red leather jumpsuit with her blonde hair twisted tightly on top of her head. My feet started working before my brain caught up, pushing myself away from her knowing deep down inside there was no way I was going to get away. I rolled over and pushed myself to a standing position, but Elaina grabbed me by my hair and pulled me back across the stone floor. In one flowing movement she grabbed me around the throat and held me up against the wall. Her dark eyes were fierce against her pale skin and light hair, but her face was calm as if we were just having a light conversation between friends. She brought her face nose to nose with mine as she spoke in a high-pitched coo.

"Little, bitty, Brianna. The woman who changes everything. Isn't that what they've told you?"

I felt the blood rushing from my head as I pulled at Elaina's fingers, trying to get even the slightest amount of air, but my struggles were simply making it more difficult to breathe. I could feel my body burning with my power, but I struggled to get it to flow to my head with Elaina's hands squeezing my throat closed.

Elaina smiled wickedly at me as she said, "Now that we are actually face to face, I find myself a little disappointed. After all my effort to prepare my hybrids and vampires for the battle of their lives, and you come to me wrapped up in a pretty, little, breakable bow. It is delightful and dreadfully boring at the same time. I hope you said goodbye to your lover. Won't he and Victor be devastated that I was able to take you right from the great Warrior palace. Cameron might go right ahead and kill himself after having failed to save yet another wife of his."

At the sound of Cameron's name, the burning in my body became an explosion. Every nerve ending felt exposed as I pushed the burning from deep within my abdomen up through my head. The pain was excruciating while I fought against Elaina's crushing grip around my throat. Suddenly remembering what happened to Cameron the day before, I grabbed Elaina's face with both hands and projected with my mind as forcibly as was possible, *Elaina. Courtyard. Now!*

It wasn't the most coherent message, but I was bordering on unconsciousness. Elaina screamed loudly in my face as my mind projection reverberated in her head, and the power of it burned her face under my fingers. Her hand released me immediately and I fell clumsily onto the stone floor. My lungs burned as I coughed and gagged for air, but I had enough wit to press the button on my watch, the watch that Cameron had made me promise to wear every day, the watch that would hopefully alert Alex to my whereabouts since I had no idea if my message reached anyone in the manor.

I pulled myself along the wall, trying to reach the stairs that were only a few feet away when Elaina's arms came around the front of me. Her left arm stretched across my chest while the other forcibly tilted my head, exposing my neck to her. Before I could scream, I felt her fangs pierce my neck and rip the skin across to my shoulder.

"CAMERON!" I screamed in agony as Elaina dug her fangs in deeper and feed from deep inside me. The stairwell in front of me began filling with black smoke along with the sound of the house alarm echoing throughout. My Warriors had come, and it didn't take long to recognize who was in front, my Cam.

Elaina lifted her mouth from my wound, not bothering to lick away the blood that was smeared all over her mouth and chin. She laughed wickedly as Cameron slowly stepped toward us with Devin and Alex close behind him.

"Let her go," he growled through his fangs.

I screamed painfully when Elaina pressed two of her fingers knuckles-deep into my gaping wound. Cameron stopped his approach abruptly as tears streamed down my face from the pain. Elaina removed her blood-covered fingers and seductively licked them clean.

"To think, little Warrior, you get all of this sweetness to yourself. That's not really fair now, is it?" Cameron didn't answer, but Devin and Alex were keeping the other Warriors steady as my blood began streaming down the front of my shirt. "I leave with her, or I break her neck right in front of you."

"You need her, Elaina," Cameron said calmly. "You will not hurt her more than you already have. What good is her power if she is dead? We both know you did not come here to kill her. That has never been your plan."

"You know nothing of my plan, little Warrior," Elaina snapped back, laughing like the villain she was.

Just then, the three walls of the courtyard were overtaken by Elaina's vampires, some even carrying others I assumed were hybrids. All the Warriors with the exception of Cameron turned to view the enemy filling the courtyard. The Warriors were beat in numbers, and all the visions that I had of this battle flooded into my head, reminding me of everything I needed to prevent.

Cameron began inching forward again; looking at me fiercely and nodding his head only the slightest bit. He began speaking to Elaina again, but his words were lost on me while I concentrated on slowly moving my arm to my back and feeling for my dagger that hung from its holder. After I wrapped my hand around the silver handle, I took one last breath and looked at Elaina through the side of my eye to ensure Cameron still had her attention. In a quick move I drew my dagger and ripped it down the length of her forearm. She let go of me quickly and before I fell, I plunged the dagger over my shoulder and into the space at the base of her neck. As she screamed, I ducked to the ground just in time to see Cameron lunge for her and tackle her into the Council Hall door, breaking it in two.

The Warriors broke ranks from within the stairwell and fled into the courtyard in a blur. I pushed myself to a seated position and felt a cool hand tilt my chin up to see Kyla kneeling in front of me.

"We need to stop the bleeding," she shouted over the battle cries behind us. With quick hands she ripped Cameron's T-shirt from my body, wadded it up and pressed it tightly to my neck.

"Kyla look..." I started to scream but before I could finish, Kyla sidestepped a hybrid swinging a heavy medieval ax that just missed her head.

"Oh, no you did not!" she shouted at the hybrid. The hybrid looked like a crazed dog as he lunged for Kyla again, whipping his ax wildly around. Kyla grabbed him by the shirt and threw him back out into the courtyard. "I'll be right back," she shouted back at me and then fled into the middle of the fighting.

"Kyla, wait!" I shouted while pushing myself painfully off of the floor causing the bloody shirt to fall from my neck as I ran onto the grass. In a blur, someone came in front of me and pushed me back into the breezeway causing my head to hit the wall behind me with extreme force. Before my eyes opened, I felt hands around my throat squeezing my already bruised and torn tissue. Gasping for air, I stretched my eyes open knowing I would come face to face with Elaina again. Instead, I shut my eyes tight and opened them again thinking I was hallucinating.

"H-hannah?"

"I'm surprised you even remember my name," Hannah replied scathingly. She was just as small as I remembered her being, but she was a million times stronger and her once tame wavy hair was wild and matted against her face.

"You're...alive," I sputtered through the pain in my throat.

"No thanks to you. Was it your plan all along, Brianna? Sending me to your room so they would take me instead of you?" she hissed. "Is that why you insisted I go on ahead! Answer me!"

"No...no I tried to...stop them."

"I saw you! I saw you do nothing!"

"Dev...Devin stopped me. Hannah...p-please," I cried, pulling desperately at her hands. "You were my...friend."

Hannah's fingers relaxed slightly while she shook her head wildly from side to side. When she looked back up at me her expression had softened.

"They've done horrible things to me, to all of us," she said slowly in a completely different voice.

"We'll help you, Hannah. I promise I never wanted anything to happen to you. Let me help you," I pleaded, feeling her fingers continue to relax.

Her eyes fluttered, as if she was breaking from a spell, but then her whole body flinched violently. Her fingers tightened around my throat again as her face sank back into a crazed expression. She pulled a knife from her pocket and thrust it toward my stomach. I grabbed her wrist and struggled to hold it away from me, and then heard the voice of the person I was praying wouldn't come down those stairs.

"Bibi!" Jared yelled as he stepped down the shadowed stairs holding his gun at the ready.

"Jared, no!"

My grip on Hannah's wrist slipped slightly and Jared pulled his trigger just as Hannah turned to face him. In another blur, Hannah leapt to the side but the bullet still hit her in the shoulder. This was wrong, this was all wrong. That was supposed to be Elaina, not Hannah. Hannah was never in the picture. Everything was jumbling up…again! For goodness' sake, why give me prophetic dreams if they don't unfold like they're supposed to.

Jared stood in place on the steps, shock wiped across his face as he watched Hannah rise from the floor, holding her wounded shoulder with her opposite hand. Her expression had softened once again, revealing more of the Hannah that we both knew. In another blur she was standing in front of Jared, gently caressing his face and streaking it slightly with blood.

"It can't be. I saw you. I saw you on the gate, burned and…"

"You saw a woman," she corrected. "They made me put her there. You saw what they wanted you to see."

Jared shook his head in disbelief. "But I would have seen you on the tape."

"They've made me faster. You wouldn't have seen anything. Oh, Jared. Jer…" she said softly, allowing him to sink his face into her hand. "I'm sorry."

The world seemed to move in slow motion as I watched Hannah push Jared into the bright sun, somehow launching him into the air. And that's when I saw him, the big evil vampire from Flagstaff, standing in a pocket of open space and laughing wickedly as he eyed Jared flying toward him. The evil Vamp ran a few steps forward and caught Jared in midair, pulling him down to the ground and holding him there while he screamed in agony.

Fury raged within me at the sight of the gray and black smoke rising from Jared's skin and the sound of his cries. Hannah took a step toward the stairs so I quickly tackled her from behind and we both fell to the floor. She wiggled her way out from under me but I grabbed her again while I unsheathed my remaining dagger and held it up against her neck.

"Don't think I won't cut your throat after what you just did. I want to know why! Why, Hannah!"

Her expression softened, showing me little Hannah again with a tear streaking down her cheek. "They have control over us. You have no idea what they've done to us. I don't want to be this, please help me. Kill me, Brianna, please. Just kill me," she sobbed.

My breathing was fast and I was completely conflicted at seeing little Hannah, my friend who I let this happen to, begging me to kill her.

"I-I can't."

"Please!" she screamed. "I won't be able to stop myself from hurting you. Please put me out of this misery," she pleaded and pressed the skin of her neck into my dagger's blade.

In my moment's hesitation, I saw her body flinch again and the Hannah I knew was gone. Both of her hands suddenly made contact with my chest, launching me back into one of the archways behind me. As stars danced around my eyes, I saw the glint of Hannah's knife coming at me. Just when she was inches away from me, I held up my dagger and allowed it to disappear deep within her stomach. Her face flinched with shock but then melted and she became Hannah for one last spilt second before she collapsed in my arms. I laid her to the ground and watched as she smiled at me and then took her last bloody breath.

I had killed her, I had killed my friend. This time I was certain she wouldn't return. But before the grief could consume me, I heard Jared's screams behind me. I took my dagger out of Hannah's body and turned to the courtyard to see Warriors being overtaken by Elaina's Vamps and hybrids. It was mayhem as blood and bodies were strewn everywhere. In the middle of it was Jared, his body smoldering in the sun while the big Vamp stood over him, laughing and ripping Jared's shirt away to expose even more skin. It was up to me to help him. Everyone else was taking on more than they could handle, but suddenly I began to feel light-headed from my blood loss. My wound was large and deep and still bleeding. I needed help, but Jared needed it more. Push through it, Brianna. Wasn't that what Devin always told me? Push through it, be the Warrior who kicked Eris's ass.

I took a step onto the grass and to my left I saw a blur of orange flying across the courtyard.

"Kyla! Archway!" I screamed just in time for her to Project herself to the other side. Kyla looked up to me and gave me a thankful nod before she ran back out to fight.

Unfortunately, my shout out to Kyla alerted my Flagstaff foe of my presence and he licked his lips when I made eye contact with him. Taking a deep breath, I closed my eyes and let my guard down enough to feel the essences of those around me. When I opened my eyes, I concentrated on the evil Vamp's light and pushed away the sight of everyone else's. I heard Jared shouting at me to run, but I flipped my dagger in my hand to hold it by its tip and flung it at the evil Vamp while I pulled his light toward it.

Either because I was bleeding and fatigued, or he had been able to resist my weak pull on him, my aim was bad. I had been aiming for his heart but instead got him just above the collar bone. He fell to the ground trying to pull the dagger from his chest though his hands were burning from the silver handle. I didn't know what else to do. Both my daggers were gone and I wasn't strong enough to do anything else. Jared was going to die. Think Brianna, think!

"Brianna!"

My eyes shot up at the sound of my name. It was Devin. He was fighting against four vampires, flying and kicking at unimaginable speeds.

"Two things!" he yelled.

I shook my head not understanding. My head was aching and I couldn't process anything. Two things? What two things? Shit. Shit. Shit. What two things? Oh, duh you stupid idiot.

"My daggers are gone."

"What else," he struggled to say as one of the vampires clamped his arms around Devin's neck only to have Devin grab him by the shoulders and fling him over onto the ground.

"I'm not a vampire!"

"Alex, give her a vampire!" Devin yelled to Alex who was fighting against six vampires with a hybrid hanging off his back. Alex roared as he ripped the hybrid from his back and flung her against the stone wall next to him. Then as one of the vampires grabbed him around the throat, Alex grabbed the Vamp's arm, ripped it from his body, and tossed it in my direction. I scurried away just as the arm of the vampire flopped to the ground in front of me.

"You have got to be kidding!" I screamed as I watched the fingers of the arm flinch.

"Help Jared!" Devin screamed at me again as another vampire joined the others fighting against him.

A little bit of bile climbed up my throat while I reached down for the bloody vampire arm at my feet. The evil Vamp was still on his knees trying to remove my dagger from his chest when I held the dismembered arm up like a baseball bat and ran towards him screaming, "I'M GOING TO PUKE!"

The evil vampire turned in my direction just before I crushed his face with the rock-hard vampire arm. He fell to the ground but then tried to push himself up. I hit him in the face again, seeing pieces of it fly across the grass. He lay flat out on the ground while I continued to beat him while I shouted, "Don't! Touch! My! Brother!"

But even after the beating, the evil Vamp still stirred. I knew there was only one way to finish him. I grabbed my dagger from his chest, held his head by his hair, and sliced his neck clean. I dropped his head on the ground and turned to vomit on the grass. When I was done, I wiped my mouth, still hearing Jared's moans behind me. I turned to find him lying face down, his skin black and charred and still burning. I knelt beside him and whispered in his ear, "I'm here, Jer."

"Your breath stinks."

"I just cut off a guy's head, give me a break," I snapped at him but then began to cry at the sight of his burned and cracked body. I put my arm around his shoulder, rolled him over to face me, and brought his mouth to my still bleeding wound.

"Drink it, Jared."

"No, Beebs."

"It'll help you from burning."

Thank you, Hybrid 101. Hybrid blood can prevent young vampires from burning in the sun. It wouldn't help his current burns, but it would hopefully stop him from burning even more while I got him to safety. I felt his fangs sink weakly into the area closest to my neck and could feel the blood being pulled from my body.

"Come on, baby brother, I need to get you out of here," I said after only a minute or so and pulled Jared's face gently from my neck. Thankfully, he didn't resist.

Jared groaned as I pulled him across my back and held his severely burnt arms around the front of my chest. His weight was a little much for me, but I was able to slowly run him across the courtyard towards the shelter of the breezeway. I had no idea what I was going to do once I got him there, no way could I carry him up the stairs. But just as I reached the stone floor, Jared's weight was suddenly lifted from me. I panicked and looked up, fearful one of Elaina's vampires was taking him from me.

"Hey Dad," Jared whispered as Victor pulled him up into his arms. "I forgot the sun block again," he said lightly and trying to smile, but his lips cracked open and began to bleed.

Victor had a fierce calm about him while he held his youngest child in his arms, surveying his extensive burns. Quickly he turned his attention to me, on my hands and knees and gasping for air while the blood from my wound dripped onto the floor.

"You can stop this, Brianna," he said firmly. My head jerked up at his words; the words that I had heard Elaina say to me in my dream. "It is your choice. You're choosing to let them die. Your family, your lover, everyone you care about. Is that what you want? You want them to die when their salvation is so simple?"

"What do you want me to do?"

"You have all the power to stop this. You are the only one who can stop them all at once."

"I can't," I panted, shaking my head vigorously. "I'm too weak, I'll hit them all."

"Then hit them all!" he shouted. "We'll capture who we can. Brianna, you must do this."

"I can't do it, Victor," I cried.

"If you don't, you'll never forgive yourself. So do it now!" Victor screamed.

Tears of exhaustion and pain trickled down my cheeks as I pulled myself up to a standing position. The familiar burning in my stomach grew and stretched into every cell of my body while Victor stared me down, challenging me to say no again.

"Run then," I sighed and looked out into the courtyard. I stepped out onto the grass and held my hands out, taking in all the vampire lights around me and concentrating on not hitting the two on my right that were fleeing up the stairs; noticing full well that Jared's essence was dimmer than all the others.

With all my strength I pushed everything I had within me to the halos in the courtyard. As my mind projection left me, so did my consciousness. The battle had ended, but I neither knew who won, nor whom I'd lost.

Chapter Fifty-nine

Cameron

I had Elaina pinned when I saw Brianna scamper across the courtyard with a badly burned Jared stretched across her back. I was thankful she was alive, but terrified that she had not fled. She could be taken at any moment, and specifically by the female vampire I was holding to the ground. Elaina's chin had Brianna's dried blood smeared across her face; the sight of which infuriated me. Her fangs sank into my forearm just as two of her hybrids jumped me from behind causing me to fall forward onto Elaina as they clawed my back and neck.

I was amazed at the fact that they could penetrate my skin, which meant they had also ripped through my shirt. Knowing I would lose Elaina as soon as I stood up, but knowing it would be the only way to get the hybrids off of me, I launched myself backwards into the wall behind me, crushing both of them and hearing multiple bones break. Even though they were dazed they began crawling along the grass toward me again. I kicked the closest one in the face, breaking his nose up into his head and then twisted the other's neck until it snapped in my hands. While both of them lay dead at my feet, I felt the breeze flow through the large tears in the back of my shirt.

"Damn you," I shouted and kicked one of them for ruining my shirt before launching myself up onto Elaina who was now trying to climb over the stone wall. I grabbed her by her waist and pulled her roughly down to the ground, holding her head tightly between my hands.

"Before I kill you, tell me what you want with her?"

Elaina's blood-streaked mouth stretched into an evil grin.

"I could care less about Brianna, you foolish Warrior. It is what's inside her that I want."

I squeezed her head tightly between my hands, enjoying her screams of pain.

"What is it about her blood that you want so badly?"

"Blood? You thought this was about blood!"

"Then what!"

But before Elaina could answer, I looked up just in time to see Brianna step to the edge of the courtyard and extend her arms. Suddenly a wave of energy burst from her body, hitting every vampire in its path. It felt as if a bomb had gone off in my head as the wave hit me, throwing me back against the stone wall with Elaina landing a few feet away from me. Although I was dazed like the others around me, I could see several of Elaina's hybrids pulling her to her feet. I pushed myself up, ready to go after her when I noticed Brianna lying face down in the grass. Knowing I was letting Elaina slip through my fingers, I rushed over to Brianna and rolled her over to check for a pulse. It was weak and her breathing was ragged. The wound she had sustained from Elaina was incredibly deep and still oozing blood. There was literally a hole stretching across my angel's neck, chest, and shoulder.

"Devin!" I screamed over my shoulder and within seconds he and Alexander were next to me along with Kyla. All of us had wounds of our own that were healing, leaving behind only rips and tears in our clothing with thin scars beneath, but Brianna was not so lucky. "Devin, what do we do? This is more than just a few stitches."

Devin nodded. "It's too extensive. She doesn't have time for a doctor. You'll have to give her your blood. It's the only way..."

"No," I said quickly, "she would not want that."

"Brother, she's not awake to make the choice. She's lost a lot of blood already between being fed on twice and bleeding out from the wound itself."

"Twice?"

"She gave her blood to Jared. I saw her do it just before she carried him away. She was smart to think of it, but it didn't help her in any way. Now stop arguing with me and give her your blood, Brother, that is now an order. Kyla, bring down some medical supplies. I am going to go check on Jared and speak with Father on what he wants to do. I want to see fang marks in your arm by the time I get back, Brother," Devin said firmly before Projecting away while Kyla ran up the stairs in a blur.

I looked down at Brianna whose face had lost its color and I could hear that her heartbeat had slowed slightly.

"She is going to kill me," I whispered to Alexander, but without a moment's more hesitation, I bit into my wrist and put it to her mouth. When the fang marks closed, I bit into my arm again and began squeezing the blood onto Brianna's gaping wound while Alexander began taking stock of the scene around us.

"Cam?" he said a few feet from me. "That is Hannah Berkshire."

I turned to face him and noticed he was standing over the body of a small brunette who was bleeding from multiple wounds and remembered hearing Jared's gun go off in this vicinity.

"Was she shot?"

Alexander nodded. "Yes, in the shoulder. Jared must have missed."

"No wonder. He was probably in shock since she was supposedly dead."

"She has a knife wound, too," he said, looking at her abdomen and then looking in Brianna's direction.

I licked my bleeding wrist closed and gently caressed Brianna's face knowing how devastating it must have been to realize her friend was alive, and then have to kill her in self-defense. And still afterwards she was able to find the strength to put her life in danger to save my youngest brother. I loved her so much, and was even more terrified at everything she had sacrificed today. While my fingers trailed down her face, I saw the hint of pink coming back into her cheeks just as the blood seeping from her large wound began to slow.

Seconds later Kyla came down with bandages and solutions and immediately began working on Bri. But even after she was bandaged up, Brianna still laid unconscious in my arms. I kept thinking to myself that I could not bear if she went into another coma for two days, or longer. I was so focused on watching Brianna that I did not hear my brother calling me until he snapped his fingers in front of my face.

"Brother!" Devin yelled. "Did you hear me?"

"Sssorry, no," I stuttered.

Devin sighed with impatience. "Jared is critical, but healing. Father has given him a significant amount of blood, but it will be several hours before he is fully healed. A few more minutes and he would have been dust without Brianna's blood. She's the hero today."

"That she is," I replied softly as I brushed the hair from her eyes.

"Father wants the prisoners taken downstairs and everyone to convene in the Council Hall."

"What about Bri?" I asked, rising to my feet with her hanging limply from my arms. "I do not want her to wake without me."

"Alex and I will take her," Kyla said. "We'll keep her with us and if she wakes, you'll be right there to see her."

Alexander extended his arms to me and reluctantly I shifted my angel into his arms. I kissed her gently on the cheek and then her forehead, feeling the warmth returning to her skin. When I turned away, I was once again torn by my love for her and my duty to my family. Devin stepped in line with me and we walked toward the broken doors of the Council Hall.

Devin patted me roughly on the shoulder and said, "I think you have finally found a way to balance your responsibilities, Brother."

"Shut up, Devin."

Chapter Sixty

Brianna

"*Mama, wake up,*" *I heard a little boy's voice whisper in my ear, but I didn't budge.*

"*Yeah, Mama, Gampa said you has to wake up,*" *a little girl said in my other ear.*

"*Maybe she's sick,*" *the little boy said and placed his small hand flat against my cheek.*

"*Let me see,*" *the little girl said as she placed her hand on my other cheek. "She don't feel sick. Mama, you sick?*"

My eyes fluttered opened to see the two little faces I expected - my little fraternal twins, mirror images of their father with their dark eyes and curly black hair. Both of them were nestled on top of my chest staring intently at me with curious faces.

"*Don't worry, little ones, I am not sick. Where are we?*" *I asked looking around the room, but quickly recognizing the interior.*

"*At Gampa's house. He says it's time to wake up,*" *my son said to me.*

"*But I am awake.*"

"*No, Mama,*" *my daughter replied. "You has to wake up, wake up. For real, wake up. That's what Gampa wants.*"

I could feel the pull of my heart seeing both of them in front of me. Their sweet innocent eyes and bright smiling faces were too much to want to leave behind.

"*But I don't want to. I want to stay here with you.*"

"*Yes, but you will be seeing them eventually,*" *Eris said as he stepped into the white bedroom.*

The children giggled at their grandfather and quickly scurried past him out of the room.

"You know it's cruel to use them against me already. They're not even born yet," I mumbled.

"Yet, being the operative word. But regardless of my methods, my message is still the same, you need to wake. There are many pieces about today that need your help in putting together."

"You know what happened?"

"Yes," he replied as he sat next to me on the fluffy turquoise comforter. "Victor informed me of everything that you did today. If I could only have been there to see it," he said in a prideful tone.

"It was awful," I said, feeling the tears leak from my eyes and down my cheeks.

"That is war, Brianna, and it has only just begun. You must stay strong, for yourself, for Cameron, and most importantly for your future children. From this point on, everything is a test of your strength and faith. It will be difficult, but you will persevere. I know you will. After all, you are a daughter of the great Eris."

"Thanks, Dad. No pressure or anything."

Eris smiled at me as he patted my hand. "Ah, Brianna Marilena, how I love hearing you call me that." He paused for a moment, looking pensive in his thoughts before he continued with, "But I must insist that you wake. It is imperative."

I sighed knowing that I would wake up to pain both physical and mental. Neither of which I was ready to face.

"Do you think I could see them just one last time? Just for a few more minutes and then you can wake me up yourself."

My father twisted his lips together, debating whether he should give in to me or not. But seconds later, my little darlings ran back into the room and jumped onto my chest. Their laughter made my heart sing and the joy it brought me was over way too soon...

"Julian, it is your responsibility to see that prisoners stay alive unless otherwise ordered," Victor yelled from somewhere.

My eyes were still closed, but I could hear everything. Seriously, I mean *everything*. I could hear the rustles of shoes against a hard floor, the sound of someone whispering in the distance that Julian was getting what he deserved, and even the sound of my own heartbeat was like a bass drum in my ears.

My eyes shot open trying to figure out where the hell I was and why my hearing had gone supersonic. Carefully I pushed myself up a little to find that I had been leaning against Alex's arm. When I looked up at him sleepily, he gave me a warm smile and helped me rise to a sitting position. My left shoulder was aching, but not as bad as I expected. I looked down and noticed a large bandage covering my neck and shoulder, the tape of which was thoroughly irritating my skin. Still getting my bearings, I could barely see anything past the rows of Warriors sitting in front of me, only that we were surrounded by grey stone – the walls, the ceiling, even the wide steps we were sitting on. Since it was pretty much the only room I hadn't been in, I assumed we were in the Council Hall. Just then I felt someone tap me on the other shoulder and when I looked to my right, I found Kyla smiling widely and pointing to Cameron who was sitting down at the front of the hall behind Victor's king-like chair. His hands gripped both armrests tightly at the sight of me.

Victor cleared his throat loudly, looking sternly over at Cameron before turning his attention to me. "Welcome back, Brianna," he said and nodded in my direction.

"Thank you…ah, sir," I replied weakly.

"Let us continue, then," he said forcefully, turning his focus back onto Julian who stood in front of him. "Now Julian, I want an explanation as to how the prisoner died under your supervision."

"Ky," I whispered, "who died?"

Kyla leaned in tightly and for the first time I noticed that Kyla's hair wasn't really orange, but a plethora of amber, ocher, tangerine, and pumpkin-colored strands, of which I could see individually. She whispered into my ear and it was so loud that I had to lean back from the pain. "The prisoner Jazlyn brought in yesterday. They found him dead when they brought the other prisoners down a little while ago."

I looked back down at Julian, who for the first time wasn't his usual cocky self while he was being yelled at by Victor. Served him right, I thought evilly to myself.

"Step down, Julian. We'll deal with you later," Victor growled when Julian couldn't provide an explanation for the death. "Devin, if you would please give us a statistical account of today's events."

Devin rose from his chair on the other side of Victor and stood in the same place Julian had just vacated.

"We have captured ten hybrids and eight vampires from Elaina's coven, though we do not expect the hybrids to live long from their injuries, many of which they have inflicted upon themselves. So far there have been forty confirmed dead. None of which are ours," he said proudly. "We have one Warrior injured, but healing, and one Warrior missing."

I shot a glance up to Alex. "Who's missing?"

"Jazlyn," he muttered under his breath.

Jazlyn. Jazlyn, who I had seen just before the whole nightmare began, was missing. While Devin continued his debrief, my head swam with dozens of images. They were, oddly enough, extremely clear and organized, unlike the usual mess I had when my brain was overloaded. Suddenly an image came into my head of a past dream where Jazlyn was cackling next to me while my onyx ring burned my finger and arm with poison. When she actually gave me the ring in real life, no such poison existed. I looked down at Cameron's ring on my left hand. No, the ring Jazlyn had given me.

"Jazlyn's not missing," I said under my breath.

I felt Kyla's and Alex's eyes on me and everyone followed suit when Victor said, "Brianna, do you have something to share?"

I felt the blood rush to my face while my heart began to thump out of my chest. "Sorry, I was accidently thinking out loud."

"Then why don't you think out loud purposely in front of us," Victor said with a raised eyebrow.

Kyla pushed me up from my seat and helped me down to stand in the center of the room that was now all mine since Devin retreated back to his seat. I was terrified standing in front of everyone, seeing skeptical eyes on me. My only saving grace was Cameron sitting a few feet away giving me his most encouraging and loving eyes when he noticed my hands shaking at my sides.

"Brianna?" Victor prodded.

"Oh…yeah…I was only saying that I didn't think Jazlyn was missing."

"And what would make you think that?"

Nervously I picked at the medical tape pulling on my skin and answered, "Because she is part of Elaina's coven. She's your traitor."

Gasps and murmurs echoed around the stone room, but it was Julian who shouted, "That is outrageous! Accusing one of our own Warriors without any proof is inexcusable."

"Who says I don't have proof, ya jerk?"

Victor cleared his throat, once again bringing my attention to him. "Let us watch our tone, Brianna, as well as our words."

"Sorry," I replied, feeling my cheeks burn with embarrassment. "But I do have proof. At least I'm pretty sure I do."

Victor nodded and flicked his fingers at Julian to sit back down, which Cameron seemed to enjoy.

After a big exhale and a satisfying scratch of my shoulder, I clasped my hands tightly in front of me in order to stop their shaking while I said, "First, I need to ask if there is any other way to get to the prison cells other than through this room?" I said looking to Julian.

"No," he muttered.

"Okay, then. You see, this morning while you were all on restriction, I couldn't sleep so I decided to work out, but I had this aching feeling to talk to the guy Jazlyn brought in. Now I know it was probably a bad decision," I said defensively and put my hands up to Cameron who shifted in his seat, "but I wanted answers. Only when I got to the door of this room, Jazlyn was coming out. Now why else would Jazlyn be coming through this door if it wasn't that she had just killed the prisoner?"

"Impossible," Julian yelled as he stood. "My guards would have seen her."

"Yes, but couldn't she have Projected in? She's been down there before, hasn't she?"

"But why, Brianna?" Victor asked. "Why would Jazlyn kill the man she herself brought to us?"

Julian scoffed when I didn't respond right away. "She doesn't have the proof to back up her claims. Father, this is a waste of time."

"Oh for fuck sake, were you screwing her or something?" I wanted to rip my tongue out of my mouth as the words passed my lips. Victor raised his brow at me again. "I apologize. What I was about to say was that the reason Jazlyn would kill him would be to tie up any loose ends. She brought this guy to you on a silver platter and he came in singing like a Jaybird about an attack on the Facility, which I think we can all agree was never going to happen. Elaina probably promised this guy money or power to get captured and then throw you all off track. But when the real attack occurred today, I'll bet you Cameron's wardrobe that they had no intention on rescuing him. If and when he realized he'd been duped, he would have told you all the truth about Elaina's operations, which of course they couldn't have that happen. So Jazlyn killed him before he could say anything. Whew, can I get a glass of water or something?" I said breathlessly and desperately scratching my shoulder.

The room was silent except for the sound of Kyla's whispering feet running out of the room and then returning with a cool glass of water a few seconds later. How on Earth I had even heard her leave and come back was a mystery, but it wasn't something I could concentrate on right now.

"Father, this is all speculation," Julian said snidely. "We cannot condemn one of our own without substantial proof."

Victor tapped his fingers on the arm of his chair as he pondered my explanation before finally saying, "Brianna, I have to agree that most of what you have said is speculation. Is there anything else you could provide that would convince me that my sire of over three hundred years betrayed me?"

"Well, let me think," I said before taking a large gulp of water. "Okay, so before Eris came to you, no one knew my whereabouts, is that correct?"

"That is correct. Only Cameron and I knew you were located in Connecticut."

"And then when I left Connecticut, I forced Cameron to take me to my grandfather's home in North Carolina. Now somehow Jazlyn found us there, whether it was through the Gatherers or you guys. And Alex, correct me if I'm wrong, but there was no evidence that Elaina's coven was anywhere near North Carolina until the night Cameron and I fled from there. Right?"

"That's correct," Alex announced from his seat in the crowd. "I called Cameron as soon as we received information that she was in the area, but by then the two of you had already left."

"See! The night that Elaina was in North Carolina was the same night Jazlyn came to Daddy O's..."

"Who?" Victor interrupted.

"Oh sorry, my grandfather's house. *And* shortly after that, Cameron and I were attacked at a mall in Flagstaff *where* we eventually found that a tracker had been placed on our SUV. Jazlyn could have easily put the tracker on our truck, right Cam?" Cameron nodded slowly, obviously overwhelmed like everyone else in the room as the pieces began to fit together. "And furthermore, the day that the Facility was attacked happened to be the same day that Jazlyn visited with Devin. How would Elaina's Vamps know exactly which room was mine if Jazlyn didn't tell them?

"And come to think of it, when the explosions came, she was the one who told me to go to my room. Devin, remember? When you finally found me, you said that going to my room was the opposite of what I should have done. And don't forget when we found Jazlyn, she was leaving through the emergency exit. I doubt she was really looking for us like she said she was."

Devin nodded his head. "I have to agree that I had my doubts about her logic that day."

"There is still no concrete proof," Julian shouted, definitely getting on my last nerve.

"Then here," I snapped as I ripped the onyx ring from my finger. "This is the ring Jazlyn gave me at my claiming ceremony. She told me Cameron had given it to her a while ago, and she knew that I would most likely accept anything that was associated with him. I'll bet if Jared took this apart, he would find some kind of tracker or transmitter. Cam, you said yourself the setting had been changed. Something could have been easily inserted into it."

Julian took the ring from my fingers. "And what does this ring have to do with anything?"

"How else did Elaina find me today? Within this entire place, she found me exactly where I was, right outside these doors. She wasn't roaming the halls searching every room. No, she knew exactly where I was because that ring showed her where to find me. And I'll bet that Jazlyn told Elaina exactly how to get into the manor without being seen. You can't deny that at every turn there has been one common thread, and that's Jazlyn."

"Father," Cameron began tentatively, "we knew when those hybrids were left on Warriors' doorsteps that we had a traitor. Jazlyn could have easily provided Elaina with that information. Although it is difficult to admit, Brianna's theory has merit."

The room was thick with tension as the Warriors began realizing and believing that Jazlyn had most likely betrayed them. Unable to take the scratchy tape any longer, I ripped the large bandage from my shoulder and revealed a wide, raw, red scar that ached and pulled from within the more I moved my arm. Elaina had done a number on me, I thought, and then a sudden image of Elaina carving up my stomach flashed in my head.

It was then that the final piece fell into place.

"Just one last point before I finally collapse here. Victor, every vampire in this room has seen Jazlyn's deceit with their own eyes." I took a deep breath and looked apologetically at Cameron. "Yesterday the alarm in the manor was set off because all the vampires in the house suddenly had a forced vision of being stabbed by Elaina. What probably surprised and scared many of you was that you viewed yourself as a pregnant woman being held down while Elaina sliced you opened. Now if you think back to that vision, try and remember the face of the woman who held you down. It never registered before because I was always in so much pain, but if you really think back, you might see that the woman has some similarities to Jazlyn."

I caught Devin looking at Cameron through the side of his eyes knowing what I would eventually admit in front of Victor and the other Warriors.

"Brianna," Victor began calmly, "may I ask how you know this since you said yourself that only the vampires had this vision?"

I took a big drink of water before I answered, "I know because it was my vision. I dreamt it. And yesterday morning I discovered that unfortunately I can project my dreams."

"Brianna, a dream is not proof. And not to point out an obvious fact, but you are not pregnant. The event from your dream has not occurred."

"Not yet," I rebutted. "But it might, unfortunately. You see, Victor, my dreams tend to come true, like today for instance. I have dreamt about today's battle several times, and with a few exceptions everything that happened today occurred in my dreams."

Victor blinked several times while he rubbed his bottom lip with his index finger. "So Brianna, you are saying you have had several visions about the battle we fought today, and took no care in sharing this information with us?"

"That is correct," I announced to the sound of grumblings from the crowd. "But in my defense, although many of my dreams come true, I never know when they will happen."

Victor stood and rounded on Cameron as he shouted, "You knew about this, didn't you! You knew and negated to inform your own father, your maker, of this vital information. Yesterday when you spoke of Elaina's coven attacking us here versus at the Facility you *knew* that was the plan because Brianna had told you. How could you keep this from me, child? How could you!"

Cameron opened his mouth to speak, but I interjected, "There is only one person in this room who knew about my dream of the battle and that's me."

Victor whipped back around to face me, anger and resentment plastered on his face from what he deemed as yet another betrayal.

"Victor, I'm sorry. My dreams are new to me, and my lack of confidence in myself prevented me from telling anyone, including Cameron," I lied, and hopefully he believed me. "Like I said, I don't know when these things will happen, and sometimes they don't happen exactly the way I saw them because, well, things change, people's choices change. But I will say that my dreams only involve things that'll happen to me." I reached down for my glass of water and once I brought it to my lips, I realized it was empty and sighed loudly. "I'm sorry I didn't tell anyone. I just hope you understand why I didn't," I said taking a step back to return to my place next to Kyla and Alex.

"Brianna, please wait," Victor said firmly as he sat back down in his chair, but then his tone became light-hearted and kind. "We have all been scared by new gifts and powers. In the future, I would like to encourage you to share your visions with me or any Warrior in your coven because it is indeed your coven. A danger that affects you, affects us all since we are first and foremost one family, and we protect our own. I hope that in your father's absence, you feel that you can come to me with any fears or concerns you may have about what you are experiencing, for you are a member of my family, Brianna, a daughter so to speak."

I must have looked like the village idiot standing in front of Victor slack jawed and bug eyed. It was Devin who coughed suddenly and shook me back into reality.

"Th-thank you, sir. I will."

Victor stood from his chair and lifted his arms high as he addressed the Warriors that sat behind me.

"Brianna Morgan has presented us with the possibility that a sister of ours has betrayed us. It will be the responsibility of the Elite Warrior Council to decide how we progress from here. Therefore, I would like to excuse everyone else for some well-deserved recuperation time. But before we depart, I would like us all to honor the newest member of our coven, Brianna Morgan, for her quick wit in alerting us of our intruders, sacrificing her own safety and health to save a fallen brother, and lastly for saving us all in the end with powers greater than any hybrid in our history. Stand, my Warriors, and salute Brianna Morgan this day!"

The room erupted with cheers as everyone leapt to their feet although Julian was a little slow on the uptake. When I turned to face the crowd behind me, I saw that many were beating the left side of their chest with their fists while others merely placed it over their heart and lowered their heads to me. It was their salute. All this time and I never knew how meaningful that gesture truly was. I was an equal, to the Warriors and to Cameron, and I was unable to contain the emotions that I felt in that moment.

Cameron stepped down from his chair and wrapped his arms around me, nuzzling his lips near my ear as he said, "I will never be able to express how much love I have for you, my angel." His words caused more emotions to erupt from within me as I squeezed him tightly around the neck. "Love me?"

I lifted my head back to see his loving dark eyes and said emphatically, "Always."

The view from my father's home was truly spectacular. I leaned over the wide stone railing that revealed a two-hundred-foot drop onto craggy rocks below that expanded into miles and miles of stunning blue ocean. I loved being here in my big floppy hat and white sarong with a frozen peachy drink in my hand. I could feel the breeze blowing through my hair and the refreshing sea spray gently misting my face. It was amazing how real my dreams had become since my activation, and in cases like this I didn't mind. Other dreams, however, I could live without the extra reality.

As I looked out at the ocean, watching the sun bounce off the cresting waves, I heard a familiar voice call to me.

"Bonjour, ma petite chute," Seraphina said as she shuffled out onto the terrace in a brightly colored sundress and a hat that challenged mine in size.

I gave my stepmother the traditional two kisses on the cheeks before I said, "I was expecting Eris, so this is definitely a nice surprise."

"Zhat is good to know. Your fazer is actually bringing our dreams togezer. It is why he isn't here, it takes a lot of energy out of him."

"You're saying he can meld two people's dreams together?"

Sera nodded as she took my hand and lowered the two of us down onto one of the couches behind us.

"Your fazer is very powerful. As are you, petite, I heard you saved the day."

"I guess," I answered shyly while sinking back into the couch cushions. "I was surprised I didn't hear from you earlier today. I thought you always knew when I was in trouble."

"We did try. But zhe numbers went to zhe voicemails."

"Oh, probably because everyone was on restriction this morning. That's something that should definitely be thought through a little more."

Sera smiled and looked out at the ocean, but continued with, "I am glad you are okay, petite. I am happy zhat we will have more time togezer."

"Me too, Sera. So does this mean that the nightmare is over?"

"I am afraid not," she replied and patted my hand. "Your journey has just started."

"Yeah, that's what I was afraid of," I moaned. "But if you know the outcome, can't you just tell me everything I should do along the way?"

Sera sighed, and I suddenly felt guilty even asking. "It is a tricky path to balance. You need to be able to live your life. Your fazer and I argue about zhis all zhe time, but I know I am right. Look at all you have done in so little time."

"Only because I had a lot of help."

"Oui, but don't we all? Trust your instincts, ma petite chute, zhey have led you here."

We sat, me and my stepmother, and listened to the waves crash against the rocks below. The sound was relaxing in some ways, but almost deafening in another. It was like I was dreaming in surround sound and watching on a super Hi-Def television.

"Why can't my other dreams be this vivid? Seriously, I can see the fish in the water from here."

Sera smiled. "Ah, zhat is zhe vampire blood from Cameron. It has zhat effect."

"Is this really what people are so addicted to? I honestly can't stand it. I can't believe Shelby wanted to feel like this all the time...oh, sorry. I know you've...sampled. I didn't mean to bring Shelby up either, that must be weird for you."

"She is your mozer. Without her, we would not have you. And I am very zhankful for you."

"As I am for you, Sera. Really, I mean it."

Sera's smile stretched from one side of her face to the other, but I noticed that the scene around us was beginning to shimmer and blur.

"Oh, your fazer must be getting weak. Zhat means our time has come to an end. Je t'aime, ma petite chute," Sera said, hugging me tightly and kissing me on the cheek.

"Juh tame, Sera?"

She laughed at my poor attempt at French and took my chin between her fingers.

"Zhe only zhing I will tell you is zhat you should refrain from zhis," she said as she took my drink from my hand, "and from having much more of Cameron's blood. At least for a little while."

"No problem with the blood thing, but why..." I said to her as she stood from the couch and then vanished inside the house.

The scene around me began to fade, and in the background I could hear rambunctious laughter in the distance...

I stretched my eyes open, knowing I would find myself tucked firmly in my bed in the Warrior manor. I looked at the clock and noticed it was almost 4:00 a.m. and couldn't believe that Cameron was still gathered with his family in the sitting room. But hey, after a battle like today, they get to celebrate too, even if it happens to be the same night that I had to deal with this awful vampire hearing shit.

I threw the comforter off of me, and stepped into my fluffy slippers that were next to the bed where I had left them. The cold stone floor had been too much to handle with my enhanced tactile senses thanks to *Blood-au-Cameron*, but even the soft material of my slippers felt odd against my skin as I padded across the room.

When I opened the door to the sitting room the laughter immediately died down and Cameron stepped over to me from the far wall.

"Oh, I am sorry, love, did we wake you?"

"Kind of hard not to be awake with this freakin' bat hearing I have because of you."

Cameron smiled crookedly as he placed his arm around my shoulder and kissed me gently on the forehead.

"I apologize for that as well. I am sorry we woke you, it was just that Jared was saying..."

"Jared!" I shouted, pushing myself away from Cam. "Where?"

"Behind the ginormous vampire," Jared laughed.

Alex stepped aside to reveal my youngest vampire brother smiling up at me. He was paler than usual, and had red blotches all over his body from where his burns were still healing.

"Jared was here! Why didn't you wake me," I shouted at Cameron as I fled from his side into Jared's arms. I had cried a lot today and really thought I had used up all my stores of tears. But as I squeezed Jared tightly, they came in full force leaking down my face and his neck. "Ohmygod, Jerry," I wept.

"Listen, woman, if you start calling me Jerry, I'm gonna bring back Bri Bri, or B-na, or something worse."

We both laughed at each other as I pulled away, wiping my eyes and nose with the tissue that Cameron handed me over my shoulder.

"I'm just glad you're okay."

"Hell ya I'm okay. I had like a gallon of Dad's blood, and that mixed with yours, seriously pow! Oh and by the way, your kids are freakin' gorgeous."

"What kids!" Kyla said excitedly, bouncing up and down.

"These two's," Jared replied and gestured to me and Cameron.

"Jared, that's enough," Cameron warned as he pulled me into his chest.

"Come on, that's like totally awesome that you already know what your kids'll look like. I mean, damn, twins? Holy shit, bro."

"Twins!" Kyla shouted again. "When, when, when!"

"Jer, enough, please. Ky, I don't know. Maybe never." Kyla's cheering and jumping stopped immediately. When she started to pout, I quickly asked, "So what were you guys laughing about before I came in?" Everyone in the room looked sheepishly down at the floor. "You were laughing about me, weren't you?"

Jared exploded into laughter, with Alex trying hard not to give in.

"Sorry, sis, I was just telling them about how I was burning like crazy with this asshole Vamp screaming next to me trying to get your dagger out of him when here you come running up holding this big ass arm and start beatin' the crap out of him. With an arm! An arm! That's classic! Nothing will *ever* top that, Beebs."

Alex and Jared held each other for balance as they laughed hysterically, whereas Devin smirked, Kyla still pouted, and Cameron tried hard to keep his composure.

"Okay, fine. The next time you feel like getting extra crispy, I'll leave you there."

"Oh come on now, you know we're just joshin' you."

"No, I'm serious," I replied. "Next time, I don't care who in this room is in trouble, I refuse to use a *body part* to help you."

But even I couldn't help but laugh a little, and the entire room erupted again in laughter, including Cameron who squeezed me lovingly into his chest.

"Oh yeah, Bibi, by the way, the Warriors are talking about adopting a new battle cry."

"Really? What's it going to be?"

I should have just kept my friggin' mouth shut since everyone in the room shouted together, "I'm going to puke!" and then erupted again in thunderous laughter. Alex even fell to the floor holding his sides. I looked up to see that Cameron was holding his hand in front of his face, unable to restrain himself.

"I am sorry, love. It is funny, and totally you," he laughed, but after a few seconds he stopped and his face changed to one of concern. "Bri, are you feeling all right? You look pale all of a sudden."

In a quick movement, Kyla moved a chair from my path and opened the door for me as I pushed my way through the room with Cameron behind me. Unfortunately, I didn't make it to the bathroom before the taste of burning bile rose quickly from my stomach and I suddenly vomited all over the floor of our bedroom. I glared up at Cameron as I wiped my mouth.

"You've got to be freakin' kidding. Cameron Burke, what the hell did you do to me?"

THE BLOOD-BORNE SERIES CONTINUES
WITH

A Blinding Winter

GET YOUR COPY TODAY AT **WWW.CR-QUINN.COM**

FOLLOW ME ON FACEBOOK AND TWITTER!

Acknowledgments

The scariest thing I have ever done in my life is decide to write a book. The best thing I have ever done in my life is decide to write a book. But in no way could I have done this without the support of my husband, John. For three years he has dealt with the crying, the anxiety, and the countless times I wanted to give up. Although the words are mine, no one else would see them if he hadn't been driving me to do this crazy thing.

I'd also like to thank Ashley Hughson, Kelsey Floyd, Nina Allbert, Marion Pattison, and Ivette Sanchez for being my readers, and frankly not laughing at me.

And thanks to Deb Faulkner for patiently walking me through this step by step, by painstaking step.

About the Author

C.R. Quinn is a first-time author whose prior accomplishments include a bachelor's degree in Biology, surviving the corporate world for over fifteen years, and a singer/dancer/actor in community theatre. She lives in Connecticut with her husband, and is lucky to be the stepmother to two wonderful children. *A Midnight Bloom* is one of three books in the *Blood-Borne Series*, with many more to come.